I0602821

Betrayal

Beverly Taylor

Copyright © 2024 by Beverly Taylor

All rights reserved.

Published by Red Penguin Books

Bellerose Village, New York

ISBN

Print 978-1-63777-611-7

Digital 978-1-63777-612-4

No part of this book may be reproduced in any form or by any electronic or mechanical means, including information storage and retrieval systems, without written permission from the author, except for the use of brief quotations in a book review.

LIST OF CHARACTERS

BECKY
MENDEL
GOLDFARB
MISS O'LEARY
POPPA
OFFICER OF THE BARON
MOMMA
POPPA
BASHA
BENJAMIN
THE BARON
ROSELE
RABBI
SCHLOMO
LAZAR
FRIEDELE
CHAVELE
RABBI AKIBA
JACOB
LABAN
MORRIS
RACHEL
MOSHE GINZE
MOTEL
PINTCHEIK
HAIME
HANNAH
ELLA
HARRY
ELIZABETH
PINCOS PERNIK
BASHEVA
DEVORAH
SIMON
MANDELBAUM
CHAIM
RABBI HERSCHBEIN
MOLKE
RIVKE
MOP
PYOTOR
IVAN
PINSKY
TOVAH

BURCHKOFF
CELIA
THE MATCHMAKER
BRINDEL
MIRIAM
LEON
VILNA RABBI
MRS. MITZER
ELI
MRS. METZGER
ROSKOV
MARVA
BECKY BROMSKY
AARON MINTZ
BASHEVA MINTZ
DR. PIEDHOFT
BESSIE
PINTELE
ROSE
MORRIS
EITAN
GUNTER EITMAN
GUSTAV
SHLOMO
PHILLIP
MIRELE
ZISME
DOV
MR. LATO
MR. EPSTEIN
PESACH-PERSIE
LOTTE BRUHL
DR. APPLE
DOROTHY
RUTHIE
MRS. NOVIE
EVELYN HENRY
DR. RAFFEL
DONNA
EDITH
MR. HERB
MR. BALL
PUNJI
LOUIE
BERNSTEIN

MRS. HANEKE
MAY
MABEL
ROSEMARIE
BILLY
JOSE
MOLLIE
LEONA
SERGE
TESSIE WURSTER
SKI
JACK
MAY LOU
TOMMY TROTSKY
LOTTIE
AUNT MARION
MRS. HAUS
MRS. JENKINS
ZEKE
BILL
IRVING
HEATHCLIFF
PANCHO VILLA
FRED
MRS. DOUGLAS
WILLIE
HAL KEACHER
HERBIE
HARRY FONTE
FLORENCE
THE CHAIRMAN
ORLANDO GUARDUCCI
EMMA GOLDMAN
MILT
GIAN
LEBEN KINTSLER
JOHNATHAN
ENZO
FUSCO
GUISEPPE
MR. SILVER
STUCKER
MR. STERN
AUNT ROSE
LEAH

Chapter One

A gentle soul turns. Becoming another. Suddenly, a crack of lightning splits the earth. Gone: the careful planting and tending of years.

Becky laments, "How could I?"

And wondering, too. An old habit, thinking probing, digging for the tangled roots of things. Trying to remember. Then asking, 'what is there to remember?' And the answer? Wanting to grow up as fast as she could and not remember anything at all. It seems now it was mostly... being cold, being lectured, being hit. The times were hard and hungry, then. And the fairy tales were heavy, too...stretching a long hand into the future.

Imagine going to school <u>twice</u> in the morning! In the first, talking of Paradise on earth in a cold, drafty little room behind a fish store., the bright sun is just a dull gray on that grimy little window. A class of sleepy ten-year-old's, hands under their chins to keep their heads up, or sleeping on the desk with their arms hanging limp by their sides, mouths open, breathing smoky little curls in the air. Only Becky and a few others are doing what they're supposed to do:

straining hard to sing as loud as they could, of hunger, and the working man.

Arise, ye prisoners of starvation!
*Arise, ye wretched of the earth!**

But Becky sang without anger: colorless, plodding, wooden. More like 'Old MacDonald's Farm,' than a call to revolution. She was never angry. The girls knew that, so they gave her a hit whenever they felt like it. And she was heavy, too... from all the bread she ate... and potatoes. The others lived on bread, too. But it didn't show on them. Only Becky looked foolish singing of want and hunger. The others didn't. Pale and puny, most of them. But they teased and taunted. Picking, like the beaks of birds, just where it hurts, "Fatty!" And the pain bursting. Hot tears gushing. 'Sticks and stones...words will never harm me... A lie! Better to have broken bones.'

From time to time, they'd give her a good sock in the belly, too. And watch it shake. Becky would bend her head, look down ashamed and crying... and watching, too.

It never mattered to the teacher how you sang the song – angry or not angry – as long as you repeated the words over and over, so you remembered them deep down, when the time comes.

Mr. Goldfarb was a very serious young man. He had the look of a man being hunted by a pursuer. And he cowered, like someone was raining blows on him. Soft spoken, whispering almost, 'til he began his lecture. Then, slamming a volume of 'Das Kapital' on the table and shouting, 'Vanguards of the Revolution!' His head shooting up, and in his eyes a look of praying, though he did not Believe, he thundered, bellowed, and screamed... like he wanted the world to hear him... in all the four corners.

He's walking back and forth, taking big steps, his back bent, like he's carrying a heavy load, and, from time to time, pounding his fist in the air...<u>battering the ghost of an old memory</u>.

It was rumored he worked in a mine and never straightened up

---

* ***Russian National Anthem after the Revolution - The International***

again. Others said it was because he thought he was carrying the world on his shoulders. But neither was true.

He'd rave on and on. A few heads snapped up, but the others slept, in spite of all the noise he made. Mendel Goldfarb, shouting poor talk: rage, protest, revenge... and pain.

"Why are you in torn coats and shoes? Without heat and light? And with angry poppas? And nagging mommas? Or no poppas? And no mommas? Or sick ones? Or dying ones? CAUSE OF THE RICH! If they're buying, we sell them our arms and backs for bread, a piece of candy or a baseball ticket. So, what's the answer to all those questions, children?"

"They're not buying."

"Exactly."

Then he pulled a crumpled flag out of his pocket, the size of a handkerchief. Waving it back and forth, glaring and accusing: "For this rag, the rich send us to war." "Why?" "Cause they want more... or there's too many of us... Or they're bored. If we live, we get a parade. If we die, we're forgotten about altogether... after the speeches, bugle blowing, and lowering us into the ground."

Then his arm would make a wide swoop around, pinpointing, cornering...

"Becky! Who is the capitalist, exploiter, warmonger?"

"America."

"Speak up!"

"AMERICA!"

"And who is the GIVER of peace and security from THE CRADLE TO THE GRAVE?"

"Mother Russia."

"Speak up!"

"MOTHER RUSSIA!"

"But the old sounds of Mother Russia, Mr. Goldfarb?"

When she turned a deaf ear to the whimpering of children: Mendel, age 12, worker, grinding out life at a job. Bent to the machine by day. Chained to it by night, so you could start work at sunrise, without wasting a minute. That terrible night the machine dropped oil. A black pool all around you. You could have put a finger, reached up and turned a screw. But you didn't. Just let the drops fall. Slow. On the same spot at the back of your head and streaming down over your face, the black tears. All night, listening and waiting for each drop to fall, 'til the morning. Then the boss screamed, "God!" Over and over, stepping gingerly around a spreading pool of wasted kopeks... and threatening.

"Not a kopeck pays 'til it was all paid back! You couldn't be trusted! Worse than a thief!"

And in the Czar's newspapers...perfidious too. Caricatured...the hooknose Jew clutching bags of money, his boot on the Russian neck, eating matzoh dripping with Christian blood. And Mendel frantic, now...to run, breathe air and see stars, terror driving him on and holding him back. Nowhere to go. No one to go to. But the wildness inside presses and presses... 'til it pushes you out!

Too cold. Too raw. They let you go. Nobody's looking. But you don't know it. The fear is too deep inside, claiming you. And always will.

At the end of his lecture, hope bursting, he'd shout, 'No more war!' Then he'd pause...a look on his face of heavy thinking; thumb and forefinger, rubbing his eyebrows. At that very moment, the heavy breathing of deep sleep, and sometimes, a snore. But they were the first to jump and scamper out, the sleepers and snorers, hands cupped to their mouths, breathing warm on them, as soon as he barked, "Dismissed!" Outside the lines: bread, soup, sometimes milk. Men, women, and children, too... desperate, numbed, shifting from side to side, like people do when their feet are icy cold.

And standing in a place where he couldn't see her, so she wouldn't embarrass him, Becky would watch Mr. Goldfarb cross the street and quietly take his place in line.

And the revolutionary vanguard went to Public School 100, a wooden one-room schoolhouse, with a smaller version in the back (if you know what I mean). The Polly stove in the corner tried hard, but it just about managed to go 'round Miss O'Leary, the teacher. She was warm because she was never more than a step away from it. The class shivering in coats and hats and galoshes, the pencils tapping on the paper, their hands trembling so, when they tried to write. They were so stiff. It was eerie, sometimes; like it was a class for the blind.

Miss O'Leary had flaming red hair, a square chin that looked horsey because her lower teeth protruded over the upper, instead of the other way around, with big splotchy freckles all over; one on the tip of her nose that looked like a fly. When Becky first saw her, she remembered waiting for Miss O'Leary to brush it off, and wondered why she didn't. She wore the same dress every day, a tight yellowish green silk.

And her stomach sloped in it, like the side of a mountain, from the place where her waist might once have been. There was a band of small circles rounding that mountain like a chain. Becky played a game guessing how many there were, counting and recounting, but Miss O'Leary always managed to turn just when Becky rounded the curve on the way to the bone. She waved a flag and shouted, too.

"What is the land of opportunity, freedom and God?"

"Becky?"

"America."

"Speak up!"

"AMERICA!"

"And what country is a tyranny...Anti-God...Anti-Christ?"

"Where all the good Christians are, in Siberia? Do you know how cold it is there?"

"Eighty degrees below zero! That's how cold! And that country is..."

"Becky?"

"Russia."

"Speak up!"

"RUSSIA!"

Then the class pledged allegiance to the flag and sang, '*My country 'tis of thee, the Star-Spangled Banner, American, America the*

Beautiful, and God Bless America.' After the bell rang, and the class was stomping out the door, her voice pursued them. She looked very stern, like she was carting them off to prison herself, warning them about traitors, revolutionaries, and Commies. The class never saw her smile except when the principal visited. She gushed all over him. He was fat, too, and they'd watch his stomach go up and down when he laughed. Hers couldn't, because her corset was too tight.

Becky came home from school, hands and feet insensible, eyes tearing, fires both out... if no one was home. The cold fastened itself on her, pursued her into the house. She crawled into bed wearing her winter coat, pulling the covers over her head, as if you could hide from the cold in the dark. But it continued to pursue her... under coat, covers, and all ... and stayed there, in her blood and bones, 'til Poppa came home. She didn't know how to make a fire. And they'd talk. Always the same thing. Like people today talk of money, poppa talked politics. It was his life. There was no other.

Nothing else moved. Life stood still in those days. He never got anywhere. Things always went wrong. Except when he lectured Becky. Then, something went right. He told her she was the only one in his life who doesn't have a hard head.

About Miss O'Leary's lecture, he warned, "Don't believe everything you hear."

"What should I believe, Poppa?"

"Simple," he said.

And he stood straight, turning his eyes to the far place where his dreams were... of love and happiness for all. On his face, the looks of excitement. And he'd talk of the people... born good 'til they were divided by the cross and brutalized by the dollar. In Russia, they're both gone. No groveling to money and God. It's enough! All those years. First, being afraid of trees and bushes (and they didn't even give rain after all that begging). Then, afraid of statues. And then, the worst... A God from nothing. For trees and bushes and statues, they didn't kill. But for *Nothing?* They kill. Who needs it?

"Not even Jews, Poppa?"

"Not even."

Heritage: Shuffling, jailing, burning, degrading, burying, bleeding pogroms, living in huts with chickens, steerage. Now, hunger. Stretching out arms and selling themselves and nobody buying. <u>But still talking of faith in Man</u> and <u>in his Goodness</u>.

"A person is a person, Becky. Remember that. Not where he comes from or where he's going. You love him for what's here," and Poppa would put his hand on his heart, his face would flush, and there'd be desperation in his eyes; the closest he ever came to a look of love. So near, yet so far, the Worker's Paradise...if only...

Then singing. Comrade songs... he sang in the old country. A song that binds. These were their love songs, passion songs, willing to die songs.

On my grave, the red flag
With her colors
The blood of the working man

Becky's thin voice joined his and exulted, too.

<u>In the Old World:</u>

The revolutionaries, the prisoners and the purged... they're burying. And the Cossacks sit proud on restless horses... their whips flying, scarring the mourners. But they're singing still... of freedom and the nobility of man.*

The In-ter-national So-vi-et[†] sh-a-ll be th-e hu-man race. Hopesongs.

<u>In the New World:</u>

Grown old now, the mourners gather in Becky's kitchen, waving tattered arms and clenched fists with arthritic fingers, names flying and clashing with other names, ideas scorned and shouted down with other ideas. Debating ists and isms... all the tailors, pressers, and shoemakers ... out of work. Socialists, Communists, Marxists... thumping on the table, slamming doors and swearing never to speak to each other

---

* ***Cossacks - Czar's army***
† ***International Soviet - Russia***

ever again! And frantic with worry if, the following night, there was an empty chair. Was he sick? If not, where was he?

They were radicals who talked revolution... but they wouldn't hurt a fly. The screaming and declaiming, protests, threats, and ultimatums... so the cries wouldn't break through. Poppa called himself an Ethical Marxist. "People are like flowers," he'd say, and make a tight fist, then open it slowly, his thick, heavy fingers bending over his palm, and "with love and care, they bloom."

Chapter Two

The night, lit with abandon and straight back going in and out of that room calmly, confidently, an officer of the Baron.

The sun was shining, earth and sky stretching as far her eyes could see. Basha couldn't remember when she lay down at midday, lazing in the sun, enjoying the land, (instead of toiling on it), the gentle curves of hills, majestic trees framed against the sky. Basha, exultant, looked up and followed a cloud. It was her favorite game when she was a child. How many faces and shapes she imagined she saw as it gently moved this way and that.

The wagon jolted. Her head fell. The muddy little river. The entrance to *Batyevka*. She was frantic now and couldn't wait to see the familiar sights on the way to her home. They arranged themselves in order in her brain... the butcher, the tailor, the baker, the old tree, the temple, the Beth Midrash, the Mikvah, the dirt road, another tree, Mendel's house, and then.... Home.

The streets were deserted. Everyone was in hiding. The whole town became one ear when the lord's wagon creaked into Batyevka. Not even daring to peek, they all seemed to hear it at once... and fled.

The horse stalled in the muddy streets. Straight back yelled and whipped the struggling animals into obedience. The wagon neared the house and stopped at last. She wanted to leap out and fly through the door... but she restrained herself.

Straight back jumped gracefully from his seat.

"Get out", he barked, grabbing her by the arm and discarding her at the door like something unclean and contagious.

The door was flung open. They were all there, her dearest friend Roselle with them, all huddled around the stove.

"Momma!"

They jumped up in unison. Ten little fingers clung to her while she sobbed a flood of tears into her apron. She had to drag them along with Benjamin's bed. They wouldn't let her go.

"You're home, Basha."

She bent down to hear him.

"Thank God," he whispered.

"How do you feel?" she asked tenderly, anxiously, bending over his bed to hear him.

"Better. Thank God. Much better."

Managing a weak smile.

"What happened, Basha?"

"Nothing, Benjamin."

"Nothing happened?"

Benjamin was satisfied. He closed his eyes and returned to his private thoughts. He was weighing a question that had been examined and re-examined but there was still another detail. The smaller the detail, the more important it became. "One could never be too careful," he always said. Becky turned. She knew the conversation was over. In the moment, how often had Benjamin quoted to her from the Mishnah* and talk not overmuch with women, even with thy own wife, and with the fellow's wife. For so long as a man talks

____

* **Mishn – Holy book**

overmuch with women, he brings evil upon himself, neglects the study of Torah, and in the end 'Gehenna* is his portion.'

Basha embraced her dear friend, Rosele, who was sobbing and thanking God, Basha was back.

"What happened, Bashele? Tell me."

Roselle sat taut, attentive, while Basha re-lived her nightmare.

She hesitantly asked the next question, "What will happen, now?" She brightened when Basha reassured her, "I think it'll be alright."

Roselle wanted Basha to continue. The questions continued in her mind but she refrained. She was too delicate to intrude on her friend any further. Basha, remembering his gaze, her face flushed. Sensing Basha's embarrassment, she didn't ask, 'how do you know?' She decided Basha would tell her in her own time. Roselle put Basha at ease like a mother comforts a child. She diverted her attention.

"Let me tell you what happened here after you were taken away," she said Basha was very tired, but her curiosity roused her.

She was instantly alert and attentive. How much she wanted to know. She didn't dare think, until this moment, that she might cause trouble to others in the town.

"Tell me, Roselle," she prodded gently.

Roselle plunged into her story, talking quickly for fear she would forget the slightest thing.

"As soon as you were gone, the Rabbi called an emergency meeting. Everyone came. He told us to fast and pray until you came home."

"But if Basha didn't come home", Mendel demanded. "Then what?"

"Then, we fast and pray some more. We're being punished for our sins."

"What sins!" Schlomo shouted...and they all joined in babble,

---

* ***Gehenna – Hell***

everyone protesting in his own way, so no one was heard above the din. Tumult.

The Rabbi had pounded the table.

A moment of silence...and Mendel shouted again, "What have we done to deserve losing Basha?"

The Rabbi was stunned. They had never questioned him before.

"Quiet!" thundered the Rabbi.

"Only God knows, and when God speaks in his mysterious way, we listen! Are you questioning God's wisdom?"

His voice rose, shaking with rage, "Do you dare!"

Not even a whisper was heard in the room.

"Now go on home and do as God will," he said quietly.

They shuffled out of the meeting like children who had their faces slapped forcing themselves to be quiet. But, as soon as they were a little bit away from the shul, they started debating all over again, same for the Rabbi, taking his side, and some against him They all gathered again, Mendel asking for a vote...those for the Rabbi... aye...those against...nay. He counted and recounted. "The ayes have it. We will fast and pray."

Becky, sighing now, "Thank God I'm home."

"Enough fasting. Go, Rosele, tell the Rabbi."

Roselle was out the door before Basha could finish the sentence. That's how Rosele was. She knew what to do without having to be told.

Basha thought she had to show God she was grateful. Tomorrow, she would fast and pray, too. The children were in bed. Lazar had seen to that. She looked fondly at Benjamin. It was the time of the full moon, shining on his face through the window, it's light encircling them as she joined him in the bed, nestling her head close to him. She touched him gently. He didn't stir. She put her arm around him and peacefully fell asleep.

Chapter Three

The neighbors found her and dragged her home, screaming and kicking. When they opened the door, the women fainted, the men raised their eyes upward.

What was once laps and knees and hugging arms throwing her lovingly in the air and spinning her around, and laughing and singing her to sleep, and soothing and rocking and talking soft, was now a bloodied pile in the middle of the floor... mouths open, arms limp with helpless succumbing. A pair of hands quickly covered Rosele's eye...but she saw and heard...all around her...the hum of all the beloved voices...their prayers still in the air...never reaching heaven.

Roselle was terrified for the rest of her life. She talked with her eyes looking into the distance... too timid to even go so far as to meet a friend's eye... not even Basha's. She had a tic in her face that quickened with embarrassment, her cheeks bouncing more and more rapidly until she had to excuse herself and leave the room. She had two dresses... one for every day... and one for Shabbos. They were like her; brown, colorless, shapeless; they were too big for her body, hanging on her as if they were thrown over her head as she passed by. She had a long, narrow face, so homely that nobody wanted her. She never married. It is said that she never said a cross word and made peace wherever she could. She was kind, sympathetic, helpful and couldn't imagine being any other way. Didn't know how. Couldn't if she had to. Even if her life depended on it.

When she reached the rabbi's door, she wanted to tap gently so as not to frighten him, but she was too miserable, the cold wind tearing. She started softly but heard nothing until she rapped so hard her knuckles were breaking. The sound of rushing footsteps behind the door. Once inside, she groped for a seat in the darkness.

"What happened, Roselle? Tell me."

The rabbi always conveyed an air of concern, but confidence.

"God will take care..." he told himself and them.

He believed it. Made them believe it. They had a friend in the Universe.

He was a small, thin man with a friendly face and gentle eyes. His scraggly beard grew in long points with a huge space in the middle. But he was fierce when he was angry. Then, the Rabbi became another person. Cold. Unreachable. Determined. He would stroke the few hairs on his beard quickly, nervously...ready to the one or the other...depending on the situation... kindly friend... stubborn authoritarian.

He was ever alert to the slightest faltering in faith or ritual... believing like Benjamin, "You can't be too careful."

At first, he was always gentle and sympathetic.

"Tell me Roselle." He repeated. "Basha's home!" whispering as mightily as she could.

The rabbi spun around on one foot in the darkness.

"Tell me more, Rosele." And she told him as much as she knew.... Taking pride that the Rabbi was listening to her.

"God's miracle," he said, clasping his hands and bowing forehead to meet them. "Will you tell everybody as soon as you can? Basha doesn't want them to fast for her. For her, they're fasting!"

The Rabbi wheeled on her, cold and angry.

"For God they're fasting. Now, they should fast, to show Him they're grateful. Foolish girl!"

The rabbi couldn't stop himself. If he had his way, he went on, giving a sermon in the darkness to a congregation of one. There would be more sacrifice to God's goodness, now that He had been so generous to the unworthy sinners of Batyevka.

Roselle waited patiently for the rage to subside. It was over as suddenly as it began. "Never mind how Basha feels," he said quietly, "She's just a woman. Leave it to me, Roselle. I will take care."

He left the room and returned with an old blanket that he carefully spread on the floor.

"You'll sleep here, Rosele," he said and groped his way out of the room.

Roselle awoke very early the next morning and already, the noise of a bustling household, footsteps clicking back and forth, the snap of linens folded for airing, children crying and being hushed, dishes clattering, pans rattling, the hum of prayer. Rosele jumped up and carefully folded her blanket.

The rabbi rushed in, picked it up and threw it carelessly in a corner, undoing all her careful folds. "Don't worry," he said, "the Rebbetzin will take care."

Roselle was hungry. The Rabbi made no mention of food. He is still fasting, she thought. He must be. The Rabbi would have shared a piece of bread with her. He rushed her into the cold morning. She was still wearing her coat having slept with it on, all night.

"You tell Basha's family," he said, "I will take care of the rest."

Roselle, tired, hungry, and sleepy, trudged the mile through muddy paths, unsteady on her feet, rushed on by her eagerness to bring the news, impeded by her fear of falling. She slipped and slithered her tortuous way to her destination where her news was received with a tumultuous greeting. She was promptly forgotten, as the family, in their enthusiasm, flew out the door. Roselle trudged her weary way home. There was no need for her now. The family circle closed again, for now. Now and again, it opened. Roselle drifted in and out at those times... in, when she was needed... out, when she wasn't. At least, that's how she saw it. It hurt... but that's the way it is with those who don't have it. You wait... like the donation box, for a donation.

Rosele returned to her little routine that was interrupted by caring for Basha's children, making a living from the little box of needles, pins, and notions on which she attached her little sign. Look in the basket. A piece of dried bread, still on the table where she left it. Desperately, plunging it into her mouth and looking around guiltily, although there was no one there, she reddened, choked and gasped. She swept her sleeve over her face and fled out the door.

Outside, people were scurrying to the Schule. The Rabbi had called an emergency meeting. Roselle joined them, hurrying too. In Schule, they sat down quietly. The Rabbi looked cold. All eyes were riveted on him. It was unlike the usual head turnings and babble that preceded his lectures.

He burst out, "Basha is home."

The people erupted, jubilant.

"Silence!" he ordered, thumping the table and thundering... "What does this mean?" Asking the question and answering it... "It means...God has wrought a miracle. We must show Him we're grateful. If Jacob was willing to sacrifice his only son, then we can fast, at least, one more day."

The Rabbi was firming the faith, testing their obedience. He was concerned. Yesterday, they questioned him. Tomorrow, they might (Heaven forbid) question God. With all the thousands of questions, there were two that were absolutely forbidden. They would have dangerous consequences. The Baron and the Rabbi had this rule in common. They understood each other. One was a test for the power of the other. As long as they feared and obeyed the Rabbi, they would fear and obey the Baron. The only difference between the two was the Rabbi's conviction that God wanted it that way. The Baron knew the Rabbi wanted it that way.

The congregation was stunned. They had always fasted for the bad...sins, misfortunes...in the past and present...but for the good? The Rabbi was going too far!

Mendel shouted, "And if she's arrested again tomorrow, Rabbi? Do we fast again? When do we stop fasting?"

And then the schnorrer demanded – "Aren't we fasting enough already?" What does God want?"

He collapsed in his seat, trembling. What had he said! What possessed him to say it!

One by one, a few rose silently and walked out of the temple. Some others followed meekly, the Rabbi's voice pursuing them, shouting, like a prophet of doom. The few remaining sat cowed in their seats.

As the others were slowly going down the street, each lost in his own thoughts, the Baron's wagon separated them as it went hurtling down the street. They fell on each other trying to jump out of the way, then froze wherever they were, stiff like an old photograph... as if they were firming themselves for the blows to come. But they were ignored. The wagon stopped at the pole where the Baron posted his orders. A new poster was hastily put over the preceding ones. There were so many rules made and unmade; no one even wondered why anymore. When they left, the one in the town who could read, broke from the group, and rushed to the poster, the others crowded behind him.

<u>By Order of the Baron:</u>
Candles can be lit through the night.

Again, they were anxious and questioning... Did he mean it? How often the Baron amused himself with them. Making orders only to unmake them. Keeping them in confusion. He changes orders in the middle of the night, then punishes them for disobedience. Should they take a chance this time? Pride settled the issue. The men were ashamed. Basha, a mere woman, had courage. They would too!

In the heat of the discussion, they hadn't noticed that Mendel had silently crept away. He had a fat face, whose features disappeared in a circle of round cheeks and several chins. His stomach preceded him, and he waddled when he walked. He always looked wide eyed and innocent. Unlike the others, he was 'immaculately' frayed. His wife worked night and day... washing, pressing, and sewing Mendel's garments.

No one knew how he managed to get all the food to fill such a stomach, but no one dared ask questions. Mendel made it clear he wouldn't tolerate them. He was so big, no one dared intrude against his wishes. But he loved the glint of admiration he saw in the eyes of some, when he made his rebellious pronouncement in the Schule. Mendel loved attention. He sometimes suspected his tongue had more courage than his heart, but he quickly dismissed these suspicions. His words were never really put to the test, and he knew they never would be. Mendel lived in the glory of battles he never fought. That night when candles remained lit far into the night, Mendel's window remained dark.

Chapter Four

Basha was unaware that she was in the eye of a dispute. Lazar was dispatched at dawn to tell the family. He arrived at an empty house. They were already informed and, on their way...momma, poppa, sister, brother-in-law...embracing, hugging, crying; the fiercely close emotions of people who have lost and found each other again; that moment of pure love and need before the familiar tensions quickly replace them...the high point of meetings... only to be repeated again at partings.

Basha told the story again, minimizing, reassuring, comforting...as much as she could. "I think everything will be all right now."

"But he warned you," Friedele reminded her.

"Yes, but he didn't mean it," Basha mysteriously replied.

She sounded more confident that she felt... or was it numbness? She really didn't know.

Friedele's face was as plain as Basha's was beautiful. She envied Basha and waited for the lines to come, for the great equalizer... time... to do its work. Gangly, tall, shaped like a pole, kinky red hair, and freckles 'til she married and covered the hair; tiny eyes always squinting with curiosity and suspicion. Again and again, she asked

Basha to describe the palace. What she wouldn't give to have seen such a room! Friedele's days were spent figuring out how to arouse the envy of others. Never a direct attack, but always going in the opposite direction as far as she could and hitting the target dead center.

Her cardinal rule was, 'Never let anyone triumph,' especially in matters of health. It led invariably to other triumphs: self-pity, center stage, etc.

"My Beryl did almost the best in cheder. I'm so upset. He should have done the best." or... "People are always complimenting Esther for her beauty. I'm afraid it will go to her head... or... "My Beryl is so smart, but it worries me. He studies so hard. It's bad for his health."

Whatever anyone had or did, she had or did...better.

But Basha's experience was her first really challenge. When the rush of warmth was over, Frieda returned to the well-worn path her mind loved to travel. He sister would be a heroine, now. How could she compete with that honor? Basha was still the bone in her throat.

Even her husband, she considered to be nothing when compared to Basha's.

"Basha is married to a scholar," their mother often said... proud and puffing. She never even mentioned Jacob. He even looked foolish and always embarrassed her. He had tufts of blonde hair that stood up on each side of his head like wings, with a bald spot in the middle. In his eyes, a look of innocence, though he couldn't be trusted. People learned that too late.

He never debated, having neither patience or time for it. Every morning, he filled four boxes with vegetables, stood on a corner haggling with customers. He seemed to have a price to fit everyone.

Periodically, he'd shout, "Don't touch the tomatoes!"

His tomatoes were like him. The good ones were neatly piled on the top to make a good impression. His hands were so deft, the hapless customers never noticed that he never touched the top tomato. They were for show. He spent the day straightening his yarmulke and his tomatoes. He had no interest in learning. Benjamin often tried. He had a simple vocabulary that settled the most complex questions, "You're a fool" or "That's stupid". He was too busy making a living, he always said, to waste time talking. First you eat, then you debate. He claimed he was too busy trying to get past the first hurdle to waste time on the second. The only part of Basha's story that really touched him was her description of the palace. That's what matters, he told himself. You can't feel a debate with your fingers, look at it, and most of all, put it in your pocket. Can you pay for anything with words? If you want a suit on your back, the tailor doesn't care how well you debate. He wants his money.

Basha's parents remained long after the others left, fearfully obsessed with what might have been. Poppa placed his arm gently around Basha. She sobbed for the first time since she'd been home as she did so many times when she was a little girl. Taller than him now, she had to bend to find his thin little shoulder.

"You're a good girl, Basha," patting her gently, "but be careful."

"I was so frightened, Poppa," she sobbed.

"I know," he said, his shoulders aching under the weight of her head, still shaking with sobs.

His body wiry and fragile, his face small, the skin stretched to its limits over a bony frame, the eyes alert, ever watchful. But the voice that boomed out of that tiny figure was still young and commanding. Basha imagined the prophets had such a voice, hypnotic, gathering followers, leading them on soothing, guiding, protecting. The Schule counted on him to make one voice out of many when the babble was leading them nowhere.

"I have to go now, mien kind."

It was time for Schule. Basha dried her tears and turned to her mother.

Momma's face was all wrinkles now. It was said she was a great beauty in her time, like Basha. Momma often said she was still pretty and could turn heads. Poppa agreed. She had always wanted to learn; yearned to read and write. She'd begged him. "No time now," he always said. "Some other time."

Through the years she waited, asking again and again, when she thought it was the right time. One day she just stopped asking. He never noticed. She never forgave him.

Basha sensed her mother wanted to speak to her alone. She sent the children out to play. Benjamin had thought himself into unconsciousness.

"What did Benjamin ask you?" Basha told her.

"He asks a million questions and only has one for you?"

"A woman shouldn't ask questions," Basha replied gently.

"Why not?" Momma persisted.

"Because," she replied and shrugged her shoulders.

"Would it be so terrible if he thought about this world, once in a while? A table, a chair?"

Momma looked around the room, making a list of Basha's world of bent and broken. And concluding with, "Maybe, God forbid, money! How can you see your own son, poor Lazar, bending over those old books, hungry because he's studying, and studying to forget he's hungry."

"If it's God's will," Basha replied calmly. But her mother couldn't be soothed.

"Can you see little Chavele with ten hands on her apron?"

"She should be so lucky."

"Davis, Saul, Borush, Abraham...children and books...books and children...That's all they'll ever know if Benjamin had his way..." her voice becoming louder and angrier.

"That's more than enough," Basha quietly reminded her. "Poppa always said you can't have it both ways...wealth from scholarship and wealth...but Momma wanted them both."

It was embarrassing...poverty...ignorance...the second more than the first. But she pitied herself. 'What did she have from her children after all? And she pitied them, too. She lusted and didn't have any. Would never have.'

Basha had something. She was proud. She was content. Friedele was neither. Basha carried the tradition. She didn't know where it was written...but it didn't matter...the message was somewhere deep in her heart.

"In the future at the judgment, Rabbi Akiba will put all the poor in a guilty light."

For, if they are asked, "Why did you not study Torah; and they say, "because we were poor", they shall be told.

"Indeed, was not Rabbi Akiba even poorer and in more wretched circumstances?"

And if they say, "Because of our children, they shall be asked, and did not Rabbi Akiba have sons and daughters?"

But they are told: "Because Rachel, his wife had merit."

Chapter Five

The people could talk of nothing but Basha. Her story flew from hovel to hovel, town to town, city to city, and finally, salon to salon. The few rich Jews in the city filled their living rooms with the tale of the little country girl. Some were curious to see her in Pale.

So many visitors came to the town to see her that the scribe posted a little sign at the edge of town that read 'Basha's Home' with an arrow pointing. He had to post a few of them later on, as later on, as people still lost their way. Crowds gathered outside her house to peer at the fancy carriages, the well-dressed men and women, graceful and dignified, their noses pointed in the air as if to purify it before they deigned to draw a breath. They usually came rushing out after a brief visit, as if they'd made a duty call to the sick. They came to see Basha and hear the story themselves.

Basha greeted them awkwardly, embarrassed that there was no place to sit, hardly any place to stand. They had to pull up a bed and sit down.

Benjamin, who recovered as the days went by, returned to his studies with even greater diligence. The rabbi told him that it was a miracle he was well. Benjamin agreed. He would glance at the visitors as they arrived, nod to welcome them, and bend over his books again. The visitors listened carefully, but in spite of their extreme caution, each one added a little spice to the retelling until the story grew into a heroic tale, having a tiny resemblance to the original, if any. Jacob became a celebrity for the first time in his life. He tasted fame. He was singled out as the brother-in-law, the maven, the authority for the details of the true story. He sold ten times as many tomatoes in the telling and re-telling. The customers were so absorbed, they didn't think to notice his little tricks of the trade. They paid without thinking, as Jacob poured detail after detail – some real, some imaginary – into their hungry ears. The customers became increasingly respectful, as Jacob created Basha into a larger-than-life heroine. They believed him when he said she shortened the story due to her extreme modesty.

Friedele gave in too. In the darkness of the people's lives, they craved a little magic. She gave it to them, and they gave her the praise she always wanted. After all, wasn't she the sister of a celebrity? It went to her head. She became irresponsible... adding and changing, unaware that her story was subtly becoming a challenge.

The men, in their eternal debates, soon overlooked the original story and debated the new one. Basha asserting her right to light a candle through the night for a sick husband, thought it was forbidden, and the Baron, admiring her loyalty, independence of spirit, and especially her beauty, sets her free.

"Ask Jacob and Friedele," they would say, when a doubtful voice was raised... "They'll tell you."

Memories disappeared under an avalanche of myth. They needed a heroine. Their wise men made them feel they were smart. A heroine made them feel they were brave. Her courage became theirs, even if they had to create one to have the other. They imagined what had happened, created it, and from there, it was a short leap to thoughts of what <u>could</u> happen <u>if</u>. Basha was shielded from the fracas. The town concluded she has suffered enough. But life was steadily worsening for them. They began thinking it was because they were giving in too much to the tyrant. They had to show him they had some backbone. The Rabbi feared for them. Their bravado was growing, their caution diminishing. And Jacob swelled the tide. The Rabbi had carefully built a mountain of prayers and miracles to shield and guide them. It was crumbling and crashing about him. Jacob appealed to their pride., their hunger, their greed. The Rabbi came down from the mountain and found them worshiping the Golden Calf.

Jacob cried, "Why are you giving the Baron the whole loaf and leaving a few crumbs for yourselves. Ask for more! What can he do but refuse! We know it's no crime to ask for a little more! And besides, Joseph was thinking, If they made more, he'd make more. "He's right!" They shouted in union.

But the Rabbi understood power. If the slave is rewarded by the whim of the master, he's grateful. If he's rewarded by his request, the master fears the seed of arrogance is planted in his slavish heart and it will grow. First, the slave humbly requests, and then...he arrogantly demands...and then...and then...Heaven forbid...the slave becomes the master. That's why the master is ever alert to the slightest wavering in abject obedience. It offends him...and...when he's offended...he, God forbid...strikes!

The Rabbi easily guided them because they were innocent. He carefully nurtured that innocence. Now, he realized his error.

Even Basha's father was shouted down, "You've forgotten what really happened," he cried desperately to ears that wouldn't hear him.

"You're not giving your daughter enough credit." Jacob cried.

"That's right."

The congregation responded. They were insisting on being passionately involved; resented being forcefully returned to the realm of calm reason. They were carried away and wanted to remain in the clouds. It was exhilarating; To be brave men and free! Basha had shown them the way, they reasoned. She'd done something for herself. Then they could do something for themselves. God helps those who help themselves! They quickly appointed a small group to manage the details, Mendel the leader. He had explained his light was not lit on the nights before because he went to bed early. They believed him. The small select group huddled in a corner and painstakingly evolved a plan. At first, they started with a mini revolution, then they whittled it down to something more manageable. They decided they would make a small request; the village scribe would write it nicely and Mendel would present it to the Baron respectively.

The Scribe wrote as follows:

Your Honor, your very obedient servants respectfully request that you consider our humble petition.

As you know, we are only able to produce twenty bushels of potatoes a day, and we would like to do more for your illustrious highness, but our women and children are hungry so that they are not able to work for as long or as hard as we would like.

Your Illustrious Highness, we beg you to consider the possibility that we could keep two bushels instead of one, so we could eat a little more, be stronger and work harder. Please accept our eternal gratitude.

Your Humble Servants,
The People of The Village

Jacob's eyes shone with elation as he heard these words; Jacob the unsmiling, the pessimist, the cynic... was a happy man. Overnight, he thought he'd be called a Tzadik (wise man). Never again, Jacob the Nar fool. He even pictured himself with his own pushcart... maybe a shop even. Only God knew what could come of this! Hopeful anticipation overcame him, his excitement knew no bounds.

Mendel was quietly sobered for the first time. He was a loudmouth, but not a hero. He knew would have to take the message. The town would compare him to Basha, now. He was no longer on centrestage alone. How would it look; a woman braver than he? They would find him out. *Mendel the Joker,* they would call him, and laugh. He was afraid to be a bearer of bad news. The Baron might get it into his head to punish him. How to turn this to his advantage? The answer? Simple, of course. Tell the Baron he'd come to warn him. Mendel had visions, now of bowing very low, while the Baron's praises flowed over his bent back.

He left the following morning, rehearsing his performance before the Baron on the way, his speech, his mannerisms, the expression on his face, the tone in his voice when he was summoned before the Baron.

In front of the guard, he managed to look conspiratorial. They both performed for each other ... the guard as menacing and as humiliating as he could manage... and Mendel as obsequious as he could. "Tell him I have important information for him", Mendel offered as a bribe. The guard, too, had visions of praise flowing over his back and motioned him to wait. And he waited... hour after hour. When he was finally summoned, he almost forgot what to say. The Baron ordered him to state his case quickly. Mendel plunged in... he was too nervous to remember where he'd planned to begin. He was too nervous to remember where he'd planned to begin. "I have some information that may be helpful to your honor", he haltingly began, taking the letter out of his pocket and handing it to the lackey.

The Baron exploded, "Insurrection! Revolution!"

Mendel stood silent...in tacit agreement.

"Who started this? Basha!"

Mendel nodded ever so slightly.

The Baron felt like a man betrayed...but he also savored this moment. <u>He would show her</u>! He would show them all' Nothing he enjoyed more than <u>showing them all</u>. The Baron was bored. He needed to be amused. The Jew needed a lesson. He needed to be put back in his place. How dare they be so forward! The Baron always found his cruelty more pleasurable when he had an excuse like righteous indignation. He screamed for the guard.

Mendel was ashamed and regretting now. The Baron shouted, "Take him away." He hated traitors. They could turn on anyone...

even him. He had more subtle ways of obtaining information. Mendel collapsed and had to be carried out. He was never seen again.

At sundown, the royal wagon came tearing into the streets of the village, the horses driven at top speed, spurred on by uniformed drivers shouting at them to run even faster. Stopping in front of Basha's house, breaking down the door, forcing their way in with weapons drawn. The children were dragged out, screaming, and kicking and thrown into the wagon. Their screams could be heard for miles, as the wagon sped away. The townspeople rushed in. Benjamin was bent over his little table. He looked like he was studying. When they called his name, he made no reply. Then he slumped over the table into a pile of torn pages. The books he lovingly tended were savaged. Benjamin died with them.

He didn't resist or struggle...didn't even realize they were there - the Baron's men. He heard no one when he studied. They thought he was ignoring them, so it enraged them all the more. One of them took aim at his small back, pointed the knife from a distance and hit the mark.

Benjamin's hand was still clutching a paper. One of the townspeople removed it gently and handed it to the scribe.

"What does it say? Tell us."

"You can't be too careful," he whispered hoarsely.

Chapter Six

They found Laban crouched and hiding in a corner. He was stuck on the head and he had fallen unconscious and was left for dead. When sympathetic hands tried to lift him, kind and gentle voices tried to coax him, he screamed and hugged his little corner all the more. They finally left him alone with Rosele... and waited. An hour passed; Laban was quiet. The townspeople put their noses to the window and saw them crouching in the corner together, Rosele's arm around him and his arm around her...and both weeping together. The people watched and waited 'til dark. When they returned at dawn, both were gone. They were found in Roselle's house.... both asleep. They parted months later when they could hide their pain... even from each other. Lazar went home to his grandparents. Roselle crept deeper into her own heart.

At Benjamin's funeral, the people wept for him and themselves. There was a fear of death. Husbands and wives clutched each other and their children and the petty resentment that helped pass their days disappeared into the mouth of this black and terrible cloud. They could deal with God. He occasionally heard their prayers. But the Czar....never. Their heads were full of terrible disasters that could be heaped upon them while they were mourning for Basha and Benjamin.

Their condolences were self-conscious and clumsy. They said them hurriedly, guiltily, looked away when they held Morris's or Basha's hand. Some embraced him so they wouldn't have to face him...and sped away without daring to look at him.

The Rabbi remembered Benjamin's numberless virtues and weeping and wailing followed his words. "How I need him now!" the Rabbi raising his arms and pleading with the Heavens.

The town faithfully gathered all Benjamin's papers. They scoured the ground for every note they could find and put them to rest with him.

The Heavens, to which Benjamin had devoted his life, were indifferent to him to the last. The sun shone brightly, birds scampered gaily, the sky was bright and blue overhead. Even the winds were calm and gently caressed the trees. It was a day to make the heart sing. Benjamin was nonchalantly erased from the universe like a misplaced comma.

Since Benjamin had no family, shiva was to be held at Basha's parent's home.

They posted a sign in the shul, "We will sit shiva alone. No visitors if you please."

Every day they found little packages outside the door.

And every morning, Rachel asked, "Maybe you would like to see someone today?"

"What for?"

"So maybe you'll feel better?

"How can I feel better when I've lost my heart and buried my dearest friend?"

Morris suffered a wound that only tears would help, and people would only take him from his tears. He wanted no comfort now. No hidden tears in quiet corners of his heart to wait their turn in time. Besides, he couldn't face the town. He hated them so. But now was a time for mourning. He would hate later. It was unfair to the dead to hate while you were crying for them, loving them. This was their time, Basha's and Benjamin's. He wouldn't let them be robbed of this, too. Enough had been taken from them. Rachel's hurt turned to bitterness. She mourned for Benjamin. And blamed him. And most of all.... she blamed herself. It was she, after all, who made the shidduch. Morris had always balanced his world and hers by finding another side to a question... a reassuring one. But this time there was no answer for so deep a wound ... so deep that the other questions and answers ceased to matter.

Rachel cried, "All those books...what use have they been...the books she'd tenderly cherished throughout the years...how often she would open them, turn the pages, stop at one of them and pretend she was reading. Those books were filled with wonder for her. What couldn't they do, now, she felt they'd betrayed her. She despised them. Morris spent his life devouring, quoting, searching them day and night. The books told him he was a 'chochim'...and she believed. He knew <u>everything</u>...<u>once</u>. Now, he knew <u>nothing</u>. If the books knew nothing...what could <u>he</u> know? He joined Rachel in her ignorance. Thousands of years of pouring over millions of words...the wisdom of countless sages...couldn't save his daughter."

"And where was God?" The ultimate question...the final and last one he asked over and over...and she, too...asking bitterly...where was He? Lazar heard their anguished discussions and started asking the forbidden questions.

Chapter Seven

The sign to Basha's house remained on the road. Mournful visitors came to pay their respects. Her house became a shrine by day. At night, a candle was sometimes seen in the window. Three men were seen coming and going mysteriously, sometimes carrying papers. Lazar was with them. No one knew what was going on. The men were strangers and Lazar wouldn't talk to anyone. When they greeted him, he'd reply, "You killed my father." He had one question for the town. They had no answer for him. "Where were they when they killed his father, and he lost his mother and the little ones?" Lazar was asking questions to which he knew the answer. Those were kinds of questions he would ask from now on; the questions that had answers.

As for Jacob and Friedele, that's a story in itself.

They were forbidden to come to the house. They were declared dead and Morris and Rachel sat shiva on them.

They both declared, "She's not the daughter we knew since she married that scoundrel."

They made an impossible decision and clung to it...having to renew it every day, resurrecting and burying...again and again. They couldn't bring back the dead that God had buried...but they could bring back the dead they had buried? Relenting from time to time and reaffirming again and again. Jacob, with his short memory and shorter temper forgot the part he played in the tragedy. He heaped abuse on Friedele, on her parents, on the town and Friedele heaped abuse on him. They fought at home, in the street. They fought in the morning. They fought at night. He finally screamed at her, "I'm going to America." "Go ahead," screaming louder. "I will!" Louder still.

Each one out-shouted the other, hoping the other would relent and save them from the final rift. But neither one did.

Jacob was shunned. His business suffered. A relative in America sent him the fare to come to the U.S, Friedele declared, at the last moment, that she was coming too. She had hoarded money behind his back, made all her preparations secretly and sailed with him. They never exchanged a word with each other on the trip, divorced in America and never set eyes on each other again.

Rumors flew about Basha and other children. Someone said that the children were converted and placed in Christian homes and that Basha went mad and there were reports ever after from far flung places that she was seen wandering at midnight in a long white flowing gown carrying a candle.

Now to return to Batyevka, the town, soon after Benjamin's death, was ashamed, blaming, justifying, reproving, praying, and questioning their praying. What to do? This was the second time they asked that question. All other times they'd left it in God's hands. The people were grateful for the endless chores and backbreaking labor that stopped their minds from turning and turning. The women blamed the men for bringing a curse on their heads. That's all they talked about with each other day after day.

But their conversations ended as they always did, "What would they cook for supper?"

At night, when the men were leaving for a meeting, each one looked very important, some brought down a peg by the wife's final warning as the door slammed behind them, "Do something!" Each one depended on someone else to come up with a good idea...with which they could then differ. They gathered in the shul early for a change, each one alert and watching the door, impatient, wondering if this one or that one decided not to come and leave the doing to them. They were finally all accounted for and sat quietly for a change, each one locked on his own thoughts.

The Rabbi mounted the podium...and began.

"You see," he thundered, "what you've done." (Not as forcefully as usual)

The Rabbi could only be forceful with an obedient flock. A few men wept. A few yarmulkes turned. The Rabbi couldn't see their eyes glowering.

A man shouting, "The time for weeping is past."

A plea anguished, angry, "We have to do something!" The Czar will kill us all!"

Others shouted agreement.

The schnorrer* rises and asks in full performance (pitiful, despairing, staring hungrily at the congregation) "What should we do? What can we do? We made a mistake, that's all."

Others are shouting now, "No, we didn't." And throwing their prepared speeches at one another; the Rabbi thumping for order. Then suddenly it was quiet.

Basha's father ascended the podium and stood near the Rabbi. Heads bending in shame, yarmulkes slipped to the ground. They're grateful not to have to meet his eyes. They bend their heads slowly, returning the yarmulkes, slowly fitting them again to their heads. Morris looks down on the collective face of shame. They stood quietly, straining to listen for the forgiveness or the punishment they wanted. He simply removed from his pocket a drawing of a bushel of potatoes and held it up saying, "<u>Look</u>, for <u>this</u> you destroyed my Basha, my Benjamin, my grandchildren, my wife, and last, and least of all...me. Flinging it into their midst, he hurried out of the shul. No

---

* ***Schnorrer – Beggar***

one stirred. The drawing remained on the floor. No one dared to touch it.

Then, a voice shouting; the schnorrer, "He's right!" And another, "What do you know? How many potatoes do <u>you</u> dig a day?

Shmuel, the speaker, was a man who looked like his potatoes. A long, dark beard, scraggly hair that he never cleaned. He was always dusty and dirty, and looked like he slept in his clothes. His features were tiny, pinpoint eyes in a tiny head and a small forehead with his hair hanging over it so he looked like a shaggy dog. No one knew how he managed to see through that hair. He snarled when he talked and looked down on everyone even though he had no reason except the satisfaction of snarling.

Chapter Eight

When the packages that were left outside the door when the family was sitting shiva was one with a note from Moshe Ginze, a relative of Benjamin's who lived in Suvalk. The note read:

Dear Lazar,

We have for you a bed, three meals a day and cheder if you want it...Our door is open...Our hearts are broken.

Your sorrow is ours,

Moshe

Lazar read over and over. "Our door is open." He decided to go; to take his few belongings: the clothes on his back, a few of Benjamin's books to keep his beloved father with him, the drawing of a candle and the whereabouts of the mysterious strangers. They were near Suvalk. He feared even repeating their whereabouts to himself. He traced it in memory ... the trees, the stream, the lookout, the pass-words, the cabin with a barrel outside covered with a red bandanna. He reviewed the events of the past weeks. His nightly visits to his home where Benjamin sat among the rubble and mourned Basha. He searched for her by day, waited for her at night. The door was gone.

He sat and stared at that open doorway, mesmerized with impatience and hope, until his eyes could no longer keep their vigil. He met her in his dreams and lost her again to the day. He hoped he could sleep and dream forever. He put a few broken boards together, made a circle on a hill of debris and ate and slept and dreamed and hopped on that board. One day, he heard a familiar creak when he was between sleep and waking. He jumped up, his eyes blinded with tears, his arms flung open, he embraced the figure that stood in the doorway. But it wasn't Basha. It was a tall, hard muscular giant. Lazar collapsed at his feet, his body heaving with sobs. The stranger lifted him gently, helped him stumble over the debris of his little island, sat down with him and cradled him in his arms.

The huge hand patted his little shoulders and hugged him gently the big chest Lazar's pillow until he was spent and dared to look upon the stranger's face.

"Forgive me," he said, "I thought you were someone else."

The stranger nodded his head in silence. He wasn't a talker. He looked up and Lazar followed his eyes. There were two other men in the doorway.

"Is anyone here besides you?", the stranger asked, suddenly suspicious.

"No one. The house is empty."

The stranger ordered 'come in' to the others and to Lazar, who looked very frightened, "Don't worry. We won't hurt you."

But Lazar was worried. They didn't look like the men of Batyevka. The man who comforted him was the largest. They all had beards and looked almost alike. You could hardly distinguish one from another.

"Laban," one of them said to Laban's comforter, "did you ask the boy if anyone came to her?"

"I did. The boy says, no one."

"That's good."

They seemed guarded, cautious. Laban decided he would listen and not speak. Laban had dark, large angry eyes, he gritted his teeth when he spoke and thumped his legs with his palms when he was at a loss for words. He had a wide mouth with large teeth that had spaces between them and even when he smiled, he still looked angry. His laughter was cynical, sarcastic, and cutting.

Motel, the other stranger was a smaller man with a quizzical look on his face, as if he were constantly wondering about something. His eyebrows were always raised, his eyes as wide open as he could manage them. But he had a powerful frame, hard and stocky and seemed taller than he was. He talked in quiet but determined tones; his head turning nervously from one to the other. He made his points. They gave their opinions.

The third, Pintcheik, was handsome. He was also tall and powerful. His huge arms twisted around his bent legs seemed like they could strangle a horse. He had a chiseled face, high cheekbones, dreamy eyes that seemed to look far into the distance to a place that only he could see. Lazar thought he seemed to be dreaming with his eyes open.

Motel asked Laban, "Do you think this place has enough privacy?"

"Of course, can't you see?"

"You need pictures I should draw for you?"

"What do you think, Pintcheik?"

Pintcheik had his head turned, looking out the window... and thinking, 'Toil and trouble, that's what you are, for the little scraps you give us for a reward. You're a tyrant like the rest... Give a little. Take everything.'

"Yes." He answered absentmindedly, as if he had heard.

"You're not listening", Motel said gently, "Now is not the time for philosophy."

"That's right," Laban shouting, "Always dreaming the new world needs work, work, work."

And he thumped his hand on his leg three times vigorously.

The question drifted belatedly into Pintcheik's brain. He turned to Motel, "Yes I think it has enough privacy and he turned his head again to the window." Laban shouted furiously, "lives are at stake" so pay attention. Pintcheik turned and paid attention". Laban thinks it's always the same. He has to see my blood first. Then he listens. But we need him. He's a dreamer. Dreamers will do anything. The bigger and more foolish the dreams, the more useful they are for my purposes.

They were all in their twenties. Pintcheik was a university student and so was Motel. Laban, a factory worker. "Those damned intellectuals, "Laban would say. If all the pencils and pens disappeared overnight, what would they do with themselves, "Without us, they're nothing!" Pintcheik came from a home where all the dreams were centered on him. He would be a famous fiddler. He looked out the window at the earth and sun and when he took his lessons he gazed over his fiddle at the flowers when the teacher wasn't looking. He was finally packed off to school in another town in disgust where the family was told he did well with window watching. He was labeled an indifferent student, a dreamer, and sent back home.

Motel went to school on the charity of others. He slept on a bench in the synagogue. Sometimes, with families who fed him. He was rankled with the injustice of it all. When he'd glimpse the maid going upstairs to turn down the master's covers to prepare for bedtime, he returned to his bench. He felt guilty because of his ungratefulness, but quickly reasoned himself out of it. They met in the tea house on the day of Pintcheik's dismissal from school. Motel reasoned Pintcheik into accepting his fate and turning it to good advantage. Motel said, "We'll return to Suvalk and work together to free them from ignorance and faith. We'll work together. Pintcheik, you'll wake up their hearts to long for a better life on earth. I'll do the rest."

"But I'm a luftmensch."

The luftmenschen made God. So, the Luftmenschen can unmake Him, and I can reason out a way to keep him there... out of mind is my job, out of heart is yours. You're wasting your dreams, Pintcheik. And I'm wasting my reason. Motel was the only person in

Pintcheik's life who encouraged him to dream. And Pintcheik dreamed and told his dreams to Motel and Motel reasoned Pintcheik's dreams and told his reasons to Pintcheik and two revolutionaries were born. Pintcheik dreamed, he confided to Motel. Of a world without tyranny and hunger, everyone the same: a world, most importantly without work... a world suited to him.

Motel reasoned...machines can do the work if men were free from exploiters on the land and in the shop.

Pintcheik went on, "The machines would do all the work. Men would be free to sing, and play music and love, to live in beauty, make poems and travel to distant lands."

Motel's reason was to go to work. The best place to start was at home. They visit Motel's parents. Motel reasoned while Pintcheik gazed out the window. Then Pintcheik told of his dreams while Motel thought of more reasons.

"Who needs dreams? And ideas, we have plenty. Everyone who has a mouth, has an idea. We need bread. That's what we need!"

Motel's parents, they decided, were not the right people to start with. Too practical... no vision... no imagination... too frightened. Unintelligent. In the tea house, they met Laban, a factory worker. Ignorant, loutish and easily provoked, hea had earned a reputation as an angry man; angry about things that mattered to Motel and Pintcheik. Motel approached him, quietly. "Mr. Laban."

"What do you want?"

Motel sat down without invitation.

"You work in a factory?"

"Why are you interested? It bores me to death."

"And your boss? You like him... or no?"

"He should be killed or worse."

Motel couldn't think of anything worse, but he nodded in agreement.

"Why are you asking these questions?"

Motel knew he had his man. He harangued him with reasons; Pintcheik with dreams until he declared, "You're right. If there were no bosses and everyone had their money... if there were no Barons and everyone owned their land... we'd all be rich and free... Paradise on earth."

Laban hated his boss and all bosses. He wanted to bury him and put on his gravestone, 'So you were fired!' the boss' favorite threat.

"Tell me, Motel, how to kill him and I'll do it."

Motel wasn't ready to tell, not yet. But they were not so successful with the others.

"We have 5000 years of God, and Motel and Pintcheik have a few years of school and they're telling us?!" the faithful raged. "The Messiah will come, and you'll have your songs and poems and music."

Laban was feared...even by the bosses, unbeknownst to him; his violent temper, waiting to spring into action. The boss enjoyed provoking him, knowing he was impotent, that he could only go so far. After all, he needed the job. The boss knew it was a dangerous game; pushing him, fighting him, and watching him bend. Laban had to bend. He had a wife and three children he ruled with an iron hand. His word was law in the home...if he was ever home. He came home only to eat...and left. No one knew exactly where. He couldn't stand to be inside at night when he'd been in all day. The wife and children were glad to see the door slam behind him. He was nervous at the table.

When he came into the house, he demanded "What's to eat?" Then he ordered the wife... bring in this and that. He'd slap the children across the face at will. They seldom knew why. Reasons could vary from, 'Sit straight in your seat, I told you,' to 'shut up while I'm talking.'

When the news reached Suvalk about Basha's candle, the murder of the family, the three revolutionaries, who always talked of the same thing, talked differently. "He should be killed, the Baron," Laban said. Since Laban was always 'killing' someone, they ceased paying attention to his one solution for all problems. But tonight was different. Pintcheik saw himself a hero in the town.

"Yes," Motel heard himself saying quietly. "I agree."

They both stared at him in shock.

"I agree," he repeated. "Here's what we do." And he reasoned a plan. "Reason, without action, he reasoned is empty reasoning. Dreams without action, idle dreams. Action without reason, without dream...absurd."

They met every night and the more they talked and listened and planned it all so it seemed more right and more sensible. The day finally arrived when they were to take the first step. They met at the railroad station, Laban carrying the propaganda. They boarded a train for Batyevka. There, they followed the sign, 'To Basha's house,' and were surprised to find Lazar. They thought the house was abandoned. Pintcheik imagined it was, Motel reasoned it out and concluded it was and Laban planned to do the necessary work to make it livable.

Motel, asking Lazar, "We're here to help our people so this won't happen again. Will you help us?"

Lazar nodded in agreement. "You see these drawings," he told Lazar, "We want every house to have one...so they'll never forget what happened here. This candle...the symbol now of our struggle. And attached to it, a piece of paper in which it is written, 'Tyrants must go!' If you agree, hang this picture on your wall. We will know our friends."

The following day, the villagers found a message under their door, the first of many...exhorting them to have courage, to be strong, to unite against the enemy, the Baron.

After a few weeks, they sent Lazar home. "We'll be gone tomorrow, so we want to say goodbye to you now. Say nothing to no one... whatever happens. You had nothing to do with it. Lazar was puzzled but didn't ask questions. They told him where to find them if he needed them. They'd been watching the Baron's routine for weeks. He rode a horse every morning at 7. Motel and Pintcheik waited in the bushes. Laban, in a tree. He sprang on him, put his large hands about him and strangled him, mumbling, "I wish all the bosses had one neck...this one." Laban wouldn't let go, they had to pull away.

"Are you sure he's dead, Laban?"

"More than that. By now, he's in hell where he belongs."

They all returned to Suvalk as quickly as they could. Lazar left to find them before the disaster struck Batyevka. And then, he hated even more...and mourned even more. He became a dreamer and a reasoner. He didn't know if he could become a killer. After a tearful goodbye to Roselle and his grandparents, he boarded a train and left his innocence behind in Batyevka.

Chapter Nine

Lazar took the ride to Moishe's house to Suwalk in Haime's wagon. Haime was the town peddler. He was out in all kinds of weather. His old horse was a bony as he was.

It obeyed him, he said, "because it was too thin and weak to do otherwise. They were both very tired and slow."

Lazar was impatient but Haime couldn't be hurried. Lazar sat amongst old pots, worn clothing, clothes of the growing, the young... the old, the dead...tools, medicines...a sample of everything...birth, illness...death...even a bridal veil and an old Bar Mitzvah suit.

He made the customer feel so important. To the servile and obsequious, he was more servile and obsequious. To the ladies, he removed his old hat. To the men, he would ask how he could help them as if he would willingly give up his life. No one trusted him. They called him 'weasel'. He was always selling... "even the tears in his eyes for salt water," they said, you had to be careful even to talk about the weather. If you said it was going to be cold, out came a sweater from the wagon.

"You're smart to leave Batyevka," he said. "Too much trouble there."

He babbled on asking questions, maybe he could sell him something.

"Where are you going?"

"To my uncle," Lazar answered absentmindedly, hoping Haime would stop asking... even talking.

Haime was mercifully distracted by a stone in the road and turned to watch the horse who was unsteady on his *feet*. Lazar was wondering about his new home. Would he have friends? How would he do in his studies? It excited him to think of himself as a free man of adventure, scheming, plotting, and doing daring things. The wagon passed field after field, the farmers pitching hay and singing. Lazar loved the Christian songs. They were so vibrant, so vivacious. When he heard them, he wanted to dance, jump as high as he could, and embrace everyone. Then the guilt would come bursting, too, when he'd think about the singers of these songs...killers...Jew-haters. He just couldn't put the Christian soul that made this music together with the Christian heart that hated him. How can the music of love and life spring from hate and death? How can they live together side by side? Wouldn't you think one would drive out the other?

Haime was growing impatient with Lazar. Thinkers weren't buyers. A boy his age, already with wrinkles on the brow. Haime busied himself with only two questions. 'How much does it cost? How much can I sell it for?' He concluded Lazar would be a captzen (poor man) all his life, 'All head and no pockets'.

"How much further is it?" Lazar asking to be polite.

He felt the time had come to say something...

Haime brightens, anticipating more conversation, "About seven miles."

Lazar turned inward again; not even aware he was doing it.

"Giddyap," an angry shout from Haime...the poor horse suffering his frustration.

They traveled the last mile in silence. Haime finally announced, "We are here."

Lazar wordlessly gathered <u>his</u> hooks, put <u>a few coins in</u> Haime's extended hand and jumped off the wagon. He forgot to say good-bye.

It was dusk. Suvalk in front of him. He had never seen such a big town. He was excited. There were little shops on each side of the street, and lots of people hurrying back and forth from one to the other. Lazar found himself stepping lively. He stopped a passerby for directions. The man was annoyed to be stopped in mid-flight scurrying somewhere. He pointed straight in the air and fled on. Lazar was lost and bewildered.

He entered a store and asked the merchant who painfully and meticulously drew a map. He followed the map in and out of circuitous alleys until he arrived at a muddy country road, the house at the end of it. A face was staring out of one of the windows.

Lazar shouted, "Moishe Ginze!"

The figure opened the window and pointed to the door.

Lazar mounted the stairs and banged on the first door. He feared he'd trip in the darkness. He could hear children crying, a woman yelling from behind the door. He hoped this was not the place.

A loud, angry voice, "Who is it?"

"We're not buying anything today. Try us next week!"

He lit a match. It went out. He stumbled and **fell,** picked himself up and fell again, feeling his way in the dark on hands and knees to another door, He rapped gently.

"Just a minute. Who is it?"

"Lazar."

The door opened just enough to let a crack of light through; an anxious female face, half a nose, one eye, one cheek and then, the door flinging open, "It's Benjamin's son!"

Two arms embraced him, lips kissed him, a hand pulled his arm into the apartment.

"I'm Moishe's wife. We were waiting for you." Her eyes searched his face, warm and joyous. Her hair hung in braids in front of her. They danced on her shoulders as she ran to fetch Moishe and Lazar's heart danced with them, reminding him, for the first time in a long time, that he was young, and life was ahead of him. Lazar scanned the room. It looked comfortable. A sofa that was once plump, had deep bends in it now. Tables, lamps, a real desk and everything covered with doilies.

"Lazar."

Moishe shook his hand, reserved, a bit distant.

He did the polite thing, but didn't think Lazar would accept his offer. Where would they put him, now that he's here? Moishe loved the grand gesture. The sofa, of course; the end of the living room. Moishe was the cleanest, neatest man Lazar ever saw - blonde hair, blue eyes but looking very stern, in spite of the gentle complexion. Every **hair** in place, pants, and jacket with patches but not a crease to be seen. 'Nice to see you, Lazar," he lied.

"Make yourself at home."

"Hannah! What's the matter with you? Why are you standing there like a fool? Can't you see he's tired? Offer him some tea."

The smile was wiped from Hannah's face. She was humiliated, stuttering and bowing: "Yes, sit down, please, let me get you some tea."

Moshe was childless. He was secretly glad as he never really wanted them, but he took every occasion to blame Hannah. It was easy. She already blamed herself. But this only confirmed her stupidity in his eyes. He pleaded with her father on bended knee to have her hand in marriage and he never forgave her for it,

The father's words were still burning, "A beautiful girl like my daughter for a-nothing like you!"

And he'd been waved out the door like he was a door-to-door peddler. But he knew how to win her. He looked sorrowful. She had a soft heart. It didn't take much to melt it. He cried for her and, finally, she cried for him. He told her he couldn't live without her. It frightened her, though she couldn't really believe she was that important to anyone.

She pleaded for him. "Drop by drop, the stone melted, her father later said," to my regret.

"Before the marriage, she could do nothing wrong. After the marriage, she could do nothing right. She became a babbler, a stutterer, a crier."

His mother wanted grandchildren. "One crier in the house is enough." And Hannah's father, "Without children, you made my daughter a prostitute." he told him.

Nonsense, Moishe thought. He wants to bounce grandchildren on his knee over my back. I'll be slaving to put bread in their mouths.

And he'll brag, "Mein enichlach." (My nephews.)

Moishe suddenly realized he hadn't smiled once since Lazar came in the door. "How nice to see you." He showed his teeth in a forced smile. "You'll tell us everything when we sit down to eat."

Moishe was a fixer. If not for Hannah, he might have been something, he told himself. He blamed her for everything. He corrected her throughout the meal. Lazar was very uncomfortable. The dinner was disturbed by a knock at the door. Moishe ordered her to see who it was. She opened the door slightly and was nearly pushed into the table. The visitor, a huge man, flailing his arms and repeating Moishe's name in alarm, "I have terrible news!"

Moishe, annoyed, swallowed the piece of fish in his mouth, calmly put his napkin on the table and asked in a superior, detached tone, "What's the matter, now?"

"Batyevka! They've killed everyone in the village! Revenge... for killing the Baron!"

Lazar shouting, "What!"

Trembling, sinking to his knees and into a merciful blackness.

He awoke to hear voices, Moishe whispering, "Who needs this headache. It's written, 'Ask and you shall receive.'"

"Asking I do plenty and receive nothing. This time, I figured, also the same. So, of tsaluchus (spite), I ask and receive...what I don't want...him."

"Shhh..." Hannah warning, "He'll hear us..."

Her index finger pressed to her mouth. Lazar slowly opened his eyes, remembered where he was, what he had heard. And he was anguished. A terrible guilt tearing.

"Those men...they'd killed the Baron...and I helped them...to kill him...and...the town."

Lazar put himself on trial. One voice answering another.

"But you were only standby."

"I watched and did nothing."

"But you didn't know how to stop them."

"Ignorance is no excuse."

"I should have made it my business to know."

Lazar stood condemned in his own eyes. What would be his expiation?

Lazar's eyes fell on Benjamin's books. 'God,' he answered. I have to ask God's forgiveness. He sat down at the table, opened Benjamin's hook, bent over it with his elbow on the table - his thumb and forefinger over his mouth, Moishe and Hannah talking to him, but he didn't hear. Nodding up and down and mumbling, stroking an invisible beard 'til the candle went out and he slumped over the table, sleeping until the morning...when he opened the book again to the morning prayer...stumbled into the kitchen, groggy and very weak. Hannah was sitting at the table.

He looked up at her and said, "I'm leaving."

Basha was trundled into the wagon for the long ride home. It was uncovered. She looked anxiously at the sky, hoping it wouldn't rain, lay down in the wagon, leaned on her elbow, using her arm for a pillow, and covered herself with the horse blanket. Her head was buzzing with questions about Benjamin and the children. Were they all, right? Were they well? For distraction, she turned to face the drivers and forced herself to think about their backs. The one on the right sat rigid, his back as straight as a stick. She didn't remember when she'd seen a straight back. The men of Batyevka were all bent from peering over books, or ploughs, or paying homage to Christians. They looked like they were always saying, "Your honor."

51

Her reflections turned again to the <u>straight back</u>. It intrigued her. It was so commanding. She recalled the face in front of that back - trim, barbered hair; overbearing, stupid, cruel, a mouth so small, it was visible only when it barked commands and then seemed to disappear; shoes shined, jackets well-fitting and pressed, with shiny buttons, leather belts with fancy buckles, <u>immaculate </u>....unlike the shoddy army of baggy pants bound with twine, shoes with holes, torn jackets that lost all their buttons....that scurried about in Batyevka. Her mind wandered on from them to the palace where she'd seen – a room full of silks and satins, soft, pink, and shiny, lighted by hundreds of candles that flickered through the night.

"You believe, Becky?"

"I do."

The Believers warn their flock, "You shall be tested."

<u>We had no such warning, poppa, and I."</u>

Remembering is harder now. Becky was struggling with images. Not wanting to see. Not wanting to know. They struggle through the sheltering and excusing, through the <u>understanding</u>; through the heavy cloak over evil: compassion. And the heavier one still... tolerance. The second war to end all wars....and its crush of numbers. Thousands are dead. Millions. In Russia, too... the camps and Jew killers.

Poppa grieves. But he blames Stalin; still clinging.

The <u>people</u> Becky, like flowers...<u>good</u> like bread.

Becky is living alone now and needing friends, even meeting someone who likes her. A German girl. Ella and Harry: Once comrades...now just friends, Liberals, (since Stalin disenchanted them and Harry was now in business making a good living). Once lovers of all humanity, now, witless with shock, "How can you be friends with a German!" And Becky defending, "How <u>can</u> you blame a -person for the sins of others? She was just a 12-year-old child. What did *she* know?"

"And her parents?"

"They were little people. What did they know? And afraid. What could they do?"

Friends for just a month 'til Elizabeth went back to Germany to medical school. But Becky had to explain and explain as if it were a lifetime.

Another test. More severe, this time. Years later. Eichmann *on* trial. The crimes. The Pictures. And historians, accusing. <u>The people knew</u>. The little ordinary ones. Poppa's explanations: poverty, hunger, unemployment, inflation, the Versailles treaty, Nietzhe, Wagner. He dismissed them all.

"No excuse, Becky. <u>They should throw them all in the sea – the Germans</u>."

A terrible truth breaking over him. Lost: innocence, pride. Even the songs. The dream: only for forgetting. Ashamed now of what he said... what he believed. Especially about religion. His own. Becky, too. Guilty... and ashamed... of her friend. Elizabeth returned, recently.

"What do you think, Elizabeth? We know now that the people knew!"

"Forced, Becky."

Krieg! Ja! Ja! A roar like an ocean gone mad. Thousands. Delirious. Ecstatic. Strutting. Posturing. Fists in the air. Bloodlust. Germany will be free when Jewish blood runs from the knife.

Ja Vohl!

***Horst Wessel song. German national anthem until the end of the war.**

"Going to war, Elizabeth. They were so eager." Her voice rising.

Brisk, succinct. "DUTY!"

And Becky thinking: '<u>Guerra! Mussolini shouting and strutting, the people...silent, heads bowed, glum.</u>' Becky, wanting to say, '<u>That's the difference, Elizabeth. The people.</u>' But she just said, "I guess."

And then Elizabeth saying, "By the way, did you hear that Goering's daughter is trying to clear his name?"

Becky mumbling, "If he was my father. I'd change mine."

"But he's her FA-THER!"

And snapping to attention, commanding and very stern. Becky hurrying away. Frightened. Regretting her invitation to Elizabeth for dinner, tomorrow. Odious, now, just to <u>think</u> of serving her. Ella and Harry would be there, too. They'll talk to her. Even when they were revolutionaries, they were mannerly. The following night, Becky is in the kitchen, peeling and scraping. Words drift in from the other room. There is talk of an abortion. Ella saying, "How awful the poor girl died. What a horrid man! That doctor. Trying to get rid of that body.*" Her poor mother would be left with nothing to bury."

Then Elizabeth saying, "He should have used lye. After all, he's a DO-CT-OR!" Piercing. Crisp. Punctuated.

Becky remembered thinking, "So Goebbels was a doctor." It was suddenly very cold, like death and evil were at the table as long as she was there.

Becky saying, "He should have done...what!"

And Elizabeth repeating: Used lye. After all, he's a DO-CT-OR!"

A rage inside Becky. Pressing. Exploding. "What! Get out!" A shaky arm points to the door. The hand hangs limp.

Ella: "I'm surprised at you. You're ov-er-re-acting. Control yourself!"

***A true story: Before abortion was realized.**

Elizabeth lunging out of the chair. Her plate clattering to the ground, breaking in pieces. She steps on it and crunches it deep into the floor. Then, a triumphant march down the hall. Becky follows. It's dark. The bulb is out. Elizabeth turns at the head of the stairs, calm, cold as stone, "I demand an apology!"

Becky feels faint. Ella's hand creeping on hers, then gripping it hard, insisting, "Let me hold you." Then numbness and the haze...the sinking...the unreal...that seemed so real.

Mr. Goldfarb pointing a finger and saying, "<u>This to hold: Brotherhood, Faith, Belief, Innocence.</u>"

And Poppa there too. A father and his little girl standing together in the kitchen, rubbing hands over a crackling stove. Their eyes are turned to a hope in the far distance. Then, strength flowing, shooting fists in the air, they march round and round. The chin pointing proud and sing:

America, America
God shed his grace on thee.
Father and Elizabeth say, "She fled out!"
Father shakes Becky's hand.

Chapter Ten

Lazar hadn't the slightest idea where he was going when he announced his intentions, but he heard Moishe's words and decided he wouldn't stay where he wasn't wanted. He wondered why Moishe wrote him a note of welcome he didn't mean. But there was no time for wondering. He would find a shul. The Rabbi would help him.

He looked at the passersby. Some didn't look as debagged as others. There was a man with a matching suit that looked new. He had an air about him... straight, confident. People tipped their hat as they walked by. Lazar decided to ask him. He looked like he would know. He approached him shyly and blurted out gruffly, "Excuse me, can I ask you a question?" and looked at him deferentially.

"Of course," a cold, polite, disdainful reply.

"I'm a stranger in town. I've left home and I can't go back. You see, my town was Batyevka. Can you tell me where I might stay..." He wiped a tear from his eye with his sleeve.

The man looked wordless. A homeless, fatherless, adolescent boy who, he thought had said much more than he intended but couldn't stop himself. Lazar listed his offerings. "I'm a good student. I can read, write, and learn," he said, between sobs. "My father was Benjamin Berger."

"Who?" The man lifted a curious eyebrow. He'd never heard of him, but he guessed he must have been considered a learned man in Batyevka. In those towns, anyone who can spell is learned.

"What...question do you want to ask?" Uncomfortable now; a crowd gathering. They thought the boy was bothering him or something. The crowd embarrassed him. He was at a loss at what to do. He had to get the boy along and then he would decide what to do with him.

"Come with me," Taking the boy by the arm, "we'll find a place to sit down and calm yourself."

Lazar did as he was told. It was a comfort to have someone take command.

"Where are your parents?"

"My father died. My mother's gone."

"Gone where?"

"I don't know."

Lazar was on the verge of tears again, but he was trying hard not to antagonize the man with more tears but, the more he tried, the less he was able, until he was again incoherent.

The man suddenly turned impatient and barked, "I've had enough! Wait here. I'll get my sister."

The man was a well-known writer who came to Suvalk for 'material'. He was a distinguished, cultured man who left Suvalk years ago to see the world. He was urbane, well-traveled. He had never married as he enjoyed his privacy and felt it a burden to have someone impose on him a periodic need for attention. He turned to others only when the mood seized him. He then demanded they be available. He could not abide the same demand being made on him. His sister Basheva took care of his major and minor problems. She was proud to do it for an 'artist.'

Pinchos Pernik was dapper, everything carefully matched, even the shoelaces and the head of his cane. It was said he thought he was above life itself. His whole existence was dedicated to artfully dodging the demands of life and arrogantly looking down on those caught in its commonplaces. He was handsome, commanding, a presence...but the only thing he ever really managed to command was a pencil. He commanded people by default. They stood in awe of him because of who he was. He wouldn't permit them close enough to find a flaw. To such a one, Lazar poured out his heart and mind, and was hopefully waiting for rescue; quietly, patiently, calmer now, that he'd found, what he was supposed to be...a friend. Lazar had never been in a world of strangers before. In Batyevka, he'd said 'Hello' a hundred times a day. Here, for the first time, he silently watched a parade of strange faces... but he was saved from desolate loneliness by his new friend, who, he was sure, was coming back.

Lazar didn't know how long he sat there, straining, and looking in the direction the stranger had gone. He realized he didn't ever know his name. The day turned to dusk. No one came. He continued waiting. The darkness came. He could see lights being lit, and imagined meals on the table. He was hungry and homesick and repeating desperately to himself that his new friend wasn't coming. He tried to go straight to the Rabbi, but couldn't he be too ashamed of what he'd done. The Rabbi wouldn't want one such as him in his presence. He'd questioned God, consorted with criminals. He wasn't worthy.

He just sat on the bench immobilized, starting into space, dazed. Two figures emerged in the darkness, one a man, the others, a woman in a flowered dress.

"Are you still here?" Abraham hoped he would be gone by now. He'd waited all day to tell his sister Devorah. She had to do her chores first. The rhythm of his household could be disturbed by nothing.

She'd asked him "Why didn't you tell me before?"

"I didn't want to tire you with more problems." He always said that before adding on another one.

She added, "I could have looked in on him, while I went to see Hymie about your manuscript... "Let's go see if he's still there. Maybe he needs someone, she was about to say, but didn't ...Pincho scowling. He didn't like to see her preoccupied with anyone else but him...not even for a moment.

Devorah was a big girl. She loved to cook and eat; went to bed at night thinking what she would eat the next morning... She had a huge round face and several chins and soft, tender eyes that felt sorry for everyone. They were somehow all worse off than she was. She heaped so many favors, gratuities, kindnesses, and considerations on her friends that they sometimes found her incessant hovering unbearable. Only Pinchos never tired of her limitless concern with his comfort. Sometimes, he felt he could sit down in her lap and stay there. Devorah sat down next to Lazar, frantic... a young boy... alone. Her brain was burning with concerned questions which she fired at Lazar and which he dutifully answered. He needed his mother. Devorah was only too happy to step into her shoes.

"Come home with us. We have plenty of room." She held him and was gently nudging him while she whispered her invitation.

Pinchos knew she'd say that and dreaded it, but what could he do? The boy would not stay in his room... of that's what she meant by plenty of room. Pinchos lived too much with the characters he created. He couldn't stand real people. His characters gave him fame and money... and asked for nothing. People were always needing, asking... and ... worst of all... contending. Pinchos couldn't bear contention. It wasn't dignified.

Basheva helped Lazar to his feet. He was so sleepy; he could barely stand up. She put an arm around him and practically carried him home, his books and belongings too.

Devorah's home was comfortable, soft, plump chairs all around, bright curtains, flowers, a huge samovar in the corner for the endless glasses of tea she consumed during the day. Devorah had one small area of self-indulgence. She would not permit the slightest disruption in her parlor.

Pinchos suggested, "Let him sleep on the sofa."

"No, we'll put a bed in the storeroom."

Devorah and Lazar struggled cleaning, emptying, and carrying. Pinchos sat in the kitchen, <u>thinking</u>.

Lazar couldn't stop eating when Devorah served the dinner. She was delighted. Pinchos scowled thinking that he eats like a horse and who could afford him?

After dinner, Abraham started questioning Lazar ... maybe he'd find some material. Pinchos seldom spoke to children and expected them to be adults when he did. Children's prattle bored him. Tears exasperated him.

"What books have you read?"

"Only the cheder books."

Pinchos concluded, "Same as nothing. What do they teach them in cheder?"

"What did you do with your spare time?"

"I didn't have any."

Pinchos realized material from this boy was pain and tears but he would have to wait... It was too soon. There was a story here, but it would take some time to pull it all out. No longer needing to speak to Lazar, he rose brusquely, clapped his hands, "It's time to go to bed."

Basheva tucked him in, singing a lullaby, then tiptoeing out of the room. When the door clicked behind her, he muffled his head in his pillow and cried himself to sleep.

Chapter Eleven

Lazar had only planned to stay a few days, but Devorah prevailed on him. Weeks turned into months. They had a secret. Lazar told Devorah his story. She comforted him and helped him search for Basha and her sisters and brothers. Rumors flew. She was seen here or there, and they would track each one down. As the months passed, the reports were more infrequent... but they hunted them down... everyone.

Pinchos was becoming restive. The boy was taking too much of Devorah's time. Material or no material...he had to go! Besides, he needed the storeroom for his manuscripts.

"He can't stay with us forever!"

"Why not?"

That's it! Lazar has to go! An emergency is one thing. A permanent fixture...another. Pinchos wanted no permanent fixtures other than the ones he was unfortunate enough to be born into...a hassle of cousins, uncles, aunts who were forever trying to marry him off.

Together, in the kitchen at night after Lazar went to bed, Pinchos broached the subject.

"Does he have any family at all that we can send him to?"

"Yes, he has a family. He misses them so much that he cries himself to sleep every night. He thinks no one can hear them...but I do. He needs a companion, wouldn't you say? Someone his age. Someone like Pearl, Esther's daughter, a good, strong, dependable girl, cooks, cleans, will give him lots of children. He needs his own family." And she told him the story.

Pinchos' face twisted with sorrow, pity, then rage that he was forced to feel sorry when he wanted only to throw him out.

"Where is the drawing?"

"He keeps it under his pillow."

Finally, he had his <u>material</u>. Basha's candle, a story full of dramatic possibilities...and more. Revolutionary potential...an inflamer of hearts. Pinchos enjoyed watching the radicals taunt and rave while he watched comfortably on the sidelines. They needed an audience and thought he was an appreciative and admiring one. Pinchos was already savoring the explosion. But first, the problem of Lazar. He couldn't stand the boy.

Lazar wonders, "Why doesn't he like me?"

Devorah reassures, "Of course, he does."

"But he doesn't. I can tell."

Devorah's palliatives and white lies were to no avail. Her benevolent smile turned serious. She left the stage for a moment and gave in.

"Maybe because you cry too much," she told him, one day, quietly.

Basha always comforted him when he cried. Benjamin turned his head from his book only for Lazar's tears. Only the teachers were offended by tears.

"I won't cry anymore then."

Lazar didn't want to offend his benefactors. He thought adults were very strange. They said things they don't mean, dislike you for strange reasons. There was no commandment that said, 'Thou shalt not cry.' What rule was he breaking? He thought his world was becoming much too complicated. The answer must be in Benjamin's books. Lazar decided to try harder to make a friend of Pinchos. Wednesday was visitor's day. Pinchos entertained callers in the afternoon. He never contented himself, but he invited people of different points of view to these gatherings.

Each competed with the other to appear the most brilliant in his eyes. A slight nod from him of approval to one of the contenders' competitive struggles. This afternoon, a hot head and a Rabbinical student were invited. Neither knew the other was coming.

Simon, the hot head was a so-called because he had a <u>tail of straw</u>, ready to ignite at the slightest spark. He had a profound sense of injustice coupled with an intense need to right all wrongs. He was dropped as a baby from an open window into the street and suffered a life-long disability. He limped badly...but he was always running ahead of everyone to prove he could walk faster than they could. He was always in a hurry...even for a revolution. If anyone walking with him went rushing ahead, he considered it a personal affront. They were rushing away from <u>him</u>. He wanted to equalize. Everyone should be able to move at the same pace. No one should be crippled at birth by poverty, religion, whatever. He made it his life's work to rescue all the cripples. What God made; he would unmake.

Mandelbaum, the student, profoundly disagreed. If a man was a spiritual cripple, his twisted soul would torment him on two good legs, a back as straight as string, a pocket full of groschen.

Simon had a round face that was always sneering. He would scream at his opponent and offend him, storm out, his face red with anger. He was never at rest, hands waving, shouting, grimacing. His favorite phrase was, "What's the matter with you?" Shouting, accusing, sarcastic; his answer to Mandelbaum's argument when he was unable to think of anything else...or...God Forbid...Mandelbaum was right. Mandelbaum, on the other hand, took his shouting with good humor and argued logically...which only made Simon more furious. He considered him a liar, a hypocrite, a snake, and Mandelbaum considered Simon an idiot, though he never told him to his face.

Mandelbaum's calmness infuriated Simon all the more and

Simon's fury only made Mandelbaum withdraw into calmness all the more. They were perfectly matched to amuse Pinchos, who quietly kept score. Both knew it and performed for Pinchos.

Lazar screaming, "Where was God when I was dropped!"

"Why don't you ask Him?"

"I do. Every day of my life!"

"God works in mysterious ways."

"Not even a hint? Give me something to go on? I dare you! Something! Anything!"

"You have to find out for yourself. I can't do the work for you."

"Then do it for someone else...the poor, the hungry."

Simon reviewed for the hundredth time, his litany of misfortunes, Mandelbaum referred him to the book of Job.

Lazar interrupting, surprising even himself. "May I say a word?"

And he told them the story of Basha's candle. They all listened quietly, attentively.

Simon answered, "I don't understand."

And Mandelbaum echoing him, "I don't understand."

Pinchos sober, reflecting, "I understand."

Simon asking, "What do you understand, Pinchos?"

Pinchos asking, "Tell them, Lazar."

And Lazar replying, "I understand that I don't understand."

Mandelbaum, nervous, grabs his coat and hurries out without a goodbye. Lazar hurrying too and slamming the door behind him.

"Lazar."

"Yes, Pinchos," Lazar looking hopeful.

Maybe he'd be a little pleased with him now that he had confided in him, crying.

Cold and distant now, "Leave the room, now. I have work to do." Lazar left the room quickly before the hurt would show. Abraham furiously scribbled Lazar's story. It was so unlike his own. He was the adored only boy in a family of women who doted on him; spoiled and indulged, every whim gratified as they competed for his affection. His father died when he was young and left money from a factory he owned. He abandoned religion early as he couldn't bear the discipline of ritual and he saw no need for the polemic and debate that raged around him. *If they have no answer to all these arguments by now, after all these years, they never will.*

At the University, he discovered he had a talent for writing. He visited the shtetls and satirized them, considering any belief that infringed on the freedom of life, an <u>absurdity</u>. One of these impingements was the emotions; tyrannical, unpredictable, uncontrollable.

As a writer, he was a confidante to all friends, their sleepless nights, humiliations, loss of dignity...all in the name of love. Imagine, pleading to the beloved, crying...and...worst of all...begging. He wanted none of that...ever. He had one affair in his entire lifetime, a widow who cried her heart out to him...her loneliness, her despair. He visited her for one week at appointed hours set by her. One evening, her sobbing touched him. He stroked her hair, put her head on his chest, and was ashamed that she should hear the wild thumping of his heart. He placed a trembling hand on her bosom. She didn't move. His fingers slowly moved to the buttons on her dress then retreated in panic. The flirtatious, submissive look on her face quickly turned to scorn. He embarrassed her. He desperately wanted to flee. She wanted him out as quickly as possible so she could make a victory of the shambles: he abandoned her...but she had reduced him...the great writer...not even half a man.

Since that day, Pinchos couldn't stand the sight of tears.

Chapter Twelve

Lazar went to bed as he was told but his mind refused to lie down with his body. It was tossing and turning with angry questions and turned into hatred...tossing his little body out of bed and into Pincho's study.

Standing at his desk, trembling, "I want to talk to you!" On his face, fear and hate, submission and defiance taking their turn.

Pinchos is calm, indifferent. "About what?"

No one dared interrupt him at his study before. "I thought I sent you to bed."

"I poured myself out to you and your only response is to send my whole life to bed...is that all you have to say? I'm standing a foot deep in my own blood and you're sending me to bed...with my mother, my father, my sisters, my brother, my town! We're all sent to bed!"

"What do you expect? You've been an unpaid, unwelcome guest in my home for three months. You're eating my bread...but that's not enough. You want to eat my heart out as well."

Lazar hadn't seen it that way. Devorah made him feel welcome. She needed him. That clouded the fact that Pinchos didn't.

"Think Lazar, in all these months have you ever once said, "I'm leaving on such a date to such a place...you want the truth, Lazar. Here it is: Your sad story is a convenience. I don't have a sad story so I never had that convenience. You will tell your story over and over. If and when you leave here, you'll tell it to someone else who will do as Devorah did. Your sad story will be your life annuity to be taken care of forever."

"How do you know?" Lazar demanding.

"I know, because you concluded your story with, 'I don't understand. Damn it! Pick an <u>understanding</u>. The Talmud is full of them. Pick one and act on it. If you don't <u>understand</u>, you'll sit forever, pondering over Devorah to keep the <u>poor child</u>. But when you're a man already, this story won't open any more doors for you or put someone else's bread in your mouth.'

Pinchos reached up and pulled down a pile of manuscripts. "This is Suvalk," he said, "All stories. If my heart, which you probably think I don't have anyhow, but just, for instance, let's say I had one, went out to all these stories, I'd be left with nothing, beating, right here."

He rose and waved a finger in Lazar's face, screaming, "Get out of here! And I mean now!"

"No, I won't! You think that's all you have to do is order me out! I'm not leaving 'til you answer one question! How do you manage to be a writer without a heart...without a soul!"

"I have a mind!" He spat out at him. "And you would be well served to develop one, too!"

Lazar felt like he was struck with a red, hot poker. He wanted to crush Pinchos, stamp on him, wipe him out...if only he would stop trembling.

Devorah rushes in hysterically. "What's going on here?"

She embraces Lazar, pulling him out of the room.

Pinchos shouting, "Him! You're worried out! Before me! From me, you slob, from me, comes your Kavet*...you prance with pride in this world because of me! Who are you without me! I scribbled my

---

* ***Kavet – Pride***

guts out night and day and you toss a few pots and pans and dust rags around all day. If not for me, you'd be nothing, nobody...and it's <u>him</u> you're comforting and chuckling over. You both deserve each other. Without me, you'd be two stray dogs without a master!"

"You're right," Devorah shaking her head sadly, "We're two dogs howling in our loneliness for a loving master."

Pinchos throws up his hands in disgust, "What do you think you'd had!" Sarcastic, now. "How much love do you two deserve! That I permit you in my presence is enough...an ignorant house-keeper and a parasite!"

He grabs a sheaf of papers and waves it in their faces. "Letters from heads of state, professors, all asking for a few minutes of my precious time...and here, you alone have the luxury and you're prating about love!

And turning to Devorah, "I chose your home in preference to others. That's more love than anyone has around you. My presence brings you honor. That's love!"

And he listed on each finger the wives and husbands and children in the rest of the family...heartache...misery...even degradation.

"That's what their love brought them. And to you, they bow and tip their hat...everybody."

Devorah nods her shamed head, agreeing. Pinchos was her career. He sent her to the stars. Without him, her life would be drab and undistinguished. Because of him, the town was at her feet, a victory by association...effortless.

"Go Lazar, go to bed. Pinchos and I have to talk about something."

Lazar felt betrayed, though he told himself he had no right to. After all, they were brother and sister. He turned and left.

"Pinchos, let's talk a little. I want to explain."

"Don't bother me now. I'm writing the story of Basha's candle. That flame will spread, Devorah. Mark my words...it's spread already."

"Not enough."

His eyes shining with greed and power. He saw himself in history.

Alone again, Lazar's rebellion ended as quickly as it began. Pinchos was right, he argued. Lazar had made it his life's work to search for Basha and his brothers and sisters. He never thought beyond that. Occasionally, a fleeting thought about his future, quickly set aside. He'd been wanted for so long that he had to get used to the idea of not being wanted.

He cherished a fantasy that he'd find Basha, and she'd take care of him. Hard words turning new in his unwilling head. Basha was gone. He may never find her. What would she want him to do? She wouldn't be proud of the token interest he was taking in learning, carrying around Benjamin's books. When was the last time he turned a page in any of these books? He couldn't remember. The answer was clear. She would want him to be a Rabbi...and he wanted her to be proud of him when he found her. Lazar doubted a little...but feared much more and reasoned that he must believe in Him if he feared Him. Pinchos was right, he concluded. "I am ignorant." Then, talking to Benjamin, as often as he did, "You'll be proud of me, then, maybe you'll forgive me..."

That night, Lazar, dreamed of Benjamin. "Nothing to forgive, Lazar, mien kind," he said. "But if you must hear it, I forgive you."

Lazar replying, "Not yet, Poppa, I have to earn it first."

"Not for me you have to study, Lazar. For God."

"You still believe in God, Poppa?"

"I do, mien kind. I do.

Chapter Thirteen

Devorah crept softly into Pinchos's room the following morning. Sunlight was peering through the windows. It would wake him...she pulled the doors closer and soundlessly tiptoed out again.

Pinchos in a raspy voice, "Devorah come here..."

"I disturbed you. I'm sorry." Craven submission in her voice.

Pinchos ignores her apology, "I want to talk to you."

He sits up, raised his pillow behind him, and slaps the bed with his hand. Rubbing his eyes and yawning.

Then, "Sit down."

Pinchos was never awake so early. Devorah waited anxiously.

"That boy has to go...into marriage, the Rabbinate, the army. You'll tell him today; such emphasis on the last word meant...no appeal."

"It's not necessary to tell him."

Putting her hand in her apron pocket, handing him a note which read:

.   .   .

Dear Devorah and Pinchos,

As you can see, my bed is empty. I'm sure you know what that means without me telling you. Let me explain first that I stayed as long as I could because I couldn't face my aloneness. I still can't. I'm going to the Rabbi if he'll have me. I know I will try to be his son the way I tried to be yours...you and I both wanted to be my mother, father, brothers, and sisters. That's not really a very big desire. Pinchos, you want the world at your feet so you could kick them when you felt like it. I just wanted to come in from the cold for a little while longer, but your foot was too restless and impatient. It was kicking time, and I was unfortunately there. Lazar never said goodbye, couldn't even say, "Thank you. He didn't know why. Devorah was hurt but she forgave him...felt too sorry for him not to.

Lazar never said goodbye, couldn't even say, 'Thank you.' He didn't know why. Devorah was hurt but she forgave him...felt too sorry for him not to. When children lost their parents in Batyevka, Lazar would ask Benjamin who would be their parents now, and their parents now, and their brothers and sisters too.

And Benjamin always said, "We will all be their family. We're all brothers...and all sisters."

He walked to the park after writing his note and creeping down the stairs barefoot, found a bench, put his knapsack under his head and fell asleep...he awoke to find everyone rushing; women pushing baby carriages, carrying bundles and dragging other children, young women wearing wigs, legs swollen, pregnant; a tug of war between the generations erupting from time to time, 'Momma, I want.' 'No!' Children and mommas...the park was no place for Lazar. The winter had exerted it's final tyranny. It had finally acquiesced to spring. Life was beginning everywhere. Lazar thought, 'Maybe for me, too.' He wanted to jump and run and do foolish things. He hopped along on one foot, then the other, the bundle bouncing behind him, the books precariously slipping under his arm, he started running. He knew not where or why. He was a boy again, running to and from cheder, running home, running errands, running...like everyone else...to somewhere...from somewhere else. The <u>somewhere</u> for Lazar, now, was the next tree, the next bush, the next flower. He leaped as high as he could, testing himself on one hurdle, then another, running faster to one place than he has the one before and then, repeating himself, running the same circle over and over, faster, faster. He felt light and heady as if he was lifted and carried through the air, happy, wildly, joyous, and carefree...laughing and jumping in rhythm...the laughing a melodic accompaniment to the bouncing and beating of happy feet...a wild stallion...Pegasus...flying to the clouds.

Then, just as suddenly, his will-less body was thrown on the ground. He lay on the grass, panting. His bones ached. He was tired, he was hungry...and he was remembering. Reality, that had lost sight of him for a little while, seized him again with a vengeance, furious that he had managed to escape it's careful surveillance, planted itself heavily on his small shoulders once again. He rose...bent, treading slowly and wearily...ashes all around...the branches all fingers pointing accusing fingers at him. He put one foot in front of another heavily, resignedly. Lazar was an old man again.

Chapter Fourteen

After the assassination, Motel, Pintcheik, and Lazar fled to their haven in the forest. It was to be a refuge and the center of the propaganda machine. They shared a common faith in the power of words on paper. Their families received no word of them. Lazar was relieved to be rid of his burdens. The other two would reveal themselves when the storm was passed...they huddled night and day in heated discussion...what to write...how to phrase it and what words to choose to inflame the people. They would light a fire in town after town. On the right-hand corner of every declamation, they printed was to be a drawing of Basha's candle. They planned it carefully. Every pamphlet had her story, followed by an appeal to righteous indignation, and then, united action against the tyrant...action...underlined. They decided the coming Passover was the best time to start their campaign...another release from bondage if the people listened to them. They worked feverishly night and day. Lazar found food.

The dreamer wrote, "Everywhere death is giving way to life. Deep down, in every dead, brown, bent, ugly branch there is life waiting it's moment, pink, purple, gray, yellow, red..." That saddened him. "Red...waiting too. How much more blood?"

And Lazar answering, "The blood of tyrants. Who cares?"

"That's right," Motel says, "Who cares."

"That's right," the dreamer repeated mechanically.

"Who cares."

He envied their ability not to care. He wished he could wake up one morning and it was all over...like the end of winter.

"The facts are," Motel would say, "you have to fight a battle at a time."

"A battle at a time? We'll never see the end. What are we fighting for?"

"A good beginning."

Motel lit a match in the fireplace. It's tiny flame danced from twig to twig until they were all united in one roaring fire.

"That's what we are fighting for."

Lazar stared suspiciously at the dreamer. Lately, he had to restrain himself, more and more, from putting his hands around his throat... "What could come out of that head but rainbows?" he chided him. Soft, pink hands that spent most of their time knuckled under his chin staring into nowhere. Lazar resented his soft, pink gentle arrogance. Now, he's questioning! Now, it's too late for questions!

"And what would fall out of your head, Lazar?"

Lazar never asked himself questions. "What would fall out of my head," he stormed... "what you're busy staring at all day...when you should be thinking...a mountain of shoes! I'm going swimming. The water and I get along good. Better than people."

There was a small lake near the cabin. He loved it. It calmed him. Nothing else could, jumping, swimming, diving, shaking his massive head and pounding the water...it healed and revived. His keen ears heard the leaves rustling above the splashing. He stopped...all aware-ness...like a hunter's dog, didn't move a muscle, slipped soundlessly into the water, hid behind a bush jutting out...all ears, all eyes, all muscle...ready to spring. He saw a male figure approaching the door.

He could barely see the outline, and couldn't recognize him. He knocked softly. Alone, thought Lazar, at this time of night. Must be a spy. Then, the door opens. Laughter...and squeals of recognition, Lazar jumps out, looks carefully through the window. The man had his back to him. Maybe they were all conspiring against him. They were talking on and on, God, how they talked! These so-called intellectuals, Lazar fumed. How they loved finger waving and opinions. Lazar could never figure out how they could dig into that basket on top of their shoulders that was always full of a million words and manage to put their tongues on just the right ones that happened, of course, to be different from the ones the other fellow pulled out of his basket. The stranger sat down, made himself comfortable. They were good for a whole night, Lazar thought, of talking. The show was on.

It was getting cold. Lazar thought Spring was like a woman, warm and teasing by day, a cold stranger again...at night, can't stand here shivering. May as well go inside. Lazar opened the door. He came up behind him and faced the stranger. He saw desperate, watchful, angry eyes staring out of a hard, lined bitter face, nervous scrawny hands that followed the rhythm of his talk and he cracked his knuckles while he spoke.

"Lazar, I want you to meet to Chaim," Motel introduces the two men.

Then he slunk back in his chair glumly staring into space like Pintcheik, both stricken with guilt and panic.

Motel orders, "Sit down, Lazar. We have something to tell you..."

The stranger told them about Batyevka. He was one of the few who escaped into the forests. They became brigands and had been watching their cabin to rob them, but they were seen delivering propaganda, so they decided to send Chaim to explore further.

"What!" Lazar roaring at the conclusion of the story. "Kill them all!" Screaming over and over, "Kill them all!"

He threw a chair against the wall, slammed his fist into the table, stalked the room like a caged tiger and stamped his boots as hard as he could.

"Kill them all!" And he held his hands around an imaginary neck. "All! The czar, the barons, the lords, the ladies...Vermin...all of them!"

And he dug his boots into the earth as if they were beneath his feet.

Chaim agreed, "He's right." And he turned to Motel and Pintcheik... "Are you with us?"

Lazar knew the answer in the heavy silence that hung on the desperate question. He put a big hand into his own <u>basket</u> this time and touched the words that were hidden at the bottom, sulking, angry, vengeful words he hadn't dare touch 'til now. <u>I hate you both. I didn't realize 'til now how much I hated you</u>. They kept their hands clean. Only he still felt the neck between his fingers and wanted more. He felt he was losing them already. Worse, they would betray him.

Motel crying. "We're killing out own. How many were there? How many did they kill?"

"Too many."

The dream of rebellion came to a sudden end for Motel and Pintcheik...and became a nightmare; Pintcheik tearing at himself, Fool! His vision of a grateful people raising him on a pedestal now a grim and terrible one...dead men, women and children cursing him in their graves and beyond. Pintcheik repeating again and again in his head...the facts...desperate, inconsolable facts. He knew the pain would never leave him. It came from a place deep inside that he'd always cover with dreams. And those facts would tear now... brutally...like voracious bees on gentle buds...night and day...and forever.

A bitter, despondent, "I'll take a walk," from Pintcheik.

Motel and Lazar suspicious, ask where he is going.

He repeats, "For a walk," and reassures them, "I'll be back soon."

Lazar threatens, "We'll come for you if you're not."

An hour has passed. He has not returned.

Lazar directed Motel, "You take that path. I'll take this."

No one. Then, Lazar hears the sound of creaking wood above.

"Good God, no!"

Pintcheik's body above him, swaying in the wind.

Lazar tender now, gently took him in his arms and carried back to the cabin, Chaim helping. Lazar mourned. He knew the words by heart. He'd heard them so many times...from his earliest beginning, Death took his mother when he was born.

"We can't bury him here, Lazar. Let's take him to the Rabbi. His family should know."

They left him at the Rabbi's door and returned to the cabin. "Come with me, Lazar. I want you to meet my comrades...you should leave here now, anyway, it's not good to stay in one place too long. Besides, we must work together to spread the word...be strong, fight back, remember Basha. There were no introductions. They remained nameless, their faces had hardened, masks of bitterness and hate. They were killers. Lazar felt at home.

Chapter Fifteen

Pintcheik and Motel were left at the doorstep of the fanciest shul in town, like foundling children. Even in death, Laban was conscious of class. No little shtiebele for the intellectuals, Laban was consigned to those. Even his prayers, he thought, weren't good enough to travel the same exalted path to heaven as theirs. They had to take a back road. Maybe that's why God couldn't find them, Laban often concluded wryly. He ceased praying at an early age, deciding that his back breaking labor was enough praying. His path to Heaven would be strewn with countless numbers he helped all his life that would reach to the stars.

Chaim pinned a note to Pintcheik's jacket and fled. The porter was the first to find them, to scream his grim message 'til a crowd gathered, and hands lifted and carried and prepared them for burial. The rabbi was besieged by family and friends for answers. He examined the note over and over. "They died for a cause. Give them your gratitude. Remember them!"

Lazar asking, "What did you write on that note? And exploding, "Gratitude? Died for a cause? They died for themselves! They were cowards! You don't understand. Don't you see? We have two martyrs now. The power of tyrants can only be matched by the power of martyrs."

Motel and Pintcheik had beaten Lazar even in death. Their names would be on everyone's tongue. Laban wasn't even an afterthought. He resented bitterly. They lured him on, then abandoned him when he needed them most and...they would be rewarded for it. How many cups of wine would be raised in their honor and how many times would their names be whispered in hushed respect?

The rabbi made an eloquent speech. He had already heard about the "cause" and was in complete agreement. He was known as a "strange one." He was very short, thin, with a large head that had no relation to his body. He hated his body, all his life. All the relatives were tyrants whose favorite amusement was dictating to him.

"Eat! You look like you're disappearing."

He often wished he could. As much as he ate, it made no difference. The bullies in school beat him mercilessly. He could never defend himself, so they laughed at him. The more frightened he looked, the more they laughed. He didn't remember when he decided to become a Rabbi, but he knew he would love the sense of power. He was smugly satisfied when he could rant and rave at the grown bullies in the shule. He looked so tall and powerful when he stood on the dias and shouted at them like they were recalcitrant children. Years of venom burst forth on Yom Kippur especially, when he warned them about their sins. He had them quaking; delighted to see the cringing fear on the faces of his old enemies.

"These two men were martyred by the enemy," he shouted, "It was they who were trying to unite us in protest by slipping those notes under our door. They were found out...and...you can see the Czar's justice. This was their last message to us...and he held up a paper which read, Death to Tyrants!"

The women wailed, lamented, and beat their chests. The rabbi concluded from this that he had concocted a good story.

He knew about the ferment in the Christian world, as well. The Jews use them and then take power, he reasoned. Their brawn needs

Jewish brains. The <u>cause</u> was going somewhere. Wherever it went, he would follow, and, when all the scrambling was over, he would make sure to come out on top...as he did in Suwalk...he manipulated and maneuvered 'til he occupied the highest rabbinical seat in the town. He was a consummate actor...hypnotizing his hearers. He saw that Motel and Pintcheik gave him the chance to unite the town and he wasn't losing a minute. He started his campaign at the funeral. The Rabbi was using God for his purposes now and was ready to abandon Him for a more profitable calling when the opportunity arose. Outwardly, he performed his duties well, comforting, sympathizing, fathering. Inwardly, he was planning. How many times had he stood at the mouths of open graves? How many times had he been reminded that he had to make the most of his life? He had ceased believing in his own sermons on these sorrowful occasions. It surprised him, still, that the congregation believed him. Rabbi Herschbein no longer believed in God, but he had to make a living. God had mistreated, disappointed, too many times. Molke, his wife, had a soft, tender, lovely face, but a razor-sharp tongue. Only she could still hurt him, cut him to pieces, even.

"You think you're so smart," he shouted sarcastically, when the Warsaw Rabbi came and left.

"He, she'd remind him, has brains."

Of the six rooms in the house, not one piece of new furniture was bought in years. Every time she'd look at the frayed edges of the soft chair, the holes in the sofa, the old drapes crumbling with age, it was a reproof to him. They were the judge and jury to whom she constantly appealed.

"You see," she'd say, pounding the bulging spring in the middle pillow of the sofa, "how stingy he is?"

Then turning to him, "Aren't you ashamed of the people?"

"Aren't you ashamed! A Rabbi's wife with her head in the store windows."

He enumerated duties that she had sorely neglected.

"And where is your money going? To the family?"

And she pointed to the sofa for the thousandth time.

"To the poor!"

"What money!"

"You know!"

"I know nothing."

Round and round, the same words repeated a thousand times like it was the first time. And she was summing up with, 'I could have married...' And repeating a familiar list...each name still stinging again and again. She had married beneath her.

"I'm descended from a long line of Rabbis and don't you forget it!"

He couldn't for a moment, of course. She could never forgive him for the great promise she thought he had.

"It disappeared in thin air like all other promises you make!"

He even thought her nature conspired against him...he desperately wanted a boy. She had one girl after another...and showered them with love, some of it for spite, he thought. He envied the little girls, watching them frolic amongst the goodies while he had his nose pressed to the window, longing; his eyes begging for the kisses and hugs, the soft words she gave and gave to them without their asking. At night, his arms aching for a warm touch, he'd reach out to her. She'd turn from his outstretched hand. He took her in spite. She gave herself in duty. She would turn from him after they were together as if she had cleared the dishes from the table. His arms ached to hold her...just a few moments more, but he wouldn't dare touch her. He also turned. And back-to-back, they fell asleep, she wearily thinking she'd finally completed her chores for the day. He declared firmly to himself that he couldn't go on like this any longer. Later, to such a household came Lazar, knocking at the door.

Chapter Sixteen

Lazar shuffled along. Dejected. Pushing peddles into cracks... and thinks... 'I'm like a pebble, too, some bigfoot is kicking me.'

A wagon suddenly came bearing down on him. "Yold!*" the driver screaming. "Don't you watch where you're going?"

And Lazar thinking, "Where am I going, that I have to watch?"

And too numbed to care about what he narrowly missed. When the dust of the speeding wagon cleared, Lazar saw the shul where he was going. He crossed the street, mounted the stairs, climbed down again, deciding and undeciding with each step up and down to knock...not to knock. When a passerby stopped to watch him, he started feeling foolish...and decided. He knocked once. No answer. The second knock was less timid. Still no answer.

A passerby encouraged him, shouting, "Louder!" He rapped harder...nothing.

In frustration and anger, he kicked the door and heard, "Who is it?"

---

* **Yold – Fool**

"Lazar," he shouted. "Let me in."

"Lazar who?"

"Berger...Lazar Berger!"

"Just a minute."

Suddenly his determination left him as rapidly it came. His body turned to descend the stairs. When he heard, "What do you want?" He looked in...and saw the smallest man he'd ever seen holding a broom whose handle reached over his head. He had the shape of the size of a boy with the face of an old man.

"Don't just stand there. Come on in."

He wiped his hand on his apron and extended it to Lazar. When he came close, the man smiled a toothless grin while he practically pulled me into the entrance with his powerful hands.

He was the Rabbi's slave in residence, swept, cleaned, dusted, lit the fire, the first one up in the morning...the last one to bed at night. He was moody and temperamental, was hard of hearing or pretended to be when he rebelled at the constant din of his name being called. No one knew anything about him. He asked for a little, did too much, so the Rabbi was endeared to him. He had wandered into town one day like Lazar, made inquiries of the Rabbi and remained there. He kept to himself, had no friends, and was therefore to be trusted. He shared secrets with no one, not even the rabbi, fielded all the rabbi's questions very cleverly.

"I was a thief," he'd say smiling. "My family found out and left for America. Don't know where they are."

The rabbi knew he was lying, but years passed, and he never added or subtracted one additional fact.

"Where did you come from?"

"Here and there."

The rabbi's curiosity grew boundless, demanding to know. He fancied threatening to fire him...but then, he would never know.

Asking him from time to time, "Are you a murderer?"

He would pucker his small mouth, wink and reply, "Maybe."

He'd search his face for some small sign that his barrage of questions touched him...at least...one. Nothing...not even a wrinkle in spite of his years. Only his eyes; sad, old, tired, his eyebrows, a continuous black line across his forehead. Nothing could be read on that face. He never even raised his eyebrows. The rabbi taunted him mercilessly at times, plied him his wine, was in turn sympathetic, brotherly, fatherly, a friend, a confidante...nothing.

At the door, Jacob leaned on his broom and questioned Lazar.

"What do you want?"

"I want to see the Rabbi."

"At this hour? What is your business?"

"I can only tell him."

"You'll have to wait. Sit down."

And he finished sweeping a little pile of dust into a corner, put the broom against the wall, and left.

Returning shortly, "The rabbi will see you soon."

Then he continued sweeping without a word. The sound of the broom swishing across the floor calmed Lazar. It was like home.

A loud voice commanding, "Jacob, tell the boy to come in."

Jacob pointed and Lazar followed the finger. The Rabbi was sitting at his desk and motioned him to sit down. Books everywhere; the desk, the chair, the floor. The rabbi removed a few books from the chair. Lazar sat down. The rabbi knew no one or where to begin, so he began for them...the usual questions. Always arranged, the jumble of thoughts in some order.

He started with, "Where are you from?"

"Batyevka."

Startled. The rabbi knew of ten men from Batyevka. He didn't know about Lazar. Sympathetic...but cautious. After all, he could be a spy.

"I know about Batyevka."

He shook his head sadly and asked God the same silent question, "Where were you then?"

Lazar talked on and on. The rabbi listened, though somewhere deep down he already knew his story... and could tell it himself. It was in his first cry the moment he was born. It would be in his last one. Lazar was determined not to cry, staring fixedly at the rabbi's shoe through the whole recitation. He knew if he faced him, he couldn't control himself.

When he finished, the rabbi said softly, "Look at me."

"I can't. Please don't make me."

The rabbi usually said, 'God will help you.' The congregant was grateful for his blessing and dropped a donation on the way out. But not this time. The boy wanted a home and the rabbi said to himself, 'I want a boy.'

"Lazar," he said, "you'll stay with me."

Lazar's head snapped up to meet his eyes. He jumped from his seat, embraced the rabbi and sobbed his heart out shamelessly into his beard.

Then, the rabbi gently removed his arms from around his neck, "Come with me. You must be tired."

"I am sleepy," staggering to his feet.

The rabbi picked him up, cradled him in his arms. Lazar's head resting on his shoulder and carried him to bed, covered him and tip-toed out of the room. 'I have a son at last.' He walked slowly to the kitchen preparing his speech to his wife. After breakfast, the children went out of the kitchen and he told her the story of Batyevka. A few tears fell. He saved Lazar to the last.

She exploded. "What? You claim you don't have to give us and you'll give to a stranger. What do you mean, <u>your son</u>? He's not your son. Your son comes from here." And she pounded her belly. "Who's supposed to mother him? Me! Or do you just pick mothers off the street nowadays!"

Softly now, an offering. "I'll buy you a new sofa if you let the boy stay."

"You mean it?"

"I mean it."

"All right then, he can stay."

The rabbi was thinking wryly... 'At least he's worth a sofa.' And he glanced about all her complaints. He calculated that there were about ten years worth of replacements in one room alone. He could bribe her indefinitely. It would cost him. But it was worth it. Already, the boy felt like his son. He was making a sacrifice for him...like a father should...he happily told himself.

Chapter Seventeen

L
ater, he called the children together.

"I have something to tell you. Now, listen carefully. Yesterday, a boy came to me without a home. He has no mother or father, sisters or brothers."

Rivke interrupting. "No mother or father?"

She was unable to imagine anyone without at least a mother.

"How does he eat if there's no one to cook for him? Where does he sleep if he has no home?"

"Good girl. That's the point I'm coming to. Momma will cook for him and we will give him a bed to sleep. He will live with us."

They received the news without a murmur. And then the questions:

"What's his name?"

"Where is he now?"

"He's sleeping."

The rabbi left them to attend his studies for a while. His debates with the Warsaw Rabbi demanded constant application if he were to have the last wave of the finger in a complex point and stun him into a pensive stroking of his beard and nod of his head...he needed that kuvid*...especially when his wife was present.

Lazar awoke in the bare room; a bed, a dresser, his belongings in the corner. He couldn't believe his good luck. 'But I must be careful not to hope too much.' He would hope a little. A little hope, a little disappointment. A big hope...he couldn't even bear to think about it. The rabbi found it difficult to concentrate. On all the pages, he saw and heard Lazar. His head buzzing with plans for him and then...the questions. 'What do I know about being a father to a boy? The girls were different. They were their mother's, but a boy was his father's.'

His real father disappeared when he was child. He'd never known him. He was never even discussed. His mother used to say, 'I have to be a mother and a father to that boy.' As a child, it puzzled him. 'When was she a mother and a father?' But he would learn to be a father. Lazar would teach him and he would teach Lazar, teaching and learning together. That's fathering a boy. But does he have a kop? The rabbi panicked. A boy without a kop...he couldn't tolerate. Why was he so precipitous? He must test him right away.

Lazar was reading his father's book when the Rabbi opened the door. He dropped the book on the bed and jumped up immediately.

"Sit down my son."

A bit cooler than the day before. The rabbi was already rehearsing a goodbye speech just in case.

"Let me see the book you're reading." And turning the pages swiftly he added, "This book is very difficult. Do you understand it?"

"I know it by heart."

"And what else do you know by heart?"

Lazar remembered now that the rule in cheder when the answer was 'nothing' and he shrank as though from a blow...

"Nothing," he answered.

The rabbi thinking, 'A genius he isn't. I'll settle for a little talent. At least he can read and write.' The rabbi asked him a few questions.

---

* **Kuvid – Praise**

From the answers he decided his reasoning was good. He beamed. Lazar thought, 'He's laughing at me, I'm stupid. At least he's not beating me.' The rabbi grabbed Lazar joyously and pulled him nearer.

"Come mien kind, we must get something for you to wear. But first you must meet the family."

****Kop – Head***

They descended the stairs, the rabbi first, Lazar timidly behind him, anxiously wondering if the others would welcome him and painfully aware his clothes were wrinkled and ill-fitting, he was not clean. He imagined his wife saying, "What did you drag into this house?" The rabbi apologizing and himself saying "That's all right. I'll go." He sighs wearily.

The rabbi turned and asked him what's the matter.

Lazar replied, "Nothing."

"Molke! Children! I want you to meet Lazar!"

Five children's eyes turned to stare at him.

And Molke saying, "Don't stand there with two feet in one shoe. Come here so we can take a good look at you." She pulled him into the center of the room. "Hm...a handsome boy."

The rabbi fuming, 'Why did she have to parade him around like a prize bull?' She knew what she was doing. She would make it hard for him. But he had no fear. He glanced at the hole in the lampshade. No fear at all.

"Sit down," she ordered.

She introduced the girls. They were too shy to look at him and averted their heads.

Then suddenly, a warm mothering, "Tell me about yourself."

The rabbi didn't know what to make of this tactic.

Lazar repeated his story. It was just as hard every time. A tear slid down her cheek when he finished. 'Means nothing,' the rabbi thought. 'She always cries easily. Ice melting. That's all it is. Melting or not. It's still ice.' The rabbi watched them carefully. Lazar impulsively placed a comforting hand on her arm, the words rushing out, "Forgive me. I'm sorry I made you cry." Her hands softly covered his. And both remained in silent communication.

'So that was it! She's going to take him away from me!'

'Come Lazar. We have some work to do.'

"Don't trouble yourself," Molke softly replying, "We'll go together, won't we Lazar?"

Lazar looked up at her and silently assented.

Chapter Eighteen

The rabbi was interrupted by Jacob, who handed him a message. There was to be an emergency meeting of the 10. Would he be available? He folded the message into a triangle which meant 'yes' and returned it to Jacob, dressed hurriedly and fled to the meeting place, loudly announcing he was making a sick call as he left. Though he'd committed the directions to the cabin to memory, he still had difficulty finding it. The country was anathema to him. Hidden enemies lurking everywhere; flies, mosquitos...even snakes. He reviewed the directions in his mind including the vital turn. He'd be lost in the forest forever. That's the trouble with rebellion, he mused, it's just so uncomfortable...struggling, panting on the uneven terrain...a contrast to the friendly smooth underfoot of civilization.

Finally, the clearing of...the cabin. He rapped twice and slid a paper under the door. Laban opened the door, embraced the rabbi, who drew back offended by his familiarity. The others sat on the floor in a circle. The rabbi had never seen them smile. Their greetings were perfunctory as usual. This was not a social call, they always said. He was startled to find two new faces...Goyim? Both clean shaven, wearing the same peasant hats, blonde hair sticking out over both sets of ears. Blue eyes turned on him coldly. The rabbi's hands were wet now but thinking too, maybe they can be trusted more than Jews.

Laban explained, "They're here to spread the message among the Christians."

The rabbi understood. They were also tired of waiting for their Messiah. But he remained uncomfortable. Too much exposure to outsiders. Laban asked the others to leave and took the rabbi aside.

"We need help to spread the word...someone with a pen of fire and blood...to wake the sleeping and the dead. In short...we need...the writer...and we need you to convince."

"Him! He's interested only in his cuff links and seeing that his tie matches his socks."

Laban had watched the writer in the tea house. He knew him well.

"No," Laban said, "he likes to be the master puppeteer. He's a cold fish with no heart at all but he likes to push his characters around, our hearts in them so he can watch them bleed. He plays that game in real life too, lights the match and stands back to watch the flames roaring, an arsonist with life...as long as the flames don't touch him."

A pleading tone in Laban's voice. The rabbi liked the feeling; even Laban, the savage, recognized his superiority, came to him to solve a problem, depended on him. Power creeping over him conquering the last trace of caution. Under thousands of years of Talmud, Bacchus, the Greek goddess, still making men drunk lusting for the supreme intoxication...power.

"All right. I'll do it."

He'd conquer the writer; the final finger waving would be his... the acquiescent thoughtful nod and stroking of the chin...the writer's. He saw himself in history. Pilpul figuring were for the others...not for him, Laban called the other in and nodded. The rabbi loved the obeisant, grateful admiration in their eyes...even the goyim. That pleased him the most. The conquerors bowing to the conquered. He left abruptly, gave a note to Jacob to give to the writer that he had to see him at once.

It was Spring. Jacob was not rush-able in the Spring. There were too many distractions and he was distractible. The weather was not one of those few perfect days...like all of life, he thought, a few perfect days if you're lucky. He saw his own reflection in a window as he passed by. Jacob's room had no mirror. It wasn't much of a day when I was born. Maybe it was night. Lucky for mother...she couldn't see too well or she would have left me where I came from. She plied him with everything...to make him grow. He was always being measured. It was always the same. The tape measured unrolled down the back of his spine. His mother nudging him in the back of the neck with her index finger, "stand up straight."

He wondered why there wasn't a hole there from years of measuring and poking. Only his mother's impatience grew, but he didn't. He'd stretch himself in front of the mirror to no avail. When he breathed and brought his arms down, he shrunk again to his real self. The one value his size had for him as there were children and townspeople...ranging from the usual midget to poppy seed, pea pod, and pinhead.

As he neared the writer's house, he dawdled, slowing his footsteps and prolonging his time in the fresh bright day...his little chest expanded, a smile crossed his face. He was not accustomed to freedom during the day. He lived his life at the Rabbi's window.

"How is it outside today?" Mop suspended while he inquired.

"Nice...very nice."

He took a last look at the bright sun before entering the dark hallway...like a man returning to jail. He rapped on the door preparing himself for the usual scene when he was an unexpected stranger. Who is it? Then a look through the peephole.

"I can't see you." He couldn't reach it. "Where are you?"

"I don't see anyone," he called out.

"Look through the keyhole."

Eye would meet eye and, for some reason, they'd open the door, having seen only his eye. Then they'd look down and recognize him. The writer's sisters answered the door. She was sure he was here for more money from the shul. She was always saying 'enough' but gave anyway. There was an invisible string from conscience to her hand. Pull on one and the other snapped up palm open with a handful of money.

"What is it?" he asked cautiously.

This was the first time Jacob came personally. The rabbi must really need money, this or that family...this or that charity. Probably meaning his family and him...the writer often said, "Oh no!" He smiled, talking with such pleasure in putting a crack in her ideals and the most joy when he succeeded in smashing them completely. Jacob said right away he wants to see the writer. She was relieved and rushed to comply. He told her to wait. She returned to Jacob.

"What's new?"

And he told her about Lazar. She returned to the writer to tell him. She knew he'd want to know. Writers are curious. When he finally came out to greet Jacob, he bent down to shake his hand.

"What brings you here?"

"The Rabbi wants to see you about something urgent."

He quickly concluded, "It must be about Lazar."

"Okay, I'm coming up."

Jacob was accustomed to such speedy acquiescence. 'No matter what he says,' the writer thought, I'm not taking him back.'

Chapter Nineteen

The rabbi anxiously awaited the writer, pacing back and forth, biting his nails, waving the children away, brushing them away like flies. He wanted only to see the writer... anyone else was an intrusion in the dialogue that was already proceeding in his mind and any interruption was a distraction that could not be tolerated. He was girded for battle and had the impatience of a warrior. Jacob plodded in with his heavy feet, the only part of him that was too big.

"He is here."

"Good. Show him in."

Both uncomfortably tugged each other's hand's while exchanging greetings.

"Why am I here?"

"To put it briefly, we need you."

"Just a minute. I want to make it clear; we have no room in our room for a third party."

"A third party?"

The rabbi was confused.

"I understand," he said. Not understanding at all but letting him reveal himself first. Maybe then it wouldn't be so hard to convince him.

"I'm glad you understand. I'm a writer. I need my privacy. My living depends on it. Lazar can find a home with someone else with other children around."

'So, that's it' the rabbi thought. He thinks I want him to take Lazar.

"But he's a bright boy and you would be a good influence on him...it's a shame. The boy will be in the street."

"Why don't you take him?"

"Me! I have three of my own already. What will I do with a fourth?"

"He'll be a son to you."

"I need a son. Another mouth to feed?"

"I am fond of him," he lied, "but...between being fond and keeping him..."

"Well, you think about it. You can't make a hasty decision in a matter like this."

"Let's change the subject."

After all, to have it known, he turned out a homeless boy, even in his reputation as a writer couldn't prevent the scandal. They would love to have an excuse to scorn him. Hats wouldn't tip for him any longer. He couldn't really bear that...he never dwelt too long on anything that was too uncomfortable. His sister would find a way out for him...the only problem on which he dwelt were the ones he created and uncreated. The ones that life created, he couldn't handle.

Why couldn't they leave him alone! They were there to amuse him...with obeisance, with respect, with rage, with action.

"I'll think about it and let you know."

"So, tell me, what are you writing about now?"

"I'm not too fertile, struggling to find a vital subject I haven't written about..."

"Like what?"

The rabbi knew these intellectuals. Let them talk. They loved it. Make them think you're very impressed with every word and they expand themselves with their own hot air...like a balloon...when it's all laid out in front of you with careful and interested listening, then you find the weak point and strike so gently and deviously they think they've outwitted you.

"How about the political situation, there's plenty of material there. The town is bubbling."

"I know," smug with satisfaction. "Thanks to me."

"Thanks to you? How?"

"I know how to steam them up. Get them going...so they'll do something."

"What would you have them do?"

"Just like a Rabbi. Pray, of course. But pray and win, Moses smote the Egyptian. Time again for smiting."

"But how can you make them ready for such action, no one can do it."

"I can."

"How?"

The writer saw his new book. Those hot heads would live it for him. He would write it.

"I would spur them on. They act."

"With talk that they forget when they leave the tea house, most of them."

"No. talk, they forget, but...put that talk into print. Send it home with them in their pockets..."

"What do you mean?" struggling to be calm.

"I'll be the propagandist."

"I'll write the material."

"But why do you tell me this?" the rabbi asked, frightened now.

"Because I know."

The guy in one of his drunken moments told him. And he led him on and on to tell him more.

"Bah," He said to him, "how can a rag-tag group of renegades turn the path of history. You're all just providing an amusement for yourselves with big dreams for small lives."

"Rag-tag!" And he lurched nearer, his wet mouth whispering, "Is the rabbi rag-tag?"

"Revulsion and mockery, the rabbi, what has he got to do with it?"

The goy's pride touched by the writer's interest; he couldn't stop himself.

"If you don't believe me, ask him."

"I'm asking you."

"Well, I'm telling you," cautious now.

The writer chose to believe him, relishing the drama of a secret. Like turning a page in one of his books and finding himself. The writer now confident, arrogant, watching the taunt face and hard eyes of the rabbi twitching, "I know everything."

"Only God knows everything."

It was a standoff. Each had a secret to control the other, loaded, and ready to fire if necessary.

"Well, rabbi, I have to go now. I think we understand each other. Lazar will be comfortable with you, I hope."

"And the revolution with you," the rabbi replied.

"Jacob!" The rabbi screamed when he heard the door closing on the writer.

"Give me a three-cornered paper and drop it at the tea house when I tell you..."

This meant, "Our man is ready. Contact him."

Chapter Twenty

When the winter left, the Rabbi locked himself in his study. Slumped over his chair, elbows on the desk, his palm cradled the brow of his bent head. The Rabbi's mind, accustomed to an infinity of questions, answers leading to more questions, a mind ever alert to more questions and more answers, finally stumbled into a question he didn't want to entertain and an answer he feared to find. How did the writer know...if...he knew? How...how...how? He folded his hand into a fist and pounded his head with it as if the mere force of pounding would hammer the answer out of his brain. Of course! The answer was simple. He was one of them, too, and had sworn them to secrecy like the Rabbi had. He must have seen him the day he visited the cabin. The Rabbi was accustomed to wild conjecturing. He'd done it all his life. After all, it wasn't all religion-based on a wild conjecture? So why not a small accident...a tiny coincidence, a likely possibility.

He'd been assured by Laban that the men in the group were well-tested. They needed each other and knew each other's secrets.

The rabbi was interrupted by a knock on the door.

"Who is it?" Angry, shouting. No one ever dared intrude when the door was closed.

"Lazar. I want to show you my new suit."

'My God,' the rabbi thought, 'It's Shabbos already!'

"Alright, I'm coming."

He rapidly composed himself, prepared a warm, welcoming benign smile and opened the door.

Lazar had never had a new suit before. He stood straight as a string, afraid to move for fear of making a wrinkle. The rabbi had to suppress his laughter. Lazar looked stiff...as if he were posing for a picture or facing an execution.

A roar of approval, "You look so handsome!"

And the rabbi grabbed him by both arms. When he removed his hands, Lazar glanced quickly at both arms to see if he had made a wrinkle. He had.

"You really like it?" Lazar's eyes widened, searching.

The rabbi nodding his head, "You really liked it! I said I liked it."

Lazar heard impatience in his voice. He didn't dare question him further. He realized very quickly that he couldn't play the same games with the Rabbi that he had with Basha.

"Do you like it Momma?" he'd say.

"Yes," she said. "I like it."

"Really?" he'd say.

He loved to hear her repeat, over and over, 'I like it.' Whatever it was he did that pleased her. She would give him as many, 'I like it' for as many 'reallys.'

There were no more 'reallys' with the rabbi. Lazar relinquished the game of 'really' on that Shabbos with the rabbi. But he played it with Rebbetzin. She was a better player.

"How does Rebbetzin like the suit," the rabbi asked.

"She loves it. She told me over and over. She chose it."

"She did?" The rabbi suddenly noticed a few flaws here and there.

"It could fit a little better, etc. etc. You have a fine shape, Lazar... or that suit would have had some problems."

Lazar grasped at these few words.

"The rabbi thinks I have a fine shape. It made him proud."

"Thank you, Rabbi. I won't disturb you any further."

"You're not disturbing me," he lied. "I'll see you at the table."

The Shabbos was not a restful time for the rabbi, his restless mind anxious, 'How many others knew about him?'

For the first time he looked forward to his wife's nagging as a welcome distraction, but she was strangely quiet. She was herself obsessed with a question. 'How to handle this boy?' Her first decision was to create a good image...the quiet beleaguered wife of a tyrant. Sympathy for her from Lazar...a good beginning. She would appeal to the need of everyone, from childhood on, to take sides...and she was determined it would be hers that Lazar took.

The rabbi was weakened as he was battling on two fronts. She had only one...and all of nature had generously provided her with it's weapons...motherhood. She just had to follow her instincts.

Both were distracted during the evening meal. The children were noisier than usual...like all children...quick to sense the slightest relaxation in authority. The rabbi suddenly found it impossible to continue sitting at the table. He needed to be alone...and yet...being alone now was too distressing for him. He chose to be alone with Lazar.

"Come with me. I want to talk to you."

Lazar feared he'd displeased the rabbi and prepared himself for the farewell speech...sympathetic, warm...the 'I have something to tell you' speech that ends in, "You understand, Lazar. You'll have to go." And Lazar replied, "I understand," which he really didn't.

"Oh no, nothing like that. Lazar, I want to know what you have concluded from all that you've been through."

Lazar puzzled, "About what?"

"About tyrants, I hate them. God forgive me, I should like to see them all dead. And the people who killed them. I hate them too.

Everyone dear to me is gone because of them. And me...I hate me too."

"Why you!"

Lazar told the story. The rabbi listened gravely...without interruption 'til Lazar feels silent.

"They are not gone because of you...they're gone because of the tyrants...not the people...never them...you...or anyone else. The tyrants killed your dear ones."

"But they wouldn't have if we didn't kill one of them."

"Yes, they would have...but they would have found another excuse. They make you <u>think</u> they have a reason...a killing for a killing...but that's not true. They kill us for the sake of killing us. First, they decide to kill...and then...they find a reason...or make one up."

And the rabbi talked to Lazar and reviewed with him the trumped-up reasons and the real reasons, the deep pain and hate in his own heart swelled...the ritual murders, the pogroms, the wanton killings...thousands of years.

And Lazar's rage grew and grew as the rabbi talked.

"Maybe there's a chance for us."

Lazar grasping, "What chance?"

"Maybe if we join the rest of the condemned in their struggle, kill their tyrants, they'll respect us. Maybe if their bellies and minds are full, instead of empty, they'll leave us alone!"

Lazar stammering now...overcome by the Rabbi's talking to him man to man.

"What can I do to help?"

"You're already helping...by talking together, listening together, and I hope...agreeing together."

"I agree. I want revenge, Rabbi."

Putting words for the first time what he hadn't even dared to think. And felt strong, purposeful, powerful...like gentle words never had. It wasn't the Jewish way, maybe...but better. It was God's way... Noah and the Ark, Sodom, and Gomorrah.

"When do we start?" Savoring the 'we.'

"Now, my boy. Right now. But everything I tell you is...and he put his index finger in his mouth. Lazar put his finger in his mouth. The pact was sealed...a shared secret of love. For the first time, the rabbi found another side to a secret...love...not power. And he told Lazar his secret...feeling a bond he'd never known before...stronger than any he'd ever felt of necessity of instinct...a bond honed by choice.

"You realize what's involved here, Lazar?"

"Yes, I can stay here...with you. We can live together."

"And die together."

Rather die with you than live with anyone else. What can I do? How can I help?"

"Remember what you did before, putting papers under the door, a picture of Basha's candle and 'other things?' That's what I want you to do now."

The rabbi quickly planning again...all brisk efficiency now. He was controlling events, and he was not alone. His equilibrium was now fully restored.

Lazar's head nodded in agreement far into the night while the rabbi outlined his plan to put 'Basha's candle' under every Russian door.

Chapter Twenty-One

The Rabbi woke the next morning feeling refreshed though he only had a few hours of sleep. He'd never been to bed that late before. The Rebbetzin was furious that he was spending all that time with Lazar, but she also had to admit she missed the Rabbi a little. She'd so often wished for his absence but now the bed seemed big and lonely.

That boy was becoming a nuisance now. At night, the rabbi made up for lost time. The hours she spent with Lazar during the day, he made up with the boy at night. The rabbi's good humor annoyed her. In his enthusiasm over gaining ground in this battle, the rabbi forgot his feud with the Rebbetzin. After all, he couldn't fight on two fronts at once.

One morning at the breakfast table, "Nu," the rabbi asking, "What do you think you will do with yourself, Lazar?"

The Rebbetzin sieged her opportunity.

"Leave the boy alone," she said, "Let him rest a minute. He's been through so much."

The rabbi saw her ploy and responded, "I meant how he was going to enjoy his day? And was going to offer suggestions."

Lazar, still hearing the writer's speech in his ears, was determined he wasn't going to be twice condemned for the same crime. The penalty was too high. He had been thinking about the future... thinking and thinking.

"I want to study...to be a Rabbi."

The rabbi would teach him during the day, and he could work for him at night...

"Settled!" the rabbi thundered, "Today, we begin. Come with me."

The Rebbetzin crestfallen. He took Lazar into his study where he handed him a pile of books.

"You'll review these today and we'll review them tomorrow. And don't say, 'Today,'" the rabbi warned.

Suddenly with the tone of a teacher with that '*do as you're told*' ring in his voice.

Lazar suppressed all protest and questions and, staggering under the load, he repaired to his room. The rabbi's slogan was 'give them too much and they'll do <u>something</u>.'

"You want the door open or closed?"

The rabbi smiled as he watched Lazar to the door, the struggle to close the door behind him. 'He had to learn to do things for himself, starting with the impossible.' Lazar wouldn't dare to let any of the holy books fall. He also wouldn't dare to presume to ask the rabbi to close the door, the rabbi watched him struggle with this dilemma. How would he solve a difficult problem, even of a trivial nature? The rabbi wanted to know. Lazar raised his foot to the doorknob and pulled it toward him. The door closed with a loud bang.

'Good boy,' the Rabbi mused. 'Has respect and uses his own head...I like that...I like that very much. Tomorrow we'll see what's he done. Today he's already made a good beginning. Thinking without doing is like a hammer without a nail. Lazar would be very busy thinking by day; doing by night.'

The rabbi, by habit, raised his eyes to God...grateful. The Rebbetzin mounted her campaign immediately. Calling him from his room she found chore after chore after chore for him. The rabbi would be disenchanted with him if he proved to be a fool.

A weary Lazar did not join the family for supper that night, pleading he had a headache and plunged into his books. Throughout the night he read and read till he collapsed in his chair and rose after two hours of sleep at dawn to read again. He watched the pile of books recede somewhat, but it was a grain of sand. He approached the rabbi timidly the next morning.

"What have you done? That's all?"

"I guess I could have done more."

"Not at all. I just wanted you to realize the first rule of learning...the little you know...and how much there is to know...that big pile of books in front of you teaches you that lesson like nothing else can."

"But no one can ever know all there is to know, Rabbi."

"That's exactly the point. That's the secret of learning because if you feel you know all there is to know..."

Lazar completed the sentence, "then you stop learning."

"Exactly. Now let's begin."

And he questioned him, and Lazar answered.

"Well done," the Rabbi said, "But it could be better."

Lazar shrunk expecting a blow. But the rabbi didn't need a stick. Lazar would do anything to hear him say, 'Well done.' And the rabbi knew it.

"The lesson is over," the Rabbi said and handed him another book.

"Thank you."

The Rabbi did not reply.

His mind was already turned to other matters. He was expecting visitors and had his own studying to do before they came. The Rebbetzin greeted him outside the rabbi's door.

"How did it go?"

Lazar shrinking, expecting more chores.

"It went well, thank you."

The Rebbetzin unbelieving, "When did you manage to study?"

"All night. I don't really need that much sleep."

The Rebbetzin decided on another tactic. The boy was too frightened of the rabbi to displease him. He had a hard life, she thought. He had to earn his love every day from him and me. Nothing given freely and easily like his own children. Lazar didn't realize he couldn't learn it from him because he couldn't and from her because she wouldn't. But he's a tryer. Doesn't know much else to cope with life but try and hope. She would resort to her old ways...the oldest known to women.

"What would you like to eat?"

And she listed the delectable food...kasha, flaken, etc. Lazar's mouth watered. He didn't dare choose.

He nodded to everything and said, "Anything."

At dinner, she fussed over him especially. The rabbi scowled. Motel announced a package had been left at the door for him. The rabbi rushed from the table and disappeared in his room with the package...tore it open. Five hundred circulars. He decided Lazar would start that night.

"Lazar, come here."

"Let him finish his meal."

"He'll finish it later. Meals don't have wings."

"But it'll get cold."

"It's better cold."

Lazar rose. The Rebbetzin nodded. She'd made her point. The rabbi explained to Lazar.

"What do I do if they catch me?"

"Pray. That's all you can do. Pray for us all."

Chapter Twenty-Two

Lazar worked day and night, studying, working...he had little time for anything else...not that he'd want anyway. He lived for the future for the future...for the world...his career...all in the golden tomorrow...a rabbinical seat for him in a just and peaceful world. He would sleep tomorrow. He never gave a thought to play, occasionally to some more rest and sleep but there was really no time for either. He had two worlds to conquer...the Talmud by day, the tyrants at night. He had no doubt he would conquer them both. There were more and more groups forming...the word was spreading...beyond Warsaw...beyond and beyond...Lazar was grateful for an excuse to stay awake. As soon as his head touched the pillow, he was greeted by his nightly visitor.

"I have seen Basha."

"Where?"

"Everywhere" was his answer...and he would disappear.

Lazar would awake shaken...shouting, "Where, where, where!"

He was grateful to see the dawn of day, light to immerse himself in study and avoid the anxious question that always hovered beyond the others. And during the day, another one behind all the rest.

'Where was God?' he asked the rabbi when he reviewed the history of blood and pain and 'Where is momma?' he'd ask at night.

When he first asked the question and the Rabbi answered, "I don't know here God was, Lazar."

He was astonished. He expected a blow, for even daring to ask the question.

And when he asked, "Where's my mother?" the rabbi answered, "I don't know, but we'll find out."

He never said, 'We'll find out' about God. Lazar sometimes wondered if the rabbi really believed in the Messiah.

As the months passed, the rabbi seemed more preoccupied than ever, but not with Talmudic questions and God. He was immersing himself more and more in the idea of paradise on earth. He remained invisible to the group, but they depended on him for leadership, 'Like God,' Lazar thought. Messages flew back and forth continuously, and Lazar was sent further and further with his leaflets. Sometimes he had to stay overnight and each time he came to a new town he questioned if anyone had seen Basha. But each town had its madwoman, broken by life, sleeping in hallways and fields. Lazar would wait for them as they came down the main street, talking or singing to themselves, shouting sometimes, always in rags and carrying a few pitiful belongings. He would approach them carefully, slowly, so as not to frighten them, and looked hard under their bandanas and kerchiefs. Sometimes they were frightened and laughed at him...or slapped and kicked him. He would drop a bun into their rags and run. Some cursed or spat at his fleeing figure while devouring it. At first, he had pursued rumors of a lovely vision seen fleetingly at night with a candle. He'd camped on a dark hilltop at night and waited...for nothing. Lazar became known as 'Friend of the Misugoyim.' Like a stray cat will rub it's head against the trousers of a loving stranger, these ladies, who would flee from, ignore, or attack anyone else, would approach him, stand timidly by and wait, submitted their faces to his scrutiny without being asked and then, sensing his disappointment, would extend a scrawny, dirty hand to comfort him. He would press his little offering on them which they would greedily devour and retreat again into their private worlds where Lazar could no longer reach them.

In the new world, Lazar dreamed, they would be taken care of, and somewhere in the new and gentle world, someone would tend to Basha. In a world without hunger, people would be kind. Sometimes, he wished he could bring them all home with him and clean and clothe and feed them...home for the homeless.

He talked about it one day to the Rabbi, who impatiently turned on him and raged, "One meshuga woman in this house is enough!"

He dropped the subject and the Rabbi, just as suddenly, dropped from his pedestal in Lazar's eyes...Lazar had also accidentally stumbled on a domestic problem he'd been too absorbed in his work to notice.

Misugoyim - Crazies

From now on, he decided, he would pay attention. He didn't want to be caught in a crossfire. Who would be a more convenient scapegoat than Lazar? He would step gingerly between them. Above all, take no sides. Lazar learned an excellent lesson today from the rabbi. The Gods are only in heaven. The rest of us are only human...the rabbi included.

Till now, Lazar was blinded by the glare of idolatry. Today, the rabbi did him a favor. He emerged from the blinding light with just a few ill-chosen words. It was as impossible to rekindle that dazzling light as it was to put the words back in his mouth. The Rabbi's fall from the heavens was total. Lazar was too young to make gradations and fine distinctions.

He looked all the way up or all the way down. When he had looked up, the rabbi didn't have a blemish, now that he looked down, the rabbi didn't have a virtue. Lazar found his brain spinning now with criticism and judgements. Like a sunken ship which floats with its debris to the surface, the light shining on it for the first time, so Lazar was now remembering old words of the Rabbi's that he'd swept down under and were now plunging to the surface. Lazar greeted them harshly and tasted power for the first time...the power to wound like the Rabbi...with words. Lazar had been wounded out of his gentle obeisance. The cage door was suddenly flung open, and Lazar surveyed the tactics of offense...what had he feared most about the Rabbi? His rage...displeasing him...and his criticism... 'You're stupid.' Those were the rabbi's two weapons. He would have to forge them for himself. By becoming as smart or smarter than the Rabbi, he had the right to use those words, and, when he was free of the rabbi's bed and table, he would be a man that the world around would concern itself with pacifying...when the time came.

"Nu, Lazar," the rabbi asking, "are you ready for today's lesson?"

"Oh yes, Rabbi," Lazar replied obsequiously, "I am."

For the first time, he noticed how pleased the rabbi was with his submissiveness. He hated him for it, but he smiled graciously and obediently and turned to his prayers. He kept turning pages until he was sure he could press down the tremble from his voice. The lesson proceeded. At one point in his discourse with the Rabbi, Lazar tried his new weapon. The rabbi's argument was not very profound. Stupid, Lazar thought. It felt so good to call the Rabbi stupid. Stupid. Stupid. Stupid. The word rolled around his head. Rolled and rolled. Made him glow with such satisfaction that throughout the lesson he applied the word whether the rabbi deserved it or not...just for the pleasure it gave him. The lesson was suddenly interrupted by Jacob... a three-cornered message was handed to the Rabbi. He grabbed his coat, the hanger clattered to the floor. He didn't bother to pick it up. He perched his hat on his head and fled out the door.

"Something wrong, Jacob?" Lazar asking, curious.

"Not necessarily," a grin on his face, "the Rabbi is often rushing here and there. It looks like an emergency, the way he grabs his hat and runs but it usually isn't...maybe the pond overflowed a little, but not the ocean like he makes it seem..."

"So why does he rush about like the world will go under if he's not there to hold fast for the last string?"

"Makes him feel important to go rushing around," and he winked at Lazar.

It was such a shock. Until now, the conversation between them consisted of, "Stay out of that room, it's just been mopped. Give me your shirt. I'll have it pressed..."

And another trivia of this kind. Jacob was suddenly talking to him as if he were a secret ally...or he was imagining things?

"But the Rabbi is important. Why does he need to do anything more than feel important?"

"It's never enough. No one ever feels important enough. Or money, Lazar. No one ever feels rich enough. Or love. No one ever feels loved enough."

"Or powerful enough?"

"Or even powerful enough. Only troubles. That's the only thing that's enough."

"How about you, Jacob?"

"I have nothing. Not even troubles. That's worse than not having enough."

"Who needs troubles?"

"That's what I asked myself once."

Weary. Anguished. Touching his face and quickly disappearing... giving way again to a vacuous smile.

"Sometimes that's a dangerous question," he said, and quickly changed the subject, "Stuffy in here, don't you think? I think I'd better open a window."

He rushed away breathing heavily. Lazar had just learned to relish the word 'stupid.' Like a poor man with new money, he was ready to squander it wherever he could. But he had to admit Jacob was not as dumb as he thought...maybe. Impatient with himself...he cruelly dashed that moment of tolerance against the new wall he erected inside himself and smashed it into pieces. 'Stupid talk. That's just stupid talk. Troubles, we need. What is he talking about? Upset because he has no troubles? I'll be glad to change places with him. Any day, that is, without the rag and the broom...'

"One more question, Lazar, I forgot to ask you. You were gone for two days," his face fixed stiff now, too stiff, Lazar thought.

"Nothing much."

"I couldn't help overhearing as I passed by. The door was open, you know. Those ladies..."

"Yes?" Lazar was ready to spring on him if he dared say one word out of the way about them.

"Those ladies," Jacob repeating, the grin fixed on his face, his eyes suddenly filled with pain, his voice pleading, "Was there one for them, a hunchback, a hokey on the back," and he swept his arm in an arc over his back and about so high, flattening his other hand in air at the point of his chin.

"Why do you ask?"

"Just asking."

"No, I don't think so."

Jacob turned his back and walked slowly to the door, Lazar couldn't see the grin leave his face, but he sensed it still. And Lazar thinking, 'maybe I know what you mean Jacob...what you said about troubles. They come and go, new ones replace old ones, and old ones are quickly forgotten but old sorrows dig in tenaciously touching a raw nerve whenever the fancy strikes them to make you scream with pain inside.' Maybe Jacob has such sorrow...like me. Maybe that's what he meant. And despite his new self, his heart went out to Jacob.

Chapter Twenty-Three

Lazar heard the Rebbetzin call his name. He quickly sat down and bent his head over a book, hardly knowing to what page he was turning. As she approached the door, he raised his head as if he were deep in heavy thought just a moment before.

"Excuse me," he said, rising from the chair, "I didn't hear from you."

"Let me not interrupt you."

'Thank God,' he thought, 'no chores.'

"What can I do for you, Rebbetzin," hoping she'd refuse.

"Just be as smart as you are, you're so smart Lazar," shaking her head to and fro, "So smart."

The three children ran up behind her. "Momma, can we play with Lazar?"

"Sha," she warned without answering, "go out and play, children."

Lazar was pleased. Just like Basha. Women were like that. Every question didn't have to be answered for them like the men, whose whole life was absorbed with that game. 'What would men do,' he thought, 'if all questions were asked and all the answers answered?' An inward smile on his face. He was even asking a question, about questions.

Lazar was distant from the rabbi's children. He loved his brothers and sisters when he had them and he couldn't fill their little places with substitutes from the womb of a stranger. It would be a betrayal. His heart wouldn't permit it. It refused to let them in, though they tried very hard...as children often do with recalcitrant adults. Lazar's responses to all their efforts to please and impress him were proper but perfunctory. 'That's very nice' or 'thank you,' were the limits of his exchanges with them.

"Lazar," the Rebbetzin asked when the children left, "I have to ask you something. It's hard for me to say and I hope you won't take it wrongly."

Lazar was already taking it wrongly. He was now anxious and alert with preparatory speeches.

"Tell me, have I been good to you these past few months?"

"Very good."

"I can't help wondering why you're so distant. I thought maybe I offended you."

"Oh no! What made you think that?"

"You're so distant, so much inside yourself. I thought, in time, we could love each other, like mother and son. I feel like you're my own son," and she drew nearer.

He instinctively withdrew, an image of the ladies flashing. The Rebbetzin was embarrassed and angry. 'In this house, I do the rejecting,' she thought. She hoped she wasn't being too forceful. She had waited for months for some sign and had to know. She had fussed over him, flattered him, expressed concern over his health, his appearance, showered him endearments; mien son, mien kind; in short...had exhausted her maternal repertoire to no avail. Lazar remained distant and enigmatic. In her lonely, silent monologues at night when the Rabbi was snoring beside her in bed, she pondered and reviewed over and over. Her error, she decided, was trying to respond to what she assumed was his need for her. Today, she would try another tack: her need for him.

"Lazar," her tone warm, confiding.

He stepped back.

"Why can't we be friends? I don't ask that you be my son. But can we be friends?"

"What do you mean?"

"I mean, I would like you to talk to me...about yourself."

"With the Rabbi, you talk about the world. I want to know about you, how can I help you, what troubles you?"

"But why should I burden you?" Lazar incredulous.

"But that's the point. It's not a burden. The Rabbi is always busy with his studies, the children with their play. I need a friend in the house."

A confidence of hers to a friend usually led to a large return. She waited for an avalanche, an outpouring. It never came.

Lazar bitter inside, sarcastic, 'She needs a friend!' And remembering now the ladies with the mottled hair, cold, hungry, despised, derided, and alone.

The Rebbetzin stood before him more elegantly dressed every month since he came. How often a feeling deepens from a small beginning. 'How nice you look!'

Lonely! Lazar's poor head was still bitter; mocking. What does she know of loneliness that closes a door on a chorus of familiar and reluctant goodbyes and opens a door to a chorus of welcome hellos? No, she doesn't need a friend. She needs an ally. But so did he. He needed both. But the Rabbi and Rebbetzin were both too clever for him. They'd been honing their weapons a long time. What part was he to play? He didn't know. One thing he did know. He didn't want to wander like the ladies. He was the only one who called them 'ladies.' To everyone else, they were 'mishigoyim*.'

---

* ***Mishigoyim – Nuts***

"Rebbetzin, forgive me if I'm a little distant. It's just that it's painful to think about myself. Everything is too fresh in my mind."

Regret gnawing now. He gave her too much. Told her a partial truth.

She came nearer. He withdrew further. This time she was pleased; a benign smile on her face, the maternal glow she affected so well.

"That's what people are for," she said, "to help each other to stop hurting."

"But I don't want to stop hurting. I owe it to my mother and father, and sisters to hurt for them as long as I live." And dreamy now, "The only bond left to us is to hurt for each other. That's all we have left of one another."

He looked into the distance, no longer talking to her but to someone far away, "All we have left."

She turned and left him without another word. She knew he'd forgotten she was there, looking at her but no longer seeing. She heard him mumbling as she walked the long hall back to the parlor. She knew she hadn't touched him.

He was in love with ghosts, the missing and the wandering and the dead. The Rebbetzin was mellowed for a moment by his sadness, but she was also content now. The battle with the Rabbi was over. He doesn't know it, but we're both losers. She would watch the rabbi struggling, not knowing the battle was no longer against her. She would like to be there when the Rabbi found out. Her eyes involuntarily glanced around the room. 'Ah! I need another lamp for that corner. I'll have to speak to him tonight.' And she sprang out of her chair. She called the children, "Get ready. We're going out!"

Lazar, numbed, stared at the page he opened and read with his eyes only, despair now and fatigue. He drops his head on the page to rest a minute and succumbs to sleep. The dream was full of books as large as people. He turned pages and found another person...not print...but people. He was terrified, tried to stop, but couldn't. The ladies! On each page, a misshapen figure in a bundle of multi-colored rags; eyes protruding from faces or sunken hollow, bellies swollen or emaciated, bony hands extended, smiling, toothless, twisted mouths, introducing themselves with screaming, sardonic laughter, pirouetting and lifting the skirt, prancing away in a wild dance laughing as they went, faster and faster at a more feverish pace. Lazar thinking, 'Maybe! Good God! Maybe! He stopped at the next to the last page and prayed...closed his eyes and slowly turned the page.

He heard the cackling. No introduction.

"It's me!" He opened his eyes. Felt the blood leave his face, "Roselle!"

"Roselle, my darling, forgive me."

He extended a hand but she, like all the others pirouetted clumsily, did her little dance for him, not seeing...not hearing.

"Roselle!" he was still shouting when the rabbi nudged him.

"Lazar, wake up." Gently nudging him, "Who is Roselle?"

"Nobody."

Lazar remained in his room for two days without eating or sleeping. He saw no one. He couldn't face the Rabbi. The Rebbetzin, clean and meticulous, the children; starched, clean, pudgy. The Rebbetzin's concern about the crumbs on the floor. He wondered what she did on Pesach. How do you eat Matzo without crumbs? Poor Jacob spent his life cleaning them from the floor, brushing them from the table, searching for more in case he missed any by order of the Rebbetzin.

When Lazar finally left his room, the rabbi greeted him as he came down the stairs and then asked again, "Who is Roselle?"

And Lazar repeating, "Nobody."

"But she has to be somebody."

"She was my mother."

"But I thought Basha was your mother."

"I have two mothers. Roselle nursed and tended us all."

"What happened to her?"

"I don't know," he told the Rabbi, but to himself he said, "I forgot about her."

Like most people, except Basha, Roselle was only remembered when she could be of some use. She was there when there was trouble, then forgotten 'til the next time a helping hand was needed or a listening ear...

"You see, Rabbi, Roselle was a 'nobody' except to us. Momma loved her, I loved her...and even I forgot her, too."

Lazar is guilty and ashamed now. But the Rabbi pressed on.

"What do you think happened to her?"

Lazar wouldn't dare tell him. Couldn't bear to hear him saying, "You think she's meshuga?"

He repeated, "I don't know."

"So, you have two mothers, Lazar?"

"You could say that. Of course, Basha is dearest."

"Of course, I understand."

And he thought, 'If he has two mothers, what need does he have for three?'

"Of course, you miss being mothered?" Hesitant, the Rabbi asking.

Lazar, sensing a trap, replies, "I miss who they were, not what they gave me."

The rabbi nodded his head, understanding and content, too.

"The Rebbetzin is wasting her time," he concluded.

And he cautiously asked another question, "And your father?"

"The same."

"Then I'm wasting my time," the rabbi unhappily concluded.

Like all mankind, Lazar had a yearning for the simple past and his was Basha, Benjamin, Roselle. He had made a covenant with them and would keep it pure forever.

"The battle is over for us both," the Rabbi mused. He hadn't used those words together in such a long time.

"I suppose this is the only time in years we've shared anything; a loss for us both."

Chapter Twenty-Four

The Rabbi had received a three-cornered message with one bent corner which meant, 'Come to the cabin.' He was expecting such a message. The movement had grown. There were groups of *'havayrim'** all over the land. A major move was being planned. He didn't know the details yet. The rabbi would be called for high level consultation when the time was right to strike. They would require his approval and guidance. The rabbi had a sense of timing and history, and they needed both. If their plan turned into a fiasco, they would love what they've gained. If it succeeded, they would gain and gain. The movement was gaining strength. They had their adherents, noisy and quiet ones and...the music that binds and inspires; they had songs.

Laban was singing one of the songs lustily when the Rabbi arrived at the cabin. He imperiously waved the others out the door. He liked the feeling of being in the supreme council, no matter how small and unimportant it was in the world. He couldn't dream of sitting near the Eastern wall in shul. But here, he sat right by the

---

* *Havayrim – Friends*

rabbi's hand, and best of all, the Rabbi struggled his way to him... Laban. Already, the revolution was worth its weight in gold. The two wasted no time on formalities. Laban didn't even inquire about his family this time. The discussion proceeded instantly, as if the two had never left each other's side, even though it had been months since their last meeting.

"The plan is this," Laban talking, his eyes glowing, face shining with excitement and anticipation. He'd felt so confined here. The very words released him from the walls of the cabin.

"The people are cold and hungry, and ignorant, Rabbi...and we've made promises. They're growing impatient with talk. We have to show him we can make the tyrant listen."

The rabbi agreed. "If we can get him to listen once, he'll listen again."

"But he can't listen and hear, Rabbi, if he doesn't know there's something to hear. We have to come out of our corners and show ourselves."

"I agree. The tyrant is only as strong as he thinks the people are weak. What have you planned, Laban? Tell me...it's enough talking. You don't have to convince me. I've already convinced myself...we have enough people to make an impression on the Czar..."

"The plan is this: At an appointed time in the night, all the groups of activists and sympathizers and their friends throughout the land will light candles and march silently through their villages and towns and cities."

"Basha's candle would become a thousand, then five thousand, a hundred thousand candles."

Laban's voice rising, passion growing, "We will send a message to the Czar. We can do these things," and he showed the Rabbi a list of demands, "and snuff out the candles. Or, he can ignore these demands and the lights will join together 'til they become a roaring flame."

"Whose idea was this?"

"The writer's."

"I thought so. He loves the idea of roaring flames."

"I guess, I like it too."

"When would be the best time, Rabbi?"

"After Lent."

"Why Lent?"

"That's when the Christians are hungriest. They have nothing to give up in the first place and they've asked to give up something more."

"You're right. After Lent."

The rabbi rushed out the door. Evening fell, and he feared the night in the forest but tonight, he was even more fearful. To dream... to plot and plan...is one thing...but to change the course of history is another. To do that, he thought, 'you have to have martyrs...and any one of us may be chosen...even me!' The march of candles appealed to the dreamer in him...the romantic. We'll reverse the heavenly design. We'll repay a little debt to them, he mused. For millennia, they've been winking at us. For once, we'll be winking at them.

Lent passed quickly. The rabbi only spoke a few words to Lazar in that time. He told him of the plan, told him he would have to work harder than ever, piled his little wagon high with material and sent him on his way.

Lazar traveled as far as he could, allowing enough time to return on the evening of the march of the candles. His first stop in every town was the baker, where he bought a bag of buns. He searched by day and nursed his bruises at night as some of the ladies were more frightened than others and hurt him...and bent under doorways all night while the town slept...careful not to be seen. Here and there, he snatched a bit of sleep...but he did whatever he could to avoid dreaming...since the last time.

But sleep captured him when it could, standing, sitting, reading, he would suddenly 'chap a dremel*.' He never knew when it was happening and was surprised to find himself where he was when he

---

* ***Dremel - Dream***

awoke. He didn't dream then. He was getting too clever for the dreams, he thought. He was running away from them, and they couldn't find him.

A weary Lazar returned to the town with an empty wagon. He could feel the tension in the air. Tomorrow was the big night. The people, as usual, rushing to and fro performing their survival chores for this earth, then rushing to and from shuls to ensure their future in the next...but he saw, too, the fear on some faces, heightened courage on others, or maybe, he thought, it was his imagination that the town looked and felt different.

The rabbi motioned him into his study as soon as he entered the house.

He showed Lazar the diagram.

"The people will start from here."

And he went on drawing and explaining.

Then, Lazar, asking softly, "And where will you be, Rabbi?"

"I'll be here."

And Lazar thinking, 'I thought so.' "And me, where do you want me, Rabbi?"

"You're a leader too, Lazar. You'll stay with me."

Lazar turned his head, guilty. He had to admit he was relieved.

"Besides," the Rabbi continued, "we've already taken enough risks. It's time the others put their hands to the wheel."

Lazar thought the rabbi was right. The rabbi went to bed early that night. The Rebbetzin was grateful to be left alone. The rabbi didn't tell his wife. He didn't dare. Her tongue was too loose. Besides, he didn't trust her. What wouldn't she do with this knowledge? Refurnish the whole house, God Forbid! And bring all her relatives to stay and be sponges.

The rabbi remained in his study all day refusing to see anyone. He was obsessed with a vision of the night's event; the heavens looking down on a carpet of flickering candles. The whole world, he thought, marching someday in a huge procession, the rabbi leading and holding the biggest and brightest candle of them all. And then, men would light their own way, the heavens smiling now that the vast darkness below them was no more, especially on him.

He had clearly seen the alternative; grinding out his days on pilpuls, advice to tearful women, delivering sermons he hardly believed in himself anymore, breathing new life away into dying traditions, burying the dead, reading his life away on five thousand years of sermons which never made a difference. They didn't even help him to keep his wife from nagging. The Cossacks sword dispensed with five thousand years of wisdom in the flick of an eyelash. He had delicately discussed this with Lazar and planted a small seed in his brain. The Rabbi debated with himself: 'What am I after all, but a small man leading a small people?' Even to his own he was small. Even they gave more respect to the Warsaw Rabbi than to him. The Rabbi was fired with ambition. In this business there wasn't much opportunity for promotion.

A new world was being born. He didn't want to be a spoke on the wheel. He would be formidable. The new books he had recently read, the old ones he knew so well, a wedding of past and future, a perfect union...and he would be the matchmaker. He was born to be a leader of men and thought it was about time he assumed his birthright. After all, he argued, 'who remembered the rabbi who fasted day and night?' No one. Maybe a few fanatics...that's all. As the train approached, he grew more impatient. The Rabbi had a foot poised on history for too long. He was feverishly anxious to take the first step. He paced back and forth, looking at his watch every hour, then, every half hour. Thirty-five minutes more...he rushed even more, circling the room, counting the trips he made, running a race against himself and timing himself to see how much faster he could spin around the room. Finally, he heard the gong ponderously making it's announcement...but the noise continued...as if the clock had announced a visitor...louder and more insistent...then, a scream; the Rebbetzin, all fear now. He flung open the door and saw three uniforms facing him, hands on their sabers, and behind them, through the open front door, a contingent of mounted police.

"You're under arrest!" the uniform standing next to him, crisp and commanding.

He was grabbed by both arms and shoved out the door, a bayonet at his back.

"You're coming with us!"

In the wagon, the rabbi dug his nails into his flesh to keep his hands from trembling. He asked himself, 'How did this happen?'

And he asked them, "What did I do?"

"Conspiring against the state! No more questions!"

The rabbi remained silent until the wagon stopped. "Where are we?"

"I said, no more questions!"

And he was slapped across the face and pulled out of the wagon, thrown on the floor of a small cell. Mice and roaches scurrying as he entered their domain. 'Nu, my temple now as he looked around the cell...and my congregation'...as he looked at them.

He tried a few more quips, a pathetic attempt to rise above the situation, he couldn't go on. The state, is the only area where it has been completely efficient, had reduced him to a small, trembling frightened being who, in a moment, had ceased to dream of conquering worlds and was reduced to pleading for mercy.

"God help me!"

And he beat his fist against the jagged stone walls until they were bloody, then he crumpled in a corner, with his knees drawn up in front of him, hand his mouth and sucking his bloodied fingers for comfort. Soon, he heard footsteps approaching. He pulled his hand out of his mouth and stood up, ashamed that anyone should see him that way.

The jailer shouting, "We have some company for you," and one by one, they were thrown in, stumbling and tripping, the comrades, not daring to show a sign of recognition until they were alone.

The Rabbi sprung on Laban, "Tell me what happened! For God's sake, tell me!"

Chapter Twenty-Five

It was easy to arrest and jail these few protestors...and kill and maim hundreds more to bring the lesson home. The writer secretly made plans before the march and fled the country.

In the rabbi's home, a state of mourning. Jacob's face lost its grin. His work was slow and heavy, his face sorrowful...with no attempt to hide it.

Laban continued with his story, "I was to leave a little earlier to lead them, so I took down 12 candles."

"You only need 10," Pyotor said, "we're not going, Ivan and me."

"Not going!"

"No."

"But why! You were pushing and pushing, hounding us day and night that we should do something!"

"We thought it over. You're just using us so you can control the world."

"I knew that wasn't the real reason. Tell me the truth! Now, you tell me. Why now! Tell me the truth or I'll kill you!"

"You'll never know if you kill me."

"They know. We told them."

"Why?"

"Because we needed your brains. We can do the rest ourselves. We don't want Jews taking over."

"But how about the other Christians?"

"They know. We spread the word...there'll be no Christians marching tonight."

"The goy knew my plan. We would use their brawn."

"But" Laban smirking, "we were supposed to be brothers, comrades. You wanted to use them too, didn't you, Rabbi?"

"Yes, but not betray them."

Jacob visited the rabbi every day. The Rebbetzin cried and beat her breast day and night, "Why did this have to happen to me?!" Lazar barricaded the front door.

"Don't worry," he said, "Rebbetzin. No one can come in now."

He thought this futile symbolic act would comfort her. And it did.

Lazar hated and raged more every day, more intensely because it was silent. A few times he lost control of himself and raged at the children in front of the Rebbetzin. It frightened her. Lazar knew then that his rage was frightening and tried harder to control himself.

The trial was well publicized. They were called, "The Jewish Ten." Everyone knew the outcome, but they needed an excuse to bring the rabbi back and forth in chains every day.

The goyim testified. The chains tightened. He sometimes wished he could return to his faith, but this convinced him more than ever that it was, at best, an indifferent universe. Finally, the day came for the sentence to be pronounced. He had rehearsed the scene to himself many times, but it was still like an earthquake when he heard it. He and the others were to be shot in ten days. He shuffled out of the courtroom. The clanking of the chains couldn't be heard above the din of excitement. Crimes against the state, the judge roared again and again. But the state's crimes against God doesn't matter, the Rabbi thought.

He found a note in his cell when he returned. 'We will continue the fight.' He was a martyr already. He was in history, after all, he thought. He decided not to pray, or fast, or ask for forgiveness. The last few says left to him, he decided he would live as much as he could. The jailer reported there was singing and dancing and carousing in the cell. He thought they must be mad. He had heard they were made and now he was convinced of it. On the last day, they smiled at each other, clasped hands, walked slowly like soldiers, and singing, the rabbi's deep voice above the rest. The ordeal of months had maddened them. None of them really conceived of their own deaths. It wasn't real.

"And this too shall pass," the Rabbi said.

They thought they would hear a noise, fall, and then, when the smoke settled, they would get up and walk away. Laban was even planning what he would do tomorrow when a bullet interrupted his plans forever...the noisy crowd behind them was resistant and angry and tearful. They refused to leave and had to be forcefully dispersed. When they were gone, they found a flag on the ground, embroidered with a candle.

"Now, they even have a flag," the commandant roared.

"Good! It'll be engraved in their coffins!"

Lazar and Jacob rushed to cradle the rabbi in their arms. The Rebbetzin was moaning and weeping at home.

Jacob suddenly commanded, "Don't him touch, Lazar," the sobbing hysterically, helplessly while he rocked back and forth in such anguish it seemed his little body would break. The men came to prepare the Rabbi. Jacob wouldn't let go. He had to be pulled away by force. At the funeral he occupied a place that was only for the immediate family and remained at the gravesite after everyone left. He kept a lonely vigil night and day for a week, sleeping on the ground and fasting. He returned home looking downcast, haunted. When Lazar approached him, he turned his head, picked up a broom and began sweeping listlessly. Lazar didn't go near him again. For weeks, the only noise in the house were the Rebbetzin's moaning, the children crying and the sound of Jacob's broom. Lazar pondered what to do, drumming on the table. How long could he live on the Rebbetzin's charity?

He heard a gentle tap on the door one day, while meditating in circles as usual. It was Jacob. No longer bowing and grinning.

"May I come in?"

"Come in and close the door."

"I want to tell you a story because I must," he began. "It's been inside for so long, and I trust you," he said. "I trust you to listen and to be kind. I've watched you all these months and I know you'll be kind. Now, I need someone to know. It's too heavy for me to carry any longer."

Lazar was all attention and tender concern.

"Tell me, I'm listening."

"Let me begin from the beginning, so you'll understand. I was the son of a schnorrer, who was the son of a schnorrer. I was a child who never grew so my father could put me to good use for money years beyond my childhood. We stood together, Poppa and I, he was also very small. Who didn't feel sorry for us? We looked like two forlorn children. My father and I were a wonderful team. We'd practice for hours in front of a mirror on all the ways to look sorrowful. We had a list...and some worked better than others. My father insisted I join him...not so much for the money. I was so small that he would rather people have pity on me, then laugh at me. My mother, I don't remember. She was also very tiny. She fell ill one day, and we lost her the next. Just like that."

And he snapped his fingers.

"When I was old enough to think a little about girls: 'Who would have me Poppa?' I said, a schnorrer, the son of a beggar...and so small I'd have to jump into her arms and be lifted to the mouth to kiss her."
'Nonsense,' Poppa said. 'The matchmaker has just the girl for you.'

'What's wrong with her?'

'She has a little pimple on her face.'

'How big?'

'This big.'

The arch grew wider.

'Never!'

'Beggars can't be choosers. You'll marry in the team of Pinsk and soon the team will be dissolved, and you'll struggle in business for yourself.'

That scared me, I'd never been in business alone...without Poppa. The following day the matchmaker was called. He had spoken to the girl's parents. They were glad to find a man. Even me for Minna, the hunchback was deformed, poor girl, since birth...and what's worse... ugly. The schatchen charged half-price which was still overcharging as he didn't have to work even half as hard as he usually did. In fact, he did practically nothing in the way of convincing. 'I have a girl for you,' he told my father. 'I have a man for you,' he told her father. 'Well, half a man, that is.' 'Set the date,' her father said. My father said the same. It was as short and as simple as that before the wedding. But after...I would come home from work from a hard day only to find her waiting for me...eager to please...grateful for my attention. Can you imagine? An excuse for a man, no money, no education, no family...not even a good heart...and she's grateful for my attention. I was stingy. Somehow, I couldn't take money that was put in my hand and put it in hers. But she didn't mind."

His face reddened.

"I'm ashamed to tell you this. Forgive me...but I didn't want her. She was a burden, a responsibility. When she was ill, I left the house with some excuse or other. Somehow, she and a neighbor always managed. She was trouble. I couldn't bear troubles. Poppa cared for me. I liked that. He couldn't stand anyone fussing over him. I liked that too. But she wanted fussing, and I couldn't give it to her. I wanted to be left alone except when I needed care. Then, I'd tolerate her. It made her happy to take care of me, I told myself. And, to my amazement, it did. As long as I walked in the door, she was content. She asked for nothing more. She never dreamed anyone would marry her. Every day she showed me how grateful she was. It went to my head. I tested my power. At times, I became indifferent, intractable for no reason, even tyrannical, sometimes cruel. I frightened even myself. I started questioning myself. Who and what was I? I couldn't stand what I was becoming. But she could, poor thing. I'll never know how. I found myself silently asking her...begging her...to tame me... discipline me...even frighten me a little. But she couldn't. She didn't know how. I don't think it ever occurred to her. I was ten feet fall when I opened the door to my house...and shrunk again the minute I opened the door to leave it. I was a beggar to the world...and she was a beggar to me, for the paltry, miserly scraps of attention, I occasion- ally gave her because I was guilty...just like the scraps given to me... the few kopeks I brought home every day. 'We'll find a way. Life will be better...easier.' And I'd scream, 'That's woman's talk! For us, there is no way. You understand!' And I'd grab her by the neck, shaking her. I wanted to choke her. What I meant was, 'I don't want the burden. I don't want the trouble of finding ways. You're too much already!' She fell back as if I hit her. 'I'm trouble, Jacob? I won't trouble you anymore.' And she humbly bent her head and left the room. Later, when I went to bed, I fell asleep with the sound of her muffled sobs on the pillow.

One day, I remember coming home and, for the first time, she looked almost human to me. Her face had repelled me from the beginning...but you know...a man is a man. She looked like a rabbit...a receding chin, a long nose, two front teeth protruding, a small fore- head, and tiny hands. I sometimes shriveled when they touched me. I always took her in the darkness when she was sleeping, so, God forgive me, I didn't have to look at her. But tonight, there was some- thing special. She had a new tablecloth, candles on the table, fresh flowers.

'Are we having a party?'

'Yes.' And she smiled warmly.

'What's the occasion? Somebody coming?'

'Yes.' Eyes shining, flushed, embarrassed.

'We're going to have a baby.' And she looked at me loving and tender.

'A what?!' I was barely able to breathe. I was so horrified. Her poor face twisted from a small to anxious desperation.

'You don't want a baby?'

And she lay down holding her stomach like it was hearing and she was closing it's little ears.

'Absolutely not! What will we ever do with a baby?'

I wanted to flee...to run...as fast as I could...far away. That night I waited. I heard her heavy breathing, crept silently out of the house after packing a small bag. I couldn't write, so there was no note.

I could make a living anywhere. A beggar takes his business with him wherever he goes. His face and his hands had plenty of patience and no pride. I wandered from town to town. No one told me anyone was looking for me. It was strange, I thought, letting me go...just like that. Well, you see, you never can tell. Years passed. Lonely, terrible years. I had a small taste of home, and I must admit, I began to miss it. And my child. Whatever happened to him...or maybe...her? I'd had a scribe write to my father. He wrote back, 'You are no longer my son. I am no longer your father.'

Ten years passed. Twenty. I was the wandering boarder...a room in good days, the streets in bad...the day came when I could stand it no longer and I returned to Suvalk. First, to my father. I passed the corner where we stood together for years. There was another couple there...father and son. I approached them.

'Do you know Pinsky? Pinsky the schnorrer?'

'Yes,' they said. 'We bought this corner from him. Best corner in town. Near the funeral home. The mourners are reminded they may be next...so they give.'

'Where is he living now? Do you know?! I've been out of town so long I lost touch.'

The one with the bent leg and the crutch looked around to see if anyone was coming. No one. He straightened his leg, pulled a piece of paper out of the cuff, and wrote. Beggars could write! I was amazed.

He told me, 'I went to the university, came back and there was nothing to do to make a living.'

I found the address. Poppa was still a boarder, as always...it was a shock to see him after all those years, gray, almost blind, carrying a cane for real. We cried, embraced each other. He had forgotten our argument. Almost forgot me. We talked on and on. His mind wandered. At times, he called me by another name.

'What happened to Tovah?'

'Tovah? Who is Tovah?'

'My wife. Your daughter-in-law.'

'Tovah,' he said, 'poor Tovah. She had a son and lost her mind. She wears a pillow under her skirt as if she were pregnant, eats from garbage pails, sometimes she steals. The shopkeeper knows she's stealing but they turn their backs. She wanders from town to town.'

'How can I find her?'

'You can't. she hides in her room, just runs out to find food, and disappears again.'

I was never as small as I felt then. A twisted ball of shame inside.

'And the child?'

'They gave him to a prominent Rabbi who educated him and raised him well. He's a prominent Rabbi himself, now.'

'Where?'

'Here in Suvalk.'

I had to see him, to be near him, to tend to him. To make up for all the years I'd shunned him. And Tovah, I want to find her too."

Jacob shuddered. He had to admit he didn't want to find her. He didn't want that kind of trouble.

"My God," Lazar exploding, "The Rabbi was your son! Why didn't you tell him?"

"I didn't want him to be ashamed of me...a schnorrer for a father."

Chapter Twenty-Six

Laban's voice was that of a dead man. He was the only one who talked. The others sat huddled against the wall...their hands around their knees, their heads bowed, like they were about to be born...but they knew they were dying. There was nothing left but their bodies. A man is dead when he leaves his dreams behind a jail door. That's all that's left is to bury him. The only comfort after the numbness...self-pity and martyrdom. Laban was now, mercifully numb. I have no strength to talk but I'll tell you, you have a right to know.

Sadly, philosophically, the rabbi repeating, "We were all ready." And he pictured, in home after home, a pair of trembling hands lighting their little candle, and the army of candles growing as each left his home and joined the others, the comradery and numbers allaying their fears. Someone would be singing, and the others would join in...and they would all feel and look invincible. Laban told his story. Pyotor and Ivan were spies.

"You wanted to use them, didn't you, Rabbi?" Laban smirking.

"Yes, but not betray them."

The mass march the rabbi envisaged did not happen that night. A few brave and foolhardy men marched in front of the town halls in a small circle round and round...all Jews. No one noticed the Christians were strangely absent. They found an excuse and stayed home. A flicker here and there. Heaven was not impressed.

In the confined little cell, each man chose a spot where he could be <u>alone</u>. When he was sitting there, no one spoke to him. He needed his few moments of <u>privacy</u>.

In one of those moments, looking at Laban, the Rabbi couldn't contain himself. He sprung up.

"Tell me, Laban, are you sure the country was ready to join us in a mass march?" He emphasized the word, mass. "I have to know...if it was worth it..." a despairing look around, "to come to this."

"Of course." Laban reassuring. "Don't we have enough problems? Do you have to look for them under the rug?" He looked wryly at the bare floor.

"That's nothing new, Rabbi...that the likes of you did very little looking at the likes of me...you left me to do the dirty work while you were content with consulting. I'm consulting you again, Rabbi. What do we do now?"

"I have to understand first what I have done before I can figure out what to do..."

It was true the Rabbi thought he had been lazy, above a battle in which he was, or, thought he was...the central figure. He left the details to Laban, conflicts, personality clashes, obstructions. The Rabbi was inspired, but Laban perspired...with recrimination to please his God...me. The rabbi had never realized his power before. Laban, a dangerous man...who could still be cowed by his need for praise. 'Just like me...the Warsaw Rabbi. Solomon was right...but... there is vanity with a mission and vanity without one...the Rebbetzin was vanity without one. Laban was vanity with one. The Rebbetzin's vanity destroyed him slowly and his own and Laban's completed the job.

Laban was a more serious contender than the Warsaw Rabbi. He lived in the world. The rabbi lived with words...Laban lived with people, fought with them, commanded them, manipulated them. The rabbi couldn't even handle his own wife. Every day, Laban struggled with the world. The rabbi struggled with the world. The rabbi struggled with himself. Laban lived in a world of words without experience. To him, the world was an idea. It was not difficult to make the brief trip from the world as an idea to the movement.

"You tell me," The Rabbi said to Laban, "what do we do now?" And he meant it.

"No, you're the man of ideas. You're just tired."

The Rabbi was the perfect foil for Laban. He needed him to depend on, even to scorn or deceive, but he must lead. Laban had to feel he had a leader...to keep his fear at bay. If he differed with him, fought with him, was even indifferent to him, it was all right. As long as he was <u>there</u>. The rabbi had performed that one function for Laban, unbeknownst to him. He was <u>there</u>. Laban really didn't need much else from him, though he pretended he did.

Laban would call him after all the meetings, the frantic rushing about from one town leader to another, the shouting...was over. The conflicts, the clashes...the rabbi knew none of this. Above all...the risks. Laban needed the rabbi for praise, approval, recognition, or to reconfirm his sense of security. Laban enjoyed the battles. He was a man of war. He shared none of this with the rabbi whom he gave the illusion of authority to please him when necessary. Part of him couldn't tolerate the rabbi but he would be terribly lonely without him. He needed the rabbi as a leader on his own terms. He seldom examined himself, searching for motives. He considered it too confusing...but now he had too much time and couldn't help it. He could really revere no one. Was too realistic for that. But he needed a father...a friend...that he took for granted...that he could ask what to do and then give himself the answer. But he couldn't take this...the rabbi asking <u>him</u> what to do. Laban wanted to, at least, do the asking. In this area, the revolutionaries demanded a status quo.

"You forgot, Rabbi, I ask you and you ask God."

"I can't ask him, Laban."

"You can't ask me, either."

"There was to be a trial, and a lawyer was needed. 'Who would defend them?' Even a trial needs a 'show of defense.'"

After two days incommunicado, the jailer announced a visitor for the Rabbi. He was not up to visitors. His stomach ached. He'd spent a sleepless night worrying about the Rebbetzin and the children, he was still in shock, dazed in the sudden shift from life to death. He was led to a small room. At a table, a thin, spectacled, serious young man with an arrogant importance of the newly arrived professional. His whole face, a studied mannerism. The rabbi thought he looked like a lawyer. His head was slightly bent to the left, his long, bony fingers searching for a paper in his briefcase...shiny new. He didn't look up 'til his search was completed, and thought he knew he'd come in. He pulled out a paper and turned to the rabbi.

"My name is Burchkoff, I'm your lawyer," he said, without extending a hand. "Be seated."

The rabbi sat down.

"I'm your counsel, assigned by the state," and his nostrils flared as if he were smelling something evil.

"I will plead you guilty, of course, and throw you on the mercy of the state."

"Guilty of what?"

"Of instigating an insurrection, rebelling against the state, in short, Revolution!"

His face purple with rage. The rabbi could see the veins in the forehead. His nose, red from too much drinking, had little veins converging on the tip that almost made the rabbi laugh but he controlled himself thinking, 'A man who takes himself that seriously has no sense of humor.'

"What evidence do you have?"

"Evidence! Two God-fearing Christians have admitted everything."

"That's evidence! We're Jews. Have Jews admitted anything?"

"Jews don't have to. We know they're plotters."

"But do you have any concrete evidence?"

"This is a Christian court of law. We have faith in our God-fearing Christians to tell the truth."

"Well, I don't. and I will defend myself and the others..."

"You will have a fool for a lawyer!"

"Better a Jewish fool than a Christian fool."

"Guard! Remove the prisoner!"

A cold rage filled with command, the rabbi thinking as they led him away. 'He would be a good sergeant in the Czar's army. He likes to strut, pose, command, shout orders and he's stupid. And I...with the Jewish brains...to what avail? He's out...and I'm in.'

Now that he said he'd defend himself, he regretted it. 'What do I know about defending myself? I couldn't even do a good job of it with the Rebbetzin. But then...what other choice was there?'

The others leaped on him with questions and concluded, 'We're doomed, what's the use?'

Laban, excited by the prospect of a coming battle pressing, "What's the use! Do you want to die the way you've lived!"

It was true. They never had a choice how they would live but they were determined now to have a choice how they would die.

"Let's stir them up a little," they said. "Let's show them we can make trouble for them even from here. They put us into corners in the Pale and we weren't quiet. Let's show them they can put us into an even tighter corner and we're still not quiet. The tighter the corner, the more noise we'll make. They huddled and whispered for days...planning.

The night before the trial no one slept. They awakened each other, some crying, some trembling, comfortless, lonely, anguished crying of lost and frightened children. They couldn't go to the Rabbi. He was with them. The age-old comforter was himself in need of comfort. At times, he cried and trembled and moaned, 'why me?'... more than the rest. Even Laban, found himself in the palm of the hand of the state, its fingers around his throat, and broke down and cried, "Momma help me!" Against this might stood the state. They were ashamed of themselves for their weakness. The state was not ashamed of itself for the it's strength.

Laban had cut the state down to size in his imagination. The state had enlarged him in theirs. It might be said that Laban was foolish; the state was mad. The following day there would be a trial; foolishness prosecuted by madness.

They were all awake early, eyes red, bleary, hesitating to leave the cell for the blare of the outside. They were carried through the streets in a wagon...a show for the public. On exhibit...the state as power...the Jew as menace. As they were led into the courtroom, some jeered, some were grimly silent and exchanged meaningful glances with them. The rabbi thought, 'We have friends out there. We'll have more when it's over. It's almost worth it already.'

The proceedings began. The prosecutor read the indictment. The rabbi asked who would be representing the defendants and declared himself defender.

"So be it," the judge said.

The prosecutor called the two witnesses, Pyotor and Ivan. They said they'd seen the rabbi twice, three times, described the plan, the propaganda. The state rested its case.

"Tell me," the Rabbi asking Ivan, "What was the plan?"

"To have a march of candles."

"Were there any guns? Did anyone carry a weapon? Did we have a gun in one head, a candle in the other?"

"No, but this was to be the beginning of an armed revolution."

"Who said so?"

"Laban."

"Your honor, the witness is only talking about what could have been...what he heard...there is not even a shred of evidence that a march was being planned."

Pyotor came to the stand and repeated Ivan's story.

The rabbi asked him, "What evidence do you have that a march was planned?"

He pulled out a three-cornered triangle with a bent edge.

"This," and he smiled. "Isn't this the way messages were sent to you from Laban? Why the secrecy if there was nothing to hide?"

The Judge interrupts, "Let me ask you, what was that?"

"I don't know. I've never seen it before. Is a three-cornered paper enough to make a revolution?"

The rabbi saw a cloud of suspicion on the judge's face. He didn't believe him. The judge knew conspirators were always careful not to write anything. The rabbi knew suspicion was enough to convict in this court of <u>law</u>.

Then, the prosecutor rose and called witnesses; Christian after Christian describing the march, detail for detail.

"How did they know?" the Rabbi asked, "Were they also part of the plan?"

"No. they were guarding themselves against a Jewish plot."

The rabbi could only throw himself on the mercy of the court. But the court had no mercy. And he didn't want to throw himself at the feet of Christians, anyway. They would do enough of that themselves. He didn't have to help them.

The judge addressed the rabbi.

"Have you anything to say?"

"Do I have your permission to say what I want to?" he asked the others.

They nodded wearily. "What difference does it make?"

"Your honor," he began, "I am not an eloquent man, so I ask you to bear with me while I state, not of a march, your honor. That's the least of my crimes. I am guilty of ambition and naivete. I wanted to enter your world. Mine was too small for me and I thought we could trust those who suffered our afflictions. Together we could make a better world. My crime was not against your people. My crime was against my own...that I trusted the Ivans and Pyotors...so their hungry bellies could betray ours. I thought if the Ivans and Pyotors lived with us, ate with us, fought with us, they couldn't help but see us as real people...not love us...I don't ask for that...but see we don't have horns. That was what this march was all about, your honor...brotherhood!

We thought we could help them and ourselves...and incidentally, the Czar...because if things keep going the way they are, the people will be holding a gun instead of a candle. If men can light their way to betterment, they won't resort to shooting their way in. a man only kicks down a door when he knocks and gets no answer." The rabbi's voice rising now, "raps louder and gets no answer, shouts and screams and begs," the rabbi desperate, shouting now, "and gets no answer! I rest my case."

He collapsed against the rail, pale and exhausted. The judge responds, firm, cold, disinterested, "Sentence will be imposed tomorrow. Bailiff, remove the prisoner!"

The rabbi collapsed and was carried from the courtroom. He slept until the morning. The others, exhausted from a desperate day, collapsed with him.

In the morning, they attacked him. Why had he said what he said? He was right. He was wrong. They were quarrelsome and argumentative; frightened men attacking each other. Who else was there?

Chapter Twenty-Seven

Lazar awoke the following morning, opened his sleepy eyes, then, startled, open them wider. The pillow next to him was empty. He looked down and saw the blanket in a little heap beside him. He gently raised the blanket and peeked under it. He could see her snuggly curled...like a little kitten. He tenderly tucked her in again in her little retreat, feeling strangely like he opened a door that said, 'Do Not Enter.' He crooked his arm on his pillow, his hand under his cheek and gazed tenderly at the blanket moving up and down with her breathing, and calmly thinking, 'my wife.' She wasn't so frightening now that she was just a little heap under a blanket, and he didn't have to imagine, when he looked into her eyes, that they were mocking him, or anxiously wonder what she was thinking of him.

Unbeknownst to him, she had opened her eyes. Through a fold in the blanket, she could see the chair. He had carelessly thrown his jacket over it the night before. She spoke silently to the jacket. She knew he was awake, could feel his eyes watching her.

"How should I greet you this morning?" she asked the jacket. It was her first morning as a bride.

"I can't hide under the jacket all day," she told the jacket. Lazar saw the heap turning again towards him, her head still under the blanket. He felt her hand reaching for him, He took her hand in his and guided it around him. With the other, he pulled the blanket over his head and found her mouth in the darkness.

In their little shelter, hidden even from each other's eyes, they found the courage to let their secrets be known to each other.

The following day, the house was in turmoil. Visitors were expected and the Rebbetzin was screaming at Mendel. Nothing had been done in weeks. The Rebbetzin saw schmutz* everywhere. Despite death and disaster, the Rebbetzin was embarrassed if the house was not spic and span when the important guests arrived.

During the shiva period, she was in a kind of daze. People came and went. She hardly saw or heard them. The first sign of recovery was when she moved a candy dish on the buffet table and found, heaven forbid, a circle.

"Mendel, this place is a mess!"

Mendel was relieved to hear her screaming. It meant she was improving. He was concerned about his grandchildren. Throughout the years, they loved the games he played with them with his rags and brooms. He would dance with the broom like it was a lady, makes cats and dogs with his fingers in the rags. He even had names for the raggedy puppets. Mendel took the children aside and told them their father went far away and answered their innocent questions as best as he could. The Rebbetzin was too distraught to comfort them. 'Left a widow so young,' she repeated over and over. Mendel was so busy comforting her and the children, he neglected his duties.

"I'm coming," Mendel said, rag in hand and swished an arc.

'Clean like a mirror.' She continued berating him, nevertheless. He let her go on. It relieved her so.

The Warsaw Rabbi was coming with his wife and her parents. Mendel was grateful that the Rebbetzin could distract herself with

---

* ***Schmutz – Dust***

chores. After all, they'd helped him to distract himself. He'd advanced a little in life from schnorrer to servant, he told himself. At least now, he earned his keep even though he had to ask for his few kopeks every week. The Rebbetzin was forgetful when she had to part with money, but remembered well when it was coming to her.

"You pay for what you break," she told Mendel, his first day in the house.

He had her make a list of everything that was broken already, so he wouldn't be charged for breaks she'd forgotten were there. The things he broke throughout the years were instantly removed from his pay.

The few minutes before the Warsaw Rabbi arrived were fraught with tension. Nothing was right. The Rebbetzin moved chairs to and fro, checked the soup, the flanken. When they finally arrived, she greeted them calmly, without a hint of what transpired before. She had an appropriate expression on her face, sad, a few tears, suffering... but brave. They all rushed to comfort, commiserate, and praise her courage. The praise continued throughout the dinner. The meal was excellent, she looked well in spite of her ordeal, her father was hovering, apologetic, obsequious...tortured by his thoughts. What had he done to his daughter! Married her to a man who was a poor provider, a foolish dreamer, and, above all, a non-believer, masquerading as a believer, who was punished for his sins and brought his daughter down to disgrace with him...then...left her alone, a widow with children. Didn't he think of his family when he was busy with his wild ideas? And he answered his own questions. A man with wild ideas doesn't think of family, like a man in love. Who can reason with him?

Lazar sat quietly throughout the meal, the Warsaw Rabbi looking at him very hard. He was an impressive looking man himself. A long, black beard, deep set eyes, a forehead lined eyes questioning and impatient...a man thinking and rethinking and a heart that felt deeply for everyone. The Rebbetzin; kindly, maternal, generous...reflective too and intelligent. She had studied in the university, knew several languages...but had no airs. Everyone was welcome in her home...day and night. They stayed as long as they wished, and she always said they were leaving too soon. Students came from all over to study with the rabbi and she was mother and friend to all of them. After dinner, the Warsaw Rabbi approached Lazar.

"I want to talk to you alone."

With that, he turned, and Lazar followed him into the rabbi's study. It was the first time he's been there since the rabbi was gone.

"I'll be brief and to the point. I know everything that happened, but I want you to tell me."

"Why?"

"Because I have a good reason. Trust me."

Lazar told him what he knew, the planned march of the candles, the betrayal by the goyim*.

"That's all foolishness! There was no such plan. A few stragglers here and there...but the whole country!"

"But Laban said there were groups across the country ready to march!"

"Laban lied."

"How do you know?"

"Because we have our own meshuga† in town. They came to us for a good meal, a warm bed, and they talk, and I listen. Me...they think they can trust. The leader I see every day. One day he tells me Laban is propagandizing for a mass march, but it'll never get off the ground. A few fools will be out there, but from what I hear, he'll be lucky if he has a minion‡. He told me we'll get more by saying it'll be a mass turnout. He insisted we try."

"You know what that trying will mean."

"Yes, martyrs. We need them."

"But why should Laban lie?"

---

* ***Goyim – Christians***
† ***Meshuga – Crazies***
‡ ***Minion – Ten people***

"To impress the Rabbi with his accomplishment and because he was impatient. Martyrs would relieve him of years of waiting."

"But why didn't you warn the Rabbi?"

"I didn't know he was involved. He was so secretive with me. Afraid I'd take a piece of glory away from him if I knew."

"But why did the goyim betray him?"

"They saw no future with Laban and a future suddenly opening for them with the state...for their services. In yesterday's papers...for distinguished service to the state, Pyotor and Ivan are awarded positions in the Ministry of Culture."

"What position? They couldn't read or write. Probably bootblacks...for which they're well suited. They can clean boots with their tongues forever. But how could the Rabbi have been so foolish? So naïve? The Rabbi was a dreamer, I know...a passionate one. Wasn't God enough...or Zion?"

"I shouldn't tell you this, Lazar, but I will. We all chipped away at those dreams, heaven help me, even God. The Rebbetzin would compare him to me, he would compare himself with me, and I did nothing to balance the scale. I enjoyed the favorable comparison. It pleased me that she thought me to be more handsome, brilliant, accomplished, smarter, wiser.

It embittered him. Somehow, he remained a child in relation to God. He asked questions and wasn't rewarded, what was the sense of being good? He became ambitious. He had to reach the top of the mountain with a passion and love what he found when he got there. The Rebbetzin and he, as you probably know, had no life together. She spurned him for years. The Rabbi was a passionate man. His passions had nowhere to go. The Idea was all he had left. And the passions are blind and foolish. That's their nature if they're bound to a wild idea. And me, too, I also chipped away at him."

"What do you mean?"

"He wanted a son, and I insisted on remaining a boarder. That was another foolish dream. A boy can't come in from the street and become your son. We can't pick up sons by chance. Hundreds of students have visited me, lived with me. Do I have an army of sons!"

"Was the Rabbi mad?"

"Yes, he had the Jewish madness; a curious mixture of egotistical ambition, foolish romantic idealism, incalculable naivete and an unhappy wife...a dangerous combination."

"But I want to do the same thing, Rabbi. I want to change the world."

"You mean you've learned nothing from all of this?"

"I've learned...you can't trust the goyim."

"Then you've learned something...very important. These are considered <u>enlightened times</u>...in simple language meaning...trust the goyim. The rabbi said we have to join the others. They must be wondering what we're doing here for so long."

The rabbi turned to Lazar, "Would you like to come with us, study with me?"

Stunned...he could only nod.

"We'll leave tomorrow. Mendel will stay and help the Rebbetzin. A quick parting and on with the boy's life," the rabbi explained later. "Or he would sink into self-pity and remorse. We'll never be able to pull him out of it. It can become a way of life, brooding, and asking... why me?"

Lazar brightened but guilty...realizing he would be glad to leave the Rebbetzin and her noisy children. But he would miss Mendel for a little while. The future held some promise now. He was anxious to start moving again.

The following morning, packing his belongings, sadness, closing the door to an empty room. When he came down to breakfast, they were all at the table, absorbed in the details of moving, and glad to be. The wagon picked them up at the door a while later. Everyone hastily grabbed their belongings.

Lazar lingering. "Hurry up, Lazar. They won't wait for us," the Rabbi was shouting.

"I'm coming," but he didn't budge.

Softly to the Rebbetzin, "I hope you remember me kindly, and, maybe someday, we'll see each other again in better times."

He had rehearsed that speech. He didn't really care how she remembered him and never really wanted to see her again. But after all, she was in mourning. He addressed his speech to her sadness.

"I know you don't really mean that," a wry smile, "but I'm glad you said it."

He turned swiftly, acutely embarrassed to be discovered and fled out the door.

Chapter Twenty-Eight

It's always a wrench to tear yourself from the familiar. Lazar looked out the window lost in his own reverie, daydreaming. He couldn't remember when he had done that. He hadn't had any time or inclination. He guessed the inclination came with time. The others talked and mercifully left him to himself. They passed a fallen tree in the middle of a gently sloping valley. It disturbed the symmetry of the landscape, jagged, torn, where it was broken, flowing and graceful where it wasn't.

Lazar thinking, 'just like me.' He could feel the jagged edges, the hardness in him, the discontent, the rage. He'd been broken many times...away from dear ones and those not so dear. The breaks left their mark. How many more were waiting for him? One is never really prepared for them. It was a balmy day, gentle winds caressing delicate flowers and waving grass. Everything seemed fragile, pliable, color everywhere, nature generous and giving. Lazar was content to see it at a distance. It was safe that way. Nature was devious, he thought. You come too close, and you find the predators waiting. Maybe there's a lesson in that. But then, again he thought, there is time enough for lessons and he willfully snapped his mouth shut and let his eyes feat undisturbed as far as he could see.

"Warsaw," the Rabbi said, "we're almost there, Lazar."

In the corner, someone had drawn a small candle. Mercifully, Lazar didn't see it. The outskirts of the city; houses like any other. Then...Warsaw! More than Lazar had ever imagined. Tall buildings, more people than he'd ever seen, well-dressed, urbane, sophisticated. Lazar looked at the suit the Rabbi bought him and was ashamed. Then he was ashamed. The wagon stopped.

The Rabbi grabbed bags, "Let's go!"

Lazar rushed in behind him and stopped inside the drawer as if a hand had suddenly descended on his shoulder. He stood in awe, silent respect of things...not God now...but rugs, silver, shining mahogany furniture, soft chairs.

"I'll show you your room."

Lazar stood outside the room and looked in without daring to step inside.

"This is mine!"

"Who else? Go in, Lazar. There's nothing that will jump out and bite you."

Lazar rubbed his hand over the satin spreads and drapes, the night table, the desk, the bookcase full of books...just to make sure it was real.

"This was my son's room. It's yours now. He's married and gone, but we kept his room as it was."

The rabbi closed the door quietly behind him. Lazar sat down on the bed, careful at first to roll back the green satin cover and stared at the desk unbelieving. His own desk, his own room, the soft under his foot...a rug. While he was musing, the Rabbi and the Rebbetzin were planning his future. They had even decided when and whom he would marry. The last was very important. Lazar needed his own home. He'd wandered long enough. He was attracted to wild ideas because he wasn't settled. A rolling stone picks up anything that sticks to it. He was still a hobo.

"A rich hobo," said the Rebbetzin, "but still a hobo."

The bedspread, the desk, someone else's. Lazar had nothing of his own. He needs something of his own. A wife, and if God's will, a family. He can't adopt them willy-nilly as they fall from the skies on his way through life. Too many such families have dropped on his head already.

"I'll discuss it with him tomorrow."

"Wait a few mornings. He'll think you're trying to get rid of him."

"You're right," and never one to waste time, "tomorrow, we start learning."

The Rebbetzin compromised. She knew <u>something</u> had to happen tomorrow.

The rabbi forgot about the *shidduch** as he taught Lazar. The boy was a wonder. He enjoyed his quick mind. 'Not a genius like me, but quick, alert, searching.' He thought.

Then, one day, the rabbi asked, "Let me hear you sing."

No one had ever asked him that before. He panicked. His mouth opened. Nothing.

"You have to do something besides open your mouth. You can sing. Everybody can. Especially the ones with no voice. They sing the loudest. Come, Lazar, sing loud in a bad voice. I even like bad singing."

"What do you want me to sing?" Lazar stalling, "I don't know Rabbi. If I want to be a rabbi or a revolutionary."

"It's easy to be a revolutionary who knows nothing or a scholar who does nothing. But a man who knows and does...that's difficult. First, you'll know and then you'll decide. A carpenter has to learn first how to drive a nail before he builds a house. A revolution is more than carrying a flag, singing and polemic. You can't bang nails when the impulse hits you, just for the pleasure of banging."

"What do you believe in after years of study?"

------

* ***Shidduch – Marriage***

"I don't want to influence you. I'll tell you after I'm sure you've made up your own mind. Sing Ofyn Pripitchuk."

Lazar knew that simple song from childhood. He drifted off to sleep with it many a night. He took a deep breath, looking very solemn, stood up, started off key softly, then, blasting ponderously the next few words, he sang louder and louder, faster, and faster, the nervousness pushing him on and on, out of control. The more he tried to impress the rabbi, the more ludicrous he became...stentorian tones bellowing forth in a grand manner. The rabbi couldn't contain himself. He burst out laughing. Lazar was mortified. He started fleeing to the door. The rabbi grabbed his hand.

"I told you I couldn't sing!" Tears bursting.

The rabbi struggled to control himself. "Ofyn Pripitchuk is not an opera. But that's beside the point. You have an excellent voice. But you don't know what to do with it. The chosen will teach you. Now I have to go."

He rose brusquely, Lazar walked out of the room in a happy daze, bounded up the stairs to his room, would have floated out the window onto a passing cloud and beyond if he could. He could now say he was a <u>singer</u>!

A year passed. The students came and went. The house was always full and ringing with their endless debates. Sometimes, he would join the group as a listener, but he was always on guard against himself. He could so easily become enamored of an idea. After a brief courtship, he fell passionately in love with it and was hurtled into a dream. He often wondered about the Jewish leap from words to dreams...and then...to visions. Millennia of disappointed visions from high sounding words and they were still trusting the words and the vision.

One morning he awoke very distraught. He realized he hadn't dreamed about Basha for several months. Did something happen to her? Was she gone? He tried to remember when he last dreamed of her, he couldn't. Those dreams frightened him when he had them but despaired him more when he didn't. After all, what else did he have left of her?

He heard a knock at the door. The servant with a message.

"The Rabbi wants to see you."

The rabbi was in study with a stranger.

"Lazar, I want you to meet Sergei Deitch."

The stranger was young, impeccably dressed, confident, strong face, immaculately trimmed beard, peering eyes that stared coldly. Lazar nodded slightly as he was introduced.

"Solomon is visiting us from Moscow. He's here to study with me. He'll be staying in the room next to you."

Lazar was suddenly aware he felt intimidated. Solomon was rich. His family had to bribe the officials so they could remain in Moscow. He was the son of a rich merchant. Lazar heard they usually spent their days on a horse at balls. 'What was he doing here?'

That night, Lazar left his books early and joined the group. He'd heard Solomon leaving his room, so he decided to follow. There ensued a heated discussion about the coming of the Messiah, why He wasn't coming, the Jewish sins that prevented his coming...Solomon growing increasingly impatient...even angry.

Lazar daring to ask, "What do you think, Solomon?"

For some reason, he feared his contempt.

"What sins!" Solomon exploding, his detachment suddenly disappearing and a passionate orator declaring now, "Aren't you more sinned against, than sinning? And can't the tyrant always depend on your being so busy condemning yourself that you have little time and energy left to condemn him! We don't even have the brains to learn from the animals. Have you ever seen a cat wait for his master, counting its good deeds and repenting for the bad ones when a dog appears? No! it runs to safety or attacks when it's cornered! It doesn't just sit there with a book and wait to be saved. A wolf runs with its own, hunts with its own, attacks with its own. It doesn't sit among lions and wait for deliverance. The Christians run in packs and each pack has its own name. They're very careful to guard the demarcation point which each pack must not cross and if they do, they fight like the devil to get those few inches back that belong to them. But we sit like little puppies amongst the wolves, grateful they pass only snarling or biting...without devouring. And if they devour us, we count our sins, instead of theirs or we try to copy their ways, a few of us wearing wolves' clothing, biting, and snarling. This makes them even more furious. Arrogance is never permissible in a little man. The rulers always consider their exclusive domain. Don't you see! We have to make our own pack, out own line, and we have to stand at that line with our fangs bared."

Lazar exclaimed, "Where do we put that line?"

"In the promised land. In Zion, of course. Where else?"

The others joined in. There were so many interruptions...

The rabbi interrupted, "Time for bed."

They all left for their rooms; Lazar followed Solomon into his. They continued to talk...in whispers; Lazar astounded at the neatness; not a book out of place. He wondered, too, how Solomon, the impeccably spoiled rich man had become so angry. He'd thought only the poor were angry because they were hungry.

Solomon explained, "My eyes opened when I left home on business. I had a Russian name. They didn't know I was Jewish. I was invited to wealthy homes where Grace was said. I didn't bend my head. The invitations ceased...in country after country. I accepted, as a fact, Russian barbarism, but Germany, France...the homes of culture, philosophy, music. I came home an angry man and isolated myself to think...which was for me...a rare experience. Culture, I realized, had nothing to do with hate. The rich delivered the message with polite but searing indifference or used our brain, then the poor beat our heads in."

"But don't we betray our own, too?"

"Better to be betrayed by our own. At least, we can protect our innocence. The state uses and abuses but takes care, too."

But Lazar was still not satisfied with Serge's argument. 'How does a broken weed, floating on a perilous river, driven here and there and bending with the tide, turn into a dagger hacking its way through a jungle, determined, purposive, firm...to draw his line?' Lazar felt the excitement of a new dream...but with the responsibility of a heavy and burdensome task, the guilt already settled on his shoulders. If Serge was right, he should be there in Zion, instead of resting comfortably in the rabbi's bed at night and poring comfortably over his books by day. He was still bloodied from the last encounter and already, another one facing him. 'Was he such a naïve fool?' he asked himself. One tirade and his head was already turned.

"But isn't it hard for the comfortable to be pioneers?"

"I don't know, but I have to."

And Lazar knew he had to, too. Dreams and visions, needing to suffer and sacrifice swept over all the doubts and questions.

"You're not really here to study, are you, Serge?"

"Not really."

"A propagandist. I attract them somehow."

"Well," extending his hand, "I think you have one follower. I'll discuss it with the Rabbi tomorrow."

"Don't."

"Why?"

"The Rabbi had heard these discussions many times. He doesn't like the definite ideas falling out of untutored heads. He doesn't want to lead fools. When the time is ripe and the Rabbi thinks you've learned enough to make sense, he'll discuss it with you. I know because I've asked him. Right now, the Promised Land is sitting on your desk. Every day your job is to draw the line further than the distance you traveled in those pages the day before."

"But you're impatient."

"Yes, but humoring the Rabbi is one of the hurdles I have to pass. There'll be many more after him."

He wondered now whether he was convinced because he was

ready or ready because he was convinced...but too weary for further thinking and rethinking. He bid his friend goodnight and yawned all the way to his bed where he collapsed with his clothes on and woke a committed Zionist...fervent and proud just thinking of the hardships he would valiantly endure.

Chapter Twenty-Nine

A year passed. Two. Lazar grew into manhood. He was very impressive, tall, well built, black fiery eyes, large bony face and generous mouth, a full black beard that parted in the middle. He looked like an angry prophet even when he wasn't. The day came when the rabbi announced him ready for the pulpit. A small shul needed a rabbi...Lazar consented gladly. What greater compliment than the Rabbi should think he was ready.

And the rabbi concluded, "I have a shidduch for you. With a girl," he stammered.

"What else? A horse?"

The rabbi smiled. "I didn't mean that."

"I know you didn't."

"Who is she?"

"From a good family. The father is a tailor, and works hard. She is what you need, a homemaker, a good cook, honest, clean, and hard-working."

Lazar wanted to ask, 'is she pretty?' but he didn't. The rabbi would think him frivolous.

"I will arrange a meeting," the rabbi said, "I don't like introductions under her canopy. She and her parents will be here tomorrow night for one hour so you can get to know each other."

Reb Pinsky had four sons and two daughters. His wife was pregnant, it seems, continuously, since they married, but only six children survived. The oldest daughter Celia was a 'good girl' which means she worked like a slave without complaining. She bossed the younger children with an iron hand so they wouldn't upset their mother in her 'delicate condition.' Since Momma was always in a 'delicate condition,' she gave Celia a free hand. So, Celia raged at them continuously, not realizing she was upsetting her mother herself. But they kept their hands out of mischief because they were always covering their ears with them. When Momma discovered she could no longer become pregnant due to a complication from the last one, she decided it was time Celia married.

"Let her marry already," Momma said, "I can't stand anymore of her screaming. Besides, the younger ones can already take her place. Thirteen is enough already to be in the house."

Until the meeting, the rabbi continued to impress on Lazar, Celia's virtues.

"Well built, a good bearer of children. Modern women were too flighty and lazy; their heads in books that twist their minds, their faces in mirrors that turned their heads; too thin, spoiled to make a good home for a man. Celia was perfect."

They arrived on time. The matchmaker, a small man with a pointy beard that he rubbed when he calculated as if it helped him to count, small quick eyes that dated from one to the other to assess progress or lack of it. He had tiny fingers on which he calculated with the speed of lightning and the obsequious smile of a man bent on making a sale.

Lazar arose when the prospective bride and her father entered. He dared to glance at her briefly before she looked at him. She had long brown hair tied in a bun at the back and one braid around her head. Her face was round and soft, her eyes blue and tender. She was a little heavy, but he liked what he saw. She seemed shy and, he thought, malleable. Reb Pinsky didn't recognize his own daughter. Was this blushing flower the same screamer he'd heard just a moment ago? Momma, too, was stunned, but didn't show it. They had never seen this side of Celia. They were also introduced to someone new.

The rabbi said, "We'll leave them to talk a little."

They all left except for the Rebbetzin who sat in between them. Lazar stared into space, crossed, and uncrossed his legs, felt himself blushing from tip to toe. 'A revolutionary afraid of a girl!' He had paid them no attention until now.

She stared in the opposite direction. Suddenly being overcome with shyness was a surprise even to her. She had commanded a family only this morning and was now asking herself a dozen frightening questions she'd never thought of. Did she think she was pretty? Her eyes, her hair, her hands. She was suddenly conscious of her broken nails and hid them.

Like a small child, who, a moment before the stranger comes, is disobeying its mother, or arrogantly commanding its younger brother...is suddenly hiding its face in its mother's apron when a stranger says, "Hello."

Lazar had read thousands of words. Not one came to his rescue. He stared at her dumbly...the silence aching.

Suddenly both heads turned to the Rebbetzin and in unison, "Rebbetzin, do you think the sun will come out?"

The Rebbetzin smiled, "I'm sure it will. I know it will."

They both returned to staring into space, stricter than ever. He was thinking, 'is that all she thinks I can say?' and Celia thinking miserably, 'is that all she thinks I can say?' They both expected the other to graciously decline. But Lazar wanted her the most as he thought she was turning from him. It unnerved him so to look at her hat he couldn't even search her face for a sign. And she...despairing now, certain that there would be...no shidduch.

The rabbi burst in with the other, returning to what looked like a shiva ceremony. Both sets of eyes were riveted to the rabbi.

"Come children. We've set the date!"

She looked up and smiled. Lazar too looked up, hesitant at first, then joined her in a smile. Lazar, sent for his grandparents, his only family now.

Under the canopy, he was trembling. She was calm. He hoped their life would be like Basha's and Benjamin's...warm and peaceful. He didn't notice a face peering at them, bulging eyes, twisted, smiled, flaming redhead band, a flower in her hand. After the ceremony, she hastily put the flower on the stoop and fled.

No one noticed it as they went into the hall to dance. Lazar, young and flying now...one with the music. But the dance ended. Time to go home. He started trembling again. Going home...to be a husband. He'd never known a woman before.

The shul was not ready yet. They thought it would be but there were unexpected delays. They would have to stay with the rebbe for a few more days. As they left the hall, he spotted the flower, gently picked it up and handed it to his new bride...and she pressed to her bosom...grateful. They went silently up the stairs to his room, Celia patting the bowed head of the flower as if it were human...murmuring sweetness. His trembling increased. It was dark. The moonlight shone on her face through the window. She was lovely. He trembled even more. She stood quietly and waited for him, then she turned into the darkness. He averted his eyes while she carefully folded her veil, her gown, her underthings and dutifully sat down on the edge of the bed. He remained clothed. He had removed his clothing without a thought thousands of times in his life. His jacket was now an impossible hurdle; his fingers were shaking so. He approached her, put both trembling hands on her shoulders. She fell back taking him with her. She helped him to come to her. Ashamed, he turned and buried his head in his pillow. She turned and pretended to sleep. He arose and undressed very quietly so as not to disturb her. He found her arm welcoming him as he returned to the bed. He found her mouth, kissed her and took her again. They fell asleep in each other's arms.

Chapter Thirty

L azar said, "I'll get the pillows."

Celia pleading, "No, let me."

He watched her as she rose and performed a domestic chore. Twinges of embarrassment as he watched her walking nude for the first time. He helped her tuck in the sheets, he on one end, he on the other. When they were done, they admired their handiwork. They'd made their first bed together.

They jumped back into bed, pulled the covers over their heads, and closed their eyes, pretending to be asleep so they could think their own private thoughts without disturbing the other and snuggled under the two pillows above their heads. Their eyes and ears had been so attuned only to one another; they were unaware of the quiet stillness in the house. He was the first to notice and luxuriate in the peace and calm...'til... 'I wonder if something is wrong.'

He tenderly disengaged her arms. She pretended again to be asleep. She needed to be alone in a little cocoon of her own, even for a few moments, so she could welcome him again. He dressed carefully and quietly and tiptoed out the door and down the stairs. He saw and heard no one. He went into the kitchen. On the table was a note to Lazar from the rabbi.

Dear Lazar,

The Rebbetzin and I have taken the students on a trip to the Minske rebbe. We will be gone for the entire week. If you will be already gone to your new place when we come back, we will see you in shul.

Lazar thought, 'he wanted to leave us alone, bless him.' He loved him too, and he Rebbetzin and the students and even Solomon. Lazar felt he loved the world...and what's more...he would love her. He counted his blessings and raised his eyes to God.

Lazar came back into the bedroom and came to Celia. He, frantic, clumsy; she submits calm, turning this way and that way to please him. He hurt her but she gave no sign. And hungering, devouring, taking...then turning his mouth from her mouth, he lay his cheek beside her, and sobbed heavy horse cries of pain, his tears streaming down her cheeks. She took his head in her arms and placed gently, protectively, on her breast.

Lazar's love is deep, touching pain. He hid them both for so long, they found each other to grow side by side, growing more and more impatient until now, bursting and nearly rendering him in two. It flattered Celia that she could affect him so deeply, gladdened her heart that she pleased him. But she was concerned too. Would she be able to continue to please him? Could she keep him? She covered their heads again. Warm, and safe with him under the blanket. But she couldn't sleep. She waited until he awoke. He smiled at her. She smiled at him, playful, teasing. They tossed away the cover, sat up and looked at each other and were ashamed. She flipped the blanket over her head again, laughing coyly to hide her shame, to comfort him in his shame. He tossed the blanket playfully over his head, his spirits suddenly exuberant and bouncing and they rolled and tossed and tumbled and laughed into each other's eyes and laughing and unashamed of their nakedness.

On the floor, a pile of tangled sheets, two pillows and a blanket. Fatigued now, "I'm tired."

"Me too," she said eagerly. They were delighted to find they both shared a common feeling at the same time.

She nestled in a corner, curled up and closed her eyes, stiff and unapproachable, a ball of shame. Lazar thought she was angry with him. He liked that. She was challenging him to court her...to win her affections. She had spirit. She heard him rise from the bed and then, a groan of pain.

She turned and jumped out of bed kneeling beside him, concerned and anxious now, "What happened!"

"You hurt me here," pointing to his heart.

"You can't see the bruise. Right here," he pointed, "you have to kiss it and make it better."

She shyly did as she was told, a quick peck, and bent her head again.

"Now kiss me," he said, "and I'll be even better."

And he raised her face to his and kissed her.

"I'm sorry I hurt you, Lazar." A gentle whisper.

"You should be," he whispered too.

"And I'm sorry I hurt you," he added.

"You should be."

He thought, 'I should have tiptoed out the room again.' And she thought she shouldn't have shown him she was so upset. They decided in the future, to dance a delicate ballet around each other's feelings.

A gentle tap at the door; the rabbi's servant. "Driver is ready," he said, "Hurry up, the soup is getting cold."

How many times had she said that, wiping her hands on her apron and shouting. She shuddered at the sudden intrusion of reality.

Celia, in bed alone and in pain, felt her spirits fall from a great height, like a trap door suddenly opened and flung her out of heaven. Her body ached so much. She would ache again tomorrow and for how many tomorrows. With him beside her, she had pleasure in his pleasure. Receiving his love enchanted with herself. She was adored and petted and the center of his world. Alone, she was an aching body, looking back and watching him love her. He didn't know she was watching him. Would he ever find out that she loved him loving her? But then, she would love him in her way. She would be his eyes and ears, hands, and feet. She would serve him, tend him, worship at his feet if that's what he wanted. The closest door was open. She glanced lovingly at his clothing. Her eyes caressed his jacket. She rose and stumbled to the closet and lovingly ran the tips of her fingers over his jacket. Then, embracing it tightly, "Oh, I'm so happy," and raising her grateful eyes to God. Lazar tiptoed to the room and stood silently behind her, then whispered to the gentle curve of her neck, "What are you doing?"

She turned, her face crimson, embarrassed that he'd discovered her in a private ritual...thinking, 'he must think I'm foolish, suddenly releasing the jacket and bending her head in shame. He put his hand under her chin and raised her face to his, "I love you, too," he whispered gently. She bent her head again in shame.

"Look at me," he insisted tenderly. She couldn't. He picked her up in his arms.

She was planning their first meal. Lazar saw the contented smile brighten her face. Spoiled already, he thought. He would handle that when the time comes. It will come soon enough, for both.

She dressed behind the closet door and hand and hand they scampered down the stairs. They sat together as close as possible, holding hands with one hand, eating with the other. After the meal was over, Celia disengaged her hand and did what she always did at the end of a meal, without thinking. She was like a robot, piling one dish on top of another.

The servant stopped her. "I'll do that."

She sat down and watched the dishes disappearing, felt uncomfortable, guilty as if she was disobeying a commandment. She forcibly restrained her hands and sat rigidly in her seat. Lazar thought 'Looks like a queen already. How easy it is to spoil a woman.' And she was thinking, 'What use am I?'

Lazar asked timorously, "You'd like to live like this always, wouldn't you?"

"Oh no, I'd like you to live like this always, but not me."

Lazar smiled at her, relieved, an image dancing in his head, Celia bringing him a cup of tea. She smiled, relieved too, an image dancing in his head, bringing him a cup of tea. She looked forward to asking herself the daily question, 'What will I cook for him tonight?' And suddenly she was terrified. Like a young pony, unharnessed and without the whip of daily chores, suddenly let out to pasture, running this way and that. Frenzied seeking its master, Celia's life without its daily chores, had no purpose. She quickly calmed herself with a vision of an old familiar task; what she would cook for dinner in her home.

Chapter Thirty-One

For a week there was silence in the great house, the
conversations of students raised in debate, visitors coming
and going, tradesmen bickering with the servant, irate
couples fighting before...and sometimes after...seeing the Rabbi.
Lazar and Celia in exile behind their door, a magic and unreality in a
careless nonchalance about time. Day becomes night and night
becomes day; Celia's hands idle, Lazar's book unopened...remem-
bering only prayer. Lazar never talked so much. He had an enraptured, attentive listener for the first time. Sometimes Lazar pretended
he was on the diaz, addressing his congregation, waving his arms,
pounding the air, power, and command in his voice. One time he
sang to her, cantorial songs of lamentations and tears and infinite
longing. His lyrical, powerful voice could not be contained by walls
and doors. It traveled quickly to the ears of strangers. A small crowd
collected outside his window, listening respectably, nodding their
approval...and some with awe. Celia, sitting on the bed, a congregation of one, hypnotized by its dramatic force, its intensity...its passion.
At other times, after they'd loved, Lazar caressed her with his voice;
softly, gently, building an altar to her, they flowed from his heart,

words magical, ethereal, mystical words unknown and unexpected... even to him. They came to his lips and made poems.

At other times, he would sing her to sleep...a sweet and tender lullaby, Celia crooked in his arm, nurtured, and protected, in a mythical kingdom of gentle perfection, harmony of mind that flowed without will or design, a perfection that was given without striving or searching...effortless...enchanting.

The servant was as invisible as possible. They were barely aware of his presence...wanting to pretend he didn't even exist. One morning they were awakened by a squeaking of wheels, doors slamming open and shut, voices shouting.

"My God," Lazar jumped up startled, "the Rabbi is back. What day is it?"

"It must be Friday."

"Of course."

They dressed hurriedly and fled down the stairs to greet the Rabbi. They pretended they were delighted to see everyone, helped with the luggage, both suddenly ashamed to be caught in idleness. They wearied themselves to the point of exhaustion until mealtime. Sitting around the table, the regret they dealt as the rabbi's return disappeared. They were glad to be in the world again...around a Shabbos table with friendly faces. Tomorrow would be his last Sabbath in the rabbi's home. He was beginning a new life...but he wasn't alone this time and he looked lovingly at Celia. She was embarrassed in front of the others and quickly looked away. They politely remained at the table until they could excuse themselves. They both tacitly understood now there was a new kind of talking to be done. The practical, functional talking of daily life.

That night, they went to bed early to attend shul the following morning. Lazar, his head churning with myriad details, turned his back on Celia, closed his eyes and pretended to sleep while he did some heavy thinking. But she knew he wasn't sleeping. She was accustomed to falling asleep in his arms, endearments whispered in her ears. She waited in silent anguish for him to return to her...but he didn't. She wanted to come to him...but couldn't. her arm...that found him so easily and carelessly so many times in response to his remained stiff, unbending while he seemed unreachable in a distant land. She was restless, turning and tossing...feeling in turn despairing and angry, alone, and unloved. She tried to get his attention. He remained oblivious to her tossing and turning and jumping out of bed. If only she could get him to turn around! When she dropped her shoe very loudly on her fourth trip in and out of bed, he responded.

A mechanical, "What's the matter?" with his back still turned.

"With me? Nothing."

"What are you thinking of?"

"Thinking? What do you think I'm thinking?"

Timid now, "How can I know?"

Lazar impatient, "I'm thinking of what I have to do the day after tomorrow," and he enumerated in a mechanical voice she heard for the first time.

In these few moments, Celia stepped from center stage; the spotlight moved from her to the grubby realities of life. She sighed, turned her back and prayed for sleep.

Lazar was frightened. From Sunday on he would...The Rabbi. They would come to him as he had come to others. He had a vision... expectant faces turned up to him and then, turning away in disappointment. That image tormented him...but he couldn't tell Celia. She looked up to him. He didn't want to give that up and be mothered like a frightened child, her eyes looking down at his. Shabbos would not be a day of rest for him. He would be in a fever of expectancy. He was suffering from stage fright. That night he dreamed he was looking at a sea of faces with mouths slightly slanted upwards smiling and smirking at him. He woke at dawn, relieved to find himself in the rabbi's room...no one looking at him. But the relief was momentary. Was this the other choice...oblivion? He decided it was not for him. He would be cast into it perhaps, but he wasn't rushing into it voluntarily. Desolate...to be the only one awake...in the house...the town.

Not a soul of life anywhere. The silence he'd welcomed the day before was now a void he found unbearable. Fear robbed him of patience. When Celia awoke, he was dressed and waiting.

"Hurry up, Celia. We have to go to shul."

He waited while she dressed behind the closet door, pacing, turning a few pages, sitting down, and getting up again to look out the window.

"Hurry up."

Pressing and pressing. She primped, though she looked lovely, turned hoping to see him gazing at her in approval.

"You ready? Let's go!"

He rushed down the stairs. She followed slowly, despondent. She'd thought they should go down the stairs together...hand and hand.

When he opened the front door, the sun shone brightly on his face and startled him. He felt uneasy...like he was opening a strange door for the first time to a strange, distant city. Only one week and he felt he had to renew his acquaintance with the townspeople, the shops, even the streets. When he entered the synagogue, he felt at home again, the warm books, the familiar prayers calmed him. And Celia too. Both were calmer when they returned home. God would help, Celia thought. He would see to it that Lazar came back to her. Even if he didn't, she wasn't really that important. She had borrowed his heart for a little while. Now, it was where it rightfully belonged... with God.

After all, what happened to the woman who, just last week, was thinking she'd be grateful to bring him a glass of tea. But you can't base a whole life on one week, she would store it in her memory box and open it like a treasured heirloom to be taken out on special occasions to be remembered. Like the admirer when she was 12...the baker's son. He would stare at her from behind the curtain at the rear of the shop. One day she found a note from him at the bottom of a bag of rolls. 'You're so beautiful. I love you.'

His father had seen him sneaking in the note and forced him to reveal what he had written. He was forbidden to look at her again.

'Already, she mused sadly, her life with Lazar was a memory.' But maybe they would make new ones? She hoped they would. That night they went to bed early. Celia turned before Lazar did. Somehow, it hurt her less that way.

They awoke early the next morning, packed their meager belongings, Lazar; irritable and anxious, rushing and flinging his clothes carelessly into the bag.

"Well Celia," putting his hand on hers, "we're going home."

She could feel his hand trembling, but she paid little attention. 'I wonder what the house looks like.' She hoped the bed was comfortable.

Chapter Thirty-Two

They rode in silence, each addressing their own concerns, without being aware they weren't saying a word to each other. They were on their way to Vitebsk, a house she never saw, Lazar addressing a congregation that existed only in his head.

The driver said, "We're here."

They both turned towards the window.

"Where?" Lazar saying.

"Where?" Celia echoing.

"The shul," the driver said. "Where else?"

In front of them stood a small wooden building in the center of an empty lot, the front door hanging upon on one hinge, the Jewish star faded and barely visible. It looked scarred and abandoned. The thoughts that preoccupied them swept away as if they ever existed. Both united in shock.

Lazar asked the driver, "Are you sure?"

The driver repeated the address. Lazar mumbled his despair. 'An excuse for a shul and not even a congregation. No one here even to greet him.' And she thought, 'Could there be a kitchen here? And how will we close the door?'

The wagon left. They both had an impulse to go after him, but instead, stood silent, watching the wagon until it disappeared. They turned and stared desperately at the shul both feeling a simultaneous affection for it. It seemed as lonely and abandoned as they were; seemed to need protection and care...as they did. They entered slowly and cautiously; disbelief and horror growing as they wandered; benches and walls hacked, they walked numbly through the chapel. Behind it was two smalls, one, a stove, a table and four chairs still standing, and the other, two mattresses on the floor, the door between the rooms on the ground. Lazar moaning, 'What will we do?'

"The first thing we have to do is close the front door."

"What door!" Lazar suddenly shouting, his face crimson, eyes glaring hate and rage.

"This," he kicked the door lying at his feet, "or that," he roared, pointing furiously at the empty frame of the front door. Frightened by his outburst, she stepped back, stumbled over the door and fell, sitting on one foot, the other sprawled in front of her, knee on the doorknob. Her terror left as she burst into laughter at the foolishness of her position and at the place of injury.

"Did you hurt yourself?"

Lazar screamed unsympathetically, more enraged at the interruption.

"No," she laughed harder, too embarrassed to tell him where it was but unable to stop laughing, the laughter tinged with hope that he would join her, but he didn't. his rage intensified because she didn't join him.

The laughter left her face, vanishing suddenly without a trace, when she realized Lazar's rage would not be appeased or pacified. She had exhausted her tiny repertoire to deal with it; she could deal with angry children, but not angry men. And Lazar could not be reduced to a child. His was not a reaction to a trivial frustration. It was the rage of the betrayed lover, aching for revenge, yet not knowing where or how to strike...or worse...not being able to strike. Lazar was attacked where he was most vulnerable...in his sense of justice. Lazar's mind was tormented with reasons, one after the other that he discarded, only to reconsider for this outrage. Some rational... others, in his despair, almost irrational. And finally, he settled on...the goyim. His mouth quivering, his eyes cold with hate, he swore revenge. He would get them for this. He would rouse the town. They would see. He would get them for this. He would rouse the town. They would see. He would lead an army. Celia, who'd been an enraptured congregant of one in his imaginary congregation, was now a timorous soldier of one in his imaginary army.

"You agree, Celia!" staring and glowering at her.

She had no choice but to nod her head in tactic agreement.

"You agree or not!" she nodded her head with more vigor. "That's good, Celia! Now come with me!"

She willingly followed him, not even daring to ask where they were going, though she anxiously wondered where he was bound with such fierce determination as if he really knew. They trudged on a dirt road till they saw a small path leading to a house. Lazar walked up to the door, his face still rigid and unsmiling and pounded on it authoritatively in cadence. The door was rapidly opened by a tall, bearded man whose fear vanished when he saw Lazar and turned to anger. His wife, standing timidly behind him when he opened the door, now stood beside him, her hand on her waist.

"Who are you?" the man demanded.

"And what do you want?" from the wife.

"I am the new Rabbi and I want an explanation!"

He was too angry for an exchange of courtesies. Nevertheless, they extended a hand, insisted he enter, now respectful. Lazar entered a house that reminded him, painfully, of home, all beds, and children.

"Sit down," the wife said, and removed several garments. Lazar noted a fiddle hanging on a wall.

"Who plays the fiddle?"

"I do," the man said.

There was a hat hanging on a nail next to the fiddle, battered, worn, dirty.

"That's my business," he said, banging on the wall, the fiddle, and the hat. "I went to school, graduated from the university, came back here and the only use I had for the diploma was a lining for the hat. I play in the street, in hallways and in backyards. I pick a place, put down my hat and I'm in business. Sometimes," he quipped, "I bring home a few potatoes. Not everyone likes music. Last week, one hit me on the head," and he pointed to the spot.

Lazar saw the fine, sensitive hands in this gross tall, clumsy looking man as he raised his head, his face close to Lazar, friendly face, sad eyes behind the long, scraggly beard. The man was sturdy in contrast. The body of a laborer, the head of a poet. His wife, a stocky woman, looked somewhat like a bulldog, the loose flesh on her cheeks hanging down on each side, a snub nose, a thin curved mouth between the jowls frozen in a perpetual scowl and two arms that never seemed to leave her hips. She was in a perpetual stance of giving orders. While Lazar was talking to Brindel, she provided the background music, a steady stream of staccato commands to the children. Lazar thought she would have made an excellent drill sergeant.

"Brindel," she snapped at him, "stop talking nonsense and explain to the Rabbi what happened. After all, that's why he came here, isn't it? Not to look at your head?"

"You're right, Miriam."

"Tell me what happened, Mr..."

"Brindel."

They all introduced themselves now, the children rushing up as they were named....and dispatched again.

"I've already guessed what's happened to the shul. Goyim... bored, goading him on...the restlessness 'til he grabs a weapon and pursues the shul like he's lusting after a woman, tears, ravages, mutilates, 'til he's spent...then struggles home to his grubby wife who's grateful, for once, he returned home drunk, without beating her."

"No, Rabbi, this time it didn't happen like that. You know, Rabbi, we have hotheads in the town; radicals who say, 'Religion is the opiate of the people; the churches and the shuls teach submission to God and the Czar to enslave the working man. The Jewish and Christian leaders joined yesterday and decided to 'demystify' the churches and the shuls. They were going to start with the crying saints in the churches. They called a mass meeting in front of the church, harangued the people calling the church a fraud, rousing them to such a pitch, they stormed the church door, pulled out the body of the saint that was in a glass cage, threw it in the street, opened the case and cried, 'You see, the saint is made of wax,' and turning it over, they exposed a tangle of wires and shouted, 'You see, fake tears!' The people were enraged, felt betrayed. The leaders then marched them to the shul...the Jewish leader spoke. Here, too, is a symbol of decadence. We must realize our common enemy; we must unite against our exploiters. In unity there is strength. The religionists divide us! 'Let's show them,' one of them shouted. And the Jews watched in horror while the goyim, their comrades and brothers stormed in the shul like it was an enemy fort and hocked its innards with their bare hands. The shul was empty. The old Rabbi died a month ago. They took everything they could, even a pair of his old eyeglasses. Of what use were they to anyone? The Jews fled afraid the goyim would turn on them. No one was there to greet you because, I suppose, they were too frightened or ashamed to come near the shul."

Lazar screaming, "The Vilna Rabbi, the march, and now this. Another betrayal. We are leading the brothers to our burial place, showing them the way so they could dance on our graves."

His rage frightened Brindel.

"But maybe they don't understand," Brindel offered sympathetically.

"That's no excuse!"

"What do you think we should do?"

Lazar thinking, Miriam silent and he shrugged his shoulders. It's as hard to make the good into evil as to make the evil into good. He had an army equipped with shrugs and understanding and brotherhood. They were equipped to disarm the enemy. How could he teach them to arm themselves?

Chapter Thirty-Three

"Maybe you should return to the Vilna Rabbi, maybe he has another place for you."

"No, I'll stay. We'll fix up this one. The people aren't here to greet me, so I'll go to them and introduce myself. First, to the men who can paint and hammer."

Brindel grabbed his overcoat, delighted the Rabbi changed the subject. He wondered if the rabbi was a dangerous man. He frightened him a little.

Lazar ordered Celia, "Wait for me here."

She reluctantly sat down. It was the first time he'd left her since their wedding. Brindel took Lazar from door to door, introduced him to the men hammered and painted, fixed, and patched. They followed Lazar and Brindel back to the shul.

"Go home and fix your fiddle," Lazar demanded Brindel.

While they worked, the congregation gathered to watch. Lazar gave his first sermon in the street in front of the shul with the sound of banging and clopping behind him. His voice soared above all the tumult. He controlled his anger so they wouldn't be frightened, reviewed the events of the night before and ended with a quote from

Isaiah, 'The righteous perisheth and no man layeth it to heart, and merciful men are taken away, none considering the righteous is taken away from the evil to come.'

Lazar could feel the shudder through them all as if they were asking themselves the same question, 'What evil yet to come and how to take ourselves away from it.' Lazar didn't intend to upset them yet, but he was carried away by his own words.

"Brindel, pick up your fiddle. I will sing and then you'll play what I'm singing."

He sang and the men stopped work to listen to the cantorial song. Brindel put his fiddle to his chin and joined him. Everyone was enchanted, hypnotized. He concluded with a rousing Hatikvah, and the crowd joined him singing of a homeland that didn't exist. The song transformed them from bent shufflers to men. Lazar suddenly knew what Solomon the Zionist was talking about. The answer was here in front of his eyes. He had two purposes, to save their dignity now, his people later. His aim...a homeland in Zion. God does work in strange ways, he concluded. After the sermon and many repetitions or Hatikvah, each one louder than the rest, he was besieged with outstretched hands and praises...as if he was the Messiah.

Brindel, the first to notice how tired he was, played a few notes on the fiddle, gained their attention, and announced it was time to leave the Rabbi in peace. They quietened down. After he left, he made the following announcement, 'All those who can and will contribute the following,' and he listed, 'beds, pillows, sheets, pots and pans etc. Go home and bring them to shul. I'll collect them and the Rebbetzin and I will know what to do with them. The crowd dispersed rapidly to make a home for their Rabbi.'

Brindel sat down on a chair at the entrance to the shul to collect the items as they came in. Lazar, happy to see the door to the bedroom was repaired, closed it behind them, curled up on the mattress and fell asleep.

All day, people could be seen scurrying to and fro with whatever they could spare to make the rabbi comfortable, a pot, a pan, a pillow.

The pile mounted and mounted. Brindel collected the offerings and the Rebbetzin happily directed him where to put them. Someone even contributed two sets of curtains so they could have some privacy. And another brought food. At the end of the day, Celia had a kitchen and a bedroom. She was to cook her first meal. She carefully prepared and tasted, and when it was done to her satisfaction, she tenderly awoke Lazar with a kiss.

"Supper ready," she whispered.

A sleepy, "I'm coming."

He arose, washed his hands, sat down at the table, prayed, and waited to be served. Celia placed the soup before him and anxiously awaited his judgement. He pushed the plate towards her. She felt like she'd been pushed but he wanted only to adjust the chair. He hadn't noticed she was still standing.

"Is it good?" she finally asked, excited.

"Of course," he said. "Why do you ask? It's delicious."

And he looked at her like a grateful, submissive child. Celia sat down like a queen; haughty and confident. She had established her domain. They ate in silence, Celia rising only to bring the next course and they lapsed again into silence. Lazar was thinking of the sermon he delivered that day. He longed to discuss it; started talking on and on. Celia listened. As the days passed, at mealtimes he eagerly told her of his ideas and dreams. He talked and talked far into the night. He decided he would tell the people the story of Basha. He saw himself as a charismatic leader, exciting and disturbing them, goading them on. He was a man who couldn't wait, even for the Messiah. He wanted his people to meet Him halfway. If they continued to wait, he reasoned who would be there to greet Him when He came? Only a remnant of a remnant if that. Celia was titillated and flattered watching and listening to him. He gave her a private performance every night; his subtle, intricate mind, from the strand of a thought, weaving and weighing, growing more excited and flamboyant, mounting excitement until the triumphant conclusion when he would fill the house with song.

At night, Celia waited for him to come to her. She would watch him as he courted her, a touch, a word, a look, from subtle beginnings to intense, devouring and when he'd loved her, he would hold her close to him and caress her with words of yearning and adoration as if he were courting her from afar, warm words that came from a grateful heart that she let him love her. Sometimes, she'd be awakened in the middle of the night, Lazar sitting at his desk reading by candlelight. Those were the nights he dreamed of Basha's return. He would awake startled and fear closing his eyes again. These dreams were known to Celia. She never urged him to return to bed. She would find him in the morning asleep at his desk.

The days were hectic for him. The visitors who sought his advice were a problem for him in the beginning. He was amazed they were putting that much confidence in him. But then he learned why; his presence and interest soothed them. The words came, as they always did, from an infinity of words in his head. The right ones magically found each other when he needed to advise or comfort or both. Then the night came...for the Basha story. After the prayers, to comfort and release tears, he told them the story, his magnificent voice, crescendo and diminuendo heightening the drama and excitement. They were watching a master storyteller. At the end, his voice rising, higher and higher, feverish, burning with moral outrage. At the conclusion, he paused...and peered at the parishioners. They were overcome...with sadness. He was stunned to see that he could not find one angry face. A sea of despairing faces was looking up into his burning, flashing eyes. His shoulders drooped. His head fell. They had missed the point. He had failed. Instead of angry mutterings, he looked down on white handkerchiefs dabbing at tearing eyes. It was something that just died in him, and he was watching his own funeral. All his life, he would be enraged with people who wouldn't let him rescue them.

Chapter Thirty-Four

As the years passed, Lazar's fame spread...of his rhetorical and musical brilliance. Celia bore him seven children, the last one carrying with him a family secret that was never discussed. He became an awe-inspiring figure; his face broadened, his dark eyes deeper and blacker. His beard grew to his waist and was parted in the middle. He was very tall, and when he walked through the town, men stepped aside, women's hearts' quickened. On Yom Kippur, the Christians stood in the rear of the shul to hear him sing the Kol Nidre. He worked tirelessly for Zionism, traveling from town to town, speaking for the cause. His fame spread as an orator. He was known to Christian and Jew alike and earned the respect of both.

A story is told that, on one occasion, he decided to lecture in Moscow, a city forbidden for Jews to enter without a permit. It was somehow discovered that he was in a hotel room there. When he heard the command, "Open the door – police!" he crawled under the bed and was easily found, of course, in this undignified position, taken to the station house and jailed. The chief of police, to whom his arrest was reported, ordered his immediate release, shouting, "Him, you arrested." He'd heard Lazar speaking and singing. He was a lover of music. He personally released Lazar from his cell, and to his astonishment, apologized for the 'abysmal stupidity of his men.' Lazar looked so imperious, even behind bars, that the police chief was humbled. Lazar thanked him stiffly, retaining an erect and rigid posture. He could never humble himself to inferiors or superiors and decided the police chief was definitely the former.

But, despite his successes, Lazar remained a discontent and restless man. He was a visionary who compared himself to the giants; Moses, Isaiah; demanded the impossible of himself and of life and, compared to his visions, his accomplishments seemed to him, puny and barely deserving of notice. People came to listen. He was a great performer. Lazar put on a great show when he spoke. He was witty, sarcastic, brilliant, told stories to illustrate his point and then, they turned not to him, but to each other, to mumble about mundane affairs when the show was over. There were some who confronted him, arguing he had to wait for the Messiah. It was against God to be a Zionist.

Lazar had an army of listeners, but no followers. He disputed with them furiously. His oratory finally opened doors for him. The rich Jews who were bribed to stay in Moscow, vied for his presence. But they also listened and did not follow. The seas parted and Lazar was marching alone to the Promised Land. The poor were waiting. The rich were too comfortable...or thought his ideas were interesting...but impractical. He was named Benjamin after Lazar's father. With the birth of the child, Lazar's nightly soliloquies were met with, "I have to tend the child." The music of his golden tongue was often lost in the competition with the baby's squalling until Lazar realized he'd lost the battle and morosely contemplated the purpose of life or some other unanswerable question. He noticed the changes in Celia's face; the face that inspired him to poetry and song; whose absorption with every word encouraged his alert mind was not the face of a homemaker and mother; preoccupied, harried, tense and, worst of all; commanding and efficient. She sat at the table with him but was listening to the child. At night, when he loved her, she would, at times, briskly jump out of bed in an intimate moment...the baby. At other times, after they'd loved, his heart filled with poetry, aching to share loving words with her...shattered by the din of the child. When she returned to bed, she turned her body toward the child.

"Celia," he said tenderly.

"What," she'd reply, annoyed and tired.

"Nothing," sulking.

And the flow of love ceased. He felt the child was Celia's. It was too young to interest him. He resented its intrusion on his poetic senses. Lazar lived in a world of dreams and verbal battles and causes. Music was in his body, its rage and its tenderness, its explosions and lyricisms. Celia's world was bottles, diapers, and the kitchen. As her kingdom grew and more children came, her power grew, and she ruled with an iron hand. The Celia of old, the child who ruled other children, reasserted herself, once again. Lazar raged at the world and Celia raged at the children...but she was fiercely devoted to them. She was a dutiful mother, and they were dutiful children. Lazar's gifts lay strewn about her, neglected, and discarded.

When the children grew up, Lazar too turned to them...old enough to sing with him. He would line them up and conduct his little chorus, four boys, not the girls. Some had a voice, but were not in tune, others were in tune but had no voice. Eli and Leon were his favorite. The other two, he decided, were not too smart.

The girls he smiled at and patted on the head in his tender moments. They waited eagerly for his smiles and pats, each one jealously watching the other. If he patted one, the others quickly surrounded him and submitted their heads.

One night, Lazar took Celia aside for a private conversation. It was very difficult to reserve a few moments with her during the week, but this was pressing. Leon was 12, a powerfully built boy, a broad face, large brown eyes, always very serious and loved to engage in polemics with his father.

"Celia, I'm afraid Leon is running with a bad crowd."

"What! Why didn't you tell me?"

"I'm telling you now."

He'd been noticing Leon getting up at night reading by candlelight. One morning, he examined the book. It was a copy of Karl Marx 'Capital' and he was using an old drawing of Basha's candle as a bookmark. Lazar didn't know how he'd found it and when he'd questioned him the next day. It seems he'd known about it for a long time, and he wondered why no one fought back. He told the story to a friend of his who revealed to him that he was a follower of Karl Marx and that their group was inspired by her story to an interest in Marx, a dedication to revolution.

So, he asked him, "Why not Zionism?"

"That's running away," he said.

"We have to stay here and help change the world for everybody."

"But you're a Jew. How about your world?"

"If we help them, they'll love us too. Besides, you believe in fighting, standing up for your rights."

"But that's a godless revolution."

"No, liquor is an opiate, not God."

"What's the difference? What is an opiate, a painkiller so you don't know it hurts. And what is God? Also, a painkiller so you bury the hurt, do nothing about it."

"Wrong! Your father knows what hurts, knows what to do about it, is doing it."

"You're right," Leon said respectably, in awe of his father, "but a dreamer like him and excited by his own vision."

He was captured by the idea of living a secret life that flowed from his ideas. Unbeknownst to Lazar, Benjamin was the 'lookout' for a group of revolutionaries who had their meetings in the forest at night. He sat high in a tree where he could see for miles around and warn them to disperse if he saw police searching the area for revolutionaries.

A week after Lazar's discussion with them, he spied a search party. He shouted to the others, then clambered hurriedly down the tree himself. But he was too slow. The other escaped; he was captured, marched behind a horse for seven miles and hailed. At 2AM, he was brought before the chief of police.

"What were you doing in the trees? Who were you with?"

"Nothing, no one."

The chief of police slapped, punched, kicked him for lying, then ordered him released due to his youth. Benjamin trudged wearily home in the darkness. Celia was waiting for him, frantic, having a thousand trips to the window, peering in the distance for him to emerge from the darkness and praying hard as she could that was unharmed. Lazar fell asleep. When Benjamin reached home, his terror of the police they'd both fallen asleep. He decided to rap gently on the window to wake brother Phil to let him in. Celia was sitting on her bed in the darkness, wide awake.

She screamed, "Lazar!" and was out of control as soon as he was in the door. Attacked him instantly, "Where have you been?"

He had no chance to even answer with the lie he prepared. She slapped and punched him adding more bruises to those he already had and ordered him to bed...forthwith. The following morning, grueling questions by Celia and Lazar. He repeated the story over and over; how he got lost in the forest, couldn't find his way home in the dark, fell asleep from fatigue. When he woke up it was dark, and he managed to guess his way home by a hit and miss method. It took a week of shouting of Benjamin before she could calm the fear that mounted in her that night. Someone speedier than Benjamin was chosen as a lookout, and he was given another assignment.

The Turks, who could be helpful allies if they could be swerved, had to be convinced, somehow. They loved the Turkish baths and Benjamin reasoned that they could most easily be approached there, without clothing or weapons, calm, soothed by the waters. Benjamin would approach them in friendly conversation and then, at the opportune moment, when he saw that they liked him, were chatting with him in a genial manner, he would ask them if they'd ever seen a Jew.

'No,' they'd say, 'I'm a Jew,' he'd say. 'You're a Jew!'

Incredulous, they'd peer hard at his head, some, rubbing it, with the palm of their hands.

'Where are your horns?' 'You see, we don't have horns.'

And then, he'd lecture...and win converts to Marx and respect for Jews. In addition, he was assigned to the committee on army propaganda. He had to sneak into the army barracks unobserved and leave a package of propaganda for them to read. On the top of the page was a small candle. 'They would be grateful to the Jews when they learned they had helped them to a better world. They'll love us, be kind to us,' Benjamin told his father one day. Lazar then told him the story of the Vilna Rabbi.

Benjamin pondered the story and replied, "It was the wrong time. The time was not ripe."

And Lazar replied, "It was always the wrong time for us."

Benjamin had no reply. Their discussion was interrupted by a shout from Brindel. He burst in the door shouting,

"Rabbi, you must come. There's trouble in town."

"I'm coming too," Benjamin said, before Lazar could ask, "What's the matter?"

In the town square, there was an angry crowd gathered around a group of Cossacks on horseback waving the pressing crowd back with their whips. Benjamin saw his comrades in the crowd, he quickly left Lazar's side to ask them what happened and was determined to join them...no matter what. Benjamin darted away so quickly; Lazar lost sight of him in the crowd. The Cossacks finally pushed and beat the people into making a path. From a distance, the sound of singing could be heard. Benjamin recognized the words. It was one of their songs, a worker's song of exploitation and degradation of the Jew at the hands of the many. Those voices, Benjamin thought, were familiar. The leaders of his cell, a man, and a woman, walking proud, heads high, hands tied behind their back. Behind them, ten armed men; the firing squad. As they sang, the crowds joined them, the martyrs sang ever more lustily, their eyes glowing with the hoy of self-sacrifice and a surge of overwhelming love for the people who were suffering with them and for whom they were willingly giving their lives. The young man, in his early twenties, pale blue eyes and blonde hair, beardless, boyish innocence, his hair cropped short, a small, thin wiry body. His wife, a head taller than he, short, cropped hair, a face hard and determined, her eyes looking into the distance at nowhere as she sang the music that gave meaning to her life and death. They both marched in rhythm to their own music; proudly, heroically. They turned when they reached the wall and defiantly stood even more erect, protesting to the very end with the only weapon they had left, their pride. They were offered a blindfold and refused.

The captain barked, "Ready, aim!"

Their heads slightly turned for one last glance at each other before the order to fire. The men in the squad were surprised to see them fall. Each one had decided they'd shoot above their heads. The angry crowd refused to leave. Cossacks whips were flailing everywhere, beating, and scarring whomever they could. Benjamin was struck several times on the back. The crowd was finally dispersed by the might of the Czar's army. They went home, each to mourn their loss in their own way, some to sob and flail their arms in impotent desperation, others to angrily pound the walls with their fists 'til they were even more bloodied; others...to coldly plan the tyrant's end.

"Why don't you do something?" Celia pleading with Lazar nursing Benjamin's wounds.

"What can I do? He's like me. Nothing can be done with me. How can I expect to do anything with him?"

The Cossacks whips found Benjamin's back again and again as he joined angry crowds at the death of his comrades. He carried those scars on his backs to the end of his days.

Chapter Thirty-Five

Lazar, deep in the study, had his hands to his ears to muffle the din of Celia's shouting at the children. He felt sorry for her. Sometimes, he thought he had given her too many of them. She feared for them all and tried to protect all seven as if they were one. They had so many enemies: illness, accident, goyim, the Army. She was afraid of <u>life</u> happening to her children, so afraid that she became a weapon herself.

She couldn't scream at life and be heard, so she screamed at them instead, 'Watch yourself! Don't go there! Why did you go there? What's the matter with you? Didn't I tell you!'

Her voice soaring higher and higher. Lazar waited for it to crack, but it never did. He looked forward, more and more, to his trips for the cause to avoid the ruckus at home. 'This house is full of causes,' he thought, 'Mine, Zionism, Benjamin's communism, Celia's, the children.' Lazar was to speak in shul and was invited for a reception afterward to the home of Mrs. Mitzer. Unlike many others, she had no interest in making her living room into a salon. She had initiated some correspondence with Lazar, was interested in his ideas and assured him she was not in the habit of inviting strangers to her home for vain and shallow reasons.

"She had no need," she said, "to fill her living room with names that she could flatter herself so they came to her table and that others could envy her for having."

She would be at the shul to hear his speech. He was surprised at the frankness of her letter. She seemed desirous of convincing him she was sincere.

Lazar was intrigued.

He was anxiously counting the days 'til his departure. The speech would be very special, he decided. He went to bed at night distracted, reviewing, and correcting his discourse and woke up the next morning correcting what he had written the night before. Lazar spoke extemporaneously and required no notes once he had made the final decision in his head what he was going to say. His conversation with Celia at bedtime became more and more perfunctory until it was reduced to a mechanical good night before each turned their backs to the other. He continued performing his marital duties strictly prescribed in the Talmud. Not a whit more. Celia was too harassed to notice and somewhat grateful. She had neither time nor energy to lose in 'romance' anymore. But Lazar knew that despite her attitude, she would feel neglected if he didn't, at least, do his duty. And then, God forbid, she might become more demanding. He was careful not to neglect her. She knew the rules and would be alert to any deviation from them.

On the day of his leaving, she admonished him tearfully to be careful, as she always did. He hugged her and the children as he always did. And scurried back and forth, forgetting, and returning and forgetting again...as he always did. And Celia plunged into her chores, the moment he left, as she always did.

Lazar boarded a crowded and dusty train. It was midsummer, hot. He was dreadfully uncomfortable. He tried to read, couldn't concentrate, but read anyhow. The heat was overpowering. Good humor turned to irritation. The train stalled, unplanned delays. After an interminable few hours, he arrived at his destination and became even more impatient, the closer he came to the evening's event. He was to be picked up by a friend in a tavern, Eli, with whom he was going to stay for a few days. Eli was waiting. Called a wagon while they chatted. When they arrived at the shul, the crowd was standing outside to greet him. He entered the shul amidst the outstretched hands and greetings. He began his speech the way he always did in a new setting...with the story of Basha. It was his way of saying, 'This is who I am and this is what I come from.' This time, after the tears came, instead of engaging in his polemic, he told them another story; one he'd never told in public before; the true story of the Vilna Rabbi and his betrayal. For the first time, he heard an angry crowd muttering in indignation to each other. He concluded with the usual soul stirring polemic.

"You must go home again and build your own land."

And the congregation answered, for the first time in unison, "Amen."

Lazar was jubilant. He stepped down from the podium and had to restrain the crowd from raising him on their shoulders and parading him around the room like a new groom.

Eli wrestled him by the arm and managed to pull him out of the clutches of the crowd into the carriage waiting nearby. He fell on his seat trembling with exhaustion, his head in his hands, his eyes closed.

From the seat opposite him he heard, "Good evening, Rabbi," said a feminine voice.

He looked startled. A woman in the carriage...alone...with him, in the moonlight, he could see one side of her face. Her hair perfectly coiffed in the latest fashion, high cheekbones, a tiny, delicate nose, ear lobes glistening with diamonds, a full, sensuous mouth. She sat upright, erect, and proud, the bearing of a queen. Lazar thought, 'What is she doing here with me?'

"Who are you?" he asked.

"I'm Mrs. Metzger. I told Eli to rescue you from the crowd."

Her tone was soft, distant. She spoke slowly and evenly; a voice and manner trained to reveal nothing to the casual observer.

"Thank you," Lazar stammered, "I am, how should I say it, humbly grateful."

Lazar surprised even himself. He couldn't remember the last time he felt humble. 'So imperious,' Lazar thought. He felt himself humbling even further. He was aching to know what she thought of his speech. But he feared to ask. The answer might not be what he wanted to hear. Besides, he didn't even know if she'd heard him talk.

As if reading his mind, she said, "I heard your speech."

He was in anguish waiting for a sentence to be pronounced.

"It was excellent," she said.

Without enthusiasm but with a slight emphasis that convinced him she wasn't being 'polite.' He welcomed the darkness.

"How much further do we have to go?"

"A few more minutes."

He dreaded their coming into the light. He didn't want her to see his embarrassment. He knew somehow that when he stepped out of the carriage, all the years would suddenly vanish and Lazar, the Yeshiva boy, would be standing before her. The man on the podium vanished.

"I'm having a small reception in your honor...a few like-minded people who require just a bit more prodding to convince them fully to Zionism."

The carriage stopped. The driver opened the door and she slighted gracefully. Lazar stumbled after her, tripping and nearly falling as he tried to maintain a precarious balance on the small stones made more difficult by the excitement taking over him. She led the way to a small villa that was her home. He entered a room that was pink and soft, and everywhere the eye alighted, there was beauty. She liked the small and graceful furnishings, impractical but tasteful, everything in the room in delicate balance with everything else. In the living room, a fireplace flanked by two soft pink sofas covered with roses, a small grouping of white chairs, a pink, covered table, a vase with fresh pink flowers at its center, paintings of gentle Victorian ladies holding graceful hands to their bosoms, bowing cavaliers extending bouquets to haughty ladies in silhouette. There was an air of tender romance as if she created a tiny island of beauty for eyes and heart, almost, it seemed, a refuge, where, as far as the eye could see, and wherever it chanced to fall, it met beauty and tenderness and love. All her paintings were of man and woman, reading, courting, or of woman alone...but not alone. The painting that dominated the room was a woman, in fashionable evening dress, seated at her vanity, looking in the mirror, surrounded by roses, pinning one to her bodice. The expression on her face, one of anticipation. Lazar thought she looked like she was going to meet her beloved.

"That's my favorite," she said, "Do you like it?"

"Very much."

"If you like drawings, I can show some others you might like."

They sat down, one on each sofa, and she passed the drawings to him. They all had the same theme; the martyr facing the fire squad, dying for his cause. 'She's a romantic,' he thought. She wants to live a romantic life and fancies a romantic death.

"Who made these drawings?"

"A friend."

She was not elaborating any further. As they exchanged pictures, he had an opportunity to look at her face, shyly, at first, then more confidently. Her small pert face, delicate pointed chin, deep dark brown eyes, the pale green silk dress which flowed about her small voluptuous form, a pink flower on her neck...an exquisite combination.

Lazar was confused. She was a study in contrast. The face; fragile and sensitive, the eyes strong and intense, the voice calm, modulated, controlled, her hands gentle, small, the light in the room soft, not one jarring note of indelicacy, every flower in place, every accent muted in gentle harmony with another as if to surround one with poetry, as if she'd decided to live on a pink cloud. But, in the drawings, violence, extremism, fanaticism, love of sacrifice, even death.

The butler interrupts, "Dinner is ready."

"Are there others here?" Lazar asks.

"No, they canceled."

He wondered if that was true. He was very uncomfortable. The only woman he'd ever eaten alone with was Celia. He sat beside her at the long table, they ate in silence. Lazar, never at a loss for words, was speechless. He'd never been in an environment before without an undercurrent of babble. The silence intimidated him. Even the servants came and went without a sound. They retired to the parlor following the meal.

"I suppose you're wondering why I asked you to my home."

"I am."

"Well, I can't tell you that, but I can tell you that I want to help you. I believe in you and your cause."

"But why?" Lazar pressing, unable to restrain himself.

"Because I need *a tomorrow*. My life has no tomorrow."

"Meaning?"

Lazar wondered if she had read this somewhere in a French novel that the fashionable ladies were reading...or...one of her amusements was the dropping of subtle phrases that created a mystique about her. He had to admit he was further intrigued. Being a performer himself, he immediately recognized this trait in others, and adored it. A man of poetic sensibilities himself, he loved to be in the presence of another who also had a sense of drama and lifted him out of a mundane reality. They subtly entered another sphere together, Lazar finding himself responding to her allusion and mystery with his own innuendos and subtleties. He sensed an unwritten drama. The script called for more questions from him. He didn't supply them. He waited for her to question him...and she did.

"Why did you accept my invitation; a single woman extending an invitation to a Rabbi?"

He suddenly found himself saying, "Maybe, in a way, the same is true for me. I have no tomorrow; I need a tomorrow."

"What do you mean by that?"

He couldn't reply. He couldn't dare tell her what he meant.

"I suppose you're wondering how I came to know you." She was suddenly formal.

"That's not what I was wondering."

"What were you wondering?"

A haunting, mysterious look clouds on her face as she stared into the distance. 'She's now playing the tragic heroine,' he thought, 'the result of her evenings in the theater.'

"I was wondering why your eyes are so sad," he said, staring into them as hard and sincere as he could.

She moved back, startled, uncomfortable. She had ensnared her audience, but, unlike the actors on the stage, she was not protected from the audience by the darkness. The heroine was not herself. She'd crossed the boundary unreal to real. The unreal wasn't as comfortable as it appeared from a box seat. He continued the theme of the tragic heroine; soft, compassionate.

"You must have suffered a great deal."

She turned away, gazing further into the distance to hide the pleasure, tinged with self-pity, she felt at hearing these words. No one before had ever realized how much she'd suffered. Lazar, the director, and she, now, the consummate tragic heroine. She needed a tragic hero. Lazar thought she must have chosen him for that role. But why him? A rabbi? A married man? First, he was unattainable. That should heighten the drama. But so were many others. Why him? A poor rabbi, a reputation...but little money, too impatient to be mannerly, rages that gave him the reputation of being a little 'mad.' And how about him? Why did he accept an invitation. He knew it was different. He could sense it. Yet, he took it.

She slowly rose and turned regally, summoned the servant. He appeared quickly, as if he'd been a ghost in the room and suddenly materialized.

"It's late. Roskov will show you out."

She was imperious now, unapproachable, dismissing.

Lazar was humbled again, uncomfortable, shy. He thanked her, hurriedly opened the door without waiting for the servant in his sudden desire to flee. As soon as the door closed behind him, he was overcome with guilt. He hailed a passing carriage and busied himself with directions...peering out the window, craving distraction. He hoped Eli wouldn't demand sociability. He needed to be alone...God forgive him...to relive those few moments with her. 'Forgive me Celia, God forgive me,' he prayed fervently. He couldn't bear asking the children's forgiveness. He didn't even think of them. He couldn't.

He was enthusiastically greeted by Eli, his obese and frum wife, whom he adored and their five children who were mercilessly in bed. He smiled appropriately, barely heard the conversation, said yes and no when he deemed it appropriate and pleaded when he was tired and thought it was inoffensive to do so. He was grateful to be alone for a few moments when tormented again with guilt. He couldn't sleep. Her neck, her eyes, her breasts, her soft voice. He grappled with these images...but the more he fought, the more the army increased. She besieged his fortress again and again. He turned and twisted, praying for sleep, until he capitulated in his desire for her. He sat up in bed breathing heavily as if he'd been pursued by a dangerous apparition. His burning body ached for her. He was torn between fleeing in the morning or dashing to her door that moment and pounding on it until she let him in...and ravishing her. He dismissed them both as 'ridiculous.' He decided to leave for home that following morning...if he could. He prayed that the decision made at night would not be unmade in the morning. But then, again, if he was to pursue her, how would he bring her to him? Create an obstacle, he decided. Her indulged life had none.

Chapter Thirty-Six

Marva rose the next morning in her pink bedroom. She loved this room. It comforted her every morning; the satin drapes, the vanity covered in white organdy, the lamps covered in fluff and fringes, the pink rug...a garden of green leaves and pink roses. The maid brought breakfast. She dangled her feet over the bed while she slowly ate a spare breakfast to keep her figure. While sipping her coffee, she indulged herself in the memory of last night and decided she'd planned it splendidly; her sudden mysterious entrance into his life and her equally mysterious dismissal of him. She knew he would be gone this morning. The married ones were all the same; especially a Rabbi she mused. She was certain he was rushing home to forget her. In a few days she would know. She would receive a note, neutral in tone, suggesting he would be in town for just a brief time. Could she spare a few moments in her hectic schedule? Did she have some suggestions for help with the cause?

She remembered when she first saw and heard him. She had gone to his presentation at the urging of a friend. She was between lovers. Life was unendurably dull without one. Aaron and Basheva Mintz, her parents, were themselves indulged children who carried on the family tradition. They indulged their only daughter, Marva. Her father, a wealthy merchant, often took her on trips with him to buy whatever she wanted. His eyes would light up with glee whenever she wanted something. Momma waited for them at home. She always eagerly awaited her surprise. Poppa always came home with something in his hand.

"See and do as much as you can, Marva," Poppa would always say. "There should always be something new around the corner."

And he took her everywhere, a new city, town, village, people.

"You'll be forever young," he'd say.

The trips were always exciting, except for Poppa's business appointments when she was left with the maid. He was stern only about one thing, she had to go to bed early as he had business appointments for dinner. She would rise very early in the morning and often wonder why there were candles on the table that had burned down to the rim of the silver candlesticks surrounded by faded flowers and a smell of perfume lingering in the air. Once she asked Poppa if there were any women in business.

"No, only men."

She was puzzled but didn't ask any more questions. Poppa didn't like questions.

One night, she woke in the middle of the night, and heard voices, the gay sound of a woman's laughter...then silence. Her heart pounded just thinking what she was about to do. Trembling, she tiptoed to the door, peeked through the keyhole as hard as she could, one eye, then the other, then both. She dared to put her hand on the huge doorknob and suddenly realized that if Poppa came towards the door, she couldn't hear his footsteps on the soft, thick rug. She wished the woman would laugh again so she could be sure she wasn't dreaming. She scurried back to bed and lay awake, her eyes wide open, her ears straining in the darkness.

There it was again, a woman's laughter. Marva wondered. 'Who was the woman with the laugh?' She tip-toed to the door again and pressed her ear tight against it. She heard nothing. Suddenly, a faint sound above her head. She looked up and saw the doorknob slightly moving. She hurriedly pressed her eye to the keyhole again and saw Poppa putting on his jacket and smoothing his hair. She couldn't see the laughing lady. Poppa was standing in front of the keyhole whispering. Then, the sound of the door closing. If she could have seen more through the keyhole, she would have seen Poppa walking to the mirror, smiling at a man who looked very pleased with himself. She hurried back to bed and pretended to be asleep...just in case. Sunday was her favorite day. Poppa would take her to a 'business lunch.' He would let her pick his business outfit for the day. He always dressed elegantly, in the height of fashion, looking very distinguished, a square face that inspired confidence, a combination of arrogance and humility, superior but not offensive, intimidating, but not rude...an excellent merchant. His eyes were always laughing, and Marva never really knew if he was serious about anything...except being young. He was very serious about that. He wouldn't even tell his age. She always had to wait while he paraded himself this way and that before the mirror, making sure everything matched perfectly, and, most important of all, the outfit made him look 'youthful.'

He always took her to a different restaurant, but Marva noticed that there was always a table reserved next to theirs for a woman alone. It was always a beautiful woman. Sometimes Marva recognized her. She'd seen her on other Sundays. Sometimes, it was a new face. Poppa always sat at the table where he could face them; Marva sitting with her back to the lady, facing Poppa. She often wondered about those coincidences, but never dared to ask questions. Poppa believed children had no business prying into the affairs of adults. He wouldn't even hear questions about other things. He would grow impatient and hand her over to her mother or the maid. He hated questions since his days in the Yeshiva where he was ceaselessly tortured with questions in whose answers he had no interest. He married a religious woman and always said he would keep them secure in this world and she would take care of them in the next. He attended synagogue on required formal occasions, did what he was supposed to do to be above criticism, always contributed more than the others to charity, to the synagogue. He was an honored and respected man, and an example to others in his devotion to his wife. She was a frail and delicate creature, very thin, small, pert face, eyes bright and shining with joyful optimism. He said he was very distraught that he had to leave her so often and it was said he didn't insist she join him out of his consideration for her fragility. He couldn't bear to see her tiring herself out on trains. It was much too hectic.

Marva noticed that Poppa was not as distraught as he claimed when he left Momma, and his traveling was not all that hectic and tiring. He seemed to be enjoying himself enormously. He would often leave Marva of course, to buy her a surprise. He always explained it took a long time because he was so particular. She stills remembers the day of her fourteenth birthday. He said he was going to buy her a surprise and would be gone quite a while as he wanted to get something special. She sat by the window and watched and waited for him impatiently. She saw him entering a store across the street from the hotel, a young ladies' shop. After several moments, he hurried out carrying a special package. She thought he was returning immediately. Instead, he hailed a carriage. He returned several hours later with the same package, claiming he'd spent all afternoon searching for it in various shops.

For the past several years, Poppa had no business meetings in the suite at night. She could hear the door softly closing and the sound of his footsteps down the hall as he hurried out after she pretended that she was sleeping. Marva found explanations for all of Poppa's behaviors, but the unasked questions pressured, mounting through the years. The day came when the questions came tumbling out. Unbeknownst to her, they'd be forged into a weapon with which she attacked him mercilessly.

His arm extended, holding the bag, but his smile froze on his face as she hurled one question after at him with the cold hard burst of a machine gun. 'Who was the laughing woman? Who were the ladies at the adjoining tables? Who do you see at night when you go sneaking down the hall? Why do you tell me you spent the day looking for a gift that I saw you buy three minutes after you left me?' Her face was cold, hard, demanding, ruthless. Aaron was stunned into realizing his error. She had been deprived of nothing...except an answer. Marva could not tolerate his daring to leave one empty corner in her life. He saw her whole being as one large, grasping, greedy hand reaching out for the one thing he had not given her. And he was powerless to resist...now that he knew what that was. She was pacing back and forth like a hungry tiger stalking her prey, hands gripping her waist, staring at the floor. His knees couldn't hold him. And he fell. She suddenly stopped, standing over him like a colossus.

Waving her finger in his face and screaming, "Answer me! Any answer at all! Just give me an answer!"

Soft, apologetic, "Sit down and I'll give you an answer."

Glaring at him, her hands tightly clenched on the arms of her chair, head bent, back hunched as if she were about to spring. God had fallen from the Heavens and become a man...obsequious, uncomfortable, embarrassed...man. And Marva's awe turned to contempt as she looked down at her father...sneering.

"What do you think the answer is?"

And she lashed out, "Women!"

Aaron won the first round. She'd given him the answer.

"And suppose it is...women. What will you do with this information? Tell Momma?"

Still unable to confront her father, she hadn't realized the tables were turned.

"Never! Why should I break her heart?"

Poppa rose from the floor, kneeled beside Marva, put his hand in hers and looked up at her tearful face and she said softly, "I didn't mean to hurt our Momma."

She rose abruptly from her seat, "Leave me alone!"

Tearing into her room, throwing herself on the bed, sobbing; the unanswered question, the question she hadn't dared to ask, wracking her little body with terrible sobs, 'What did he want with others when he has me!' That was the question she longed to ask him.

She finally fell asleep and woke early the next morning. This time, for the first time, Poppa brought her breakfast on a tray.

With strained exuberance, "Good morning, Marva."

'Strange,' she thought, 'he isn't already out on a business breakfast as he usually is.' The maid generally informed Marva he was already gone on a business meeting no matter how early she rose. 'How stupid I've been,' Marva thought. 'He was just out all night. Hotel maids keep their secrets well.' The following night, after she'd heard him leave, she sat in a chair and waited...'til the dawn came. She heard the clatter of horses, the clinking of bottles; the milkman, the church bells ringing, 8 o'clock. She returned to her bed.

When the maid came with the breakfast, Marva asked, "Where's my father?"

The maid informed her he had already left for a business meeting. She dressed and returned to her vigil at the chair. She opened the door at 11, startled to see her there.

"Poppa, I'm going home."

She waited for his protest. None came. "That's a good idea if it'll make you feel better."

She sensed he was relieved.

"Alright," she said, crestfallen, "I'll pack."

He eagerly offered, "Let me help you."

Marva still remembers how his offer devastated her.

She mumbles, "I can manage myself."

She couldn't bear to see him helping her pack. He rushed her out of the hotel room, into a cab, snapping his wrist every minute to check the time. He didn't want her to miss the train; seemed desperately anxious that she shouldn't. When they arrived at the station, he became frantically obsessed with details, luggage, and departure times. It seemed he couldn't even look at her.

The train was about to leave momentarily. He fought her way to the window, but it was closed. He was waving his arms up and down frantically, signaling her to open the window...but she wouldn't. she looked at him glumly, thinking how ridiculous he looked. She could still see him, his arms frantically waving up and down, opening wider and wider to articulate them...as the train left the station. She turned from the window and sank wearily down next to her luggage. She was alone in the compartment. She put her hand on the large, soft brown case and held it tightly as if it were a companion, comforting her in her desolation. Poppa's seat, the seat next to her, was empty. She had never traveled alone before. Thank heaven, she wasn't too far from home this time. Just across the border. What would she do now to amuse herself, she thought, as the train went on, the rhythmic sound and increasing distance calming, slowly lifting her spirits. Strange, she thought, she wasn't concerned about Momma. In a way, she always felt Momma was an outsider...as she should be. Now, Poppa and she had another bond between them that Momma couldn't share. Only Marva knew Poppa's secret. No, she'd never tell Momma. But then, without going on trips with Poppa, how would she amuse herself?

Studies were boring. She'd always said she'd learned more traveling with Poppa, everything, in fact, there was to know. Of course, the answer was simple. She'd do what Poppa does. Just turn the tables. Amuse herself with men. Poppa was a good teacher, after all.

Chapter Thirty-Seven

Momma was home when Marva arrived unexpectedly.

"Home so soon?" Momma asked, worried. "And Poppa?"

She looked past the door, "Where is he?"

"I was too tired to go on this time."

"I understand."

Marva noted Momma was not too happy to see her as she expected. But then she thought maybe she was imagining things.

Poppa also returned sooner than expected. He entered the house subdued and quiet, without the usual, "Where is everyone?"

He hesitantly greeted Momma, then smiled warm and confident when he saw no sign of change in her. He also explained he was too tired to go on...and for the first time...he was empty handed. Marva was waiting to be welcomed, too. He averted his eyes.

"I have another kind of surprise for you tonight, Bessie," he said. "It's Friday night and I am going to shul with you."

He thought she'd be ecstatic. For years she hoped he'd attend every Friday night.

"That's fine Aaron," she said, "but you really don't have to. It's not necessary. You're so tired."

"I'll go," he said emphatically.

"Poppa, how nice to see you home so soon," she said cool and distant.

"I have a surprise for you, too. Next trip I've planned for Sorrento."

He knew she'd always yearned to go there.

"I'm not going on any trips for a while, Poppa."

"I understand."

Momma said, "She's so tired. You're running her into the ground. Look how thin she's getting."

"How long will you be staying this time?"

"Just a few days."

He couldn't tell her he'd returned home to assure himself that Marva kept her promise and didn't tell Momma. Aaron loved changes the moment he stepped out of the door, but at home he wanted everything in place, especially Bessie. He adored Bessie. He never wanted her as much as he wanted other women, but he adored her more than no other woman. Bessie was special. He first saw her at a distance, fell in love with her at a distance, and kept her at a distance all these years so he could continue his adoration as it was in the beginning. Everyone wondered why they'd returned home from their honeymoon after a week. They were to be gone in a month. Aaron explained he had to rush back to business. Bessie was pregnant a month after the marriage so all speculation about 'difficulties' in their honeymoon abruptly ceased. The meadow around their little honeymoon cottage was strewn with pink petals that had fallen from the dogwood trees as if nature had seen to it that everywhere they looked and tread they would be surrounded by a romantic haze of pink petals.

"Let's go for a walk," Bessie urged.

"I'd rather not."

"Why not?" she insisted, jumping on the window, "It's so beautiful!"

"That's why not."

"I don't understand." The smile faded from her face.

"I've disappointed you already."

Without explaining, he said brusquely, "All right, we'll go."

Bessie hugged his arm while he looked doggedly down at each step he took. It seemed painfully symbolic to him, crushing the fragile petals underneath his boots; an alien intrusion into the gentle carpet that caressed the earth below like a tender mist. He saw himself making a trial of gashes and rents, felt the petals being crushed under his feet and he was overcome with nausea.

Bessie walked along beside him, gazing into the distance as far as her eye could see, ecstatically repeating over and over that it was beautiful. Aaron gazes at Bessie in wonder. She was glowing, as pink and as fragile as the display that nature had put before her. At dusk, they returned to the cottage holding hands. When they closed the door behind them, Aaron abruptly dropped her hand, fled to the farthest corner of the room and sat down, his head hanging, staring at the floor, spinning his thumbs in circles.

"Are you ill?"

A distracted, "Yes."

Jerking his head abruptly to answer her, then returning to staring at the floor and making circles with his thumbs.

"I'll be alright after I've rested a minute."

"Why don't you go and make yourself comfortable?"

Bessie shyly acquiesced, picked up a piece of her luggage and took it to the adjoining room. Aaron's anguish mounted, knowing she was dressing for him. He heard the door opening, the swish of her gown as she walked toward him. He couldn't lift his head. He saw one silk slipper, then another. She turned her little feet; two satin pink slippers pointed toward him. His eyes were glued to the slippers.

Gaily she said, "Look at me. Don't you think this gown is pretty?"

And the two pink slippers pirouetted around once, revealing the delicate ankles, then stood still together, both pointed towards him. He slowly raised his head. Bessie's tiny body in satin and lace, both pink, and delicately flowing around her body like the petals on the soft earth. He could only gaze adoringly at her as she turned this way and that as he directed. She danced a minuet with an imaginary partner, pirouetted and bowed and fell on the bed laughing. Aaron was enchanted...but he couldn't rise from his seat. At that moment, she was pink petals and moonbeams. He couldn't bear to touch either. Her head fell on the pillow and instantly sank into sleep. He watched her as she slept and then joined her...lying down as far from her as he could so as not to disturb her. He awoke before her. When she awoke, the servant was coming through the door with breakfast for them. After breakfast, he suggested they go riding. She gleefully accepted.

He opened the door...the petals again. He tried to walk in his footsteps from the night before so he could avoid crushing new ones underfoot. But he couldn't. The squishing of those tender petals under his boots...sickened him. They spent the day racing, subdued at sunset, and cantering slowly and rhythmically back together. They had a leisurely dinner and fell to bed, happy though exhausted.

As he was falling asleep, at a distance from her, as the night before she gave him a quick peck on the back of the head, plumped her pillow and cheeringly said, "Goodnight."

He felt the hem of the pink nightgown touching his leg and quickly moved it away. They awoke together the next morning. She was cheery in the morning, bouncing out of bed, teasing him mercilessly with a peckish grin about the funny way his hair stood straight up on his head in the morning. The night made a mockery of all the meticulous care he expended on it during the day. He suddenly looked desperate and determined, not being able to bear the weight of deciding any longer. She thought he was upset because she was teasing him. He suddenly grabbed her white arm and flung her on the bed. The laughter left her eyes and face. She closed her eyes tightly and lay stiff in his arms. He ripped her pink gown, nausea rising in him as he forced himself to touch her breast and her waist...and then, he invaded her...feeling brutal and unclean...as if he had torn and sundered savagely a gentle, pink, delicate, fragile flower that had it's trusting, gentle face turned toward him. The nausea grew and he felt he had to separate from her. He dated to look at her. Her body remained stiff and unyielding; her eyes were still tightly closed. Her face was a rigid mask, determined to endure. Her lips which she inverted into her clenched mouth were a thin invisible line.

He was breathing heavy but managed to say, "Forgive me, Bessie. I'll never do that again."

"You promise?"

Tenderly, "I do."

His outstretched hand was near her.

They fell asleep, their fingertips touching, "I love you," he said.

She nodded her head up and down on the pillow which meant 'I love you too.'

The following morning, they packed for home. He never touched her again...but he was an ardent suitor throughout the years, and she remained, in his eyes, a young unattainable girl, courted, ardently wooed, but never won.

Their marriage had a brief period of suffering as Aaron watched her frail, delicately formed body growing deformed and misshapen with child, he loathed himself, for, as he saw it, the crime he'd committed against her. When she was enduring the pain of child-birth, he raged against God and nature that Bessie, whose tiny eats were made for music and poetry, her gentle eyes to gaze upon beauty, her graceful body to be touched only by the caress of his adoring eyes, was suffering excruciating pain, her legs apart like some dumb animal, her secrets exposed to strangers, being examined by a cold, detached eye...like a biological specimen, the rude reaching in that precious body that he feared to touch even with a flower, then the final wrenching from it...a screaming child...and a fountain of her blood.

He was hiding in his room since she started screaming. He'd

never known her voice to be other than calm and soothing. It was so soft he often had to tell her to speak up so he could hear her. They never argued.

He opened his closet door and banged it again and again to muffle her sounds but he could still hear her. Two of her gowns were hanging on each side of him. He grabbed them and put them to his ears, hiding in the dark closet until he heard a banging at the door. He rushed to open it.

"Congratulations! It's a girl!"

"Bessie? How is she?"

"Fine. Tired but fine. You can see her now if you wish."

"I'll wait 'til the morning."

He didn't think she'd want him to see her like that. The following morning, Bessie's personal maid primped and dressed her, so she looked like she'd suffered from nothing more than a headache the night before, that she was temporarily inconvenienced.

The following morning, he dressed very carefully, elegantly, suit and tie, his new shoes, handpicked a bouquet of flowers in the yard, and bounded up the stairs, gently knocked on the door, "Bessie."

"Come in."

He walked in the door like a bashful suitor; doting looks at Bessie, bouquet in hand. She extended a hand from under her pink wrap, shyly smiled up at him while she accepted the flowers, put them down on the bed and embraced them by her side.

"They're beautiful. The baby, Aaron. The nurse is coming with the baby."

He turned and looked down at the smallest human he'd ever seen. He kept his hands clenched behind his back, afraid to touch it.

He lied, "She's beautiful. What shall we call her?"

"I want to call her Marva."

"Marva, you're beautiful."

Chapter Thirty-Eight

Aaron created a private world at home, sweet, pure, and most of all, calmly serene. He walked into a poetic sanctuary from his strife-ridden life in the marketplace. But as the years passed, he stayed away longer and longer on his business trips, but Bessie never questioned or scolded him. It would have never occurred to her to do either. She was secure in the knowledge that he adored her. Often, away from home in lovely cities; Aaron would read voraciously. He loved poetry, especially romantic ones and could recite lengthy poems from memory. One evening, a year after his marriage, finding it too hot to remain in his hotel room, unable to concentrate on his reading, he decided to visit a coffee house. He ordered a coffee, lit by a lady of the night. She asked him the familiar question in seven languages. He continued to stare at her dumbly. She was very young, had a large, beautiful face, long black hair, her full lips painted vivid red, her nails long and perfectly manicured, red like her mouth. His eyes were riveted to her nails. He had a wild impulse to have those nails sink into his flesh until they drew blood. She talked on and on in a language he couldn't understand, waving her hands as he talked, her fingernails glistening in the darkness. He suddenly grabbed her hands and dug her nails into his palm. She sprang up and grabbed him by the arm, beckoning with one hand and pulling with the other. He followed her in a daze, wondering what came over him, but knowing he had to follow her. She led him into a dingy room, ripped off his shirt and dug her nails into his chest, ripping his body. She bit his breast, his neck, until he felt the need for her and took her brutally. When he was done, he left her as suddenly as he had taken her. The sheet was wet with sweat and his blood when she had torn his flesh. At the sight of his own blood, he lusted for her again...and took her again and again and until the morning... when he separated from her and stood at the window, staring, numb, watching the sun rise.

He took the wallet from his pocket, "How much do I owe you?"

He flipped the bills like playing cards and asking her to choose.

"Nothing," she replied, "I'm not one of those. I was just lonely."

But he didn't understand her. He took a random number of bills and handed it to her when he saw her resisting payment.

She calmly placed the money on the table. When he left the room to dress, she quietly slipped it into his jacket pocket that was hanging on the chair. He hurriedly put on his jacket, parted his hair without combing it, rushed out the door and fled down the stairs without even saying goodbye. She waved at his fleeing back through the window knowing he wouldn't look back, but hoped he would. But he didn't. They seldom did. He didn't even know her name. She didn't know him. She listed him in her little book. Her fingers went down the list under "N"...Norman, Nathan, Nathaniel...she wrote, "Nameless." Then she put on 'something more comfortable.' She set the table for two, chatted gaily with 'Nameless' through breakfast. In the empty chair, on the other side of the table was her 'companion,' the memory of Aaron.

Aaron hurdled down the street like a blinded, wounded beast, not knowing or caring where he was going, twisting this way and that...each time the humiliation burned him again. He flailed at the imageless pain, the self-loathing and remorse. His body ached where she bruised him...and he yearned to flagellate himself the more...to ease the pain she inflicted on him with pain he'd inflict on himself. He wandered the streets for hours, head bent, gazing at the sidewalks. He couldn't bear to be alone in his room and couldn't bear to face anyone. He'd besmirched himself...and worse than that, besmirched his wife. How could he face her again knowing who he was? But what was he? He asked himself...but couldn't bear to search for an answer. His legs were aching. He was very hot and thirsty. His clothes were clammy and wet. The simple, human discomforts interrupted his obsessive weighing of the intricacies and consequences of his behavior. He suddenly decided to return to his hotel room...if he could find his way back. He was grateful that he had an excuse to focus on externals...tracing his way home. As he neared his hotel, he found he was growing feverishly eager to be in his room alone. He was beginning to feel aroused again. His hand searched his chest for the bruises she'd left on him, and finding them, he traced them with his fingertips gently, until he was on fire to see them. He was breathing heavily when he saw the front entrance to his hotel. He rushed through the door, grabbed the key from the extended arm of the room captain, filed up the stairs two at a time, opened the door quickly and slammed the door behind him. He tore his shirt open and stood bare-chested in front of the mirror, caressing the rents and gashes 'til the passion returned, overcoming the shame and self-flagellation...even the questions until he was drained of every other thought but one...the woman...every other feeling but one...the desire for her. He dressed again and left the room, found the café, seated himself at the same table and waited for her. He was so overcome when he left her, he couldn't possibly find her again. He was certain she would search for him and find him. He waited for her every night, the craving for her overcoming every pain, the guilt no match for the glint of her fingernails. He was obsessed with them, dreaded looking at a woman's hands for fear he might not be able to resist jumping out of his seat and...he couldn't bear to think.

He continued his nightly vigil, imagining so many times, it was

<u>she</u> he saw emerging from the darkness, coming towards him. He'd strained forward eagerly so many times, a profile, a walk. He was sure...but then...as she came closer, he knew he'd created her out of bits and parts...and overcome again with pain and longing. He decided to search for her, straining his memory from detail, a glimmer to lead him...at least...in her direction. He chose a street at random, hoping he'd be lucky. Searching was a comfort after the agony of waiting. But suppose there was someone with her! What would he do? He brushed that thought quickly aside. 'I'll pretend to have made a mistake.' It was late. The streets were deserted. He recognized nothing. He assailed himself why he'd paid no attention to where he was going. Didn't he see anything? Why doesn't he remember one thing! He repeated over and over, 'I must think,' but he couldn't. He could only race madly through those streets, growing more and more frantic as he yearned to burst into freedom and break the bars of his cage. He peered into lighted windows, hoping for a glimpse of her, playing a little game with himself...it had to be that window...or the next one... from hope to disappointment in a twinkling. His legs aching, he finally collapsed on a dark, cement stairway, not caring that he would dirty his light suit. His head sunk in his hands, panting, grateful for the exhaustion numbing the pain. Then thinking, 'What had he come to? A man in his position!' Overcome with self-disgust...a man in his position sitting on a dirty stairway like a bum.

Two lovers passed giggling. He was mortified. He thought they must be laughing at him. 'He must get up and pull himself together. He probably looked ridiculous.' He arose staggering and stumbling, looked in the direction of the lovers...then quickly looked again. They were standing in front of a house with a white rail. He suddenly remembered that rail. 'Don't touch it,' she'd say. 'It's been freshly painted.' He remembered how careful he'd been to balance himself up those steep stairs without touching the rails. She held his hand tightly digging her nails into his wrist while he was being verbally solicitous. He stumbled even more so she would tighten her grip. He forced himself now to amble slowly towards the house, his heart pounding.

"Excuse me," he mumbled, as he pounced on the rails and bounded up the stairs.

The building looked familiar. He pushed the creaking door open, felt his way through the dark hallway and up the rickety stairs and he saw a sliver of light under a door. He tapped lightly, she opened the door, he looked up at her beseeching. She was wearing a blue satin negligee. He saw the table set for two, the candles lit.

He turned, mumbling, "I'm sorry, I didn't know you were engaged."

"Come in!" Smiling, radiant, "I've been expecting you."

Chapter Thirty-Nine

She was the first of many of his escapades, and, as he remembered later, 'the best of the lot.' He married and left her one day, without a farewell. He'd prepared her from the beginning. He never said he'd see her again. She always assumed 'this time might be the last.' It was an unspoken agreement between them. There'd never be a word of love. He knew nothing about her. Not even how she survived. He never asked her. She never told him. They remained nameless, without past or future. They had pet names for each other that they remembered for a little while until they forgot what each other looked like. But those who came after her made demands and that's when he started taking his daughter with him...so they could see for themselves when he took her to lunch.

"I couldn't hurt an innocent child," they'd always say, nobly.

The only woman who never wore him out was Bessie. He continued to leave her reluctantly and return to her eagerly. The titanic struggles he inwardly waged with others wearied him...and so he tired of them, hoping each one would be the last...but it never was. First, the red long fingernails waving gracefully, following words he seldom heard, hoping the stem of a glass, putting a dainty morsel in the red mouth, his craving would be in anew. The anxiety of the pursuit, the need for them to ravage him, the pain of their ferocity, burning, stinging, the pangs of remorse and self-flagellation.

Bessie was a soft, constant sweetness, a mild rhythm in their days, no peaks, and valleys. He had no mountains to scale; the ground was level beneath his feet.

"Bessie," he'd say softly, "I'm home."

"I'm glad," she'd answer.

Soft. Warm. Content. But this time, he sensed a subtle difference. 'She didn't expect him,' he told himself. Unlike the others, she didn't welcome the unexpected. Surprise didn't titillate her.

"I didn't expect you home so soon."

He tried to catch her eye, but she wasn't looking at him as she usually did, lingering, welcome. She summoned the servant.

"Help me with the luggage," she said, and averted her eyes.

'I wonder if she knows...if she was told.' He panicked, dismissing one question after another in his head. 'Should he inquire if anything's wrong? Should he wait for her to ask her a question? If only she'd ask him a question.' It would comfort him. He'd know where the danger lay. Without questions, he felt he was in a mine-field...for the first time in his life with Bessie. He decided to pretend as if everything was the same as always. It was like seeing the very first line on the face of a beautiful woman.

She says at first, "It's nothing."

But she returns to the mirror again and again to reassure herself it's really <u>nothing</u>. And then, the denials...it'll go away, too much sun, too little rest; every moment of panic quickly allayed with a comforting explanation.

The following morning, he awoke late. She was not fussing over the table as usual, preparing his breakfast. Instead, she had her coat on and was preparing to leave.

"Good morning, Aaron. I have to go now. I'll be back soon."

And she rushed out the door before he could reply.

'Maybe,' he thought wryly, 'she has a boyfriend.' He immediately disciplined himself not to be so ridiculous and vulgar. The first time he'd ever questioned his life at home and his feeble imagination was capable of nothing else but ugly explanations, searing alternatives. He was even soiling his own home with the depravity he'd been eagerly seeking outside the door, and it burst into his home at the first opportunity. He'd never permitted himself an evil thought at home before. It unnerved him. Marva found him glowering at his morning toast and muttering to himself when she joined him for breakfast.

She chided him. "Having an argument with the toast?"

He looked up. Smiled.

"Good morning."

"You don't have to be cheery for me. What's wrong?"

Serious now, "I don't know. I'm worried about Momma. She's been avoiding me, been cross with me since I came home."

"You're worried about yourself. Worried you've lost another worshiper? First me...now her. Too much for you. A man who degrades himself needs to balance the scales, laughing, and mocking. How else to cleanse all that self-contempt if not with worshiping admiration? You came to the door, ascended the throne, and all was well...until paradise falls."

She leered at him, "isn't that so, Poppa?"

He'd betrayed her, too, he thought. She hated him most for that.

"And you," he said, "wanted to share that throne with me. We both wanted no other Gods before us. Only God can make that request. The rest of us have competition."

She quickly changed the subject. 'I'm not going on trips with you anymore,' she hoped he'd say, 'I'll miss you.'

Instead, he said, "How will we explain this to Momma?"

"You created this mess!" she cried angrily. "You explain yourself out of it!"

And she fled out the room. He remained where she'd left him; too weak to pursue her, too numbed to think. His head sunk in his hands; he didn't even hear the quiet approach of Bessie's steps behind him. She didn't stop. Passed him wordlessly and went quietly up the stairs to her room. He raised his head and saw her back as she was going up the stairs to her room. 'Good God,' he thought. 'She saw me like this and didn't even ask, "What's the matter?" Unconcerned if I live or die?' He tore up the stairs, livid with rage, stopped caring about the infinite subtleties that had stopped his hand. He burst into the room. She had her back to him, removing her hat.

"What's the matter?" he shouted. "What's wrong! Tell me! What have I done?"

"You?" quietly. Wearily, "You've done nothing wrong."

"Then why are you so..." he stumbled for the right word wanting to say, 'lacking in admiration, in worship.'

But how could he say that? Instead, he mumbled, "So different?"

Before she could reply, the maid knocked on the door to announce a caller.

"Dr. Pledhoff is here. He wants to talk to Mr. Pearl."

"Here?" Momma gasped. "What is he doing here?"

"I'll see him in the parlor," Poppa said.

And his officious, business-like face returned immediately, and Poppa went to meet him. Dr. Pledhoff was a man of definite utterances, a commanding voice that brooked no questions. He was kind, serious about his work, and concerned about his patients. He was a handsome man with a fat, ugly wife to whom he was devoted.

"I will be brief," he said. "Sorry to disturb you at this hour. I am violating the confidentiality of my patient, but the time has when you must know."

"What patient? Know what?"

"You must know your wife has multiple sclerosis."

Panicked. "Which is that?"

"A deteriorating disease. Haven't you noticed how she's been looking?"

He'd been away, busy. Seldom home. He mumbled explanations. Dr. Pledhoff heard Bessie's voice from the top of the stairs.

"Why are you here?" her voice trembling.

Bessie had never questioned a doctor before.

"You know why I'm here," he said. "Aaron has to know. I told him. It's that simple."

'That simple,' Aaron thought. To men of science, the sudden wrenching of a gentle subtle harmony, of the poetry of a life is 'that simple. Bessie, deteriorate. Impossible!' Bessie was eternal, the essence of beauty, of truth. That could never deteriorate. Bessie was a pure spirit. He'd created an enchanted bubble around them. Nothing real ever dared to enter. Only flesh deteriorated. Dreams and fantasies remained forever untouched.

Aaron was determined to battle his enemy. He would devote all his days to courting her, admiring her, writing poems to her. Did Venus deteriorate...or Cupid? Inconceivable! Goddesses did not deteriorate. As time passed, his devotion increased. He neglected his business, his daughter, and his other life. Bessie loved one of his little games best of all. Only he knew it was a game. She didn't. she believed him; trusted him completely.

If she was gone too long, on an errand, he would confront her when she came home, pretending to be in a jealous rage, "Where have you been! With a lover?"

"No," a cagey reply, blushing and very pleased...and then... explain carefully where she'd been every moment. It soon became a neck and neck race between Aaron and the incurable. It was left to Marva to face the word, 'deterioration.' 'Let Poppa live his dreams. Deny life. Let him have his comfort.' For herself, there was no comfort. She became Momma to Mamma. Imperceptibly, their roles changed. Aaron courted her, while Marva tended to her and faced her 'deterioration,' day by day, crying herself to sleep every night until, at last, there was no sleep, anxious days, and tearful nights. 'It's so bizarre,' she thought sometimes, as she watched Momma, stumbling, more aged and in pain and poppa gazing at her as if she were descending a staircase, all youthful radiance and grace, taking his arm to dance a pirouette when they met.

"Don't you see, Poppa, that you're losing the battle!"

And she heard him as he whispered to her willing his words into her body.

"Your limbs are white, as graceful as a nymph."

Droning on and on...to no avail. All the poems, the books, the tender romanticism that nourished their life throughout the years was no match for the relentless onslaught of grim reality. Bessie succumbed. Aaron was defeated. A tidal wave burst through the gentle, gossamer veil of their lives and tore it asunder.

He stood in the temple unseeing, whispering, "How do I love thee, let me count my ways."

And he counted...over and over...and continued counting on the slow, mournful journey to her resting place.

"Yis Kadal, Yis Kadash," the Rabbi intoned.

Aaron whispering, "I love you, Bessie. My dearest Bessie. Your gentle eyes that light my way. A rose for a rose!"

An anguished cry. And he bent down and tore a handful of dandelions and threw them, one by one atop the small box as it was lowered into the earth.

"Your path shall be strewn with flowers. Bessie, we must rush home. You'll warm your little feet by the fire. The beauty of your face in the glow of the fire. I want to see that."

Marva whispers, "Poppa, Momma's gone."

He didn't hear her.

She repeated, "Don't you hear me? Momma's gone. Gone," she screamed, "you hear? Gone!"

"Bessie," Aaron went on, dropping to one knee, whispering softly, gazing adoringly into nowhere, "How do I love thee? Let me count the ways."

Louder and louder, Marva shouting, "She's gone, you hear!"

Not to see or hear that Aaron, too, was gone...and had been... since the doctor made his fatal announcement. She screamed until she had no voice. Wept until she had no tears.

And then, in the stillness, she heard Aaron repeating again, his favorite poem to Bessie, "How do I love thee? Let me count the ways."

In a gentle singsong, warm, endearing, as if he were kneeling by her side removing one shoe, then another, then gently putting a pillow under her head.

Even death couldn't make Momma real for Poppa. She was always his dream. Nothing could take Poppa's dream away from him. Not even Momma.

Chapter Forty

In her room next to his bed he kept, in a drawer, a lock of her hair, her combs, her perfumes. Before retiring, it was his nightly ritual to brush tenderly, the little lock of hair, a stubborn little curl that resisted his brush. He enjoyed seeing it snap into place rebelliously. He would smell her perfume, his eyes closing, enraptured, adoring as if he'd just gazed at the curve of her lovely neck and was savoring its beauty in his mind's eye. And finally, he would imagine he was combing her long hair, his hand moving slowly, carefully, 'Don't worry, I won't hurt you,' he would reassure her from time to time...until hide arm, growing weary, would reluctantly replace the brush, the comb, the perfume in the drawer. Then he'd bend over her bed raising the sheets to where her dear head once rested, tucking her in, 'Goodnight sweet Bessie, until tomorrow,' and he would tiptoe to the door and return to his room. In the morning, Marva would see him at breakfast, solicitously buttering her toast, chatting with her, amiably nodding his head. He would then repair to the garden and return smiling with an armful of flowers.

"I chose them for you" he'd say, smiling gaily.

The vase was always on the table waiting, empty...in readiness for his flowers. And then, he would sit at the piano and sing the old love songs, in Yiddish, in Russian, some in Hebrew. With these songs, the house became a temple. The tears and lamentations, the anguish of loss and prayer for return. Aaron could only express through cantorial songs which he'd never sung before and rarely heard, but now, needing to mourn, unable to face his loss, he cried for a lost temple and longed for a distant land. Sometimes, he would weep for Israel and rend his garments. Marva would take him in her arms and comfort him.

"Bessie is coming," she would say, "Bessie is here Poppa."

"Where?" he'd say hopefully. "Bessele," he'd say, "is that you? I have a poem for you, Bessele. Listen. How do I love thee? Let me count the ways."

Day after day, month after month, Marva watched and heard him performing his daily ritual, hoping one day, he would turn to her as if he were old and say, "Marva, let's take a little trip."

Yet, she feared what would happen to him if he fully realized his loss. Sometimes, she feared him. He would pack a suitcase and go to the other end of the house with it as if he were leaving for a trip. There was a guest room there with red satin wallpaper. There he would unpack his suitcase, look around furtively to see that no one was there, his excitement growing to frenzy, open his shirt and scrape his nails across his chest. Then he would again repack the suitcase, climb out the window to the front door, ring the doorbell. A sigh of relief when Marva opened the door.

"Bessie," he'd say, "I'm home," as if he'd been on a dangerous journey and was home safe...at last. Marva determined he'd never known Bessie was gone. All visitors were forbidden, servants discharged.

Only she could play this game with him without patronizing or sympathizing. Only she could fasten the door tighter and tighter against reality. Instinctively, everyone else fought his flight into fancy. They wanted to snap him out of it. 'You have to face facts,' was their message, 'I don't want to,' was his.

Marva questioned, 'Is he crazy because he won't face facts or are we crazy because we do?' she decided it was better he not face them...and for her too. He had run away from them in better times. How could he possibly face them in the worst of times? The arguments went on, familiar, worn and repeated, 'He'll meet another...make a good life again, he'll need someone, what kind of life...for you...for him?'

How could she explain? For her, an ideal life, in a way. Finally, <u>being</u> Bessie. For years, she'd watch Aaron adoring her, beseeching, courting her with poems and songs. If there weren't enough occasions as an excuse for writing her poem, he would create an occasion, the fourth day of her sofa, the fifth day of her new shoes...writing an ode to: how lovely the sofa framed her and the petite loveliness of her tiny feet. The very sight of Bessie and a poem danced off his tongue. This was Marva's secret now. He gazed at <u>her</u>, and wrote <u>her</u> poems, and adored <u>her</u>.

"Bessie," he'd say, adoring and Marva would reply to a tender, lilting, "Yes?"

She always felt left out, jealous...but no more. He seemed to have forgotten his daughter entirely. But it didn't matter. She'd rather be Bessie, anyhow. That's why she looked forward to their trips. It was the only time she had him all to herself.

At home, he had eyes only for Bessie. Even in death, she still had him all to herself. 'He must never snap out of it. It's better for us both.'

But who can make decisions for the vagaries of a mind that can't even decide for itself? A year passed, two...all others had finally turned away; the Rabbi, the doctor...they'd been most persistent urging their help. 'Nothing more obnoxious to her than unsolicited help. She finally shouted and slammed the door on the two of them, "She'd be sorry," they warned her.

"Just wanting to punish me for not letting you meddle in my life... both of you!" she shouted after them.

She started noticing, one day, that Aaron's poems lacked their usual ardor. He recited them with the same frequency, but they lacked originality, spontaneity, spark. She supposed he was fatigued, the weariness of age. He ceased his daily singing and occasionally sang a few plaintive, Yiddish love songs, looking in the distance, not at Marva as he had been. He'd ceased buttering Bessie's 'toast,' left it untouched, muttered to himself instead of chatting with her. Marva thought it must be a new phase of his malady. One night, she watched his nightly ritual to see if there'd been any changes. She noticed there had been a few. He opened Bessie's drawer, touched the lock of her hair, put the perfume bottle to his chest, replaced them both, closed the door and left. 'He'd forgotten to tuck her in,' Marva thought. He didn't tip-toe to the door as he usually did and carefully close it softly behind him, but walked heavily, morose to the door and carelessly left it open on the way to his room. She waited a few minutes for the sounds he made before retiring, and, satisfying herself that he was readying himself for bed, she retired for the night.

The following morning, he was not at the table as usual. She looked quickly towards the piano. No one. She hurried upstairs to his room. Knocked gently. No reply. She opened the door. His head was bent over. His face, in the palm of his hand. She touched him. He fell back, eyes staring straight ahead...at nowhere...blank. She ran down the stairs and grabbed the first passerby, a bewildered and frightened man.

"Get a doctor," she said, "quickly!"

She waited at the open door, afraid to return. The doctor only confirmed what she knew already. And then she saw the note on Aaron's pillow, "BESSIE'S GONE."

Aaron returned to reality as suddenly and mysteriously as he had left it and he kept the charade going for Marva as long as he could for her sake.

"You see," she wept bitterly to the doctor, "he came back without your help. What <u>help</u> would it have been if he came back sooner."

"You're right," the doctor said, "he would have died sooner of a broken heart."

Chapter Forty-One

Marva mourned Aaron by secluding herself in his library, surrounded by the books his hands had touched throughout the years, his friends, and comforters. Maybe they would also be hers. Aaron was a man of enlightenment. He loved the 'goyishe' writers, as Bessie used to call them. He had once told her that his Bible, the guiding principle of his life, was in the room. Now she wondered which one of these was his Bible. Each one of them was capable of being his Bible. She needed a clue. Something or someone to direct her considering there was no one here. She looked carefully around the room again and again, staring, focusing, glad to have a purpose to relieve the pain for a moment. Aaron was not a careless man. Books were carefully ordered, neatly piled. Somewhere in all this was the key to Aaron's life...which would be the key to hers. How else could she keep him alive? A gentle rap at the door... the servant with a tray; came and left silently. Suddenly, the memory of old dinner table conversations between her father and the Rabbi intruded in her thoughts. She quietly dismissed them; remembering the gay times now. But they refused to be banished. Scraps of conversation returned until she was recounting them ad verbatim, first on one side, then, the other.

"But the Bible says, 'be fruitful and multiply,'" the Rabbi said.

"Who will take care of all this progeny," Poppa asked.

"God will take care," the Rabbi answered.

"Maybe in your family he takes care. In mine, I take care."

"The woman is the queen of the house."

"How can she be a queen, being fruitful and multiplying? Only a bee can do that. The woman standing on swollen feet with varicose veins, Friday night after being fruitful and multiplying is suddenly a queen because she's praying over candles?'

Marva thought it was strange she should be remembering that now. Through all the loud and sometimes bitter debates Aaron had with the men of religion, she remembered only this...and why now?

"Even philosophers," she saw Aaron laughing as he quipped, "sometimes have children."

She remembered the Rabbi angrily replying, "That's not original!"

And Aaron countering with, "why do I have to be original? Rabbis spend their lives quoting. Why not me...on occasion?"

"Is he worth quoting! A man embittered with life, a pessimist, a cynic, a non-believer."

The rabbi redder and redder with rage.

Soft now, "How can you say that? He's the eternal spring."

"What do you mean by that?"

"Asking me a question, Rabbi. It's of no use. You'll never understand the answer. If you don't accept him, then you can't understand him."

"You compare that German toad to our Sages!"

"I make no comparison, Rabbi. I can simply say, in my mind, the others came and went, and he came and stayed and will remain with me to the end of my days..."

Marva found a clue. A German philosopher. She examined the German philosopher books, struggling with the huge volumes remembering one as it clattered to the floor. She'd seen Poppa bent over it and came on him several times unawares.

"What are you reading, Poppa?"

"Philosophy. Do you want me to read you a few paragraphs?"

"No. It's too heavy for me."

"Someday, I'll make you stay and listen when the time comes," he said once, half-joking, half serious.

"Well, Poppa, the time has come, hasn't it?"

"You've made me stay and listen."

She knew, somehow, she'd found what she was looking for. Pages dogeared, sometimes underlined, unlike the others that were untouched, pages like new, not a mark in them. She read quickly, turning the pages hastily, reading only the under linings. Hospitals, nature, and women.

Poppa fought reality as long as he could, lived his life with Bessie always, 'in the beginning,' shutting the door as best he could against time, and nature. Marva would do the same. She felt closer to her father than she had ever been. She saw him as a man protecting a fragile sensitivity against the pain he saw around him, especially of the one dearest to him, his beloved Bessie. Marva agreed with her father wholeheartedly. He would be her mentor as well. Who would protect her against life? What man? Only Poppa could do it. He was a man. What could a woman do? A man sang the songs and wrote the poems and wooed and courted and whispered and sighed. What could she do when he was tired of the game and wanted to rush her to the next step, further and further away from the magic of the beginning? Leave him, she decided as soon as she sensed a change in key. Leave him and begin again, 'from the beginning' with another troubadour. How else to be courted for the rest of her life and never won...unless she found an Aaron that would court her forever. She had little hope of finding such a one again.

As the years passed, she became an expert in the art of courtship, knowing when to start refusing a caller before he refused to call; married and unmarried...it made little difference...even though she preferred the married ones. They missed the sweet agony of courtship...and she never had enough of it. They were perfectly mated...for a little while. She gave dinner parties for one reason... admirers...present, past, or future. She had to be surrounded by romantic admirers she'd left while they were still alive, and those who were courting and yearning for her were always room for another one of <u>those</u>. She had once found herself, for a brief period, without all three. The experience was so terrifying, she was determined never to repeat it and so spent her days guarding scrupulously against a possible vacuum occurring again.

It was at one of her parties that Lazar was mentioned in the agony of courtship...and she never had enough of it. They were perfectly mated...for a little while. She gave dinner parties for one reason...admirers...present, past, or future. She had to be surrounded by romantic admirers she'd left while they still yearned for her, those who were courting and yearning for her now, and those in the wings to be ready 'just in case.' There was always room for another one of <u>those</u>. She had once found herself, for a brief period, without all three. The experience was so terrifying, she was determined never to repeat it and so spent her days guarding scrupulously against a possible vacuum occurring again.

It was at one of her parties that Lazar was mentioned. The current amusement among members of her class was a romantic involvement with ideas. Marva was too busily preoccupied with romantic involvements of the other kind to pay much attention. Besides, she found it difficult to compete with ideas, so she left these young men alone as a rule as she found their poetry and song reserved mainly for their ideas. Zionists, Socialists, Communists, she found them all very exhausting, but it was becoming more and more difficult nowadays to find men who were 'ists' or some type or another. Politics meant little to her, and she became an ardent 'ist' of whatever persuasion to help the romance along whenever necessary. One evening she had some Zionists for dinner to make things interesting. Lazar was described by him as spellbinding, magical, poetic.

Marva asked, "Where can we hear him, the Zionist? His ideas interest me."

She went to hear him. Fell under his spell as did everyone...and determined to know him.

To such a one was Lazar rushing. His heart was warm with poetry and music...and love for Marva. Somehow, he knew she needed to hear his songs as much as he needed to sing them. He'd been a troubadour without a song for too long. There'd been no one to hear him. Marva would listen and hear, Lazar thought. Listen and hear...like no one ever had before.

Chapter Forty-Two

For the first time in his life, Lazar wondered about the other rabbis. He'd always found validation before custom, the Talmud, support, agreement, encouragement had come from somewhere. He had never felt that he was committing an act that no one in his position had ever done, conceived of, even been tempted. No one. Not one rabbi. It made the shame intolerable to wear. How many times had he lectured, advised, cajoled, on the dangerous temptations of sin to others and now, he found himself looking up quietly at his own accusing index finger shaking menacingly at his frightened eyes. He was being sentenced. With or without her, he was to be sentenced. Without her, by God. With her, by the Devil.

He had always prided himself that he was above the rest. And suddenly, he yearned to know they shared his weakness...at least... one. He couldn't admit that his reasons were as mundane as the others. It was the desperate search for reasons that kept him sitting resolutely in his seat, preventing him from jumping off the train and running home by foot if necessary. Why her? Why me? Why now? What am I doing? And what if someone were to find out. Lazar had

never asked that question in shame before. Arrogantly, conspiratori-
ally, desperately, fearfully...but not guilty and in shame. And yet, that
part, <u>Pintele</u> thought it was at that moment, powerless as it was, knew
that he couldn't turn back. Lazar was a tenacious man, who held tight
as hard as he could, tighter and tighter, straining harder and harder.
Marva was like an angry wind that roars wild and arrogant through
puny obstacles sweeping him along through the wreckage of his questions, his conscience. The train pulled into her station, and he was
hurrying to greet her. There was no other thought in a head that overflowed with them night and day...but one. How would he greet her?
How would he say, 'hello?'

Marva had taken his years from him. She wanted a 'man of the
world' and would find herself with a shy little boy. He would lose her.
Worse. She would find him contemptible. He must say 'hello' from a
position of command. He must force her to do anything. He could
not be found in Moscow. A Rabbi was a criminal there. He could be
in her house. Nowhere else. And no one must find him there.

Arriving at her door, the servant ushered him in, motioned him to
a chair and left. It was time for prayer. He opened his suitcase,
tenderly removed his Talis, placed it around his shoulders, gently
wrapped the tefillin around his forearm to his heart, closed his eyes
and prayed. He prayed the traditional evening prayer...and more...he
prayed to be released from her. He prayed to god to help him to be
righteous...and forgive him if he was not. As a humble penitent, he
still stood very proud, still Rabbi of the shul...in command. He
opened his eyes. She was seated shyly, humbly, looking up at him as
he stood towering over her, majestically lost in a private world which
excluded her. The exclusion humbled and excited her. He was her
God talking to his God. He looked down at her, desire having left
him as suddenly as it came. He felt confident, powerful...the Rabbi
again, a mentor, a guide, a mighty arm on which the 'frail, frightened
hand of Marva can rest.

He removed his Talis and tefillin and slowly replaced them,
prolonging the task until he would have to face her and address her,

unprotected by the voice and dress of the rabbi, the convenience of distant warmth created by them both, the protectors of dignity and pride, the shield.

A small smile darted across Marva's face as he said, 'hello.' Deep, resonant, distant, reserved. Still the rabbi.

"Glad you could come."

Everything was going according to plan. She adored him at a distance. Unlike the other men, he wasn't reduced to flesh and blood when he stepped off the podium, weak, malleable, undesirable. He remained on the podium. But now, his black eyes only saw her. She just had to put out her arm and she could touch him. But she couldn't. He just had to extend his arm to touch her. But he couldn't. It was so strange, he thought. He wanted to be with her, but he didn't want her. She wanted to be with him...but she didn't want him; the only difference being, she had never wanted him. He had wanted her...but only for a brief while. Now, he yearned to be with her. Between him and her, it seemed, there was a magic circle. And he again asked forgiveness, it was like the magic circle between him and God, him, and Zion, him, and Marva.

It was a mystical feeling of awe. He felt that from the first moment he saw her...and it drew her to him again. He saw that she was equally in awe of him. He knew only that he wanted to stand with her on that treacherous pinnacle, subtly balancing on the tip of a fine point where the slightest slip of a fatal plunge from the aery graces of the beginning, the subtle glance, the sigh, the words of music, the music in words, the fears, the reverence in poetry and song. Lazar needed to live in an ethereal world on earth. He needed to sing hymns to God, and praises to Zion and poems to women. The words fell halting from his mouth. He had forgotten for so long that women were beauty and magic and inspiration. How easily his own words once flowed. How, he barely managed to stumble on someone else's.

"How do I love thee?" he haltingly began.

"Let me count the ways."

She joined him and they recited softly together. Silence between them as they looked at each other. 'But I don't love her,' he thought, 'but I needed to tell her so.' 'But he didn't love me,' Marva thought, 'but I needed to hear it.'

"Did you know I was coming back?"

"Yes."

"Even though I'm a Rabbi, a married man? What made you think that?"

"Don't you ask enough questions, Rabbi? Besides, you don't really want the answer to that one.

"Let's not make the mistake of answering for each other."

"But I want an answer to that question."

"Why, <u>that</u> question, Rabbi, out of all the questions in the universe? Why that question?" Flirtations, smiling, her eyes large and innocent.

'She was clever,' Lazar thought, but with charm and sweetness... as if she's asking my permission to be clever, he was charmed.

"I won't answer that question," he smiled in mock victory, "because <u>you</u> don't want an answer to that one."

She teased, "You see Rabbi, you tell me not to do something, and then you go ahead and do it yourself."

"I'm the Rabbi here."

Indulgent, fatherly twinkle in his eye, a gentle smile on his lips. "A Rabbi had privileges."

He enjoyed the repartees, the lightness, the exchange of wit.

"What's the answer to both questions, Rabbi? Let's see how bright you are."

"Simple, the answer is very simple to both questions, but let's see whether you can tell me."

"All right, Rabbi. Give me a few days and I'll tell you."

Stumbling, "You know I have to stay here. I will, of course, be as discreet as possible."

He stood as erect and rigid as a Prussian.

Marva had to suppress a smile.

"Come," she turned, "I'll show you your room."

As he followed, the questions started again. What was he doing here? Where was he? He was suddenly very tired. His shoulders slumped, the questions ceased...and with them...the anxiety. He was mercifully numb while she chatted gaily. 'Do you agree?' he heard from time to time. 'Yes,' he would mumble. She was encouraged to further chatter. At the end of what seemed an interminable hall, she opened the door to a small room, single bed, sparsely furnished. He understood. It was the farthest room from hers. Not because she feared him but to maintain the distance, they both required. They both needed to create what didn't exist, to embellish and dignify. They were still in a situation where Lazar had 'come to call.' The house was larger than five in his town. Her apartment was across the hall that stretched as far as the eye could see in the direction her finger pointed. He could at 11am, she said. The maid would permit him to the waiting room. He would wait his turn to see her. He agreed.

"Tomorrow, I'll show you the library," she said.

"Tomorrow is Shabbos."

"So, it is."

The word sounded so strange in this house, out of place. Lazar had never been happy with orthodox ritualists, 'narrow-minded, dictatorial, petty' he called them. Since the death of his parents, the destruction of his town, he scorned their explanations and often had to suppress doubts about his own faith in God. He had a secret admiration for free thinkers, free of trivial dogmatisms. 'What kind of Rabbi are you?' Celia would rage at him when he nonchalantly treated a dogma with which she tyrannized the family. That's what he resented the most...the tyranny, the narrowmindedness, with which the rituals were adhered to and sadistically imposed on others. Yet here, where he suddenly found himself without one religious' symbol, not one ritual, not one dogma, one Yiddish word, not even Shabbos...he thought he would feel liberated...but he didn't. he felt strange and uncomfortable to be 'A Jew among Jews' who are not

Jews and profess to be Zionists. Lazar believed in Zionism, not because he believed the land was given to the Jews by God, but because he felt for his people. He was a Jew feeling for his people. How can she be a Zionist if she wasn't a Jew? Who were her people? Even though the bed was strange and uncomfortable, Lazar was strangely content. To Lazar, strange and uncomfortable was a life pattern he never relinquished. The familiar and uncomfortable would suddenly disquiet him and he'd find himself driven to wandering and searching. Lazar was an unfortunate man. Unlike the other rabbis, faith Talmud, family, children, did not content him.

"A life thirsty only for Talmud and the search is over," the rabbi said. "The secret of life's fulfillment," he went on, "is to drink at the fountain of Talmud every day."

Lazar thirsted and read and thirsted more and studied and read more and somewhere deep inside, he felt the desert widening, a spirit parched, dry, and cracking, a desperate thirst that no Talmud or study...or even God could tender and nourish and bring to life once more. When those times came upon him, Lazar did what he could... to run, to shout, to declaim on the pain of his people, and underneath that, his own pain that was seeking a painless promised land. He would arrange another lecture tour in new territory, more dangerous than the last, hiding, subterfuge to enter the town, deliver his message and get out. He craved these challenges. Marva was the most uncharted land, the strangest. He didn't fear her or want her. That was not the challenge. The challenge was discovering what he wanted from her, what she wanted from him, perhaps, but mostly... what he wanted from her. They pretended to know each other that they knew the answer to the earlier question. Perhaps that was the beginning of knowing. They were pretending to know each other. Lazar mulled the phrase over and over in his brain. Perhaps, that's what they wanted.

Chapter Forty-Three

Lazar awoke the following morning to an enchanted scene. He'd discovered another reason why he'd been placed in this room. From his window, the sun streaming into the room, red colors dancing on the walls reflected by the sun from the red glass lampshade on the dresser drawer. Wherever he looked in his room there were shafts of sunlight. He was surrounded by light and color. There were three windows in his tiny room, the leaves and branches of tall trees pressing against them. He had the magical feeling of awakening in a treehouse in the forest. Lazar's heart filled to overflowing with joy. When he heard the gentle knock, he heard himself saying, 'come in.' The manservant entered with breakfast. Lazar grabbed a pencil from his apron and started scribbling on his apron while he stood there frightened, startled, thinking surely Lazar must be mad. Lazar wrote a poem of grateful, hearty joy to Marva, feverishly in haste, while he was inspired, fearful he would forget, if he didn't grab the moment. When he reached the bottom of the apron, he pulled it off the neck of the immobilized servant and turned the apron over to write the final stanza, then dismissed the servant. He then carefully copied his creation in florid script, revising here, exaggerating there, and falsifying for poetic effect. He would present this to her when he 'called on her,' he decided. He checked the time. Solemnity crept over to him as it usually did at this hour. Time for morning prayer. Prayer was a deep joy to some...communing with their God. To Lazar, it was always a despairing and anguishing experience. He always felt, somehow, that God wasn't hearing him. Maybe because his prayers ended with Israel and Basha. It seemed like he would never see either one.

"You're not supposed to negotiate with God," the Rabbi said.

"God is not an accountant, with a list of debits and credits."

"But I'm not negotiating," Lazar insisted.

"But you are."

"How do you know?"

"Because you're sitting in judgment of Him. You're forgetting who sits in judgment on who."

"It's a judgment to lament he doesn't hear me?"

"It is. How do you presume to know who he hears?"

Lazar inwardly railed against this kind of passivity, even to God, but he prayed and officiated, and he would be a rabbi. Lazar was a good son and wanted Basha and Benjamin to be proud of him. He hoped Benjamin wasn't watching him all the time. He wouldn't approve of all the things he did, but his disapproval was easier to bear than breaking his heart. It would make it impossible for him to rest in eternity if Lazar had not become a rabbi. Though Benjamin had long gone to his eternal rest, Lazar was still concerned he shouldn't displease him. 'I hope he isn't looking now,' he sighed, as he removed his tallis and tefillin, took his poem in hand and walked down the long, dark hall to Marva's suite. Lazar walked erect, his long beard, reaching to his waist, was parted in the middle, he wore his hat, which made him look even taller, his black eyes, forceful and determined, were even more determined than usual. He was a majestic, lonely figure, walking slowly, dignifiedly, as if he were visiting a congregant, only the poem in his hand reminding him of a mood long since gone.

He would give it to her and maybe her joy would rekindle his spirit once more. Or maybe...she would laugh at him. He discarded that thought as quickly as it came. Lazar looked so much like a Prophet. No one laughed at him when he looked and felt like Isaiah. No one would dare.

He rapped on the door gently. The maid opened it and Marva simultaneously appeared.

She waved him out as he said, "Good morning. I want to show you the library."

His plans were instantly disrupted as he had an image of how he'd present his poem...in her pink parlor, her pink dress, the room bathed in flowers, a perfect setting for his poem. But then, he shrugged inwardly, he would find another. He folded the poem and pocketed it. He followed her as she moved gracefully, the gentle curve of her neck caressed by the soft curls of a few wisps of hair, and beyond the wave of that lovely hair, her marvelous face.

"You're beautiful," he suddenly found himself saying, in that resonant, deep, rabbinical voice.

She exulted. That's what she dreamed since the first night she saw him on the podium. That voice saying, 'You're beautiful.' She continued walking silently. He took the poem from his pocket and read to her in the dim light, accompanied by the slow ambling footsteps down the hall, his voice raising and lowering to the music of his words. She didn't dare turn her head. It was an ode to the beauty of her spirit. In her absence, she had prepared for him a feast of beauty for which he was grateful. Their hearts touched. He understood her language. He had passed the severest test. It mattered not the smallness, the bareness, the spareness of the room. Lazar was moved by what moved her, the symphony of color and light, the magic that greeted him in the morning.

He had written of that in his poem. She turned and smiled, graceful.

"So, you do know why I chose that room."

"Yes."

"I'm glad."

"You made a beauty of ugliness. I like that. Just like your Zionism...also making beauty out of ugliness. The in-gathering of tortured, lonely, homeless, and abandoned exiles nestled under a protective wing...and the reality...disease, death, hardship. But they didn't mention that."

Marva thought, 'The rabbi is the man for me. Never <u>once</u>, in any of his speeches, did he mention the reality of the Promised Land, only hypnotic words that touched the dreamers...and touched her... though she dreamed other dreams. The rabbi was a courtier. He courted the congregants for his God with the Old Testament's poetry and song and promise of paradise, he courted them for Zionism with visions and dreams and appeals to their hunger for hope with a voice that was trained through the generations to hypnotize and lead and inspire...and leave it's healers will-less and malleable. Who could better court her than this rabbi? A master of his art with the outside world. Why not with her?'

She opened the door to the library. Lazar gasped, "Magnificent."

His eyes circled the walls lined with books. He rushed to the nearest wall, labeled 'Philosophy,' excitedly pulled out book after book, Heidegger, Hegel.

"I must read them all! Let me stay," he pleaded, "for a while in this room without distractions, Celia, congregants, children."

"You can stay as long as you like. My father always pleaded, 'Read with me, Marva,' I never did. I'm sorry now."

With the passing days, she confided in him more and more of her days with Aaron and he to her with memories of Basha. They only revealed to each other the memories that embellished the romantic image of each other. Marva didn't tell Lazar about her trips with Aaron, of the women with red fingernails at nearby tables, of strange whisperings in the middle of the night. She talked softly and mystically only about his eternal romance with his beloved wife.

Lazar told her of Basha's gentle beauty, the worship of her at a distance by everyone, especially by him. He didn't tell her how she was ignored by Benjamin. She didn't ask. He just let her imagine an idyll between Basha and Benjamin as he was led to imagine between her mother and Aaron. The message was clear. That's the way it would be between them, would be...indeed...had to be. Lazar had found his Basha. He held Marva's hand and talked to her far into the night, his voice resonant as she sat sleepy beside him. Half dreaming, he would recite by memory, pages of Talmudic wisdom, psalms, the Songs of Solomon. They would awake sitting on a pillow surrounded by books, sometimes, one open on their laps to the last page they'd read before their eyes could no longer grasp the words and then Lazar dipped into his memory or his own soul for more words and yet more. He adored her with his talk, and she listened and wanted to hear her more and yet more. He would lull her to sleep with his words. She listened to them as a child waits for a lullaby.

'Some people are made up of rhyme, coincidence, omen, periodicity, and presage. They meet the person they seek. If I put my hands on the North star, would it be as beautiful?'

They were both seeking purity, both fearful from the fall from grace, the first hint of the in harmonic note, the intrusion of which meant betrayal...as deep as Eve had wrought on Adam; burning shame and removal from paradise. Lazar was grateful to have found a woman of such exquisite sensibility that she not only understood but felt as finely tuned as he to the poetic nuances, the mystical, the subtle ebb and flow so fine that there was never any movement from the enchanted circle, but further refinement of the circle, a beauty so exquisite, it was painful.

Marva was grateful to have found a man who needed as deeply as she, to remain the circle, adoring and adored, because he feared, as she did, the black void on the other side of paradise into which they would fling each other and which neither could bear. A circle in hell, two tortured souls, berating each other inwardly, twisting and turning, shouting and hurling abuse and invective, the sordid pain of the degradation in reality. Lust was the trap door that awaited the unwary and plunged them into the grim circle from which there was no return. Their circle was as fragile, as beautiful as the stem of a flower, and as easily broken. They were happy to find another who would tend the flower, too, with devoted and gentle care, to keep its bloom and its freshness and its face to the sun. The hope was there that it could be kept forever, the fear that it could not. Each day, they met each other anew, each searching the face of the other for the answer to their question. Each day was a new beginning.

She asked him, "Am I still being courted?"

And he is wondering, "Was I still enchanting her?"

The library was their meeting place. There were never enough hours in the day for his devotions to God and to her. Somehow, he felt close to God since he found his Marva. He looked to her and he looked to God...with adoration, supplication and now, the first time, gratitude. There was one difference, however, he'd been angry with God, questioning Him, criticizing, judging. He was never angry, critical, or judgmental with Marva.

"Read with me, Marva," Lazar pleaded.

Marva saw 'I love you,' in his eyes, and heard, 'I love you' in his voice. She didn't reply. Lazar replied to her thinking, believing her silence meant, 'I love you too.'

"Where shall we start?"

"You start...and call me if you find something interesting."

Lazar's face fell. He couldn't bear for her to leave the room. She walked efficiently to the bell pull. The servant arrived.

"Bring a coffee for the Rabbi."

And to Lazar, "I shall wait for your signal." And left.

He quickly turned his eyes searchingly to the bookshelf to restore his dignity in front of the servant. He sat down for a moment when the servant left. 'What had happened? Nothing,' he realized. She was pretending. It was all part of the game. A romantic game, risky challenge, sometimes dangerous, but poetic and beautiful. But hadn't he also pretended? The loving, pleading in his eyes, the game of hidden message behind innocent words. But it was a very serious game to them both. They both needed the magic circle. Lazar needed the magic to bury the horrors of his being under a mystical, dreamy vision. She needed it because she's never known any other life and dreaded making it's acquaintance. She had glimpsed it from a distance and turned away quickly, like a traveler who's lost his way traveling the main road that leads again and again to a grim certainty so decides to follow a slim path, hidden, obscure, beautiful...but leading nowhere in particular. Marva walked back and forth across that road and found Lazar to make a few trips with her. He was an old hand at following paths that lead nowhere.

She was certain he wouldn't press her when the time came. She'd spend her days figuring, 'how to prolong the enchantment'...the beginning. She had no trouble with the ending. There was always the magic of a lost attainable love. She decided she would wait to be summoned by Lazar.

Lazar felt alone in the library, searching by habit for the familiar Jewish books; a novel, a short story, maybe, even a Jewish song...nothing. It was the first time he'd seen a Christian library in a Jewish home. The titles and authors intrigued him. He chose books at random and forgot about Marva until he came to a poetry book, flipped the pages, and read.

Marva had been waiting, comfortably, at first, until she could wait no longer. She crept noiselessly up behind him, his head bent intently over a book. She tapped him gently on the shoulder while he simultaneously raised his hand and pulled the bell.

He turned around and shouted joyously, "I've found a poem I want to read to you!"

"Let's read it together, earmarked by my father, one of his favorites...and mine. I found this poem after he died."

Love comforteth like sunshine after rain,
But lust's effect is tempest after sun,
Love's gentle spring doth always fresh remain,
Lust's winter comes ere' summer half be done.

She quickly turned the pages, "We must read this one."
She began and he joined her.

Sorrow on love hereafter shall attend,
It shall be waited on with jealousy,
Find sweet beginning, but unsavory end,
Never settled equally, but high or low,
That all love's pleasures shall not match his woe.

They looked up at each other like two weary soldiers suddenly stumbling on each other on a grim battlefield, surrounded by blood and pain, thinking they're alone and suddenly finding each other. They embraced and wept, deep, and buried tears shaking their bodies. Marva's head, resting on his shoulder, nestled in Lazar's large, powerful arm, Lazar's big head on her slim little shoulder, careful it should not rest too heavily, yet needing the comfort of his head nestling in her small arm stiffly touching her shoulder...careful not to hurt her.

Chapter Forty-Four

A week had passed without either being aware of the passage of time until Lazar announced, "Tomorrow is Shabbos."

Startled. "What does that mean?"

"It means I must leave today. I must be in shul tomorrow. I'll miss you." A desperate edge in his voice.

Distant, calm. "I'll help you pack."

Then from him, as he turned to day goodbye at the door, "Come with me."

"No, Lazar, don't you see? We will miss each other. Don't insist I come with you."

But she would have been upset if he hadn't. They both knew that, and each did what was right. Their unwritten code demanded he plead, and she refused. They know their parts perfectly because both were pure romantics. Each knew how to preserve that fragile mood in the other. He hurriedly turned to go.

"I'll write to you."

She watched from the window 'til he closed the coach door...and turned away. He looked back for one more glimpse. The window was empty...in his pocket, as he took out his handkerchief, his fingers touched a note she had left for him.

"<u>Song of Solomon:</u>

I opened to my beloved,

But my beloved has withdrawn himself and was gone,

My soul failed when he spoke,

I sought him but I could not find him,

I called him but he was gone and gave me no answer."

A tear dropped, blurring a word. He gently folded the note and returned it to his pocket where it was safe from his tears.

As he neared the door, he heard a voice screaming, "Rose, remember the potatoes and a fresh loaf of bread. You hear? Fresh!"

He didn't hear the soft reply, "Yes momma," as Rose opened the door.

"Poppa," she said smiling, Lazar patted her on the head.

Without him realizing it, it remained there while Celia shouted, "Lazar is that you?"

And she suddenly appeared, staring at him in surprise.

"Who else?"

The black void again, the other side of paradise, the other circle.

"Of course, I'm back!" shouting now, "Didn't I say I would be back today!"

She retreated into silence. Not because she feared him as did almost everyone else, but because, mercifully for Lazar, she couldn't think of a snappy, stinging reply just then. That occasionally happened. All day, the children had been 'on her nerves.' She was angry. She was preparing for Shabbos, and he was late, and she was late. He never showed the anxiety about Shabbos as she had. She asked herself the same question over and over about Lazar, 'what kind of rabbi was he?' Sometimes he thought the one factor, above and beyond the world's tribulations and his own, that made him question his faith was Celia. God, above all other issues, had become an issue between them. She zealously bombarded the children with her rules and regulations, keeping an ever-watchful eye of their souls. He would whisper, 'Pay no attention. It's not that important.' He couldn't bear her screaming, but couldn't bear giving in to her, either. Even Sabbath dinner could not contain her. Lazar's fantasy of a peaceful dinner, solemn and obedient wife praying over candlelight shining on her face, children reading the siddur around the table and then all joining together in song. Celia and the children were never realized.

This was Lazar's deepest heartache, the magic, the peace of Shabbos, somehow managed to quiet the tongue, the heart, remove the scowl from the face of the worst shrews. His congregants, who complained interminably about their noisy wives looked forward to Shabbos when peace mercifully descended on them at sundown, the eve of Shabbos. But not Lazar. For him, there was not much expectation. Celia's voice...on and on to the children, 'Read slowly, don't muffle your words, don't wolf your food'...on and on.

His trips away from home increased in frequency, and she revenged herself with the increasingly stridency of her voice. On Shabbos, more orders, more interruptions. Lazar found every mood, every nerve shattered, the battering on his senses ceaseless and scarring as her voice ripped through them time and time again. A bitter circle at home; the assault of the high-pitched venomous voice, the running away, only to meet more of the same, worse even, when he returned. And above all, she had grown ugly in his eyes. And more, she had committed the worst crime of all in Lazar's eyes. She was uninteresting. She'd become a bore. She screamed, not about the human condition. Her screams were the noise and rumble of the trivia of life under which all thought and reflection was buried; trivial chores, trivial joys, trivial despairs...even trivial religion.

"Be careful," he heard her screaming, "don't spot your dress!"

'Could it be,' he asked himself, she didn't know how miserable she and Lazar were? 'Could it be that he'd never really reflected on that before. It would make him too miserable to reflect on his misery. He couldn't bear the pain of facing his pain. He rose to leave the table.

She shouted "Where are you going? Sit a minute with the children!"

He sat down will-less for a moment. He suddenly rose again, turned to her, his face blazing with rage, slammed his fist on the table, the Shabbos candle shaking, flickering. Morbid, frightened, put his hand to steady them. The other children started crying in unison. Lazar stormed out of the room. She sat, hushed and quiet, touched the table with her open hand where he had struck it as if it were a blow, he had visited over her face...and her hand reflexively snapped to the spot to touch the <u>wound</u>. She knew that blow was meant for her. How dare he! She pursued him into his room. He was sitting, his back to her.

Before she could release another stream of righteous indignation, the kind she loved best, he said quietly, without daring to face her, in a voice deadly quiet, "I'm going to leave you."

Fuming, "So, what's new about that?"

"I'm not coming back."

Screaming now, "To a wife and seven children, you're not coming back?"

There was no stopping her now. She had all her weapons arrayed and ready. In the midst of the storms, Lazar asked himself, 'What was the drama in her life? My imperfections and the children. What would she do if we were perfect, and life was fair to her? She would go mad. There would be nothing else to fill her days...without a reason for churning.' She was goading him now. He knew she was seeing the dramatic possibilities...the ultimate drama, the quintessential heroine...left with seven children...abandoned: Lazar, the quintessential villain...the abandoner of a good wife and innocent children. She was too blind with rage now to realize the danger; the scandal if they knew. He would lose his home, his temple. That was the only appeal possible now, the appeal of bread. She would never see her children go hungry. He turned without a word, put on his tallis and tefillin and prayed. She sat down quietly and stared at him. He was still and awesome sight to her in his tallis and tefillin. He prayed for strength to tell her what he'd decided he would tell her. He continued a rhythmic, fervent shaking, back and forth, accompanying his thoughts and his heart. He had run away again, away again, away from her in a private communion with God, the only way he found that he could be left alone in peace, for a while, in his own home.

Chapter Forty-Five

Lazar prayed silently until Celia's eyes started closing, her head nodding. He knew she would soon rise to check the children and he would raise his head from the prayer book and prepare for bed. He would pretend he was sleeping while his head whirled with images. Celia was brave now, but suppose she thought he meant what he said. 'What then?' He asked himself. He would howl in pain and Celia never listened. She would <u>whisper</u> in pain, and he heard. Suddenly, her part, in the long years of martial travail would disappear. Asking, "What have I done?" and crying, "I don't understand!" in anguish and disbelief. It would be no use explaining as she would still maintain, more and more stridently, that she doesn't understand and then, the tearful accusations would follow. He was cowed before all that. 'Was it worth it?' he asked no one in particular. How many times had he imagined that such a time would come to pass in his life? How many times had guilt stayed on his tongue? Guilt, and he must admit, convenience.

He had nowhere else to go. It seemed so ironic that domestic scenes had the same tawdry sameness, the same pattern, regardless of how many years of wisdom and Torah learning lay between them.

Whether the man was a plumber, a tinkerer, or a rabbi, the martial pain of dissolution had the same language, the same pattern. How many Celias had he heard from the congregants? The loud rat-a-tat of the machine gun mouth, the words pouring forth the authority of a drill sergeant without cadence, period, comma, expecting the other, with his brain shattered by the onslaught and the volume to provide the periods and commas and ground under the avalanche of the words of a woman needing desperately to be right.

And the Lazars twisting and turning, this way and that, shrinking more and more the daily assaults labeled, 'How can you do this to me?' the rope getting tighter and tighter with every year, every child. Which group was Lazar to join? Those that complained but never even mentioned leaving, those that complained and sighed, someday, all of their lives, those that broke the bonds and fled, with a chorus of condemnation behind them and desperate dreams in front of them, desperate because they're not the fresh, innocent dreams had turned to shambles, but the guilt-ridden ones of those whose dreams had turned to shambles, and they're still driven to pursue another despite of it, carrying with them, however, the images of their victims. Youth has no victims, exacts no price for its illusions. Age exacts a price in the dream and the realization. Both tainted and tempered. The dream needs the props of endless explanations and apologies, beset by fears and doubts. Youth plunges into its dreams looking ahead. Age walks hesitantly, slowly, looking forward and backward every step of the way, feeling its direction bound by the decision of another...not a romantic decision, but a guilty decision. <u>If only I'd be thrown out</u>. And they wait to find the lock changed when they come home, trying to get in and refused. Only to hear later, 'You left me.' 'But you threw me out!' 'You would have come back if you really wanted to be with me!'

The guilty one knows the other is right and the guilt returns, more powerful than ever. The victim knows he is guilty. Her despair is tinged with satisfaction. She can torture him. Lazar had seen this so many times...and now...he too? Forever the weapons of torment, a dash of tears, the wide-eyed helpless look, the chest pounding. 'Was the universe so brilliantly constructed,' thought Lazar, 'that even marital pain can be a pleasure to the sufferer, a torment to the villain? He would be pilloried!' Lazar thought, 'I would welcome that.' 'Good lord,' he begged, 'pillory me.' That's why the old Rabbi warned Lazar, 'Don't turn your eyes from the book!' A few poems, a little moment in man's paradise? They were right. Better to wait for God's paradise. All of life was arrayed against man's paradise in this life and beyond. Lazar feared, most of all, that all his endless and infinite reasoning and weighing would be helpless in this situation. He would be unable to guard against his temper. His wild impulsive outbursts when his wife goaded him on. It had not really mattered at this point. But now it mattered. One unguarded moment that passed, the one to come, Lazar was swinging helplessly between them both. In his darkest moments, sleep came to him...but not this time. He tossed and turned, pleading to be rescued. The dawn came, his eyes still staring into the darkness.

Sometimes, during the night, his wife crept into bed beside him and fell asleep. He could hear her snoring, shook her several times to no avail. Her snoring increased his desperation, to erase the sound of her and the thought of her...and failed abysmally in both. Even in sleep, she defeats me and torments me. Even in sleep, she can't be quiet. He pretended to be asleep when she awoke at dawn, prayed the morning prayer. She would not disturb him 'til after breakfast. He savored the few remaining moments of peace. After all, he couldn't wear tallis and tefillin all day, just to keep her quiet. He arose when he heard the door closing.

He went down to breakfast. She had her back turned to him as he descended the stairs. He sat down at the table, and she served him in suffering silence, her martyred face staring at the bowl and teaspoon, but accusing him. 'Aha,' he thought, 'the assault had begun already.' She appeared to be busy with other chores, but he knew she was watching, like a hungry tiger, every move made by the prey and choosing her time to strike. She always waited 'till he finished his meal. 'No sense cooking for nothing,' she always said. She wouldn't give him the satisfaction of leaving her cooking untouched, or worse, have him push a full plate away from him. Oh no! She waited... usually, 'til he finished his tea. This time, she couldn't wait that long. Still half a cup remaining, she attacked him.

"Nu, Lazar," wiping her hand on her apron as if she were preparing to strangle him, "Nu," she screamed, "what are you going to do! Did you mean what you said about leaving? When is it going to be!"

"No,' he thought, 'he hadn't meant it. But he meant it now.'"

"Now!" the word exploded from his lips.

"Now!" he repeated, as he rose abruptly from the table, the chair falling to the floor as he rushed wildly to the door. She followed him, screaming, "Where are you going!"

"I'll let you know when I get there!"

Pursuing him into the other room, "What are you going to do?"

"I don't know what you're going to do but I know what I'm going to do! I'm getting a divorce! Do you hear? A divorce! And I'm going to marry someone else. You hear? Someone else!"

"What?" she burst into tears. "So that's what you are...a...a..."

He couldn't hear the words through the tears. "And what will I tell people?"

"Tell them I'm lecturing!"

Sobbing now, "And how will we eat? We'll go hungry!"

"You won't go hungry. Don't worry. I'll make the arrangements."

Suddenly quiet.

"What arrangements?"

Quiet, too.

"Arrangements. Now I have to go."

He was astounded to realize he was still determined to go even though his rage subsided. Has his pride taken over? Certainly not. Whatever it was, he was going, the impetus, the momentum...was there and couldn't be stopped. She watched him in silence as he methodically packed his belongings. Without being aware of it, she had been catapulted into a state of numbed shock. Her hands, always busy, now hung listlessly by her side. She heard the luggage snap closed. He walked briskly down the stairs. She heard, 'Morris, come here, I have something to tell you.'

Then the front door snapped shut...and she fainted. As he hurried down the street, his directions hid purpose became clearer and clearer. He took a coach to the station...one way to Warsaw. His excitement mounted as the train pulled away from the station. He could hardly wait. The train seemed slow, the trip so long.

He hurriedly scribbled a note and gave it to one of his congregants traveling with him on the train, "Give this to the Rebbetzin," he told him, "When you come back."

It said, 'Go to Rabbi Pincus if you need anything.'

He didn't even ask himself what he would find when he arrived. The train stalled when he was a few minutes from his destination, and he was frantic with impatience when he finally arrived at his destination, his heart beating so fast, his hands trembling, 'Lazar, the veldt mensch*, behaving like a schoolboy,' he thought.

The servant answered the bell.

"Tell your mistress, the rabbi is here."

"Come in," the servant replied, calmly, imperiously. Lazar rushed in.

"You may be seated," the servant said. Lazar stood.

"Lazar, what are you doing here? Back so soon!"

He thrust out his hand to welcome her, rushed closer, and stood near her.

"Marva," he whispered, repeated again, and again, adoring her with the deep warmth of his voice.

"I want to marry you."

"But you're married already!"

She fell back. The welcoming smile disappeared, the face hardening.

---

* **_Veldt Mensch – Worldly Person_**

"Sit down," she said coldly, "and tell me about the children."

He was so shaken by her coldness; he obeyed her without thinking.

"I'm arranging to take care of them. We'll discuss that later."

"You mean you left your wife and children...to marry me?"

"Who else would I leave my wife and children to marry?"

He suddenly quipped and became deadly earnest again.

"I left my wife years ago for many reasons. This is the first time I ever left her to get married. My children, I haven't left. They're used to my coming and going. I'll be coming and going out of their lives as usual. The only thing that will really change, my darling, is that I can open my eyes and see you as often as I can and hear you...and you'll hear me...and I'll want to...and you'll want to...and then there'll be nothing between us but a book and that book will only serve to bind us closer."

Cowering, like a child about to be beaten and begging, "No, Lazar, please, I don't want to be married."

"But why, Marva?"

Gentle now, and rising to pat her head, "Don't you love me? Don't you want me?" and suddenly snapping, "Don't you?" as he suddenly doubted, she did.

Desperate, "I love you, but I don't want you! I don't want anyone! Only Poppa! I want Poppa like Momma had Poppa. Like I had him! Don't you understand Lazar? I don't want to be like the ladies with the long, red fingernails! He took them and left them. He only adored Momma...who he never had. No one is going to do that to me, Lazar. No one!"

"How do you know what went on between your momma and poppa?"

Screaming, "I know! I know!"

"What are you saying? What ladies' nails? Tell me the story."

She sat down on the floor. Mumbling, "I'm ashamed." Her head leaned on her knees.

"Tell me. I've heard every story."

She told him, halting, fearful, looking up at him when she'd finished. All her haughtiness and sophistication swept away.

"Alright, I understand. You can't marry. I won't pressure you."

"Why don't you rest and stay for dinner?" she said casually, detached. "You can take the night train home."

He was pained but relieved. He didn't want another hysterical woman in his hands.

"She knows," he concluded, "what she wants to know. As I did. We both made the same mistake."

She pulled the bell and turned as the servant appeared. He knew the discussion was over. He'd lost his case.

The servant appeared. "Someone to see the Rabbi."

A woman with a young boy. He fled to the door. Celia and his eldest son, Phil, age 16. The head rabbi had directed them here. They traveled all night, practically falling into the big room. Celia's eyes searching Lazar's face.

He could only manage to say, "What are you doing here?"

Her face fell.

"I want to talk to you alone, Poppa."

Celia stood outside the doorway strangely quiet, turned and closed the door behind her.

"Momma says you're leaving us for another woman. Is that true?" his mouth trembling, his legs apart, defiant.

He was prepared for a battle with Lazar, yet petrified to confront him.

"It's true," Lazar said quietly.

Phillip crumbled.

He walked slowly to the chair, his legs suddenly too weak to hold him and sobbing, "Why!"

Lazar sat down beside him, put an arm around his shoulder, comforting. The first time in their lives they felt so close to each other, a guilty father and accusing son.

"Because Celia is a good mother to you, but not a wife to me. But it doesn't matter anymore," he said wearily. "I'm coming home."

"You are?" a smile struggling through the tears. Then cautious and disbelieving, "How come?"

He thought wryly, 'How could he tell his son he was rejected by the other woman?'

"Enough questions, Phillip. You've already had one explanation too many. Poppas don't explain certain things to sons, only to other poppas. We'll discuss this again in ten years when you'll understand something. Now, you'll understand nothing. It will just be a lesson in that's above your head. Go tell your mother and leave us alone."

Celia came in quickly, "I'm coming home. You came for me and I'm coming home."

Celia wanted to say, 'What's the matter? She didn't want you. But she didn't...not because of any conscious subterfuge.' She was too numbed and tired even to talk. Lazar misunderstood. He thought she was chastened. He thought he'd long ago given up hope, but he discovered that he hadn't. He looked at her sympathetically. He hadn't done that for a long time, and had almost forgotten what she looked like. He tried to remember their early days. Her mouth thickened now, the high cheekbones bulging jowls, her chin doubled, her body...all mother, breasts for feeding, large stomach and hips for bearing, legs veiny and swollen from tending.

He was revolted, but said gently, "Come Celia. We're going home."

He opened the door for her. She was discomforted, hesitant for a moment. The graces embarrassed her. Her pace was frantic, rushing, dashing, plunging in and out, scurrying like a mole. There was no time to pause for niceties. No one there to perform them. Spinning and spinning, the daily momentum rushing her more and more. Lazar slept through it all. 'Closed to life. Do not disturb.' He came and went and left her alone through it all. He came to sing, to converse with them, bid them goodbye as he left for his trips. The idea was his chore, his romance, his duty, and, she began to grimly realize, his escape from her and the children. She prided herself that she could see through it all. Lazar, a poor rabbi, with seven children, had delusions of grandeur. 'He was already trying to make her into the woman to whom she nearly lost him, a lady, and an aristocrat…a bum, a tramp, a curve,' she thought, glaring at him. The smile disappeared from his face. He glowered back at her as if to say, 'Watch yourself. I'll change my mind.'

She bent her head, stared at the floor, and scurried to the front door, flinging it open before he could reach it and jumping into the wagon shouting, "Phil!"

He followed them slowly out the door, the servant shutting it behind him. Celia took the reins and prodded the horse on. They traveled in silence to the long-distance home. When the wagon rocked on the uneven road from side to side, their bodies touched. It was their only contact on the long journey home. Lazar stared straight ahead without one backward glance. 'He would weep later,' he thought when he was alone.

Marva watched the wagon as it ambled down the road from a window where she could not be seen. She was glowing with pride. Even in that humble, rickety wagon, the Rabbi had dignity. He was an awesome figure no matter where he was, she, Marva, had conquered him. She had arranged a dinner for that night and was particularly glowing, remembering how skillfully she'd maneuvered herself out of this one. It ended just the way she liked it.

He would remember her nostalgically, even yearn for her at times. Yes, she'd performed well enough to be convincing, even to a Talmudic scholar, a sage. She'd convinced him she was a frightened child. How important that must have made him feel, frightened of him. And it was the beginning, too, of his desire to flee. The rabbi didn't want to live with problems. He preferred to be remembered. As she did. She'd pretend to hysteria. 'It worked. He left her. I'll always be with him, always when he's alone. I like that. Very much.' When the Rabbi reached home and fell into bed, his body that had been touching Celia's was near her again.

Celia turned from him lamenting, "You don't want me. You're here because you can't have her."

Lazar pleading, "But I do want you."

A gentle lie.

"Come here." He ordered softly, and turned her around, loving her dutifully, without passion, dutifully...as she had been accustomed. And she submitted dutifully...as she had been accustomed. A child was born from their union on this night, and they named him, Eitan. When he found out the truth of this story in later life, he called himself a love child. And all his days, he considered himself living proof that their love was rekindled.

Chapter Forty-Six

Lazar rose the following morning to the familiar sound of Celia's shouting, the children's wailing. The sounds jarred his ears. He could never understand how people could say they were inured to the sound of clack and discord of wife and children. He'd long ago concluded there must be two differing human systems, both discernable by their reaction to sound. His was a poetic, musical system that found human jangle a painful experience. Celia's judgment, 'too sensitive.' No one took his complaint seriously. Marva lived in tranquility, an invisible world around her, the murmur, the whisper, the sigh. Loud, passionate oratory...only at a distance, passionate declaration...the soft plea, insistent, of the ardent romantic. The world intruded only at her invitation...even its sounds. Those that had no respect for barriers, assault, and retreat at will, ungovernable, anarchic, barging in ruthlessly when unwanted wouldn't dare to enter. Even the sound respected her boundaries, asking her permission.

Lazar concluded that was a dignified and poetic life. A world that falls gently on the ears. It was as simple as that. He was suddenly aware that the noise had stopped. Silence in a noisy household is as startling as sudden ruckus in a silent one.

He dressed hurriedly, rushed down the stairs. "What's wrong?"

The tinkerer Brindel at the door, the children and Celia surrounding him, curiosity overcoming everything else, they were quiet...and listening.

Lazar shouting, "What's wrong?"

"A pogrom is coming."

"In where! How do you know!"

"Send the children out. It'll show you."

And he removed a picture of a candle from his back pocket. Lazar collapsed in a chair.

"This picture was slipped under my door in the middle of the night. On the back was written, 'A pogrom is coming in Koltchik. Do something.'"

Lazar demanded, "Why your door and not mine!"

"I don't know, Rabbi. I think they made a mistake. I'm not one of them."

"No, they don't make these kinds of mistakes. The situation must be very serious. They're trying to rouse everyone. There will be others soon. Maybe they thought I knew."

'But how could I have known,' he thought, the shame deep, accusing, 'I was so busy with myself.' He remembered now Celia telling him, before he fell asleep, that the head rabbi had been sending urgent messages, that he had to see him immediately.

"Where's the Rabbis' messages," he demanded now, and she pointed to them. In the pile was an envelope with a different hand-writing. He tore it open. Inside was a picture of a candle. On the back, the same message.

"I have one too," he told Brindel.

"Don't worry," Lazar heard himself saying. "I'm going there myself. I want to see what's going on. And Celia, you don't worry," he patted her head to reassure her. "I'll see for myself and let you know."

"Don't go. It's dangerous. You'll be killed." And she grabbed both his arms with her hands, "Don't go."

To Brindel, "Did you even hear a Jew going into a pogrom!"

"Yes," Brindel replying, "every Jew that's born is going into a pogrom."

"What kind of talk is that! Remember, you're a tinkerer...not a philosopher. Now, you're tinkering even with philosophy! You're not a philosopher. Lazar is not a tinkerer. Don't answer for the Rabbi."

Lazar brusquely disengaged himself from Celia, grateful that Brindel's interference caused her to loosen her grip. 'I have no time,' he thought, 'he debates between hysterical women and illiterates.'

"I must do what I need to do! We must protect our children."

He knew that would quiet Celia. It had no real meaning at the moment, but that sentence had a magical charm. It silenced her immediately. He used it sparingly when he thought she might make some connection between it and the point about which she was screaming. He hated packing and unpacking. Celia was too slow and there was more bickering, so he did himself. He winced as he heard the door slam behind him.

Basha, his brothers and sisters, his town, his youth, Rosele, his in-laws...maybe this time, he could save them. What Jew rushes to a pogrom? The answer is simple...the guilty. Who ran away from home, who cursed one, who lost his near and dear, who wants the new family to live the unlived life of the old one. Lazar felt he owed them all a life...to tear them back from the Christians and bring them home...to safety...to the land where they belonged...not like his brothers and sisters...condemned to walk through eternity in a land of strangers. They were all his brothers and sisters now and he was bringing them all home. Why weren't they listening? He was always impatient in trains and coaches. They were a torture; waiting in depots, reading in crowded cars, children laughing at him, deriding his beard, the occasional, 'zhid*.' But most of all, he was impatient.

---

* **Zhid – Jew**

He couldn't wait to be where he was going. He arrived at night and was to take a train to the Kisner Rabbi.

He dozed a bit and suddenly heard the coachman barking at him, "Run zhid, the town is burning! Get out! I don't want to be found with a Jew in my coach!"

He flung Lazar out and sped away. Lazar rushed behind an embankment and watched in horror...the savage cruelty of man when it's drunk with the freedom to vent itself however it sees fit, when it feels under it's whip, helplessness and passivity...in a people never taught to defend itself...or even feel the right to be angry without qualification or explanation.

"How can you be angry with all Christians, the congregants asked. Some of them are so good."

The truth was they weren't angry with any of them. The good gave them an excuse for never being angry. Nothing put more fury in Lazar's heart than their lack of it. Lazar watched as the arrogant, advancing, uniformed struck with clubs and whips, babies torn from their mothers and exultantly raised in the air with the point of their swords.

Anguished screams rent the air mingled with the rhythm of military cadence, of shouts of order shouted from the leaders urging them to more and more barbarism and bloodletting...a cacophony in hell. The pitiful huts, the people rushing heedlessly with small bundles of possessions, scurrying in circles, the bundles dropping as they're clubbed or stabbed or stomped by the horse of an indifferent rider. Their lust for excitement, their boredom, the emptiness of their lives...was received for a moment. It mattered little that they had vanquished the unarmed. Death all around them. There was no one left to kill or maim.

"On to the next town!" the leader shouted, as his horse tread carefully over the bodies. Lazar crept out of hiding as the sound of their horses receded into the silence.

His task was a grim one. He searched for one who was breathing. He felt each one from one to the other, embracing each with his hand on the heart, turning his ear to their chest, searching for a sign of life, their blood covering him as he went from one to the other. No matter how scarred they were, he bent down and embraced them...hoping to find one that would breathe as he touched him. He found no one.

In the darkness, he crept back to the encampment. He understood now why Basha and Roselle left this world for a private one of their own. Right now, he felt he could do the same...if he let himself cross that narrow path...but something held him back. The mission he had to fulfill. He was afraid to weep, to give in to the anguish he knew would overwhelm him if he dared open his breast to it, even a crack. 'No, he wouldn't weep, moan, or lament.'

"I'd rather kill, God forgive me, I'd rather kill! No, I ask for forgiveness. Give me the strength," he pleaded to God, "give me the strength to kill...and lead others to do the same. Give them the courage to join me in hate."

Lazar's journey home, surreptitious, guarded, 'til he fell into the house managing to say, "Don't worry," as he collapsed on the bed.

He awoke to the familiar sounds and was grateful to them for the first time.

Rose by his bedside, "Poppa."

"I'm alright, any messages?"

"Just this from the head Rabbi."

She read, "You all know about the pogrom in...we must show them. We must fast."

"I don't want to hear it anymore. What do we show them if we fast? That we're hungry. That they know already."

"Blood on your face, clothing! Where did it come from? We were frantic. We thought it was your blood!"

"It is."

"But you're not hurt anywhere!"

"But I __am__ hurt, __everywhere__! Call Momma now."

Celia rushed in, hovering, adjusting his pillow, question followed question, remedy after remedy suggested.

"I want you to announce an emergency meeting for tomorrow."

Celia protested. He protested her protests. She finally agreed.

There was full attendance at the temple. He told the story of what he had seen. He knew he'd never recover from this experience. As he talked, the people wept.

"The head Rabbi insists we fast in protest."

He saw a sea of heads resignedly nodding in agreement.

"I say NO!"

The heads all remained fixed and staring.

"Fasting is not a protest! I say, arm yourselves! If they come to touch a hair on a Jewish head...kill them! Maybe they'll think twice before killing us if they know they might not have a head to pour their vodka in celebration that night!"

Lazar committed a fatal error. He had forgotten how vicious the frightened can be to <u>their</u> scapegoat.

"What are you suggesting! He's trying to get us all killed!"

A chorus of "yes!" from the whole congregation. Pandemonium.

"Get out, Rabbi! You have one day to get out or we'll kill you!"

Fists raised, they rose in unison, menacing.

Lazar was not a foolish hero. He'd been a mistaken one...trusting in their passivity to follow him. A trusting flock had turned into a mob before his eyes. To be angry with <u>them</u>...<u>impossible</u>. To be angry with their own...that was possible...even welcome. Lazar panicked. He turned to run and hide again...yesterday from the goyim...today from the yiddin*.

Shouting now, "Run, Rabbi, as far as you can!" "Murderer!" one shouted.

"They come to kill us if we do nothing...so if we do something!"

He fled behind the Bima. They laughed at him derisively, wanting to humiliate him...those who knew how he felt about their ignorance, his arrogance, his handsome imposing appearance, those who envied his stature above others, had known his contempt for their mediocrity and the gnash of his temper. Those watching him

------

* ***Yiddin - Jews***

leaping frenziedly, undignified, like a hunted criminal, watched him and savored his defeat. The tinkerer waited for Lazar as he crawled out of the shul, rushed him into his house, bolted the door.

The mob advanced shouting, "We want Lazar!"

Brindel came out and confronted them.

"Quiet! I have a message from the Rabbi!"

"We have one for him!"

"You really want him dead! Don't you want him, at least, alive!"

"Neither! We want him out of town, or we'll tar and feather him and throw him out ourselves."

"The Rabbi's message is that he has already left."

"We don't believe you!"

"He took my horse and is running as fast as he can! Now, you'll go as fast as you can, if you please, from my door!"

Mumbling is heard, "Enough wasting time with the Rabbi's foolishness!"

Another yelled at him, "Why don't you let us get our hands on him for just a minute, to squeeze that arrogant throat!"

"What could I do? I begged him not to come to my house and involve me but he was like a crazy man, running through my house, taking my horse. What could I do?"

His palms upward, a supplicant.

"What will we do with his wife and children!"

And another, "He should have thought of them, and, incidentally, our wives and children before he came up with his crazy notions."

"Who will tell them what happened tonight?"

"You tell them Brindel."

"Alright, I'll tell them. Now go home."

And then, thinking, 'No one else can face them. Tonight, they made a widow and seven fatherless children. And now, they're going too fast. All their days, they fast. How much hungrier can they get? Can't they see, it hasn't made much of a difference? The Czar is not interested. He will kill...hungry or not hungry...fasting or not fasting.

What does he care about the condition of our bellies? Our souls, they want. Not our bellies. The only thing is that we're fasting, it's easier, we're weaker, less resistant. We go down fast under the club because we're limp already. That should please him. That should make the Czar very happy indeed.'

Chapter Forty-Seven

Lazar had never been on a horse before. He was suddenly frightened of everything, the blackness, the forest in which he found himself with no sense of direction. He was frightened even of the horse...especially...the horse. It seemed to him the horse sensed he was without a master for the first time...someone who could control him. It galloped wildly, struggling, and winning against Lazar's meager effort to restrain him. He continued to gallop at high speed when he was released from danger. In his desperation, he pulled the reins as hard as he could. The horse threw Lazar to the ground, galloping away as fast as it could. He lay where he was thrown battered by fear and fatigue, he fell into an unconscious stupor and awoke the following moment...on a grassy bed where the horse had thrown him. Lazar thought, at least, the horse had some consideration. It picked a soft spot for me. He rose painfully and slowly. 'Battered, but not broken, Thank God. Betrayed by everyone, even the horse.'

He shouted to the trees, "Be my witness, I will not rest until I have convinced these people, with the help of God, without it if I must, that they must leave their accursed places. If they cannot fight in them, they must leave them. I will pursue them with this message, no matter how many times I'm defiled, threatened, insulted, abused. I will prevail! My body may falter! My will... never! He felt himself succumbing again to fatigue. I have no time to waste on resting. My wife, my children, my future...where are we all going? Why did I have so many children and still behave like a bachelor? Can I afford the luxury of being a revolutionary, a Zionist? A leader without followers? A Rabbi without a congregation? Who will feed us, clothe us? My God, what have I done? Because of me, we'll all be in the forest. The first thing to do is get out of this forest. Follow the horse and hope he knows better than me."

If the horse was not dependable in Lazar's presence, he could be counted on in his absence. He led Lazar right back to Brindel's house, and Brindel pulled him in as soon as he heard his knock at the door.

"I don't want to endanger you, Brindel."

"Don't worry. How can I help you?"

"I don't know myself right now."

Brindel pulled a picture of a candle out of the drawer.

"They're rebels and they're starting another march. They'll help you. They like fighters."

Lazar grabbed both arms to hold back the tears.

"I'm a Zionist because of them. Believe me, they're no good for us!"

"If you say so. But where do we turn?"

"To ourselves. Let me think."

"Brindel! I have an answer! I have been corresponding with a Zionist in Germany. He offered to help me if I consented to leave Russia and lecture for the cause. I'll take Morris with me, so he'll avoid the draft and I'll send for everyone else later. Celia wept uncontrollably, no matter how gentle they were in telling the news."

'My husband, a fugitive, was abandoned with seven children. He'll never send for me. And you know why. It would happen again and again, now that he'd be completely free in a strange land.'

Lazar pleading, "Let's be nice to each other now. Who knows. This may be our last meeting," beseeching, asking forgiveness.

His home was suddenly dear to him, even leaving Celia was a wrench. He felt so alone, for the first time since he'd married. 'Why was he being so selfish? Not even concerned how she'd manage without him. Strangely, he wasn't concerned. Celia would manage. She was made of iron. For the children, she'd do anything; even manage without him.'

"I have to go now," she said abruptly. "I have to feed the children. You forgot about them, but I never do."

Angry now, "I'll feed them!"

A soft reply, "I'll feed them. I'll find a way, and I'll feed them."

She was about to say, 'Don't worry,' but thought, 'No never mind, let him worry.' Morris cried. The embrace. She pushed him away from her.

"Go with Poppa. God help you."

She motioned to the children to follow. They formed a line behind her. Her head high, every nerve taut, stiff. She left wordlessly, without looking right or left. Morris begged to see his girlfriend before leaving. Lazar agreed...and he fled to her house. She had been ill and was still in bed. He tapped on the window. She recognized him and beckoned him in. he told her he would be leaving with his father and swore her to secrecy, his finger to his mouth. She put her finger to her mouth in agreement. They whispered excitedly, like two conspirators. Morris noticed suddenly that she had a hole in her nightgown where he could see the delicate, pink nipple. He tried hard to not look but his eyes travelled back to the forbidden spot despite all his efforts. Suddenly her eyes followed him. She jerked the blanket to her chest as fast as she could.

"You saw!" groaning and fighting the tears, "You saw!"

"Yes, and I'd never seen anything so beautiful."

Soothed, he diverted by telling her he had to leave. She buried her face in her hands. He patted her gently on the shoulder, tiptoed to the window.

Before he lowered it again for the final time, he whispered aloud, "We'll see each other soon."

But he never did. He remembered her to the end of his days; his first and only girlfriend. He would tell her story from time to time and always conclude with, 'I wonder what happened to her.' He left with his father that night, arriving in Germany after a wearying journey by train. It was exciting when he left the train and took his first ride by coach. He felt so important, stared at the well-dressed passerby, the world full of wonder everywhere he looked. A boy passed hawking papers. Lazar had an impulse to call him, but he remembered he couldn't read German and waved the boy away. But a picture caught his eyes, and he beckoned the boy to come back to him again. A picture of a candlelight parade. He couldn't read the text but wondered if it was the parade, the march, that was talked about before he left home. There had been a last night while Lazar was on his way to Germany. They were brutally dispersed, as they knew they would be, but they increased in numbers as they knew they were not alone. A photographer was called. This march would be flashed around the world. Basha inadvertently found herself at the head...leading the march.

"Disperse! An order from the commandment."

They all fled but Basha.

"Arrest her!"

She submitted silently but refused to relinquish her candle.

"Give us the candle! You've caused enough trouble with it!"

It was torn from her grasp, but she cupped her fingers around an invisible candle.

Then the judge demanded, "What is your name?"

"Basha," a soft reply.

"The infamous Basha! What do you plead? Guilty or not guilty!"

She gazed silently at the judge, tears streaming down her face.

"Guilty, your honor. Guilty! I only wanted to sleep. I'm guilty, your honor, of candle lighting."

"You'll sleep, alright. Longer than you think! The prisoner is to be shot immediately. Remove the prisoner!"

The bailiff shouted, "Next wave!"

Basha was in between two other enemies of the state at the firing line. On her left, a young boy in his teens, passionately in love with his idea of the better world to come. On her right, a lean, hungry, old man, who, finding himself homeless, sneaked into a building and fell asleep on a pile of books. When the building was raided for revolutionaries and sabreurs, he was arrested and charged with 'guarding revolutionary propaganda.' They both turned to Basha.

"Momma," the boy wept as he clutched her.

"Sha, mien kind," as she embraced him.

"Rest, Benjamin," she told the old man as he embraced her.

The three, who lived as strangers, died, as a loving family.

Chapter Forty-Eight

Gunter Eitman, the distinguished Zionist that Lazar was hurrying to see, was unaware he was about to receive a visitor. He was checking the last-minute arrangements for dinner for 12 this evening. He was a tall man, blonder hair, blue eyes, pert nose, hair cut shot, close cropped to his head like the military. He secretly prided himself that he didn't look Jewish. He resented the Christian stereotype of the Jew; bearded, shuffling, bent, filthy, scurrying, rude. Reacting against that image, he affected a military gait; slow, erect, dignified. He was immaculate. He didn't even know he was Jewish until the age of 8 when he was called 'a dirty Jew' by a nanny after she undressed him to take his bath. She had been a wealthy lady who found herself in reduced circumstances but, 'not so reduced,' she said, when she announced her departure to his father, 'that she would not serve Jews.'

He then tearfully asked his father, "What's a Jew?"

"A Jew is someone who's circumcised," his father replied gruffly, impatiently, waving him away to terminate the discussion.

"And what's that?"

"What you are."

"And what am I?"

"Circumcised."

"Does that mean I'm Jewish?"

"Yes, it means you're Jewish," a wearily reply.

Gustav was more confused than ever but knew when to stop pressing. Besides, he forgot about it the instant his mother came in and diverted him to his favorite game, hand clapping with his mother while she accompanied him clapping, and singing a song, making strange words that sounded like German, but weren't. 'Patche kichelech,' (slap) 'Patche kichalach,' (clap hands) (slap.)

And his father shouting, "Be quiet! I don't want that language spoken in this house! Do you hear? Spoken, sung, or even whispered!"

"I'm sorry," Momma would say weakly. "I forgot myself."

"Don't let it happen again!"

Gustav was so frightened by his father's anger that the strange words began to appall him. He would keep his hands tightly clenched in his pocket when she knelt beside him with her palms open facing him, her signal to begin the game without singing, 'Patche kichalach.'

She tried to coax the hand out of his pocket at first button, as he defied her, even more resolutely, she discontinued the game. His father prided himself that there was no religion in his house. He had suffered unspeakable indignities as a poor Jewish boy in a religious household. He was degraded by the Christians who beat him and forced him to submit to their sadistic whims. At home, his father degraded and abused him because he wasn't behaving like a Jewish son should...not sufficiently religious...or brilliant. He still remembered the beating his father gave him because he said he wanted to be a businessman. He fled his home, his past, his heritage...that night. When asked the question, 'What does it profit a man if he gains the world and loses his own soul?' He would answer, 'Plenty.' He had no use for soul. It had brought him only blue marks and bruises to his body. His soul, he noticed, was much more comfortable, less anguished since he had gained the world. He had a flair for trading, a good head for figures. More than wealth, he wanted to be a Junker, A Von. But such titles were never bestowed upon Jews. Besides the misfortune of birth, he had another contradiction in his nature, a fatal attraction to Jewish women...and only those who spoke the unmentionable tongue...Yiddish.

He met his future wife in Poland, having gone there on a business trip. He was invited to dinner...and he could hear her in contention with the guest seated nearby. As usual, the table was wracked with religious debate. "Soon, there would be as many Jewish religions as there were Jews," he noted wryly.

'Nowadays, every Jew has his own Judaism.' He wondered what hers was. He noted she spoke Yiddish but didn't look Jewish. That was important. Dark eyes, long, aquiline noses...not for him. Blonde hair, blue eyes, pert nose, speaking Yiddish...that was for him. And what was more important, what she was saying. Her father, a devout Jew, was glowering. She was a rebel, like himself, but a Yiddish speaking one. She delivered her argument to her father and turned in Gustav's direction. He nodded approval. Her father, intent on his reply, didn't notice. She stared at him while her father shouted to the back of her head. She barely heard his harangue. She'd fallen in love with Gustav. A Jew who looked like a Christian...and a rebel like herself. He slipped her a note. They met secretly. He insisted she speak to him of love in Yiddish. That was the only thing he missed at home. His mother said tenderly, 'Mien kind*.' He never spoke of love in German. Or it would sound like his father...who he despised.

Her father refused to consent to the marriage unless they were married in a synagogue. He notified his mother that he was married and enclosed a picture of the bride. His father refused to even see the picture. They settled in Berlin. The marriage proceeded fairly smoothly for a little while 'til she became homesick, so he invited her relatives to visit. He was suddenly surrounded by a gaggle of Yiddish.

---

* ***Mien kind – My child***

What had previously entranced and touched him deeply began to repel him more and more. Even the songs, unbearable. More, they seemed alien to him, and he started to hear them as if they were in a strange tongue with the revulsion, he imagined he sounds must provoke in a Christian. He began to strike out at her when she spoke Yiddish, interruptions at first then rudeness, the orders, commands...not to. Surrounded by a strange tongue, she'd carried home with her...longing for it more and more. She missed the candle lighting and even found she was peering into the door of the shul as she passed by. When she became pregnant, she secretly harbored a wish that he would relent if she had a son. She leaped far ahead, fancying a bris, a bar mitzvah...and in between...years of learning...a Talmud Scholar...perhaps.

But when Gunther was born, a crisis was born with him. Her parents, alerted she was about to give birth, wrote that they were coming to stay with the rabbi until the bris.

"Bris! Absolutely not!"

Gustav wild with rage, tossing the letter on the bed and fleeing out of the room. His parents, he decided, were not to be notified 'til at least a month after the birth. There was to be no battling over a bris. Before she could reply to her parents, they were on their way to the rabbi, the child was on his way into the world. Poor Gunther was in a dilemma at the moment of birth.

The boy was finally 'kidnapped' by his grandfather and the ceremony performed without his father's knowledge. His mother learned of it when he was out. The boy was finally 'kidnapped' by his grandfather and the ceremony performed without his father's knowledge. His mother learned of it when he was out in her arms with a note pinned to him in Yiddish that she was to look at her son carefully. From that day forward, relatives were forbidden to visit.

A bar mitzvah was not performed. It was heatedly discussed behind the parents' bedroom door; Momma's impassioned pleading, Poppa's angry refusals to even hear the word mentioned. Religion was never discussed with Gunther.

Father waved him away when he asked, "What am I?"

Mother said plaintively, "Speak to your father."

When he was asked what he was by others, he replied defensively that he was German. When his father received an irate letter from his father-in-law demanding the boy prepare himself for his entrance into Jewish manhood, he was seized with an uncontrollable impulse for revenge, marched the boy determinedly into the Lutheran church, had the boy and himself baptized.

"Alright," he announced, as he rushed the boy into his mother's room, stood him in front of her and loudly said, "From now on, if anyone asks you what you are, you're a Lutheran, you understand!"

Gunther wanted to ask his father what that was since he couldn't understand the ceremony, but he didn't dare.

Gunther's subsequent conversion to Zionism was just as sudden and unexpected...especially by him. For public consumption, he attributed his conversion to the pogroms of 1905, which allegedly sent him off to confrontations with his father and subsequent rekindling of the Jewish faith. The shameful secret he would reveal to no one was marked differently. His grandfather's plotting had borne fruit 20 years later. He had visited a friend in Paris and was smitten with a guest at his party. They were seated near each other at dinner. She chatted gaily on and on, charming feminine pattern. He listed with an external calm, detached and polite air. By the time the dessert arrived, he decided he would marry her, and further, that his father would be pleased with the match. He called on her whenever he was in the city, courted her with daily notes and flowers. She knew she 'loved' him when he missed a day of flowers and she 'nearly died' 'til the following day when two bouquets arrived.

He assured her it was the florist's error, and she hadn't realized how much he meant to her 'til then. She told him all this later when he pleaded with her to say she loved him, and she permitted herself a slight confessional...but not too much...for fear she would cool his ardor. They discussed children. She said she wanted five boys and five girls and that she'd often dreamed of walking down the church aisle on their communion day, each one looking like a little bride or groom.

"Wouldn't that just be precious?" she asked, looking up at him, wide-eyed, innocent, vulnerable.

She had practiced that look to perfection. No, that image didn't please him. For some reason, it upset him deeply, but how could he not agree with her?

He smiled benignly, "Of course," he replied warmly, his voice cracking with tenderness.

He pleaded with her to marry him. She silently agreed, suddenly overcome with such shyness, she couldn't utter a word. She'd rehearsed this scene so many times in her reveries, she was overcome by fright when her moment on stage finally arrived. He was even more enchanted and announced his intention to return home immediately to arrange for the necessary meetings.

First, he had to tell his father. He rushed home, planning to tell him at dinner time when he was mellowed with food and wine.

"She's Lutheran," he told him, before describing her beauty or money.

"Good," his father said. "Marry her in town...in church."

Momma's hand trembled. She said nothing. Then, she dared.

"My son is getting married in a church?! He thinks he can put religion on and off like a new hat?"

"Why not!" his father spat the words out at her.

"If there is a pogrom on Lutherans, you can convert to the religion of the pogromists...whichever one is in Vogue at the moment... which means...whoever is bigger than you."

"But how about beliefs?"

"They're all the same. What's the difference? The people get down on their knees, the plate is passed, and they have an excellent excuse to defile and torment their neighbor."

"Then why not be Jewish? If it's all the same?"

"Because in that religion, you never get off your knees!"

"What do you mean?"

"Enough! Do as I say!"

"But why? Why can't we, at least, have a Jewish wedding?"

"Because...to have a Jewish wedding, you have to be Jew. You are baptized as a Lutheran," he shouted, as he threw the wine at her face and stormed out of the room.

She remained sitting numbly, while crimson tears covered her face, falling in her hands that remained folded, as well to receive them. Gunther gently wiped her face with his napkin. He suddenly stopped, his tender concern swept away by rage and revulsion.

"Stop crying!" an angry command and he fled from the room, up the stairs to his room and throwing the blanket over his head not to hear. 'Why did she behave like that? Abused by him, degraded by me. What else are those tears but an army of beggars beseeching him and poppa for mercy. Disgusting! Disgusting!' He hated that meek face that never got angry. Poppa was right. That was Jewish. Always on its knees. He was grateful to his father that he wasn't Jewish anymore. His father had seen to that! He fell asleep, rose the following morning, and announced to his indifferent father and his grieving mother that his mind was made up. He was marrying in church. He returned to Paris and posted the ban.

'Now that the bans are posted, I can press my case.' He was secretly tortured by a nagging doubt. He had never forgotten the scene with his Christian nanny. Would his intended respond the same way? He had to know. Now that he had publicly declared his intention, she would be less resistant. He decided he had to know whether she loved him...completely.

That night, in the garden, they romped and played and teased each other, touched and fondled and caressed 'til she slowly removed her clothing and revealed herself to him. In his eagerness to join in her nakedness, he tore his garments carelessly from his body, then frenziedly. They stood together, seriously intent on each other's bodies. He touched her and sighed deeply, yearning and wanting her so much. She touched him and suddenly grew cold wend distant and withdrew from him...abruptly. Her shame returned and she quickly covered herself with her dress, hiding from him as best as she could, crouching behind the garment that shielded her from him.

"What's the matter? What happened!"

"I don't know myself. You're Jewish. I can't stand you now that I know."

"I...I...I'm...what!"

'<u>Poppa, what is circumcised?</u>'

"Let's get dressed," mumbling, mortified with shame.

She knew what he was...and worse...he knew it too...now. They turned from each other, dressing quickly. He offered to help her as she stumbled in the uneven earth in the dark. She repulsed him, disgusted.

"Forgive me," she pleaded, "I don't know why. I don't mean to... but I can't help it. Don't...touch me. Don't...come near me. I never want to see you again. You...make me...sick."

And she bowed her head. He turned without a word. Alone in his room, he undressed and looked down at himself. 'That's what a Jew is,' he concluded...not a man like other men. And he wept bitterly. How could he tell anyone why there would be no wedding? The shame of it. He wept until he fell asleep.

The following morning, he awoke to buzzing in the house. A visitor had come and gone announcing there would be no wedding. It had been canceled. He was greeted with a chorus of questions.

"I want to speak with you, alone, Poppa."

And he repeated his childish question and received the same answer.

"But the girl I want to marry turned away from me in revulsion. If I'm still Jewish, what did my conversion mean? Is that what it means! I'm missing my manhood! I'm not a woman. Not a man! I'm nothing!"

"No, Gunther," Poppa said, stunned and saddened.

All his life's precautions have gone to naught. Judaism was a many-headed snake he could not kill. It was here again...killing his son...killing him. Practicing or not practicing...a speck...a trace...of the despised religion and you shall suffer unto your children's children. Poppa talked far into the night about Judaism and by the time he'd finished he'd almost talked himself back into the faith. The news spread in the town that the wedding was canceled. Gunner barricaded himself in his room...hating...first Christians...then himself...in that order. His father bought him books on Judaism. As time went on, Gunther the playboy became a Jewish scholar of sorts. After the 1905 pogrom, he declared himself an ardent Zionist.

Chapter Forty-Nine

At first, he became an intellectual, philosophical Zionist with his Jewish friends and a silent, spiteful, angry one with the Christian world. 'We should leave and take our gifts with us. It would serve them right. Then, maybe they'll appreciate us, but it will be too late.' He was sulking like a betrayed lover and Zionism was his revenge...a hurt child who was running away so 'they'll be sorry.' It wasn't until the pogrom of 1905 that he became a fearful Zionist...wanting to run away for safety...and a protective one...take those with him who wanted to go. He carefully spread the word, and soon, there were scrawny, filthy beggars with beards and side-curls coming to his door for funds to go to the promised land. He burned with shame and reluctantly but firmly gave orders that they be advised to use the side entrance where they would not be seen. He couldn't bear that his Christian neighbors or even his servant should in any way identify him with those people. He gave them money, fed them, they slept in the basement...and left.

Lazar had rushed so he had not been able to contact his liaison for specific instructions. He rushed out of the wagon and rapped on the front door without even noticing the bell. The servant slowly opened the door, her face changing from polite condescension to arrogant revulsion as he waved him imperiously towards the small door marked 'Servants Entrance,' erecting the final barrier between Lazar and the front door, then quickly shutting the door in his face. Lazar was stunned, and checked the address again. Correct. The servant must have made an error. Maybe they were expecting a tradesman. He would knock again. The servant looked at him through the window and walked. Lazar was too tired to feel anything but compliant. He would clarify later. 'The servant would get a good dressing down for his error,' he thought. But the door opened again, this time by a young woman who extended a hand to him. She was wearing an apron. Her coarse skin embarrassed him as she pulled him inside. He had the smooth hands of an idler. She lit a lamp.

"Won't you sit down? I'll make you some tea if you'd like." She asked him in Yiddish.

"Don't bother. I'd like to ask you some questions. She sat down compliant. In the dim light he saw a thin, bony face, lined, hollows in her cheeks, then a passive, expectant look of those who wait for orders without protest, eager to comply, fearful only to displease.

"Ask me," she said...and sat up straight in her chair...and waited... listening intently.

"Who are you?'

"I'm the scullery maid. I'm here to welcome the travelers because I'm the only servant in the house who speaks Yiddish."

"Why didn't they let me in the front door?"

"I can't answer that question. I assure you; you'll find out."

Lazar was irritated and surprised to find a streak of snobbery in his character. To be greeted by a scullery maid!

"When will I be able to see someone in charge?"

"Soon. He knows you're here. But tonight, there was dinner for 12. He'll be down when the last guest leaves."

"And I'm not a guest! And this is a Jewish home! ...that puts a Rabbi and a guest in the cellar! ...with a scullery maid!"

"Let me give you some tea and let me take your things."

He had been holding the paper and hadn't even unbuttoned his coat. He stood a moment, as he always did, when he was distraught, stared into space and stroked his divided beard which was thick and long. How majestic he appeared as he stroked it slowly in harmony with the heaviness of his mood. He sat down when he heard her returning with tea. She took the paper from his hand, helped him off with his coat. He was homesick already. He missed the samovar in the middle of the table; 30 glasses of tea, always hot and ready. And here, this drop of water in an absurd little cup. Ten glasses of tea a night was nothing for Lazar. He could just imagine the poor maid running back and forth a hundred times with those little cups that looked like they were filled with eye droppers. Lazar could already see the world was different here. Not painted with broad strokes in the Russian manner, large, sweeping, grand, like he was used to. Here, there was a more subdued rhythm of life. They called it <u>refinement</u>. He could sense the restrictions already. He kept the left hand on his lap, talked slowly, in quiet tones.

"Am I keeping you?"

"No?"

She asked no questions.

"How long are you here? Where do you come from?"

All his curiosity having nowhere else to go fell in a heap on the poor scullery maid."

But the big questions remained, an unbudgeable heap. There were no answers. Lazar filled the silences with another question and another. She remained discreetly silent 'til he exhausted himself with nervous questions.

"I'm sorry, I didn't mean to pry."

"There's very little to answer. I'm afraid I'm not very interesting. If you're rich and your life is dull, it's still interesting to others because you're rich. If you're poor and your life is dull, no one is interested."

Lazar thought she was telling him she didn't want to answer any more questions and was doing so very politely...and cleverly.

"Hannah," a male voice calling.

"Yes sir," she stood at attention obediently.

"Do we have a guest?"

"We do."

"I'll be right down in a few minutes. You tell him that."

She relayed the message to Lazar.

"I thought he knew I was here."

"He does, but he always asks anyway."

"I understand," he said. But he didn't.

"Would you join me?

"No thank you."

They sat in silence, Lazar no longer feeling it necessary to speak. He looked around at his surroundings. This was the biggest kitchen he'd ever seen.

"Am I keeping you from your work?"

"No," she lied.

He knew she lied, rushing to protect him from discomfort on her account.

"I work quickly when everyone is gone. I'll start as soon as I'm alone."

"How long does it take you?"

"About three hours. When it's an elegant party like this one, the glasses are so delicate, I have to pray with each one, that I don't, God Forbid, break it. But I love those glasses."

Her voice faded. She was silent, musing, once again. How often at midnight, when the last dish was put away, she set the table for herself elegantly and sipped non-existent wine from an empty wine glass that she held by the stem with thumb and forefinger, pinky extended, smiling, chatting, and nodding, head turning from side to side like an elegant guest at dinner.

"You'd think you'd want to smash them one by one."

Such a violent act never even occurred to her. She had accidentally broken one once and trembled at the sound of glass shattering ever since.

"Why? They're beautiful."

A bitter reply, "But so much work."

"If we smashed all the beautiful things in life that are, as you say, so much work, we'd have nothing left to enjoy."

"But they enjoy it upstairs, not you."

"Oh, but I do too."

"How?"

"I just do."

And she turned from him, alerted by the sound of a door opening.

"I have to go now. Mr. Eitman will talk to you now."

He extended his hand, but she avoided it. My hand is too rough and scratchy. Once is enough. God help you."

And she disappeared into the darkness, opened a door to another mountain of crockery, dishes. Lazar had never seen so many before... and this little woman was going into battle!

Lazar looked up and Gunther standing over him. He extended his hand in greeting. Gunther always dreaded those first few moments with its mandatory handshaking. He could see no reason for the Jewish custom of the enthusiastic bounding of one palm into another and the intertwining of fingers of someone you've never seen...or known...with the requisite amount of warmth generated for an occasion no one could really feel. Besides, the revulsion he felt for them precluded this activity entirely.

Lazar's hand remained open and extended in the air. Gunther bowed his head slightly but politely. Lazar's hand, extended by habit as a sign of good feeling, suddenly turned into an aggressive fist and became a weapon.

Humiliated and pained, he wanted to strike Gunther but struck the table instead, bloodying his hand and shouting, "How dare you! Do you know who I am? Reb Lazar...the man who's been who's been writing here for months, invited to come," and he tore the letter of invitation from his pocket, "Do you invite scholars to come here and then consign them to the kitchen to debate with scullery maids, then it's an anathema even to the touch their hand!"

Lazar didn't even wince on Gunther's clean shaven, well controlled, aristocratic face.

"Read the letter of invitation again, Reb Lazar," Gunther in icy tones. "You were instructed to contact Herr Bock and advise when you were coming...if you were coming. Nothing else was included in the invitation. Our relations with Jewish and Christian neighbors are good. We cannot imperil them by unpleasant associations of Jew as Jew...as a Zionist, I have provoked them both already. I will alienate them altogether if it is brought into clear view for whom I am fighting. It is hard enough suggesting this cause. Even harder if we treated your kind as an equal. That would be an unforgivable crime that would react badly to the cause. My colleagues are not interested in sitting across a dinner table from the people being saved...and neither am I...Rabbi...quite truthfully."

"I see. This is a convenient Zionism for you and your class. We battle malaria, mosquitoes, and starvation so you have an oasis for yourself if and when you need one. We are your scullery maids, hidden in the dark corners and put to work to clean up before the guests arrive; the guests in this case being...yourself."

"Exactly!"

"And you arrogantly imagine you have the right to this service because you pay."

"Right again Rabbi. I'm sorry you hit upon the truth. The others comply without embarrassment. They may think these things, but they don't go so far as to confirm them with me. Once confirmed, Rabbi, twice humiliating..." a sardonic smile. "Am I right?"

Lazar gasping, shouting hoarsely, "Aren't you ashamed to be treating your own people this way! Your own people!"

"How have my own people treated me...vilification, scorn, ridicule...when I give my message...go to Zion."

"Do you know why I'm here? Not for your largesse and a ticket to Eretz, Israel but because I'm a refugee from my own shul...do you hear! I'm ashamed, too. Not of their beards and their ill-fitting clothes but of their narrow, petty little minds and now I'm more ashamed of you and your arrogance."

"What makes you so arrogant that you think you have the right to judge both of us from your exalted height and find us both wanting."

"I have the right and I do judge."

And he questioned Gunther's impertinence in daring to put that question to him.

"Alright," Gunther said. "Now let's get down to the issue before us which we may be able to settle."

"Remember, when you are in trouble with the Christians, they will not be nice to you because you don't have a beard and a few more groschen in your pocket."

***Groschen – Money**

"But they are now, for exactly that reason."

"And when they're not, you'll grow a beard if necessary, and come to Zion. By that time, you figure we'll have cleaned the swamps and built a fancy hotel to accommodate you."

"Exactly," Gunther said, and clicked his heels.

"But you need me now, so use me now. I'll use you later if necessary. It's all part of life's game."

"I'm your money in the bank, so to speak," said Lazar.

"So, to speak," said Gunther.

"Since we're being so truthful, let me see if you can bear a little truth. If I put on your suit and shaved my beard, I would still be Lazar. If you put on my beard and my suit, what would you be, Gunther?"

Gunther grew weak and sat down. He couldn't answer. The very image nauseated him.

"Yes, you'd be Jewish: a suit, a beard, a few wrinkles, God forbid, a patch, a bent shoulder. That, to you, is Jewish. You think you put it on and off with a beard, or a suit, or an erect shoulder. You think it's political, philosophical, debatable. It is not debatable. You're born into, you die in it. It's not debatable! You'll be a Zionist when you can come and shake my hand and not until then. Until then, you're an idea collector, an attention getter, a dispenser of charity. If you get bored with Zionism tomorrow, you'll embrace another idea to amuse you because, worst of all Gunther, you're a traitor. You were my dream. You sustained me through all the hardships of the struggle to exchange an old idea for a new one. You sustained me because I thought you really believed as I did...and would be waiting to welcome me if I needed you."

Gunther submissive now, "You need me now!"

"No, Gunther, not me...the people, the future victims in a world full of pogromists. I want to go to America and spread these ideas. America is fertile ground for new ideas."

"Now, you need some rest."

They faced each other like two tired warriors.

"I'll show you to your room."

And he led him to a small room behind the kitchen. Lazar entered unprotestingly, thinking, 'Gunther, a Zionist, who could not be converted to Judaism.'

Lazar had spent years battling with Jews who could not be converted to Zionism. He was condemned to being on the other side of the fence no matter where he was, sadly concluded. He put down his bag and paper, prayed and fell asleep on a small cot. In the morning he found the scullery maid at the kitchen table, wiping her eyes with her apron and his paper by her side.

"What's the matter?"

"My son. They killed my son."

And she collapsed on the table, weeping. Between sobs, she explained she had come to Germany to work and send home enough money to bring her son and husband out of their accursed land where her son was threatened with 25 years of Army Service...and she was frightened because he was involved with radical elements. She was saving money for a ticket to America and had almost enough when she read in the Rabbi's paper that her son was shot for revolutionary activity. She was going to leave immediately for home to find her son's grave and comfort her husband.

Lazar comforted her, then took out his siddur, put on his tallis and tefillin, and intoned a memorial service for her alone while he sat at the kitchen table and wept. Then he sat down beside her mute, in silent commiseration. She rose and walked stiffly upstairs, to tell the master. Lazar returned to his room, and then, he heard the sound of farewell, of departure, came out to say goodbye, saw the paper and tenderly placed it under her arm. When all was quiet again, he heard a rapping at the door. The butler, requesting his presence upstairs. He followed him to the parlor, gilt, satin, chandeliers. Gunther nodded his head and Lazar, likewise. He kept his hands in his pockets.

"Arrangements are to be made," he was told. "You will leave on a ship tomorrow. When you arrive, you'll be on your own."

Cold, distant, "No problem. Can I go now?"

"If you wish."

Lazar knew Gunther was grateful. His vanity demanded he show Lazar his luxurious surroundings but he didn't want him to stay too long for fear there would be guests and Lazar would be seen and have to be explained. The following day, Lazar was busily involved in his departure. A nice cabin was given to him...second class. He was the only bearded Jew there and he was avoided by everyone. Children taunted him and laughed at him. He spent the trip in steerage ministering to the sick and the dying.

A fetid, black hole, black with filth, disease, and fear; fear of all they'd left still with them, fear of authority, uniform, orders...and now, fear of the new. Non-persons, all ticketed like a piece of luggage. He thought of Gunther and hated him for his good fortune. But then, he thought, 'thanks to him, I'm here, helping the little he can.' Truth was a hard and bitter pill to swallow sometimes, and Lazar hoped he could, at times, be less truthful and a little more merciful with himself. The ship docked and Lazar was sure he was in Bedlam. He somehow survived the questions, examinations, indignities. He was finally released and on his way to a cousin's house where he climbed endless stairs 'til he reached the top and tapped softly on the door. No answer. He opened the door on a disheveled lady in an apron carrying a mop and a pail of water.

She dropped the pail shrieking, "Lazar! What are you doing here! People are starving in the street!"

Then, she embraced him.

"Can I at least come in so I can keep from drowning!"

"Of course."

"I'll only stay for an hour or two. I have to see another cousin."

Four children came clacketing into the room; thin, undernourished. 'She can't feed me,' Lazar thought.

"A letter came for you."

He took it without looking and put it in his pocket. 'She was the same age as Marva,' he thought. Her hair graying, her face worn with care and poverty. She looked like her mother.

"I'm sorry, I have to leave before it gets dark, or I won't find my way."

He remembered he passed a shul on the way here.

"Won't you stay?" she insisted.

He declined, as was expected. The Rabbi welcomed him, proud of Lazar's presence in his shul.

"I'll stay a day or two," Lazar said, having no idea where he was going.

The rabbi led him to a small room in his apartment behind the shul. Lazar sat down, took the letter from his pocket, and saw it was from the scullery maid. He read, stared in shock, and read again. 'My son died with a woman, Basha.' She had enclosed the article. Lazar beat the wall 'til his hands were bloody.

"You died alone, without me."

He collapsed in a coma for several days. When he awoke, he refused all food and prayed, and mourned the loss of another dream... of someday finding Basha.

Chapter Fifty

Lazar was not a man of blind faith. With every tragedy in his life, he questioned his faith again. God was always in the witness box, it seemed, with Lazar steadily losing his case. The rabbi told him that God was testing his faith.

"Well," Lazar replied.

It was becoming clearer and clearer to Lazar that he could not pass God's test and God could not pass Lazar's test. Each was deaf and blind to the other. Lazar decided, many years ago, that he would struggle to unlock His secret. But now, he was growing weary of the world of the struggle. He doubted, now, that the world had a Friend in the universe to whom an appeal could be made, who could make order from disorder, justice from injustice to the deserving suppli-cant. Despite Lazar's sophistication in his deepest heart, his faith was founded on that simple formula. Reb Shlomo tried to help Lazar in his titanic wrestling with his anguish and his conscience...but he was not able to cope with either...Lazar's rage overwhelmed him, at times, when Shlomo questioned Lazar's questioning. Shlomo repeated the stock arguments enraging Lazar even more until he realized what the

Rabbi was doing. On the one hand to reinforce God's argument and on the other to ease the pain of his loss. God and me, the scapegoats now. He'll stop beating us both when his pain is dulled.

Shlomo was right...to a point. Lazar turned from questioning his faith to a silent battle with Celia and her fanaticism. She was more severe in her judgments than he. She would say he was being punished, for not paying attention to the rituals as seriously as he should. He hated her for that! In the final analysis, it was Celia who was his scapegoat. His internal argument with her, his passionate rage with her when she imagined his reply...veered him from his dialogue with God. As he began wearing her down in his mind, he grew calmer. The victory he never had with her calmed him in his mind without her. Shlomo noticed he became calmer as the weeks wore on.

He wondered what Lazar planned to do and broached the subject one morning at breakfast.

"I've contacted many people for you for a shul, but I've had no luck."

"I must make a living. I must find something to do here."

Repeating the obvious for want of anything better to offer.

"I will try the out-of-towners in Baltimore, but I must warn you, they are very orthodox."

"Don't worry."

"I won't."

Lazar replied...but he didn't mean it. Shlomo pegged Lazar, a troublemaker and wanted to be rid of him. Out of town was a good idea. Shlomo had patiently borne him out of compassion for his tragedy...but now that he appeared in control, Shlomo found he irritated him, even feared him a little. He was too wild. There was something primitive and uncontrollable about him, a place where even God had never reached, a place untouched, untouchable, and ready to spring like an unleashed tiger. He was an antagonizer, a troublemaker. Shlomo had a hard enough time making a piece of bread in his shul. There were more rabbis than shuls...but enough believers to keep all the shuls full...but...there were more non-believers than rabbis; Socialists, Communists, even Zionists...who believed in Israel...but not in God. Lazar would excite the young with his Godless passion. Even in Israel, they would find a Jewish state without God. Reb Shlomo was horrified. In his home was an incipient incendiary. Lazar had to go! As far away as possible. There were enough people infected here already. Lazar disturbed him, bringing *isms* so close to him. He was a dangerous combination.

Skepticism and cynicism on the one hand, Zionism on the other... a man locked in an inner struggle between personal reality and political illusion and not realizing his inner contradiction. Or, he does realize it, letting them exist in dialectical opposition. Reb Shlomo took out his map.

"This is Baltimore, there'll be an eight o'clock train leaving tomorrow."

"I'll be on it."

Anxious to be on his way, to resume his occupation for his own purposes. He needed a daily regimen. Strange, he thought, what was once a holy purpose had suddenly become a job. Maybe it had always been one, while his real purpose was Zionism, the promised land. He was fated to be a lonely prophet; discarded, maligned, enraged, but seeing the truth others will not see. So be it. 'I must fulfill my destiny and...along the way...attend to mundane matters like finding my wife and children. Even a man of destiny must think to pay the landlord and the grocer, he thought wryly.

The following morning, they embraced each other, the two rabbis; their desire to be rid of each other turned to instant regret as the moment of parting came, and they whispered to each other hoarsely, "I'll miss you" ...and, at that moment, heartily meant it.

Lazar rushed on the train, not daring to think. His first train in a strange land. The babble of a strange tongue, children staring at him, tugging at their mother's skirt, and Momma staring at him tugging at their husband's sleeve. Smiling, laughter, derision. 'They were the same in any language,' Lazar thought. 'Was it the beard? Jesus had a beard.' They knelt to Him and laughed at Lazar. He took out his prayer book and read and prayed. He was alone, he needed to pray. This encampment on the train alone turned more people to God than all the scholars debating. 'Yes, he needed Him.' But did he believe in him. Lazar didn't really know. He looked up. The child in the seat across from him was mimicking him stroking his beard and reading. His hand stopped in mid-air as Lazar caught him in the act. His child's face turned nasty, feigned innocence preparing to deny the obvious. Lazar bent his head once again, his eyes shut tight, his palm on his forehead, his elbow resting on his body, his head rocking back and forth. 'Mocking me, Oh Lord, while I'm praying.' He rocked his head back and forth, harder, and harder, while he silently screamed, louder and louder... 'While I'm praying!' He opened his eyes and looked across the aisle. The seat was empty. He'd frightened them. They were sitting in another car and telling a passenger sitting next to them about the 'crazy kike' in the next car.

"Where?" Curiously avid for something to relieve their boredom.

"In the next car. You can't miss him. Long beard down to here," a palm put against the waist to illustrate and a space in the middle like this and wearing a funny hat and rocking back and forth like a drunk on the edge of a bridge over water."

"I want to see that," said one.

"Yeah!" said the other, "Me too!"

And a third rose to join them and they rushed to the adjoining car, the women's crosses bouncing on their necks. Lazar's head was again bent over his prayer book.

"Ha, ha, look at the belly! Look at the head. Who does he think he is...God or something."

He looked up slowly, uncomprehending. There were several others in the car. They rose and joined the hecklers. Another, a small man bent in his seat and crouched even lower and covered his face with the long nose. Lazar did not understand what they were shouting, but he saw the snide look on their faces, heard the cruel derision in their voices.

"Kike," they shouted in unison. "Go home."

"Where are you from?" one asked him.

He poked through his slips of English phrases and found one that said, "Don't understand English."

He held it up while they all examined it.

"A furriner besides. A Jew furriner. We don't need another one of them. Go home!" They shouted in unison.

"He doesn't understand what you're saying," one said.

"He'll understand. I'll make him understand," said another.

And he grabbed Lazar's beard, pulled one side, then the other.

"This is called milking the Jew!" and he cackled.

Lazar rose suddenly, his mouth twitching, his body taut and wound his beard around the young man's throat.

He paled and sank to his knees, pleading, "Let me go."

There was a sudden silence. The young man gasped for breath. Lazar held the young man and looked up at the crowd. Derision was now fear. Both glared at each other tongue-tied. Both wanting to say the necessary words, but unable.

The little man in the corner rose and said to one, "Will you leave him alone if he releases that boy."

"We will."

In Yiddish, he gave the message to Lazar. He released the boy with disgust, throwing him at the others. They turned and left conversing with the victim and commiserating with him as he leaned on the others stumbling and breathless.

The little man continued talking to Lazar, "You must shave your beard or you're inviting trouble with a beard like that."

"Never, for them I will shave my beard." Shouting, quivering.

"You will join me and grow a beard. We'll show them. Every one of them who touches a beard is enough to make them tremble. Not us...that we rush to the barber. Them! Not us! Do you hear!"

The sound of the wheels rhythmically joined him as he shouted, "Them! Not us!" over and over.

The stranger left him. Lazar didn't realize he'd gone, and he was shouting alone to an empty car...shouting in Yiddish in an empty train as it rushed past barren fields. There was no one to hear him.

He turned to face the window and shouted into that vast, silent emptiness, imploring God, "Them! Not us!"

He turned from the window, looked around the car and saw no one, realizing his was a lone voice with no one to hear him. He needed God after all...though he didn't believe in him. He would beseech Him, but he knew he wouldn't help him. Lazar had lost faith in Divine Providence. He sat near the window staring numbly into the blackness. He was met at the station and taken to his shul. The following morning, at service, he looked down at his congregation, meek, passive, gentle, beaten faces eyeing him timidly. 'Good God,' he thought, 'worse than the old country. I'm home again. I've traveled 6,000 miles to be home again.' Just looking at them infuriated him. Spineless, beardless, probably witless as well.

He read from Isaiah:

'And I will lead the blind into the ways which they know not.

And in the paths which they were ignorant of, I will make them walk.

I will make darkness light before them and crooked things straight.

These things have I done to them and not forsaken them.'

Lazar's hypnotic voice flowed over them, carrying his message he would protect them. This was all he could expect from them at first. His other mission is to be their father.

After the sermon, he was surrounded by eager hands and hearts rushing to embrace him. Lazar's charisma, his magic, was capturing hearts in the new country...as it had in the old. He looked at his flock as they surrounded him and was overcome with loathing of them and himself. Was this to be his army after so many years of struggling? He thought, in free air, the heads would be higher, the backs straighter, the gaze firmer. And what did he find? Innocent, shy, timid children who would be grateful to him for helping them to study, for a bit of advice, for a well-delivered sermon...and that's all. They wanted no more. And Lazar sadly knew, while he was welcoming his flock, shaking hands with warmth but unsmiling, that the day would come when he would spill over, when he could no longer bear the humiliation of leading fools daily; their very being an affront to him. He was bound on both ends by humiliation; the Christians who derided him; the Jews who took it, their weaknesses and submission equally humiliating. Reb Printz, the former Rabbi, rescued him from the crowd. Lazar gratefully fled to his room behind the shul, sat down on a chair and stared out the window; a grimy alleyway faced the window of the joining building.

He could hardly see out of his window. He rubbed a circle on the window so he could see better, his eyes narrowing. No light would penetrate that narrow little alleyway. He discerned a window facing him, it had long ago lost its purpose, the layers of grime and dust having made them as impenetrable as the wall. Lazar turned and examined his room, bare walls, a cot, a curtainless window.

He draped his jacket over two hooks in the center of the window frame, his shirt over to hooks on the wall and sat down with a weary philosophical sigh, bowed his head and lamented.

'He hath led me and brought me into darkness, not light,
Only against me hath turned, and turned again,
His hand all day,
My skin and my flesh he had made old,
He hath broken my bones.

The Lamentations purred forth from his memory and he recited, rocking to and fro,

His head resting on his hands,
He hath broken me into pieces,
He hath made me desolate.
He hath filled me with bitterness.'

And he remembered, Reb Shlomo, who said, 'It was good to wait in silence for the salvation of God.'

"I can't wait in silence," he shouted.

The very word unnerved him.

"I can't wait in silence!"

And he pounded the pillow again and again, "I can't...and I won't...wait in silence!"

Chapter Fifty-One

After Lazar left, Celia had to leave the shul for the new Rabbi. She instantly obtained employment flicking chickens. The rituals in Judaism provided for bedside dietary health conditions, employment for its people. Chicken plucking had been for many a widow and divorces, and now Celia had a job where she could not only make some money, but observe at close hand, whether a chicken was indeed kosher. A chicken who died, who had 'guzzles*' and chicken freshly killed...now Celia would know for sure. The butchers were thieves. The butchers needed her but quaked at her judgment. A Celia chicken was a sure seller. The customers lined up when Celia was plucking. The number of children dwindled as time passed. They fled...from pogroms, drafts into the army, infatuation with Christians.

When the time came to join Lazar in America, there were three left. In Ellis Island, she and the children were lined up in front of a doctor, tongues, chests, exposed, turned, pounded...shamed...then beckoned away from the door marked, 'Exit.' The others were

---

* ***Guzzles – Marks/Wounds***

welcomed, embraced, and led through the door. Their ordeal was over. She and the children were put into a room marked, 'Isolation.' A nurse told them in Yiddish that they would have to return. They had...Celia was bewildered.

"God! How can I go back!"

But the nurse had left. She was too beleaguered to do anything but deliver a message. A uniformed man beckoned her to follow him. Celia was too intimidated to do anything but sob hysterically and do as she was told. Besides, if she made a scene, they'd never let her in, never! As she mounted the stairway with the children to the gangplank, she saw Lazar's anxious face and his arms frantically waving at them. The children didn't see him. She marched them along ordering eyes straight ahead, fearing they would create a disturbance. Celia was deathly afraid of a uniform. They would arrest her and the children if they disobeyed...or caused a disturbance. They might run to Lazar against orders.

"Go, go hurry, the ship is leaving. It can't leave without us."

"But Momma, why are you crying?"

"Don't ask questions. Do as I say. Do as I say. Be quiet."

Lazar fled to his office.

"My wife and children! Why are they going?"

All around him, wives and children were embracing husbands. 'Why were his arms empty?' By way of explanation, they handed him a booklet, translated in several languages. The official made a check mark next to the paragraph that related to his case.

It read: 'Arrivals returned for the following reasons...a list of illnesses and one checked.'

He waved away as the official had to attend to other duties. Lazar stood rooted, numbed, bewildered. The day had begun as a joyous celebration and became a day of mourning and loss.

Through the years, Lazar's eloquence had brought him a better shul. His difficult personality had prevented a rise to the top of a prosperous shul, but he improved his situation somewhat. He had prepared the home for Celia's coming. The congregation waited with him, eagerly looking forward to the Rebbetzin. When returned with the news, anticipation turned to mourning once again. He'd been lonely for his children, yearned to see them. Celia and the children endured again, the dark journey home. They sought medical treatment immediately so they could apply for return as soon as they were well, but history decreed otherwise. The war came and reached deep into the town where Celia and the children were struggling to survive, and the family was caught in the maelstrom of armies hounding each other.

As their casualties mounted, their fear of innocents grew. The children were seen as spies, the adults as traitors. The family was ordered to evacuate far into the interior. Celia and the children were trundled into a box car; dark, airless, thick with humanity, just like the ship...only worse. There were no pleasant anticipations...only dread. Small children succumbed all around them, women with sick children in their arms. At each stop, the doors opened for more. Finally, the door opened to orders of, '*Get out!*' Celia and the children fought their way through the others to a breath of fresh air. The need was so intense that they shoved and trampled, a Darwinian struggle in that car. The fittest and strongest were the first to reach the sun. But it was bitter cold, and they were ordered to march. Many fell by the wayside and were left. The human chain struggled on, hands interlocked, bodies close to each other for warmth now. The children pleaded they couldn't go on.

"Shut up!" Celia muttered ruthless... "Cry! You'll have to deal with me!"

They finally arrived at a huge dormitory, surrounded by snow, as far as the eye could see. An egg-shaped dome in the middle of a vast expanse of nothingness. They were all assigned a cot. Celia was grateful she could, at last, sit down.

She didn't know where she was, nor did the others. They were forbidden to write or receive letters. No one knew where they were.

As the years passed without a word, Lazar thought they'd surely perished in the war. But a Jewish organization found them. Another dark, bitter journey and they found themselves on Ellis Island again. And again, they were told to wait while the others went ahead. They panicked. They could not endure another journey. She would not budge this time. They'd have to jail them all.

A well-dressed lady came in and asked her in Yiddish for her nearest relative. They had to contact someone to pick her up. Celia beaming for the first time in years, reached into her apron and pulled out an old phone number...Lazar's cousin. Anxiety returning...

"I hope he's still there."

"Don't worry, we'll find him."

The cousin was still there. He was called to the phone and, for the first time in his life, he fainted. At Ellis Island, there was a tearing and loving reunion...joy for the first time in many years...and the last. She was worse than ever...from years of suffering alone, and immediately got down to her task...bringing the other two children to America.

Lazar didn't earn enough money. She would flick chickens again. Day after day for two years, Celia flicked...thousands of feathers until she had the money secretly tucked away on her person...safe from burglars, she always said. Lazar was becoming restless again...going further and further to lecture on Zionism. His differences with his congregation reached explosive proportions and he had to get away to cool down...before he found himself again exiled from his own people, his shul, and of equal importance...Celia...who was ever more explosive. Their combined rages could not survive in the household for long. Someone had to go. Finally, it was said of him that he was seldom home. He was enraged by the anti-Semitism...children tarred and feathered by jeering Christians, one house on the block sold to a Jew and 'For Sale' signs appeared on all the other houses the following morning.

"Fight back...or leave!" he shouted.

No one listened, the placates, the supplicants, those who willfully lived like the legendary little monkeys...evil deaf, evil blind, evil dumb. They stood in awe of Lazar, his appearance...like a prophet, his wisdom, the hypnotic personality. It frustrated him deeply that they admired him but wouldn't follow him.

"Fight back or leave for the Promised Land!" he shouted.

But they wouldn't do either. To the children of Christians, Lazar was the funny man with the beard who they jeered and derided mercilessly. He strode through the streets like a colossus, nevertheless. His contempt knew no bounds when he began to see the clean shaven gentle looking Jew avoiding him. <u>They</u> were ashamed of <u>his</u> beard. A few supporters here and there sustained him as his reputation as a lecturer spread. If he had no adherents, he was known to put on a good show...all for free.

The shuls were always turning people away from the door when Lazar was on the podium. He lectured and chastised them. They came and listened and respected him and went home debating and discussing...but...the following morning...didn't remember a word he said. One or two tried to rekindle the flame he started but they were unsuccessful. Those that were ready for having their spirits kindled for militancy and battle were not in shul. They were learning Marx and dreaming of the promised land...Russia: rising against the capitalists and fighting for the exploited. But he went on, fulfilling a promise that he would not be silent. Only death would silence him...but only for a little while. He had a score to settle even <u>there</u>. He would demand answers to all the questions that plagued him all his life. Demand more than answers! Demand...an explanation. The Almighty would have to come to terms with him. He would make tumult even in Heaven. How dare they be so peaceful while the earth raged and twisted in torment below?

Chapter Fifty-Two

Phillip, the oldest son came off the boat without a beard, tallis or tefillin, a belief in America or even God. He believed in Karl Marx and work. 'Arbet macht dus leben zees.' Everything about him was big and broad. His head, his eyes large and wide, a long nose that flared across his upper lip, a wide and generous mouth, powerful shoulders, bugling muscles, hands with fingers that had skin like leather, and each finger like small hammers, hard and powerful, thick, and stubby, hands yearning for work that could never find it. The doctor who examined him first at Ellis Island found him fit to work like a mule.

"You are the strongest man I've ever seen come off this ship, but America will destroy you," he said.

And it did. There were lines then for the chance to sweeten the life with work. He jumped into the race eagerly craving for the chance to swing a hammer on old shoes with a mouthful of nails in his small even teeth. He didn't like to be exploited. But...not to work... he didn't like more.

Though he knew capitalism had no morality, he expected it anyway, face to face. Three in the morning, he was on the line for a job. The men were ordered to raise their arms so the muscle feeler would go down the line to see which one was the strongest. Phillip was chosen. 7 days, 14 hours, 2.50. At the end of the week, he opened the envelope...2 dollars...take it or leave it. He left it. Wouldn't work for a word breaker. An agreement was an agreement. Phillip lived in a house with a distant cousin Mirele and her mother. They had a bread and milk store and an apartment behind the store, that was full of beds and immigrants newly arrived and not so new. Every one of Mirele's friends from the old country came there first. There were weddings, heartbreaks, quarrels, jealousies, and, it was whispered, even a baby once.

Mirele was a tiny woman whose body was twisted around a limp. She had broken a hip in the old country, punishment for playing on Yom Kippur. The old woman said who saw her playing. She had never been to school as the Christian boys threw stones on the first day, so she was too frightened to go again. Her one dream was to become an American citizen someday. She mothered the world with an intense, devoted concern. Unlike her own mother Zisme, who, it was said, married for the third time and threw Mirele out on crutches in the snow to fend for herself. No one knew why. A neighbor told her to go home and told Zisme it was against the law to throw a 12-year-old on the street. Zisme was afraid of the law, so she took her back...reluctantly. All her life, Mirele tried to please Zisme...impossible! Though she couldn't even sign her name, she dominated Mirele and her brother with an iron hand. Zisme preferred her son, but it mattered not to Mirele. She was obsessed with the need to protect everyone in an ever-widening circle of protectiveness. Whoever needs...take...whatever she had...or could give.

She sometimes mentioned that she never heard from some who grew up rich and forgot her. Not in anger or reproach. Only the listeners would get furious. But she never did. Her brother, Dov, was also a-man-in-a-hurry who lived in a shul and worked. He also had a small face, a very long nose, quick, jumping, nervous eyes. Four in the morning, he went to shul to make a minyan, always carrying a black bag with machinist tools. They said he had lots of money, but you could never tell that looking at him. He would come to visit bursting in the door like a shot, calling every name in the family as he could never remember names, until he came upon the one he wanted and making jokes as he flew around the apartment, and often, if the mood struck him, he'd come bursting through the door singing in a lyric tenor voice, like he was entering upon a stage. All the neighbors stopped whatever they were doing and listened. Everyone said it was a pity he never trained his voice, and it was, but then, so many things were a pity in those days, you couldn't keep up with all of them and singing lessons, for a grown man way down on the list. Way, way down. But Mirele, of course, offered to give him lessons. He refused. He was stingy, he couldn't even bear to spend <u>her</u> money. But she was willing to spend hers, so he wouldn't spend his. She was just there doing it, like a soft cushion on an old mattress. Nobody thought much about it anymore. You don't say 'Thank you,' every time you flop down on the sofa. You just flop down on it and expect to be <u>there</u>.

Phillip slept on a surplus army cot, a piece of canvas with six sticks under it holding it up, in a room that was furthest from the kitchen stove. He was put there because he could stand the cold. The heat never reached that room, but it didn't matter to him.

"It's not good for you to be in such a cold," Mirele told him when she showed him his room. "The lady upstairs had a warm room if you want."

"It's alright," he said. "I'll take this one."

"You'll pay when you can," she told him, and brought him a roll and a glass of milk.

"You'll eat supper with us," she told him. "A good piece of flanken will warm you up. It's no good, the cold, you'll get sick. And then, what will be? Your mother will say we didn't take good care of you."

He heard her every morning, scraping the floor with her left foot, the bad one that was bent at the knee, very thin and much shorter than the other.

Phillip took the room at the beginning of the week and was fired at the end of it. Every night he crept out of the window at 2AM, stood on the line, and offered his arm to be squeezed like a loaf of bread when his turn came to test his <u>qualifications</u>. Then, the arrogant speech at the end, when they gave him less money than they promised, 'Take it or leave it!' And he left it.

Phillip's large, earnest eyes, his square face with hollow cheeks, his despair and talking like a poet-philosopher made him very attractive to women. He was hardly aware of it. The shikhas* in the shop, when he worked, brought him little things from home and there was so much wriggling and sashaying around, unwrapping an apple or sharing a salami sandwich, no amount of refusing or objecting making the slightest difference.

The factory smelled like a restaurant 'til he left.

The other men were shocked, "What's the matter with you! Don't you realize the shikhas are mad for you!"

"With me, nothing! You want her to get pregnant with a little *shiksele?* Not me! Babies! God forbid!"

Phillip found purity infinitely preferable. He was just not of a mind to bother himself with women. Work, books, the revolution, <u>that</u> was different. Shaking his head, mocking in despair, 'women, women, women,' was all he ever said about them when they did something foolish, which was most of the time as far as he was concerned.

The lines were growing longer, men fainting on the line and shoved aside, another taking his place, glad to move ahead, hoping they'll find all faint and he can kick then aside so he can be the first. And then, no matter how early he arrived on the line, there was somebody always ahead. Some bosses just kept them waiting, picking one, sometimes at random from the back of the line.

---

* ***Shikhas – Christian girls***

You'll be grateful then to work for almost nothing...just to be picked. The others were jealous of the one who was picked...like it was an honor. And the day came when the foreman went down the line slowly and Phillip found himself hoping like a dog wagging his tail for a bone...<u>just to be picked</u>. Craving, standing at attention, like it was a prize, like he was about to receive the medal of honor, and the humiliation, the blow to his pride, when the man examined him for head to toe and <u>passed him by</u>.

"You!" The foreman pointed to a head he could barely see.

Three men jump forward.

"No, you!"

They were still confused and stepped ahead.

"The one with the blond hair! Yeah, you!"

The unwanted ones are embarrassed and stumble back. They leave when the line breaks. All the Czars Cossacks with their whips and guns couldn't break Phillip but now? 'What have I come to? I thought a life lived at the bottom has a limit even they can't sink below.' Phillip had been pushed far beyond his lowest limit. The working man turns in his own, the revolutionary songs sung only with his father, of dead days and hopes in Russian tongue.

He writes to his brother in Paris, 'America is a country of free slaves who devour one another.' And he'd remember, 'Comrade, brother, a glass of tea from the samovar, one heart with the chavurah, hurt one, hurt all, we will break the chains that bind us.'

Phillip was homesick. 'Life was once something I took for granted, like air or water. Now I look at it hard and closely, asking it, every day, to account for itself and make it worth my while. It was once full of reasons to go on, but lately, I ask and get no answer. Like it has nothing more to say. Life, it's asking me to just keep moving... just because it's pushing, whether I have any place to go or not.'

It was a hot night. He'd climbed the stairs to the very top, stepped out on the roof and looked around. There was no one. 'I'm tired of being pushed. In line, out of line, all my life to stand on lines. And what was I hoping for now? Only to change places with the picker?

Afraid, can you imagine, not to be picked.' The future was clear to him now: to climb out of dark windows to peddle himself, a little timorous now and more later. Fear grows fat on itself. Now that he tested it, he'd have to stand at attention before it, too. That's what all the slogans and songs and comradery and dreams were for...the hold terror at bay. Now the snarling dogs are circling and baring their teeth, and he was sniveling and crying and wanting to die. All of life's endless wanting...and not being able even to die. Not even picked for that. The old anger returned. He would pick and choose now, this day, this moment, this place. He jumped on the parapet.

"Phillip!"

Two arms circled him round the waist. He couldn't jump without taking her with him. He fell back.

"Mirele, what are you doing? Leave me..."

But he couldn't say 'alone.' Heavy sobs wracking his huge body, his large fists pounding the rhythm of defeat, his feet stomping huge gashes into the black roof, his huge head beating Mirele's little chest as if it were a solid wall...and she let him, raising herself each time he threw her down so he would find comfort on her breast and then...his head never left his body...and his sobs grew fainter and fainter 'til he fell asleep, cradled in her arms. She wouldn't leave his side 'til Zisme found them in the morning and told Mirele, she should be ashamed of herself. She rushed to tell Celia the story. She said there should be a shidduch. Mirele was a fine girl and Phillip needed her.

Phillip crying, "But she's a cripple."

And Celia shouting, "No! you're the cripple! If you can do a thing like that, you're the cripple!"

Chapter Fifty-Three

Mirele worked before the wedding, took a day off to get married, and returned to work the following day. Zisme prided herself on baking and cooking, Mirele doing the work, and Zisme directing and stretching her neck with pride as if she were a goose. Mirele had a simple formula for marital success... sacrifice. She would do everything. Phillip could do nothing...if he wanted...if that's what is necessary to keep him healthy. Health was something that could be lost suddenly, once, and for all of time. T.B, people dying. Once and for all time...these afflictions. Zisme had two kitchens, milchig[*] and flashing[†]. The milchig one was closed for days in preparation for the wedding. Phillip was wretchedly uncomfortable. Mirele rented a suit for him, Zisme borrowed a ring for the ceremony which was returned to its rightful owner. Phillip had contempt for the ceremony but just couldn't flaunt his ideas before his religious relatives out of respect, though he said he didn't respect them. There

---

[*] *Milchig - Dairy*
[†] *Flashing - Meat*

were friends who joined free love colonies but he ever even entertains such an idea for himself.

After all, didn't they fight, were jealous and miserable like married people so why bother to pick potatoes to fool yourself. He couldn't admit that in certain things he was still old fashioned, a good suit on Shabbos, and fasting on Yom Kippur. After the wedding, he took her to his room. She submitted to the pain without a sound. A man should have a woman. It was good for his health. The following morning, she joined Zisme in the kitchen and cooked her first meal for Phillip. For the first time, he slept late in honor of the occasion, greeted her at the table with a nod of the head, and sat down at the head of the table while she served him like they were, already, an old married couple. Phillip was a talkative man at breakfast, offering opinions on everything, yesterday's news, tomorrows, whatever. She offered an opinion to please him.

"What did she know?" He asked her. His answer in the tone of the question.

She agreed, "Not much."

"So shut up!"

Mirele's eyes shone with pride. To her, this was love. To be married to such a smart man. She couldn't imagine how she'd been so lucky. Lazar's son! After breakfast, he pushed the chair back.

Mirele asked, "Where are you going?"

"To bring back the suit."

"I'll do it. You should rest."

Phillip covered his face with the forward and poured over the 'Help Wanted' column, looking displeased. He lowered the paper to say, 'goodbye.' She thought he must be upset over the world situation and admired him even more for it. But she was wrong.

When she returned, he decided he would tell her. He wanted her to cook like his mother...a tagacht*...and everyday like that.

---

* ***Tagacht - Pudding***

"Why aren't you davening, Phillip?" The first question from Zisme.

"You daven Zisme," and he slapped the paper and stormed out, vigorously scratching his head with his thumb and his forefinger several times, and rubbing his forehead, exasperated.

"When God gives me a job, I'll daven...not before."

And he slammed the door.

She got on a chair and hollered through the transom, "You don't tell God what to do."

"He doesn't tell me what to do either!"

"Yes, he does!"

The pot was boiling over.

She climbed off the chair, rushed to the stove, and quickly returned, stood on the chair, and shouted even louder, but Phillip shut the transom in her face and climbed out the window while she screamed even louder, kicking the door and demanding to be let in, "The room, after all," she screamed, "was hers! You're still a boarder, and you're not paying rent. Besides, you'll be in the street, you hear! Mirele brings me a Communist for a husband who pays no rent!"

She had a defiant threat through the door.

"You will burn in Hell!"

Nothing Zisme feared more than hell. Every penny she threw into her apron went to the temples to assure her place in Heaven. Every time a new shul opened, Zisme made her contribution. She had every shul covered just in case God listened to one better than the other. You never can tell.

Apart from her craven fear of Hell, Zisme was fiercely independent. In her final years, she bought one half of a nursing home and went right in at the first sign of decrepitude. No one has to plead, beg or trick her into going in. There she sparked romantic rivalries and jealousies, men pursuing her even there. She had two graves, one in New York, one in Florida...just in case. She never had a moment's doubt about anything except the placement of furniture. She was always moving it about, hers and everyone else's. She shocked many a relative into thinking they opened the door to the wrong apartment. They came home to find nothing in it's place when they were permitted to stay a few days. It was rumored she was a beauty in her youth. She still thought she was one and bragged that the men still turned to look at her though her skin was wrinkled like a prune. And she had to have her way, no matter what. Years later, when she had a house in Brownsville, and her daughter-in-law, whom she detested, moved in, and wouldn't leave, she knocked the house down. Her nephew came home for lunch from school and there was no house.

Zisme was still shouting and waving a fist at the wall when Mirele would return from work and wheel on her, "I want you to get this mamser* out of the house," waving a finger covered with challah dough. "When are you leaving, I want to know."

Mirele rushed to her side as if she was stuck by a fatal disease, "What happened?"

"He's a bum, I can live with, maybe. But he doesn't believe it! Not in my house!"

"What should I do, Momma? He's my husband."

"You'll *bench licht*† tonight with that husband here!"

"I will!"

"How!"

"Like I always do."

"But he'll protest and make trouble."

"We'll see."

That night Phillip refused to sit at the table with Zisme. Mirele carried his meal to his room. He ate on a chair. Only once he got up... to drive Zisme out of the kitchen. When he saw Mirele praying, he barked, "Foolishness!" and returned to his room.

From then on, every Friday night, he argued with Zisme about lighting candles and praying. Every Friday night, Mirele was ordered

---

* ***Mamser – Bum***
† ***Licht – Candles***

to throw him out of the house. Every Friday night, she lit candles and prayed, and he barked, "Foolishness!"

After that, another furious argument erupted, "Who would sit at the table?"

One or the other would finally stalk out...depending on who was hungrier. No eating was done until the issue at the table was settled. During the week, Phillip read the papers to them both at the table. Mirele enjoying, Zisme barking, "But he can't make a living."

She was not impressed with his mind. Her favorite song was, '*Vu bist du given, ven di gelt is given, un der leben is geven tzuker zees?*'

Phillip wrote 40-page letters to his brother, poems he'd written, songs, political opinions, friends came, and Phillip talked the longest and was listened to with respect and he played the concertina and the fiddle. Mirele was so proud. He was an amateur, but she didn't know it. She pressured him to play whenever visitors came. Sometimes, she even danced with the company...a little like a penguin waddling but the friends indulged her.

"Doesn't matter who makes the money," she always said, "As long as we have it. Rent, food, a music lesson for Phillip, the doctor...what else?"

She cooked tagachts every day for months at his insistence. It was too rich, too heavy, and besides, she got tired of it. He would insist on the same thing being cooked for him for months 'til one day he'd tire of it and declare there was to be 'no more in it in this house!' she waited for that day with the tagachts. But it never came. She tried to nag him out of it, but he threatened, 'I'm leaving this house.' She schemed. Made the tagachts extra heavy one night.

He pushed the chair away and said, "No more tagachts in this house!"

Mirele was delighted. Mirele was content just to hear him talking, playing, near her, healthy! It was true he criticized her, 'What did she know?' But, she thought, too, 'What <u>did</u> she know...nothing.' Right is right. She shouldn't offer opinions if she doesn't know. Mirele worked in the store, then at home. He never washed a dish or pushed a broom. It was not 'manly.' Mirele agreed. Mirele never questioned that she had to work from sunup to sundown and beyond, if necessary, to <u>protect</u> everyone and was eager to do it. A man, especially, should not overwork himself. <u>He</u> was fragile. Zisme never knew where Mirele got those ideas from. She couldn't read it so it couldn't be from a book.

"From you, Momma," Mirele would tell Zisme. "You're so strong and Poppa so weak, and so scared.

"So, it's my job to protect him!"

"No, it's mine!"

"Your job is to get him out of my house already."

Mirele was always caught between Zisme throwing her out of the house and Phillip threatening to leave the house, she thanked God they settled on the house to bludgeon each other with. Phillip continued his nightly forays into the job market and occasionally found a place to earn. He was picked up and discarded like a stray cat. A few days here and there.

And every day devouring the papers and calmly announcing "I'm leaving this house."

"But why! What have I done? You don't mean it!"

"I mean it, and you did nothing. I see an article here. They want men to work in the mines. Think of it Mirele...a good job. They pay and give me a place to live. I'll go first and then you'll come."

"You're sure the work won't be too hard Phillip? I'm afraid it will be too hard."

"Hard, shmard, what are you talking about! How long can I climb out of windows at three in the morning? And listen to your mother call me a bum and then pull-out empty pockets! You're ridiculous! As usual, you know nothing, and you talk!"

"I know that men go into holes in the dark and bitter a whole day and sometimes they come and sometimes they don't come up again."

"You know everything!"

"I know nothing...but I sometimes know something."

All night, she nagged, and he threatened. In the morning, he was packing.

"You're going already?"

"You wouldn't let me tell you. The first group is leaving this morning."

"You'll be sorry," shouting at his back as he's leaving, limping after him as fast as she can, calling after him, "If you need anything, call me right away."

His scarf was still hanging on a chair. He forgot to take it.

She opened the window, "Phillip, your scarf. It'll be cold out there."

He turned an annoyed and impatient face. She threw it and it fell on his hat. He bent to pick them both up, hat and scarf. The wind blowing them both down the street, out of reach. He looked up at her again...furious. Her little face was frowned in the window.

"Phillip, a sweater you'll need. Did you take a sweater?"

He scratched his forehead with his fingers, "No, what do you do with such a woman," shook his head with a sigh, dramatizing a little, feeling sorry for himself, for her, his 'philosophic' look.

Impatient again, he swiftly turned. The sweater hit him in the back. He turned again and picked it up, waved, a sad smile that marked the end of anger and the beginning of the pain of separation. She waved back and kept waving 'til he rounded the corner out of sight, though he couldn't see her.

"Mirele! The shock of Zisme's voice. "I need you at the counter. The bum left already. Come on down!"

"I'm coming."

That night Zisme says, "I'm leaving too. The butcher is going to open a restaurant next door and give me half. I do the cooking. Maybe I can make some money for a change. You can keep the store. Slave and slave and have to eat the profits. What's the use?"

Mirele was sorry to see her go. She would miss her. Mirele wanted everyone in the family near at hand so she could keep an eye on them. Arguing, mistreating, judging, exploiting...no matter.

Family is family. Love, shmuv. They did. They didn't. No matter. Family is family. A month later, the business was signed over to Mirele with an X and the signature of a witness.

Zisme's last words as she left were, "That atheist should be here to help you. His own wife isn't a comrade?"

Mirele touched her letter tucked in her pocket from Phillip. And later, a reader read over and over again. She paid for each reading willingly until she memorized it.

Dear Mirele,

I am in a terrible situation. The work is very hard, but I don't mind. I work every day for a whole month. But it's like I'm in jail. All around the mine camp, there is a fence with barbed wire, and I can't get out. The capitalist swine! How I know them! What did I expect? I can't leave this place without money. They say I owe them for food and a roof over my head...I sleep in a big room with 50 others and for these 6 feet and two inches where my head is, they say I have to pay. They say I owe two hundred dollars. Where will I get this money? A fortune, Mirele. It's like I committed a crime and they put me in jail for life. They say they freed the slaves in America. But they didn't. Tell somebody. Tell somebody who should tell the president. Maybe he doesn't know. To keep someone in jail for no reason is against the law. The president is not a lawbreaker. In this country you can write the president. Write to him, Mirele, and tell him.

Phillip

She knew, right away, what she had to do. She would sell the store right away! A small counter, a place for a few baskets for rolls, an ice box for milk and a few customers that could manage their way down the treacherous stairs to the basement. She was paid 150 dollars for the store and fixtures, borrowed 50 dollars from the Hebrew Free Loan Society and sent it to Phillip. The following morning, she went to the better neighborhoods, banged on doors, and told them she was available for house cleaning. In one of them, she rented a room for them both.

When Phillip came home, Mirele greeted him with, "Phillip, you're so thin."

Embarrassed, looking away, "It's alright. Bothering me already."

"What do you mean, 'bothering'?"

"Why did you seal the business, Mirele? Now, we have nothing."

"What else could I do? Leave you in jail?"

Phillip looked around, cautious, as if he were afraid to be overheard.

"What's the matter Phillip? You look frightened. What are you afraid of?"

His eyes, shifty, evasive now. We never knew when something would fall down, or cave in, or collapse. He looked gray, without color in his face, but for his eyes...as if he wanted to disappear and become part of the dark landscape. The blackness of the mine was in his heart; dull and empty now...so long without singing and hoping and dreaming.

"Friends are coming to see you, Phillip. Any minute now, Pincus is coming."

"Pincus is coming!"

A small light flickered...and went out again.

"He'll see me like this."

"What's the difference, he'll see you."

"Still stupid, Mirele."

And he turned from her.

"You're right. It's good he's coming. A man understands."

Religion to her was empty of all principles...except two; keep kosher, give money to the shul. The prayers will lift you to heaven and keep you there. She gave more and more as the years went by to store as much insurance as she could. Cooking, boarders, peddling, everything from lollipops and ice cream to religious artifacts she made enough money to buy a place in heaven for herself. Even though they lost eventually. Brownsville went from slum to hell. The shuls moved and the homes followed.

The first Baptist Congregational church was nailed above the Mogen David. Mirele learned nothing or practicality from her mother, her ethics from her father; a small timid little man, Zisme's second husband, whom she divorced, she said, because his breath smelled. He always lived around the corner from Mirele in terror of meeting Zisme all his life. He ran like a cat before she spotted him. In later years, when Phillip was cornered on the 5th floor, with no window to sneak out of, the war of Zisme raged in the living room. Neither gave an inch, Mirele placating to no avail. Pincus came with his concertina and Phillip took his and they played and sang the revolutionary songs from the old country while in the background, the landlady cursed her husband.

"His cuts should twist like a spring; he should grow like a turnip with his head in the ground and his feet in the air."

Phillip was so happy when his friend left, he embraced Mirele, took her...as he always did...without love...with need. She was glad because it meant he was healthy. Of course, she wouldn't let him come to her too often. It wouldn't be healthy. He thought she was probably right. After all, it's written, 'Too much of anything, isn't healthy.'

Chapter Fifty-Four

"We'll always be poor, Mirele. For ourselves, maybe, maybe..." he repeated.

His index finger in the air, and his eyes to God.

"We can eat, but the children..." his voice rose, as if he were addressing a crowd, "with children! What will we do with no gelt and more open mouths."

Mirele nodded quietly but disagreed. The rabbi told her to have a child. One...at least.

"Now he doesn't want Phillip, but he will get used. You'll see, Phillip. You'll get used too. And don't worry. I'll take care. I'll make the money, just don't worry."

"Phillip!" Zisme said shouting as she entered the house.

"You must open a business. You're a shoemaker! A shoemaker needs a store to bang and pound. You have to make a little living. How long can you be a boarder for your wife?"

Phillip in center stage now, eyes looking in the distance at the fates, the tragic figure, put upon. Even Zisme was touched when Phillip performed.

"I'll see what I can do, I don't have much, but maybe I can do something. A business maybe, Phillip."

A soft maybe from him was considered a triumph. Zisme could be very generous if she had to revenge herself, prove a point or win a brownie pie in Heaven.

For two weeks they didn't see Zisme and Mirele hoped she'd come and say she found something...just so Phillip would get to do something. Rest wasn't helping. She thought it would, but it wasn't. In the morning, he would jump out of bed and hear a sound no one else heard.

"It'd be blowing, Mirele, the whistle. I have to run to work."

"But there's nothing Phillip. No whistle. Listen. No whistle."

"Let me out. They'll come for me and beat me if I'm not standing outside when the whistle stops blowing. And he'd hurry to get dressed and run out the door and stand there...waiting...in the dark."

When the daylight came, he'd come back in the house, "No work today, Mirele, but I was ready, anyway."

"There's no one there. You're home. There's no work. There's nothing. You must see a doctor! You're sick!"

"I'm sick? You're sick! Crazy one! You're sick!"

And would take off his shoes, struggling as if they were heavy boots, fall asleep again and wake up like nothing happened.

Mirele screaming, "Don't you remember!" a desperate wail.

"Terrified of sick. People die early then, so quickly."

"I'm not sick!"

And so, the circle went round and round until the ultimatum.

"I'm leaving the house!"

"But Phillip, you're sick!"

"Leave me alone!"

But she wouldn't leave him alone. Fear nagged at her, so she nagged 'til he went to the doctor...who prescribed...rest.

"He needs to work, doctor."

"So let him work. Why do you come to me if you're a doctor, too?"

"I'm sorry."

But she couldn't let him rest. She prescribed fresh air, vegetables, tea, watched and advised as if she could make him well by telling him over and over again and watching...like you watch the dying, every minute...so they won't go while you're not looking.

He was afraid of night and blackness. The light burned all night so he could see, the moment he opened his eyes...everything...it was so black down there. Blackness, untouchable, still, working even now...never enough light...or water. A blackness deep, like the night sky in Phillip's heart. The living is forbidden to be with the dead...in the deep of the earth, robbing what is theirs. If they do, the living must pay, in torn bodies and ravaged nights. Phillip went in black and came out blacker. The streets black with hollow men...like crawling again in the center of chaos...before sun and light warmed and heightened...where it all began...in the center of punishing earth...the clawing for survival.

The stars look gently down on the poem makers to help them delude us while we tear and stumble...work made holy when you put it rhyme and song...but foraging underground like a hungry mole, the beast comes up for air when he wants too, but man can't. The boss's time is more rigid than nature's. 'Air, I must have air!' Running to the window and breathing in deep, hungry breaths, coughing the miner's cough, a cry in the throat as if he were being beaten, cursing life, and gasping for one more breath of air. Breathe, Phillip. The mule breathing hard in and out, showing <u>him</u>. Mirele thanking God, 'we have to go back to the doctor!' frantic rushing for something, to eat, to drink, to rub, to take care, care, care.

"We have to see the doctor again!"

"What for?!"

She repeats, just to say something.

"What for?!"

"He knows what to do! Doctors know, and teachers know everything...and would do something."

Zisme finally came in the morning with the good news. She

found a store, three months' rent fee to start the business. No one was paying rent anyway. Landlords were saying, 'Better give it to a person, than the mice and the thieves.'

"When you can pay, you pay," the landlord told him.

"And the machines?" Phillip asked Zisme, "also free? How do I pay for them?"

"The machines you'll pay out a dollar per week."

"A dollar a week. I'm already a millionaire by her!"

Zisme haggled with the machine company, bought the furnishings, some old chairs for waiting customers and a Big Ben clock to hang near the front window, an unnecessary extravagance to please. He loved clocks. He said they had 'character.' He hung it high on the wall above his head, once a week he wound it, gently, carefully. His one possession was a man who scorned them. He looked at it with love, as if he expected it to jump on his lap and wag its tail. His greatest pleasure was a visit to the clock store. He knew them all, how they sounded, when they needed help. He and the fellow who owned the shop would level and fuss together like two midwives at a birth when a new arrival came in.

The customers came to Phillip's shop at first, and then dwindled. He worked in rhythm, like a fine drummer, a month full of nails, boom, with the hammer. The store smelled of fresh leather. The first week, he didn't make the dollar. Fifty cents for Shabbos, he told Mirele. Rushing to the store before sundown, she lost it in the snow. They ate again at Zisme's and argued.

"You must close on Shabbos. You're losing customers."

"So, when will I keep it open? On Sunday? It's against the law!"

"Don't worry. They won't bother you. What's the crime? Working?!"

"And you know what? The machines are no good!"

"Then don't pay and sue!"

The following day, he saw a lawyer and promised to fix his shoes forever. There was one policeman for miles around who had nothing to do with his summons book. The streets were empty. No cars. Just children in the street playing ball. He was busy only in summer, chasing peddlers on the beach.

"Zisme finds a store for me here to force me to keep Shabbos, or I'm without bread!"

Mirele shouting, "Bread has nothing to do. It's your soul!"

"Zisme has a soul?! Your mother has a <u>soul</u>?! Ha-ha. A soul, she's got? What she has, ha-ha, I don't want. Ha-ha, not ever!"

And the world struggled out painfully "A soul!"

"Phillip! Sit down! Gottenu!"

A rock determination on her tiny face, set, rigid, banging her head against the wall.

"An ockshen! What can I do, Gottenu[*], with such an ockshen[†]?"

There is a terrible noise. A shoe banging in the wall; the neighbor.

"Quiet, already!"

Mirele takes Phillip's shaking hand in hers and whispers, "Come to the doctor."

"I'm leaving the house!"

All the way to the doctor he repeated he was leaving the house. The next day, she consulted Zisme. The store is not making money. The landlord is still waiting for the rent. Six months already.

"He's so proud of his work." He says, "When a customer passes by, he 'kevels.' Still good, the sole, never wear out, like the side of a house. But around the corner, he charges cheaper than shuster[‡], and he's making money. He puts paper, the gonif. So, they wear out and come soon again. The lousy capitalist! Not me!" he says. "He's special. That's true. Leave it to me. I'll find out. I told you," she called out after her, "No, so you told me. So, tell me something else."

"So, you'll listen."

"Depending."

------

[*] ***Gottenu – God***
[†] ***Ockshen – Stubborn man***
[‡] ***Shuster – Shoemaker***

And she scurried on 'to prepare.' When she arrived home, Phillip was looking cross.

"Zisme was here and said you should come right away."

"She's sick."

"In the head, yes."

"But she's a stone otherwise. She'll outlive all of us."

"So, what does she want?"

"She wouldn't tell me."

"I'll be back soon."

Zisme was not one to keep the hearer in suspense by keeping the climax before him.

"He's a fool, your husband. Just like I told you."

"You dragged me here to tell me what you told me?"

"What you told me, I know already. Tell me something else."

"He went to the back of the store for a minute, so I sneaked in and put a piece of his leather in my apron and took it to another shuster. Tell me, I asked him, if he charges 50 cents a pair, can he make a living?"

"Not only he can't make a living, but he's losing money. It cost him to put on his kind of leather shoes. He's crazy. Here's the piece I took. You can sneak it back for me. So, what will you do now, Mirele."

"I'll have to help him. I'll have to go to work myself."

"What work? Where will you find work?"

"I'm not ashamed. I'll do housework."

"And Phillip? What will you do with him?"

"I don't know. He works too hard. That's the trouble."

And she looked down at the ground like she was talking to a spot right near her foot.

"I'm worried about him."

"Ach!"

Zisme waving a frustrated hand, disgusted with too much goodness, the same way that people are angered by evil.

Mirele turned to leave with Zisme spitting insults at her, "You're a worse fool than I thought. Don't bother me with your troubles!"

Mirele paid no attention, too tired to answer just then. Outside, it was bitter cold, beat her like a whip on her house, faster, faster, pushing her hard into a pole and she held on fast, afraid it would lift her off the ground.

She could feel a hand holding her, "Let go, I'll help you. You can hold onto me. Where are you going?"

"The shoe store on 5th and Ocean."

"Me, too," he yelled. "We'll go there together."

Her hand hesitantly left the post. They stumbled on together 'til they reached Phillip's door. He had just closed the light and opened it again when he saw them...a customer maybe.

Mirele stumbled in first...gasping, "Thank you. He helped me."

"Why don't you sit down and rest a minute."

"As a matter of fact, I was coming to see you."

"Me?"

"I want a job."

"A job? I don't have work for myself. What made you think I had extra?!"

"The talk in the neighborhood. They say you have so much, nobody could even count your money."

Phillip laughs now, "You listening to that?"

"I need, at least, one day's work please. I can't remember when I ate last."

"No, alright, you'll come tomorrow morning."

"Where will I sleep tonight?"

Phillip pointed to two chairs, "Make yourself comfortable."

Late that night, Mirele asked, "What work, Phillip?"

"It's your business."

"He'll take it from our mouth. From our mouth, he'll take."

She was right. He took. From the table, he was paid his wages. He wasn't invited to eat that night. There was nothing. Phillip was too ashamed even to go to Zisme. Enough already, to give her satisfaction. Tomorrow is the court case. He coughed hard all night, Mirele sitting close to him and 'hocking with her fist on his back' 'til she fell asleep, her head rolling from side to side on his back, Phillip still coughing, a tortured hacking. When she awoke, he was coughing still and didn't stop 'til they arrived at the courthouse. Defeat, like a hand around his throat, strangling, tightening, leaving him a helpless bundle of heaving spasms, eyes bulging in protest, face red with rage. The coughing stopped when it had a mind to, and not before. It released him and he was grateful he could breathe again. A moment more of distrust and watchful waiting and it was over. Every Monday, he was in court, but this time, it was different. He was the accuser. Made him feel...important now 'til, he saw the lawyer for the company and...by his side...the fool he hired, and he knew, then and there, he didn't have a chance.

"Remember Phillip, the stone you threw in the air, and it hit the old ladies window."

She came down with such a smile and said, "Which little boy threw that stone so high that it could hit a window?"

"Which one of you did such an amazing thing?"

Phillip proudly, "I did!"

The smiling face is hard and vengeful now, "Your mother will hear about this!"

Wrenching his arm, dragging him all the way, though she didn't have to. He still remembered the beating and now, smiling again, like that lady, preparing him for the kill. The lawyer smiling at the judge, the judge and the company's lawyer and Phillip's lawyer...a shlepper. The company lawyer; smooth, confident, and pronouncing each letter correctly, 'English not Henglish.' He argued that Phillip is a poor businessman and a swindler, scheming...not to pay. Phillip, to the stand explaining he had been swindled. The machines don't work.

"I've been swindled, me!"

No more questions. Schlepper had no more witnesses, "Attorney for the company calling a witness, Salvatore Latarro to the stand."

Phillip turned to his lawyer and moaned, "He's a witness...for them? How can it be? He's the one I helped."

"Quiet." The schlepper ordered. "Let's hear. Anything can be."

"And tell the court, how did you find the machines?"

"Perfect working order."

Bloodless mouths talking clam, even the schlepper..

"Please don't tell my mother, please."

The judged were terrified. No appeal. Not even a tear. Denied. Denied. Denied.

In the hallways, the company attorney slips a ten-dollar bill in Mr. Lato's pocket, the company appreciates. The schlepper hurries out...another case. Phillip picks up his hat and holds it above his head. It shakes up and down while he scratches his head with his finger... unbelieving. <u>The meek shall inherit the earth, the International Proletariat shall be the human race. God loved the little people because he made so many of them</u>.

Now you'll be dragged home to mother. Then wait and see. Just you wait. Phillip couldn't pay. The machines didn't work. The company sent four husky men to 'get the machines the hell out of here!' And he owed rent. Philip sold all he could, whatever he wanted from the store. He climbed up on a chair and took the clock. Phillip dropped the key into his pocket and closed the door for the last time, looking at the clock under Mr. Epstein's arm. A sob torn from the heart. Terrible loneliness of...cry...and nobody listening. Cry without appeal.

Chapter Fifty-Five

For a month afterward, he'd get up every morning and go to the store like it was still his, peer through the glass door through his cupped hands, 'just looking,' he said, when Mirele came behind him one day unexpectedly.

"What are you looking at?!" He turned swiftly, his face raw, twisted, "You're following me, watching! Why don't you mind your own business? I'm looking because I'm looking! Can't I even look without saying what I'm looking for? A crime...looking?"

He stopped going when there was a freshly painted sign, 'Shoe Repair, cheap.'

Phillip took a pair to be fixed, "Paper!" he told Mirele.

"That man is a thief!"

He was angry, but a little proud, too. He was still something special. Mirele agreed. But to Zisme, an honest man was a fool living in dreams.

"How many floors have you scrubbed already so he can be honest?"

"For him, why not? He's my husband."

"You should have a child, Mirele. It's not right, he doesn't give you a child."

"Children he doesn't want. He's afraid he won't be able to feed them. He won't be able."

"You'll feed them. You'll be like Mrs. Bunyan who had a baby and the next day she hung out the wash for the neighbors who paid her a quarter a week."

"But how can I have a baby if he doesn't want to?"

"Remind him. Lazar wanted a grandchild from him. Lazar can't refuse. How can you refuse the dead?"

That night Mirele cooked his favorite, flanken and potatoes and served him while he read the paper to her, the political news on which he thought himself a knowledgeable commentator. From time to time, she offered an opinion, and he'd slam the paper with his hand, making a derisive rattle meaning, 'Be quiet' and 'What do you know?' She was proud to agree she knew nothing, and Phillip knew everything. Her left foot shuffled, dragged across the broken linoleum floor like it was dragging a heavy chain.

Phillip shouting, "Sit down already! How can I read with all that noise?"

She scurried faster. "In a minute Phillip, in a minute," the glass of tea burning her hands.

"You forgot the lemon."

She repeated after him, "I forgot the lemon," and dropped it into his glass, watched as he pushed it down with his spoon, the juices swirling the glass, the pits floating to the top, "Give me the spoon, Phillip, I'll take them out."

They slid away from her while she followed them with the spoon. Finally, one remained, and the more and more she poked and poked, the more it eluded her, her face hard and intent now on the little struggle she was determined to win.

Phillip laughed watching her, "You'll break the glass, silly woman."

Furious, "I don't care!"

He laughed even more. She thought now was the time to ask him. He's in a good mood.

"Phillip, I want a baby. Remember, your father wanted a grandson."

The glass went sprawling across the floor with one violent shove.

"Are you crazy?"

"Don't get angry like that, Phillip. It's not good for you, it's not healthy."

"So, what's healthy? Having babies is healthy?!"

"Your father said!"

"My father will take care!"

"I'll take care! I'll take care! Your father told me, before he died, to have a baby. I'm not afraid to listen to him."

"Afraid? Of my father?!"

"It's a sin he told me not to have."

And the tears came and the frantic cries to God for help and then, the sound of her heart thudding again and again, harder, and harder, Phillip crouching as if it was hitting his chest.

"What'll it be, a baby that we make, you and me...a stupid a cripple like you or a beggar slave like me...or both?! Can you imagine that combination?! All he'll need is a tin cup! What's the matter? No argument now? It doesn't matter, does it? You win! That's all that matters! I warn you! I want no complaints! Not like these yentas, for nine months complaining and making everybody's life miserable after, just like before. If I hear just one complaint...just one...do you hear?! You'll pay! I'll leave the house, that's all, you hear?! Say something. Stupid, I know it'll be but your quiet is more stupid than your noise!"

"I should be pregnant and have a baby and not complain?"

Weeping now, eyes wide, return to childhood innocence, asking Poppa.

"That's what I said!"

A resigned, "No."

And she complained for nine months, all the tears inside her. He didn't say a word to her until the baby was born. The only sounds he made...the paper rattling, scraping his plate clen, shoving his glass toward her when he wanted more tea, a loud yawn before bedtime, and then snoring. She complained sometimes just to hear the sound of her own voice...the knot of pain in her belly. She let him know it hurt, at least, that. Every morning, they went separate ways, he to look for work and her to work. Sometimes he softened, but the fear came and hardened his heart again. He hated her for making him even more afraid, like something pushing out inside him too, a terror that would grow beside him like a wild horse loosed, stamping and rampaging beside him while he stood by, helpless, just able to shut his eyes, put his hands above his head and hope it's all over real soon. But he knows it'll never be over.

Sound of Zisme's voice, screaming, "Anybody home?!"

"Anybody is home. What do you want?"

"Your wife had a baby."

"Are you interested if it's a boy or a girl?"

"What is it?"

"It's him. It's a boy. What do you want, what should we name it?"

"What I care about. Let her name it."

"No, you want to see the wife, or no?"

"The wife I see enough. I'll see the baby. That's at least something new."

There was light snow falling. It was pleasant, the flakes blown by the wind against his face, calming steadying him.

"I don't know what to do with a baby, Zisme. How do I even begin?"

He was talking quietly now, friendly.

"Nobody knows how to begin or middle, Phillip. Only the end, we know."

Terrible, the dark thoughts in his brain... 'I wish it was not the end, instead of the beginning. It happens to people all the time. Why not to me? They'll tell me how sorry they are. I'll be glad. I know I'll be glad.' A savage inner voice rudely interfered. 'Stop it. Enough! You should be ashamed! God, what am I thinking?'

She was holding the baby when he arrived, looking already protective and hovering. Revulsion sweeping over him again. How he hated that look. And that horrible ugly little thing beside her that she thinks is such an accomplishment. Already, a fierce possessiveness in those small, dark eyes of her.

"Someday, he'll look like a person. Not now, but soon. We all look like this when we're born."

"I didn't say anything. Why are you explaining?"

"He's ugly."

"He's not ugly."

Anyway, what's his name? we can't call him 'ugly.' Even if it fits now. Later, he'll be handsome like his father."

"So, we'll call him 'Handsome'."

"And if he's not handsome? Just good looking? We'll call him 'Pesach' after your uncle, he should rest in peace. He was a good man."

Phillip told the nurse to write 'Pesach' for 'Name of Baby.'

"What do you mean, 'Pesach.' What do you call it in English? That's Percy in English and she spelled it 'P-e-r-s-i-e.' Looks good."

Mirele agreed. "Sounds like a name!"

And she called him Persie.

Chapter Fifty-Six

The frigid cold hung dead in the house when they brought the baby home. The big, black cold in the kitchen without a fire roaring, big red tongues lapping round the crackling wood. Phillip loved to lift the lid and watched the roaring and the snapping, the fire swirling, desperate, trapped, searching desperately for a way to run wild and Phillip in control...and dreaming...a gentle haze numbing his mind and comforting. They took the subway train home from the hospital. No one could even see the baby, but everyone was beaming, just seeing Mirele hold the rolled blanket. There could have been God-knows what in there, but the very thought of a baby was enough to make them all look foolish...even the nickel riders in the train with nowhere in particular to go. Once they were carried home in rolled blankets, cooing, and rocking and Mazel Tov, Mazel Tov, Mazel Tov.

"Now little Pesach, it's your turn...to be welcomed when you don't know from nothing...and turned aside when you know from something...of life. You see the people in the train...Pesach-Persie? They don't look straight in the face. They look away a little because they must look away first a little before the other fellow looks away a lot. You'll learn, too, Pesach-Persie."

You're making a fire in the stove, maybe Phillip? You can die here from the cold?

"This cold?"

And he'd go on with his lecture about Russian winters that she heard so many times before. Mazel Tov and Mazel Tov...the heavy smell of sour milk and diapers and Mirele bending over the small scrub board in the kitchen rubbing hard with her small fists, a frenzied little machine keeping a greedy, demanding life alive. At night, he would hear her, the fire out, shoes scuffing the cold floor, leaving the warm body. He let her. What else could he do? Sometimes she wouldn't come back for hours. He'd wake up for a moment and see her huddled in a blanket, shivering beside the cot, the distant moon shining cold in the curtainless window. Sheets hanging on the bottom of the windows, an enamel covered table with two leaves that sprang up when they had company, chipped, black scars from too many dogmatic pointed made with knife handles. Nothing extra or trivial in this kitchen-bedroom. Phillip and Mirele in a bed at one wall, the nursery in the corner, a bathroom in the hall. Seldom time to take a bath. But you don't have to worry about that, yet Pesach-Persie.

The wind, in rage, tears a shutter somewhere. It flaps, cracked against the wall. The baby cries. Mirele hides her head under the covers. Tucked in so the cold can't be found here.

"Phil," a sleepy Mirele pleads. "Phillip."

A frenzied rattling of the wind against the windows. Not one of them giving up, the wind, Phillip, the baby.

Mirele, "I'm coming," and her body begging for warmth and sleep. Limp with sleep and still warm, flinging her blanket to one side, the cold attacked and sent her trembling, her bare feet searching the cold floor desperately for her shoes, wrapping the blanket around her.

Then at the crib, "Sha, mien kind, sha."

A plea to the window, the wind...anybody, anything. The wind hurling itself, the window clacketing. Stubborn and unyielding the world around her.

To the wind, "Please don't hurt the baby."

Pesach-Persie, born into such nights...the brutal wind stayed inside somewhere, tearing and gnashing and nothing Mirele did could stop his crying.

In the morning, Zisme comes to watch the baby, Mirele goes to work, complaining about work. Phillip goes to look for work, complaining about no work and Zisme complaining, too...that Mirele is working, and Phillip is not working.

Phillip shouted, in one of their bitter quarrels, "When she worked for you, it was OK, but for me, it's a shame!"

"You remember, God threw us both out of Paradise, not just Adam...Eve, too. We should both work. He said both. And it was her fault, remember? She wanted the baby!"

"With you, she was in Paradise before the baby?"

"Compared to now? Yes!"

"Compared to now...no! And before that and before that, no, no, no! Never! First, you have to live before you can go to Paradise. With you she lived? When?"

"And with you?"

"What's your business...with me? And so, it went. Mirele the placate and peacemaker. Over her and God, there was war without end."

"Let him win, Momma, once in a while. Once in a while a man has to win something."

"He'll win when he deserves...not before...not after!"

Mirele did all her duties at a frantic pace...always rushing after them. She had no rush of warmth for the child...needing to hold and kiss and fondle. The word 'love' was never used by Zisme or her. Being good was the highest virtue and the way to be good was to sacrifice, sacrifice, sacrifice. Love was an indulgence for which there was no time even if she knew and felt it's urgings. Just room in her little heart for all the needing and sacrifice. The baby needed and she provided. Phillip needed and she provided. The grind never stopped so love could burst in her. And if it did, it would be in vain. After all, there were no arms ready to receive her. There never have been.

An old concertina was left to Phillip, and he learned to play it by himself. He could read music. Lazar taught him. And he played the Yiddish songs from the old country. Mirele thought he was an artist. 'Play, Phillip,' urging and proud when company came. She would dance when he played, her face shining with joy while the friend put his arm around her and she put her feet apart and together and everyone lied and said how nice she was dancing and she believed them and tried to move her legs even quicker to keep up, looking down and watching her friend's feet so she wouldn't step on them, being double careful. Dancing always made her particularly happy. But even in happiness, her eyes watched. She never lost that look of an anxious mother hovering over a sick child, looking deep and hard... with fear.

"You can't watch over life, Mirele," but she thought she could.

Had to watch it every minute, so it doesn't strike suddenly from behind and take and carelessly throw to the winds Pesach-Persie, Phillip, Zisme...what she lived for. She had so much <u>watching</u> in her that it spread to friends and neighbors...even strangers. If they needed, she begged and cajoled and...got. Grocery bags were left at the door, no one knew where they came from.

For those who needed clothing, she gave hand-me-downs from her customers. She is always from her customers. She always had more than enough closets. Nothing much to hang in them. Never any time for shopping. No interest. She was proud of her long hair. Said it was healthy because she didn't ruin it in beauty parlors...never wore makeup, 'it's bad for the skin. Polish...no good for the nails.' Mirele distrusted the natural...disease and death...and the unnatural, 'poisons in the paint and powder.' Mirele moved in an intense circle... goaded by fear. 'Eat...eat...eat,' the small face hardens. Pesach-Persie, not a good eater. Those who are defied and mocked by life, demand instant respect and obedience from their children, 'after all they've done!' Too much to bear. An indifferent turn...even from a little one. Pesach-Persie, five now.

An angry fist crashing down, "Eat I said!" Eyes burrowing into the little mouth as if an act of will, can put hand to mouth.

"And God, have mercy, please!"

"Eat what your mother said, damn you!"

Phillip slams the table hard and the dish clatters to the floor. The boy clambers from down the chair...rushing now to pick up his plate.

"Eat, damn you! Eat where you are! Off the floor if you have to... but eat!" Phillip shouts while his legs straddled the floor, and he loosened his belt. Between frightened sobs, his body shaking, he ate.

For the first time, Phillip tasted power, and it was sweet. Mirele was watching to see he finished everything on his plate. He finished.

"No, sit up and eat at the table like a person," Mirele said.

But he refused...crawled under the table, and ran to his bed, put his covers over his head to hide. Phillip slid off his belt. He ran. Phillip chased him, covering his desperate little legs with welts 'til he fell off the bed crying.

Mirele covered him saying, "You can't live if you don't eat, Pesach. You must understand, that's all. You'll eat, you hear! From now on, you'll eat! I have no money or time for a particular eater. In this house, there's no particular people."

And then they agreed they mustn't spoil him. For some reason, this is always a fear of the poor. Never the rich. Nothing to spoil with, really. But where there is only one...two is spoiling.

Chapter Fifty-Seven

Pesach-Persie whispering, moaning, not crying anymore but making the sound anyway like he was...so he'd get a petting and know everything was alright again. They made up with him.

"Shut up, or you'll get more!"

He stopped and stared in the darkness, waited 'til he heard Poppa's snoring and Momma's hard, tired breathing. They were deep asleep. He crept out of bed quietly, careful not to roll on the place where it squeaks, then softly, on his bare feet to their bed and put his cheek on Momma's hand, then Poppa's...then curled his little body in a corner of the bed and fell asleep. They found him the next morning with his head cupped in Phillip's hand, his body warm on him. Phillip shook him. He awoke for one moment, large, frightened eyes staring at Phillip.

"Go into your own bed. Go, or you'll get broken bones sleeping like that in the corner. You have a bed. Why should you sleep with us, a big boy with his own bed..."

But he couldn't lift himself. Too sleepy. He stretched...and fell asleep again. The last words he heard were Phillip muttering, "Doesn't listen."

Mirele screaming, "School! Pesach, today is the first day of school!"

He had to be on time. On time, to Mirele, was early. He didn't like getting up early in the morning. It was so bitter cold. 'Why don't they have school in the summer?' She fought with Phillip all the time, never agreeing on anything...but in ultimatums to Pesach-Persie, they found common ground. There was no appeal. Pesach had to be healthy, strong and <u>something</u>. Now, he had to go to school and the warm, dark, under the covers was especially sweet. His whole head was under the covers, his eyes even. It happened so quickly...the buckle clinking...and then the hurt...singing through the soft, warm, and tearing him out of bed, clawing at Phillip's arm to 'please stop,' and then dropping to the floor while Philip stood like a colossus over him.

"Stop Poppa, please, I'm going to school!" the words struggling through a cry.

"Get up and be quiet and put these on."

The last instructions were, "And listen to your teacher. Whatever she says, you listen."

Kindergarten was one big room with lots of chairs around in a circle. Some new, and most, old.

The teacher ordered, "Take your chairs now, children."

They all scrambled for the new chairs, except Pesach. He couldn't <u>scramble</u> and never sat in a new chair...just yearned and hoped and looked. The children giggled when he first told the teacher his name, 'Persie Popsky.' Even the teacher shook her head and smiled.

"The airs of some of them!"

He didn't know what she meant... 'airs?' What did she mean by 'airs?' He asked Phillip when he got home, and he didn't know either.

"Airs-schmairs, don't worry, you'll find out someday. And besides, if the teacher wanted you to know, she'd tell you. Maybe she was just talking to herself."

But Phillip knew what she meant by 'airs.' No...there were worse tragedies in life. So, his name is not so perfect...so what?! If it's in you, you can make any name proud. Jasha and Mendel weren't so beautiful, but they made them proud...fiddling and writing. Pesach wouldn't dare tell Phillip the children laughed at him. They teased him so hard; he'd cry sometimes...in front of them even...hoping they'd be sorry for him and stop...but it made them laugh even harder and make poems, 'Persie-hursy, pudding and pie, touched a girl and made her die...ha-ha-ha, Persie-hursy. Can't even spell his own name, Persie-hursy. How do you spell your own name Persie-hursy? Spell!' They'd force him to his knees at the beach near the water...and they'd bend one arm back, his nose in the mud spelling.

"Spell Persie, 'til it's right."

He wrote, and the water came and washed it over again...and again 'til they tired of the game and decided even if he could spell, it was a silly game anyway, so what's the difference how it was spelled anyway.

It all started one day in class when the teacher told him to spell his name on the blackboard...and he did...and he was the only one in class who spelled his name wrong. Even the kids who were dumb in spelling could do that! Spell their own name! He sat down in his seat, bent his head, and stared down at his desk. 'Can't even spell my own name. Stupid! That's what I am! Stupid!'

The report cards were never good...and the diagnosis and the remedy, quick and certain. He's lazy. Needs a good beating. They each had their own reason for beating some sense into him. But Phillip had more reason. His whole life was a reason. He needed... and Pesach needed. Phillip couldn't stand anyone else in the house... needing it. He beat his son for needing.

"Another pair of shoes?! What are we, millionaires?! It says in the report card – can't read, can't spell. Think! What can you do?! What?

Wear out shoes and scrape plates and cry?! I'll give you something to cry about!"

And every night, a crying, tearful boy chasing an angry belt with desperate hands to protect his little body and Phillip swinging his weapon, agile, swifter, eluding the boy's little hands deftly. He didn't dare run. It would only make Phillip angrier.

"Defying me?!"

So, he could only fly his arms around and beg and tremble, cringe, and cry for help like an anguished soul at the gate of Hell...or...turn to God. All night he could hear them fighting.

"I want him to have a Jewish education!"

"Not in this house! Friday, you have, that's all and Friday he can have too!"

Pesach loved Friday night, the only night there was peace and quiet in the house. When he went to visit Zisme, she showed him *siddurs* and he prayed. He liked praying, talking to God. And he thought, maybe God liked him...too. Pesach had no friends. Everyone laughed at him, so no one was brave enough to be his friend...or they'd be laughed at too, but God wasn't laughing. He was nice. One night He even came when everyone was asleep and visited him. Of course, he wouldn't tell anyone. But he was very grateful, so he read the prayer book as much as he could at Zisme's house. Even at night, when everyone was asleep, he'd recite what he remembered. 'God, I love you,' he whispered every night before falling asleep. 'I love you God; do you love me?'

And Zisme bought him tallis and tefillin and he wrapped the shawl around him...and was safe and protected. 'I love you, God.'

Mirele complained to Phillip, "Zisme tells me he's praying all the time over there. He's becoming a religious fanatic."

"I told you!"

And that Friday night, Phillip ripped the siddurim, broke the candles, wiped the walls with the tallow and waved a match threatening to burn the house down, screaming, "That's what you're good for! Nothing else!" And to Mirele, "You get out of my sight! Making more of a fool out of that boy than he is already!"

Back to Pesach, "And you, remove the schmattes!"

Pesach swaying back and forth, his eyes closed, "Help me, God."

"Take off the schmattes*!"

Hands loosening his belt. Pesach's head sinking further and further into the prayer shawl, holding it tight around him.

"Let go...or I'll strangle you with that shawl! Come out of there!"

The belt hits Pesach's back while he's idling behind the shawl.

Mirele screaming, "Stop Phillip."

Pesach sobbing, "God help me," a pool of blood spreading across his back.

"Stop it, Phillip!" Mirele screams, "You'll kill him!"

"He's removing the tallis, yes, or no?"

And he stood still, the belt dangling, touching the floor...waiting.

"No! I'm not going to lose you...to Pesach...and to God! I am not! Pesach, do you hear?" And he jabbed him hard in the back with his hand.

Pesach turned around slowly, his body huddled and trembling, "God will be mad at me on Friday night, Poppa, without a tallis. God will be mad at me and he won't talk to me anymore."

"God talks to you? To you, he talks? Who are you that he should talk to you?! You see, Mirele, he's crazy! That's right. God talks to crazies and fools. My son is one and my wife the other."

To Mirele, "He talks to you, too...God?" And not giving her a chance to answer, "To you, he talks, but me, he punishes. That's the difference. To me, he hasn't talked since I'm born. Take off the tallis, Pesach. Maybe He'll talk to me too."

"Maybe," the boy's eyes brightened.

And he painfully straightened, took the shawl from around his body and handed it to him.

"Maybe."

---

* ***Schmattes – Rags***

And he stumbled to his bed...Mirele hobbled after him, rubbing his back with peroxide and putting a rag where it was still bleeding.

Pesach waited until they were both asleep, then crept out of the house and ran to Zisme, banging desperately at her door, "Bubbe, let me in!"

"What's the matter, Pesach?"

"I'm afraid to go home. I'm afraid of Poppa. I want to stay with you, Bubbe...with you and God. Please, let me."

"It's alright with me if you stay with me Pesach, but first, I'll have to ask God. He says to honor your father and mother remember?"

"Ask him, Bubbe, ask him."

"You know you'll have to do what He says."

"I will, Bubbe. Whatever he says. But ask him...right away."

"We'll wait till morning, it's too late to bother God."

"I understand Bubbe."

Chapter Fifty-Eight

At dawn, the first train of the morning woke Zisme. She could almost touch it from her window. Taking people to work. "Only one of them was Phillip. Maybe it would help if once, he could get up in the morning going somewhere where they especially wanted him...and even pay him for it. Ah...nothing will help him. He needs it too hard. And Pesach...nothing to do now...just run and hide...or...if you can wait that long...just grow up bigger and stronger and very mean. God, what am I thinking? Forgive me. No, don't forgive me. I should only live to see it. When Phillip should be afraid and come to me in the middle of the night. And I'll remind him. I tell you...I'll remind him good.``

"No, tattele*," she lifted the covers gently.

He was fast asleep. He opened startled eyes and sprang from the bed, the blanket wrapped around him, bare feet on the icy floor, shouting, "I'm going to school, please don't hit me."

"Go back to sleep. Today is Shabbos. There is no school."

---

* ***Tattele – Dear***

They sat down on the bed together, his head falling on her shoulder. She took his head in her hands and lowered it to the pillow.

"Bubbe?"

"Yes, tattele?"

"Why are you up so early?"

"I have to talk to God, remember? I have to be up early. There's always a long line waiting. I want to be first."

She dressed quickly. It was cold and she learned to dress and undress without baring an inch of skin. She slipped her dress over her feet and inched it up...sliding down her nightgown over her head.

She had to get into the bathroom quick before Lotte Bruhl. She bathed every morning, imagine? Once a week wasn't good enough. Zisme complained to the landlord. But he said, 'What can I do? Pull her out of the tub? There's no law against it.' Lotte wasn't up yet. For once, she'd wait for Zisme. But she didn't wait long. Zisme slapped cold water on her face to wake her up, make her brain tingle, so she could talk to Phillip. To him, you had to know how to talk.

Back in the kitchen, she poured a glass of hot tea to warm her hands. Helped her to think, she always said, rolling the warm glass back and forth between her hands. When she made her mind up, she thumped the glass down hard on the table after drinking the tea down with a gulp.

'I'll tell him the boy is twisted, that he can stay with me. It'll cost him less. Why should he complain? I'll tell him I'll keep him for nothing...So Mirele will slip me a couple of dollars. What will he know? From money, he knows nothing anyway. Only not to give the boy. That...he knows. No, we'll see who's smarter. Him...or me. A stupid question. How smart can he be? In business...nothing. A husband... nothing...a father...nothing. The boy came to me. Now his legs are long. If he takes him, he'll come back to me again. Only next time, he'll run faster. Pesach is also afraid of me. Of whom is he not afraid? poor Pesach! But it's a different *afraid*. With me, he knows because. I hit him because why? Because this or that. But with Phillip, there's no because and not why. Just like that...from nowhere.'

She bent her lips into a thin line and out her hand on her hip as she came to Phillip's door.

Phillip shouting, "Who is it? Mirele...it could be the devil. I'll go see."

"It is the devil."

Zisme asking, "Where is your son?"

Phillip shouting, "In shul, where else?"

Mirele pounding the bed, knowing it's empty and still pounding.

"You took my son."

"You gave him to me."

Phillip talking softly now, "Keep him. Don't let him come back. I need to hurt him. I don't know why. It's not I can, or I can't. I have to. If he was ten feet tall, I'd break him in two. And even broken as he is, I have to break him more. It doesn't matter Zisme. Love is blind. My meanness is my blinder. It has no reasons. He can be good. He can be bad. It makes no difference. I don't want him here, Zisme. I don't want anyone to see me in the house...a witness that I do nothing but sit and wait...for what, I don't know. You know, Zisme what I do all day? In the morning, for an hour, I look in the papers for work. Then I look out the window for another hour. Sometimes, I make a little tea. Then I read the rest of the paper. Then, I eat a little something. Sometimes, I write a letter to my brother in Europe, forty pages, sometimes, these letters, so it feels like I'm doing something. I don't want to finish sometimes so I keep adding P's and more and more 'til I have to force it into the envelope it's so fat the letter and then I remember something else, so I spend more time struggling to take it out of the envelope and write some more. If I have no news, I write some poems I made up...anything to fill up more paper, spend some more time so it's not there waiting for me, and I don't know what else to do with it. Sometimes, I play a little concertina...and then, I'm tired. When Pesach comes home from school, he used to tell me what happened until I told him I don't want to hear. Pesach had a place to go. I was even jealous when he did his homework. He'd pull out his books as soon as he finished his glass of milk, looking busy. Me...I'm sitting, looking, and Mirele running in the house and quick to the stove, in her winter coat sometimes, and me, already at the table, looking important. But with Pesach, how could I look important, or look anything...just sitting and looking, giving him his milk? Zisme, go tell him it's all right. He can stay as long as he wants, even longer than that."

And he turned, a martyred look in his eye, rubbing his head with his big thumb and finger.

Zisme thinking, 'He's playing tragedy now. Well, I'll let him. He has such a talent for finding a good excuse.

Mirele shouting, "You can't help...what? What do you mean you can't help? Terror sweeping her this way and that...pacing the floor back and forth in wild circles."

"Let me talk to him, Zisme. I won't force him to come home. But to talk to him, at least."

"Wait until tomorrow. He needs a few hours to come to himself. And you to yourself. And Phillip to himself...and...you know something...me to myself."

"You'll come and tell me Zisme when it's all right. Phillip is a good man. He doesn't mean the bad things he says about himself. He means well. It's my fault. I have two men here and I'm not taking care. Men are weak. They're not strong like women. Phillip is too nervous. Maybe he needs a better diet. I'm not feeding him in the right way. And Pesach too. He needs to see a doctor. It's been a long time, Zisme, that I didn't take them. What do I know about what they eat when I'm not home? I know. I must prepare in the morning before I go, Zisme."

"Alright Mirele. From now on, you prepare. But I think, maybe Phillip needs a little business again...to occupy him. Maybe he'd learned a little now. We'll try, Mirele...again. Now, I'll go back to Pesach. He'll wonder why I'm so long."

Pesach had a death pallor on his face when she returned. He looked through the window first before opening the door. She was alone.

"Tell me, Bubbe. Quick, tell me. What did God say?"

"It's alright, Pesach. You can stay. God said it's alright with Him if it's alright with me. And I told him that you're 100% welcome. Now, be a good boy and fix your bed and make some tea. Pesach scurried to the bed, then the kettle to do her bidding as quickly as he could. At dinner, he scraped three smears of butter on his bread.

"Be careful with the butter," she told him. "One smear is enough."

After all, Mirele didn't give her anything for him. 'We're not millionaires.'

He carefully scraped two smears from his slice of bread and put it back on the plate...crumbs and all.

Chapter Fifty-Nine

Zisme tried to remember, in later years, when it was that he left her, too, or he didn't sneak out again in the middle of the night. this time, it was different. It was always the middle of the night. He lived in darkness when it was light. There was no day for him. All day, he sat at the table, the candles lit, reading his siddur like it was Shabbos night. He would light one with the other, so they'd never go out. And sometimes Zisme says, 'It's not always Shabbos. Today is Shabbos. You see, the sun is shining.' And he'd turn, with a terrible flame in his black eyes.

"There is no sun, Bubbe. I put it out, see…"

And he'd put his finger on the candle and snuff it out…

"I'll put out the sun, the world has no eyes, now, Bubbe. I made it blind. I made it so it can't see what I'm doing."

"What are you doing, Pesach?"

"Nothing."

And he retreated behind his tallis so deep, you couldn't even see his eyes.

"Let me see your eyes, Pesach. Look at your Bubbe."

The muffled saying, "No, I don't want you to see. Eyes tell...and then you'll know."

"What Pesach?"

"Nothing?"

And he sat mute, no matter how much gentle coaxing, to 'tell me.'

When she left the table, she could hear him again, mumbling his prayers, the chair creaking back and forth, louder, and louder, swaying back and forth, falling asleep at the table, waking, and lighting the candles again. The house smelled of burnt candles.

Mirele pleaded to see her son. "Not yet, he doesn't even ask for you. Not even once, like you never were. Like he was born now. From the air."

"Talk to the born, I'm going to have a baby!"

"You? Pregnant again?"

"What can I do? It happened."

"And Phillip? What is he doing with this news?"

"Choking on it. A woman is a burden. What can I tell you?"

"So, how is he, Pesach?"

Weary now. Asking the question, just to ask. Impatient with him. Whining.

"Why can't he stop this nonsense and come home and be like other boys?"

"Lennie threw his son out in the street, in the cold. For a week, he wouldn't let him in the house. And they say, when he gets mad, he throws on his son whatever he can lay his hands on. But the boy stays home. All the children I know are home. Except mine. Tell him, Zisme. Maybe it'll help. Tell him he may have a baby sister."

That night, she told him.

"Your momma tells me she's in a family way."

He turned from his books.

Anxiously, "Will the baby cry, Bubbe? Poppa won't like it if the baby cries."

And he turned back to his siddur.

"God," he whispered, "help the baby he shouldn't cry. Poppa doesn't like crying…I'm not crying, Poppa."

A sob broke from his heart, a scream exploding, then…a quiet whimper, sobbing, clutching tears in the throat, trying not to be heard, only the mouth stiff, stark, crying silent now, under a wet palm.

She took him in her arms, put his head on her shoulder, and he curled to her and gurgled, and she patted him gently, "Sha, mien kind," and he cried and cried, rocking back and forth, "Sha, sha mien kind," until he fell asleep in her arms.

Sometimes Phillip would shyly ask, "How is he?"

"Fine," Zisme would say, and he'd quickly turn to other things, relieved he'd done his duty and nothing was asked of him.

Zisme thinking, "I don't know why he even bothers to ask. He cares?"

"He cares!" Mirele defending.

"But what can he do? The boy doesn't want him. Can you blame him?"

"Why not? He's his father, no? A father is a father. And that's all! Like a husband is a husband! And a mother is a mother. You take what God gives."

Zisme nodded her head, philosophically, in agreement.

"I need some help now, Zisme."

Mirele twisted body bent even more to one side as the months went by. Like a small ship in stormy waters, she'd almost brush the floor, then spring up again miraculously.

"You see how hard it is for me to walk. Tell him."

'What help?' Mirele will let herself take help. 'She wants him home, that's all.'

"I'll tell him. Maybe he'll go home. Maybe he'll be better at home. No matter how hard it is. Home is home."

Zisme never listened to Mirele's worship of doctors. She didn't trust them. Zisme had never been to school but was convinced she knew everything and they, doctors especially…knew nothing. She knew plenty of people that got sicker from them and poorer. 'No. no doctors! Pesach will go home. That's all he needs and doesn't know it. A grandma visits and goes home, but not with this grandchild. Nine months with Bubbe! Enough!'

That night...with determination, "Pesach, it's time you went home. Momma needs you."

Without a word, he let the tallis slide of his back, unwrapped his tefillin, put a torn piece of paper in the place of where he was reading the siddur to mark his place, brushed his black hair from his forehead with his thin, bony, hair hands, blew out one candle, then the other, took a knife from the drawee, the one he used to cut the bread, and carved a word into the darkness on the table. Zisme couldn't see. Then, he plunged the knife so deep in the table, the handle was still shaking when he walked calmly to the door and left without a goodbye or thank you. For the first time, Zisme felt terror in her hands and her body trembling.

Not able to walk, she remained sitting in the chair where he left her, with her finger, she traced the scar on the table moving it slowly and carefully up and down around the knife, she traced the word, B-A-B-Y.

"I have to tell Mirele! We'll have to take him to a doctor!"

Someone banging on the door and shouting, "Zisme, open up!"

Following orders, she opened the door a crack, fearful it was Pesach, grateful, for the first time to see Phillip. He pushed the door in, nearly knocking her down.

"Mirele! She's having the baby now! The doctor's in the house, with her. It happened so quick! Come with me. I don't want to stay alone! Where's Pesach?"

"He's home. I sent him home."

"He must have left when I was coming. Mirele needs him now, or maybe he needs her now. I don't know what he needs. But he needs something. Hurry up. We'll talk later."

She dashed out, then rushed back to check the door. It was locked.

"What have you got in there to lock, Mrs. Rockefeller?"

"None of your business."

She was not happy in the house when Zisme came, Mirele complaining her breasts hurt and she couldn't stand the baby near her, she was in such pain.

They'd put the baby in a small crib near Pesach's bed. Zisme moved it away from him as lose to Phillip as she could...but he moved it back.

"How will I be able to sleep, if it cries in my ear?"

Pesach stood in a corner, his back to everyone praying. Once in a while, he turned and looked at the baby, sullen, morose, as if he hoped she'd be gone each time he looked...and she wasn't...and he was disappointed, she wasn't, like he expected...prayed for it even. God let him down. Even God. Zisme shuddered. Pesach looked evil... like a savage fury deep under sloping, gentle hills and soft flowers, to crack the earth Zisme would stay awake all night, watch him, and tell them tomorrow. Phillip greeted him and tried to make small talk. He didn't answer. Mirele told him to look at the baby. He looked quickly and turned away. Phillip, angry now. 'I'll settle this with him tomorrow. If he doesn't talk. Who needs him if he keeps this up? A piece of furniture I have in the house already...and it doesn't even cost.'

Mirele was glad to see him, talk or no talk. Phillip dimmed the lights and crept into bed carefully on the farthest side of the bed, Mirele was complaining so. Zisme on a pillow and quilt on the floor, pretending to be asleep, but watching Pesach. She could see him in the dark, sitting, his head turned, staring at the baby, it happened so quickly. He suddenly sprang like an angry tiger and put both hands around the baby's throat.

"Pesach!" Zisme screaming.

He fled out the door and down the stairs and disappeared down the street. They never found him that night and all trudged home wearily at dawn, hoping to find him asleep in the hallway like all the other runways. But he wasn't.

Pesach ran through the streets like a frightened animal, scurrying in one direction, then another, breathing frantic like a dying man, fleeing shadows, clutching his throat with both hands and pressing harder and harder, his nails digging deep and hurting, and digging deeper and deeper until the blood ran down his fingers...and still he tore. Under a streetlamp, swinging a club, he saw a policeman, relief flitting across his tortured face. A light flicker in doomed eyes. Lurching toward him, the officer stiffens, cautious.

Pesach, trembling, clutching him with both arms, pleading, "Lock me up, please, lock me up. I tried to kill...my sister."

Chapter Sixty

Zisme with a secret, watching by the window. Mirele asking, "Do you see him coming?"

And Zisme hoped to tear him from the street by an act of will or counting numbers in a strange roulette...the next one had to be him. And if he does come up those stairs, how would she tell them what she would say? She rehearsed repeatedly at the window. 'It was terrible, Mirele. I could see the shadow of his hands, those long fingers bent and the nails he never cut coming down like the claws of a big, black bird, coming down in a circle. I knew what he was going to do when his head bent over the crib, looking for the little one, for the little neck, making bigger and smaller circles with his hands...and then Mirele would scream, 'My son?! Never! You're imagining things! My son, he's a good boy!' only good boys kill sisters, Mirele. Bad boys kill strangers, anybody, everyday...so that's no argument.'

Only Phillip going to the police...and thinking, 'Why would they bother with a poor boy running away from home?'

"Try Phillip," Mirele pressed.

The baby red from crying. Mirele's breast ungiving. With one hand at the sink rinsing dishes, the other patting a squirming bundle of life protesting already, the only way it can.

Zisme saying, "Let me help you."

"Watch the window, that's all!"

Mirele wouldn't let Zisme take her eyes from the window for a minute, even set up a chair and served her breakfast on it.

"You're removing!"

"Just to get to my glasses. I can't see so far, but I think I see something."

"Here's your glasses," Mirele putting the baby in the crib, pushing Zisme aside, "Let me see."

"Pesach and Phillip and...and...a policeman. My God, he's arrested! My Pesach with a policeman. What's a boy like Pesach doing with a policeman?!"

"A boy like Pesach," Zisme bursting, but holding the flood back, "You'll find out."

"What is there I should find out? I don't know my own boy?"

"No!"

"They're at my door already," Mirele's face numb with terror, a stiff smile as she opens the door, "Come in officer. Pesach, what happened? You're arrested?"

"Sit down Mirele," Phillip's voice, an undertone of taking charge, of protection that Mirele obeyed without question.

The family was in trouble with the government. She fell into the chair. The baby yelling louder and louder. Mirele sitting, unable to move. Zisme took the baby. It was spurred on to more crying.

"She's frightened, Mirele. I can't stop crying."

"Let her cry."

"Tell me officer, my son did something he shouldn't?"

The baby was crying louder, Mirele shouting, "My son did something, God forbid?!"

The policeman didn't like this one. From the first day he took his oath, he was assigned to frighten such immigrants in quiet streets where he strode like a colossus to keep them that way. The following morning, she went to see Pesach and returned home only to pick up her clothing.

Phillip asking, "Where are you going Mirele? What happened?"

"I have to hold on strong to the rope. Pesach is drowning. I can't let him drown. I'm going to a hospital to sit with him. Night and day I'll sit with him. That life is mine. God gave it to me and he's not getting it back!"

Her eyes searching voraciously for the things she came to take with her. Hurrying, not to let a moment go by that she's not clutching and insisting on that life.

"It's not time, it will never be time!"

Phillip watched her while she flings a few things into a paper bag, an old night gown, a pair of lisle stockings, salt to mix with water for rinsing her teeth, fruit for Pesach. She carried fruit with her to the last...ready to feed him when he came to.

She gave him instructions before leaving, "What to eat that was good for him, not to tire himself, above all to take care...a man is not very strong you know."

Her instructions annoyed him, "Get out of this house already and leave me alone!"

"You'll be alone, you'll see! Bury me and be alone!"

As she hurried out the door, the bag plopping down the stairs behind her. He opened the door and shouted after her, "Pick up the bag! It'll break and then what will you do?!"

She picked up the bag and did not answer him. There was only the uneven sound of her feet, the slow off-beat short sound of the lame foot and hard, long one of the good foot. He listened 'til he was sure she'd reached the bottom. He couldn't see her, but he could hear the quick rhythm and fast little shuffle when she was on certain ground. He closed the door and appealed to God for the first time since the cheder* days.

"Help them God, help them."

____

* ***Cheder - School***

Mirele sat at Pesach's bedside night and day, watching, and waiting. The struggle between them was coming to an end. Pesach gave up his life. Mirele, insisting he hold onto it.

"Pesach, Momma's here. Do it for me."

The mind that refused to come out of hiding and come home was now the body, eyes and ears that wouldn't see or hear. The bag of food dutifully brought, was carried away untouched. All Mirele's shoes rested on a piece of fruit, watching his weight in ounces like a baby. She sat vigil by his bedside, his breath so soft she could barely hear, her hand desperately searching for his chest and finding his heart. She bent her head and listened very hard. He was still with her. Sometimes, she thought she was imagining. It was so faint, she grabbed another's hand, whoever was nearby and rushed it to his chest, under the sheets, "Listen, please." And they'd nod, 'Yes,' and she'd be sure for a little while until it grew even harder to hear him.

Thinner and thinner...the will and death hollowing the cheeks and eyes. In the early hours of the night, dusky lights in the bare room, gray walls and a striped mattress without sheets, the desolate quiet of the world asleep, forgetting even to pray, forgetting everything, seeing nothing, her whole world, only the tiny little mound going up and down watching as if it would stop if she took her eyes away, even for a moment. Early in the morningshe was keeping the desolate vigil, watching that spot where the sheet was going up and down.

The nurse came in quietly, bent over him, "I'm so sorry, Miss..."

"It's not true! Can't you see? It's still going up and down! That spot...still...going up and down."

"What spot?"

"There, can't you see? Give me your hand and I'll put it on the spot."

"Where? you tell me?"

She takes Mirele's hand. "You see. Your hand. It's staying in one place."

Mirele screaming, "Let go of my hand! Let go of my hand!

Phillip, Zisme, somebody...tell me...or you'll send me to my grave! You want that I should go to my grave not knowing?! You want that I should go to my grave...now?! What is there to tell me? My Pesach is home. The policeman found you and brought you home. You got lost, and he found you, isn't it, Pesach? He's 15 years old. Policeman don't bring big boys home, only little one. Pesach is a big boy."

Pesach, softly, "Yes, Momma, you're right. I'm a big boy lost. No one understands. Just you, Momma. The boy is lost. I'm an old man... now," and he stroked a long, imaginary beard, and shook his head ponderously up and down.

"I have to find him, Momma, that boy. We mustn't let him get away. The policeman is taking me to a place where there are all little boys hiding and waiting to be found..." his voice rising with hope.

He could almost see that boy now, free, without mommas and poppas.

"I have to find him, Momma. you understand. Mr. Policeman, you promised to take me to that place, remember?"

"I remember."

Phillip shouting, "What place?"

Zisme, "You know, already, what place."

The horror touched Mirele, and she shut her ears, "Don't tell me!"

And she shut her eyes and shut her mouth tight and shook her head from side to side.

"Don't tell me! First, he runs away from me, I don't know why. Then, he comes back, I don't know why."

Sometimes he had a little trouble here, nothing serious, but enough to infuriate him so he's boxed an ear or gave one of his lectures numbered 1-9, 'when I was a lad' or 'you don't know how lucky you are' speech for every occasion. Cruelty fed by power, too much imbibing after a hard day lecturing, getting his lunch wherever he wanted, slapping an angry summons on a seller who wouldn't 'play ball.' But this was different, this boy was beyond command, lecturing. Worse yet, he frightened him. There was a devil in this boy.

He talked to God, but the devil was in him. He could feel it. The father told him the boy was very religious, but there was something deep inside, wild and out of control. And, worst of all, he comes right out, right away and admits to something awful. No yammering, 'didn't do it.' No hiding behind phony innocence. The cruel eyes softened, the mouth twitching, touched with mercy, struggling with a painful self-consciousness being kind, in uniform.

"You want to tell your mother what happened, why am I here?"

Phillip stood behind the policeman. Pesach would not walk beside him.

Zisme urged, and stood guard in front of the crib, "Tell her, Pesach."

Mirele screamed, "Tell me, Pesach. So, tell me, already. Do you want me to come Pesach?"

Mirele hopefully taking his arm. He tears it away.

"No! The policeman will take me now!"

When they were out of sight, Pesach, his head sunk to his chest, said, "Will I have to tell them what I did?"

"If you want them to help you."

"I'll never tell."

Cruelty spreading again over the policeman's face. He doesn't like to be despised by the younger generation.

"You'll tell them, boy! That's an order! Or you'll get this," his hand waving in the air, "You hear? Better hold on to this one after all," snapping the handcuffs on his wrists.

Pesach, craven, pleading now, "Is it far, the school, Poppa? Will the teacher hit me?"

That night, Pesach disappeared behind the walls of the place where the secrets are. The relatives in one talk about, sons, daughters, husbands, wives, whose names are never mentioned, generations after dropping the name or rapidly changing the subject. His was a life sentence. The door clanged shut behind him and all the years he was there, he thought he was in school. He hated being in school but didn't want to go home. When the bell rang for a bed check at 3PM, he thought his class was being dismissed and ran into hiding under his bed 'til the ringing was over.

"Now he wants to go again and still I don't know why. It's my fault, I should know why.

That's what we have to take special care of. To know why our children come and go again."

Phillip takes her by the arm, "Come with me, Mirele. I want to talk to you."

And he takes her into the other room.

"Listen to me, Mirele. Pesach is a sick boy. Be still, Mirele, a minute, and listen very hard. Pesach wants to go to the hospital. Himself, he wants to go, no one is telling him. He's afraid, Mirele, of himself."

"What do you say, Phillip?"

"I think he's right, Mirele. After all, who knows himself better? They'll help him, I know."

Hoping too, now, "Alright, Phillip, if you say so, they'll help."

"Why not? He's young. The young heal quickly. Their wounds are fresh."

"You're right, Phillip," while she moaned, and beat her breast and wailed...a flood of pain that 'she didn't take care.'

In feverish haste, she tore open the bag of oranges and threw them in the air. They fell, hitting her on the chest and arms while she submitted to them, willingly.

"It's like it was. You and I remember." She repeated over and over.

Mirele came home and wailed and beat her head on the wall and Phillip stood by helpless watching life flay Mirele. The years he hadn't seen his son. 'Poppa don't hit me. I'll go to school.' Phillip said that to his father and his father to him before that and before that. 'So did Pesach do so bad?'

Phillip came to see him for the first time...and the last. He heavily shook his head giving an appropriate face to tragedy. That struggle at the door. How he pushed, Pesach's frail little body pushing back and the terror crawling on his face when the belt reached around the door and burned him, 'Poppa!'

A dry, tearless moan, like the cry of a leashed dog, escaped unbidden and quickly caged again. It was the first and last time Becky ever heard Poppa cry.

Mirele blamed no one. Her lifelong enemy from now on was bad food and Becky was doomed to receive all the doctoring, pills, that Pesach consumed, and with the right food, she thought, she would have saved him.

They returned to a policeman who is impatient now... complaining he doesn't have all day. They had to make up their mind or he'd have to leave the matter in their hands and 'go all together.' Of course, he didn't mean a word of it. The boy was dangerous.

"In now!" to Mirele, he said, "The sooner the better, he needs care now."

Shaking her head wearily, "He needs. He needs. What lives and doesn't need? Of course, he needs."

Phillip saying, "Come, we're going."

Pesach saying, "No, just you Momma. Don't hit me, Poppa. Please, don't hit me. I'm going to school..." and he crossed both arms across his face and looked out the door.

Phillip touched his arm and whispered heavily, "It's alright, Pesach, today you don't have to go to school."

It happened so quickly. He struck so swiftly; Phillip couldn't even see the hand as it swept across his face.

"You go to school, Poppa! Now you go to school!"

Soft now, "I'll go to school, Pesach. Maybe we'll go together. You and me in school."

"No! you'll go! Just you. I've already been going," sullen, stubborn. "When you catch up, I'll go!"

"Alright, Pesach, when I catch up. Now, you have to catch up. He's going, the policeman."

"Wait for me, Mr. Policeman." He takes his arm.

Phillip was forbidden to come...ever. Pesach never even asked about him. Mirele would come every week, bringing fruit, and taking him for ice cream. He especially loved the icecream. Sometimes, a terrible black storm, somewhere deep inside breaking over him and he would spring, like a loose tiger grabbing the fruit from Mirele and ripping it to small pieces while the other fruit rolled on the floor around him. Then he'd pick up the nearest one, enrage at it's daring to try to escape him, and throw it at her, another, and another as fast as he could. And she'd just...stand there...crying...the fruit rolling down her shoulders, over her head, under her legs...some missing her...some hurting...hurting her badly. No one came to help. They didn't even notice. Told her so many times not to bring anything, but she wouldn't listen.

"How else do I know he's still sick if he doesn't hurt me? I think he's well, so I take him home, and he hurts Poppa, Zisme and the baby? Hurt me Pesach if it helps you. It helps me, too. I didn't watch it well enough. I should be hurt. I deserve it. If I could do it again, I'd take you to the doctor every month, every day if I had to, to see how you were. Maybe you were sick for a long time and I don't know. But...he has doctors now everywhere he turns, and it doesn't help. Are there good ones over there, Phillip? Who knows if they're good ones. A good one, Phillip...helps! But who knows...like they say about religion. With it, it's terrible. Without it, it's worse. They explain it to me, it's hard to know what's in their mind. But I think, maybe, if he had a better diet. It's all in what you eat, Phillip. Too much artificial stuff is now in food here, it's no good for him. The doctors ask me about you all the time. I tell them how you sing and play and make poems. They don't understand, then, they tell me, why he hates you so much, I tell them I don't either. You were strict, but for his own good. He should be smart like you. Smarter even. Not to work in a shop like an animal...or worse...not to work even like an animal...just to look like one...with hungry eyes...looking to work like an animal."

Mirele was proud she never sat in a circle on a porch with the other ladies and complained about her husband like they did about theirs. Not her Phillip...throw into their mouths. Besides, what was there to say? They wish they had one like him! They wish!

Doctors <u>conferring</u>. How to tell Mirele, Pesach has TB. His second year in the hospital deteriorating rapidly. They can't send him home even if he were well.

Mother: Borderline Psychotic

Father: Unknown – But according to the boy's report in his clear moments...Serious Mental Incapacity with violence.

Doctor, "Pesach, do you want to stay in school or go home?"

"I want to stay in school."

<u>He doesn't want to go on. That's what's he saying. This boy is going to die because he wants to so badly. God forbids it the open way. So, he's doing it the hidden way, so even he doesn't know it. But we know it</u>. And the mother, didn't she see? Or hear? Her own son begging for mercy like a beaten dog? What's the first thing we do when something comes hurtling down on us? We close our eyes and ears and stand there...hoping it won't happen...hoping we'll be missed. What's been hurtling down on her? Judgment. One or the other. She can't. she wouldn't dare.

And Phillip? What's hurtling down on him? He wants life to love him a little...to care...and it doesn't. It eludes him no matter how hard he runs...coquette...erases and runs...and makes him hunger more...so he grabs the first thing he can and beats and beats his hunger into it 'til it chokes and begs for mercy...then <u>it</u> is his son. And Pesach knows he can't be sane and defy his father...or be insane and stay in school... so he chooses the only way left for him.

"Is it that simple?"

"No, I made it that simple. You see, I'm blind and deaf, too, to all the other little voices that are trying to tell me something more and more. I don't want to hear or see anymore. It's too much already... having to make do with what I've allowed myself to know. I too can't stand it anymore."

"How can we tell her, the mother?"

"We'll tell her so she can hope. For our sake. So, she doesn't disturb us with her tears."

So, they told her with hope. And she hoped...through all the lies that professionals have practiced, for generations, to soothe the simple and trusting, potions, incantations and rabbit's feet. Mirele was grateful to the doctors, even when they just passed by and nodded. It meant he was getting better. Everything meant he was getting better. She didn't even she he was getting worse. Didn't want to. And couldn't.

Quote Report Here:

The hospital needed the bed. That's all the room he took up in the world at the end...and even that couldn't be spared. Pesach...a boy who lived without a life. Nothing to take in the end that wasn't given in the beginning.

Mirele pounding her head against the wall, so hard it hurt, tearing and scarring wherever she could, ripping flesh and smearing the walls with her own blood. The mourners came. Phillip disappears into the other room.

And Phillip, taking down an old paper bag upside down and all the family pictures fluttering to the ground and searching and tearing whatever he could find...of Pesach...into little pieces...and threw them in the bag...an old pair of shoes, an undershirt, a notebook, two pencils he'd chewed on while doing his homework, one glove, the other he'd lost, then he pulled his tallis and tefillin out of his drawer and crushed them into the bag, working quickly, like a thief, afraid someone will catch him. Then he looked under the bed, and again in the drawers, nothing else left...a thread from his coat...or a hair on his head. Leaving the drawers open so he wouldn't make any noise. The bag shaking in his hand, he held it tight to his chest so he wouldn't make a sound, opened the door a crack, the mourners had their backs turned surrounding Mirele, so no one could see him. He slipped out the front door quickly, ran and kept running on to the beach and into the water. He dropped the bag, turned his back, and struggled out again. It followed him, but when he reached the shore and turned around again, it was gone. <u>Mirele will be alright because it'll be like it never was</u>.

The boardwalk, desolate at that hour too. He was too weak to stand, sat down on a bench and looked out at the sea again at the very spot where he dropped the bag. Though he saw it still floating and wanted it back. Frantic, he ran into the water again, pursued it, but it deftly eluded him and drifted further and further away. A few scraps drifted towards him. He grasped them with his fingers. Part of a picture. He caught the corner of his mouth and one eye. When he reached the shore again, he put them in his pocket. Later, he forgot to take them out again. Mirele, cleaning his pockets, threw them out. The tallis floated to the beach. A family was happy to find it. They dried it in the sun, then sat on it with their wet bathing suits while their little children played with the fringes.

The tefillin were found in the water by an excited little boy who wondered what the box was for. His mother thought she could use it for safety pins and clips if she found a way to open it...and the rest of it she would 'wrap around his neck if he didn't shut up!' He was nagging her to tell him what it was, and she didn't know and kept nagging.

When Phillip returned home, Mirele was in bed surrounded by women scurrying back and forth tending and soothing. One said she feared Mirele would die of grief.

Another shook her head sadly and said, "She'd never be that kind to herself."

No one saw or heard Phillip as he slipped past them into the bedroom. Huddled in the dark in a corner, Becky, staring at him.

"Poppa, you're wet."

"I went to get the paper, it rained."

Mirele's wailing frightened Becky. She sneaked into the bedroom. There was a card on the floor. Pesach's report card. She put it in the drawer carefully and didn't tell anyone she found it. She didn't know why she didn't tell, but she didn't.

"Go out from here, Becky. I have to dress myself."

She went into the other room, stood in the corner, and watched. No one even remembered she was there.

At the funeral, one anguished cry came out of Phillip. The only one she ever heard come tearing out of him. Then Momma's head banging against the wall night after night. Becky would tell herself not to hear. Be dead, Becky...like Pesach. He doesn't hear anymore. No one told her what death was, so she figured it out herself. Death is...to be put in a deep, dark hole and you don't see or hear anymore. He must have been a bad boy to be put in such a place. Becky couldn't sleep 'til the knocking stopped, 'til she learned to play dead. She was glad when Mirele was better, and she sat on the bed beside her sliding her two fingers up and down Mirele's nose 'til she fell asleep.

And then Mirele comforted him as soon as she was able to wake without a sob and fall asleep without tears...he sighs and shakes his head significantly up and down.

"Play a little," she'd coax him gently. "Play a little concertina. You'll feel better."

"No," he'd looked down as if he hadn't heard you, "No, that's how life is."

"So, play a little, Phillip. It'll help."

Phillip erupting, "What'll help?! What do you know?! You know from nothing! What helps?! You play because you play. Sing songs... not because it helps! It doesn't help! Life...nothing helps! It's a disease that's incurable. No one asks the important questions so you can decide. 'Do you want to be born? To get sick? To die?' But everyone has remedies when the damage is done. You're born...sing, play...like a stupid. It's a big drug store, the world...for what hurts. Life hurts...so play! How long can I play?! Forever! Till I die! I play?!"

Phillip was hollering again. Maybe it's good for him, he should holler. 'Holler, Phillip, Holler. That's the best remedy.'

Phillip, quietly, "Sit down, Mirele. I'll tell you what's the best remedy. I don't want to hear of him again, talk about him, cry about him, like he never was Mirele, or I'll go crazy, and you will, too."

He was never mentioned again.

Occasionally, Mirele would open the drawer and sneak a look at his report card. He was really real, the report card said so. Spelling, reading and conduct...D, D, A.

Mirele moved quickly, running all the time, hurrying away quickly from sitting, even for a minute, frightened of trouble or sickness, more frightened without it, so she filled the empty spaces worrying about it. Never leaving any room for anything to sneak past the barriers. Filling up the spaces. That was Mirele's madness. Always filling.

And Phillip...did what he always did...only this time Becky took Pesach's place. They both turned to her and she joined them willingly...eager to touch love, even if it's mad...and Mirele not knowing but being mad. And no one else knows either. There was no delirious or talk of things no one could see but themselves or fists in air crashing into innocent faces. None of that. Just a lot of little things and a few big ones that seemed right but weren't. it took years to see they weren't. and then it was too late. For Becky, that is. But then, we're getting ahead of our story.

Chained, held fast, choked memories, rock hard like Prometheus on his tortured rock. Sanity laid bare, stripped, and flawed. Madness, like a great protector, like a hovering mother tending to her young, tucking him in tighter and tighter, then wrapping him in her arms and holding fast against till a wind comes. Pesach's madness was like a wild beast to be put in a cage. You had to guess if that was there. Pesach's eyes could cut like a knife. How she moved quick, rushing all the time. Hurrying away quickly.

Chapter Sixty-One

Pesach's death made Mirele a fanatic preserver of life. She didn't have to wait for old age to realize it's fragility. Every day, <u>life</u> was under threat...every hour, every minute and Mirele watched over it, eyes and ears in a continuing and frantic search for it's enemies, to battle and conquer it before it has a chance to do its damage. Every month Becky was dragged to the doctor, Becky hating him and in a temper tantrum all the way, sitting down stubbornly refusing to move on every corner, but her little arm was no match for the determined force of Mirele's...and Mirele's face hardened with determination, sometimes, even hate. Those who sacrifice and mean well deal most horribly with those who will not let them. Mirele was caring and protecting. How dare Becky not let her?! How dare she?! The waiting room was always full and they waited for many hours. They were always the last ones called. The doctor had to chase Becky, drag her from under the table to give her the needles that protected and cared; Mirele, helping him. They were so much bigger and stronger. She never once got away. They had a point to prove. Grown-ups need to show who is boss in times like these. It wasn't really protecting and caring in the end when she was slipping and wriggling, and their faces looked meaner and meaner as they struggled to grab that arm and hold it firm while hurting her so badly.

The doctor's office smelled and looked funny. Like nothing she ever saw before. And it was all so scary. Metal shapes of all kinds, it seemed with points that hurt, bottles that looked like they were made of bitter things that made your face screw up and your tongue burn. And he was Momma's God. And she couldn't stand Momma's God. He frightened her so, that when the needling was over, she sat as quiet as she could and didn't make a sound, wouldn't dare! 'There's a fright before and after. The fright before is courageous and springing, striking little fists out and wriggling when you're caught, struggling so, that big fingers tightening harder and harder, hurting too, and Momma's face growing fiercer and the doctor's colder but she wriggled on and he held firm 'til he could plunge <u>health</u> into tender flesh, digging and riveting 'til she screamed in pain, Momma's determined face clenched so hard helping the doctor. Learn, my child, early. Sick is pain and health is pain, and the doctor gives pain and Momma helps him and you're little and they're big, if you give in, it hurts now, and if you don't give in, it hurts later, so give in quick, so it hurts now and be over with later. And then, you can be afraid too, but they'll be kind, because it's a different afraid when it's over, it's whimpering and crying softly in a corner and hiding your eyes on your hand that getting wet with tears because you're rubbing them away and they keep coming and coming. Rubbing them away, trying to be good. They're saying, 'Stop crying now,' so you're holding the cry back and it's forcing its way out quick, clumsy bursts, cause you're holding your breath hard, but the cries still come, the little chest heaving silent and then another hacking, quieter and quieter.'

They were becoming a little gentle then, the doctors and Ma...so she pretended and went on heaving her chest and making little sounds as long as she could...until...the order came, "That's enough now."

Momma grabbed her hand quickly and pulled her up. The doctor officially opened the door and Momma gratefully shuffling out.

Momma depended totally on Dr. Appel's medicines to preserve Becky. His what she called, 'prusiks*,' bitter powders dissolved in water, tonics, pills, and Becky, knowing she had to be healthy, was sick all the time, anyhow. Measles, mumps, chicken pox...Momma always worried, would she get well, and when she was well, would she get sick.

"Tzu gezunt, always. Tzu gezunt†."

Mirele reminding Phillip, always reminding Phillip, "You remember when Becky was born? How she was dying until I found Dr. A? I told him I have a son in the hospital. And every day I see more bones on his face. Sometimes, I think, he's dying too. Why does life come from me but stays for so little a time? God wants my children. Becky was only just born and Pesach is not even a man yet. Why Doctor, tell me why! He wanted mine when he has so many already, born, and unborn, and lived and grew old and died already. And on me, no mercy at all? Pesach, I schlepped to see in a hospital, and Becky I schlep here. This is my life, with children. Other mothers show me pictures of boys, healthy, going to school, marrying, having babies, smiling fat, happy looking. They got to bounce grandchildren on their laps."

Dr. A was a doctor when things were much simpler for the medical profession. They didn't have to treat patients as whole persons as they weren't expected to be whole, themselves.

He'd worked his way through childhood and medical school in a coal mine and knew illness, death and dying before he knew there were any cures. Black life around him and black death since he could remember. the darkness still on his face, even now, a cold shadow between him and the world around and a colder, calmer silence in his heart. He gave no comfort and asked for none. He didn't need any. There was nothing to comfort him to comfort. The fear and pain froze when he was a child. The men who picked him up and danced

---

* ***Prusiks – Pills***
† ***Tzu Gezunt – To life***

with him and swung him in their arms and brought him goodies for his birthday...that he knew only by their hands and voices sometimes, because he couldn't see their because they were quiet now.

The busy hands that tore the earth's secrets and loved and punished were suddenly taken and silenced, his father among them. Then, he would run away from the new men.

"What's the matter with you, Harry? Say 'hello' to the new man. You're going to work beside him, so you best be friendly, you hear?!"

He didn't hear. He was courteous, but not friendly. The men tried so hard to woo him, wanting him to care just because he didn't. People are funny that way. Fall all over them and they turn away but act like you don't care a fig and they're panting over you. But he knew it was a trap. Touching him, even his face, like his father did.

"I'll never leave you, son."

He thought, like all children, that daddies never die. The other maybe, but not his. He would live forever. After all, he said so, didn't he? And Daddy always kept his word. And after they lowered him into the ground, he dreamed that night he dug deep into the mine and there, he tore out of the earth all by himself, was his father.

"Aren't you coming home now, Pa?"

"Go along son and leave me alone."

"But you said you'd never leave me. You promised."

Angry now. "Do as I say, damn you! Get out of here! And put all that stuff you tore right back and now! Do you hear?"

And all night he labored, until his arm gave out shoveling it all back, his father shouting, "Come on boy, there's still more to go," until his name was just a whisper, and he couldn't hear him anymore.

"Daddy! Are you still there?"

Momma standing over him. "Wake up, dear."

"I don't hear Poppa anymore."

"No one does, dear. Now be quiet."

Turning from him to her inward talks with Poppa. She had a look then...tight, like she was all curled and stiff and waiting to spring. 'Gave me all these children and went and left, me waiting for you to come for me but you never did, still got me waiting, waiting for you to come home from somewhere deep down, only and God knows where. You were down in a grave living. Nothing changed for you. You are still down in that hole...waiting for your children to be born...then waiting for them to come home out of their graves, waiting for you still. Or maybe now, you're waiting for me?

"You're going to grow up, Harry."

And she thought out loud, "What are you going to grow up for?"

"For people to look up to me. Way, way up, not down so deep they had to bury Poppa to find him."

"How son, how are they going to look up? Tell me how."

Worn eyes looking at hope, distrustful.

"I'm going to be a doctor."

"But you cry too easily. How are you going to stand all that misery people got and you have to do something for them?"

"I ain't gonna cry, Momma...and to cry you have to feel bad, and I ain't gonna feel no more nothing. Just doctoring."

"And you gonna pay the school?"

"I'm gonna work...like Poppa...but not for children and women like him. I'm gonna work for myself. Gonna be something."

"Yes, son, you're gonna be, but now, you are late for school...and work and eating and all."

He jumped up from bed, "You're right Ma. I'll never be late for nothing."

And he never was. He ordered his life...or rather...life ordered him...with punctuality. He was on a pendulum, swinging between two spheres, the filth, the blackness, the smell of death in the mine in the morning and then, the sterile, healing, whiteness of his laboratory. The clock ruled him tyrannically. There were no men, women, children, or dogs in his life. Nothing close to him is sick and dying...not even a plant. He made the necessary gestures with the brothers and sisters he lost all around him...but then felt nothing except that it was good they were out of their misery. He saw them all going their different ways...the women to childbirth...the men to scrounge in the earth...and he would heal them, so they'd scrounge longer and have more babies. He left home after receiving his diploma and never returned, never longed for the past, opened an office in a good part of town, charging exorbitant fees for a visit. He wanted to even score with death, one life for each one he'd lost. But the balance sheet cruelly weighed on the negative side of the ledger. He was losing the battle. Couldn't even save the little ones. Death was still taking from him.

Armed as he was, with all the bottles and pills and chemical equations he'd drilled into his head by the hundreds...until Becky. Becky was his miracle, and he wanted to go on making miracles with her. No one else knew why she was dying. Only he. His pictures appeared in Medical Journals...and his office was full from then on... though the statistics remained the same. Mirele paid her bills promptly. Five dollars pressed eagerly into the doctor's hand. Grateful that he designed to take her money and that it was enough to have this gift of his time and attention. Unlike the other women whose husbands doled out money to them to be doled out to others and kept the doctor dangling with promises and guilt. How could he turn away a sick child. 'Next week I'll pay,' Mirele feared he would turn away a sick child. The others knew he couldn't, wouldn't. Mirele had one sick child turned away already, why not another? She often thought now, maybe if she paid Pesach's doctors herself, they would have tried harder.

And Dr. Apple used Mirele to shame his patients into paying. 'The poorest among you,' he'd say, 'and she pays on time religiously.' And Mirele would proudly tell friends, 'He tells everyone about me,' unaware she was a useful example.

Sometimes, after the struggle between Becky and the doctor, she'd dress quickly, and he'd motion to follow him to his office. She loved his office, the prettiest room she'd ever seen. A rug on the floor, a soft lamp, the only light in the dark room. He would order them to sit down, then take out his fiddle and play, just for them. They couldn't see his face in the darkness. He played very poorly, but

Mirele thought he was Jasha Heifetz. And Becky could only wonder at it all. He wanted someone to hear him. For years, he'd played alone, the tuneless drawing of a bow, dancing on a string clumsily, scratchy, discordant. He'd taught himself. He wanted no one to see the look on his face when he played...enraptured...only Mirele and Becky, he knew, would be content to hear without seeing, would tell him what he wanted to hear. 'It's a wonderful, Doctor! Such a talent!'

Becky could only see the white of his robe. It was like a ghost playing. She was even more afraid of him then. He always played the same pieces, and, when he was done, he would plunk the string several times and turn the little knobs on the side, tuning the fiddle...'til she could hear them creaking. But it sounded the same to Becky no matter how much plunking and turning he did. But he was finally satisfied for some mysterious reason that Becky couldn't understand. She didn't dare question Dr. Apple. She couldn't remember even saying a word to him, glad to hear the door close behind her when they were leaving even though he said 'Goodbye.' Momma nagging was a numb, shy stare. And him saying, 'See you next month.' Momma began her first visit with 'I want to go to the hospital to see a boy who is wasting away, and this baby is also disappearing before my eyes.' Her eyes shrunk so far, I don't know already what's the color of her eyes, if they're black or brown or what...or even if I have a baby or an old woman already. Her skin was so wrinkled. He motioned to the chair, and she scurried to obey. Turning, punching, feeling and then, 'know what's wrong.'

In flat, dead, monotonous tones, "Your milk is no good. I'll tell you what to feed her. And she'll be well."

Mirele believed. No one ever told her Pesach would be well.

Jasha Heifetz – Master Fiddler

He scribbled quickly and in frigid tones replied, "Give her this, three times a day."

Mirele held the piece carefully, put it into her pocket and held it there with her hand all the way to the drug store.

Becky was soon well and when she was 12 pounds, they bought wine and a dozen rugelach, one for each pound. Phillip made music singing and danced with Mirele, she is dragging her foot while he complained she couldn't keep time. But it didn't matter. She wasn't the least bit shy about dancing, bad foot, and all...and accused him of being jealous...that she was doing better than he. Even Becky cried in rhythm...short wailing to the beat of a fox trot. Phillip knew how to get down on his knees to do a kazatske, but he'd never learned the new dances. Not interested, the music bored him.

"Nothing happened," he said. No spirit.

So, he waddled from side to side like a duck and Mirele did what she wanted. She'd hold the baby between them, rocked her back and forth while Phillip held Mirele with one hand and sipped wine with the other.

Chapter Sixty-Two

augh...little girl. Little girls are for laughing and knee bouncing and throwing in air, pretending to frighten them and squeals of honeyed laughter rounding the room, bringing a flush to everyone's cheeks and warm blood to their hands, little fingers grasping appreciation, dolls and homemade little hats with bouncing balls on pointy tops and sweaters handmade by grandma and hiding a shy face in her apron when everyone says how pretty she is.

"Come and say hello little girl," burying her face deeper.

"Let me see how pretty you are. How pretty."

And little girls tattling on each other, so she'll play with them. Other little girls. Not Becky. Becky stood aside, begging, and hoping and watching. They knew she was there and let her wait...and watch...'til they <u>wanted</u>.

"Becky, can you buy something at Baker's? Take us to Baker's. We'll let you play with us."

And each time Becky thought, they'd let her play with them forever. She'd shake her head up and down...unsmiling. Becky never smiled.

"Poppa, give me a nickel."

"What for? If I give you a nickel, that's all for the week! The whole week! And what do you want it for? Candy?! Fat as you are, you need 5 cents for candy! A penny isn't enough? Two cents! Not a penny more! I have no more money!"

"Another penny, Poppa, please...or they won't play with me."

Angry now, threatening a blow. Two pennies torn from the pocket, fell from his hand, rolled on the ground. She found one. Couldn't find the other. He slammed down another penny. She grabbed it and fled. The three girls were waiting. They followed her to Baker's Candy Store. She opened the door for them, and they sped past her to the candy counter. A heavy odor of cigar smoke in the air. He had a small, dark shop that seemed all yellow and brown like his face. There were no windows, that musty odor clinging everywhere. Behind curved, glass windows, were little trays of penny candies, some two or three for a penny.

"How much ya got, Beck?"

She opened her hand, the two pennies sticking to her sweaty palm.

Then, she waited while fingers pointed and heads shook, "No, not that one. That one. There. No, there."

More and more squealing. He finally took out a small bag and filled it with just what they wanted, three jelly beans, two peanuts. Some were bigger than the others. Dorothy handed them out as fairly as she could. Becky waited 'til they were finished to hear the magic words, 'You want to play with us, Becky?'

But they turned suddenly, cutting laughter, in unison, 'Becky fatty...fat Becky wants to play, come again another day. Ugly Becky wants to play. Two cents if you're pretty. Ugly is five cents. If Ugly wants to play, Ugly has to pay," and Ruthie scraped Becky's profile in the dirt with her shoe...a square for her head and a circle for her belly.

Becky didn't even cry. Not because she didn't want to give them satisfaction, but because she thought she could do something to make them like her. Tomorrow she would ask Poppa for a nickel. It doesn't hurt to try as long as she knows when to stop. The cruel words just circled round and round and slid away. She knew she was fat and ugly and that there was a price to be paid for it and she accepted it... without question.

"Again, you're asking?! I'm made of money?"

He gave her less. She tried it with the friends. Maybe this time... they raised the ante.

"Ten cents, Becky. For ten cents we'll play. Not a penny less."

And she'd watch them from a distance playing, hoping they'd feel sorry for her if she looked wanting and was no trouble. But they didn't. just a look of smug satisfaction, enjoying...having her just standing there.

Momma's purse laying on the table. Momma is not around! Becky groped quickly, found the change purse and opened it. Ten cents! All that was there. She shoved it in her pocket. The girls were on the corner, drawing chalk lines on the street, playing 'hospital.'

"Dorothy, look!"

Becky opened her hand.

"C'mon Becky, let's go to Nathan's and get a hotdog!"

Dorothy had soft, blonde hair, a slim body that never gained an ounce, though she ate all the time. She was always laughing, and the girls liked that. Becky was too serious, but she couldn't help it. That's the way she was. They bought two frankfurters and cut them in four parts. Each one had a couple bites.

"C'mon Becky, we're gonna play!"

"Me too?"

"Yeah, you too!"

"We are gonna play at Ruthie's house," she winked so Becky couldn't see.

Becky had never been inside her house. Her body was full of wanting now. To play with Ruthie at her house! She'd never even dreamed...she quietly followed them, the door opened on a long, dark hall, a shaft of sun from the kitchen lighting on a baby carriage, a beach ball, the smell of fish in the air. The hall painted a dark green, so dark, Becky couldn't see, only hear a door being opened and Ruthie saying, 'Follow me.' Becky followed. It was the first time she had ever seen a bathroom inside an apartment.

"Is this all just yours, Ruthie?" daring to ask.

"Yeah, dummy, who else? OK girls. Get around her. Take off your dress, Beck. Go ahead. Get it off!"

"No."

They lifted her skirt, and she grabbed it and tucked it around her legs as hard as she could. They locked the door.

"Pick it up Becky!" Grabbing her skirt and pulling it over her head. "Fat belly, Becky!" and they poked her stomach with their fingers again while they held her dress tight over her head.

"Like a watermelon in a bag!"

And they laughed and laughed. The more she pulled and squirmed, the tighter they held her.

"Pull down her panties!"

One swift efficient sweep. She could feel them round her ankles. Shame burning. Now everyone would know they're torn.

"Please, leave me alone. Please, let me go. I won't tell." Sobbing, "I won't tell. I won't tell. I won't tell."

"Look, Ruthie, let's play doctor. We'll pull her legs apart so we can see the inside of her big belly. Maybe we can find out what makes it so big. Maybe there's a balloon inside or something."

Becky is still hoping to find that place in them that feels sorry. "Please leave me alone."

"Ruthie! Is that you in there?! What are you doing in there for so long? You think you're the only one who lives here?!"

Quickly pulling her dress down...her panties up.

A nervous, whispered order, "Shut up Becky. Out in a minute, Ma!"

"I'll be back in 2 seconds!" as the steps faded down the hall, "Out, now!"

Becky was pushed out first, then the others came running down the stairs two at a time. Momma was waiting for Becky when she came home. Cruelty on her face, coiled and lusting for it's victim.

"You stole ten cents from my pocketbook! I'll teach you to steal! A crook I'm raising! I'll teach you to steal!"

Momma waving Becky's jump rope...backing her against a wall... terror, helpless and sobbing, "Stop!"

Cruelty drunk...an orgy of righting a wrong...rope cracking on flesh, arms, thighs, buttocks. Anywhere the <u>lesson</u> can be taught. And Becky, learning well. She was always a good pupil. And the following day, Poppa...in a mood, pulling his belt through his pants, sending her stumbling and rolling across the floor. Another <u>lesson</u>.

"That should teach her!" he said.

But this time, Becky was not sure what she was to learn. She went to school with welts and bruises, but, in those days, no one paid attention.

Chapter Sixty-Three

They were asked to move from the one room. Becky didn't know why. Not wanted. Not good enough, she concluded. She didn't ask why. Becky was silent...numb with shock and fear. It didn't even occur to her to ask. There was an iron rule, felt but unspoken. Don't ask questions. Terror creeping behind them. Answers too terrible. Other children are bored and digging with a fine scalpel. 'Why Daddy?' And another 'why?' graining behind every answer...and another behind that one. But not Becky. Questions remained unborn.

"A lady is coming here from the government. Don't answer any questions. Just say 'I don't know.'"

Mirele shaking a severe finger. The GOVERNMENT...they said it in capital letters like it was God...big, all seeing, all knowing, powerful and frightening.

"They give us a little money, but they'll give us nothing if they know I'm working. We can't live on my money, and we can't live on theirs...so don't tell them nothing. Remember, if someone asks you, you don't have to answer. They're terrible people. Even children, they make liars. Don't lie, Becky. Say you don't know...and you don't."

That was true. Becky never knew where her mother was exactly. They moved to a cold flat, three rooms, paid no rent, but the landlord was grateful to have someone occupy the place, so nobody broke the windows. No one could pay rent.

The investigator was a man. Becky watched him as he searched the bare rooms, two army cots in the kitchen near a big, black stove, beds in the other two rooms for Becky and friends and relatives who were down and out. He stood a moment, staring at the wainscoted walls, the spaces between them, roaches running out from between the boards and chasing each other.

Somehow, they gave him the courage to say, "Where is your mother?"

Becky is silent.

Louder, "Where's your mother?"

A hoarse whisper, "I don't know."

Sharply, "Tell her I was here. We'll let her know, tell her." And he slammed the door behind him.

Becky had to answer a million questions.

Mirele probing, "How did he look? Was he friendly? Did he look Jewish? What did he say? How did he say it?"

"I don't know. I don't know. I don't know."

Late at night, Phillip shouting, "They'll put us in jail. They'll arrest us, you'll see!"

Mirele cried, "Maybe you're right. Sha! Becky will hear!"

Becky couldn't sleep. Terrified. 'Will they arrest me, too?' She saw jail in the movies once. She was so scared that she wished she could crawl into Momma's bed, but there was no room for her and it might break like it did once, when she forgot herself and climbed on the army cot and it wouldn't hold.

"Momma, can you come here? I can't sleep."

"I'm coming," and she got up and sat near Becky.

Becky reached up and put Mirele's nose between her finger and rubbing up and down, she could feel the tears. Mirele sat there and let her nose be rubbed 'til she fell asleep like she used to when she was a little girl. Poppa was two people; the philosopher who asked, 'What's it all for?' and hid behind a sigh and a raised eyebrow and two big fingers scratching a perplexed and saddened head and the other, still fresh, and young and untouched, living with comrades, brave and shining, loving the fight to live and glorious submission to significant death. Hours everyday, songs of brave martyrdom and blood of little people. Singing with them still, and Becky joining, loving this Poppa, the working man, the revolution, the world, exuberant but serious loving. Russian instruments in the house, a concertina, accordion, Russian dancing, Russian fiddling. Momma lit the candles on Friday night, then Poppa sang Russian songs.

Becky's tuneless voice joined in. Becky loved Russia and the revolution and causes and the worker...and feared her mother and father.

"Az ich vel shtarben lieber brieder*..."

They were together singing and feeling brave like Russian music made you feel...and the Yiddish songs...pathetic, sad, of poverty and hunger and longing, nostalgic, crying...like Yiddish songs made you feel. The girls laughed hard at Becky because she played the squeezebox and funny pieces, not Frank Sinatra and Benny Goodman. Becky was the concert in synagogue. They were so anxious to help the young and so starved for music, they even appreciated Becky, whose fingers trembled so, that she was lucky if she managed to play half the piece. They applauded and bravo-ed anyway. Some out of kindness, and most because they didn't know the difference.

Every day, Mirele came home and told another story about her boss for the day.

"Not satisfied with nothing," Mirele said. "Sit's on a chair in the sun all day, stomach getting bigger, the chair smaller and comes in to tell me, just as I'm finishing that I should do here a little something and there something and this isn't clean enough and that isn't clean enough and that isn't and everywhere she goes with her eyes looking for a sour face I should charge less money even when I'm charging."

---

* ***Az ich vel shtarben lieber brieder** – **If I die beloved brothers***

"Tell them to find someone else!"

"They will! There's plenty of 'someone else's.' When Poppa's revolution comes, things will be different. The yachnes will do their own shklaferei in house. Sometimes, she'd come home much later than usual. 'I forgot what time it was,' she'd say. 'Mrs....has so much trouble, how could I leave her in the middle?' At the end of the day, when she put down her mop, broom, and apron, she was advisor, counselor and general. 'Mixer in,' as slave and domestic she 'could do better,' but what can you do? A dollar and a half per day and doesn't steal, but as a counselor, she was very smart. And she was a 'good woman.' Proud, 'I sent that family groceries and they'll never know who sent them.' But she complained later, 'they got well and rich and forgot my name, even. Much later.' They're coming Becky, to see me. He lost all his money, you heard?"

"How can you let them in the house after they treated you like this?"

Squeezebox - Accordion
Yachnes - Gossip
Shklaferei - Slavery

"Who ever said I wouldn't see them if they needed?!"

"Oh, Ma?! Where is your pride? Where are your principles?!"

"What kind of pride? What kind of principle should you walk around in the world, mad?"

"But they left you after you were so nice to them?"

"So what?! Who am I? I'm so important? Maybe they had a few other things on their mind besides me? And me, they got to, when it came my turn. Now, it's my turn."

Poppa tended to the world and Mirele to him and the neighborhood.

"Be good, Becky. Save the world, Becky."

"You see what I'm doing for you."

The others saw, too. They didn't run away because they were rich but because they couldn't stand the guilty and came back for the same reason and ran away again.

Becky wrote in her elementary school graduation book under the heading, 'Favorite Proverbs.' 'Life is to give, not to take.' And Dr. A wrote, 'To be a good girl, serious in whatever she does.' Mirele and Phillip wrote nothing. First, because they couldn't write, and then, it never occurred to Becky to include them.

A numb, dead, flat face and a huge body in a white tulle gown on graduation day, listening to the principal's words that he'd been repeating over and over for 20 years and believed. 'The world is full of hope. Get out there and get to the top! You can if you try!' He mentioned nothing about giving and sacrifice, so she put them together in her own head, Momma's words, and the principal's 'Get to the top, trying hard, giving and sacrificing.' The principal said nothing about making a worker's world.

Becky thought everybody outside the school was Jewish and Socialist and inside, Christians and Capitalists. The revolution would happen on the outside, but no one would ever touch the principal. They wouldn't dare!

Poppa enjoyed searching for wood on the beach. They started first on the boardwalk, talking politics like two grown-ups. Then, the lecture, 'Don't marry, own a house or an automobile and you'll have a peaceful life. They're all trouble. More than anyone can handle. You'll always be poor, Becky. Keep that in mind.'

Becky kept than in mind.

Becky never tattled...even on herself. Things she never told Momma and Poppa...like reading 'True Romances' after school... while eating strawberry shortcake. Gobs of whipped cream and chocolate kisses on a dark bench in the moonlight. But after he turned the last page and licked the plate clean, rubbing it on her tongue 'til it hurts, the house was silent and lonely again.

She wanted a friend...a <u>best</u> one...like the other girls had. Everybody had a best friend. It seemed so easy when they did it. Sometimes, they'd let her in. She never knew why. Then, they'd close the circle again.

"I want to go and play, Ma."

"It's not important. Practice, Beckele. That's important. Who needs friends! They're not good enough for you anyway! They'll be nothing all their life. Shopworkers! That's all. If you want so much as a friend, I'll find somebody. Leave it to me. Wait a little."

Becky waited, while knowing 'a little' meant <u>never</u>.

The girls enjoyed dangling Becky. She never got mad or hit anybody, so it was just plain fun. Becky was perfect. Just waiting there like a puppy dog, pick her up when you feel like it and kick her out when you don't. Made them feel important that she was dumb-grateful or waiting, hoping for them. And they were always changing best friends...but never to Becky. She was too willing. Anybody could <u>have</u> her. And besides, who wanted her? Never talked, too quiet, too serious, no fun. There were grown-ups to visit, but that wasn't the same. Her Aunt Fanny with long, blonde hair and three children, so pretty, high cheekbones, a slim body. Every day she visited. Aunt Fanny didn't mind her sitting there quiet, didn't nag her to say something, didn't ask a lot of questions she had to answer. Then, one day she visited, and the door was closed for the first time, no sounds of children crying, children whining, like there always was. Becky returned day after day, knocking, and listening, straining to hear a familiar sound.

Then...sound of hammers banging, smell of paint, a stranger opens the door, barking, "What do you want?"

"Fanny?"

"No Fanny here? We're busy."

Door shuts in her face. And still, he didn't dare ask. Here and there, she caught a few words.

"The children were hurt in a fire. She had a breakdown."

She must be in a place like Percy. Thinking, without pain now. Then remembering, but never asking. Then wondering, but not aloud. It died aborning...the pain that asks questions, demands an answer, raging and righteous and flailing about. The life-giving pain in two little girls hurling angry insults at each other. Not Becky. Ever. Death-silence. Void. On Pesach-Persie's holler and fight and throw things...and God punishes them. The God Momma believes in...and me, too...punishes them. 'I'll die a little, so I won't die a lot.' Deep down, where no one could see, she made that decision. Not even Becky. Kids don't want to play dead. Only sometimes. That's when they played with Becky.

One weekday, Momma and Poppa dressed in their best. They looked very sad. They'd never gotten dressed during the week before. Only on Shabbos. Even Poppa dressed on Shabbos. Respect for the neighborhood. Momma was never home during the week before, but she was home when Becky returned from school...and crying and talking to Uncle and he was crying, too. And neighbors coming in with faces.

"She was your niece?"

Momma nodded her head, "Fanny."

And more questions. "How old? How did she die?"

And then Becky couldn't hear.

Momma whispered and the neighbor saying, "Consumption."

Momma put her finger to her mouth, "Sha," but it was too late.

Becky heard. Mrs. Novie, one of Poppa's old customers, came in with her daughter, Evelyn, Becky's age, going on 12. Mrs. Novie, fat, red-faced, wide mouth, always hollering at Evelyn, and bulging blue eyes. The child had long braids and was always yelping, Mrs. Novie yanking her braids hard if she couldn't grab anything else to punch or scratch.

"Go sit with Becky," she ordered. "Children should pester each other, not grown-ups."

"Hi, my name is Evelyn. Yours Becky?"

She put out her hand. Becky looked at her numbly.

"My name is B-Becky."

The girl made her nervous. Sometimes she stammered a little when she was nervous. Evelyn's dress, stiff and new, her nails manicured, her hair shining, an arrogant confidence spread across her face, an easy smile, patent leather shoes with a small strap across the middle, white stockings...from head to toe...pretty, pretty, pretty. Becky in an unpressed blouse and skirt, practical clunky shoes that were put under a machine first to ensure a perfect fit, hair thick and wild and left to dangle about her face or tied in two little bunches on each side with a tight rubber band. She was too timid to extend her hand and ashamed, cracked nails, not too clean. Mirele didn't believe in nail polish.

"Ruins the nails," she said.

Evelyn shrugged her shoulders and withdrew her hand.

"The lady who died, your aunt?" Becky nodded.

"What from?" Becky shrugged her shoulders.

"You don't know? What do you mean you don't know?" Angry now. "You do know! You're not telling!" She pulled Becky's arm. "Tell me! What's the matter with you?! Don't you talk?! Are you a mummy or something? Are you dead too?! Let's see if you're dead!"

And she pulled Becky's hair. Becky squinted and quickly turned her head.

"I don't really know," she said quietly. "No one ever tells me anything. I'm too young."

"Oh, you can talk! Tell me, do you go to the movies?"

"Sometimes."

"Would you like to go with me? I get free passes sometimes."

Becky nodded her head slightly.

"I will, if I can give you a piece of candy."

"What kind?"

"Chocolate."

"That's my favorite. Oh Henry, I love Oh Henry."

It wouldn't be easy. A nickel all at one time. But Becky decided she wouldn't go until she saved it up, a penny at a time.

Mirele to Mrs. Novie, "Look, my Becky and your Evelyn."

Mirele thought Evelyn would be good for Becky. The Novies were somebody.

"I have a favor to ask you, Mirele, but not now."

"Anything, Mrs. Novie. Of course."

She turned a benevolent smile on Mirele.

"You know, Mirele, since he left me, that no good millionaire, the word exploding so everyone could hear, it's hard for a woman to manage alone. He gives me all the money I need to scrape by. That's not enough."

"I know," Mirele commiserating as if she really knew.

"We're all in the same boat," Mirele shaking her head as if she carried the world on it.

"I wouldn't go so far as to say that Mrs. Novie suddenly conscious of poverty, assuming equality with money and not liking it at all."

Mirele rushed to take back her words, the poor taking too many liberties.

Mrs. Novie reasserting the pecking order, "But you know, we have our troubles, too, different from most others, but it hurts, Mirele...it hurts, what can I tell you!"

"Whatever I can do to help, Mrs. Novie."

That day, there was an accord reached between them, unstated but like it was etched in stone. Mirele was to serve and Mrs. Novie was ready to be served.

"Look, Mirele at Becky and Evelyn! They're together talking. Maybe they, too, like us!"

That day, Becky, like Mirele, found a <u>best friend</u>.

Chapter Sixty-Four

Now that Becky had a best friend, she discovered she didn't know what to do with one. They went to the movies and then came home and played, 'movies.' One was Clark Gable and the other Joan Crawford but then, Evelyn would turn on her suddenly, lash out, pull her by the hair until her eyes turned red, hit her with sticks until she turned tired and ran away, wouldn't talk to her for weeks, then come to make up with her again like nothing happened. Becky always made up. She was grateful too. It never occurred to her not to. She didn't even have to give in. she was in already. Evelyn just had to find her where she left her...waiting.

Becky always came home for lunch from school, Poppa waiting for her. But one day, she came home to find the door closed. The man upstairs came down to tell her Poppa left.

"Will he be back soon?"

The man fled up the stairs quickly. That family spoke to no one. He was a ruddy faced man with flaming red hair who worked as a beer barrel roller, a good job in those days. He walked with his head down, ashamed to look at anyone for fear they heard and would shame him. His daughter, a tall heavy girl in her 30's with long, blonde braids, walking on her toes and talking loudly to herself by day and at night, screaming and stomping back and forth across the floor, then...sudden silence until dawn when she would wake Becky with the sound of a maniacal voice coming from the across the sea on the radio.

Mirele said, "Make like we don't notice. She's a sick girl."

This was the first time her father ever spoke to her. It scared her, as if she heard something forbidden. She ran down the stairs going nowhere.

"Becky!" Evelyn behind her.

"Where are you going?" Becky shrugs.

"Why aren't you home eating?"

"My father is out."

"Come home with me."

"OK, you're sure your Ma won't mind?"

"Why should she mind?"

Mrs. Novie barking, "Evelyn, you're late!"

About to close the door, "Becky! What are you doing here?"

"Poppa's not home."

"Come on in. Did you eat?"

"No."

"Would you like something?" Becky asked silently.

"You'll have something with us."

Buttering a piece of bread carefully, measuring a spoon of jelly, pouring a glass of milk for Evelyn, and putting the container back.

"We just have enough left for us for tonight. I'm sorry, Becky."

"I don't want any milk, thanks."

Later, after school, Mr. Novie grabbed her from the back and turning her around, her mouth blazing with accusations of crimes. Becky never knew she committed and concluding with, "You come to my house to eat! Come Evelyn!"

Becky could only reply inside her head, "I'll never go to eat in anyone's house again! Ever!"

They both turned and walked hand in hand down the deserted

street. This was the time she and Evelyn played 'movies.' But now, it felt like early morning in the house before there's a sound...lonely... like there's no one else in the world.

"I'll never make up this time! Never! A firm, silent declaration, but she still hoped she would. She liked to think she had a best friend, made her feel part of the world, like other people. Again and again, she'd ask Evelyn to say it, 'You're my best friend, Becky. My best friend.' And deep inside, 'Please come back, best friend...worst friend, only friend. I need you so much.' Becky went home slowly, hoping to hear those quiet steps behind her. She dawdled. Though she heard, 'Becky, wait for me.' Turned. No one. She waited anyway and stared down the street, ready to turn around if she saw them coming, so she wouldn't appear too eager, so they wouldn't go away again if they knew she was. She looked hard down the street, like waiting for a train...willing it to come so hard...it just has to.

It was growing dark. Twilight time. The fallen leaves blowing in circles round her feet, chill in the air, lights casting an eerie light and still, with narrowed eyes and bent head she stood staring hard until it was dark and she could see only the rings of light around the lamps, people scurrying home, theirs heads bent against the wind, holding their sweaters tight against their throats...huddling against the sudden cold of early autumn. Becky shivering but unable to move.

"Becky!" Mirele shouting from the window and continuing to shout 'til Becky heard her and came through the door.

"Why didn't you answer?!"

Becky didn't answer why she didn't answer. She went into the bathroom, locked the door, and wept in the darkness.

"What are you doing in there, Becky? Having a baby? Hurry up, out! Mrs. Novie and Evelyn came to hear, you hear? Your best friend! They don't have all night! They're hungry!"

Becky washed her face and dried her hands as well as she could.

"Hello, Becky! What's the matter, no tongue? You left it in the bathroom? So, say hello already!"

"Hello, Evelyn, Mrs. Novie."

"Smile a little, too." She spread her lips.

"That's a smile?" She spread them as hard as she could.

"And say 'hello' like you mean it. Loud, so we can hear you."

"Hello, Evelyn," as loud as she could. "And hello Mrs. Novie," even louder, and smiling 'til her cheeks hurt.

"That's a 'hello' Becky!"

A blushing Becky sat down and then, when the meal began, she wouldn't eat 'til she offered them what was on her plate, too, and left some over in case they wanted more...and they did.

"You're not finishing what's on your plate, Becky? It's a shame to throw it out. I'll have the potato, Evelyn, you take the chicken. It's a shame how you taught her, Mirele. Not to finish everything on her plate."

"She usually does and asks for more. I don't understand it. Maybe she doesn't feel well. Becky, you feel alright?"

"You told me not to take, Momma, and if I must, I should give back right away what I took. So that's what I'm doing. Giving back, right away, what I took. I'm not too hungry tonight, Momma."

Becky was awarded the following day. Mrs. Novie invited her to a restaurant for a chicken dinner and put into her plate only the part that goes over the fence last.

"Es mien kind," she said.

She and Evelyn walked on the boardwalk after the first snow had fallen. She showed Becky her new gloves, spread her fingers wide and turned the top over for her to see the fur inside, pushed the fingers of those gloves way up until they fit right, snug. Becky remembered in later years they were brown leather and slid them on so jaunty like in the movies and held her hands clenched in the pockets because she didn't have any. 'I don't know, to this day, why I didn't have any...whether we had no money, or Momma forgot or...I lost them. I keep losing them now. I have a drawer full of widowed gloves. Maybe I did then, too. Anyway, I can't remember ever owning a pair.'

"And once, we saw a crowd and you said, 'Let's take a look,

Becky.' You are pushing your way through, I'm letting you pull me by the hand, we could stand tip-toe and see. And you laughing so hard."

"It's your mother, Becky!"

"And me, hiding my face, behind my frozen fingers. You, Momma, standing in the snow on a beach in a bathing suit, having your picture taken by the newspaper, smiling, with only two teeth left in front, the rest you broke on a walnut. Swimming in winter. You were proud. And I heard, 'She's crazy!' I never knew you swam in winter, Ma. Crowds collected. Gaping and awing like you were another Coney Island freak show. Only no charge for this one. The first time I knew shame of you and never lost what crept into me that day, stayed and grew and twined with mine. And then you told your mother, Evelyn, and both of you bursting into laughter and scorn, telling, and retelling the story. A month later, I graduated, and you came to my party. Told my mother I'd never be anything like you would because we had no money. And the next day, when I came to show you the present my mother bought me for my graduation, a cape, a gray skirt, and purple bonnet, you both laughed and laughed and said how silly I looked. And I turned without a word because I could never say anything I shouldn't. But, on the way home, on a dirt road under the L train, I decided I would never-ever wear makeup again. And I didn't. you tried and tried...and I didn't and wouldn't... no matter what. But I had a bitter satisfaction. When we graduated, I was in the Honor Guard, got a medal, and you got nothing."

But that didn't make up for not having a best friend. Nothing could make up for that. Nothing in this world. Posters were touching her now. She was part of something that wanted and needed her.

"Only wire twisting for radios, but every wire counts," they told her.

And Mirele woke up to a nightmare. Becky went to work in a shop.

Chapter Sixty-Five

"The Russians send people to Siberia," the teacher said.

"Is that true, Poppa?"

"Don't believe everything you hear."

Newspapers saying, 'Zimonev and Kaminev accused of sabotage. Soviets purging.'"

'These people?' Phillip wondering out loud.

"Why, they suffered for the revolution. Russia was cracking a little, but not much. There was still the Red Dean of Canterbury. The Soviet Power...a benevolent miracle. Free the Negroes, Becky. Go home to the cold, hungry, desolate, humiliated flat and worry about the Negroes. The Young Communist League on the corner, dances every Saturday night, dance with a Negro, show them we think we're equal."

But Becky couldn't dance, so she settled for just talking and sitting and eating with them. One fellow just grabbed her one day and tried to pivot her around the floor. He gave up quickly, thanked her and rushed away. The struggle wasn't worth the proof of equality. Stiff, rigid with fear, she tried valiantly to do what she had been reading about all the romantic stories, light airy swaying to his rhythm...but she couldn't. Mortified, she stood on the side and watched the other with a fixed smile on her face. She hadn't the simplest gift that was so carelessly given to others. Like there was a master plan to have her forever running in the opposite direction, alone. Can't dance, talk, smile, flirt, be cute, skinny, a good revolutionary or even play Joan Crawford and Ginger Rogers like they should be. No one asked her again. They were good dancers, the Negroes. Had pride in their spinning, holding, tossing the ladies, and watching them twirl in and out of their arms. Becky cramped a man's style. Looked like it was his fault, her tripping and stumbling.

Thoughts burrowing to the surfaces, 'They don't give a damn about your proving equality, silly. They just want to dance with the white girls. So why don't they dance with me if that's the case? Because they're men...Negroes or not. They want to hold the pretty ones. You're ugly, Becky. Fat and ugly. It does no good to them to be with the white rejects. They don't feel any better or feel they got something then. It's just one reject holding another. Oh, no! They feel equal with superiors. You just make them more miserable, Becky because they think they're scraping the bottom of the barrel and you, too because you have no other choice, and they're it."

Mirele asked, "What are you doing with your accordion? Why don't you pay attention to that instead of wasting time with people who don't appreciate you?"

"I think I'll give it up."

"Give up?"

"I just told you what. I don't think I'm any good, no one's interested in my dull music, I don't know how to play the other, I'm tired of practicing and being scared to death to play. I can't go through life scared like that."

Third street shul, where Becky gave her concert was one small room with 50 congregants, a small beam with a chair for her. She hated that lonely, little chair where she sat, ahead buried in the keyboard, breathing hard 'til it was all over.

That day, she practiced hard and made the same mistakes over and over...and the more mistakes, the more she played faster and faster 'til she couldn't even keep up with herself. So nervous, her fingers had a life of their own. She couldn't control them. 'You'll play the first accordion concert at Carnegie Hall,' the teacher said. 'Before all those people who know?! If it's getting worse in 3rd street shul? In shul, and God's not helping me! I can't sit on that chair ever again. Not today. Not ever!'

When the time came for the concert, no one could find her. She sat on a bench in the park where she could see the shul, but they couldn't see her. Momma and Poppa running in and out of the shul looking for her inside and out, giving up but still running in and out because they couldn't stand still. Then Momma alone standing outside the door, under the light, waiting, and Poppa home, also waiting, 'I hope nothing happened to her.'

When the people came streaming out of the shul and it was all over, she went home.

"What happened Becky? Mirele's eyes searching Becky head to toe and back again.

"I don't want to play for people. I'm too scared."

"Maybe you're sick. I'll have to talk to Dr. Raffel."

Mirele's dreams punctured. Becky was not in a shop. Becky 'somebody.' All those floors and sinks and garbage pails and toilets, seeing sunlight only through the window, looking down and under and in-between, on your knees breathing dust and going in and out the back door humble...for that big moment in 3rd street shul when 50 people applauded Becky's fractured playing. Dr. Raffel would solve it. He would cure her. He always did, didn't he?

"Keep after her," he said. "Insist she stay home and practice!"

Struggling under the table...he would not tolerate it! Like those stubborn veins in the mines that wouldn't yield. Defying him! He wouldn't allow it!

"Force her!" His cold eyes hardened even more. "She eats the bread on your table. Let her earn it, like I did."

"Don't be mad at her. She's still a child," Mirele pleaded.

"If you're not mad now, you'll be mad later. If she's still a child, she needs to be shown, to be guided and you have to show her and you have to go show her you're mad or she'll think you don't care... and 10 years of hard work is out the window and a lifetime of harder work coming in that same window. It's hard work to be nothing. The hardest there is. You should know."

Mirele came home to find Becky talking to a group of candy store loiterers, trying to make friends. Becky saw her watching. It embarrassed her so; she came home to practice. Every day, Mirele stood watch on that corner. Then, one day, she wasn't home nor on the corner. 'Where is she? How dare she hide from me?!' Mirele questioned the loiterers. She'd made a friend who lived down the block. Mirele opened the door to a hallway and listened. She could hear Becky laughing upstairs.

"Becky come on down!"

Becky came down. Day after day, Mirele pursued Becky in the hallway.

Flushed, crimson faced Becky fled home wiping her eyes.

"I won't practice! You won't make me!"

Mirele attacks. Becky screams.

"Stay away from me, you hear? Nobody else's mother follows her!"

Pounding Mirele's chest with her fists and Mirele digging her nails into her arms and Becky's timid grandfather suddenly opening the door and fleeing in terror, screaming for help in the street, "Police!"

Mirele tearing herself away and running after Aaron, "Poppa, it's nothing. We had an argument, that's all. It's all over."

She led him by the hand into the house. Becky was already gone. She met her friend in the street.

"Edith is having a party, and she says you're not invited but I told her I won't go if you won't go."

"I'll go," Becky pleaded hiding behind Donna's courage.

Edith greeted her with, "Who invited you?!"

"I invited her," Donna said. "If she goes, I go, too."

A grudging, "OK. Come on in."

It felt so good to be protected by Donna. Like she was someone important. Later, they played, 'spin the bottle' and when it pointed to her, she moved away. She'd never been kissed before and didn't know how and didn't want anyone to know that. And then she came home to Mirele waiting in the darkness.

"Where have you been, Becky?"

"Out."

"I've sacrificed my life for you and you're going <u>out</u>? Up...you should be going! Somewhere's up! Out is where me and Poppa are!"

"And <u>out</u> is where I want to be! I'm leaving home, you hear?!"

"You'll leave <u>school</u>? <u>School</u> you'll leave?"

"A little child hobbling on crutches to school. Raw, cruel child-scorn from behind, 'Dirty Jew, Christ-killer,' sharp pain on my back and legs and blood from the stones they threw on me. Never got to school that day. Never went again. It was my first day...and my last."

"Leave me alone!"

"I'll ask Dr. Raffel."

"And don't ask Dr. Raffel! I don't care what he says!

Later Becky asked, "I want to do something for the war, Poppa."

"What do you want to do?"

"I want to work in a defense plant."

"Leave school?!"

"If we lose the war, there'll be no school."

"They'll be no anything if we lose the war."

Becky waited outside the Dean's office for two hours. Dean Aspen came from Connecticut and spoke with a broad 'A.' She was never seen except in very special circumstances.

"Miss Popov," cool, with disdain, "Be seated. What do you want?"

"I want to leave school."

"What term are you in?"

"Eleventh."

"No problem. You can leave whenever you want. The secretary will sign you out."

And Becky was dismissed with a wave of her hand. Unwashed foreigners. What difference does it make...one more or less?

Becky's heart was filled with pride.

Chapter Sixty-Six

For the moment, the shop was her salvation. No school, no tomorrow to prepare for. Important and necessary now to something or someone. That terrible thing called 'the future' that demanded so much work...for what? An empty and terrifying present. Becky was frightened of all the listening ears and judging heads branding her again and again. College...that dreadful place it seemed one's very life depended on, and few could get into...or music...Becky Bromsky also played. But even a war couldn't sway Mirele. She cried and banged her head against the wall.

"You're not leaving school! For good. Not! Not! Not!"

And Becky crying and joining Mirele, "I am leaving school! For good. Am! Am! Am!"

And Phillip shouting, "STOP!"

Grabbing Mirele, "For God's sake, is that what you're teaching Becky? Each time she has a crisis, she bangs her head instead of using it?"

Her lower lip slid under the two yellowed front teeth, then clamped down hard on her small chin, while she choked on the sobs that were still pressing, exploding in desperate moans, "I'm s-t-o-p-p-i-n-g!" Her teeth dug two deep holes into her little chin.

Softly now, Phillip says, "Sit down, Mirele."

A dead voice complying, "I'm sitting." But she remained standing.

It didn't really matter to Phillip whether she sat or didn't sit. She was quiet. That was important.

"Now, I have something to say."

"Hurry," she whispered, "I have to light the candles. It's Shabbos. God can't wait."

Angry now. "God knows we've been waiting for him forever. He can wait for us in a minute. I'm talking. Let him wait. He's not helping. At least, to wait a little he's able. No?"

Phillip didn't really know what to say but he thought he'd improvise as he went along. Words always came to him easily, but not now. 'Why didn't Mirele's God make it hard to have children and easy to bring them up? Instead of the other way around? What does a man say to a woman when he sees her first go mad and now madder. And what does one say to oneself when he has gone mad with her?'

A scream caged inside now. It mustn't come out. Not now. Later...when it's safe. When they would be terrified quietly. Not now...when they were hungry for blood and would both spring at him. He wasn't up to it now. He wasn't sure what he feared they might say in such times. He just knew he was afraid of words he couldn't bear to hear. Words of dying. This was another dying. Mirele sitting shiva on her daughter, too. There should be a service for the aggrieved...those who bury hopes and dreams.

Mirele lurched forward, grabbing Becky's hand, pleading, "If you really want something for the war, Beckele, I'll go in your place. If I could go to school for you, I would go, but I can't. To the shop I can go, let me?"

"Everybody should go! Everybody! Poppa you're smart! Explain to her!"

"No, you explain! Why everybody's graduating…1,300 patriots… like you…and 1,299 of them are going to college if they can."

"Wrong! Only the women! Anyway, you're glad to see me go. You won't have to worry anymore if Momma is slipping me money! I'll have my own! I won't cost you anymore!"

Phillip looking inward at life's tragedy stoically, his favorite pose.

"No, what can we do, Mirele!"

A quiet philosophical acceptance…what's done is done…

"The world is not waiting for Becky to finish school. You'll be sorry Becky."

"No, I won't!"

The following morning Mirele barred the door.

"Over my dead body!"

"Don't threaten me, Ma! Get away from the door or I'll kill you! And myself too!"

"Me! You killed already! You…you're killing!"

"The dead don't bar the door! I'm late for work! Let me out!

Grabbing Mirele by the bun in the back of her head, throwing her to the ground and fleeing out, slamming the door, then turning around and kicking it hard…the door shaking, rattling after her…a sudden pounding…heavy drum beats in slow cadence…Mirele on trembling knees…weeping. Becky pleaded with Mirele when she was little, 'Don't hit me!' and still pleading now, "Leave me alone!"

Not only when you're not there, not that kind of alone. Alone is just hearing you say once…once…once…do you hear…once… "That's right. A good idea."

Not because it's better than yours…yours can still be better…but mine can be good, too…even a little bit good…Tears wiped angrily away, "Was I born to make you cry? And you make me cry? Always?"

'What could Momma say,' "That's the way we were made. I came here first so I know a little more. What's wrong with that?"

"Don't remind me every minute. Lie a little. Play. Pretend. God made us like that, too. He made us liars. Lie to me, Momma. Please lie to me. Let's make a deal. One, 'You're right Becky' for one hundred wrongs. At least, then I know I have something to look forward to. Surprise me, Ma. Pick something else every month or every six months or a year. You don't even have to say the words if you can't. Leave a note from time to time, like, for instance...you said powder could ruin my skin. 'OK I said, but maybe it could make me pretty for a while. Time ruined your skin...not powder.' 'You're wrong,' you said, 'look at me.' And I looked. 'Your face in full of wrinkles.' And you said, 'You see, healthy skin, Ma.' 'You're right, Becky. Right. Right. Right.'"

It was a brief walk to the shop. She'd passed it many times without knowing it. One flight up, Tec, Radio inc. girls wanted. Uncle Sam tacked to the door. She wiped her tears with the hem of her dress. If no one remembered her to take her handkerchief, she never had any. She was early. The boss wanted to see her first to tell her what to do. Creaky stairs, black halls, garbage pails behind the stairs.

"You're wrong, Becky. You'll see. You don't know what a shop is."

"And you don't know what playing the accordion is...alone...and for people. Loneliness...terror. We're both learning, no, Ma?"

Chapter Sixty-Seven

A window at the top of the stairs, a small arc cut out at the bottom, she sat at the top of a starched shirt, a diamond pinky ring, a voice, "What do you want?"

"I'm the new girl, Becky Bromsky."

"Who?" shouting as if she had dropped something valuable that broke into a thousand pieces.

"The new girl! The new girl!"

As loud as she could. Humiliated. Put in her place. Speaking up when told to.

The man stumbled out through a small door and thrust his hand straight out.

"I'm the boss. You can call me Herb."

"Pleased to meet you, Mr. Herb."

She let her hand be grabbed and shook and dropped. A friendly smile with lots of teeth, but she felt herself crawling. There was a compelling hardness in him...the eternal pecking order, but no struggle here and he was already beating his chest and she was padding the ground, just in the way they said 'hello.' That's the way the boss wanted it. He was a good man who sent his wife to the country, children dressed in the best, gave to charity, his smiling face always shown shaking hands with another boss...both looking benign and happy at a function for the poor. This morning too, he was with someone he was to give money to. But this was different. Becky could never understand the difference. Why he gave money to some with a smile and workers with a snarl, begrudgingly was beyond common understanding. He looked her over quickly as if he was feeling her muscles too, like they did to Poppa years ago...then looked again like he wasn't sure.

Then, like a man taking the plunge, he said, "Let's go. I'll show you the shop. You'll try us. We'll try you. We'll see if we'll both be happy. If not, only I'm happy, you'll see if you want to stay. If not, you're only happy, you'll have to go. And we'll still be friends."

He smiled...small yellow teeth, pock-marked face, dull blonde hair cut square above his ears like a German, so he looked like <u>authority</u>. It didn't matter that the workers had enough incentive to eat and pay rent. He thought...just a little more...the green taste of fear to keep them going. The question in his mind is always, 'is she afraid enough?' The rules were extra strict in the beginning to test her out. If not, there's plenty out there who are, or no are...by him... 'a worker has to work.' The sign on the door read, 'No slouchers here and I mean NO! There's a war on, remember?' He opened the door and she followed. He pointed to two rows of long tables. As far as the eye could see, shoulders crouched over long tires, fingers deftly separating the golden innards, looking hard like monkeys searching fleas. Indoors yellowed, gimpy. Not cleaned since he opened. Too distracting. It was so quiet. No one looked up.

"You see this?" He picked up a rubber hose and dug into its insides.

"These three tires you twist like this." He curled them until they were like one.

"The more you do, the more you make." He made a money sign with his fingers.

"Let me see you do a couple. You think you can?"

Faintly, "Yes."

The tires made deep marks in her fingers.

"It's like playing the guitar. At first, it hurt. Then the string digs into your fingers, but then, you make beautiful music."

And he made the money sign again with his fingers.

Watching her, "Yeah, you got the hang of it. No spaces. Tires close together. You gotta twist <u>hard</u>!"

That day, the floor lady called her out of the bathroom several times.

"Talking and smoking only after hours!"

She was timed. Daring to take five minutes each time. 'It's not your time!' the sign read in the bathroom. Neck hurting. She lifted her face several times and down again quickly. Hers as the only head up, a sudden roar at lunch time. God is no longer watching. Thirty minutes only to gossip, solve the world's problems, start a love affair... and eat.

An Indian fellow next to her, "What's your name?"

"Becky."

"Where's your lunch?"

"I'm not hungry. I don't eat lunch."

"Have some of mine." And he jumped from the bench licking his lips, sliding two fingers into a brown paper bag, rummaging. He was very short. She looked down on a head of brown curly hair, thick and unmanageable. She wondered if he ever combed it. It seemed full of so many kinks. She thought to ask him a silly question. 'Did he sleep in curlers?' But she didn't.

"Don't bother me, please," she said.

"Of course, I'll bother. I was taught it's a sin to eat alone when someone else is hungry."

"But I'm not hungry, so it's no sin."

"You just don't know if you're hungry." And he looked up and laughed.

"When you see what I have, you'll be hungry."

"Where are you from?"

"India."

"Where in India?"

Death passed his face quickly.

"Calcutta, here everyone is hungry all the time. Cows are hungry. It's a sin to kill them. And people are hungry. So, they watch each other die."

"I'm sorry. Do you ever wear a turban? Like in the movies?"

"No." He smiled again and pointed to his hat hanging on a nail in the corner...

"Or a big handkerchief around my body, either...see...this shirt..." and he pulled it to a point with his two fingers. "Pants..." and he slapped his thigh... "Tie" and he picked it up and let it fall again.

"My skin is different." And he put his hand near hers, pinky to pinky, and he tore his sandwich out of his bag.

"Try it. Delicious. Please...try it."

She dressed back quickly.

"Will you take something from me tomorrow?"

She forced herself to say, "Why not? Aren't your hands as good as mine?"

And forced herself to touch the bread his hands defiled. Dark hands...dirty...nausea wrestling with the principles. Dancing is not the same thing as eating...or...kissing.

'Would you want your daughter to marry a...no. I can't hurt his feelings. Nausea. Quick bite.'

"Good."

Eagerly, "Isn't it good? Tell me."

Choking, "Delicious."

"You want more?"

"Thank you. I can't."

In her lap he spilled the remainder of the bag. One pear, one apple. A piece of pie.

"Eat. Please. I want to see you eat. Go eat!"

Eyes ferocious now. Like a mad dog. The bell rang, but he couldn't let go.

"I'll eat it at home."

"No, I want to see."

Like a lover no, yearning to hear her say, 'I love you, too.' She looked around quickly. No one was looking. She bit, choking, forced to do it, giving him the apple, gasping.

"Take another," he whispered. "No one's looking." She looked around...a hunted animal.

"No! No! No one's looking!"

She put the apple to her mouth again...bit hard...teeth stabbing her hand, she dropped the apple. It rolled under the table while she shook her hand in pain...clenching and unclenching her fingers. Then, bowing her head over her fork again, bowing her head even lower and twisting it with her left hand. The next day she brought a chicken and tomato sandwich. He touched her fingers lightly when she gave it to him, so she went to wash her hands...and stayed to smoke a cigarette. 'I'll asked to be moved.'

"TIME!"

Shrill, hard, like the clang of old metal. Becky ambled back now slowly, pulling out another minute. Like the first time she saw Poppa back down and Mr. Ball, the history teacher retreating when she shouted and raised her hand and he timidly said, 'Yes,' and nodded his head. He'd heard the question so many times.

"Why can't we have an International Army to keep the peace?" Becky's voice is stubborn and pointed now.

"I don't know," he said quietly, flushing as if he'd been stuck.

Becky smelled fear. She pressed with another and another, louder, strident, piercing. All the hurt of her feeling now a knife at his throat...a Jewish throat...doing his best to teach well. Let them know what seems smart isn't always. Gives them confidence. He was always the first to say he didn't know. The first to let them crush him with the newness of power...rushing its victims on and on and deeper and deeper...the victim of victims. New, fresh fickle confidence... dying every day and every day needing a victim to be born again.

All the talkers in the back were not talking to her, only to each other. One day, she sat in the back too, whispering and crumpling little wads of paper notes and giggling. They never did homework, never opened a book, and passed all their tests. That's what being smart was. She stopped doing homework, studying, listening...and failed. 'I'm a dummy if I can't just pass a test.' Only Mr. Ball made her feel smart...so she badgered...pressing her smart...he is shrinking more and more while she rubbed it in...the old message still stinging...from young to old... 'What a mess grown-ups made of the world!' He agreed. Mr. Ball paid for all the messes the world made, God made.

When she came home, she tried it on Poppa. Phillip wanted her so much to be smart, he let her be. She was a high school girl now. She had to be smart. At home she shouted the same questions and he nodded with pride. Then she tried Momma. Old arguments shouted now. She remained unbending, adamant.

"Why can't I put polish on my nails?" Screaming now. "All the girls do it!"

"It's bad for your nails!"

Rock hard determination on her little face...that same look when she grabbed her arm for the doctor.

"Listen, stay in one place, damn you. Stop wriggling and squirming like a stubborn cat. Obey for your own good...and for mine."

Even Momma...self-sacrificing, chest bearing, heart bleeding Momma's demand obedience or they turn and kill.

"I gave you life. Appreciate!"

"I'm giving it back Momma! You won't let me use it! I'm giving it back! The light hurts my eyes, Momma. I'm not used to the light. Let me get used to the light. Momma, let me paint my nails!"

The deep quarrel between them dancing crazily on a painted nail.

And Phillip, "Such megillah over a nail?! God made a mistake. If he made nails red and cheeks white and hair curly, we wouldn't have to fight so much."

"I should kill myself every day, working for her and then watch while she ruins what I'm trying to build...a healthy person!"

"A little powder ruins everything?"

"Yes! It's artificial, fake, not natural!"

"What more?! Tell me!"

He gave up but she thought she won. Later, he started again.

"Is it natural for a girl not to do dishes or shop or cook or sew a button?"

"An artist doesn't do dishes or shop or cook or sew a button. Becky is an artist!"

Becky in the bathroom thinking. 'Mr. Ball taught her freedom. Rebelling is freedom and attention and being Emma Goldman. Doesn't matter what. Just don't do as your told. And attention, too. Admiration in all those eyes that stared at her lunchtime. She was suddenly Emma Goldman and Sacco and Vanzetti, and all the people Poppa talked about. The only way to be little and important is to defy the big ones for the little ones. You'll never be big, but you'll be admired by the little because you'll stay even littler. Rebellion now...five minutes more. The very rich...free from time...proud of it. The very poor...free from time...ashamed of it. In that stolen five minutes, freedom from time was Becky's...rebellion, independence and more...mother love...the world will take care...no matter what... like Momma. You don't have to be afraid.'

The bell clanged 'Lunch' again.

When she returned, Zubin asked, "What took you so long?"

"Smoking."

"You smoke?"

"One cigarette a day."

Paper bags crackling...the smell of a hundred sandwiches in the room.

"What did you get?"

"What have you got?"

He offered her fruit. She offered him another kind. The courtesies done, they ate their own.

"I have something for you."

"I'm full, thank you."

"It's not food."

"What then?" Soft, shy now.

He put his hand in his pocket and pulled out a tiny vial with a small cork that he pulled out gently.

"Smell it."

She'd never smelled perfume before.

"Pretty."

She turned it upside down on her finger.

"Put it on."

She touched the shoulder of her blouse. He reached up on tiptoe, put his nose to her shoulder and breathed hard. She jumped away.

"Please, I can't accept it."

Hurt clouding his face, "Why?"

She didn't know what to give back for perfume.

"You must take it. You must! I brought it all the way home. My sister's."

And he pulled her bag from under the counter, opened it quickly, thrust it in, put the bag back under the counter again. She pulled the bag out again, opened it wide, rummaging furiously, but she couldn't find it. It had slipped through an open seam in the lining. She poked one finger through the hole and turned it around as far as she could reach. Nothing...just tobacco, pennies, a safety pin.

"Did you really put it in here?"

He grinned, "No," and opened his palm. "Here it is. Will you take it now?"

She took it. Feeling foolish falling for such an old trick...but it tired her to go on with a battle of wills. Hers was not really that strong. And she hadn't battled really. Just hiding from that perfume like she hid from the spinning bottle.

"Don't worry, you don't have to say or do anything. Just take it, that's all. Take it, please."

Her heart was knocking hard. Something she didn't know about and never talked about, but it was there in his eyes, and it frightened her. Like the time Mr. Landau came close to the bed. An old family friend.

"Don't be afraid," he said as he bent over her.

She remembered defying him. She was afraid...to say no and hurt an old family friend and afraid of something else...she didn't know what then, either...but it terrified her. Now, only her eyes moving, she said nothing, staring at her pocketbook.

He patted her hand gently, "There, there, don't worry. Don't be afraid."

He turned again to his work. She thought he was laughing at her and wouldn't date look at him. At the end of the day, he met her at the subway and held her elbow as they went down the stairs.

"Let me tell you why I gave you the perfume. I've never given anything to a girl in my life and always wanted to. You see, I have nothing much to give. How many times have I seen in the movies that a handsome actor opens a velvet box and takes out a diamond bracelet and gives it to the lady and she smiles...happy and grateful. I wanted to give, too, and see that smile."

"Why me?"

"Forgive me, Becky, but I knew you would be happy and grateful for the little nothing I could give you. <u>You</u> would really think it's <u>something</u>. Am I right, Becky?"

And he chucked her under the chin with the point of a bent finger.

A happy grateful smile, "My train!" Shouting, "Thank you!"

And running, the people pushed her in so he could no longer see her.

The next morning, they all complained she was reeking of perfume. Even he was dizzy from the smell but thankful she liked it. All day she proved to him how much it was hovering in the air all around. That was her...being grateful. Payday today.

He asked, "You know what you're going to spend your money on?"

"Nope, do you?"

"Nope, do you?"

And they both laughed...though nothing they said was funny. Just the way they said, 'nope.' It was a funny word. The bell rang. Paychecks handed out at lunch time so they could be cashed at the bank. His first pay...ever...her first very own money...ever. Herbie's pinkie ring glittering while he handed her the envelope.

"Oh," he said, "wait a minute, something else..." and he handed her a pink slip.

"Sorry."

It was like she'd just finished playing a piece on the accordion in front of people knowing you've played badly. Humiliation inside...and smiling and bowing to the kind, attentive, considerate applause demanding an encore no one really wants to hear. But there's a contract between audience and player. The ritual of asking on their part...the ritual of giving on Becky's...only one condition...they both know when to stop. She...not too late. And they...not too soon. No contract here. Too soon. Told to go. Too soon.

"Why, Mr. Herbie?"

"Too much time talking and smoking and bath rooming and not enough working. This younger generation...what do you know from working?"

And he dismissed her with a wave of the hand.

"Go get another job where you can find the war part-time. The soldiers have no choice. For them it's full-time...for some, forever...but for people here, they choose their hours...when to fight and when not to. You're lucky, you know, but you don't appreciate it. Lucky...you're here and not there...and lucky you're a woman, not a man. Your collectors, your women...pay, insurance and veteran's pensions...the men sit in trenches and fox holes and early graves. Thousands of young men over there...life giving them every day a pink slip. They are asking only if we do a little bit of something, and you do a lot of nothing.

She turned and ran...Punji running after her, Herbie shouting, "Get out!"

Punji pleading, "Stop a second, Becky. Please, stop, I want to say something to you before you go. I love you, Becky."

Herbie shouting, "Get out! Get out of my shop!"

"I need you, Becky!"

"Out! Out! Out!"

"Becky, please, wait for me!"

He grabbed her, flung her around, and feverishly started tearing a silver bracelet from his arm. He couldn't release a clasp. He squeezed until he bled, pinching his skin, and tearing at the lock. In a frenzy, he pulled so hard, it broke. And he put it into her hand, closing it hard over the bracelet until her hand hurt, but he held fast.

"Say you'll take it. I want you to have it to remember me. Please, I don't want it. I really don't. I know I may never see you again. But that's alright. That's why I want you to have it. Tell me. What do you think? Is it beautiful? Tell me if you think it's beautiful."

"It is. Very."

"What?"

"Beautiful."

"Say it again. Again, and again."

"Beautiful. Very, very beautiful."

"You like?"

"I do."

"Say, 'I like it.'"

"I...like it...very much."

"Say...you love it."

Looking down, rubbing it over and over with her thumbs, "I do."

"You do...what?"

Whispering so he barely hears, mouth moving without a sound, he watching her lips intently, "I love it."

"Alright, you can go home now and cry. I know you want to."

"Why? What am I doing?"

"You're smiling."

"Am I?"

'Don't give a satisfactory smile, cry smile, I don't really care - just smile a relieved smile.'

"I don't want this job anymore anyway. It was hard work being heroic. Much too hard. See you, Punji."

"Yeah, Becky. I'll see you around."

Punji was arrogant now. After all, they were keeping him. He had a job. That hurt more than anything. He didn't want to see her... not even Punji. Now that she was in the discard heap, he was particular. Seething on the way home. Even he didn't want her. She banged on the door viciously.

Mirele shouting, "Who?"

"Me! Let me in!"

Slapping the door open with his hand.

"What's the matter? What happened?"

Becky opened her coat. "Hang up your coat!"

In the worst crisis, Mirele demanded coats be hung.

"Shut up!" And she flung the coat at her with such force, she was reeling into the chair.

"Give me the damn coat!"

And she flung it over her shoulder and left the house again, slamming and kicking the door, "Hang everything," she screamed. "Hang it all! Hang me too, why don't you!"

The next morning, Mirele went to see the doctor and told her anguished story interrupted by phone calls every minute, her pained face anxiously hovering over him until finished talking in his alien voice to someone else, unable to wait, terrible anxiety to tell the whole story, afraid she'll forget something.

And in the end, the eternal question, "What should I do?"

And for the first time, the doctor silent, thinking, slow to answer, then...quietly, "Let her do what she wants, Mrs. Bromsky."

And Mirele readily agreed...from now on...to let Becky do whatever she wanted. She was afraid not to. The doctor was afraid. So why shouldn't she be?

Chapter Sixty-Eight

A job wasn't just <u>working</u>. Poppa was on WPA.

"Lazy bums on relief," they said. "That's not work. Get them working! Lazy bums on the dole, making it look like they're working."

Poppa said he worked hard, and Becky believed him. He said it proud. She could tell he was feeling good all over when he said it... straightening his back...pickaxe and shovel work. Poppa loved work. They said it made life sweet and he believed it. He lived by that maxim. Work makes life sweet, and he believed it. That's why he was a Communist. Everyone would work. Everyone's life could be sweet. That's how life should be, sweet. That was Poppa's utopia. A whole world wiping sweat from it's brow at the end of the day. Even just the chance to work...even just...it's there...if you want it. Even better...it wants you. The job looking for the man. That's the perfect state.

"Phillip, you're sick. Don't do in today."

"What do you mean...sick?! I have to go in."

The job would disappear if he didn't watch it every day. Like Mirele hovered over Becky, he hovered over his job. Be perfect... never late...never sick...never tired...never rest...even for a moment.

Always willing to do more. He swung and hammered until his muscles ached and his back complained, the sun battering him in the summer, cold in the winter. His dull gray fedora bent in the middle where he pulled it down or lifted it up to scratch while it dangled, then he'd put it back with a tug in that damn spot. He never cleaned that hat. He was at work the moment he put it on in the morning. Poppa didn't drink or beat Momma. He just looked down on her and she let him...not because she knew it was the only thing he had. He'd tell her how stupid she is and what does she know? and she beamed because it meant he was smart and knew a lot and when Becky won her debates with him, he beamed because Becky was so smart. The rest of the body mattered little...just tacked on for some reason. That's all that mattered to them both was...the head...character. He loved his hat because it had 'character.' Poppa saw 'character' in everything. He always said he could tell a person's character from the way their old shoes looked when they brought them for fixing. It was a serious indictment if a person didn't have any. After all, if a book, a chair, even a dog has it. Why not a person?

Once he had a trade. Now, he was a laborer. But he didn't consider that common. No such thing as a common laborer. Nothing common about labor. But all the days Poppa spent hammering his life out on stubborn ground to force it to yield so others could take pencils and make lines on paper on fancy desks and be considered 'workers.' She saw that once in the movies. Carey Grant said he couldn't be disturbed. He was at work...architecting, looking clean, shaved, well dressed, at ease. He didn't seem to Becky to be doing anything really. Not what Poppa called...work. But that's why Mirele wanted her to go to college...so she could be in a nice place scribbling with a pencil and say she has a job. Mirele didn't look down on Poppa because he labored with his hands...but she would on Becky. But that's what work did to people. Made them confused.

"I want you to be something, Becky."

"Isn't Poppa something, Ma?"

"Of course, silly girl."

Momma's little face was rigid now, cold, too.

"No more questions."

Now Becky knew it's because she had no answers. She'd ask Poppa. But how could you ask Poppa why he was nothing and wanted you to be something. Poppa didn't even have a job, even though he was working.

Momma rubbed him every night with Bengay and slept on the floor in her room because she couldn't stand the smell. No matter how powerful he was, he still ached. They worked him so hard just to show people their money wasn't going to pay slackers. For the first time, Poppa was working with Italians, and he heard them talking open...in front of him. They thought he was Italian because he didn't have soft skin and white fingers and small shoulders like tailors and furriers.

"Hey countryman, isn't it good who Mussolini is doing to the Jew?"

"Because the Jew is stingy, that's why."

"Stingy? He sends his wife to the country in summer and his children to college paying for both of them. You send your wife to the shop and your children to shine shoes and we're stingy?!"

"What you mean, 'We're?' You Jew?!"

"And remember, you go every Sunday on your knees to beg a Jew. From us, you took him. Now beg him to forgive you, you're so stupid."

Poppa was telling the story at home now...chuckling what he said. Strange...not angry...what the man said. Only proud of what he answered. That was Poppa's classroom. People saying what they shouldn't, and he is answering them and setting them straight.

"Why weren't you angry at what he said, Poppa?"

"I was, but I'm not now. If I didn't answer him the right way, I'd still be angry...ashamed of myself that I was stupid when I shouldn't be."

Becky suspected he was prouder of his wisdom than angry with the offender.

"So, what do you think of the working man now, Poppa?"

"Ignorant, that's all. Needs to be educated. Work is not enough. After all, a donkey works and works...and...he's still a donkey!"

Poppa's eyebrows shooting up in two big arches when he was positive, he'd said the last word on the subject. It was cold, the wind touching her everywhere, breaking through easily, the flimsy coat, thin sleeves, flair skirt blowing through the coat. She pulled her hands out of her pockets to pull it tight around her legs. Then the cold stiffened her fingers, froze them until they tingled so she put them back in her pockets and the wind had it's way...pushing in, swirling around everywhere while she helplessly watched and shivered. Strange, Ma and Pa didn't feel lonely or desolate even in that bare house with sheets hanging on the window, a dim bulb in the kitchen, the other two rooms with doors open to get a little light from it, too. Winter was hard on that house and the empty lot around it with pebbles and rocks and glass. She stood on the corner where Ma used to stand watching the candy store. It didn't seem so cold when the boys and girls were there. No one was there now. The boys in the war, the girls home waiting. 'I have no one to wait for.' She looked back at the house and back again to the store. A life lived in that little black circle...the 'immy' marble holes in the dirt where she was sometimes invited to play a game or two. She fell because of them several times. That's all she could play...immies. The kids knew she had jumbo marbles and peewee marbles, and they wanted them. And across the street, Mr. Gross put the cup under the malted machine. She loved the sound when it first started spinning...rich and creamy like she liked it. It wasn't enough anymore, immies, malteds, reading True Confessions, and eating marble icecream cup with chocolate on top, and pining after Louie. Years of pining and waiting and he never ever noticed. All night, she slept on curlers and woke up with headaches, just to make her hair pretty for him. How her heart pounded, when she saw him, even at a distance. He never even said her name. Hardly ever talked to her. And she dreamed and thought of him all the time. Somehow, they knew the boys and girls on the corner teased and laughed at her. One even knocked on her door one day, pretending to be him. She quickly tore the curlers out of her hair, put a comb through it on her way to the door, opened it slowly so he wouldn't see she was so excited. And it was Benny, doubled with laughter. He knew she was primping quickly behind the door.

"I knew it wasn't Louie."

A forced smile. But it was no use. He knew how much she hoped it would be. But she kept on lying. The hurt, the humiliation, humbling...shrinking...needing the lie.

"I knew it wasn't him really."

A weak protest. Becky was not a strong liar. But he would not be merciful.

"Yeah, I'll be," he repeated.

The memory burned for years. It was later joined by another and another. Her first dance...and the last. 50 cents for a whole night of waiting to be asked for a dance. Becky never danced before, but thought she'd try at Brighton Beach Ballroom. Another leap she made into magic and blind hope. Somehow...and her mind came to an abrupt halt after that. She'd manage. It never prepared her for the clumsy steps, the awkward apologies.

"Sorry I'm fat, heavy, clumsy, hard to push and pull, turn, and spin, stiff, unbending, not yielding like I'm supposed to. How does it feel...yielding. I don't even know. She could only hope the boy would be as grateful as she and wouldn't notice.

She waited near the entrance, ready to run, just in case. She watched the others, swirling and smiling, the girls spinning into boys' arms like a top at the end of a string he caught her, and she was yielding. From the back, a tap on her shoulder, a flippant male voice. She turned to him.

"Hi," smiling.

Teeth and eyes and hair like she'd seen in the movies bending over the leading lady, looking at her laughing and confident, like he'd picked her up and was holding her and she was kicking and protesting, and he was just laughing louder.

She loved that look and always wanted to be that lady in pantaloons, kicking, while he held her tighter and laughed louder, real he-man like. Now, it was happening, and she wanted to run and hide like a cat, running and screaming inside. Outside, dead silence, tight, arms wrapped hard around her heart, holding fast, so only death shows on her face.

"I love you," he said. "You're beautiful. You know what you remind me of?"

A quick swoop of the hand into his back pocket. A little glow, her head and body bent forward, to look, to not look, pressing not to come alive...and wanting to...and not knowing what to do if she does...if she doesn't. <u>Help me somebody</u>.

Still smiling, he took a picture out of his wallet.

"See."

And he put it in front of her face, real close.

"That's what you look like."

It was dark. Hard to see. But she looked and looked. A horse! A picture of a horse! Tears springing from her eyes.

Gentle now. He whispers, "I'm sorry."

Her hands in front of her face. He pulls them away. She hides behind them again.

Pleading now, "Let me see you so you can see me and know I mean what I'm saying. I'm sorry, please forgive me."

She separated her fingers. Peeked through. His eyes warm with pleading. He pressed on. A wan smile.

He coaxes, "That's good, a little more now. I want to see your pretty teeth. They had an overlap, so she had to smile broad and push both sides of her mouth back hard.

"That's better. Now, that's talk."

And he talked and talked. She doesn't even remember what and she listened until it was closing time and she thanked him for an interesting evening.

'I learned from him to be pitiful, Momma. so at least, someone will feel something for me. Better than nothing. Oh, I forgot. Something else I'm missing, Ma...personality. Do they give lessons in it, you're asking? No lessons, Ma. You have it or you don't. Like a talent for music. It's a talent for being a person. It means talking a lot, being funny, being popular, having lots of friends. <u>That's</u> a person. Oh, I'm learning how to talk and talk and be funny, but I don't like it. It's too hard for me...like I'm going on stage with my accordion. First, I get stage fright, and while I'm putting on the act, I'm scared how long I can go on and I'm glad when it's over. So, you're asking, 'Why do you bother?' because I need to have someone to see and someone I've seen to go. It's the in-between, Momma, that's so hard. Being smart with the smart ones and dumb with the dumb ones. I'm not smart enough or dumb enough or deep enough. Not even a good audience, Ma. Can't listen enough and don't laugh enough. Only Lisa, dirty blonde permanented hair is tiny waves with scraggly ends, hand me down dressed always too big for her, fitting another shape, giving her a stomach, she didn't have and bulging out in the back where it didn't. She always had a hungry look...that wanting to be friends look that kids can spot a mile away and run away from. It must be in the blood...not wanting someone who wants you...badly. Especially those who want so you can feel it a block away...so you turn when you see them. They didn't want her because she was still sucking her fingers...like a baby. Not just one finger...but all four...at once. And she wanted me. Can you imagine? Me?! For a friend. But I wouldn't have her. Couldn't stand her. Even her dog. When she wasn't look-ing, I hit him hard with his leash whenever I could, and the little thing didn't even whimper. He quivered when I hit him. And I shouted at him like he did something wrong when he really didn't. I've heard kids who are hit like that. They beat dogs. I left school because I couldn't make it, Ma. How could I tell you that? I wanted to be 'one of the girls' and I failed. And the job? Fired me because I'm not good enough... and the music I'm playing, so scared of perform-ing, I leave out half the notes and rush through the other half, quick and loud so they won't know the difference. But I know, Momma. outside of 3rd street shul, no one's gonna appreciate half a piece. And

I'm growing up, Momma. They don't applaud big girls for the same things as little girls. The little ones they applaud for encouragement, the big ones for talent. I'm past the age of encouragement, Momma. They're gonna discourage me, now. They don't have the same mercy on big girls. I'm gonna leave home. Running away, that's what.'

Middle of the night, she wrote a note and left it on the table. Mirele saw her do it and read it at the window by the moonlight while Becky was packing. It ended with, 'I'm going to Florida to stay with grandma.' Then she quickly opened her purse, took out a few bills and slipped them in Becky's purse so she'd have running away money. The doctor told her Becky should do what she wanted. So...if that's what she wanted...her head under the covers, breathing heavy, she heard the door close softly. 'Come home soon, please Beckele. Don't go.' And she strained in the dark, listening for it to open again, but it never did.

"Phillip," nudging him with her finger, "Becky's run away from home. Wake up. Becky's gone."

But she couldn't rouse him. Then she bit the pillow hard, muffling a cry so she wouldn't wake him. 'Let him sleep. Let her go. Whatever they want. Let them.' Then she went to Becky's room, closed the kitchen door, and hit her head against the wall.

"My fault Becky, I didn't take care. Didn't. Didn't. Didn't."

And with each word, a dull thud, beating herself on the wall. Then she lay down on Becky's bed and put her hand between the sheets to catch some little warmth from her body. 'I hope soon you'll want to come home. <u>Want</u> Becky. <u>Want</u> me. Repeating over and over again...

"Want me, Becky."

And she waited in the dark for Becky to want her. It had to be now. She didn't know how long she could wait. She got up and sat on a chair waiting for it to open. And that's how Phillip found her in the morning, wrapped in a blanket.

Chapter Sixty-Nine

In places where time is reckoned in minutes and seconds, 2:42, 3:51, the air around charged with momentum and impact, people strutting about double time and looking significant in places where time is not rounded out to the nearest minute and complicated schedules are meticulously detailed though they're never adhered to. No one even notices that the 10:52 is seldom there, but the neck cranes and voices indignantly strut anyhow, savoring, for some reason, even the sound of such tyrannical punctuality.

Becky didn't even have a watch, but she was drawn into the furore of the moment she saw the sign, 'Penn Station' the very name, the beginning of a drama, heightened spirits, quickening steps, and heart. Ugly as she was, in some secret place, she thought she was beautiful and Prince Charming would see her and be struck by her beauty and carry her away. How many leading ladies had she played after she left the movies, loving the tragic heroines the most, those who love and die, Violetta, Kathy, Madame Bovary, Back Street, the other woman, mysterious, seldom seen, always dressed in negligees, and always unattainable, never tired, found boring, or nasty tempered, like wives. She would never own a housedress or put on an apron. It was all going to begin on a train. She would have joined Pesach if not for the movies. It made life bearable. Gave her hopes and dreams and when she left the movies, she was <u>somebody</u>. Life was beginning on this train. A far-off place is where Utopias are.

It was late. A few sailors slumped over the chairs sleeping, some snoring, some with red patches over their faces, lipstick or liquor, and some with hats covering their faces from the light, legs carelessly dangling over the seat, or head over the arm. No one was looking at her. No one even knew she was there. But she'd seen movies like this. Tomorrow one of them would invite her to the dining car, a black soft footed negro speaking to her in gentle tones would slide her into her seat, moving it ever so slightly until she fit perfectly and then stand at attention with a poised pencil until he had the order, being careful to repeat what the gentleman said so she wouldn't make a mistake. He'd make it seem like his very life depended on his not making a mistake. Then he'd come rolling a little carriage on wheels with a big, silver pot on it, and the gentleman and she'd say half sentences, just enough to keep him interested...mysterious...like Joan Crawford and the trees and bushes outside the window would go rushing by and she'd make witty comments while the pots and dishes clattered on the table and he would say, 'What would you say?' And she'd know he was interested.

The next morning no one invited her, so she went to the dining car alone holding on all the way, while the train jerked and rattled. She sat at a table alone and ordered only coffee. The waiter pushed her seat in, and she jumped up and down on it several times, thinking he was done, but he kept pushing. Not like the lady at the next table. Smooth. A sweep under the table and she is joining him like the yielding ladies she saw on the dance floor. She suddenly realized she didn't know how to eat. At nearby tables, people were maneuvering napkins, forks and knives and she didn't even know which handheld knife or how to dab your mouth ever so slightly with the napkin. Even putting the cup to her mouth, she felt like a criminal...she was doing something she shouldn't. The cup shook in her hand as she lowered it to the plate. The coffee spilled and burned her legs, but she wouldn't dare move. Everyone would be watching her then, if she jumped up quickly, but it hurt so, she couldn't help it, springing out of her chair so it fell over the cup and saucer clattering to the ground. The waiter, unruffled, presented the bill. She paid while bouncing from one foot to the other. She was asked if 'anything was wrong, Miss?' And she said there wasn't. How could she tell a man she was hurt? She returned to her seat and stared glumly out the window. At midnight, she had to change trains, waiting under a huge home, hundreds of weary people waiting, slouched over suitcases, pocketbooks for pillows, and Becky wanting nothing now but a bed. It seemed, no matter how she put herself, the benches were just too short. Why couldn't they make them long enough to put a whole person? Were the whole world midgets? It looked so easy in the movies, people climbing into beds and drawing curtains at night and sitting comfortably in club cars by day smoking and talking to newfound friends, private detectives or the secret criminal or the hero and heroine dressed impeccably, every hair in place...not even smudged lips. Not like this...getting up in the morning with rumpled hair, needing a bath, curling into a ball of shame when the door between the cars opened and a clean, starched, every hair in place impeccable, came through those doors. But here in the waiting room, everyone was limp and shabby and uncaring, like people are when sleep is all that matters. Slips, bloomers, showing on the ladies. The men barefoot, grimy undershirts peeping out of shirts they long outgrown, little arcs between the buttons now. The look of tired sleeplessness was dirty and unromantic. Becky was repelled by the rubbery skin and open mouths yawning and some scratching themselves like no one was there. Becky flushed red and quickly looked away, revulsion quickly followed by a shattered illusion. Children in their mothers' arms scowling, a mother slipping down in her seat as far as she can so her big stomach can be the child's pillow, her skirt climbing over her knees, her legs spread so you could see the big hole in her stockings and the folded flesh were the top of her stockings and the folded flesh were the top of her stocking dug into her thighs and darkness merci-fully hiding the rest. Babies crying, mothers running into the ladies room.

They were all the same. Dimly lit, painted gray, doors marked, 'OUT OF ORDER,' ladies grabbing the door before it closes on the ones you pay a nickel. A whole day for one nickel. Becky wondered about the first nickel. Who put it in there? Must be someone very particular. Becky would rather spend it on a candy bar. Waste it like that? Nickel or no nickel, paper in streams on the floor where they fell, always wet. Dark water always finding its way there and the women tiptoeing and lifting their feet in exaggerated ways over the little streams, and some laughing, so hungry for something to laugh at. Mothers hiding breasts behind full blouses, sleepy heads over gurgling babies, some squatting on the floor, smell of urine and diapers and warm milk gone sour.

'Two tickets to Frisco.'

And they kissed at the gate before going into the train and waved handkerchiefs 'Goodbye' to mother and father who stand waving back, happy tears in their eyes. Happy, Becky. Happy. Happy. Happy. And she wore a fancy hat that she held tight on her head while she flew to the train. And primly adjusted a tight skirt while the adoring hero sat beside her and held her hand and whispered...

The first waving palms of Florida, missing the haze of dream real-ity. South Beach was like home. Long stretches of bare, hot sand. Just the palm trees were different, that's all. On the bus, she rode through blocks of little stores, just like home. Groceries and the fruit store and stands where two oldsters sold just bread and milk, like Ma used to. Disappointment kept at bay, desperately. Not wanting to taste it now, so soon. Zisme lived in a part of Florida she called 'The Jewish Wastebasket.' Somehow, young, and oiled and tanned Parisienne in the sun was not the same as old and Jewish and bent and wrinkled in the sun. one was high living...the other, slow dying...except for Zisme. She was still wrapping an apron around an old cotton dress, hanging a tray of *chai* and mezuzahs around her neck and peddling them at the corner. In South Beach you could still sell a mezuzah. Some of the old people waited to be helped across the street by a uniformed young man who was there for that purpose. They let him. They'd given up the fight to prove they're 'independent and can do for themselves.' Moved even slower, to hold on to the uniformed man as long as they could, wanting 'He should hold me a little.' How long since someone held them? The doctor, may habe.

Some haunted his office, so he'd fuss over them. Make up a sickness you don't have right now. The beaches were lined with canes and gray beards all bent forward as if they were looking at something, like when they had eyes that could read, hands that could sew a button, bake a cake, pick a flower, or sit folded just like they wanted, not pain deciding. She asked one of them where #10 was.

"What?"

"10..." she shouted.

Then the whole beach was buzzing.

"You sure it's a house? No house there. Only stores."

"But my grandma lives there."

And they debated #10, adjoining streets, who lived there once, and disagreed who did and didn't. Grateful...minutes passed so quickly they didn't even pass. Becky noticed no one wore a watch. They couldn't bear to watch the time. They could have gone on debating all day, Becky bursting with impatience.

"Thank you."

And speeding down the street, any direction, canes waving at her, shouting, "Turn, turn."

She turned quickly and ran the other way. 2-4-6-10...a store! They were right. Pinsky's grocery. The door clanged behind her. He didn't hear.

She shouted, "Mr. Pinsky!"

The old man turned.

"Bernstein. Pinsky's dead. But everyone knows me, so I never changed the name. What do you want? Today the bread is fresh."

"I'm looking for my grandmother, Zisme."

"Oh Zisme...yeah...she's here. Follow me. Zisme! You have a visitor!"

He opened the curtain and quickly closed it again, "Excuse me."

A voice behind the curtain.

"It's alright, who is it?"

"Tell her it's Becky."

"Becky," he shouted.

"Becky who?"

"Becky, her granddaughter."

"You shout this time," he ordered. "Why am I hollering? You're a female, you can holler for yourself better than me. Holler!"

"It's me, grandma!"

"Me?"

"Becky. Mirele's Becky!"

"Mirele's Becky! Open the door. Come on in."

"What door?"

"You know what I mean. Come on in."

Zisme was sitting on the bed in her slip that was too short for her. She jumped up.

"Becky, what are you doing here? Run back. There's no place for you here. I have a bed, a bureau, and that's all. If you want, you can have half the bed and half the bureau until you find a job. Does Mirele know where you are?"

"No! I ran away!"

"So, send a telegram now and say where you are. You have money to send one?"

"I do."

"So go send it and then we'll talk. Why did you run away?"

"Because I want to <u>live</u>!"

"So, you came to where people are dying, and you want to live. <u>Live</u> where people <u>live</u>! There!"

And she pointed out the window of a huge hotel, a famous one on Collins Ave.

"That's where the young people are. The soldiers and sailors are in there now and they're living every minute they can...and they're living every minute they can...and they're worried about dying, too. This place is full of people who are dying, Becky. Go home."

"Let me stay grandma, please. I want to see the world a little. All those books Momma wanted me to read and movies I saw and everything, they made me want to see more than West 5th street."

"Here?! You'll see more than West 5th street? Foolish girl. This is West 5th Street...60 years later. The women on West 5th street bury their husbands...from the shop to the grave they carry them and on West 5th street. They bathed in the ocean and played peperino on Surf Ave. But you'll see for yourself, Becky."

Zisme was talking to herself. Becky sat on the bed and fell asleep sitting up. She was so tired. Zisme pushed her down with one finger. She awoke hours later in the dark, Zisme snoring beside her. In the morning, she left her sleeping and went to look for a job. Woolworth needed counter girls.

"Can you counter?" Ms. Deal asked.

"I guess so. What can there be to it?"

"Nothing. They'll tell you what they want. You tell somebody else. When it's ready, you pick it up and give it to the customer."

The interviewer was a thin, old lady with long, bony fingers who kept twisting her hair round and round one of them while she questioned Becky, frowning and looking very severe, and commenting from time to time as if she were listing criminal charges.

"Hmmm...never worked?! Hmmm...never finished school! Hmmm...only 17. Hmmm...here only one day...Hmmm...Hmmm... All right. On trial. Mrs. Haneke will train you. Follow me to the front of the store!"

At the head of a long, narrow counter was Mrs. Haneke, looking like she was born for the job, harsh eyes watching all the mashed potatoes and gravies, soggy peas and cutlets that were piled on plates as far as she could see, a small, pinched face, lined so deep one wondered what she ever looked like, a tight lit the mouth that accused before a crime was committed.

"Here, we put the food on the plates ourselves."

A few minutes training, just enough to show exact measurements. Not even a pea, more or less, that's knowing the job," she said proudly... "dumping a dollop of mashed potatoes on a plate...or an ounce of potato, either. In time, you'll train your eye. You see that girl over there? Perfect peas and potato eyes. She can be trusted to know what she's doing, so no one is cheated...the company or the customers. Now let me see you do a sample."

Becky carefully measured, using Mrs. Haneke's sample as a guide.

"You'll do," she said, rising.

Her first customer, an old, hungry-looking man, threads hanging from him sleeve, collar crumpled, yellow tobacco-stained fingers carefully counting his money to make sure he had enough, counting pennies several times.

"The Special," he said. "How much?"

She looked up at the sign with the picture on it. He couldn't see it.

"30 cents."

"Alright. I have this...Veal and what for vegetables?"

She looked up again. "Peas and potatoes."

"Alright, I'll have that. No gravy."

She looked about furtively. Mrs. Haneke was not around. She piled the plate high, way beyond measurements allowed for potatoes, shoveling on the peas, whispering, "Eat quick."

He slid the plate to his lap, buried his head under the counter like he was looking for something, buried his head under it, and took his head out again when he finished. Satisfied. He returned the plate to the counter when it no longer looked suspicious. Becky breathed a sigh of relief and then she thought, 'I'll fix that Barbara Hutton...' piling the food high as she could.

"Hey, Santa Clause!" One of the men called out to her. "Where have you been all this time? For the first time, we'll be walking outta here full!"

A blast from Mrs. Haneke. "What do you mean...full?! Becky... get over here! Do you see what I see?"

The evidence was damming. Plates bulging with mountains of potatoes, rivers of peas from one end of the counter to the other.

"Double portions at least! Even triple! What are you...a damn communist?! You're fired!"

Becky knew this was her moment to shine. Heroism under fire. Holding to principle, no matter what!

"And what are you? A Woolworth heiress? Is the money going into your pocket?"

And she removed her apron and flung it on the floor, turned and smiled at the customers and slowly walked out, head proudly in the air.

"Dumb girl," a customer said to Mrs. Haneke. "Lost her pay, didn't she? You can have this stuff back if it'll get you into trouble. I haven't touched it yet."

"No, it's okay, damn Jew girl! Reds! All of them! Have to be watched!"

"Yeah, you bet!"

It was lunch time. One of the girls followed her out.

"Hi Becky. My name is May. Don't worry. I have an idea. I want to quit too. They need bar girls in Key West. Money there. Want to go?"

"OK! When do we leave?"

"In the morning."

That night, Becky lingered around the hotel on Collins Ave. a sailor passed by and winked. Becky tried to win back but she couldn't. Both eyes closed, then...shyness. She turned away from him.

"Hi, pretty," he said. "Let's talk."

It was patriotic to talk to sailors. Why not? The barriers were down then. Even for one as shy as Becky...just for talking that is. Tall, blonde, blue-eyed Christian sailor. He bought her a drink and they talked, and Becky laughed and enjoyed while 90 miles out in the water a ship was waiting. 100 desperate eyes watching Collins Ave.

They escaped from Germany and were waiting for a word of welcome. While Becky frittered the night away talking about movies and authors and books and heaped flatteries on each other until Becky said goodbye happily, thinking he just wanted to talk and he furiously flung a lighted cigarette after her, his eyes hard with rage and scorn that he'd been led on and let down by a 'tomato.' Becky thought she made a big hit though he didn't ask to see her again. She wondered why. Zisme was glad to see her go. Her money was running out. Zisme was not about to spend on her. She'd started to spend on the next world, giving to the shuls to make sure she went to Heaven. She had no money left for this world or anyone in it. May took her to a bar in Key West, a small dingy circle with a sea of white hats to be serving. She came with a friend Zelda who didn't like Becky on sight.

She whispered to her while they were dressing, "You know. May called you a 'Dirty Jew.'"

Becky was terrified, "She what?! I'm leaving. I'm going back to grandma." And she left that night.

Zisme startled, "What are you doing here?"

"I'll find a job tomorrow."

"You better. You're costing already."

The next morning, Becky sent a telegram home, "Send money. Stop. I'm starving. Stop."

Mirele sent money and Becky bought a ticket home. She couldn't stay with Zisme a second longer. In the morning, she found Zisme had wet the bed.

Chapter Seventy

When Becky came home, Mirele hovered over Becky like she was just born but following Dr. Raffel's suggestion to the letter. No questions. No restrictions. Even Dr. Raffel was worried now. Violent eruptions like Pesach. All the other adolescent girls he knew were messy in their rooms but that was all. Mothers weren't afraid of and for their daughters like Mirele. She was afraid again of what she had created.

Phillip was happy about getting a job in the Navy Yard, mopping, and sweeping and they would get an apartment, too, in a housing project.

"Thank God, we'll have steam heat and a refrigerator...but...I'm afraid for Becky. There's a barracks for sailors in the building next to us. They'll bother her, Doctor. What'll you do?"

"From now on, men will bother her. She'll have to learn."

Obsequious again. "You're right. Let her do what she wants."

"Have faith in her."

Dr. Raffel had none in himself, but what else could he say?

"You're right, Doctor. She'll have to learn."

But after she left the office, the fear again, "What'll be while she's learning?"

"That's learning?"

To Mirele, learning was from a book. 'The other kind of learning, even an ignorant like her could do. But real learning, that you do from reading and thinking. And Becky thinks? God knows what she thinks. And reading? God knows what she reads. Without school? What kind of reading? No teacher telling her nothing. But then, nobody can tell her anything anymore, even me. Old as I am. I listen. You can tell me.'

But Becky...it was Mirele's biggest frustration that she couldn't <u>tell her something</u>.

Becky sat on a friend's stoop listening and trying out a new personality and what she copied from Monty Wooley's 'Man Who Came to Dinner.' Biting and cynical and worldly-wise from someone who knew nothing of the world. A world-weary gaze on the world with fresh and tender hopes from the magazine, True Confessions, and the towel scene from Millie and Thomas's morbid introspection and dramatizing himself and taunting her with the 'Octoberfest' days and days of dancing in the streets and forgetting who and where you are and being gay and laughing and, best of all, behind a mask, beautiful and mysterious and... 'How do I get Herbie to like me Momma? Or even look at me?' What would you say if you knew that's what I'm thinking?' 'Foolishness!'

Say the word with finality as if she were pronouncing a sentence. Life and death issues to Becky. Summarily dismissed and harshly judged by Mirele. 'How futile seems to me all the uses of this world?'

Becky's life purpose...no purpose. Phillip... 'Wave nothing and you'll worry from nothing.' Except Herbie. Him, she wanted. Or Lawrence Olivier types, dark-haired, black-eyed men who bent over women on dark, moonlit beaches and whispered in their eats, or Don Joses and Heathcliff's who suffered unrequited love at her hands and she, Carmen, wild, confident, daring, flirtatious. 'I want to be a Gypsy, Momma.' Like Phillip said, 'The hoboes are clever, Becky.

They complain about civilization but eat the bread it bakes.' 'I want to be a gypsy and eat bread and cake when I feel like it.'

She didn't really think beyond all the images that books and movies put in her head. That they left out one important image. Never occurred to her how to make a living, open a bank account, get a promotion, compute interest, look for and marry a rich man. Becky was sent out in the world with a few slogans and images. No wonder she couldn't budge...without a rudder, a ladder, a direction. And the philosophers lament the material world and spread their philosophies counting sold copies so they can have, of the material things they're so busy despising and telling others to scorn. Phillip believed and scorned and could barely pay his rent and Becky believed and scorn and couldn't look beyond Phillip to pay it for her when he could. Money was impossible to earn or sinful or was given with terrible punishment by the government or just there mysteriously in vast amounts like the movies...or you married a rich doctor...none of whom was available on West 5th Street. And none of them would have Becky anyway. And besides, what would she ever do with him if he found her? Be a wife? She didn't even know how to begin. Be a mother? She didn't want to. Becky went to the movies and walked home playing the part until tomorrow's feature when she had a heavy role being somebody else. She was the queen the minute she entered the movie palace.

Walking up the marble stairs with dee, red carpet, pass the renaissance paintings, gilt framed and softly lit, choosing any seat she wanted at midday in the vast, dark room with painted ceiling. Sometimes, he could see another head or two or hear a cough or sneeze or a whispered word or laughter. And sometimes, a strange man comes to sit beside her, heaving breathing and then, a cautious hand on her leg. She'd get up quickly and sometimes he followed until she found two people to sit between and he'd walk away muttering.

She never saw the faces. It repelled her even to look sideways... and frightened her. William Powell on the screen bringing a small silver tray to the heroine in a satin lined bedroom while a grubby hand took Becky's hand and scratched the middle of her palm. She didn't want to hurt him. Slowly got up and moved away. Later, she learned what that means, and she folded her hands in movies from then on. Sweaty hands, clumsy, sneaky, nauseating hands. Not at all like you touch a queen. Or they didn't touch her at all. Just looked until 'The End' when they kissed her. The rest of the time they just gazed, adoring, and Becky felt adored. She even thought sometimes, if Clark Gable saw her, he'd realize she was the lady of his dreams. Or Lawrence Olivier. She'd run to Hollywood and lie on his doorstep ill and he would open the door and find her and nurse her back to health and fall in love with her.

Becky was in love with Lawrence Olivier and Clark Gable and Herbie, and this took all her thinking, day and night...especially Herbie.

One night, the wind banging the windows so loud they thought they'd break and all shuddered in the bed while again and again they were assaulted but somehow held fast until morning when Becky's window couldn't hold anymore and shattered and the enraged air finally gotten it's way smashed and battered and whatever it could, finding its way even to Becky's bobby pins and panties, scattering them far and wide, dishes clattering to the ground, pots hurled against the wall, even shoes hiding in corners angrily dragged across the ground and hurled carelessly, one here, the other there.

"We have to move here, Phillip. To live like this, in the middle of an empty lot. This place is full of terrible surprises. To take a bath you have to take your life in your hands. When I put a match in that little hole in the water heater, I can't see anything. I'm always afraid it's going to explode. Remember the first time it made such a noise when it lit up, all those tiny holes to make one tub of water. We'll apply to the housing project, hot water, steam heat and a refrigerator."

"Steam Heat?! Who needs it?! I like to look for wood on the beach and see the fire in the stove!"

It was one of Phillip's, 'Who needs it' speeches. Phillip had his and Mirele had hers.

"I need it, more. I want to move from here. I can't stand the cold. It's always cold here. And after last night, I'm afraid. You can get killed here. I'm tired of sleeping with friends who have steam heat, having to listen to their parents arguing all night so I can have a night without my nose freezing."

"I'll talk to Poppa."

Talking...was night and day fighting. Poppa threatened to leave the house. Momma never said, 'So go already!' Becky would have. Maybe she thought he might really go.

Becky received the application, filled it out and then, the letter:

We are happy to inform you...

three rooms on the third floor...

they could inspect it if they wished.

"At least, look!" Mirele desperately insisted.

"Alright, I'll look."

The Housing Project built for the poor stood like army barracks... bare...not a tree, a curve, a flower, nothing to break the deadening monotony...minimalism for the poor. The square on square. The rules were posted in the hall. No holes in walls. Translation: No curtains, pictures, doodads...blank...white on white. Windows, rooms, buildings, arithmetic, geometric precision...nothing wasted...not a hair breath of space. Phillip touched the refrigerator reverently, opened and closed it gently. He opened the tap and put his finger under the water and left it there until it burned him. He smiled in approval.

"Hot water. Just like that. Hot water."

Mirele, "In a minute you can take a bath, Phillip!"

He liked that. Phillip loved the bath. Relaxed him.

"That's right." And he rubbed his head with his finger.

"But it's cold here too, Mirele."

"You have to turn the heat on."

She found the knob and turned it. The first hiss, the first knock...

steam…announcing itself. Every winter of her life Becky turned that knob fearing this time it won't be coming. Something will go wrong. She could never really believe winter would be warm for her all the rest of her days.

"Alright, Mirele, I'll think about it."

But when the letter arrived from the government, '10 days to say yes or no,' like it was an order, Phillip quickly checked the 'Yes' box. Must not make the government mad.

"If they're giving something, you should take it."

And he returned the letter by return mail.

"Phillip, we have no furniture."

"I'm ashamed Poppa, only beds in a new place."

"You're right, Becky."

"Phillip, we need furniture. They won't like it if we put junk in new rooms and maybe, in the new place, Becky will meet important people."

Mirele figured, why not? With steam heat rooms and refrigerators…fancy-schmancy. Mirele didn't even know where 5th Ave was. 30 years in the country. Never saw it. The subway didn't go there. How can Becky bring anybody to three naked rooms? No place to sit, nothing to eat on. They went to the furniture store for the poor. Art Deco…vulgate. Three rooms of furniture for 1,000. Three years to pay. And how he worked to pay. Laborer in the Navy Yard. A Navy Captain passed by while he was sweeping.

"Sweeping dust?! A grown man?! Can't find anything better to do than that?!"

Poppa props his broom against his chest, "You should have more respect for dust, sir. After all, from dust we come and to dust we go."

Poppa said the man looked at him with respect and called him a philosopher.

"I didn't disagree with him," Poppa said. "To an ignorant like him, I'm a philosopher."

A week later he announced he had another assignment. He would work in a refrigerator in Bayonne, New Jersey. A small increase in pay. Three hours travel there and three hours back. He would get up at 3 in the morning and get there at 6. That was okay. He had a job. He was grateful. The revolutionary Marxist was now grateful that the exploiter exploited. Without a job he couldn't even be exploited. He advanced from being a parasite to being exploited. Reduced to singing the old revolutionary songs in the living room. Eyes burning and that's all. America happened. 'Momma happened. I happened. Pesach happened. And the War. And Stalin happened.'Another government letter. Brief and to the point.

'Moving date is set for...instruct truck to appear at...we have only one elevator in the building. Good luck in your new home. NYCHA.'

Momma started packing immediately though there was a month to wait. They didn't need a truck. All their belongings fit into four boxes. Poppa carried two and Mirele carried one on the subway and Becky carried the rest in a large shopping bag. The rope cut her fingers, but she changed hands often and rested a lot. Poppa went back for the army cots, so they'd have something to sleep on and Becky slept on the floor again until her new bed came from Zimmerman's. Poppa gave orders the minute they opened the door to the new apartment. He had a thing about the refrigerator...as if it was made of glass. He showed her how to open it and close it. She'd never seen him so gentle. He nudged it open, then delicately closed it again, soundlessly...just touching the parts together. Becky made a thud a few times and he jumped on her.

"Careful how you close the ice box! You'll break it!"

And he'd show her how to close it for the umpteenth time.

And she whined, "I'm not stupid. I know how to close a door, for God's sake!"

"It's not for His sake! For your sake, dummy! So, you'll have cold when you want it! If you don't take care, it'll break! So be careful!"

"I'm going out! I can't stand walking around here on tacks!"

"What tacks?! What you talking...tacks?!"

She slammed the door viciously behind her. At the foot of the stairs, she paused and heard him opening the door. She peeked out of the shadows and saw him examining the door, then opening and closing it again quietly and then rubbing his finger here and there and shaking his head. She fled down another flight of stairs and slammed the hall door hard until it rattled. Poppa stuck his head out of the window and shook his fist at her. He was afraid to shout and draw attention to her on their first day here. God forbid, they would be thrown out. He retreated quickly before she saw him, afraid that she'd holler or something.

There were three benches in front of the building, new, all the slats in place, no knives had yet carved names and hearts and forbidden words. She sat down on one of them. Anybody. She would say, 'Hello.' In a few minutes, she heard the rustle of a grocery bag. In the light of a streetlamp, she could see a woman in a loud plaid coat, her face almost lost under unruly black hair.

"Hello?" Becky said. "I'm new here. Can I hold your package while you talk to me? Just tell me your name and I'll tell you mine. I don't know anybody here and I'd like to have a friend."

She shoved the bag in Becky's hands and pulled back her hair. Her face was full of pimples. She smiled and Becky could see her even teeth in a large, crooked mouth. Two front teeth covered with lipstick she had put on poorly.

"My name is Mabel. I just moved in yesterday. My husband just left me with a new baby for another woman. I don't know what I'm going to do. Can you come upstairs? Would you like to?"

Stunned. Becky mumbling, "Yes, I'd like to."

She was glad to find an unfortunate, one who needed help. She'd be a friend then. Becky would do. And she'd be a friend. The elevated train came by. What to say now? She didn't know. She looked up quickly like people do when they're embarrassed. The train was slowing down, making an L shaped curve, bare, yellow-lighted windows all empty but one...a fedora and shoulders, one lone man. Then, the light went out. Black now. She couldn't see the man anymore, but she looked up, hoping the lights would go on again...for his sake.

"What's your name again? I'm sorry, I was listening. When I hear a name for the first time, something happens...wiping it clean out that minute!"

"Becky. My name is Becky Bromsky."

She knew Becky was sticking, but Bromsky was gone already. That's okay. She wouldn't mind repeating. Give her something to say.

"Don't be afraid to ask me again if you forget. Doesn't matter how many times. I forget, too."

Smiling, "I'm glad. Oh, I don't mean I'm glad you forget. I'm just glad I'm not alone, if you know what I mean, because sometimes I think I'm going crazy."

"Me too. I think we all think that sometimes. And sometimes I'm glad I <u>think</u> I'm going because if I stop thinking I'm <u>going</u>, maybe it means I'm there already. They say crazy people are the last to know."

"Like done in wives."

"Oh no! I didn't mean anything like <u>that</u>! Forgive me, please. I didn't mean that at all."

Softly, "I know you didn't."

And back and forth, each pleading for the other's forgiveness. Becky didn't have to be asked too much. Both of them, like priests, poured out forgiveness. Made them feel good beating their chests, playing bad children, then soothing and comforting like good mommas. Good all over.

"Maybe it was my fault he left."

Becky plunging in. Rescuing.

"How could it be?"

"I don't know...but maybe."

"If it was, there'd be no maybe. You'd be sure...he had someone, and you don't. and you need someone, and he doesn't."

She wanted to believe. "You're right."

Becky bolder now that she was right. The words gushing. Mabel not listening anymore. Too tired but nodding her head here and there when it seemed right. They started up the stairs up to Mabel's apartment. Prolong the time. Talk some more. Get to know each other first.

"You'll have to excuse the mess," as she put the key in the door.

There was no mess, but she hurriedly picked up a paper bag and newspaper that was on the floor, rushed quickly around the room, arranging pillows and pushing a broom back in the closet that was stubbornly poking its head out.

To Becky, "Take off your coat."

Rushing into the bedroom and back again.

"The baby is still sleeping. Do you want to see her?"

Becky didn't, but she obliged and tiptoed in. babies didn't interest her. In fact, they repelled her a little. She was glad the baby was sleeping so he wouldn't have to hold her or be diapered in her presence. Becky recoiled while forcing herself to stay in the room. New mothers were so proud, Becky didn't have the heart to hurt them.

"See?"

Becky bent over the crib, the tiny hands and face repelling her. It opened its eyes a minute, wound its hand around Becky's finger and held it there. Becky stood motionless, miserable...smiling...

"Adorable...cute."

Mabel beaming. The baby yawned, body squirming in the blanket, it's face reddening... 'Arah...arah...arah.' Need cry. Mabel's face was stiffening now...in the efficient business of mothering, plunging a hand into the blanket...and...those dreaded words, "I have to change her. You know how to diaper a baby? Watch me. You'll learn."

A man's arm around me in black water under a full moon, the light touching my hair. Deep kisses on the beach. Soft violin, a voice whispering, "I love you, Becky."

She would turn like Lot's wife if she ever looked at diapers. They were for other kinds of women...like Ma or Mabel. She never saw diapers or bathrooms in the movies. They were never mentioned in the romance books. How do you look at the stars together and talk misty and soft and poetic, dream together...and diaper babies? Twirl graceful in a room full of rose bouquets and...diaper babies? Becky's mind spinning...ballrooms and lace, soft handkerchiefs on a white shoulder touching her carefully as if he's afraid she'll break, the baby digging nails into her finger...hard, hurting. She looked hard at the swinging toy above the crib while Mabel talked through a mouthful of pins.

"Delicious! Delicious! Delicious!"

Quiet now.

"Come. Let her sleep."

Becky unwound the little fingers from hers, the wetness nauseating her, and tiptoed out behind Mabel closing the door softly. Mabel turned round and opened it, again.

"Shouldn't close the door on a baby."

Becky looked round at the furnishings though she was not really interested. The sofa, a slab of foam rubber on a piece of wood, two large lamps on each side, an old, overstuffed, pregnant looking chair covered in faded, blue satin, bottom falling, spring showing. Mabel motioned toward the chair.

"Make yourself comfortable."

Becky sat down on the spring and suffered. She didn't want to embarrass Mabel. Dark. Only one light in the huge lamp. She hoped she would light the other lamp but she wouldn't dare ask.

"I'll make some coffee. Would you like some?"

"I would, thank you. Can I use your bathroom?"

"Of course."

Becky saw the diapers, swelled with air, puffed up like a balloon, floating in the sink. She couldn't go in and hide out of sight, returning before she noticed.

"Do you mind instant?"

"No, I love it."

Becky loved the sound of coffeemaking, the clink of a spoon twice on the cup. She never knew anyone who did it once. Woosh of water filling the cup and more clinking, spoon stirring.

"Milk and sugar?"

"Yes, thank you."

It wasn't light enough or sweet enough, but Becky didn't dare complain. Mabel unfolded two napkins and put a cup on each. 'To protect the table,' she said. Becky wondered if she had a tablecloth. Ma never had any. Mabel put the sugar in and stirred and kept stirring though she didn't have to anymore. When she talked, she kept turning the spoon, slow at the start and faster and faster as she was getting excited. She didn't drink. Not even a sip. Just stirred and stirred and talked. Becky could hardly see her face in the dim light, only her black eyes shining and the red lipstick all over her white teeth.

"I lost my mother when I was very little, and my father put me in a Catholic home. It's like I lost her now all over again. They were cruel to me and my sister Mary. To punish us, they made us sit on peas and stay out in the yard in a thin sweater in the winter...except when my father came to visit. Then they took a coat out from some-where and put it on me. That's the only time I ever saw that coat. He died too...a year after my mother...those nuns were meaner then. No one to watch or see."

She pounded the cup harder with the spoon.

"When I came out of there, I met this German and married him real quick. I'm Italian myself. He said I was sloppy and couldn't keep the house good."

Becky took a sip of coffee, ashamed to be drinking at a time like this. Mabel stopped stirring.

"Please. Drink your coffee. You're not drinking."

Becky, grateful and not wanting to be rude, took a big sip this time...burning her tongue and throat.

"It's hot. I'll let it cool some more."

Mabel didn't hear her.

"Then he met this girl in the office. She looks like a lady, proper and respectful. That's what hurt so much. If I could only say she's a whore. But she's not. She looks more like a lady than me. I look cheap. Not her."

"But you don't look cheap!"

Moaning now. "Cheap. I look cheap. I know I look cheap."

She did look cheap. Dyed black hair, wild around her face in little waves, bright red lipstick, black lines on her eyebrows, heavy mascara, dark rouge covering a heavy paste on her face to cover the pimples.

"But...didn't she steal your husband? Isn't that cheap?"

"No one can steal him. He pushed himself on her like he did me. I didn't like Germans. And he knew it. So, he pushed until he bent my mind out of shape, and I didn't know what I was doing. He did that to her, too, I'm sure."

The stirring stopped.

"Why am I boring you with all this?"

She got up.

"A fresh cup of coffee?"

"I haven't finished this one yet."

A cry from the other room.

"I know."

Mabel picked up Becky's cup and put it in the sink with her own, still full.

"I have to go to the baby. Will you wait? I'm only living for her now. I wouldn't want to do to her what my mother did to me. Take herself away when I needed her."

"Don't talk like that," Becky was frantic now. "Please."

"I don't usually. It's just...you're kind. I just knew you'd be scared and worrying for me and wanting to hold and comfort me like a momma would do if my face was long and I said I wanted to eat worms and die."

Mabel was talking about blood now and Becky was eager to give more, grateful she'd shown her the way.

"Don't worry, I'll worry...very hard until you're out of the woods. Your life has been so terrible, losing a mother like that...so young and no one to turn to."

They both shook their heads heavily. Becky commiserating.

Mabel in martyred agreement. Becky didn't know how to leave. She wanted to go before Mabel tired of her.

"I have to go to the baby. You can go if you want to. You don't have to wait."

Becky was mercifully dismissed.

"My mother must be worried."

"See you."

"See you."

She wondered when and if Mabel really wanted to see her again.

Mirele shouting, "Where were you?! The food is cold! Hang up your coat!"

Becky told her the story over supper.

"What is she, this Mabel?"

"Italian."

"Talener?! What kind of person is this?!"

Becky furiously pushed away the food and stormed into the bedroom...and waited...for Mirele to call her back. But she didn't. She sat there as long as she could then came out again and returned to the table. She ate in silence while Mirele nagged, admonishing her over and over again to be careful. That night, Mirele complained.

"Nice Jewish girls next door and Becky goes with goyim*."

---

* ***Goyim – Christians***

Chapter Seventy-One

Now Becky lives in a melting pot; all the insignificant people equally represented, the losers in all the minorities...Irish, Black, Puerto Rican and Jewish. The black neighbors next door with two homely daughters whose husband left her years ago and started gaining weight because it no longer made a difference. Ten years and she was still gaining. Her small mouth and eyes disappeared in a huge, round circle of fat and she panted and waddled when she walked, and could never point her feet straight ahead. Her breasts hung over her belly, and she covered the whole sorry mess with a flowered shift that was always wrinkled and dirty and slid up when she sat down so you could see the tops of her stockings rolled just under knees and she spread her legs so far when she sat down that you could see her panties. Becky wondered if she knew. She was too embarrassed to tell her. How do you tell someone such a thing? So when she saw her sitting on the bench, Becky's head snapped to the right as if she'd been slapped. She would be ashamed, Becky, not you...but she wasn't, and Becky was. So go make sense from the world. 'We should both be ashamed, her for showing...me for looking...even if it's accidental.'

Years later, Becky still saw ladies like that and wondered why they were so oblivious. Some of them had no garters and would roll the stockings below the knee making a little knot to hold them up. The knots only stayed for a little while. It seemed they were always rolling the stockings.

Becky tried it but she could never get the hang out. The knot opened right away, and the stocking went sliding down to her shoe where it flopped until she pulled it up again and rolled it and pulled one apart and twisted it round and round and tucked the point under until it bulged and walked a few steps while it was tight and then it fell down again. Sometimes, when she felt them slipping, she bent down and pulled them up again before they slipped too far. The neighbor's daughter laughed at her.

"Get a girdle, or a rubber band or something!"

She looked at their tight, straight seams and hated them. Even with a girdle, her stockings wrinkled, and rubber bands were dangerous. Bad for the heart. It stopped the circulation. And besides, aisle stockings were baggy by nature. We were at war with Japan. The rumor was that some girls were giving themselves to sailors for a pair of silk stockings. Becky couldn't talk to either of them. Not even talk. Mirele didn't mind. Friends were of no importance.

Next door, on the left there were black neighbors. A young girl with a baby and her mother. The husband was in the army. There was a rumor that she was pregnant again with a baby from another boyfriend. Becky was terrified just thinking what would happen when the husband came home and found out. But he never did. He was killed in battle. They emptied his pockets and sent everything home to his wife...whatever he had, in a big envelope. Folded in cigarette pack, a letter, 'With love and kisses, Stella. And all my love, Stella.' It was folded so you could see those words through the cellophane whenever he reached for a smoke. 'I miss you so much,' she told him and other personal things she never told anybody. She folded the letter and cried, 'Forgive me, Ben. I was just so lonely, afraid you'd never come back. And you didn't, didn't you? You said you wouldn't when you left. You had that feeling, you said. And you always kept your word, damn it! Always!'

And then above her was a Puerto Rican family, three boys and two girls, the little one just eight and very pretty, large black eyes, olive skin like her father, a tender, innocent frank gaze, a father a black shadow hovering over his face. Becky thought he was an evil man, just looking at him you could see it, the meanness. You knew just when he came home from work. Took his belt off the minute he came into the house, and all the children were screaming, while the wife stood in the corner, her head bent, holding the baby's head, and praying. The neighbor swore she saw it all from her window. Then, one night, Mabel whispered thinking that they were alone, and no one could hear.

"You know what happened, Becky?!"

"No, what?"

Mabel knew she didn't know but drew the story out so she could prolong the agony, like people do when they have juicy gossip. Mabel loved being on stage. Becky hung on every word. How else would she get attention? Who'd listen to her? She dragged it out as long as she could. Timing was important. Too long, and she'd lost her audience. The woman would get angry or revengeful or worse, having to rush away, cause it's getting late, and they have to do something for someone...kids home from school, husband home from work, dog to be fed. She became an expert at timing...like a comic knowing just when to drop the punch line.

"You mean you didn't hear?!"

Becky didn't want to appear vulgar or avid. Gossip was beneath her, she always said. But she was bursting already.

"No," she said, nonchalantly, heart pounding so she could almost see it.

After several more of the same, 'How couldn't you have heard?!', "You know the family on the corner?"

"On sight, that's all.

"Well, his little girl, sweet, you know she is, Becky..."

Terror was rising in her. Becky sensed the unspeakable about to break. She didn't know how she knew...but she did...even before she was told. Maybe the over-elaborate preamble, the hushed whisper as if something forbidden, evil, in the air, Mabel looking into the distance as if she couldn't face her with what she was about to say, didn't even know how to say it.

"He did her in, Becky, his own little girl! You know what I mean!"

She couldn't say it. The words unclean and revolting, strange and bitter in her mouth. Then she plunged in, "Raped Rosemarie."

Becky didn't even know her name until now. His own daughter! Shame creeping over Mabel. It wasn't amusing this time. Nausea now...trying to push her own story out of her mind. Too horrible to imagine, yet the imagination forced its way into her. Becky was terrified.

"Did they arrest him?"

"They did."

"Who called the police?"

"The neighbor. She saw it all. It happened so quickly that she couldn't stop it. And the mother. He beat her up before the police came because she came creeping in the child's room by accident and caught him. He said she was spying on him. It's good the neighbor saw because she told the police she didn't see anything, that they were breaking up her family. She said she fell, holding Rosemarie. He'll get 20 years, the police said!"

"They should put him away for life!"

Becky wouldn't sleep now for many nights. Tortured by images of that child and that big man splitting her. 'I can't stand thinking about it.' But nothing she could do to push them out. They came again and again for years.

"Don't tell me anymore," she pleaded. "Please, don't tell me."

But it was like she didn't hear her. She went on...about the knife. How he cut her from ear to ear, made an arc under her throat.

"She'll never be able to talk right anymore."

Becky pleaded, "Don't tell me anymore."

But nothing could stop her now. The excitement mounting. More needing to tell...and Becky cringing...groveling in pain and nausea and unable to move for fear of offending Mabel.

Suddenly, her familiar squeal, "Oh, I almost forgot, I have to feed the baby! Dismissed!"

Mabel liked that time alone. It was their time. Quiet. Intimate. Like lovers. The full, soft mouth touching her nipple, close, warm, comfortable, like loving should be...not like it was with Jim, worrisome, hurtful, silent repeating, '*and this too shall pass.*' 'Am I doing alright,' he'd ask her, grunting. 'You cum yet?' and she'd shake her head, rubbing her nose up and down on his heavy chest. 'Then it's okay now?' and he'd heave one big grunt and collapse on her. She really didn't know what he was asking, and he didn't either, but she knew somehow that she had to say 'Yes' to keep him happy. So why did he leave her? Did he find out she was lying? From someone else who knew better? Who wasn't pretending or was pretending but knew how to pretend better? She just heard how babies were made but none ever told her how love was made. Just babies. Didn't they think it's as much sin to make babies without loving as loving with babies? What's it all about without loving? Just taking and getting. Lust, that's all. And lust is what the church is against, isn't it?

Later Becky asked about Rosemarie. She married. Had two children. Her husband left her in a cold flat like Sylvia Plath...only she didn't write poetry...or become famous...or kill herself. She lost her mind altogether. Her father came to visit her in the asylum and she told him she had his baby but she'd never tell him where he was and he was stupid or crazy enough to believe her. After all, she was only eight at the time and he demanded to know where it was and she told him. He went to the building, and they say he was knifed by muggers in the hall, but they found all his money and rings on him, so it was strange...very, very strange.

There was an Italian lady on Mabel's floor with two boys that she wished were girls and she grew their hair long with curls around their faces. She waved her bleached, blonde hair in finger waves like the Flora Dora girls in the 20's. One son ended up on drugs and Sing Sing and the other in the chair for murder. She lost her mind, poor woman.

The ladies sat on the benches until supper-cooking time. Sometimes, they had dark glasses on when there was no sun. Grim, cloudy winter days when they'd come out for air and gossip...all lined up wearing dark glasses...from beatings their husbands gave them. No one left their husbands then. Just their minds went away as far as they could get. There was no crime there then, but there were policemen often rushing down the halls, curt secretive when you had the courage to ask them why. The children shushed and shunted behind doors to neighbors, mother handcuffed, carried, or pushed into an ambulance...screaming or numbed with sedation. Sick for a while. Be home when she's well. 'When?' 'Who knows?' Those were separations then and liberation...for a while. And when they returned, everyone was warned to shush and not to say anything.

The husbands were kind for a while and the children hovering and bringing and doing without being told for a little while and then, it began, all over again and we'd see her again with the dark glasses and sullen looks and children shouting from the windows, 'Maaa, Billy hit me, do something!' and the others shouting, 'Don't listen to him!' 'Shut up, both of you!' 'You shut up!' and the window slams shut. Hate twists her face. 'Wait until I get a hold of them! I'll kill them!' Her youngest flings open the door, the keys still in the lock, four others screaming, playing handball on the parlor wall, fighting. She falls. 'Ma!' She can't get up. Nothing broken, nothing hurts. The darkness embraces her again. It's quiet now.

The lady on the top floor with 6 children, very religious Catholic from the old country, 'Have a cup of tea, Becky,' she'd say, a kettle of water always warming on the stove. When she was mad with her husband, she'd call him, 'Himself,' and that was often. She complained he was 'too honest.' When the debtors came for their money, she wouldn't answer the bell, pretending not to be home.

He'd fling it wide open, invite them in for a cup of tea and explain he couldn't pay now. Next time, he certainly would pay...if he could. Once she told Becky the gremlins came in the middle of the night and washed the dishes. Mollie believed in spirits of all sorts.

Her big night out was Friday night. Becky cashed in the deposit bottles, and they went to the movies. A free dish on Friday had the place always crowded so just to be sure to get a seat, they'd sit on big wooden boxes outside a nearby grocery store until the show began. The streets were deserted then, but no one was worried. Nothing ever happened. Mollie's house was full of screaming, bickering, crumpled laundry piled everywhere that one of them was continually pressing. Becky hardened an old resolution...never to have children. There was no poetry in them.

The next building was swarming with sailors. She dated them <u>patriotically</u>. Necked a little...<u>patriotically</u>....and that's all. She stared at her face every day for some sign she was pretty. But what did it matter? Wrong place to be pretty, Becky. Black dust, trucks roaring by, shouting, screaming, a window is flung open, bare arms grabbing what she has lovingly tended and crashing it to the street below, watching it splatter, passerby cursing as they ground it under heel for getting in their way. 'That's the way of 'pretty' Becky, where it doesn't belong. They were all pretty once, Becky. Here, beauty needs to be avenged, the dark lady on the third floor, the blonde on the fourth, the Irish lady on the fifth.'

"You, see?" Mirele pointed out examples, twelve hands clutching Maria Riviera's apron.

A young face, deep lines around her mouth where the cries come and are silenced. An ordered will - the husband's.

"I can't stand a loud voice," he told her.

He was too old for her when they married. She was too old for him now. Jaunty, dapper, stiff, gray suit without a wrinkle, one foot on the chair for a final rub on the shoe.

"I want them so clean; I can see myself."

She stands by, a dress wrinkled, spotted, feeding the youngest.

"I'll be back soon," a pat on the first head that runs to him.

"Can't I come too, Poppa?"

"Later, Jose, later."

Mirele watches through the open door with Becky.

"You, see? No one knows he's married. Everyone knows she is!"

In the morning, the priest took a gentle walk around St. Edward's church. Becky and Mirele watched him from the window. While everyone else hurried, frazzled...the priest was benign, calm.

Mirele said, "You see, Becky. 'Not married.'" And she winked significantly. "No worries."

'Don't worry, Momma. who'll ever want me? Fat, ugly, and trying too hard to be smart.'

"Am I pretty, Ma?"

"You should go with a man with glasses. He can't see too well." And she'd laugh.

'My own mother can't say I'm pretty...and Poppa never...so what should someone else say?'

But sometimes Becky saw Mirele steal a few glances herself when she passed a mirror. 'Not bad Becky,' she'd say.

"You see, without powder and paint I'm still pretty," her lower lip disappearing in the gap between her two front teeth and still a good figure, and she'd pound her hard stomach that still bulged out like she was pregnant.

Mirele always looked like she was eight months pregnant.

"Good you, see?" pounding again and again.

"Hard, all muscle."

'Must be a gland,' Becky thought, 'that made you feel pretty all over. There was one that made you fat or skinny or short or tall, only not one that made you happy. She was sure she was born with wrong glands all over.'

Mirele said she wouldn't ask but she couldn't help it. The words spilled out, quick...like they were sitting on her tongue waiting to spring.

"When are you going back to school?!"

Becky left the question hanging in the air, hoping it would go away. Mirele encouraged and nags.

"No?! When?! When?! When?!"

"I just want to date boys, Ma. 700 sailors out there, and I want to date them all and maybe one of them will like me and I'll like him and...and...we'll get...married. Married, Ma! You hear? I want to get married!"

Yet even the thought of the ceremony embarrassed her. 'Why expose to the world something so personal...that two people want to be together. Why should they have to be gawked at by everybody? And foolish words said over them? When she really came down to it, she didn't know what she wanted. Well, maybe, to get married in a corner reading the ceremony to each other with no one there. Just us.'

Becky didn't meet the sailors at the fence. She went to Eddie's Tavern, a nearby bar that let you sit a whole night nursing one beer. Becky just had enough money for one beer. And the men would light her cigarette and start talking and sometimes, they'd walk her home and start talking and sometimes, they'd walk her home, or come in and stay a while...in the dark, kissing and struggling a little. She'd seldom see them again. Just once, mostly. But she could sleep 'til noon. Momma and Poppa rushing out in the morning. Fried bread that Ma left for her lunch in the pan on the stove.

"Stay home from work, Momma, a day. Just one day. One lousy day."

"I have to get to work."

And she'd hobble out the door, in a hurry. Momma lived in a hurry, and Becky slept, pushing the day away until the night...when she'd visit Mabel or have a cup of tea with Mollie or sit at Eddie's Tavern on a bar stool looking cheap and easy and being neither. The guys who knew her stayed away. The new ones came to find out. One night, she sat next to a girl with a smile like Mae West. She even moved her head in that slow, smart all-knowing way and her mouth up and down like she was teasing and taunting. A mouth soft, yielding...glowing with bright, red lipstick. Her eyes rolled wickedly when she talked, and she even rocked her hips. She had a heavy, round body, full-breasted, large-hipped and belly, but sensuous. She'd 'been around,' wasn't ignorant and backwards, like Becky, of the ways of men and women past kissing. Becky stared at her often when she wasn't looking. Always wearing a large hat with a veil, the new style, with a cowboy turn to the rim and a cleft in the middle. The men loved her hats and Becky did too, though she never had the courage to wear one.

One night they were sitting next to each other, and the bartender introduced them.

"Becky, meet Leona. Leona...Becky."

"What kind of name is Becky? You should change it to Belle."

More...and she rolled her eyes, her voice edged with authority, Becky submitting, smiling awkwardly.

"I guess you're right. You can call me Belle if you want to."

"A woman has no problem giving up her first name. It's her second one that's hard to give away. Right, Belle?"

Becky cringing, joining in the joke at her expense. A week later, Leona took her home to meet her mother. A railroad flat near Myrtle Ave.

"My father left my mother with five children and gave us nothing. Not even a thought...a birthday card once in a while, a phone call, even a death notice...nothing. We don't even know if he's still alive. But I'm madder at her than him. She's useless, fat, lazy, dependent on me, a kid, age 14 to go out and work. I watched babies, scrubbed floors. What I didn't do and she just took my money and misspent it all until I found a place to hide it and gave it to her a dollar at a time like she was the kid and I was the mother. Every time she croaks 'Leonchike' in that pathetic voice of hers, I know a touch is coming. I have to lay on floors, take abuse from drunk women who let it out on men when their hairdresser is out and someone else did a lousy job on their hair and that's all Ma has to do, is say, 'Leonchike.' A bum for a father, a parasite for a mother!"

Her voice boomed as it always did, but louder now that her mother would hear her.

"Go to work for Christ's sake! You've got nothing to do here. The place is a mess! Look at it! From here to there, she won't bend. 'Can't,' she says. More sickness than a medical library can hold…and some they never heard of!"

Her mother listened without a word, her huge, flabby face looking down at the hem of the dirty apron she was twisting… ashamed…not angry…but she was one of those who could live with shame as long as she didn't have to work.

"Please, *sha*, she'll say, begging me saying, 'I'm so tired.' Always tired! How tired can a person be?! Too tired even to die, I'll bet!"

Every time Becky visited, Leona made the same speech, then cooked and washed the dishes while her mother fiddled with her apron and looked pale. In the morning, she left her mother's money on the kitchen table and a pencil and paper to mark down what she spent. But her mother never bothered so they had a big fight at night, Leona demanded an accounting and she couldn't remember. Then, one day, she told her about the job she had in a fruit store.

"I fell in love with the boss, wanting him so much I fell on him in the back of a taxi one night and hit him so hard in the chest that he howled in pain and the taxi made a quick stop and then the driver smiled at my boss in the mirror and he smiled back and the taxi started up again and I couldn't stop loving him. That's the way it was with us. He had such a body! And then he left for the war, and I fell in love with his brother who looked just like him. I fell hard…and he did for me, too. God! He was delicious.

She put her arm between her teeth and bit hard, leaving deep marks.

"Delicious! Every bit of him!"

Becky went to sleep for months thinking about that scene in the taxi, trying to imagine waking up every morning with teeth marks deep in her arm.

"What's that, Becky? A bite? Someone bit you?"

"A dog, Momma. That's all. He didn't mean it."

She wore a nightgown with sleeves from then on.

Momma probing, "She's Jewish, your girlfriend?"

"Yeah."

"Does she go to school?"

"No."

"Does she have any talent?"

"A beautiful voice. Gorgeous!"

"So let me give her lessons."

Mirele giving the world lessons.

"She doesn't want any lessons."

"Just asking. Is it a crime to ask?"

"Sometimes, when a person is tired of being asked."

"Does she have a brother?"

"Yes."

"How old is he?"

"He'll be thirteen."

"Is he going to be Bar-Mitzvah?"

"No, there's no shuls anywhere here...for miles. Just bars, that's all. Between here and there must be 10 Jews and none of them every mention shul."

Even Mirele, the only thing she did Jewish since they moved to the Project, was to light candles on Friday night, create two sets of dishes when Zisme came back from Florida and hide her pocketbook when she went out on Shabbos though there was no one Jewish to see her, and sit on a bench Saturday doing nothing, like she was supposed to, with Poppa. Sometimes, when they were in the subway, Becky would see a very fancy lady shaking a blue can with a Star of David on it. She looked at no one, said nothing, just stuck the can full of coins. People got up sometimes to put a coin in the slot. That was the only time she ever saw them...Hadassah ladies, I mean.

Chapter Seventy-Two

Becky was grateful to people like Leona. Not much schooling. They made her feel smart. The really smart ones scared her. She never met anyone with a college diploma. She'd just close her mouth and never open it if she did. But with Leona, she could repeat the little philosophy she learned from Will Durant, just the simple stuff, of course, those few paragraphs from Schopenhauer, the cynical, worldly ones with just the right bite in her voice when she said them, and the Leona's would be so impressed.

For a whole month she did nothing but read Thomas Wolfe, and, like the movies turned her into a Garbo, Thomas Wolfe made her introspective, morbid, brooding, all the things that frightened her in somebody else, especially a man. How could you please someone who had such a heavy investment in being miserable as the core of his appeal? But it made her feel important, mysterious, so much more enticing than being a Marxist. Prince Charming would find her, and they'd live happily ever after <u>in love</u>. But then there was... love and Anna Karenina...love and Madame Bovary. She told Leona in one of their heart-to-heart conversations, how love frightened her, and no love frightened her, and money frightened her, and no money frightened her. Money means coldness, selling yourself and obeying and no money...slavery and humiliation, poverty, and degradation. And work frightened her and no work. And men frightened her because they were men and women because they were women. And dogs and cats, too. Dogs because they bite, cats because they have tantrums. And, most frightening of all, how do you take care of them? And children frightened her most of all. How do you bring them up? No one knew for sure. And marriage frightens her. And no marriage frightened her. And school was frightening 'cause she's not smart enough and no school frightened her because, 'You'll work in a shop!'

And Leona smiling that kind of smile that belittles, "You're scared because you have time to be. Your mother is out there carrying the load, so you have nothing to do but be afraid. I have no time to be afraid, for that kind of luxury, petting my fears and tending my complaints so they grow bigger, and I have more and more to be afraid of, so I have a good excuse for doing nothing."

Becky was especially afraid of Leona, but she never told her. That quick tongue, stinging. Becky said nothing back. She never could. Just stood there, hurting. So afraid to say anything that nothing ever even occurred to her to say. '<u>Lose her for a friend</u>! Afraid <u>not</u> to say anything, she'll never stop cutting and me like I'm flapping my hands all over trying to protect myself, so I don't feel, but she gets through anyway. There's no hiding from her...not for me, anyhow.'

Leona's recklessness with words and Becky's extreme care, dropping them gently, were no match for each other. Leona won. She strutted arrogantly about Becky, free and easy and Becky apprehensive, timid in a terrifying, uneasy friendship. She'd never really known any other kind.

Leona read the want ads religiously even though, "I don't know who would want my help. No schooling. Can't do anything really complicated. If the fruits and vegetables stop growing and then women do their own housework and watch their own kids, I'll be an unemployed chronic. But I look anyway, like I read the ads for penthouses I can't afford. I saw an ad for an accordion teacher at the Evans School. Why don't you try, Becky?"

"What do I know about music? I learned numbers, pieces, not music. I play pieces making the same mistakes in the same places for years, but the places I don't make mistakes in are because I've played it a million times over and over...plodding. I'm a plodder. That's all I can teach kids is plodding."

"Give it a try. What have you got to lose?"

"I don't know enough."

"Just give them ABC. For the rest of the alphabet, you'll send them to someone else or trick your way through."

"Never!"

"Does that mean you're afraid they'll find you out?"

"Maybe."

"Don't be silly. You know and you know it."

Becky waited for those crumbs.

"Alright, I'll try. But they might not hire me."

"Hiring is another story. That's a miracle. But trying...that's a must."

The next morning Becky called her old music teacher.

"I'm sure you can do it; I'll call and recommend you."

Becky was interviewed by a tall man who had a reputation as a ladies' man. He took her hand the moment she came in...and held it while he went to the other side of the desk to sit down, then moved back to the other side because he couldn't hold her hand across the desk. It was too big.

"Serge called me about you," he said. "But he didn't tell me how beautiful you are. You're hired to teach beginners. No problem. You don't have to be a Manganate to teach them. But then, you are an artist, your teacher said."

She trembled just hearing the word.

"Not really."

'Another reminder...life is not like the movies. Teaching five lines and four spaces, empty circles, and black circles, some with and some without stems. 'Mary Had a Little Lamb' over and over again. One and two and three and...over and over...and stamping the foot... stamping and stamping. 'Very good, Henry, Tad, Billy.' No matter, it was very good.'

The third week, Mr. U called her in, "I have a special treat for you. An adult lady, someone you can talk to. She's the daughter of a principal of a private high school down the block, place where you pay and pass, for kids who can afford it."

A soft knock on the door. He opened it and pulled the young lady in by the hand like he did Becky, but he looked very formal and serious now. She pulled her hand away. It dangled by her side. He let his dangle near hers.

"I want you to meet Miss Bromsky, our teacher, very fine, very fine."

Becky prayed, 'Don't build me up, please. An adult would know she didn't do much. What do kids know after all?'

Manganate – Great Accordion artist

"Can we start today? I'm anxious to start now. Can I hear you play first? I want to know what good playing sounds like."

Shaking, fingers trembling, she strapped the instrument on and played. The young lady applauded wildly.

"Wonderful! Marvelous! I wish I could play like that!"

She thought she played terribly. Forgot the final measures and just repeated the same page twice, adding a few emphatic chords at the end so it sounded like a finale. The young lady didn't know the difference. That was comforting.

At the end of the lesson, Becky said she wanted to return to school. Was her father really the principal?

"He is."

"Is school hard?"

"Very easy. For someone like you, especially. They had such dummies there, really!"

"Will they take me at my age?"

"They'll take you at any age. Especially you. You're so smart. Lots of kids there who aren't exactly in love with books, if you know what I mean...but neither is the school really. My father is one of those self-made men who runs the school for profit. He always wanted to be a captain of industry so he runs that dinky little school as if he were the head of General Motors, barking orders, terrifying everyone, seldom letting himself be seen, even by me, so he can play mysterious, and be awe inspiring, like he was God."

Becky wondered why she was telling her this, made her feel guilty, like she stumbled on something she wasn't supposed to see.

"It's no secret what I'm telling you. If you come to our school, you'll find out the first day. Everybody knows."

That night, Becky announced she was going back to school.

"I'll need 125 dollars."

"No problem," we'll borrow it from the Hebrew Free Loan Society, and we'll pay it back a dollar a week, maybe two. You'll get a diploma and be somebody."

"Who Momma? Who will I be?"

"Somebody!"

The following day, she registered.

Her pupil was at the desk answering the phone singing, "This is Evans Hall School," her voice drifting gently up and down and ending in the middle register, just the way her father ordered. Whoever answered the phone saying a mere 'Hello' was fired on the spot. He'd put a new person to the test. Call himself and if he heard, 'Hello' he'd come tearing out of his office bellowing, 'Who answered that phone?! You're fired! Now get out of here now!' And he'd throw a few bills at the offender and curse him while he scrambled to pick them up. 'You don't answer a phone around here like you've been disturbed in the tub. We're in business! The customer is king! Even though he knows that about us...how we treat him...expendables in school all their lives. They lived in ridicule and their mothers in shame. 'My son, the dummy.' But here, they're kings, from the first moment on the phone. We'll sing for our supper. Glad to do it!'

Strange about tycoons. You feel you have to watch every word or you're out, but they'd degrade and humble themselves in a minute if there was a profit in it. It was funny sometimes, to see Endicott Pilstein, chanting sweetly on the phone, smiling, like he was humoring a baby with a piece of candy, silliness spread across his face that snapped strictly as soon as he hung up the phone. He thought it was fun pulling the fools in with honey.

A lady with blonde hair and popping blue eyes too large for her face, heavy breasts, protruding stomach, and enormous legs who came into the front office to ask Elsie a question. She had a thick German accent.

Elsie introducing, "I want you to meet my teacher, Becky Bromsky, and Becky, I want you to meet your teacher, Tessie Wurstler."

Becky was still terrified by teachers, "Pleased to meet you. I have to leave now. A lesson is waiting for me...if you'll excuse me."

When Becky left, Tessie said, "They have music teachers here without a diploma from a Conservatory?!"

"She's teaching the accordion. That's not really music. It's for fun. To play folk dances...<u>oompah oompah</u> stuff. But she's very good."

"Americans! What do they know about what's good? Here it was supposed to be a good country. And they killed my father, a scholar who was German, a university professor, a writer of history books, a member of the Reichstag in the Communist party. He taught only two classes a week at the University and the rest of the time was devoted to his scholarship. He was a famous man one day and the next day...nothing. When the Communists defected, we fled to England. How many boring parties of English nobility we attended until we were worthy to send to America! And we looked to walk on gold the minute we arrived here. But my father was denied a position everywhere, even where his books were taught because he was a Communist in the old country. One small college finally accepted him and worked him to death. 12 hours a day he worked, his classes, every day, his scholarship, every day. He couldn't manage such a load. Died from overwork."

She hated America. She made not one friend in all the years since the family came here. Their politics, democracy, fairness, equality stopped at their front door. Inside, they were intangible and untangling alliances in the silly people they came from, petty vendettas and deceptions, wars, and peace treaties, fought, conquered, lost, compromised.

"Politics don't interest me, while they honed their schemes, manipulate skills like a diplomat, weaving in and out between rivalries and jealousies, pretending nobility and sacrifice and shaming both."

Tess wanted someone that was interested in politics, interested... in the world...as much as the living room. There was no one to debate with. Her mother was a 'hausfrau.' Like Becky, Tess was allied with her father.

"What did Momma know?" the two men said, while turning to their daughters.

Tess was firm in not associating with pupils. She occasionally had lunch or accepted a favor but, in Becky's case, she was considering making an exception. She was a teacher, too, after all. And maybe she knew a few men who wouldn't care about legs, wouldn't call her piano legs.

"Why don't we all go out for lunch tomorrow, Elsie, you and me, so you won't feel so strange."

Becky accepted. She had no money as she wasn't paid yet.

"I'll just have coffee."

Tess had hers without sugar, so Becky had hers without sugar too. Tess talked of Bismarck and Communists and Becky about her father and his socialism and then Tess of her father and velvet drapes and mahogany furniture and Becky bending her head and pawing the ground with one foot. Tess criticizing all the leaders arrogantly and Becky joining eagerly agreeing and sneering, too, how stupid they were. Tess liked that word, laughed so then she said it, mocking, cruel like she enjoyed so much their being stupid. Becky was terrified to think she really knows if she looks confident and is mocking and jeering, too. Different from Leona. One couldn't get away with a little borrowed cynicism from a dead philosopher. You really had to know something, and Becky didn't really think she did. Becky would die mortified if Tess laughed at her and called her stupid. She was afraid every minute that she would, or worse yet, find her boring. Becky strained to entertain, and Tess was amused...and interested. And when she asked what she did for fun and Becky said she lived near a building full of sailors, Tess was now a friend.

"Why don't you bring her home Becky?"

For the first time, Mirele was happy at the mention of a friend.

"A teacher? A person with some brains? Someone you can learn from?"

It never occurred to Mirele someone could learn from Becky. Even so, she wasn't interested in those types. Mirele lavished her gifts and goodness on others but wanted others to lavish their gifts and goodness on Becky.

Tess was eager to visit and have the sailors flirt with her too as she passed by the barracks. She heard it didn't matter to them what you looked like as long as it was a woman. They whistled and flattered 'Hello beautiful,' 'Hello cutie,' and sometimes they'd run to the fence and wait for the girls to come round and chat. There were two waiting for them that first night, both tall and blonde and blue-eyed. Becky put a cigarette in her mouth. She was so nervous as she neared the fence. Tess didn't smoke so she smiled as broad and wide as she could.

The fellow on Becky's side made a wide flourish over the fence with his arm and lit Becky's cigarette with his lighter. He watched quietly while she was intent on the light, puffing hard. A jovial, 'Hi smiley,' from the other fellow to Tess.

"My name is Ski, what's yours?"

"Is that your whole name?"

"No, I don't know you well enough to tell my whole name yet. If I tell you, I'll have to repeat it, then spell it, then repeat it again. Too much time wasted. I'd rather go on and tell you how pretty you are. Now tell me your name or do you want me to call you beautiful? I don't mind."

"My name is Tessie. Now, what's your real name? I insist."

He shakes his head 'No.'

"Okay, I'll settle for the abbreviations. Is that Sky or Ski?"

"I."

"Polish."

"And where are you from?"

"Escaped from Germany. Refugees."

"I figured as much."

Becky's fellow said, "My name is John...John Major Bell is my full name."

Becky was impressed with middle names. She never knew anyone who had any. Sounded so...fancy.

"Mine's Becky."

"Becky what?"

"Becky Bromsky."

Her face lowered, shamed. It sounded so awful next to John Major Bell."

Tess's fellow turned to Becky.

"You're a Ski, too? Imagine that. Two Pollacks. My father is from Russia."

Sounded so much more sophisticated. Everybody was a Jew from Poland, but Russia...so much more...important. Anyway, the place he came from changed hands every day from one to the other so what difference did it make, what she said.

"Where in Russia?"

Poppa came from Sevak and Ma from Minsk. Minsk was really Russia, so she said, 'Minsk.'"

"Oh," he said, as if he knew.

He really didn't and only asked because he couldn't think of anything else to say.

"We have to go now. My mother is expecting us."

"You live here?"

"Yes, with my parents."

"Are you an only child?"

"I had a brother, but he died."

"Oh," sad for a moment, for her, then himself.

"I'm an orphan myself, my aunt raised me herself."

"Oh," Becky chimed in.

"I don't know why I told you that."

"I don't know why I told you either."

"I guess we felt friendly a little too quickly. Sometimes people do, but not me. Must be something about you."

"You too," Becky lied.

She wanted his sympathy and that is what it really was. It made her feel good all over, like he cared. Maybe he did, too. Maybe that's why he told her. Because he needed her feeling sorry, like mothers do over their children.

"Can I have your phone number?" Becky nodded.

He crumpled his cigarette pack and threw it to the ground. He bent down and picked it up again, tore open the inside, smoothed it out and wrote. Next to him he was writing Tess's number on an empty matchbook.

Later, when they were alone, Tess said, "They'll probably throw them away, just did it to make us feel good."

"Maybe."

Shame. She gave her number away so easily.

"He must think I'm cheap. Just tricked me to show what he thinks of me."

How many times did Becky give her phone number on how many scraps of paper and pads and cigarette packs and match covers scribbled on by men who threw them carelessly away with the laundry or forget even who she was, but made her feel so wanted when they pleaded for it and flattered and cajoled and filled her with so much hope? But who else ever did that Becky? 'No one until now. I'm grateful for that bit of wanting. It's more than I ever had,' she said to herself while Tess smirked and smirked, how proud she was and how they couldn't fool her and all that. 'I don't care if they fool me,' she thought. 'As long as they ask, I like them asking. Suppose they never asked, Tessie? Not even <u>that</u>? How would you feel then?

But she said nothing. Gave up right away. Tess always had the last word. Becky was always terrified to say anything more when Tess was so definite. The punishment was swift and severe.

"Stop being so stupid!"

Not even a thought dared to find its way into her mind, then. Blank and terror filled. The little girls brought you to your knees Becky, then the big girls and now the women.

Mirele sprang up to greet them as soon as they came in. Poppa shook her hand and she barely sat down before he quoted the Jewish Forward. That was Poppa's way of saying, 'Hello,' discussing the Russian front.

And she heard him saying, "The Russians should go into Germany and stay there and never get out! Germany started two wars, it's dangerous. It'll start ten more!"

Tess jumped out of her seat.

"I'm sorry, I have to go."

Enraged. Becky was frightened and nervously followed her.

"I'm sorry, Ma, we have to go. Poppa called goodbye after them as they left."

In the street, Tess turned on Becky furiously.

"He's stupid, your father! He trusts the Russians to take over and thinks they'll stop there! It'll only whet their appetite!"

Becky was burrowing frantically for words, scared silent. 'Defend Poppa? He was stupid if Tess said so. Not just ashamed of me, Poppa, but you too, now. I wish I was dead!'

"We'll be too late for Eddie's Tavern, Becky. Let's hurry."

Becky rushed ahead.

'Hurry, horsey Becky. Giddyap! Giddyap! Horsey Becky. Let's play Horsey Becky. Giddyap! Fat horse!' Becky neighed and they'd slap her thighs and say, 'Faster, Becky! Faster!' And when she got so tired, she couldn't gallop anymore, she'd go 'Neigh' and toss her head and fall on all fours. The kids loved that. 'Again, Becky. Again!' 'Hurry up, Becky! Faster. It's getting later and later.'

"Sure, Tess." And she slapped her thighs and galloped and slapped and galloped.

"What are you doing Becky?" asked Tess laughing, "You think you're a horse?"

And she slapped in rhythm on her other leg…and Becky galloped faster and Tess slapped harder and harder, stinging so hard it hurt Becky badly, but she didn't make a sound because Tess was laughing so she couldn't stop and Becky was glad she was making Tess laugh.

Chapter Seventy-Three

Leona was already there when they arrived. She smiled her wickedest smile, rolled her eyes, hands on squiggling hips, her voice coming through her teeth, swaggering around the bar stool and holding a sailor's hand while she circled.

"I want you to meet my new man, Harry Dix, meet Becky Bromsky and Tess."

Dix ordered beer for all four. Then ordered more and more for himself while Tess and Becky coddled the same one for the rest of the night, refusing any offer of another. They both hated beer but had to sit with something in front of them all evening.

Tess turned to Leona, "I like your lipstick."

They exchanged tips about makeup, the sailor not really caring what they were talking about. He was downing one beer after another to show how much he could drink without getting drunk. Tess had her back turned to Becky and Leona didn't say a word to her. They forgot she was there. Becky watched while they left heartily and had a corking good time.

She put a cigarette to her mouth, two lighters flying in front of her, male laughter, then, "Can we buy you a drink?" and the other said, "You got a friend?"

Tess circled suddenly, squealing "Becky! Why didn't you say something?"

"I want you to meet my friend Tess."

He introduced himself, "Jack."

He shook her hand and held it.

"And your name?" the man beside Becky asking.

"Mine's Becky."

His right arm was in a sling. Said he fell and shook her hand with his left hand and asked to be excused. She could feel the marriage band. He was careful not to give his last name. Becky talked politics with him. He pretended to be interested. She thought all men were like Poppa. They liked women who they thought had brains. Becky strained on trying to impress him.

"You're too serious," he said, "anyone ever told you that?"

"Everyone."

He was instantly contrite, "I didn't really mean anything."

Becky responded instantly to a command and started being witty, told him a funny story, some of it true, most of it she made up. He was so much more comfortable then.

"Can I take you home, little Becky?"

She liked that, 'Little.' No one had ever called her <u>that</u>. 'But he's a married man.' She thought she shouldn't be talking to him at all. Though she hated trudging home alone, she had her principles! Poor wife waiting and he...she didn't mind talking to a lonely serviceman but...take her home! Never! What did he think she was?!

"My boyfriend is coming to pick me up."

"Oh."

He turned his back on her, shouting to the bartender, "Another whiskey and chaser over here!"

"Coming up!"

And two skilled hands poured and put the two glasses down with the care and reverence of holy water. He drank it down, taped his friend on the shoulder, and said, "I'm going. See you again, Jack."

The other nodded, still riveted on Tess. Becky alone again, watching her. Tess's eyes shining, alive and vital like she never was when she talked to Becky.

"I guess I'll go too, Tess. See you."

And she pushed the barstool, so it made a loud noise...grating the wooden floor. Lottie nodded slightly. She waited for the usual good-bye, see you tomorrow, be careful getting home, but they were both oblivious. As she opened the door, a blast of wind so fierce it nearly forced her back in but she fought her way out just to save a bit of remaining pride, her feet freezing in the open-toed shoes she wore, the cold stinging through coat. She knotted her hands into fists in her pockets and held them close to her body to keep out the wind, but it found it's way to her throat. Cold, dark, no stars, darker than fear, like the world was gone and only she was left. She never took this walk alone before. She kept her eyes on those square little lighted boxes in the distance. That was home. Then she turned and looked at the moon, remembering the game she played as a child. She'd stop and the moon would stop too. It was like it was there watching her. Moons were friendly. 'Watch me, moon,' she'd say. A car passed without headlights. She wanted to holler, 'Hey, you forgot to turn on, but she didn't,' then turned on herself for being lazy, then frightened, 'Suppose something happened to them, it would be her fault.' Another car. Lights shining right on her. She hoped they'd stop and ask if she wanted a lift, but they didn't. 'I should have put my thumb out like in the movies.' She ran after the car, but it sped out of sight. She dug her head deeper into her collar and pressed it against her ears, the bright yellow handkerchief too thin to keep out the wind, but it attacked wherever it could. 'Help me, God. Help me get home, into bed, under the covers. That's all I want. God. Please. This is <u>Hell</u>...walking in cold, dark, wine...forever on a small road between two empty lots and never getting home. The fear was growing now. 'Think good things, Becky. Communism, that was good. Rich, no good. Poor good. Black good. Roosevelt good. Beautiful, good. Skinny good. Smart good. Soon I'll have a diploma. That's good. So, what will I do with it? I'll be wandering with or without a diploma between two empty lots, with or without a sailor to take me home and neck with me until three in the morning when he gets tired and gives up or doesn't get any fresher that I let him because he hears Ma and Pa in the bedroom getting up from time to time and opening and closing the door so we know they're there. But they wouldn't say anything because the doctor said so.'

'Let her do what she wants,' he says. So, they were letting her.

'I want a diploma, but I don't really want to go to school. I just really want to date fellows and neck until 3am and get up at 3pm and get dressed up and date again and I want someone to ask me to marry them. Just say the words. I don't even know if I'll want them after they say it. Just want to hear it once. Now that's something good to think about. But I guess I never will and that's not so good.'

"Excuse me," a male voice from behind.

She was so grateful.

"Yes?"

"Can you tell me where the navy yard is?"

"Of course."

And she smiled the 'glad to be of help to a serviceman smile.' Nothing pleased her more than earning dribs and drabs of love and gratitude wherever she could. She could hardly see him until the light of a passing car flitted over his face. His sailor's hat was over his forehead touching his eyebrows, almost covering his eyes. His nose was large, his mouth huge, a big head, large round face on a small, squat body.

"Two block right and one left."

He grabbed her hand and squeezed it very tight.

"Thank you."

And he rushed off. She wished he would have stayed and walked with her, just a little. It hurt the way he ran off so quickly. As if he couldn't wait to get away from her. A car passed, splashing her coat.

She lingered on the corner. Across the street...and home. Suddenly not wanting to be there. No pictures, no curtains, a tablecloth, a doily. The bareness of a prison cell. But what have we done? She hated the house when she was the only one awake. Mirele and Phillip, not shouting at each other... now turned away from her, alone with themselves. Comfortable, snug, unknowing alone. And Becky now...child crying in the dark...alone. Mink's Bar blinking at her.

She never set foot in there again after she heard him say, "I'd never let my wife and kid in a place like this."

She walked out dragging her feet like she did when she was ashamed.

A passing sailor calling out, "Hi, honey. How about a drink?"

His 'How about it, honey' followed her around the fence, then stopped. She wanted to turn, go to Mink's, but the shame returned. She crossed the street and opened the front door.

"Hi," a man's voice in the darkness.

"Remember me?"

"Oh yes, you're the fellow who asked for directions. Did you find the Navy yard?

He grabbed her by the throat, his mouth stiff with hate, his face all eyebrows, fierce and ugly, "I want you, see!" Shaking her hard back and forth, "You're going to give me what I want, you little bitch or else."

She fell against the wall, whimpering, "Let me go. Please let me go."

He dragged her, flinging her from one side to the other. For a moment he let her free and a wild laugh burst from him as he watched her tear open the elevator door, then shoved her in.

"Let me go. Please, let me go." Crying, pleading, over and over.

His hand pressed the back of her neck hard.

"Touch me! Touch it!"

He pushed her head down and there _it_ was...in front of her... huge, hard, black, and being pushed into her face.

"Please, please, please...let me go! Lemme, lemme, lemme... GO!!!"

And he suddenly threw her head against the wall.

"Ah, to hell with you!"

Bitter, he marched out. Behind the easy smiles and flattery, jaunty white hats and...terror now, gentle kiss goodnight, 'Yes Mam,' and 'No Mam' and terror, opening and closing of doors and walking two steps behind and...terror...is a man who asks for directions. She didn't open the light when she came in the door as she usually did.

"Is that you, Becky?"

No answer.

"Are you alone?"

No answer.

She tried to make a sound but couldn't. Then a whisper.

"It's me, Ma."

She wouldn't dare open the light. Maybe he was out there looking. He'd know where she lived. He'd come back!

"I'm going to look for him! If I find him, I'll kill him!"

And her body shook with silent sobs...no one should hear, 'the first time and it had to be <u>like that</u>!' she'd always avoided, ashamed, frightened...that part of a man. But she dreamed and feared that... someday...new life, a far-off place. And <u>someday</u> suddenly came and went.

She never told Leona or Tess. Couldn't tell anyone. Later, she separated him from the rest. They were still loving and sweet like they'd always been. She hated him. Only him. Becky couldn't hate more than one. Her heart wasn't in it.

Chapter Seventy-Four

The Sergeant at arms snapped orders when he heard her story the following morning. Becky felt very important. The building emptied. The men lined up and marching before her like she was a drill sergeant, and they were being inspected. Suddenly, being a civilian was more important than being a sailor, martinets barking and snapping, not in anger, but authority... absolute...to accommodate her. But he wasn't among them. She was grateful to men again...pleased and protected. She shook her head, 'No.'

He barked, "Dismissed! If you have any more information let us know. We'll keep looking until we find him."

"I don't know how to thank you."

Trusting. Warm...again. Still trusting. That fright dumb and sleeping now. The others, still there. Afraid the men will tire of her, laugh at her, leave her for someone else, touch her where they're not supposed to...only ears, neck, and waist...never hips or God forbid... breast. If they make me shudder like he did, what's left? No magic, no flattery, no hope, no nothing. When she finally told Tess, a tirade.

"If I man did that to me, I'd find him and...kill him! Don't you want to kill him?!"

Tess narrowing her eyes and puckering her mouth and glaring at no one in particular. And Becky now hating him with her. Comrade, brother love hate, united as one...love-hate.

"Of course, I hate him."

Becky narrowing her eyes, puckering her mouth, and looking hard like Tess...who is looking at her with respect for the first time. Becky would be complaining and righteously indignant as often as he could from now on. It pleased Tess. Hating together.

Becky exulted hating with her...united...finally as one with her friend. Two against the world. Tess reveled in abstract, philosophical bloodletting and Becky joined her in an orgy of damnation...our leaders, countries, our past, present, future...but...the pecking order was still there...tearing into Becky if she needed a victim for the day.

"You better give it to the next guy who calls. If you couldn't give to the one who deserves it, you give it to the other. Long as he's a man...ha, Becky? Somebody should pay for that scoundrel what he did, no? I have to go now. A class waiting and you're in it, remember?"

She was a teacher now. Becky rushed to open the swinging door and waited for permission to speak. Tess was silent. Becky was sure she was bored with her. Frantic...for a few words to fill the empty space to the classroom door. But it was useless. A few words came to mind and rejected...too dull...too meaningless. Tess suddenly turned away.

"You'll have to excuse me. I have to see something. I'll be right back."

Becky was dumb...silent.

"Don't leave me, Tess."

Reprieved, "See you soon, Becky."

The whole lecture, Becky waited for Tess to look at her special. Becky liked being the class favorite. Yet, she didn't want to take advantage. Embarrassed her. Like she wasn't entitled if Tess looked

<u>too</u> often. The class ended. Tesswas surrounded by pupils asking questions, while Becky was waiting humbly outside the circle. Jimmy passing...a student.

Tess called out... "Jimmy, wait."

He stopped and turned, spinning round on one foot, an easy grin spreading across his face.

"At your command," smiling the words.

The students turned, forming a line. He lingered. She dismissed him.

"Tomorrow we'll discuss that in class."

He came in and sat down on her chair, swiveling from side to side. She vented over him talking softly and then they both giggled.

Becky waved, "See you tomorrow."

Tess didn't even hear her. She walked slowly wretched with jealousy. 'I have a friend that's good enough for me now, Ma, but she's killing me because I'm not good enough for her.' Her Ma is saying, 'What kind of friend is <u>that</u>?' 'Me, Ma. I'm a <u>that</u>. Not a she. A <u>that</u>! Tess told me she stood up for me. 'You have to be nice, Becky and good and smart and perfect you always said, Ma, but you didn't tell me the rest...that I had to be explained and defended and apologized for and shed tears and slam doors for. When the Lord made me, he didn't make a job to go with it, a friend. No entitlements. Not one friend, brother, sister, job...and others don't know which one they like best. There were so many. Love is...like scorns and humiliates him, betrays and abandons him. That's real love...not wanting, giving to others but being flirty and gay and reckless but still adored and waited for...always...over and over. In a haze of enchantment now until Ma came, banged on the door, 'You're smoking. I can smell it! She'll kill me this child!"

Becky jumped up, flung the cigarette out the window.

"I'm not smoking!"

"You are!"

"I'm not!"

"So, open the door and come out!"

Mirele shuffled back to the stove in her winter coat. Becky heard sounds of Ma home.

Pots clanging on the stove, water running, scraping of carrots, then hangers clacketing on the floor, Ma always in a hurry dropped it and then hung her coat on crooked anyway, then muttered in Yiddish, "To hell with it!"

Poppa threw the paper on the table, his coat on the chair.

"Hang it up!"

Poppa opened the paper.

"Mirele, the news is bad."

She strains to listen while running from sink to stove.

"Bah! What do you know? To you, I'm talking?! Where's Becky?"

He calls and Becky opens the door. Her window was wide open. Momma was sniffing hard.

"What is that draft? Close the window."

Before she reaches the window, the wind slams the door shut loud and hard. Phillip drops the paper.

"Are you crazy? You'll break the door!"

In the movies they talked so quietly to each other.

"Hell with the damned door! What are you afraid of?! Always afraid of everything! Even a door! How the timid hate the weak. A victim starved for victims turns on it's own mercilessly. Afraid of an icebox, a door, even the floor. Don't drop your shoes like that, you'll damage the floor," he warned.

At night, they counted their money in fear. If the income was too high, they'd be evicted. Momma lied. Afraid of the landlord. This one would evict you if you could pay the rent. Whether they <u>could</u> or couldn't pay, <u>rent</u> was a stone in the heart. They were still eating on the prison-gray bridge table, rickety by now. The soup spilled in little puddles around the plate because Ma filled it to the brim, then banged into the table. The phone rang. Becky eager to answer jumps up.

Mirele insisted, "Sit down. They'll call again whoever it is."

Becky is frantic and listening hard. Each ring may be the last.

Then, springing from the table, breathless, "Hello!"

Mirele mumbled, "Won't even let her finish eating."

Becky is desperate the caller shouldn't hear.

"Becky."

"Yes?"

"The caller, it's Tommy. Remember me?"

"Yes."

"I was wondering if you're busy tomorrow night. I'd like to see you. I know it's short notice for a Saturday night date...but could you?"

"I'd love to. I have nothing to do tomorrow night."

She just knew he'd like that she wasn't playing busy. Think her unusual...honest.

Later, he said, "I liked that about you. You didn't play games with me."

Men get tired of begging and waiting...just like women do.

Just like the movies, he was at the door smiling, holding a box in his hand, a white flower.

"Put it on."

She struggled with it, the little pin. Her first flower. It insisted on slanting crooked. Laughing made it alright. Then he pulled out a lighter, flicked it several times, a gray metal shiny one. She never had one. Was always out of matches.

"That, too?"

She heard Mirele coming and threw it in her bag quickly. They giggled like heavy conspirators. He was pleased that Becky worried about Mirele seeing.

"Where should we go to eat? I'm new here and I don't know too many restaurants."

She didn't know anyone either. Tommy was her first date. She'd take over a beer for hours at Eddie's Tavern and then they'd ask to take her home and she'd let them, and they'd leave at 3am, both faces smeared with lipstick and Becky's face especially red from the beard. Face burning, but she never said anything. Suffered in silence. Or she'd just talk to them across the fence, invite them home and they'd say 'Sure' and hop over. She'd never been asked to a restaurant. There was a place with a big dragon on the window near the school. It had red doors and a roof like a pagoda. She'd always wanted to go there but never dated. Couldn't afford it.

"Maybe it's too expensive, I don't know."

"Don't worry about that."

But she would anyway. Couldn't bear spending someone else's money. In her world, no one had any.

Inside, hushed silence. The waiter bowed and walked, without a sound, to the table, Becky's heavy clumping behind him. She bounced up and down several times while he slid the chair under the table. Becky ordered the same dish she ate with Mrs. Novie, the 35 cents special, chow mein, fried rice and an egg roll, 80 cents now, and egg drop soup. He ordered the same. She was careful not to slurp her soup and slanted it away from her at the end. How she hated to eat in public with strangers. How she loved to gulp her food, both sides of her mouth bulging.

"You don't eat much, do you Becky?"

She'd always wanted to be someone who doesn't eat much, who finds food a necessary evil. Not eating seemed so aristocratic. She snapped her head to the side and shrugged her shoulders. He concluded she doesn't eat much. She loved to think of herself as a small eater, picky, uninterested in food, like the fancy ladies, instead of the glutton she was. She found it easy to play-act a small eater with Tommy, so frightened she could hardly eat. He would see she had no manners. No one ever taught her any.

The fork trembled in mid-air. She wanted to gobble the food quickly and hide the fork again under her food, but she watched it tremble, miserable, but chatted gaily so he wouldn't notice. But he did. And she didn't notice. Thought she was so sweet and shy. 'Afraid of <u>me</u>. Wanting to please me and trying so hard. She's a tryer. I like that. Not one of those laying back waiting to be amused...me to amuse her. I can't do that. Amusing is not my style. I'm not like those chatty Northern Yankee men that get a girl like they're selling an automobile. I'm an old-fashioned guy who likes a tidy girl...but not too tidy...not like Texas girls, not like Aunt May Lou with a face with a permanent freeze from disapproving of everything outside the church doors and Dotty Ann who never set a foot anywhere that doesn't have a bar and has a tongue and body to match...both loose and proud of it. Both pushing it in your face and being arrogant about it. One that's never with a man and the other that's never without one. Cutting words, both, whips inside, had you cringing.'

And here with Becky...trembling...because of him, straining to be liked, all her feathers spread before him in extravagant color, vivid, alive, bursting with warmth and...humble. He tried to talk but the words died in his throat. He couldn't interrupt. He was taught it was impolite and all around him there were talkers who never stopped...so he never interrupted and became a listener. And now he wanted so much to be talking, some wit, a dash of charm. He hoped she'd ask him a question or two. That always helped.

Finally, "Where do you come from?"

"Texas. San Antonio."

He waited for another, but she didn't ask...so he did.

"Do you have brothers or sisters?"

"I had a brother, but he died. Do you have any?"

"I have a sister."

And then, the push of more words, "We're orphans. My mother died when we were born and my father soon after."

"Who brought you up? Were you in a home?"

Digging her nails in the tablecloth, making white scraggly lines.

"No, my aunt. She's unmarried. She raised us."

'Never know a mother or father. Must be awful!'

He looked up.

"I'm sorry I'm talking about myself. You were saying about Roosevelt..."

So, she went on talking about what she thought made her interesting, what Poppa and she talked about. But Poppa talked back, and he didn't. He seemed...boring. It worried her a little. 'How long could she entertain him without a little help?' They opened their fortune cookies. She read hers to him and then he read his to her. They both laughed like they really didn't believe it, but they did.

"Can I take you home?"

A scary question to Becky now. 'What did he expect for dinner? Maybe he spent as much as...four dollars if you include the tip.' Beyond necking, she knew nothing else and wondered if she really knew that...and wouldn't even if she really did. Her back arched and body turned from groping hands without her even thinking about it. Leaving the restaurant, going down the stairs, both silent, blushing. Then Becky talking, faster and faster, thinking, 'he likes me really. Not just sailor liking, but real liking.' They both walked with hands in their pockets staring at the ground. She counted cracks and jabbered on about school.

"Would you believe I'm graduating high school tomorrow?"

"I graduated but I never went on. Went to the sea because I like it. Beautiful, standing on deck at night alone, looking out at sea, just the moon and you...if there is one. If not...not."

She shuddered. 'Staring out alone at black water in a ship at night where the only sign of warm life is that little island, you're on?!'

She said, "It must have been very beautiful...but I like solid earth under my feet the most."

"That's because you don't know."

"I guess."

Then another flood of chatter spilling out. She was grateful she found a well spring that flowed and flowed until they reached the door. Then silence. She turned. A grateful smile. Determined to look friendly, warm, beaming.

"Thank you for a lovely evening."

Smiling. "Thank you."

Extending a hand. He knew she was nervous. The silence fell so sudden. She put out her hand to shake his. He was glad to see it tremble. It made him feel good. Confident. Sure, of himself. He took her hand and held it steady. She let him. He could feel the blood pulsing through his glove and hers. He was courteous. Scared her even more.

"Can I kiss you goodnight?"

She bent her head to put the key in the door. So embarrassing saying, 'Yes,' and she couldn't say, 'No.' No one had ever asked her before. They just put an arm around her in a certain way and they both knew. That's what manners are for...so you can't eat or kiss or anything, it seems.

"Can I?"

She stared at the keys. Then jingled in the lock. She couldn't turn it.

"Can I?"

Cringing. Shamed. She turned the key again. The door opened, the hall light making an arc in the dark room. She went as far as the rim of light. He followed, closed the door quietly and they were in blackness. He put a gentle arm around her, and she turned, her head up to his, and touched his mouth. He put his other arm around her and pressed her tighter. She arched her back and put her hands on his shoulder, then they parted, and she nestled her head on his chest and sighed. He opened the door again, so a sliver of light came through. She felt nothing as always, but this time, because she saw the joy on his face, she pretended, a face full of rapture, he beamed even more, relishing his power over her. She made him think he could just touch her, and she'd burst into flames. 'That's the secret, Becky, pretend.'

"Can I see you again?"

"Yes."

"When?"

"Anytime you say."

"Tomorrow night."

"Fine."

She stumbled apart from her as if she could stand with the power of emotions he released in her. He sat her down on the sofa, kissed her gently on her hair, tiptoed out the door.

The window coming through the ill-fitting window frames. Becky shivering through her coat, thinking, 'It's hard on them, having to go out in the cold like that. At least we women can stay home.' She didn't want to turn the light on. Ruin the mood. She felt her way along with her hands into her bedroom, threw her clothes on the floor, not to make a noise. The bureau drawer squeaked so, and it stopped midway to push hard. Made such a bang when it closed, it always woke Pa. 'Stop banging,' he'd holler, and fall asleep again.

Becky thought in bed, 'He's nice but he's so boring. Why doesn't he have Southern manners and Poppa's tongue? And what will I wear tomorrow? And what will we talk about?' She fell asleep and dreamed. An old dream that kept coming back since she was a little girl. She was walking on the boardwalk when the sea flowed over, and it covered the beach and the boardwalk. She was running and the sea was coming after her. She awoke fearful, her fingers dug into her pillow like she was holding on and there was nothing below.

The next morning, Mirele waited for her to get up.

"Becky, I have something to tell you. I think Poppa may be sick. Good and sick!"

Annoyed, "What's the matter?"

She didn't really want to hear that now.

"He went to the clinic this morning."

"Maybe he ate something that doesn't agree with him."

"I hope so."

"I have to go to work. I just wanted you to know."

Becky's mind turned the moment Mirele left. 'What will I wear tonight? What in the world will I wear?'

Chapter Seventy-Five

The Cossacks and the bosses and the no bosses, the wife, the children, the refrigerator at home and at work, the war. Always, the war. 'Since I'm born Becky,' he always said, 'I can't remember if there should be no war. Not a day somewhere, no war.' And Poppa worried about every war. He was taught to hope for peace and fight for it and someday it'll come, and people really want it, and all the things that made him pant for it like Tantalus after his grapes. No matter how many times he was thrown from the mountain, he still snapped his head up and dreamed, <u>if only</u>...then.

The world fits into Poppa's head so nicely, like the memory of an old love affair. The world was Poppa's passion. If he could have faith in it not betraying him time and time again, he could maybe suffer Mirele and Becky and the neighbors, the bills, and the government a little better. At least, Becky thought so. He talked of nothing else. It was the drama of his life. When the war ended, Poppa was jubilant like she'd never seen him. He liked the Morgenthau plan.

"The Germans should be farmers forever, scraping the land planting potatoes, or, better yet, kill them all. Wild packs of dogs that prey on innocent sheep, they kill once, twice, and you left them alone to kill a third time? No! you get rid of them once and for all!"

Poppa talking that way now?! Even Poppa?! And the Russian Bear swallowed Eastern Europe.

"Who cares about them? All antisemites! Let the Bear choke on them!"

"Get rid of them too, Poppa?"

He'd throw his paper on the floor, stamp on it, leaving the black imprint of his shoe, his face glaring hate.

"That's what I think of it all! The whole damn world! Fit only to wipe my feet. This is the only mark I'll ever leave on it. The Stalins walk on the world like giants. But me, walk in my living room on the Daily Forward. To me, nobody listens. Not even you anymore, Becky. You know, thank God, more than I do. Momma listens to me. What does she know? She's an example of a listener! You have to have brains even to listen good. Sometimes I ask her 'so what did I say?' And she tells me back something, not that I never said, so I holler on her. She hollers back and I holler louder and she's quiet. She listens to good things like, 'shut up already' and she shuts up...sometimes. That's listening. Listening is when you say something back like what a person says. Like you. If I talk about Europe, you're talking too about Europe. Or even shaking your head once in a while and saying nothing. With her, what I say doesn't go between the ears to the brain but between the teeth to the tongue and the tongue by itself wags and flags and runs. It doesn't know what to do with itself...like a wild horse."

"Maybe if you listened, Poppa, she'd get the point."

"I'm listening, Becky."

And she knew she changed the subject. Dread on his face now.

"Something out there, Becky. It's coming. I can feel it."

And he touched his heart, "Right there."

He sang 'Hatikvah' for years, for a land that doesn't exist. Blood in his eye when he sang it.

"You hate the British too, Poppa?"

"Them?! Of course! Even a dog they wouldn't send back to an owner who beats it, but Jews, they sent back to be beaten. Is this how God keeps a promise? He promises the land and surrounds it with crocodiles, and tells the naked and the starved, 'Now crawl there if you can.' And the Jew is grateful, at least for the promise. It tells him he's wanted somewhere."

"But you always wanted One World, Poppa."

"Yes, but I see now that everyone is invited to the table but us. We're not invited. So, if you're not invited, what do you do? You don't go, that's all. You go somewhere else by yourself. Everyone has a place to go by himself when he's not invited, but us. We have to shuffle our feet outside; they should feel sorry and let us in if we shuffle enough. Easier to be a revolutionary than a shuffler, Becky. A revolutionary has scars only on his back, but a shuffler has them on his heart. And you remember you have them...all the time...you remember."

She wanted to leave now but couldn't. She couldn't leave before he came home from the hospital. She couldn't leave before he came home...<u>if</u> he came home. She was worried...but annoyed more than worried. 'I don't want to worry about sickness, now that I want to have a good time, then attacking, I should be ashamed of myself, and then I wish you were gone, Poppa, like you said you would be, so many times, so Momma would give me money for dressed and stockings and no one would be watching us like you watch and want me out of the house like you want me so they'll be less expenses, one less mouth to feed. And now you'll be sick, too, and home all the time, watching me all the time, and more crotchety and more nervous and more hollering at me...about me. Dear God, please don't let him be sick. I want to have a good time without looking over my shoulder that I'm doing the wrong thing!'

The key turned in the lock...Poppa...looking heavy, martyred, and important, pronouncing, like he was signing the world over to the devil, "They're taking tests. I know it's not good."

"How can you know already if the doctor doesn't know yet?"

He cocked his head to the side, his way of telling her she was right. Mirele opened the door with a bag of groceries, holding it like it was a baby and standing in the doorway. Wet on the bottom, the eggs about to fall, Poppa rushed to support the bag with both hands, and they talked without once thinking to put it down. Becky pulled them both toward the sink, Mirele bobbing sideways, Poppa complaining his pants were wet and shouting why she didn't insist on double bagging. When they shouted themselves hoarse about the bag, Mirele then insisted he sit down if he was sick, Phillip shouting he wasn't sick, they were testing. They couldn't make it to the sink. The bag burst and they all went scurrying for grapefruit, apples, oranges. For weeks they welled an orange and couldn't figure out where it went, until Becky found it under the radiator, green...and threw it out. Mirele mumbled what a sin it was to do such a thing with so many people starving.

"You going out again with that boy from Texas?"

Momma said he had that 'goyim' look. Becky tried so hard to show her he's a good man.

"Better than the Jewish boys, Ma."

'Didn't she see enough Jewish men? All tyrants?'

"But he's such a nice fellow, Ma, kind and patient."

Momma had that, 'but he's not Jewish' look...and not nothing. 'An ordinary bum, sailing from one place to the other and looking over the ocean. Him, she compares to Poppa! An ocean looker. What's there to see in the water? Fish! But who can tell her anything? She already knows what I think. It means nothing what I think.'

The phone rang. Becky rushed to answer.

Mirele whispered sarcastically, "The beloved."

Becky slammed the door shut so Mirele couldn't hear...only giggling. He made her laugh. 'Goyim make her laugh and Yiddin, no.' Then the bureau drawer opened, creaking and slamming shut. Becky whizzed by her squirting perfume behind her ear.

Momma called after her, "Bad for your skin, all that paint and powder."

"I'm going, Ma."

"You're not eating first?"

"I'll eat out in a restaurant."

The boy was working hard. A restaurant. Special treatment. Like a lady.

"Come home early," to a closing door.

"Phillip, what do we do if she marries a Christian?"

"Attend the wedding, what else?"

"You! Not me! Never!"

"Without you, there can still be a wedding. As long as there's a bride."

"Then it'll go without me, the wedding. You don't care nothing!"

"What is there to care about? A nice man. Very nice. So, he won't daven in shul. Children she won't have, so what's the difference?"

"And if she does?"

"If she does, she does."

"And bring them up, God forbid, Jews? What happens, Mirele, so wonderful to Jews that it's important her children be Jewish? Better they not be. Much better."

"Better they are not at all! A boy without a Bar Mitzvah?"

"He'll be a man, don't worry. There's enough suffering in the world for a Bar Mitzvah to make him one. And if that won't make him a man, a Bar Mitzvah, of course not. What did it make me, my Bar Mitzvah? Aggravation and blows on the head from my father, my teacher and my mother, and that's all."

"You believe in nothing, Phillip."

"And you believe in everything, Mirele, in God, in Shabbos, in me...and we're both in the same leaky boat. I have nothing and you have nothing, so you see, it makes no difference. When you die, when I die, I'll see nothing and you'll see nothing and for once I'll thank God, not to see anymore this world."

"Shut up! What you talking?!"

"I'm talking, you shouldn't worry so much from Yiddin and goyim."

"Nothing more important, especially now."

Yesterday's paper behind him. He pulled it out and remembered the terrible story he read just yesterday...a Jew facing death in the camps and lighting a Shabbos candle...and he sighed and said, "Yes, Mirele, maybe you're right. I think now there is something more important."

Mirele started. She'd never been right before.

"What did you say? I'm right?"

Angry now, "You're right, that's all! Don't ask questions!"

She thought, 'He's reading the stories. I didn't need a war to know I'm right. All my life I fight a war and all the lives before me and his father before him and before and before and before. It took you so long Phillip to wake up. But what am I thinking? Phillip is smart. Much smarter than me. Always was. But with God, he's stubborn. Love man. But Man don't love us. I tell him. And he didn't believe me. Always looking to prove to me there isn't any. And I'm looking to show him there is. Like Becky with the goyim. They like us. She needs to prove to me and she's too young to know she can't convince me. And she'll try to break my heart every time to know she's still trying. Poppa wants the world to sit down and talk and here we are only three people talking and convincing nothing. I just believe in it for nagging. Not for talking anybody into anything. Just pushing until they give in, and my talking can't even do that. I still can't get Becky to hang up her coat even. For how many years I'm hollering before she throws it on the chair...so maybe if she holds it in mid-air and carries it to the closet. But now she doesn't even hold it a minute. Just let it go. Plop. 'What's the difference, I'm going to un-hang it in a minute anyway."

The difference was she'd win, but Mirele couldn't admit that even to herself.

"Mirele!" Phillip gasping in the bathroom.

"Phillip!" Mirele screaming. "Open the door! I can't get in!"

A thud. Silence. Mirele bangs her fists to break down the door.

The neighbor hearing and banging on Mirele's door, "What's the matter?!"

"Phillip may be dead in the bathroom! I can't get in!"

Someone called the police, the fire department. They hacked their way in. And there he was...keeled over the bathtub like a drunk. Mirele rushed in, put an open palm on his heart.

"He's breathing! Phillip is alive!"

Uniformed, efficient young men picked him up, carried him out on their shoulders, Mirele rushing to keep up with them, watching his shirt, ever so slightly, going up and down.

"Breathe, Phillip. Breathe...breathe...breathe."

Her eyes riveted on that one spot on his chest. That little spot going up and down. That was life. All of it came down to. 'Severe heart attack' they told her. Needed to be carefully watched when he went home. She would watch him, of course.

Midnight when she came home. Becky is not home yet. First time she ever came home to emptiness. Phillip was always home before her...or Becky. She took off her coat and dropped it on the chair, untied the shawl from her head. It slid to the floor. Took her head in both hands, banging it against the wall in slow cadence, waiting for the pain to come, more and more again and again till her arms ached and her body sobbed. Cries deep inside where old memories were still fresh and tender, untouched...waiting.

"Pesach, I didn't watch. Again, I didn't watch. Forgive me, Phillip."

A key turning in the lock. Mirele swerved quickly into her bedroom, jumped into bed with her clothes on, stuffed the corner of the sheet into her mouth so they wouldn't hear her sobs.

'Let herself enjoy herself a little longer. She'll know soon enough. And besides, I don't want that goy giving me sympathy. And besides, I want to cry, they shouldn't bother me to stop. Just cry until I can't anymore and start all over again when I can. I have plenty of tears and more tears. When God gives troubles, he gives enough tears to take care of them.'

From the living room, she could hear nothing. 'God knows what's going on in there.' Then, giggling, the door closing softly. 'He's gone. Thank God.' She took the sheet out of her mouth and put her hand... biting herself hard...hurting. She deserved, and fell asleep with her hand in her mouth, like she used to when she was a child. In the morning, her hand was full of teeth marks. She put it behind her back and banged on the wall hard with the other.

"Becky, come here quick. I have something to tell you."

But Becky was in the bathroom. She rushed out, mouth full of toothpaste.

"Wha-ah-ah...Where's Pa?"

"He's sick. In the hospital. Heart attack."

Becky wiped the paste from her mouth.

"Where is he? Can I see him?"

"We have to call. Maybe tonight."

Tonight, she had a date with Tommy. 'Why did he have to get sick _now_?!'

Chapter Seventy-Six

"But you don't have to go to the hospital, Becky. I'll go. A hospital, no one has to go. I'm afraid you should get aggravated there."

A dispirited, "I'll go, Ma."

That first step into the ward lined with beds and the condemned is fretting about no olive in the martini. In the movies she loved, the boy, always in a tuxedo, ran after the girl, always in an evening gown. Would they make up after a quarrel? Would they?! The only time anyone was sick it was a glamorous illness, a hangover after a night of carousing, fully dressed, an icepack on the head and oh how jolly it all seemed...to be glamorously sick on Art Deco sofas with the butler administering a bromide. Becky wanted life to be like that...effortless, romantic, smooth, silky, no one working or touching money, or getting paid just talking about thousands, millions when she was still pleading for a quarter for a pair of stockings. Nothing to make you ashamed, humiliated, nauseous, guilty. Just going to a night club with Cary Grant and Clark Gable and wondering which one to marry and fighting a revolution without blood and guns and politics and betrayal, just looking brave and martyred and singing songs and giving fiery speeches...not really hurting anybody.

Mirele was always serving and on call without even thinking it should be otherwise for her and glad to be of use, to serve...to live with grocery bags and dirty dishes and grumbling employers and dirt...everyone's...cleaning, mopping, scrubbing it without complaint, hers, somebody else's. then hers again, and medicine, pills, hospitals, groaning and moaning, tending, and rebelling only through Becky, but only partially. 'Don't marry, Becky, enjoy, enjoy, enjoy, visit the hospital.' Mirele, too, living in dreams. How much could she enjoy, the daughter of a laborer and a domestic. No matter how Mirele sacrificed afterward, and made penance to Becky, she could never make up for giving birth to her. If she married, Mirele wanted her to marry a scholar, even though she would have to support him. Becky had to follow Mirele's dream because that's how children are made.

Mirele didn't even know she was in a slum. She'd never known any better. This was the best. Both struggling with images and dreams to guide them and Becky running from life because it didn't fit the dream. Becky still remembered the first time she was told about cancer. How she couldn't sleep for a week and is still afraid when she hears the word mentioned. In the hospital visiting and passing the beds, the terrified wondering, does this one have it...or that one...her eyes staring straight ahead at walls and windows or down at floor counting squares. Locking every nerve in place coming to the bed and daring to look and trying not to hear the conversations in the other beds of more pain and surgical exercises on hapless people who talk with pride of their one heroic moment, surviving a frontal attack by the medical profession and the visitors eagerly listening and offering their dramas; Becky wondering how they can listen. Dark, gray, desolate, lonely...the look of death in the street leading to the hospital. Mid-morning...the men hurrying to another day at work. Better dying with work than without work. The women, who would have scrambled an egg or grabbed a hot dog if they were alone, just grab anything, we're already involved in the dinner ritual.

Every day was a test and they had to pass judgment...work for praise and punishment like school children. Time was important. Their greatest fear, it shouldn't be overdone...it shouldn't be cold...when <u>he</u> comes home. It terrified Becky to hear them talking. <u>He</u> was so particular. The tyrannical in him sat over plates. The women chopping and scraping, moving from stove to spotted cookbooks for him. The men slaving at peonage jobs come home to be tough and arrogant over string beans. In the movies, no one cooked...ever, or took out garbage. But Becky couldn't stand having a servant. It was against her principles. And she hated the rich anyhow. Feared them, too. So how do you marry. Cook, tend to someone or see them in the hospital, not be rich or poor, not do housework or bear to see someone else do it for you. Guilty. Like hiring Ma.

Becky on the way to the hospital, the glare of the sun shutting her eyes, the roar of a truck bringing her fingers to her ears. She hoped she could make the visit just like that...eyes and ears shut. She resented each step closer. Why does life have to be this way? Why? Why? Why? The hospital was large and old. In the lobby, clumps of dirt hung from the ceiling in long threads. The sun never reached the cavernous lobby. It was a hospital for the poor. The bricks like prison walls. Why did, even the bricks look different in this place than they did in villas and cottages, like the hell inside moved through the walls, the pain, torment, and tears. Even they seemed to be scowling. Becky could tell a hospital even from afar. Without seeing the name... gray etched on gray, hospitals for the poor were all the same. Cold, forbidding, green terraces grated, and sometimes you'd see a white rumpled night through the windows, or white, bony arms rolling wheelchairs on the terrace.

"Mr. Bromsky, please. What room?"

Snapping, "Ward, B6."

Snickering as Becky shuffled off.

"Room. Where does she think she is? Room! She's lucky he has a bed. Hasn't she heard? We've got people enough here to put over, under and between beds?!"

Becky passing a dark tunnel to the elevator, not looking right or left, dreading the accidental horror passed in the hall...or on the elevator. Cigarette butts crushed on the floor, open and gutless. Becky threw hers down to when the elevator stopped a little above the floor and stamped on it and rubbed it hard. Felt good to do that. Nurses passing, confident, white, efficient, eyes dead. And some standing at the desk...laughing?! 'How can anyone laugh here?'

Begging, "Excuse me. Can I ask you a question?"

Smiles leave their faces. Annoyed.

"Yes?"

"Where is ward B6?"

Pointing and quickly turning heads to each other again. The poor are never more craven than in illness. The wide gulf between the somebodies and nobodies who know their place even in a sick bed. Mustn't bother the prince with questions. The serf doesn't presume. Servants take orders, suffer quietly, meekly. There was once one king. Now there are little ones everywhere. The bosses, the bureaucrats, the doctors. The beds stretched in front of her as far as she could see and no one she dared ask. Serious faces scurrying by doing important things with arrogant faces that swept everyone aside but the horror that is hospital life, temperatures and charts, blood, and bile. Poor Becky, a spirit frozen in an eighteenth-century painting, dainty white feet on pink petals being adored by a kneeling, ardent swain in blue satin pantaloons making poetry, this was hell. There could be no other. Looking for Poppa, she had to look at faces shorn of the mask's men wear to please, honest faces in their sullenness, hopelessness, stony calm, deadened, sedated terror. They were all together here, the chronic, the newcomers, the old, the young. It seemed that everyone had that awful disease. All seemed to be wasting away... Pesach-Persie. The pleading moans of life clinging. The wild need to run down the aisle with eyes closed and hands cupped on ears so as not to hear, stop the terror in the heart pounding.

"Not to see your father?"

The smirk of self-righteousness.

"You should be ashamed of yourself not to visit him every day to make sure they do right by him!"

'Every day, Poppa? I'll die if I come here every day!'

She thought one of the men smiled at her. But she then saw he had no teeth, so he looked like he had a perpetual grin on his face. She glared at him hysterically.

"Bromsky. Where is Bromsky?"

"Phillip? I know him. He's in Heart. Around the corner. Very sick. You're his daughter? Go around the corner. By himself."

Poppa under a glass cage...connected to wires. She ran out, a woman's scream tearing after her down the aisle, sick heads turning slightly, dead eyes following her to the end and turning back with a sigh. 'Lucky girl. If that were only me and him. Only the homeless with nowhere to go, only those who were wounded themselves couldn't care less. Let her go. They were grateful. They hadn't healed yet. Comfortable here. Warm. They wished they could stay until the spring. Some came every winter but there weren't too many that were clever at faking. Just a few. They were the lucky ones.

"I can't go every day, Ma! I just can't!"

"Who's asking you to? I don't want to go every day! I'll worry about you, too. It's too much for you, Becky. You'll get sick too and then you'll both be sick. Poppa, God forbid, dying and you, crazy."

That look on Mirele's face again...dogged, fanatic, willing of life from death. Faster, faster, life pushing, cracking the whip, Mirele hobbling as fast as she could. It didn't matter to her that life drove her. It was keeping up that was important. She didn't want to see Becky mopping and cleaning. She wanted to see an artist and scholar. She couldn't bear the thought that she raised a drudge like herself, a woman like all women. That she should be not even a question. She did all the taking care willingly and eagerly. But Becky shouldn't do it. About that, there wasn't even a question either.

And still bludgeoning Becky, "You have to go to school. Look what I'm doing for you."

Becky burned with shame and anger, fled behind a slammed door but the words still tearing followed. 'I can't do it, Ma. I'm not smart enough. College was a terror, not going was a terror, to be nothing was a terror, to be something was a terror. Does sacrifice make me smart, pretty, or thin. If only it did, Ma, but it doesn't. So you're just sacrificing and sacrificing, like some primitive ritual, only you're slaughtering yourself piece by piece and begging the heavens and the sky is looking down and not caring. You sacrifice for money we don't have and me that's not worth it. One life you lost and the other you're losing. Is it more powerful that food or sleep, this need for sacrifice? Becky was thinking now that it must be else why would people have children or live the lives they do?

Mirele embraced sacrifice like a passion, the grand design, the meaning of her life, but not for Becky. It wasn't a morality for anyone else, she is sitting in judgement if they did or didn't. Just for her to do for others and remind them from time to time for their own good. Things were just temporarily with her, on the way to another. The goodies never stopped and stayed awhile with her. They were like burning hot coals until she couldn't give them away. The customers gave her dresses, coats, hats, bags. She searched frantically for someone who needed them, forgetting the first someone was Mirele herself. Now, she was touching death alone, it shouldn't touch Becky. Nothing should touch Becky. Pesach-Persie whispering over and over forever, 'You suffered me too much Momma, so I ran away where you can't find me.' And Becky knew the hold she had. Only Pesach freed her from Mirele's tentacles, from her following her everywhere. 'You had to go meshuga, it took Pesach to free me. If you didn't. If you waited for me, we'd both be there together, run away from Momma, locked up somewhere like all runaway children. Some choice you had, Pesach! To be locked up here or there. And you chose there. But don't you see? You were a good boy to the end, Pesach. You were always somewhere you could be watched. Put yourself there yourself. Didn't just run away where Momma couldn't find you. And me, I'm letting you do all the sacrificing, Ma and I'm just passing through, gentle, leaving no one after me, disappearing when the time comes.

Mirele giving Becky whatever she can. Pesach warning, 'Be careful, Mirele, or she'll end up like me. Careful. Careful. Careful. Give. Give. Give. Do. Do. Do. Sha-sha-sha. Giving so long that Becky forgot she was there, only he she was ashamed, she remembered, how she looked, old clothes hanging, how ignorant, poor, how she rushed. It seemed the Jews, the poor were always in a hurry. The Christians, the rich, slow confident, sure, and graceful. Shame doesn't melt in America. It stays hard inside. Stays and stays until you die. 'What did your father do and his father's father and mother and what school did you go to and what college? And what do you say Momma if you're not descended from generations of Rabbis, and you didn't go to Dalton school and Ivy League college. What do you say, Ma? My father was a laborer and my mother a scrubwoman and I went to P.S 100 and an academy for dropouts and Brooklyn College. It's those who don't sacrifice who sit at the grandest tables. They're just born right, Ma. Send checks through the mail, big ones to the right places. Don't even have to walk to the bank. The secretary does it for them. Don't you see, they give us poor schools and colleges as long as the poor stay where they belong and don't contaminate the environment with their presence. They give us City and Brooklyn, and keep Harvard and Swarthmore for themselves, no matter what? Nothing from nothing...is nothing!' a desperate, shaking monologue to convince.

"So, you'll still go to school. Nothing with college is still better than nothing without."

Becky hated her in that minute. Could never convince her of anything. Not like Poppa. Him, you could talk to. Got her high school diploma easily enough but was still making 10 dollars a week giving music lessons in a school and thinking to quit even that since that day when Osokin was principal, who grabbed her alone, twirled her around the room, held her close and whispered in her, 'You like men, don't you?' she pushed him away scared and trembling and...feeling foolish. 'I have a lesson now; you'll have to excuse me.' She called in sick for the next three days. She was going to call and tell him she was not coming back. He was too much for her. A sophisticated man of the world and 'I can't even kiss right.' He'd laugh at her if he knew. On the phone, 'I won't be coming in anymore, Mr. Osokin.' Paternal, soothing, 'Why?' 'Because...' and she hung up like she was holding a snake in her hand. Insistent ringing. She prays that each one is the last. Heart knocking like he was there...watching her like she was committing a crime, not answering. Like Mama calling 'Becky' and not answering, hiding in shame, hoping she'd stop, but she never stopped. A sulking, resentful, complying, halting stubborn grim little march home.

The phone stopped ringing. Then started again. Pulled her out at last, breaking her will.

"Hello."

"What's the matter? What's wrong?!"

"Nothing."

Silence. Her face twitching. He's silent, too. Waiting. Then...she heard a click. He hung up. Then the words exploding from her, shouted into a silent phone.

"Because you're too much for me! For the fat, shy girl from West 5th Street!"

And she slammed the phone hard and wept because she wished he wasn't too much. She cried until it was dark in the room. Somehow, it wasn't so lonely when the sun shone, shaky little rainbows on the ceiling, trembling, all colors jumping about, sound of children happy, playing, balls bouncing outside the window. All gone. Silence, now.

Through the door... "Ma, how's Pa doing?"

"Better."

When does it become How many betters add up to 'You can go home now, Mr. Bromsky.' I wish he was here now. Just for a while. He's always nice for a while until he gets nasty again hollering about something. Nice like when he first comes home after a long trip or saying goodbye.

"Becky, Poppa's home! Come help me!"

Poppa wasn't the type you rushed up to and kissed just like that. Becky sat him down, looked at him. His eyes wide open like a child. Innocent. Broken. Sevak*, ghetto, medieval innocence exposed again. The helping profession patched up his heart, destroyed his spirit, keeping him under glass and letting out half a man. The fingers, each one round and firm and stubby, each one had the power of a small hammer, now...long, thin, white, the chest once round and powerful, now shrunken, the shoulders broad and heavy, now bony, and thin, the broad ruddy face, hollow cheeked now and colorless.

The doctor's prophecy was fulfilled...the one made long ago on the immigrant ship. Said America would kill him. And it did. He looked now like he always dreaded. A tailor.

But he still had intact the sense of drama of the occasion, wiping his head with his index finger and looking down dramatically into nowhere and shaking his head heavy and profound.

"No...what can you do? Cursed! That's all. So how are you, Becky?"

"How are you?"

"I'm glad you didn't come. What's there to see there? You'll have time enough to see it, God forbid, you get sick."

"I saw it once, Poppa."

"You came?!"

"Once."

"That's enough."

"You didn't sleep, I'll bet, for a week."

"I didn't."

"That's capitalism. For the rich they make a private room, so they don't see anyone else's suffering, as usual!"

He didn't complain to Becky she didn't come to see him, but he would to others. He enjoyed victim stories, especially when the crimes were committed against him. Becky always found out about it later. First, he told her it didn't matter, then he told someone else it

---

* ***Sevak – A small town in Poland***

did, and they told her, 'How could you do such a thing?!' And she swallowed the words of explanation in defense. After all, how could she talk against Poppa?

Chapter Seventy-Seven

Night sounds. Phillip hacking for breath locked in the throat and Mirele tending, Becky not daring to ask what she did. Burying her head under the covers not to hear. The two doomed people in the other room, trying so hard to hold onto an agonized life, grateful for one more breath. Mirele staring at him all night like he was a sleeping child...watching. She shouldn't wake up and find him gone. Sometimes her mouth open on his, breathing her pitiful life into his tortured one. Breathe, Phillip, breathe. Her bent twisted back heaving deep as if she would give him her heart if she could and praying every night, 'God, let me. He should have the heart without pain, and he should give me his that hurts. What do I need a heart for? I don't have a head. But Phillip needs his heart. If I can be without a head, I can be without a heart, too. Take from me. Please, God. Take from me.' She'd lift her head from Phillip's mouth and turn it up to heaven, listening for an answer. 'Mirele Bromsky's heart is not up for trade. It's made especially for you. Can't fit anywhere else.' 'I understand now, forgive me.' But she'd forget and the next night she'd plead again. Sometimes earlier, sometimes later, so as not to bother in a better mood than others. Maybe tonight, she'd be lucky.

Sometimes she falls asleep sitting by the bed, her head near Phillip's side. His hand finds her in the morning. She wakes startled and opens her mouth, breathing hard on the back of his hand.

"What are you doing? Are you crazy?"

"What's crazy? What did I do?"

"You're biting my hand."

"You're crazy. What kind of biting? I must have dreamed that maybe I was eating an apple."

"Look at this hand, Mirele. What is there even to bite? Nothing... at least an apple."

She let him go on. He liked to pity himself. Why not? What other pleasure did he have now? And she agreed. At least an apple had something. Without pain, it lives. Without pain it dies.

"If I must come back here again God, make me an apple. Make us all apples. Me and Phillip and Becky, too."

That night she had a dream. They were all apples. Shining, glistening, gamboling together gaily, the wind tossing them about in the tree. She awoke laughing for the first time and Phillip asked her if she was crazy. For the first time, he moved to get out of bed.

She screamed, frantic, "Don't! You'll fall from the tree!"

Looking somewhere in the distance, unseeing, flinging her arms as wide open as she could.

"Fall and I'll catch you."

He grabbed her arm. She tore away from him.

"Apples falling all around me. God, who will save us?"

She picked up her skirt and spread it wide between her arms, so it was ready to receive, looked up, shuffled from side to side.

"Here, here, you see. I'll catch you, Phillip. Don't be afraid."

"Mirele! Stop catching apples! Wake up! Come back from wherever you think you are!"

Laughing again, like nothing happened.

"You're right Phillip. Better to be an apple."

"Put your dress down. Foolish woman."

Embarrassed now, "How did that happen?"

Her rolled stocking loosened. She knotted them again. Her hairpins on the floor. She picked them up, put them in her teeth one at a time while she rolled her hair in a bun and talked to Phillip through the pins. Still tearing at him, what he had just seen, he'd be screaming in pain. Mirele dropped the pins. They scattered all over, her long hair fell on her face, not even her eyes visible.

"A worm crawling in the dark, looking for fresh apples, that's me."

A child's game came to her and made her smile. She parted her hair and looked at Phillip, "Peek-a-boo, I see you!"

And she rocked Phillip's arm with her hand, and he let her, waving it back and forth as she rocked. Peeking a boo and rocking... and Phillip moaning, "What am I going to do? My heart, now my wife...what's next? Crazy...if she isn't already?"

He was so frightened. If he were gentle, he couldn't speak.

"Pin up your hair, Mirele! You look like a wild animal."

She parted her hair slowly, twisted it around and rolled it in the back of her head in a bun.

"That's better."

"What's better?"

"Your hair. Better than hanging it over your face, isn't it?"

The phone rang. Becky grumbling, "So early?"

Mirele wondered, 'Who's calling her so early? The Christian?"

"Who is it, Becky?" she always asked.

Becky never answered. 'Must be him.' Mirele pressed her ear against the door. Becky was saying 'Yes' and 'No' like a person does when they know someone's listening. 'Six months they're going together already.'

He put his hat on the chair when he came in. Mirele saw that same hat night after night, the light shining on the black brim, the gold braid in front, a goyish hat. Becky didn't know Mirele could see the chair from her room. It was her secret. She didn't even want to tell Phillip. He might move the chair because he couldn't stand her spying. Was it serious? It was terrible not to know. Yet she didn't want to know. What's the use of knowing if you don't want to know. But the question was asked every day...churning inside. 'What does she need him for? It's alright here at home. I give her a dollar a day sometimes when Poppa doesn't see. I even give her money to buy a good dress, so she looks nice. Goyim she needs. She needs goyim?'

Phillip wondered, 'Don't you think she should work a little, Mirele? Help us maybe or something?'

"She's looking. She can't find anything."

"Where is she looking? In a boy's eyes? There you can be sure, no work."

"You tell her."

"No, you tell her."

No one told her.

'A girl almost 21 and still in the house sneaking dollars in her pocket from her mother when I'm not looking. I hear them whispering, but I don't say anything.' It rankled him so he looked away when he talked to Becky, like she wasn't even there. It would be a burden lifted from him if she wasn't. And he used to wish Mirele wasn't there, either. Then, it seemed to him, he could straighten his back again. But now, he needed Mirele. Needed her to mend what she'd broken. After all, she wanted children, not him. They took the heart from him...Becky and...Persie. He didn't need Becky. He hoped that *goy* would take her away.

Becky knew Poppa was irritated around her...like he was screaming at her to get out and not come back, that he couldn't stand the very sight of her, like she was a guest who stayed too long and he's desperate, watching the clock and waiting for him to say he's going and the more he lingers, the more he hates him. Becky was an unwelcome guest always but now, more than ever. He was home and saw Becky being lazy, late breakfasts that Mirele prepared, waiting for phone calls, lounging, daydreaming. He'd nag more and more. 'Careful with the ice box! Don't make so much noise when you come home!' but he still came to her polite and obeisant when papers came from the government. After he'd filled in enough boxes to satisfy every Washington bureaucrat, they sent him a disability check. Poppa finally graduated...from welfare to disability. It was more honorable. It meant you were sick. Can't help being sick.

"Can't help being lazy either Poppa. It's a disease like a cracked brain or a punctured lung. Your will is paralyzed. You can't move. You have to work real hard being lazy, pushing away guilt, finding excuses and explanations, worrying about the time going by that you're wasting, changing night into day. Lazy people can't face the morning. They need their own commune where there's a law against mornings. No one stirs until it's time to dress from the ball. There are morning people and night people. Those who are desolate in the morning and those who are desolate at night. The power was now with the morning people, tyrannizing us, forcing us to follow, dragging us along into the dark cold from warm beds. But someday, we'll have a night place where it's forbidden to stir in the morning. My job now, Poppa is getting dressed for Tommy and being amused and talking and keeping him interested. That's hard work Poppa. Not like you and Ma...matched. Now we have to work hard at it. Making ourselves liked. Very hard...the smiling and being nice and coy and sweet and exciting. Be interesting, all by myself...with no help from the other side."

"So, what are you doing all this for?"

"My future. I have to think of my future. And cause I wanna! I wanna...so much...I can't think of anything else or do anything else. I'm crazy, too like you or Ma or...Persie. You're crazy with the world, Persie was crazy with himself and I'm crazy with boys...and my crazy is like drowning, gasping for air all the time or you think you'll go under. That's the trouble between me and Ma. We're both frantic, clawing hard now, she for the Jew, me for the Christian. You, for me and to get out, me for you to get out, you to stay without me, me to stay without you. And you were never alone. You had Uncle Sam and Aunt Rose and Dora and Uncle Max when you were growing up and when you left them Grandpa gave you Ma, and Persie and me. But I had nobody growing up and I have to scrounge and dance and beg inside and play outside like I don't care and clown and philosophize and dress right and think what to and how and feel right and kiss right and eat right...so maybe someone will choose me after that. Like music, practicing hour after hour, a thousand hours for one night, and trembling five of your best at the concert then hear a few claps from the kind and courteous. That's what I've been getting up to now, Pa! like hearing just how many hands are coming together for you somewhere in the dark out there while the rest have their hands on their laps. And the silence when you're waiting behind the curtain. No one wants an encore? It's been dark and silent behind that curtain until Tommy, Pa. the only raving audience I ever had screaming, 'Encore.' It's a little less lonely with him around, Pa, the part of lonely that's unwanted lonely. But there's another part of loneliness that's still desolate. He's not a companion, Poppa. I talk and he listens and doesn't talk back so I keep talking, like I do to myself, like now. Like arms walk with need and he's just sitting there and you're aching to touch him. That's how I feel about talking. Talking is love, poppa. The only kind I ever knew...he's too shy, I guess. We even have a different shyness. He can look straight into my eyes and I can't. frightens me and I have to look down or sideways. He can be quiet and I'm too shy to be. I don't know what would happen if we were both quiet at the same time. Too scared to even try it. He'd be bored, right away, I know it."

Every night Becky was terrified that he'll be bored. Boring was like a new disease she'd learned about...from the movies...from Elsie. It was her favorite word.

"For Tom it's over, Poppa, the race. For me, it's never over. Every night, I'm still running. I have to keep running in that race and I'm grateful just to be in the running. Got to keep going or I'll explode... like Pesach, Poppa."

"Like Pesach, Becky?"

Guilty. Defeated.

"Run, Becky, Run."

They were coming home earlier...Becky finding it harder and

harder to be spontaneously happily pouring out amusement, delight, wisdom, learned, quoted, so she was depending more on flattery, more hours on the sofa, necking and swooning. Becky became an expert swooner. It pleased him. Becky improvised...a tremble...a sigh. She didn't really know what to do, neither did he so her performance was convincing. He loved being a master puppeteer, a feeling that his look, his touch had magic power to arouse and inflame her. They watched each other, and he is watching him to see he was pleased with himself and he is watching her to see she was pleased with him and she knowing she's being watched but he, not knowing. Kissing and parting and holding her and listening like always...but not for words now...for little cries that she was weakened and wanting. In the half light, she could see his eyes besotted with joy, eyes shining with pride and she hated him.

"I love you, Becky. Say you love me."

She bent her head and whispered into his chest, "I love you."

Gagging, humiliated. He asked her to tell him, so she told him, like it was an order... one that was utterly resentful. She told him like she was in school, and the teacher said, 'Repeat after me, one and one makes two' and she'd repeat, shriveled up inside when she did it. It wasn't at all like she dreamed, saying, 'I love you,' all gushy and warm and romantic. It was terrible.

"Do it for me, Becky," and plunging a spoon of medicine in her mouth and Becky having to swallow.

He picked up his hat, slid his hand around the inside rim, pulled out a small black box, and...just like in the movies, he opened it and said, "Marry me."

He held her hand and slid the diamond ring on her finger. "Not very big," he said.

Bigger than she'd ever seen or dreamed. It didn't matter, big or small. Becky didn't really care about such things at all. It's what it meant that was so important. For the first time, she was like other people...like joining the whole human race for the first time. Engaged seemed to her as impossible once as being thin, or beautiful or popular...or rich and successful or a revolutionary or a martyr. Her head bent; she pressed her face against his chest...shy... hiding.

"Will you marry me? Please...please have me. I know I'm not much and have no right to ask, but we can't help wanting what's too good for us, can we? And you're too good for me, and too pretty and too smart."

And he stroked her head harder and harder while he talked until it hurt.

"Say you will, Becky. I'd be so happy."

And she rubbed her nose up and down his chest.

"Does that mean you will?"

And she rubbed her nose up and down again on his chest and twisted the ring around her finger. He picked her head up.

"Say yes."

She swiftly buried her head again on his chest...nodding quickly up and down. He forced her head up again.

"Yes," he framed the word without a sound. "Say yes."

"Yes," she framed the word, too, silent...wrapped in shame.

It was too much for him, being so happy. He was suddenly awkward, clumsy, in a hurry to leave.

"I'm getting back late tonight. Forgive me. Tonight is an early night for me."

He had them from time to time, but it was still mortifying each time he rushed out. A good excuse is a poor antidote for the easily rejected. Becky careful never to show it mattered or she'll lose him. She said nothing. Pulled away...and he lingered...and tore himself away. She was subtly attuned, like all rejects...to all the nuances. One slip...just one...and she's taken for granted. Worse...abandoned. The first commandment in the life of rejects, 'Let no one know. It invited them to do the same. No one wants the unwanted.'

With Elsie at the school the next day...recapitulating.

"But I don't know, Elsie. He's so dull!"

"No future for you if you don't. Marry him. Why not?"

If Elsie said, then she'd marry him. Elsie was right about everything.

"Take what you can from them Becky. They'll do you in if they can."

Mocking, joyless laughter. Piano legs, bulging blue eyes talking like that. Frightened her when Elsie talked like that, but she laughed with her...accommodating. Then Becky joined her in battle, punctuating the air with certainties and ultimatums, righteous indignation and finally, a monologue on the perfidy of me...none of which had ever been especially perfidious to her lately, but she feared they brought her already. She laughed harder.

"Why not turn the tables, Elsie, for once. Love them and leave them."

"Sure, just do what they do."

"If you really get tired of him, you can always pack your bags and get out. You'll marry him in the unitarian church. Me, Ski, Leona, and Dave as witnesses. Have a party afterwards."

"Who'll pay for all that?"

"Your mother of course. The mother of the bride always pays."

It was exciting already...planning a wedding.

"Congratulations, Becky. He's so good looking. Most of all, you'll keep the romance alive. Out to sea three months and home for one, then out again."

That was the best reason for Becky. There was no turning back now. That final appeal to her vanity and her fear. He's so good looking and would hardly be around to tire her. She satirized the usual wedding. too shy really to be the center of attention. all eyes turned on her, saying words she'd always scorned. Made her feel so smart...saying how silly she thought everything that everybody else thought was so important. It was the only way she felt smart playing the movie, 'The Man Who Came to Dinner,' mocking, sneering, brutal wit. She'd played it so often, she didn't when she was playing. It would just be a hint of a wedding. Barely noticeable...quick...just enough to make her respectable. Becky was a virgin revolutionary. In those days it was possible. Revolution had nothing necessarily to do with lust and temptation and loose morals and living in sin. Even Trotsky was a family man. Elsie was pleased with this marriage. Revenging herself on pretty women and handsome men. Becky wouldn't be happy and Tommy getting a wife who's not interested in him, resents and fears men in general though she needs them court-ing, admiring, pursuing her, interesting to see how it'll all turn out. Not happy, of course. Elsie couldn't bear that at all. Even if Elsie were happy, she couldn't stand anyone else being. It had to belong to her...happiness. If she suspected they were, she searched hard until she found the flaw or imagined one and made it real. For Elsie, this was an ideal beginning.

Chapter Seventy-Eight

Becky hung up her coat the minute she came home and made sure Momma noticed. Mirele said, 'Hang up your coat,' anyway out of habit. Becky was careful not to show annoyance shouting, 'I am, I am, I am!' as always...whether she did or not. So different from the movies, 'Good evening, mother. Good evening, father.' Becky never knew anyone who said, 'Mother.' Only the very rich said 'Mother' and the very poor said, 'Ma.' And the super-rich and very classy called mother by her first name and father, too. But it doesn't matter how you, 'Mirele,' it still sounds like 'Ma.'

Mirele darting back and forth from sink to stove, the scraping of carrots and potatoes, crackle of onion peels, plops of chicken in a pot of water. Shabbos sounds. 'Ma, mother, Mirele, I'll tell you Sunday that I'm marrying a goy. That's a purpose of Shabbos no one ever mentioned...a reprieve from bad news...for just a little while longer. The phone ringing. Mirele muttering...

"On Shabbos, they call?"

"Lottie!"

Mirele relieved. If it's Lottie, it's alright. Smart, from a good family, a teacher. Even if she's a goy. Momma made an exception.

"Did you tell your mother yet?"

"No."

"Let me know as soon as you tell her. Call me from the outside as soon as you can. Tell me everything."

"I will. Of course, I will."

Shouting, "What did you say?"

"I will. I will."

"Not so loud."

"OK."

"I'll wait to hear. Bye."

She hung up.

Mirele shouting, "You will...what?!"

"I told you a million times not to listen in on my conversations. A million times!"

"I wasn't listening!"

The phone was ringing again. Mirele thinking, 'The goy. I'm sure it's him.' And Becky running, slamming the door hard shut.

"It's me Tommy," he always said, as if she didn't know.

"I can't believe you said 'Yes.' I woke up this morning, and it seemed like a dream. Say it again, Becky, that you'll marry me. Say, 'I'll marry you, Tommy.' Say it. I want to hear it."

"I can't now. They don't know yet. They'll hear."

"Then say yes, at least. I'll say, 'Will you marry me?' and you'll say yes."

Even on the phone she reddened...and mumbled, 'Yes.'

"I just wanted to make sure. Let's make it quick, Becky. I can't wait. Can it be tomorrow...the day after?"

"It's Saturday tomorrow."

"Sunday then."

"I'll try."

"Well...then...Monday."

"Tuesday!" she blurted out. "Tuesday."

"I'm afraid Becky, you'll change your mind."

"Afraid? Why?"

"Can't believe I can be so lucky. Who will marry us, Becky?"

"We'll find someone."

"You find someone. I can't leave the ship until Tuesday morning. I'll call everyday though. You'll let me know soon."

"I will."

"I can't hear you."

"Yes, I will."

"I love you, Becky."

"Me, too."

"Forever, Becky. And ever."

Silence. A soft click. She walked slowly to the door, opened it. The sputter of candles being lit. Momma's face...hard and nervous over the candles...set...desperate...then hiding behind hands...all alone in her private world...praying she doesn't marry the goy. 'Please, God, please.'

Sabbath morning, a whispered call to Lottie...saving the secret now, the plot, the drama. Even a whispered word Momma could hear sometimes. She hung up quickly. She really couldn't but it seemed to Becky as if she could. Guilt having a big tongue. Wanting to tell. Not Momma's ears. Becky is very cautious now. Even her hushed 'Yes' to Tommy's pleading more brittle and more curt now. Hoarding her little secret, resenting Momma knowing until she's ready...like she'd be robbed...like when she was a little girl and Momma took away a goodie without asking...just yanked her clenched hand, pulled her fingers loosed and grabbed it and pronounced not good for her.

Sunday, a gray light in the house, cold and dark outside, people scurrying under the window being pulled by broken umbrellas. Becky staring at the raindrops on the windows, fragile, shaking tremulous at first, then sliding down quickly and disappearing. Becky loved black and storm on the outside...made it feel good being in. Not like when it was warm and sunny, beckoning outside and she had no place to go...felt alone...abandoned. She wished sometimes she could live somewhere where it always rained, snowed, thundered and no one ever went out. Just sat cozy and watched. She hated the sun since she was little, but wouldn't dare tell anyone. No excuse for being all alone then. It hurt to be alone when it was sunny. Not when it was cloudy. It didn't hurt so much then. 'Must be a place for lonely people where the sun never shines. But...maybe it'll be different when I'm married.'

The phone again. Lottie whispering as if she can be heard.

"It's all arranged, the Unitarian Church."

And she giggled. Conspiratorial glee.

"Write it down Becky, at 2PM."

"I'll remember. Getting married on Tuesday! Good God, I have to tell Momma I'm getting married."

Shouting, "Come here. I have something to tell you. Come quick!"

Her hands dripping with soap suds and water, "What is it?"

"I'm getting married on Tuesday."

"What are you saying?"

The hands to her side and the water dripping in little puddles at her feet.

Then she slaps Becky's face hard, screaming, "What are you saying? What? What? What?!"

"He's a good man. Likes you and Poppa and is good to me."

Mirele didn't even hear her. For the rest of her life, she would remember with anguish those terrible hours before she was a bride. Mirele...tears and threats...Becky reasoning, cajoling, pleading, Mirele tossing from room to room in desperate circles.

Begging, "Don't marry him, Becky," threatening, "I'll kill myself."

Whimpering on her knees and rolling her head in Becky's lap, "Don't hoist me so much. I can't stand," the bun in the back of her shaking.

Then, with her first, she pounded Becky on her breast and shoulders and legs and Becky leaned back on both arms and let her until she slid from her lap, lay on the floor...exhausted.

Poppa is shouting now. He'd been asleep.

"Mirele, I want some tea."

Becky saying, "I'll get you some tea, Pa."

Stepping over her carefully.

"I don't want from you; you should do nothing. Where's Mirele?"

"She's asleep."

"So let her sleep. I'll have tea later."

Mirele heard and was up filling the kettle.

Becky saying, "I'll make it Momma."

No answer. Sullen. She slams the kettle on the stove, pushes her aside and shouts from the doorway, "I'm making you tea, Phillip."

"I changed my mind. I don't want any."

Becky saying, "I'll have some coffee."

"No good for you, too much coffee."

Lottie calls again.

"It's bad Lottie. Very bad. Call the church," the word gagged her in the throat, "and tell them Monday. I'll get back to you later."

And hour later, Lottie again. "Monday 10 o'clock."

"Momma won't be there."

"Don't worry, we'll have coffee and cake at my house. I can hardly wait! It's so exciting! Tommy will pay the minister, I guess."

"I know he will."

Mirele trembled every time the phone rang.

"It's Monday Tommy. I had to change it. Momma's fighting me. I can't stand much more."

"I can't wait." His voice is warm and loving.

"I'll take care of you, don't worry Becky. You'll never have to worry anymore. I'll worry for the two of us."

"How do you know I'm a worrier?"

"Always talking about the world, how bad it is. You take care of the world, Becky. I'll take care of you. They're calling me. I have to go now. Bye, Becky darling, bride to, my bride to be."

She liked the world <u>bride</u>. Glad he didn't say <u>wife</u>. She hated that word. It embarrassed her practical common place. She liked mistress, lover, boyfriend, girlfriend. Wife was so...married. So final. She didn't even like the word husband. No mystery. Prosaic...like kitchens and foyers...not magical like anterooms, chambers, parlors, terraces, gables.

The rest of the day, Mirele rushed by Becky like a frightened cat, making a little cry each time she brushed past her, avoiding her, sullen, silent, cleaning the floor on hands and knees with a big, old rag, swishing it back and forth on the same spot over and over, then twisting it hard as she could, the nerves in her arms bulging, wringing out the last drop and clanking the pail as loud as she could, sliding it back and forth...the only sound in the house...over the same place, over and over until Poppa fell asleep.

Then she slipped quietly into Becky's room, "Shush," she whispered. "Poppa's sleeping."

"He's an antisemite."

"He is not!"

"All the goyim are!"

"So how can he like you and me and Poppa?"

She couldn't answer. Facing back and forth, frantic, "I'll kill myself!"

"You'll kill me!"

Over and over, she talked of killing.

"You're killing me, Momma."

"So, what kind of marriage is this? We're both killing each other. This is a way to get married?! What did I do that you should hate me like this? What! What! What! Tell me! What?! What?!"

And she tore her hair and begged God to tell her <u>what</u>.

"Ma! Stop!"

Both looking at each other, Becky hissing through her teeth, "I have no other way out, Ma!"

"I'll take care! You don't have to worry from here on...<u>out</u>!"

"It's not his fault that he's born."

"It's our fault that we're born. Always been our fault. It's his fault *what* he's born."

"What am I going to do?!"

"You're killing me, Becky."

"And you're killing me! Not goyim, or yourself! Me!"

"You, I'm killing you, Beckele? Tell me that's not true. One I already killed. Now another I'm killing? I'm a killer?"

Then suddenly, "It's late Beckele. Go to sleep. In the morning you'll be better."

Becky collapsed on the bed and fell asleep in her clothes. Three hours later, the sun shining on her face woke her up. She had to tell Poppa. He was up by now. She opened the door and recoiled in horror...Mirele laying across the threshold on her door.

"You're not going to any wedding."

Poppa shouting, "What wedding?"

"I'm getting married today, Pa."

"To whom?"

"Tommy."

"Nice boy."

Mirele shouting, "Nice goy, you mean. There aren't any."

"Shut up! You're talking stupid!"

"Becky will have to step over me if she wants to leave this room. You're not going anywhere and that's that!"

Mirele lay prone while Becky stepped over her...back and forth until she was dressed and ready...when Becky bent over for the final time to pick her bag, Becky turned her face to the floor sobbing.

Poppa calling out, "You should have mazel, Becky."

He was smiling, relieved, Becky thought. Momma prone across the threshold again, barring the front door.

"Like a dog you'll drag me from here!" Rage rising, "I'll kill her! Once and for all!"

Becky dragged her by the hair, rolled her body round and round and fled out the door, Mirele babbling after her. She ran down the street and turned round once more. Mirele staring after her like a beaten child, arms hanging helpless by her side. Becky turned and ran, the bag opening, everything tumbling out. Guilt driving her on. Run, Becky, run. Fast as you can. Faster! Mirele followed her, picked the things up that fell out and put them back in the bag. She came home and sat at the bridge table with one hand as if Becky had died and she was in mourning, and with the other hand she drummed and drummed with her fingers, staring into space, mercifully, her mind, a blank. Her heart, knocking hard, so she sat very still until it was over inside.

Phillip calling, "Come here. I want to talk to you."

And he talked. He was his most eloquent.

"I'm Jewish. Am I easy to live with?"

She didn't answer. Not listening. Not even hearing.

"What do they eat, the goyim, Phillip?"

"Chazer, what else?"

"If they come to eat, I'll have to make pork chops."

Waiting at the church, Tommy, Lottie, and Ski, all beaming on her. When the minister read the ceremony, she cried, not knowing why. The minister was paid 25 dollars for officiating. Tommy reserved a room in midtown. Becky would go on her honeymoon, without even a toothbrush.

Chapter Seventy-Nine

Behind the smiling face trembling lips harden into a fixed smile, but not hard enough. The mouth quivering ever so slightly. Only Becky knows the fear, but it seems to her like everyone can see. Her mind is in a desperate scramble to find comfort. In all the hundreds of conversations and cafeterias and coffee shops with Lottie, there must be a few remembered words to comfort her now!

"If it doesn't work, you'll divorce him," Lottie's hard-edged laughter, "just exchange one piece of paper for another. Better to be a gay divorcee than an old maid. And besides you won't see each other much. Magic...romance...every time to look forward to."

Becky's smile was a little softer now, an arm thrust around Lottie's waist, a hug, gratitude.

"Thank you, Lottie, my friend."

Lottie turns to Becky, a shy glance and laughing hysterical, though nothing funny was said.

Tommy said, "Let's go to the Chinese restaurant. The party will be on me."

"Lottie."

"But I was going to buy a big cake and have it at my house!"

"Why bother? The restaurant is right here. We'll have fortune cookies instead."

Holding hands tight with Tommy, his fingernails digging into her palm, but she said nothing. It might hurt him if she did, and he'd take his hand away. Already, marriage was peculiar. There were pains you could take, even welcome, and there are pains you won't. Pain is pain, she always thought...but now she knows it isn't."

In the restaurant, they chose the same table. It seemed so strange to share it with others. Like the movies, she always thought of it as 'their table.' They ordered more than they could eat and ate as long as they could, to prolong the party. It was all over somehow when the waiter put the check on the table.

Lottie frowning now, "I have a class."

Ski saying, "I have to return to my ship."

And both winking at each other. And Becky thinking, 'I...will be alone with a husband.'

"Where's your bag, Becky?"

Lottie winking rapidly now.

"I don't have one. I have to go shopping."

Tommy smiling now, besotted.

"Here, Becky," and slips her 100 dollars. "Buy whatever you want."

She'd lingered, so many times, at the lingerie windows. Loved the pretty nightgowns. More hugging and kissing and well-wishing from the two friends and they were alone again.

"Meet me in the hotel lobby after you've emptied the stores. And...don't run away with another man while I'm waiting and stand me up. You go first, Becky."

"No, you go first. Please."

He turned and she watched him as he glided through the tables to the door, straight, tall, confident, handsome. Felt like he was taking part with her with him. She missed him already. She waits until he was down the stairs and fled to the window. She could see the top of his white hat, the brass buttons shining. It was so exciting, seeing him at a distance. 'I know him...and he knows me. It seemed unbelievable, just then, that she would see him again and he would call her name and love her.'

"Tommy," she called from the window.

He didn't hear her and walked on. 'Don't leave me, please don't.' She watched until he turned the corner and disappeared, waiting for him to come back...but he didn't, and she wanted him to...so much. Knowing he wouldn't come back; she wanted him to. 'Surprise me. I want to be surprised. Do something like...come up behind me, over my eyes, turn me around and kiss me like in the movies. But he didn't...and disappointed her...not doing the things she imagined.

Out in the sun and having to put her face real close to the window to see, nightgowns...pink, blue, black. Black...mysterious... magical in the window. In the store, they were hanging on racks by the dozens, like aprons or housedresses. The paralysis of choice now.

She had to act quickly on impulse, or she'd just stand there, strained, staring until she heard, "Can I help you?" and fled, the intrusion on a <u>secret</u> secret...her honeymoon nightgowns.

On impulse, she pulled one out, then another and another, all colors rushed into the dressing room. A few dropped to the floor in her haste. Guilty, but she left them there and fled into the dressing room, putting one, then another under her chin, forcing herself to make a final decision <u>now</u>. She came back again and again and stood tortured and uncertain before plunging. But this time, it had to be <u>now</u>. She took them to the cashier. Stone-faced, seeing only the price tag, she slammed them on the table, removed them, stamped, and punched. Becky humiliated.

"That will be 25 dollars."

Becky, stupefied, hands her a bill. She clings the cash register, methodically counts the change without even looking at her, shoves the gowns into a bag too small, the black lace hanging out for all to see.

"You...have a...bigger...bag?"

Her back turned to Becky; she didn't even hear her. 'A honeymoon gown with wrinkles, like it was taken from the wash.'

Louder now, "A bigger bag?"

The cashier turned and pointed.

"Boxes over there...for a charge."

There was a line. Becky waited.

"Gift wrapped?"

"Yes."

All colored, pink, ribboned and bowed, she picked the package up gently and held it in both hands close to her chest like it would break. The pretty colors, satins, and pinks, a soft cloud now round her gentle, poetic, hidden...like it should be. 'A present for someone special? Yes, me? A present for me.' Special happy now. Looking forward, hoping, eager, like a child, when it's frenzied fingers are unraveling a surprise.

He was waiting in the lobby, that besotted smile on his face again as she came near...and she recoiled. He put his hand under the package, and they clutched fingers.

"Let me carry that for you."

"No!" and she jerked it away.

"No, please, I'd rather carry it myself. It's a present for me."

"I'll show you where we'll be staying for 10 days. A beautiful view of the city. An old hotel with a history."

Becky had waited on its steps many times for dates that never showed. She never dared go in the lobby before. Haughty ladies, men with white, silk scarves and gray hair comfortably walking behind luggage carts piled high with their bags. Becky was the last one in the crowded elevator and kept walking in and out of it to let people off. No one thanked her. Between floors, she stared up at the lighted numbers, uncomfortable having to be silent, not knowing what else to do.

"That's us, Becky. We're here."

And he bowed with a flourish as she walked down the corridor.

"To the right my lady." And he bowed again.

She walked on.

"Stop," he said and inserted the key, barring her entrance.

"Put down the package," he said.

She obeyed. He picked her up and carried her across the threshold of room 2010. He put her down clumsily and she fell against him.

She was heavier than he thought. He steadied her, looked at her tenderly and whispered, "Mrs. Hall."

A flash of hatred being called Mrs. such a prosaic ring to it like brooms and dustpans and scouring powder. But it passed quickly. He closed the door behind him.

"My darling."

It grew dark in the room. A ray of moonlight on the bed.

"I'll be right back," she whispered...and took the package with her behind the bathroom door.

She opened it as quietly as she could. It was scarring just to hear the rattle of the paper. She didn't want him to hear what she was doing. She wanted to appear as if by magic. Mustn't tamper with the image...appearing out of nowhere...a vision. Struggling with the bow. It had twisted itself into a tiny knot that wouldn't give. Desperate, tearing with the teeth, it shreds in her mouth. Stiff, new, shiny paper, the crackling sound of unfolding. She stops quickly...waits...then unfolds the other side. Another crack. Muffled, this time. She pauses again. Humiliated. He <u>must</u> know what she's doing <u>now</u>. Opening the box and putting the top down...ever so gently. She chooses the white gown, without stain, so she's smooth to the touch. She can't see her whole self in the bathroom mirror so she puts her hands round the curve of her waist, and slides them up and down. 'Nice.' Then notices the tag hanging on the sleeve. The girl forgot the remove this one. She slipped them inside. 10.95. Hope he doesn't notice. The door was old, stiff with layers of old paint. Pushing hard, bracing shoulder and arm and beaching the knee, the fragile fibers of the sleeve cling to the door as she pulls away. An armful of runs and snags and still...she can't get out.

Trapped, she calls out a desperate, "Tommy!"

She watches the knob turning. He's pulling harder again and again, insistent, determined and the door remains just as determined, returning to it's place, shaking and banging and unbudgeable.

"I'll have to call somebody. Hold on, Becky."

She turned out the light and waited in the dark. Then, the sound of men's voices, the clank of tools. She hid behind the shower curtain walking until they cracked the door open. More talking, laughing, and finally, a door slamming. She peered out cautiously. Tommy flung the door open and embraced her. She put her arms around his neck...grateful relieved.

"Honey," he said, "you look beautiful though it was so dark," he couldn't see her well but she didn't mind as long as he said it.

Perfume too heavy, sickening sweet but he didn't seem to mind. It was suffocating her. Embarrassing...not knowing even how to dab perfume. Used to not feeling. Not expecting to. Only grateful to be wanted, hoping to please. Tommy watching while she play-acted. Swoon, Becky. Moan and tremble. Tommy's hands free now, hesitant, touching secret, forbidden places. She could see the face smiling, even in the dark. Contented with himself. A spark of resentment flares, vanishes as quickly as it came, gives way to duty, blandness. 'We are both watching. He is watching me...me watching him. Loathing him now.' He hadn't cut his nails and wounded her, pulling, clutching as she submitted, breast, stomach, legs, and 'this too shall pass.'

He took her hand, touching him. Revolted...she drew back, fingers stiffening, and her hand opening like a claw. He insisted, demanding, and found her hand. She let him do it with he wanted. It lay limp where he put it. Kissing her, his beard growing, scraping her face now, she put her arm above her head and held fast to the bed.

"Am I hurting you?"

Breaking in two, "It's alright, Tommy."

He collapses on her body, his head on her chest, dead weight, breathing heavy. He rolled over his pillow, taking her with him.

"I love you, Becky," and kissed her.

They fell asleep touching each other's open mouth. In the morning, he woke her, holding her close and kissing. They laughed when she raised her hand to touch his face and the tags dangled above his head. She gazed up at him, looking adoring. He wanted her again and again, with that look in his eye of disbelief that she wanted him, too. The morning kiss is long, close, without passion. They have no need for it. Folded together, hands cradling, baby-need, mother-need. She lifts her small breast in his cupped hand. It is still a moment, then traces her body. Her nakedness is hungry for touching...hiding...but not alone, hiding safe, not frightened, hiding, and not waiting. His knee pushing hers. She has been tucked in, safe, warm and cuddled. There is no delirium, no frenzy, no quivering, or tears now. Pretending. Play acting to please. Magic, poetry shriveling. Pain, blood, and weariness now...and praying. 'Soon. Let it be over. Soon. And this too shall pass...like homework and practicing and concerts or a job. Tommy...proud...I love you, loving me.'

Raw and stinging deep inside, battered again and again to assure and reassure and close and curling again, but like a beaten child now until tenderness and closeness and curling one to the other and soft, sleepy words nudging, coaxing warm her again to him and she fall asleep on his shoulder, her head turned towards his, lips touching until sleep comes and waking the same way like they hadn't moved at all, arms or hands or bodies. He had her clinging to him like an innocent child. And she liked that part the best, talking baby-talk and nicknames. He called her Pudgy. She couldn't think of one for him. And then he loved her behaving like she was transported, wanted, and <u>knowing</u>. He believed her improvised playacting. But, somewhere, she yearned for a <u>knowing</u> man...but feared him, too. She wouldn't know how to love him, and he'd laugh at her and her pathetic little performance. 'I'm not really a woman if I've never really been with a man. And Tommy's not really a man if he doesn't know the difference. Just a silly, smitten, foolish boy is all he is. His uniform draped over the chair, he's just a dullard. When it's on him and he stands before her with it pressed and starched and brass buttoned while she's in a rumpled nightgown seeing him out the door...a flicker of excitement. He'd leave on one pretext so he could play house. Come back and have her there, opening the door...like a real wife.

Just two more days left before he had to return to sea. Constant coupling was becoming tiresome to Becky. Even her vanity was sated. And she was tired of other things, too. How long could she play bewitched and enchanted, overjoyed, coy, sweet and talk sprightly, witty, interesting monologues, scratching, and scrounging for topics until the next, 'I love you, Pudgy' from him. And when the silence and dullness came, the hours of nothingness. What then? He would be bored. Would leave her. Romance needs parting for long periods and coming together briefly. There was nothing else in Becky's mind that held man and woman together. Real life was intolerable. It was Momma's and Poppa's life.

The phone rang only once. It was Lottie.

"When is he leaving?"

"Tomorrow."

"How about a little party before he goes?"

"Of course."

"Leona and I and our boyfriends tonight with a bottle of champagne. Leona's with me. You want to talk to her?"

"Yes. How are you?"

"How are you!"

Heavy with meaning, embarrassed, "Fine."

"You coming to the party?"

"I'm bringing my latest. He's married, has two kids but he's separated from his wife. I'm crazy about him. What a man! What a lover! I've been looking for him all my life!"

Envious...a forced, "That's nice. I'm so glad for you."

"See you tonight, 8 o'clock."

When she hung up, she turned to Tommy nervous. What to get for the party. Her first party. She gave him a long list. Overbought.

Afraid not to have enough. Lottie came on time, Leona an hour late.

She later told Becky, "We were going out the door when he undressed me again and made love to me."

Leona and her boyfriend at the party, in a corner, kissing hard. Becky wanting to look but not daring to. 'How does a man who is a good lover kiss?' Jerry looked rough, common to Becky. She didn't think he was at all good looking but she said he was gorgeous, like Leona wanted. When the party was breaking up Leona bragging, "He can drink anyone under the table and hold it, too."

Becky revolted. What would Poppa say if he heard this stupid talk.

Later, Becky asked, "Aren't you worried he's a drunk?"

"A little."

And then Leona talked of passion and lust and wanting like it was real. And Becky wished she could kiss him just once to know how he feels, a real kiss, not just a tongue wriggling around in his head like Tommy's.

Leona asking, "Tommy doesn't drink, does he?"

"No."

"You're lucky."

"I guess I am."

"What do you mean?"

"Nothing."

The last day. She watched Tommy packing, coldly, efficiently, walking toward the door without turning back. No drawn out, reluctant goodbye, regrets, tears, remonstrances. It was like he'd eaten all the candy and thrown away the bag. Watching his back as he strode towards the door, 'Don't let me, Tommy.' But she never said a word. After he left, waiting for the pain to go and the relief to come again... and it did. She threw the nightgowns in the box and rushed out of the bare room. In the lobby she called home. Ma answered.

"Yes?"

"It's Becky. I'm coming home."

"Come."

They hung up at the same time as if another word was dangerous. Becky forgot her key when she left. Mirele opened the door even before she knocked.

"Don't wake up, Poppa. He's sleeping."

Becky walked to her room without saying a word.

"If there's something in the box you have to wash so give it to me and I'll do it with Poppa's and mine."

Mumbling, "Nothing to be washed."

She didn't want Momma to see her nightgowns. Embarrassing. Just as bare as the hotel room here but it was home. Not as lonely and desolate. Something made the difference. She wasn't sure what it was. Momma put fresh sheets on the bed and pillowcases and pressed them, too. She sank into the whiteness, the smell of soap still clinging, her face settled into a dull gaze, her stockings had runs, one toe showed through the hole, she crossed her leg and let it dangle across her knee. She dozed and then woke up startled, her mouth turning upward, smiling quickly...then relaxed again. She didn't have to smile. Free now.

The next morning, "How come you pressed the sheets, Ma. You never did that before?"

"In case you came with your beloved. I didn't want you to be ashamed. To the goyim it's important, things like that."

"What's to eat, Ma?"

"Look for yourself and take what you want."

In the freezer, behind two pieces of flanken and half a chicken, Becky found four porkchops.

Chapter Eighty

Now...the obligatory reports.

To Mirele: 'He's so kind, sweet and good and loves you and Poppa a lot.'

Begging.

Mirele: Silent, hard, unyielding.

And To Lottie: A cynical, confident, commanding presentation, scared to death of a verdict; sarcastic, crushing, wry...and worst of all...contempt. She'd be jealous.

Becky said, 'It was pleasant for a while but I'm glad he left when he did. He was becoming a bore. Even though I was running out of conversation.' Lottie was pleased. Becky was relieved. Becky crawled between the two like a hunted animal.

And Leona. 'I think there will be another wedding. Marriage is catching. Like the flu, I guess.'

Becky grabbed her hands and spread her eyes as wide as she could and gushing, 'I'm so happy for you.' And she was.

Leona: I'm marrying Ski. He asked me after your wedding. I don't want to be an old maid. And Leona, too getting married. There'll be a double wedding it looks like.

"Leona?! Isn't that man married already?"

"No, not him. The wife came to her thin, emaciated, hungry looking came to beg Leona not to take her husband from her. He was all she had beside several children he never told her about. Poor thing was so lonely and pathetic looking, Leona said okay not for her sake. It was the children, mostly. Reminded her too much of her father. Leaving wife and children. Too scary. Even though he as the love of her life. Love of your life can be frightening. Like all your eggs in one basket. Your whole life! But people aren't eggs and baskets, Lottie."

Becky dreamed love forever and beyond...heaven even...like Cathy and Heathcliff. But only for other people. It could never happen to her. She was also balancing eggs and baskets like Lottie. Only Leona, falling and plunging. She never counted or measured. They both envied her. 'I wish I could be a little wild and reckless, just once...to see how it feels. Running as fast as I could away into the farthest cloud, sit on the tallest rainbow, dangle my feet over the earth, come down whenever I want to or not at all.' And she thumbed her nose at no one in particular. 'Leona does that over and over and never even looks back when she's running. Me...I'd look back all the time...my heart knocking harder and harder when I see how far I've gone. I'd be sitting up there on that cloud worried how to get back down. But Leona wouldn't. she'd be having a jolly old time, rocking, and bouncing and singing.'

Becky was frightened now. Lottie had never spoken so open before. Lie accidentally opening a door that says, 'Do Not Disturb,' and seeing something you shouldn't. guilty. Mortified. Lottie suddenly recovers.

"Oh, I forgot, you asked me a question. Leona is marrying someone she met a week ago and he proposed already. Crazy about her."

"And she...about him?"

"She's just crazy...not about him. In general, I think." Becky agreed.

"A rebound marriage. Blonde, blue-eyed, handsome...just like she likes them, but I'm afraid he drinks. A southerner from Georgia and he likes Southern Comfort...if you know what I mean."

And she laughed.

"Isn't she worried?"

"No, she can't be. She's pregnant. Wants a father for her baby. It happened when your father first got sick. When she was five months pregnant, this thing happened with his wife, so she decided to get rid of it. A lady she knew gave her something to bring on the birth. She had the baby in the house, wrapped it up in a newspaper and put it in the garbage pail. She couldn't take care of it, she said. No money. Too poor. All her brothers and sisters still in the house and her mother not working and she's not making much and him...the father...everything they call father...you should excuse me...Lottie spat out the words out like a curse. She's not the same now Becky. The spark is gone. Something went out in her after that. Didn't you notice?"

"I haven't seen her since Tommy and me were going out. It's been months."

Pity...shock...and resentment, too. Becky thinking, 'I brought them together and they're closer to each other now, than to me. But she'd paid for it. Suffering like she did.' Becky forgave her. But not Lottie. She needed someone. An offering: Nobility. Becky waited to be included now in a platitude, 'if not for you she wouldn't have known me at all.' But Lottie said nothing. Rage erupts in Becky. Fear throttling it down hard. Becky didn't know to speak up to Lottie. Wouldn't dare. And besides, what could she say. Praise me, too? Praise is not something you ask for. She wanted so much to hear, 'You're so dear to us both Becky. More than you know.' But...Lottie took the offering without thought of return.

"I think so, Becky. Good I was there. Someone had to be, hadn't they?"

Becky all forced brightness now. A memory of something she never saw would haunt her forever. Leona and that baby. Fixed hard in her head. Like she was there. And to blame. How many times she repeated to Leona that the poor have no business having children.

Never occurred to her maybe Leona was revenging herself on that man, or, maybe he was not the father for her child she wanted.

"So, when will it be, the wedding?"

"We're eloping together, all four of us...my term ends tomorrow. They'll both get a week leave and we'll stay in the same hotel for our honeymoon. Different floors, or course."

And she giggled, embarrassed like a little girl.

Jumping up from her seat, "I have to rush now, Becky." And a meaningful, "Things to buy, you know."

Becky thinking, 'Why did she tell me this now, when I'm a new bride, warm with loving? Because she's angry with me. And Leona is too. I abandoned them both. The daily phone calls suddenly ceased. Becky not waiting like she usually did for the phone to ring and calling like always when it didn't.' Becky had somebody now whether they were there or not. They didn't like that. Up to then, they were that <u>somebody</u>. If they weren't there, there was nobody. They were secure, powerful, indispensable. Becky decided she would make up for her neglect of the two of them. She would complain about Tommy, find fault with him and align herself with them against the man. He was to be referred to from now on, as just a husband. Lottie and Leona, friends. She feared them all, Lottie, the most. She was so much above her. As long as Lottie smiled on Becky, she was somebody too...like Mirele wanted.

Becky didn't see either one for two weeks or received a card from the hotel with little arrows pointing to the square dots that were their rooms. Leona had no time to introduce her new husband, so she sent pictures, the two couples smiling on their wedding day. But the two women came alone. The men had to catch a ship. Both still in the navy...career sailors. In one of the pictures, Lottie was wearing his hat perched jauntily on her head. Becky thought, 'Trying to tell me she's having fun.' Resenting flaring again. 'Without me.' Why didn't Leona let me meet David? Afraid. Like I was...when I arranged to meet her with a boyfriend of mine...and didn't. just let her come to the house and let Ma explain we had to leave early. I just fled cause she's so pretty. Afraid she'd take him from me. Leona, too, I bet. Afraid I'd take him for her. Me...just married...husband gone...lonely. She wouldn't trust hers...not even with me.'

Mirele asks, "So what does she do with herself all day, Phillip?"

"Nothing, Mirele. Waits for letters from him, then writes him letters. One time I said to her, 'What do you find to write so much?' 'The same thing,' she said, 'over and over.'

"Like my friend Minke in the old country. For years she wrote letters to her boyfriend in America. Even after they married, they wrote letters. The marriage was so bad that for 10 years, they didn't speak...only wrote notes to each other, 'Take out the garbage,' 'Buy eggs,' even 'Drop Dead and Go to Hell,' things like that.

"How do you know?"

"She showed me the notes. I couldn't believe it myself. Thank God, I can't write...because if we depended on writing, we wouldn't be together, altogether."

"But they're so sweet, his letters. I saw a few by accident."

"That's what she tells me, he's sweet, over and over again, like he's on the market, selling him, like an overcoat,"

And her face hardened again.

"They took everything from me once and she took it again. How many times can they take everything from a person?"

"Always one more time, Mirele."

His hand clutching the heart now, "Sha, Mirele. We'll be a little quiet."

The pain is coming again. Mirele walking in the dark, no light so that he may fall asleep. Terrible moaning until Mirele collapses by his side of the bed...Becky...a blanket over her head, hands shutting out sound, tight over her eats until they hurt, hiding from the pain and the cold in the room.

The next morning, a sudden decision, "Ma, I want to move to a place of my own...and lying...Tommy wants it that way."

Mirele would try to please him now...agreeing so he wouldn't hurt Becky.

"If you want, why not? A married couple should be by themselves. And you won't hear anymore Poppa. It'll make you sick, Becky, so go, what can I tell you?"

Desperate searching the floor, then making a square with her twisted foot, over and over.

"You'll come to eat sometimes? You...and...and...him...too?"

"Of course, we'll come. But why are we talking of coming? I haven't gone yet."

"You will, Becky. When you want to go somewhere you go, isn't it? Always, you went when you said."

Lottie called a week later. Excited, bubbling. She just came home. had to see Becky. <u>Important</u>. Becky met her in the cafeteria between classes, amid clattering dishes, clanging registers. Lottie shouting and still barely being heard...the wonderful wedding, honeymoon. They all had a heavenly time.

"That's good."

"I'm leaving home, me and Ski...a place for ourselves."

"Me, too!"

"We'll find something together."

The something Lottie found was a boarding house in Coney Island with two adjoining rooms. Becky was overjoyed. She left while Mirele was at work...leaving a telephone number in for the hall phone in the new place. The first night she waited, terrified for Mirele's call...imagining Mirele crying and Becky shouting angry words that everyone could hear...and she'd be ashamed of them afterward. But she didn't call, Becky then imagining Mirele was seriously ill from her or Poppa giving her aggravation...or both.

"I have to take the train and go home and see what's wrong."

"Now? In the dark...to sit on an empty train for an hour, then an hour back, maybe more, including waiting on an empty platform? Are you crazy? That's what phones are for!"

"But no one's calling me, and no one answers there."

"Wait, Becky. I know your mother. She'll call."

The hall phone was ringing.

Becky jumped up. Out of control now and shouting anxiously into the phone, "Ma!"

"Yes, it's me. How did you know? Already homesick? I knew it. It looks good, the free life but nothing as good as it looks, ha Becky? Nothing. Am I right?"

Becky furious now whispering rage, "Better! Now what do you want? Just to talk and say hello?"

"You said it."

"Now I'll say goodbye. Poppa says hello and goodbye too."

Mirele called again...four times that night. Lonelier and lonelier as the night wore on. Becky went to sleep trembling, 'Why are mothers lonely for children when children aren't lonely for mothers? We're not created equal where it matters, always one needing more than the others and slaving under the yoke of that need.'

She fell asleep needing Tommy, the hugging, kissing and warm arms circling round her.

"I love you Tommy," she whispered, for the first time to his memory...instead of nodding 'Mhm' as she always did when he was with her.

Snuggling and hiding in darkness and finding him beside her. Becky would love him forever if they could only hide in the dark together, always...the dark of night, the dark of morning, hands finding hands, bodies deep in touching...not ever becoming cold, mechanical, ugly, primitive, unpoetical. Fragile, mysterious, a tone resting on air...that was love.

Lottie was on vacation. Together they read and swam and ate too much, Becky every watchful that Lottie should not be bored with her. Becky decided to study the guitar, gave her an excuse to be apart from Lottie. Alone, she could think of further amusements for her. Political discussions were easy. As long as she agreed loudly with Lottie. She considered Becky very clever. But the other times, needing to clown so Lottie would laugh. She loved to see Lottie laugh, especially if it was because of something Becky said...or did.

Every day a letter came from Tommy. Occasionally, from Ski, for Lottie.

"How come Tommy has all that time to write and Ski says he has no time?"

Lottie glaring jealous at all four letters in Becky's hand arrived at one time and nothing for Lottie after she'd feverishly fingered through all the letters thrown in the hall basket that day...from then on, Becky sneaked into the mail basket first, found her letters and hid then, savoring them alone in her room, then going into the hall again with Lottie and finding nothing. Becky was happy when a letter arrived for Lottie, one upmanship at the basket. Becky let her win. She was in such a jolly mood the whole day. Becky was very pleased.

"What happened to Tommy? Doesn't he write anymore?"

"It's been a long time. Maybe he found another girl."

"Maybe. You know what they say...a girl at every port."

"Maybe," Becky joins her laughing.

"Well," Lottie scowling, "Don't be so happy about it."

Becky quickly scowling, too. "Of course, I'm not happy about it."

Three months passed by quickly, Leona still honeymooning with David. She sent cards from Florida and Key West, gay, ecstatic, witty ones at first, then scrawled, polite ones just to show she remembered, weather reports mostly, signing off with a plaintive, "I miss you."

"What is that sigh telling us, Lottie? Is she sick or sorry? Or is he sick or sorry? Or both? I think she's telling us she's unhappy, disgusted she with him or he with her or both with each other."

"So why aren't they coming back?"

"To what is she coming back?"

"A new life."

"Maybe even the old one looks better now, Becky. We just don't know."

"I have some news myself. Tommy's coming home."

"When?"

"Tomorrow. I called and found out. The company had a directory."

"Great, Becky! I'll visit my mother, so I won't be in the way."

Becky relieved, "You don't have to."

She'd worried how she'd give of herself to Lottie and Tommy. She was ashamed to show Lottie how silly she was around Tommy, how lovesick and worshipful now. Never thought she would be. And, all of a sudden, it happened. Lottie was always looking for who had the upper hand.

"See Lottie, no hands."

Lottie smirking, "Impossible! You love him now, Becky," she'd say. "There's the hand, heavy and hard."

"Like yours on me, Lottie."

"Heavier."

And both degrading, humiliating, frightening. 'Then, why can't I do without them? Because I can't.' Lottie always said, 'Strength is being unafraid to be lonely. And happiness, too. Only if you can be alone.'

"How much alone, Lottie? With someone or without?"

"Without."

"Without hope, expectation...dreams?"

"Without."

"And love, too?"

"Especially love?"

"But how can you help, loving, hoping?"

"You can't Becky. That's the upper hand. That's why it's heavier than a friend's."

"Why, Lottie?"

"No dreams, no expectations, no magic, no moonbeams with me."

"You dreamed of magic and moonbeams, too, Lottie? Is that how you know?"

No answer. When he called, he didn't know she was prepared.

"Surprise Pudgy! I'm coming home."

Breathless, choking fear, "When?"

"An hour maybe."

Warmth in his voice spilling over into fat, gluttonous, self-satisfied glee. She hated the cutesy name, Pudgy. The hall seemed cold. A grim, little walk back to the room. 'Do your homework, Becky, and don't forget to practice.'

"This is the heavier hand, Becky. Not wanting to and having to. With me, we're together cause you want to. With him because he wants to and wants and wants. There's a difference between submitting because you want to and someone else wants you to."

"That's right, Lottie. He's the heavier hand. But that's because there's something wrong with me, Lottie."

"Tommy!" she squealed, delighted, as he rushed in the door and she hid, shy, in his arms, her head on his shoulder, so he wouldn't see her. He seemed like a stranger."

"Let me look at you."

Tortured...standing examination and scrutiny.

"Gorgeous!"

'What am I doing here and who is this man who's taking these rights with me as if he's entitled?' She let him love her right away, close...so she could hide even more.

"I love you, Becky. Do you love me?"

She nodded, her nose and chin rubbing hard up and down his chest.

"Heh-heh," more warm giggling, self-satisfied, smug, loving himself, not her.

He liked her being shy. Made him feel so masterful. She called Lottie as soon as he was out of sight.

"What do you do all day besides a perpetual honeymoon?"

"He loves the movies. Every day he disappears for two hours or more and then tells me that's where he's been."

"Why doesn't he take you along?"

"I don't know."

"Why don't you ask him?"

"I can't."

"Who took care of you when you had an upset stomach the other day?"

"No one. Myself."

"What was the matter with him?"

"He went to the movies. Has to go every day."

"Is he still boring like he was? Never talking?"

"That's why we're always honeymooning, I think. So, he doesn't have to talk...just love talk and baby talk. He's baby talking more and more now, the little he has to say. But he doesn't drink and he doesn't argue so I should be grateful. He's leaving tomorrow. I'm grateful for that, too. I'm too tired to go on right now."

"Yes," Lottie's voice cold now and hard, "you should be. Better be with a quiet man peacefully than a noisy, fighting drunk. I have to pick something up in my room now, so I'll be staying overnight. See you after he leaves."

And she hung up. Becky loving him again, now. Impatient with fear of losing. That's how it was when she wanted something so much. She'd already forgotten the moment before. Sweet, sad, nostalgia now. Nothing fierce. A child tugging at a mother's apron for something she wants. Getting it, happy forever until she's crying for something new. Then grabbing it and running away happily forever.

Memory: A child goes home reluctant, heavy unwilling steps to the deadness behind her door. Visited a friend, stood in front of her door, heard her quarreling with her mother, turned left. Now standing in front of her own door, having to go in. nowhere else to go. Nothing on the other side but having to go in. That was forever too. Hours pass before the phone rings...forever, too.

Now, she loved Tommy, wanted him, would be happy with him forever, but the shaky pendulum inside hovered, trembling between forever.

That night. she whispered tenderly, "Will you love me always? Forever?"

Blushing even in the dark as she said it. He looked down soft, adoring, protective.

She looked up, a timid, wide-eyed child, "You'll have a baby for me, Becky and we'll have a little house in the country, a real home like I've always dreamed, in Long Island, maybe, where we can have a garden."

Turning away, the creaky sound of the bed following her as she curled and mumbled, "I don't want any babies, Tommy...or a home in the country."

The bed is creaking now violently. Tommy jumps up, his elbow jabbing the pillow, his head propped on his hand, his voice different now, like he was a stranger.

Cold.

"I don't need your babies."

The caressing voice that would sooth her...forever.

"I never told you before, but I have a child. A girlfriend I had in England, had my child, and disappeared. I looked for her for years and couldn't find her. But I will!"

He got up, walking away slowly from the bed, dressed coolly, methodically packed those bags, and strode out the door without a goodbye or a look back.

Becky huddled in the pillow whimpering.

Chapter Eighty-One

Head under the pillow curled and hiding, wishing she could become a speck and disappear, a little ball blown into the wind by a sigh, lifted higher and higher until she couldn't be seen or heard, like she never was. And still hoping, listening for his step on the stair. It was too quick, his leaving. She wanted a lingering goodbye, it was holding and being held, being missed, and missing the sweet pain of a tender parting.

Memory: Clutching the back of Momma's legs as she's running up the subway stairs away from her. The more she cried, the crueler Momma got and crueler, pushing her hands away with her heels, pulling her legs out of her grasp, running from Becky as if she couldn't bear to see or hear or touch her just then, the tension of her wanting to be somewhere else, to see Pesach so she was annoyed with Becky, turned away from her like she never was.

Tommy too. Leaving like that. In a hurry. A sniper. Shooting in the dark and leaving her to scream...alone. He always left when it was time. Doing what he had to do when it was time. Momma...stay...just this once. Don't go to work. Tommy, stay...just this once. Don't go to work. Lottie, help me. Help me...what to do.

Lottie wasn't asleep yet. She could see the light under the door from her room. It went out just as she knocked. Lottie in her night-gown, a big shapeless orange Jersey, her yellow hair flopping around her round, pale colorless face, her blue eyes so heavy-lidded and sleepy they could barely even be seen. Forcing her eyes to focus on Becky, glaring at her, she was frightening, the stuff of children's night-mares when they've been naughty.

"Something terrible happened, Lottie. I must talk to you."

Lottie reached for the light.

"Don't turn it on. Please."

An arm around the waist.

Gentle prodding, "Come on in. Sit down. What happened?"

Eyes wide opened, concerned now and searching. Every moment well practiced, the voice, the gestures, the ritual performance begins, the concerned friend. Becky generously gives her hurt. It soothes and comforts Lottie while she paces back and forth wringing her hands... performing. Becky apologizes for upsetting her while feeling a dark pleasure too; for the first time.

Memory: She'd watch the other children.

"Tell me where it hurts."

"Here, Momma. Here and here."

Watching their mommas' head bend with worry while they made up more and more places. Becky hated that. Couldn't stand her Momma's hysteria when she was hurt, never even told her if she didn't have to. But now it was different. She was making up places, too, enjoying the hovering and the anguish even if it was made up. But the shock and the surprise were real. Becky performing in front of an appreciative audience, hanging on every word. She loved it. Becky, center stage.

Becky crawling on the bed in the dark.

"What'll I do, Lottie?"

"No problem. I have an answer. Simple. You'll go to college. Get an education. He'll pay...and you'll throw him out when you have a diploma. Not before."

Unreality settling in. She'd seen it so many times in the movies. It wasn't hard; the heroine making the strong decision, revenging herself. 'Leave Her to Heaven,' and all that. She'd wandered in and out of real and unreal so often. It was easy now. Playing determined, revengeful. Lottie liked that. Christians who teach forgiveness and check turning are also people of <u>vendetta</u>. A Jewish girl preaching passivity, humility, love and tolerance and how she thrilled secretly to the strutting, inflexible men when they put their thumbs down and really hated and revenged while she was uncomfortable even at a hint of a heated word about to be uttered, but she wouldn't show it. Lottie would never know she was wavering, guilty, scared, even for a moment. She would get her diploma, if she could, and run. It was a way out. Becky was always looking for a way out. But she told the story in later years, she was always Lady Macbeth...firm of <u>purpose</u>. And all the tolerant Christians and timid Jews loved it. And Becky, too...proud of herself. In truth, after a week, she yearned to see him... and sent him an 'I love and miss you' letter. She returned home, enrolled in college, and studied night and day, a plodder, afraid to take her eyes off the books or she'd fail.

She visited Tommy on the shop and after a night of loving, told him she was going to school to do something while he was gone. She said she would think about children after she received her diploma. He didn't argue. Didn't want to waste a minute not loving. He was too happy, didn't care right then and there about anything. Becky wouldn't dare talk heart to heart with Tommy or anyone. Hadn't looked in there for so long, she barely knew what was in there expect for moods when she was frightened or happy like a dumb beast. And when Tommy came home, she was tail-wagging and jumping and fetching sticks and happy he let her until she got tired and hoped he'd leave, then anguished when he did...and missed him. But it was a comfortable, secure missing. As long as he wasn't with her all the time, she felt he loved her. He never complained about school, except one time, when she was late coming home. He went back to the ship in a pique, and she had to call and beg him to come home. He said he wanted a place of his own, so she rented a third-floor walkup, came home, and did her homework, and wrote him a letter. She knew no neighbors. Cleaned and cleaned, made crosses on calendars, and waited. Lottie and Leona complaining. Both husbands are drunks.

Leona saying, "He came home the other night crawling on the floor on his knees."

Lottie saying, "I throw things at him, screaming, when he comes home drunk. Of course, I grab only the cheap dishes."

Leona asking, "How about Tommy?"

"He doesn't drink."

"Not even one?"

"Once in a while...one."

"That's all? You're a lucky girl. Do you ever fight?"

"He shouted at me once when we were hanging curtains the last time he was in. I was so scared; I ran out of the room. He came after me and apologized. I never had a fight with anyone."

Lottie, "Oh, I forgot to tell you. Leona and I won't be able to see you this weekend. We're going to my mother's place in the country. Just enough room for the four of us. You'll come next time with Tommy. You'll come see us when we're back."

"Have a nice time, Lottie."

A twinge of envy, resentment quickly pushed out and declared unjust, no right to, selfish etc. That weekend she cleaned very hard and bought a cookbook to surprise Tommy with something special. He'd been very patient, the Chinese restaurant or Mirele's pork chops or Becky's one dish...meatloaf, she'd learned from Lottie. He never complained. She found dishes with long lists of ingredients that seemed revolting but declared delicious by the author. Spices she never heard of, but she tried, all day Sunday, measuring exactly, stirring, mixing, sautéing. Miraculously it looked just like the picture, but it tasted terrible. She threw it all out, sighing and frowning, disgust all the way as she threw it in the garbage, the whole gooey French mess.

'Cooking is not for you,' Mirele always said. Told her to go away when she ventured near the stove to watch. She was right. It wasn't and isn't and never will be. 'What's for me, Momma?'

Her apartment if you could call it that, a huge, dark kitchen and bedroom. There wasn't any parlor until Becky put a cover on the bed so it looked like a divan. But it was fancier than she ever had before. An old, distinguished neighborhood, a brownstone, two rooms carved out of five, the WASP's long gone, taking the gracious living with them. Now, the speculators. She polished and polished the desk and two bureaus, her way of playing house, terrified not to be <u>clean</u>. The bay window three floors below, the lucky people with a terrace and garden. Becky was in the maid's room and children's quarters. It was always deathly quiet up there; the occasional sound of a car horn reached her...barely.

Every Friday was Leona's night. She made lavish dinners, and then, after eating, the five of them played cards...and the same questions always, 'So when is Tommy coming home?' and the same answer always, 'Soon.' And they waited for more, she said nothing. Whiskey bottle is already half empty at dinner and ready to open another bottle after this card game. They waited for Becky to join them in lamenting. <u>Something</u> must be wrong. Some little thing?! Between Lottie and Leona there was a fair exchange. Each could soothe the other with a comforting ache in the heart. Then, one Friday night, the four sat down at the dinner table, the same, the same question, the same answer, and this time, after dinner they started the card game without her. She wasn't asked to join as they usually did. 'Pull up a chair,' Leona always said, but not this time. She watched in quiet hell...waiting as they slammed cards on the table, shuffled and ruffled them, clicking and splitting them, loving heartily the whole ritual, excited, laughing, having fun. Becky sat wretchedly by...for hours.

And finally, "I'll have to go soon."

No one heard her.

"Bye, everybody."

Louder, this time.

"Bye," they all said in chorus, without bothering even to turn their heads and look at her. The following Friday and the Friday after that, she watched a closed circle...waiting to be invited to play.

<u>Still waiting, Becky</u>. Looking on, hungry and hurting, watching then squealing and guffawing and closing the circle tighter. Not just waiting, Becky. Begging. A handful of pain struggling to reach their hearts. Poppa begging for work. You are begging for love. The family heritage. Watch their toes while they walk and nagged all their life to hold their head up and stand smart.

The men left for the sea, both at the same time and the card game ended. Three for dinner now.

Lottie smirking, "Tommy gone so long and you're doing homework?! This American morality, so stifling, unnatural, ridiculous."

Laughing cutting.

"Especially after he did what he did. Still faithful! What for? Ridiculous! That's what it is!"

Leona nodded her head. Snickering, mocking too. Daring her, more...ordering her to earn respect. Becky thinking, 'I should betray Tommy for a place at the card table?' She would. She knew she would. Anything...only Lottie shouldn't laugh at her. Begging again, 'Don't laugh at me, Lottie.'

"What's life all about, just knowing one man, live a little, Becky."

"You're right, Lottie."

Lottie loved being right.

Leona agreeing, "Yeah. There's homework and homework, and you've done enough scribbling. Lottie and I have an assignment for you, now. You're like the fairytales, sleeping lady waiting for the right man. Tommy ain't nothing. I can tell."

Becky thought, 'She's right, of course. Tommy ain't nothing. Never will be. And me, too. I ain't nothing, either. You forget that. Or maybe I never told you.'

Together, in unison, they told her, "You haven't lived."

Squealing, delighted, two minds like one. Becky is frightened now...not to live...like Momma and Poppa and Pesach...and me, too...

going through hell and pain and not living. After all that...not living. Terror now. Worse than both laughing at her. Wasting, throwing it away, not hearing, seeing, knowing...life. It wasn't a job, revolution, a worker's world...Poppa's <u>living</u>. Now it was love...excitement, passion, a <u>you</u> and <u>me</u> living, secluded, alone, secret moments, a union they talked about now incessantly in books...that women were now feeling deprived and guiltily searching. A new market exploding...love in paperback. Make them want what they don't need and need what they don't want. The merchants, not the priests now, reaching their long arms into the bedroom. Invest in connubial bliss, sighing, moaning, touching, climax. Invest in fever and lust, adultery and broken promises, clandestine meetings and broken marriages and live-in and live-out lovers. Invest in breakdown and heartbreak, swan songs and partings and loss and suicide. Collars turned around. Beards cut. No future in God and morality, now. The negative commands are now positive. Thou shalt commit adultery. Thou shalt covet thy neighbor's wife. A poor investment now, being faithful. No return. And it was now a shame and worse, a disaster...not using every moment. Life is like money now. Had to be spent recklessly, impulsively. Whatever you want...get...whenever, however, wherever...thou shalt please your friend. Selective breeding was only practiced among the rich...the poor were now left to the vagaries of random selection, even the bounds of religion, race, nationality ripped away, the poor given the dubious gift of love and free choice. Becky dutifully obeying the commandment searched the ads in the back of the newspaper for the meeting places for such people. Becky's family...none...money none, residence none, job none, schooling insignificant, college unknown, daughter of nobody meeting son of nobody, thrown on a dance floor like bargains on a pushcart and the fates scrambling and rummaging, couplings left to chance for whatever purpose. Becky circled an ad that said, 'Continuous dancing, 3 bands.' She paid at the door and stood waiting at the sidelines, waiting...hoping someone who was a poor dancer would ask her...and wanting to run. 'What am I doing?!' then remembering

Tommy's 'I'll have a child.' And Lottie laughter and Leona's scorn and days and nights alone...wasting life.

Lottie saying, "Giving it up to what? Someone who doesn't care how he hurt you? Pay him back. Eye for an eye. Hurt for hurt. Jew and Christian together in pagan virtue. Emma Goldman at the firing line, Poppa. Fear with honor. A new age, now. Heart knocking. Knees trembling. Facing what? Not being asked, Poppa, that's what. And being asked and stumbling around the dance floor.

"Excuse me. Please, excuse me. Fear without honor, Poppa. Ashamed and humbled...fear without honor, Poppa. That you would laugh at, too."

The dance hall, a big dark room with lights swirling about rows of men lining one wall and women on the other, some men brazenly glaring, some women brazenly glaring, others looking away following the light, or looking straight ahead without seeing or hearing. The light touches them for a moment, then dances away, up and down an imaginary hill so you don't know where it will fall next. Becky watches it carefully, then steps aside quickly when she sees it coming. But not quick enough. In the dark someone takes her hand and pulls her out on the dance floor, swirls her into his arms. She stands stiffly, still careful not to get too close to strangers.

"Loosen up," he whispers.

She stiffens all the more, trying to loosen. He lifts her off the floor, spins her around his body, sits her down gently on her feet again and moves her about like he's waving a broom in the air. Stiff, rigid...and still he had her moving to the music in a way she never had before. Like a big tree floats on water, he had her floating. When the music stopped, he sat her down at a table for two. She fell against the back of the chair gasping for breath. He grabbed it or she would have toppled over, then bent down on one knee looking up at her, one arm straddling the table, the other around the back of the chair...and laughing.

"I'm a dancing teacher," he said. "With me, you dance whether you want to or not, or you can or not. With me, you can, and you do..." in a thick, Australian accent.

Her legs sprawled under the table; her dress slid above her knee. He took her hemline gently between thumb and forefinger and lowered it.

"Now let me get you a drink."

He snapped his finger. Out of the blackness a waiter appeared. He ordered ginger ale. She drank quickly and hiccupped. He told her to hold her breath, count to 10 and drink, so she did. It stopped for a moment, then returned. She was embarrassed at first, then grateful. He fussed over her. He told her to hold her head down, then to hold it up. She thought he stayed because she was tired and hiccupping. They were seated near the band. She could see his face dimly by the light of the music stand light shining on the music. Black, shiny hair, round, handsome dissolute face, sophisticated air about him, wordily, man about town, an easy, confident smile, made for cigarette holders and martinis. When the red light passed, it shone full on him. His mouth was a little too narrow for her taste, his cheeks round apple types that bulge from overeating. He lit his cigarette with an arrogant sweep, but she could see he bit his nails, and his cuff links were frayed, but most of him was what she would call...suave. The little bit that wasn't suave was to be expected. After all, what was he doing here if he was as aristocratic in pocket as he seemed in manner? He put his elbows on the table, lifted her hand and cradled it in his. It was trembling. He pretended not to notice.

"You're beautiful," he said. "Cute even when you hiccup. Most people look silly, but you...in the future, if they ask you how to charm a man, you tell them, 'Hiccup.'"

She hiccupped all the more. Couldn't stop herself now.

"I'm-hic-not -hic-doing-hic-this-hic-on-hic-purpose."

Smiling, "I know you're not."

His even white teeth gleamed in the dark.

"Ooh! Look at that thing coming towards us! Under the table! Quick!"

She slid from the chair, bowed her head, covered it with one hand, and held tight to his shoes with the other.

"OK, you can come up now."

He was laughing hard.

"You see, no more hiccups."

He was right. They were gone. Come, we'll dance now. He led her to the dance floor where they stood in one place swinging from side to side, the other couples gliding around them. Becky sparkled in crackling repartee with him, chiding, witty and his eyes glowed with admiration.

"You're an intelligent girl, unlike most Americans."

And she proudly talked to him about Marx and Earl Browder, her entire little basket of phrases and things she knew, and he listened and seemed impressed while she thought, 'He doesn't know how stupid I am, but that's good.' And she talked even more frantic now. Always happened when she made an impression. She worked harder to hold on to it.

She asked, "Where are you from?"

"Austria. Have you been there?"

"No."

But she'd seen the balls and bouffant gowns and ladies peering over fans in huge ballrooms in the movies dancing to Straus waltzes.

"Yes," she said, "in the movies. I'm the lady with the Madame Pompadour wig and the beauty mark on my chin preparing my toilette at three in the afternoon for the ball."

"So let me be Prince Consort," he whispered in her ear, "and whisk you to my secret chamber and court you on a pink divan, surround you with plump, soft, pink pillows, Mozart's music soft and gentle in our ears and we'll tinkle glasses of pink champagne."

She looked at him...silent now.

He said, "I'll get our coats."

She opened her purse, the ticket standing up. She tilted it towards him. He plucked it out and brought the coats back, careful to be slow and unhurried. She tried several times to find the sleeve while he gallantly held the coat behind her.

"Let me," he said, took her struggling, desperate arm and led it smoothly into the sleeve.

"Come with me now," he said softly. "Careful down the stairs. The ballroom was in the German town of New York, a garish, lighted street, 'Coney Island Continental, beer halls and restaurants... oompah-pah music and gooey rich pastries with forbidding names and little and big bands in most of them...where boy meets girl.

"I'm just around the corner," he said.

She was stumbling now. He knew her feet were hurting. High heels. New...each step an agony and smiling like nothing happening. All the women were that brave, didn't want men to think they went through all that trouble for them. That they were that important. Between two stores is a small doorway. He lit a match; the bulb was out. Up three flights of stairs he kept lighting matches and littering the stairs with them. A small bulb hanging from a wire on his floor. A musty smell from his room as he opened the door.

He shouts, "Wait, while I open the window."

Banging, rattling, and finally, a resolute squeal as he forced it open.

"Come on in."

He was standing near a big, grimy window that she couldn't see through even in daylight, a neon sign blinking on and off. No curtains. A kettle on the window full of water to dampen the air, a daybed in the far corner unmade, the rumpled sheets in a huge tangle on the floor, a hot plate, a small bureau, his clothing hanging on nails here and behind the bathroom door, a covered tub.

"That's all there is," he said, "my suite."

He bent down, untangled the sheets, straightened them carefully on the bed.

"Now what you expected, is it? I know you're disappointed. I told you about what I want to have...not what I have. You understand."

The Marxist...a working's man's friend, had to admit she was disappointed. She felt sorry for him, ashamed of herself. As she watched him fussing with sheets and puffing pillows, the suave man of the world disappeared. It was like being with Tommy or Momma. suave men didn't do drudge chores in grimy surroundings. But maybe that was an excuse to escape the situation. She was determined to see this through. <u>Living</u> was not easy. She'd come this far. Just a bit more and she could say she'd lived... revenged herself...was a person instead of a dishrag and know what it is, at last, to be a woman. <u>That</u>...most of all. The test was here. A man of the world. A man who <u>knows</u>. Not like Tommy who learned...even from her...a know-nothing, an amateur, a clod leading a lump.

He opened a small lamp on the table near the bed and a roach scampered quickly out that was hiding behind the leg. He stamped his foot hard in pursuit, but it eluded him. He moved the table, angry now. Clomp-clomp-clomp again and again with his heavy shoes, but it dashed to the nearest wall. He curved his foot, sole up and slid it across the wall and suddenly stopped. A triumphant smile. I have him now!

Turned to her, "I'm sorry. They seldom come out when I have guests. This one has no manners."

She smiled, so as not to embarrass him anymore than she thought he must be. He took a small ladder and put it in front of the window. The shades came clacketing down. They stopped in the middle of the window. He brought them down quickly, closed the lamp, sat down on the ladder. She could see moonlight flickering through the side of the shade. Next door, the sound of voices, a man and woman coming home, the woman laughing cruel and then the man. He waited for the quiet and then...

"Come here, Becky."

She stood paralyzed against the door...horror numbed...guilt numbed...submitting to determination, principle, cowardice, unable to displease, to please...all of them...Lottie, Leona, Tommy, herself, Marx, and Freud and now...the Austrian sitting on a ladder, arms reaching out to her, a gentle pressure. Becky sorry for him, for herself.

Then Lottie's words, "Napoleon said, 'First you ask, then you commit yourself.' That's living, Becky. Acting. And Mirele ordered her to live. Did she think it would come to this? And this poor man. That's what he is, poor...poor man. Be kind to him, Becky. You must be kind."

He prodded gentle again. A fatherly tone, now. She stepped away from the door...cautiously, shyly. Determined now to 'stay and get it over with!' and thinking 'This too shall pass.' It'll be over and she'll be looking back. That time will come. Seeing herself alone again, tomorrow, the day after, helped her take another step and another. You can't end it without...beginning. Begin Becky...so you'll end! Giving herself a firm, resolute order and coming nearer. He drew his legs up. She came near enough to stand over him and touch his knee with hers. Not even shy now. Like she'd left heart and spirit and was now only limbs and arms moving and touching. She waited for Pygmalion to work his magic on her. Truck rattled by buzz-sawing into her brain, then an ambulance screaming down the street demanding it's way. Her arms snapped up, her hands cupped over her ears, her eyes shut tight like she used to when she was a little girl. His hands like claws, he stamped them quickly on her breast, tearing on one, then the other milking her like a cow, then, leaving one hand on her breast he shoved the other, brusque, crude up her thigh pulling panties aside and brutally pushing his hand, fingers all searching, grabbing. Becky tearing at his hand and shoving her dress down. Futile gestures of habit. Aching her body and twisting this way and that. Then he pulled her toward him, ripping her panties, forcing her to straddle him like a horse...and it was all over. He was breathing heavy on her shoulder and panting. The light was still blinking behind him.

He lifted his face and looked at hers, her mouth open in shock, her body quivering with revulsion and he smiled...a pleased, contented, "You like...eh? Eh?" menacing now... "Eh?"

'My God! He never even kissed me. Not even that!'

She nodded, parted from him, and groped on the floor for her panties.

"Turn your back," she whispered, "please."

He laughed. "I won't look," and covered his eyes with the tail of his shirt.

She was putting both feet in the same leg on her panty over and over again.

"Why are you taking so long?"

She gave up and put her panties in her pocket.

"You can look now."

He put the lamp on. His eyes, unaccustomed to the light, he closed them tight, opened and closed then again, his face bloated with weariness now, the shirt hanging out of his pants wrinkled, his hair dangling over his brow in frizzy waves repelled her.

"Would you like some coffee?" Talking while he held one shoes in his hand searching for the other.

"Stay a while. The bed is big enough for two. You'll go tomorrow."

Trapped and clawing to get out.

"My mother is expecting me at home. My father is very sick and I can't leave her alone with him."

"When will I see you again?"

"Anytime you say. I'm free."

"Tomorrow. Same place. Same time."

"I'll be there."

She opened the door and fled out.

"Wait! I'll walk with you to the subway."

He insisted on walking her down the stairs.

"The train is coming in!"

He shouted, "Where do you live?"

She shouts back, "In Brooklyn!"

"Where in Brooklyn?"

The train door opened. She rushed in, hoping the door would close quickly behind her, but it didn't.

"I won't see you again, I know it!"

Looking so shoddy now, a scowl on his face.

"But you will!" Becky whining, insistent, "I promised."

"Tell me where you live!" and he puts his foot on the train.

"At least give me your phone number."

"I can't!" She blurts out. "I'm a married woman, see?"

She shows him a white circle on her finger where she'd removed her ring.

A guttural, sullen, angry, "So what?! I'm married too!"

The car door suddenly closed. He tried to force it open, his lower lip trembling with exertion, his face twisted with rage. He pulled his foot out from between the unyielding doors. She sat down with her back to the window so she wouldn't see him. His anger terrified her. Self-loathing, woman unclean, dump heap for man. And not even a man...a furnished room with bathtub in the kitchen...a no-good Nik...a bum. 'For this, I betrayed Tommy, dear Tommy, goodnight Pudgy,' trusting, kissing her to sleep. Good women were kissed. Not the other kind. She was sitting among squashed cigarette butts, crumpled candy wrappers, discarded newspapers, two lights lit, the others broken. The train was empty. The tears slid down her cheeks to her mouth and she licked them with the point of her tongue. 'Good God, he never even kissed me! Not even that!' Guilt tears, begging tars, craven tears, beaten child tears. 'Poppa, stop. Please, stop. I'll be good.' A man sits beside her.

"Can I help? Something I can do?"

"Nothing."

He puts his hand on hers. She lets him. He whispers to the stations as they come. The next one is hers. The train stops. She pushes his hand away rudely and rushes out without thanking him... then turns...and waves after him, her mouth silently framing the words, 'Thank you,' as the train shoots into the darkness and disappears.

Chapter Eighty-Two

Remorse and humiliation...wake up to it...go to bed with it... remembering. There have always been those who've been ahead of their time...Victorian ladies who did more than flutter fans and eyelashes. But Becky was not even a flutterer, a hider behind fans, hints, and innuendos, looking down and away, muted colors and shadows, love under covers and in the dark. Becky was thrust callously out of 'paradise' like Eve. Lottie's taunting to be ashamed of same, regret being sorry, guilty to be remorseful, sorry to be sorry. What would Lottie say if she told her?

"Get another."

Laughing and chiding her like she was a child. Get another and scar and burn...again and again until she'd earn, free herself, be modern, sophisticated, knowing...like Marlene Dietrich looking through half closed eyes over a cigarette holder coolly at her next victim.

"He's the victim, not you, Becky. He!"

"Marlines don't play the games. They're born to it. Nice Jewish girls aren't, Lottie. Little girls strutting in front of mirrors like women of the world and quaking when Momma says, 'Now stop that foolishness and go to bed,' then being afraid of the dark and asking the light be put on and being warned again to 'stop the foolishness' and crying yourself to sleep, afraid to put the light on behind closed doors when the house was sleeping. Afraid even to do that. You were told not to!"

The phone ringing before Becky could rub the sleep from her eyes. Lottie couldn't wait.

"Meet me after class in the usual place and tell me ev-er-y-thing! Over coffee."

Lottie, too, raping the spirit, more fragile now, torn by an enraged conscience. Fighting Momma, then joining her, and waving a whip at Becky. Momma's simple morality handed down for centuries...work, sacrifice, tend. Nothing of seducing and vamping and manipulating evil, of being clever and sarcastic and witty and subtle, of playing games of love and hate and leaving and flirting and black stockings and garter belts, secret adulterous meetings, and the new Bible... Sigmund Freud. In Mirele's world she was commanded. In Becky's they were now giving permission, on the surface that is. In a vacuum of commands, a new set rushed in...

"Be as free as you can!" Lottie adding, "You'd better be!"

'What will I tell her? The truth? God forbid! Never! My secret that she's grabbing for now. She won't dig it out tenderly, stroke and comfort me. Oh no. she'll claw into it, tear me apart with ridicule and him with venom.'

She could hear her now, 'Why did you st-a-a-y?' Not a question really. A harsh indictment. And then, what Becky should have done and what she would have done, been wiser, quicker, smarter, of course and what hurt most of all, what <u>anyone</u> would have done, <u>anyone</u> having more sense than Becky, <u>anyone at all</u>. And then, a glib solution. Try another. Like it was all a big raffle, men, and women. To Momma, there was no other, ever...no matter <u>what</u>...there was no other. To Lottie, there was an instant other at the drop of an ounce of pride.

'A nice, Jewish girl in the New Morality, Mirele, and you helped to put me there. How many times you sang, whining and chest beating, the lullaby of the dead, 'Don't be like me.' But you taught me something else. Then 'live' you said and didn't teach me how. 'Read' you said. 'You'll find out everything if you read.' You won't even get started reading books with plain paper covers, too ashamed to admit you have an interest in such things...or too ashamed to apply what you've learned anyway, even if you've learned it. And Poppa saying, 'The revolution, rebelling...that's living...fighting for a purpose.'"

Lottie scornful, "Don't make me laugh. Life with Stalin. That's living?"

And Becky now adding, "Fighting for who, Poppa? My dancing friend. Is that living?"

Lottie had her coffee on the table when she arrived...so as not to waste a minute.

"Tell me."

"I had a wonderful time, Lottie. It's very exciting to have a... rendezvous...with a stranger."

Peevish. Jealous, "I told you so."

Becky gambled. She told Lottie all the things she'd read in the romance magazines...and discovered Lottie hadn't lived either. She read the same magazines.

She believed Becky, gasping like a schoolgirl, "Will you see him again? Does he want to?"

"Yes, I will and he wants to...very much."

She pressed on. "When will you see him?"

"Next week. He's married and can only see me when his wife isn't looking."

Lottie persisted and Becky had to invent answers on the spot.

"Does he have children? How long is he in this country? Is he staying? What does he do? Did he take her home? Where does he live? Where did they go? Is he rich?"

Burrowing for faults now, Becky obliging.

"I don't think he's too smart. I think he'll be boring me after a while. Seems like a clutch type."

"How can you tell?"

"He said goodbye ten times and returned for another kiss and another. I couldn't get rid of him."

Lottie loved that.

"He'll be hard to push out when the time comes. Just stay above the situation, Becky. These types have done this before. They're too charming, these continental types, too knowing. They know just when they're wounded so they can give the final kick...and make you like it, telling you how good you are because you're not clutch...loving to see you bleed gracefully and easily revolted if you don't. just one clutch and it's all over. They turn like you never were...cold, indifferent..."

She turned away and whispered "hateful" turning back, a choked, tearful, "I'm sorry."

Now Becky thought she knew more than she'd imagined, about losing love, that is...not loving. But Becky wouldn't dare ask. She wasn't like Lottie at all.

"Now," Lottie still upset, "I'd like to talk to you about something. I don't know what to do."

Becky was terrified that she wouldn't know what to tell her, how to help her, to advise her right, to be wise so Lottie would respect her.

"It's Ski. We've been arguing lately about everything. He says there's one real reason. I say there's one, too. I say it's his drinking and he says it's...you."

"Me?!"

"He's jealous of you, Becky and he says if I give you up, he'll give up drinking. He says I like him and you equally and I come to you with all our secrets. I said it isn't true, but he doesn't believe me."

Momma winning now.

"Sacrifice, Becky. Tend and sacrifice."

A warm glow inside now. Pleased with herself.

From the shrinking, shriveled with shamed, indulged self to a proud, giving noobility, frowning, and grimacing on the surface like one does at loss and hurt, but blooming proud and full in her heart, and sighing, "Well, we'll have to do it. Marriage comes first."

All the voices screaming, 'Get away from me, Lottie, leave me alone! Can't take your sarcasm and tyranny anymore,' were quiet now so Becky could savor fully her sense of loss. This story became one of Becky's heroine tales. Lottie walked away from the table and never saw Becky again. The hurt came later. Sitting at their table in the cafeteria watching the door and later, still, asking discreet questions of Leona in passing.

"How is she?"

And meaning, 'Does she miss me?' And hoping she'd call. Just to soothe the pride, that's all. But now, it won't. Always fearing a friend. That this or that coffee cup will be the last one. She'd be condemned to the discard pile in time. Lottie's ma said Becky was boring, low class and Lottie was listening. It was easier now. She could pick and choose. 'They'll be next, Ski, Leon. They'll see!' Jealous, but soothed by sacrifice and nobility made her feel so...grand. Even losing Lottie was worth that, after all. Wanting not to have and wanting to have. Easier not to have...to dream and remember...easier not to worry how to keep.

'That's all worth collecting in life...memories...as many as you can. Poppa said it was 'learning' thumping his head every time he said the word. 'No one can take it away from you.'

'And memories, too, Poppa. No one can take that.'

'Who needs it, Becky? Thinking about what was.'

'Nice to know you once had something.'

'And if you had nothing, you have to know that, too?'

'So why do you look so important and so self-satisfied when you remember, Poppa? Like you accomplished something, being nothing?'

'What else do I have to be important and self-satisfied about Becky?'

'Me neither Poppa. I have nothing else.'

'Think of something, Becky,' Poppa is desperate now.

Poppa always had the last one in those imaginary conversations.

She guessed it was because, somewhere deep in her mind, Poppa was still Poppa.

'I'm thinking of something Poppa, that I wish was a memory, but I know I won't like it even when it's over and I'm looking back. I didn't dare tell anyone...not Tommy or Leona or anyone.'

Tomorrow she'll be graduating college. Shame just thinking about it. No honors. 'Just me in a long, black line invisible even to the man who hands out the diploma, looks on the list for her name, smiles, congratulates and wishes her luck and never even looks at her.' What college did you go to, they'll ask, and she'll tell them and they'll say, 'What's that?' 'In Brooklyn.' 'Oh.' Their eyes will wander and say, 'Excuse me.'

Momma and Poppa smiled at her when she came down the aisle with her diploma, coming to hold and touch their one achievement. Becky was now an educated girl, she was <u>somebody</u>.

"Beckele, come here," Ma hobbling after her as fast as she could, and Poppa out of bed for the day, behind her while she's clearing a path for him through embracing parents and parents kissing under three cornered hats and holding diplomas over their heads. And Becky running, frantic with shame, no one should see that Momma and Poppa belonged to her. Later, at home, she said she couldn't get through the crowd.

Both happy, Poppa repeating over and over, "A college girl," and rook the concertina and played while Becky and Mirele swayed back and forth to the music, Mirele clapping her hands while she shuffled around.

When Becky daring to say, "You see Ma? Thanks to Tommy, we see this day."

Mirele stopped clapping and smiling.

A studied smile, "So when is he coming back? Tell me. When?"

Phillip innocently saying, "You should give me credit that I told you to come straight home. We couldn't find you, Becky and Mirele said we should keep lookin for you because you were looking for us and I said to come home. Was I right or not?"

Poor Poppa clutching at straws now.

Mirele saying, "As long as Becky graduated college. And she closed her eyes and gave in to the delirious joy of the world, wanting to scream and clap her hands like little girls do when they're happy. My Becky, a college girl!"

It was a cold day though it was June. Momma poured big glasses of tea, and Pa was blowing and stirring, the spoon furiously clinking on the side of the glass. Becky liked to watch the sugar as it burst into a cloud. Dead cold in the house. Poppa warmed his fingers around the glass, smoky breath from his mouth when he breathed in hard.

"It's cold," he said.

Becky never heard him say that. Poppa was never cold. Pushing guilt down hard now. 'Both of them were like big-eyed children reaching for candy and I pulled it away from them and ran. They don't know what I took from them, but I know. You're right again, Poppa. Memories we don't need. You and Ma are already a tortured memory. The fates weren't looking, and some pure joy almost slipped through us. I'll have to pay for that. Even almost, I'll have to pay for. But what's the difference? You pay so much for nothing in life. At least, this time, I will pay for something.'

Leona dropped in to wish her well.

"So, what will you do now, Becky, still wait around reading and writing letters by yourself in furnished rooms or get that guy to come home so you can lead a normal life? Must be something he can do besides stare at water. And you have someone who comes home every night, not 90 days out of 365, it's too lonely. I'm forcing David to come home, leave the sea. I'm tired of little company and lots of boredom. A great husband he'll never be so at least I'll have some children. You can't take a piece of paper to be with you every night and look at it every morning and afternoon and over coffee at lunch. 'Get a job.' Even that word was scary."

"Haven't you heard? There's a recession on now. No jobs! So, what will you do? David leaving the sea and all that."

"Thinking of opening a candy store, maybe, the children in the back and me in the front, like the old timers. But you, Becky," and she poked her in the chest with her finger, "don't you change the subject," hard edge in her voice now, demanding.

Becky will-less, struggling to reply. 'What can I say that will please her? What does she want to hear? The truth, maybe?' she lied.

"I don't know yet."

"What's the matter? Don't you two talk to each other? Still?"

"Still."

Leona smiled, satisfied. "See you, Becky."

"See you."

They always said goodbye like that, though they seldom saw each other now. Tommy was less frightening now. She'd flirted with the temptation to have him home like a normal husband in a normal home. It was becoming like a normal husband in a normal home. It was becoming stronger and stronger...the urge to live like other people in the mainstream of life...a sort of test she was giving herself and had to pass.

She remembered asking him, one day, "Why don't you leave the sea and come home to stay?"

"What will I do, Becky?"

"I'll look for a job and send you to school like you sent me."

Words tumbling out. Excited.

"Me go to school? Yes, I'll go. Why not? Study engineering... but..."

The voice low now, shamed, whispered, "you support me? Never! You'll work part time...or something. Where are we going to find all this work, Becky?"

"First, tell me if you agree, then, I'll see what to do."

"I agree. Why not? It's easy to agree to what you'll do someday. It's when we talk of doing tomorrow. That's the hard part."

A sullen, disappointed, "I guess."

"What's the matter, Becky?"

"Nothing."

Suddenly, he picked up his hat, threw it on his head, a little turn this way and that, straightening so it was just right.

"I have to go now, Becky. Be back soon. I'm going to the movies."

Becky aching for one more talk, willing the pain to reach out and touch him and bring him back. His sock carelessly thrown on the desk.

She picks it up and holds it in her hand, fingering it's softness and staring out the window...gentle, green buds being prodded to life, birds, tails proud and high in the air, moving frantically in a life purpose, swollen little bellies. She wished she could open the window and that bird would fly in and perch on her finger, stiff and welcoming, peck on her mouth once or twice and never leave... never...ever...like the kitten who came to Poppa's store and it looked hungry so she fed it milk and when it finished, it turned over on it's back and Becky rubbed it's stomach and it purred and purred. Becky could have gone on rubbing forever. She was warm and glowing all over like she'd never been, bursting with tending and needing. Then the kitten turned on it's belly and was scurrying away and Becky grabbed her and turned her over again and put her hand between her paws and rubbed and the kitten yowled and scraped Becky's hands with her claws and slipped out the door, Becky running to catch her... aching after her to come back. But she never found her again. Another came by a week later and Becky forced her to stay on her lap and with one desperate howl, she lurched away, her ears straight, ugly, scary. Appealing, gentle innocence, turns suddenly, vicious, an ugly snarl, desperate to get away. 'All because I wanted to give it love.' Becky grieved inside...and hoped wanting would bring it back. But it just turned and stared at her while she bent over and made foolish, smiling faces and talked herself hoarse saying, 'Here kitty, kitty, kitty.' But she wouldn't budge, that kitty. Just sat there watching Becky's arms and hands needing to hold and cuddle her. '<u>Come home Tommy please.</u>' She timed the movie and the walk home. The key turned in the lock. She put on the light. He mustn't see her sitting in the dark. He flung his hat on the bed.

"Tommy!" She jumped up, hugged him hard and clung to him. He moved and she clung harder.

"Heh-heh, what's gotten into you, Becky? You'd think I just came home from the war...or something."

"Hold me tight. Tighter. Tighter."

He took her arms from around his neck.

"You're hurting me. I've had a long walk. My feet are hurting. Just let me sit a minute."

She moved quickly away. Stung, recoiling, "Sorry," and waiting for a rush of loving apology, 'I'm sorry Becky. Forgive me,' and prodding a Becky pretending to be hesitant into his loving arms like a small child so whatever happened...un-happened...like it never was... and besides, it was so nice...his being sorry and making up. She was always ready to make up. Never held a grudge. It just wouldn't stay inside no matter how hard she tried. Like a hole in the pocket. Something slips out and she pokes and pokes and never finds it again...no matter what. Like the cat...after she scampered away...tail and all arched and running like she was glad to run away from her. Becky was mad for a minute, but then she waited for her to come back... longing, like it was a person. Tommy settled in a chair.

"We'll go out to eat soon. I just want to rest for a minute."

Becky is waiting. He opened a newspaper...and she heard him saying, from behind the paper, "I can't do it Becky. I'm too afraid. Forgive me, but I can't do it."

"Ever Tommy?"

"Ever."

Chapter Eighty-Three

ecky was grateful to be talking to the back of a newspaper. It was trembling a little. He wasn't even reading. She was sure of that. Just holding it in front of him, hiding. Becky was listening hard. Was he sulking, crying, angry? She wasn't sure. Frightened, maybe. He sounded so different, so strange. She tried to imagine the look in his eyes, the mouth, turned this way or that. 'A hint, Tommy. Give me a hint. Please. She curled a piece of paper into a tight wad and tossed it playfully over the paper, a smile on her face though no one was looking as if he'd catch the spirit. She waited. The little wad fell on the floor. She hoped he'd pick it up and throw it back. But he didn't. She bent down and picked it up where it fell between his feet. He pulled the paper closer, so she wouldn't look up and see. She touched his ankle with her finger and played 'Little Piggy Went to the Market,' alternating fingers, going up to his knee and down again. He turned out the lamplight, the paper around her, bent down, pulled her up gently and kissed her. She touched his face with her hands. It was dry. He dropped the newspaper on the floor, she sat down on his lap like a child, his arm around her waist, her palm resting on his cheek, feeling the words as he spoke to them, soft, hesitant.

"I'm too afraid, Becky. Just...too afraid."

She was relieved. The thought buried so deep that it burst in her head so hard it sent her body quivering. 'He's going to see the woman and child. He's found them. That's why he's not talking about children anymore. He had one already.' She never dared ask. 'You never talk, Becky' or 'You talk too much, Becky.' Seems she never got talking 'just right.' Contempt breaking through...his not knowing where to go in life either. Two of us bouncing about willy-nilly. Him especially. That night she dreamed there was a fire all around him, his head stuck out the window just looking down at the firemen holding a net and hollering, 'Jump Tommy! For God's sake, jump!'

She awoke screaming so loud the neighbor was banging on the door with a broom handle, but he slept through it all. She turned her back to him and curled into a tight ball. He was beside her, curled too. Both wanting to be back in timelessness, in the soft, dark, unborn. Where it's all given and taken in silence. 'That's your secret that you couldn't tell and mine that I never told...even to myself. They always said we were too quiet. Somewhere we missed the crying and the yelling and screaming. Must have been afraid, even there, when are we going to yell, Tommy? Flail our arms and rouse the house. You have to scream first and can't. I have to scream first and can't. I'll run if you do, and you'll run if I do...get in the race. I want to...now...and you don't...ever you said.'

"Pudgy," a muffled voice under the blanket, baby-talking and she baby-talking back.

"Me thirsty," he said, "bring me something cold to drink, please."

'Only cold milk in the fridge. One glass left.' She was saving it for herself. She grudgingly poured half a glass. Eyes big and innocent, he looked up to her and she tipped the glass while he drank from her hand.

"More," he said.

And he looked up to her with a childlike innocence wanting in his eyes.

Loathing but looking down on him with a maternal smile, "Yes dear."

The backless slippers sliding off her feet, she drags them along, her feet half in and half out. The high-held feathered ones broke, so she bought these in a hurry instead. Didn't bother to try them on. Too lazy to bring them back. She poured the rest of the milk in the glass, pounding the container several times for the last few drops...by habit. It never really made that much difference.

He called out, "Never mind, I've changed my mind. I don't want it anymore."

She drank greedily and wanted more.

"I'll go down and buy some more milk."

He did not reply and soon, she heard heavy breathing. Asleep again. She threw a spring coat over her short nightgown, put on a pair of shoes, a shawl over her unruly hair. She kept her coat tight around her. She forgot her panties. When she returned, he didn't even know she was gone. Still sleeping. Only the tip of his nose showing under the blanket. He had such a pretty nose. Warmth for him again. The silly things that make such a difference in a shapeless world. She put the bag down by the bed, pulled the blanket from his head and kissed him tenderly on the cheek. He made a croaking sound like a contented baby...and she loathed him again. She picked up the bag, rattling, cracking, a grim look on her face.

She heard him say, "Honey, I love you."

"I love you too," she said, and meant it now.

Her moods were like that. Coming and going on a word.

He talked again, from time to time about leaving the sea, she knew now it was just something he liked to dream about, one of the few things he liked to talk about. Not to be taken seriously. Just a dream that was to remain a dream, like people talk about writing a book or taking a trip around the world that they know they'll never do but nothing contented them like thinking they can if they really want to...like giving up the sea <u>if he really wants to</u>. Made him feel good again to think that. So, she let him.

Then one day, the announcement, "Let's go to Texas, Pudgy. Maybe if we settled there a while I'd feel more at home. A smaller pond there with your education you'd be a big fish there and who knows, we might both make a big splash there someday."

"I'd have to go to school, professional school, social work, maybe, so I can get a job when I come out. There's nothing for me now."

Becky thinking, 'You want me to go to school so you have a good excuse to go out to sea.'

"You have a job, Pudgy. Looking pretty, being cute, that's the easy part, the hard part is the waiting. Hardest job of all...waiting. I know. It's hard for me, too."

She thought it couldn't be as hard for him as for her or he wouldn't wait...would he. And make her wait, too. He'd do something. Honeymoon without the waiting, that's what she wanted. Forgetting that without the waiting, she'd always said wasn't any.

Momma's hand pulling you away screaming, "I want!"

"No Becky!"

Craning. Stamping her foot.

"No Becky."

And hard slap, "No! No! No!"

A limp surrender. But then, the time she got lost and Momma was worried frantic.

Some kind stranger leading her to Momma by the hand and Ma falling on Becky with hugs and kisses, 'Thank God! Where were you, Becky?!"

And treating here right away to a goodie and a penny or two maybe in her pocket that she caresses with her two fingers until she finds something to spend it on, but she'd hold on as long as she could, feeling rich until they were gone and then she'd still poke around with her finger stabbing her nail into the seam of pocket.

"Do we have to go wandering always, lost, and found and lost again. Maybe now I can be given without asking and begging. Given, just like this. Just because I'm here."

"Maybe you won't have to go to the movies to play house?"

"What kind of house, Becky. You working and me going to school?"

"Our kind, Tommy. We don't have to play the kind everyone else does. We'll do whatever our life says to do...free to live without orders...life pointing an imperious finger, 'You! In the kitchen! You! Into the job!' Why?!"

"Because I said so' that's why."

"We'll be different, Tommy."

She never knew she never really had a fair choice, never knew the nice part of being the same and never knew anyone else that did. Being the same was slavery...diapers...and boredom. Being different with dignity and excitement. Until now, it was lonely, exciting in bits and pieces, but there was another kind, waiting to be tried. Becky was looking forward now.

"Why not? Do they still have cowboys in Texas?"

He laughed, "Plenty of hats. More hats than cowboys now."

"And guns too? People still carry them?"

"Yeah. They're just not rounding up and shooting Indians."

"So, who are they shooting?"

"Each other."

She shuddered. The revolutionary had never even seen a gun, couldn't think of anyone really having one, or...Heaven forbid... using it.

"When do you think we should go, Tommy?"

"I haven't really thought about it."

'Let's think about it now."

And they both closed their eyes and played thinking...Becky's mind blank with excitement...Tommy's just blank. Becky forgetting old resolutions on the brink of new ones. Once, the diploma was to mean the end of a marriage, now it meant the beginning of one. Becky couldn't be bent on revenge for too long. It just wore itself out...revenge, resolution, and all. It was never that strong to begin with. A lot of playacting she did for Lottie.

"You'll like Texas," he said in a dreamy voice, proud. "Especially in my town...where I come from...San Antonio...yippee-yay."

Yowling like a cowboy, he straddled a broom, and jumped around the room slapping it behind him like it was a horse. It was so good seeing him happy, jubilant.

Becky burst out, "We'll leave next week! That'll give us enough time to shop and pack and tell the landlord!"

Then the voice dropped to a whisper... "Tell Momma and Poppa."

Begging now, "You will send for them later if everything works out, okay?"

A voice full of giving, "Of course, we will. But not next week. At least a month. We have to pick a school, a place to live."

"OK, then next month. But how will I watch Ma and Pa looking at me with calves' eyes for a month? Big and hungry and accusing and innocent."

They always looked so tender when she was about to wound them.

Screaming inside, 'But you want to get rid of me anyway.'

"Until you get ready. Then I don't want to."

"And you want me to be somebody, Ma."

"Not in Texas and not with him."

And the old proverb repeated in Yiddish for the thousandth time, "Better to lose with a wise man than win with a fool."

"You don't understand, Ma!"

"And you don't understand, Becky."

Stalemate. Trembling, choking silences.

Then Becky, "And even if I did understand, a goy is still a goy, right? Even if he sent me through college, right?!"

Hysterical now, "Even that?!"

No answer. Grim-faced, her mouth swallowed in a straight, invisible line between her teeth...and moving.

"How did you have someone like me, Ma...who's always wanting to sleep, lay, and lounge, with or without dreams, doesn't matter, day or night, that doesn't matter either."

Poppa brushing his head on his finger and looking martyred, but joy fleeting quickly, imperceptibly, over his face, "So, when Becky, we're going to lose you to the cowboys and Indians."

Smiling...and Becky smiling back.

"In a month, Poppa."

Concerned eyes scanned her face.

"If I get a job and make money, I'll take care of you and Momma. it'll take time but Tommy promised."

Poppa saying, "We came to America, Mirele, to make bread. Texas isn't that far."

"We have plenty of bread."

And she turned the knob and flung down the lid of the bread box. "Bread!"

And the crumbs flew all over from the force of it. Becky stormed out of the house slamming the door, the rolls tumbling to the floor. Mirele picked them up, kissed each one, raised them to heaven before she pushed them back in the box with the lid.

"They'll fall again, Mirele."

"Let them fall," ...sighing, weary, sitting down, drumming on the table. Glaring, a dreadful, piercing look in her small, black eyes as if she were going to kill, but she wouldn't. she only looked like that when loss was claiming her again.

Laughing ghost taunting, 'We're coming, Mirele. We're coming for more.'

"Take me." The drumming stops suddenly, hands outstretching, "Take me."

And then, anger reddening their faces shouting, "We give orders here!"

Mirele whining, "Order me," and standing up at attention, shoulders straight, hands at her side. A terrible laughter, "You can't trick us. You want to know which one. We'll give you a hint. Neither now...but be grateful...foolish woman...she's only going away. Not forever. She's going to a place where she can come back. Sit down and repeat until we tell you to stop."

Mirele repeating, "I'm grateful. I'm grateful. Grateful. Grateful."

They turned and she called after them until they disappeared.

"I'm grateful, you hear."

And then Phillip calling, "Mirele, why are you so grateful?"

She hobbled over to him quickly and touched his brow with her hand.

Phillip smiling, "I didn't call you here to beat me on the head. Why are you so grateful?"

"She's coming back, Phillip. I was told she's coming back."

"By whom?"

But he knew as soon as he'd ask. She'd been away to that place she goes to sometimes...inside.

"I'm glad you're back, Mirele."

"Why? Where have I been?"

She looked at him suspiciously as if he saw her in a secret place, spying on her. She didn't want anyone to know. She lied.

"I thought you said you were out."

"So, now you're listening when I'm talking."

'That man never listens,' her head wagging from side to side... righteous...indignant. All those thousands of words in the air between them unsaid.

"Who told you to be grateful?"

"No one. Nothing. Leave me alone...leave me alone."

She's found a way not to go mad, being grateful.

At the last pork chopped dinner, Becky said, "We'll be back, Momma."

"Thank God. I'm grateful for that," Mirele said.

She slept all night lying on her stomach with clenched fists tight against her eyes, afraid to let a tear drop, so they wouldn't think she wasn't grateful, the order givers. Poppa said goodbye to her at the station, shaking his head up and down real heavy, gesturing and posturing...pitying himself. Becky knew he was performing but she could never get that look out of her mind...guilt...every time that look touched her. 'Doesn't matter, Poppa, if it's real or pretended.' All the arguments paraded before her again at the last minute...true ones, 'I can't do anything for us here. Maybe I'm not for anything.' This was his moment...center stage...the mask of heroism...at least once more and Becky wriggling at the end of that yearning for drama, a man who was reduced to finding them at night in his battles with a bad heart and now with a comforting like 'it's not the end of the world, Poppa, or I'll be back before you know it...but she didn't have the heart and let him play it out in the end...waving handkerchief and all.'

Mirele was caring for a sick baby that day and couldn't come to the station...or so she said. When he came home, he sat down and drummed at the table like Mirele. She came home and they greeted each other in silence. She sat down and drummed, too. First one... then the other.

Then Mirele saying, "So what school is she going to?!"

"Social Work school."

"What is it, social work?"

"Social work? You don't know what it is?!"

"So what school is it, tell me."

No, she wouldn't. A Catholic school, she told him. How could he tell Mirele? They were probably more foolish than the Jewish schools.

"She told me, but I forgot the name."

"No, as long as she should be happy."

That dreadful stare crept over her face again. Phillip waved his hand up and down in front of her eyes. She didn't see it.

"Good night, Mirele," he whispered.

She didn't answer. He went to bed and listened. He heard a child shouting in the street.

"Ma, throw me my jacket. I'm cold!"

Then Mirele with an adult's voice, "Come on up! It's late!"

Then a child's voice, "I don't wanna! Please...don't close the window. Ma! Open the window!"

Mirele's ghost taunting her. She grabbed one by the neck shaking and choking until it couldn't breathe. Phillip never heard her fall to the floor. He found her the next morning, hands still around her throat. She didn't even stir when he loosened them gently and put them by her sides. Her neck was black and blue for days, but he pretended not to notice. She was grateful.

Chapter Eighty-Four

There should be a special place for impractical people like Becky who dream useless dreams that make no allowance for people and happenings that don't fit in. a place where only those who have the same images need apply...never a bad word, kind, harmonious, gentle, loving, tender, good, whispering poetry and talking parables, living in a haze of mystic enchantment...not only in sleep...or in heaven...or in the back of one's mind staring in space on rainy afternoons...but a real place just set aside for those who love fairytales and want to live in them always...in love, work, money... even revolution...where they sing heroic songs, face firing squads that shoot above their heads and no one is shot, tortured or jailed. Becky knew she could never go to jail. She thought of it...her hands tightly clenched around the bars and looking defiantly out at her jailers. But the rest mortified her...searches...prison guards snapping at her, degradation, and humiliation. In her dreams, it was all without pain. We'll call the town 'Gentlefolk, USA' for those daydreamers, pipe dreamers, loungers, and lovers. In Becky's mind she was going to such a place...a place to put up hope and yearning and happy-ever-after. A new life! Becky didn't know then that there was nothing new about life. Daydreams are even more foolish than night dreams. At night, there are some others...witches, monsters, and we live with fright and hurt like we're really somewhere in the world. But daydreams are pure. Nothing there is not round and perfect. No one else around, just her and Tommy...no one, nothing to upset or disturb, dangerous in their purity, they collapse without warning and leave us shocked and grieving.

It was night when she came to San Antonio. Dirt and grime all around. Weary, unbathed. For the first time, not fresh and pretty and glowing, not gowned and bathed and perfumed when she saw Tommy. He said he'd meet her at the station. It was night. He was standing near a lamppost, the light shining on his white hat. There was a woman by his side. Was she with him or near him, it was hard to tell. Jolting inside. She'd never seen him with anyone before. Just had hers and hers...parents and friends. Nothing of his. Never even seen him with a friend. Didn't have any as far as she knew. He didn't see her when he struggled off the train, the heavy suitcase in front of her. She called to him, waving hard though he couldn't see her hand. He heard her, turned, and walked towards her, the woman following behind him.

"Becky!"

He took her hand, standing at a polite distance, then turning to the woman.

"I want you to meet my Aunt Marion."

And he relinquished Becky's hand to her. She acknowledged it limply and returned Becky's hand to Tommy.

"Pleased to meet you, I'm sure. Tommy told me so much about you."

"And you, too," Becky lying.

"He mentioned an aunt once and never talked of her again."

"Really? What did he tell you?"

Becky giggled hysterically.

"I'm not easy. If he told you that, he's lying and Tommy didn't lie, do you boy?"

"Let's get a cab," he said. "It's starting to rain."

Cabs were waiting. He opened the door quickly.

"Aunt Marion!" and he waved her with mock gallantry, bowing at the waist. Becky had never seen him so jaunty. She sat down at the far end, Tommy next to her and Becky at the other end. The two women stared ahead. The cab stopped at a white frame house with a white fence around it. It seemed simple and homey, saltbox colonial with white curtains and green window boxes and a mailbox on a post. A sign on the fence said, 'Beware of Dog' though she didn't have any. Aunt Marion lived alone, didn't like dogs so she did the next best thing. When the cabbie opened the light, Tommy leaned forward to pay the fare.

The two women turned to look at each other and quickly looked away...Aunt Marion her head stiff on her shoulders...a look on her face like this was the day before the last judgment...martyred pain on her long face, a bony jaw with lower teeth protruding, cheeks sunken in where teeth had once been. Aunt Marion waited while Tommy stumbled over Becky, walked around the car, and opened the door for Becky, putting his hand on the luggage. She held fast.

"I'll take it in, Becky. Let me have it."

"What for?"

"What do you mean, what for? We're staying with Aunt Marion. She has room for us. Mine since I was a kid. Pictures of me as a boy still in the bureau."

Aunt Marion scrounging for the door key in her bag grunted 'Hmph.' He didn't hear her.

"Give the bag, Becky. The cab can't stay here all night."

He was pulling it out of her and she was still clutching at it, still holding on, until he put it down in front of the door where she sat down on it, refusing to go in.

"Can we talk a minute?"

"Sure. What is it?"

Aunt Marion stood in the lighted hall, door open, swatting mosquitos with her bag as they buzzed around her.

"Hurry up," she said. "God knows what will be coming in next."

Becky, terrified at what that might be, rushed in, Tommy after her, slamming the door.

"So, talk," he said.

Aunt Marion stood near the door, watching a lone mosquito buzzing around the light.

"Get him Tommy, or he'll keep us up all night. Buzzing and carrying on next to your ear like they always do and disappearing quietly when the light goes on and coming again from nowhere as soon as you shut it off."

Becky fell in a chair while Tommy rolled newspaper whacking and made a bloody smear on the ceiling when he finally hit it. Aunt Marion rushed to the sink, wet a rag, put it over the broomstick, swishing it back and forth, sprinkling Tommy and Becky and herself with water until she got that spot out.

"Now let's go to bed," she ordered, "before something else happens and something always happens when you're tired. Goodnight Becky. Pleased to meet you."

"Goodnight." Becky mumbled. "Me, too."

Tommy led her up the stairs, fear growing and she trying to push it down and it getting bigger and bigger. He takes her by the hand, sliding it along the floor cautiously in the dark, feeling his way on the floor. Several times he reached up groping for the string that opens the light, but it eludes him. Becky behind him trembling, every uncertain step frightening her more.

Tommy asking, "You cold?"

"A little."

"Yeah. Nights are chilly here sometimes."

The light goes on suddenly. Aunt Marion behind them.

"Sorry, I forgot about the light. Don't want you falling and spending your time here in bed sick and helpless."

Tommy saying, "I know you have better things to do Aunt Marion than tending to broken legs," and he laughed.

Becky, her head bent, watched every step she took as if the hallway were mined.

"That's it, Tommy. Don't you remember? The door with the glass top that opens and closes. You liked to stand in a chair and play with it, remember? When you were a boy?"

"That's right."

And he opened the door slowly, like he was entering a shrine. In the corner, an iron bed with a skinny mattress, smaller than the metal spring showing under it, a bureau with a round mirror, a few pictures from Woolworth's hanging on the wall, a big pitcher on a table with a towel hanging on it, the bathroom was downstairs. Two huge windows, long and narrow. No curtains. She explained it was a boy's room, after all. Tommy didn't like curtains, 'too fussy, made it look like a girl's room.' A lamp on the night table with a white cardboard shade. Just one. Becky took the side of the bed that didn't have any... lamp or table.

Aunt Marion saying as she closed the door, "We'll have to get another light in here, I suppose."

Becky listened for her footsteps down the hall. She heard nothing. Tommy shut the lamp, his head falling on the pillow and breathing heavily in tired sleep on the instant. Becky sat on the edge of the bed staring at the transom, sure she'd see Aunt Marion peering down at them...scrutinizing. She was too ashamed even to undress before that transom and slip over it, saying it made her uncomfortable. Aunt Marion said she was pleased. It was a sign she was modest, as a young lady ought to be.

In the morning, the shock of newness through half opened eyes that no amount of rubbing and closing and opening could undo. His back was turned. She made little wake-up sounds that always curled him round to her. But this time he beckoned with little moans and a stifled yawn, and they both waited, awake, pretending to be half asleep. Becky turned and put a clumsy arm around his waist...grudging, unwillingly. It lay on him...stiff, wooden, dutiful. He moved to the edge of the bed, and it slid down and lay limp beside him.

"Pudgy, why don't you go down and make some coffee for us?"

Worried. "Of course, but where do I find anything?"

"That's right. I just forgot."

And he turned and put his hand on her open palm by his and squeezed it hard, then placed it over her waist, disentangled his fingers in hers and put his arm under his head.

He felt like a stranger already. Becky's mind clutching the past now, running hard from the present, struggling to keep the hope of freshness in the future. Regret pushing it's way in now and the cry deep inside, 'I want to go home.'

A light tap on the door. It opened slightly with a whispered, "Breakfast."

'How did she know they were up? There must be a peephole somewhere or she had an ear glued to the wall.'

Tommy chuckling, "Still the same Aunt Marion. She wants everyone up and about when she is. Two cups of coffee on the table at 8am. One is too lonely, so she'd say 'Breakfast!' and I'd be up there like a shot. Them biscuits! Makes them herself. She'll teach you how, Pudgy."

Becky reached for her robe, but Tommy frowned ever so slightly so she dressed in <u>proper</u> clothing. Aunt Marion, her clothes pressed clean and white like she hadn't even sat in a chair, just dressed and stood there like a mannequin while she baked 12 biscuits, made coffee, scrambled eggs without a spot or a wrinkle or a squirt from the grapefruit. Three cornered napkins sticking out of glasses, the table-cloth crisp and white as she was. Becky managed, with extreme care, watching every morsel from plate to mouth to consume the eggs without a mishap. But she filled her coffee cup to the brim. It spilled over onto the plate. She lifted the cup and a drop rolled around the bottom of it but she didn't notice. When she lifted the cup to her mouth it plopped on the tablecloth and Becky watched in horror while the brown spot spread and deepened.

Shaken. "I'm so sorry."

Humiliated. Penitent. Cravenly making amends.

"We'll take care of it, won't we Tommy?"

Aunt Marion looked hard at Becky, "It'll come out with bleach and rubbing."

"Bleach and rubbing, yes, thank you," Becky mumbled like a blithering idiot.

At the end of the meal, Becky cleaned the table. Tommy's and Aunt Marion's place was squeaky clean like no one ever ate there at all, but Becky's plate was surrounded by crumbs.

Aunt Marion warning, "Be careful they don't fall to the floor. Bugs, don't you know. That's what they're waiting for."

Becky was so embarrassed that she was spun around and while she was staring at the window, she could hear the scraping of the brush on the crumbs, and she stood there with her back to Aunt Marion until it was all finished. She took the tablecloth out to the lawn.

"Come here and grab hold of the other end and help me shake it out."

Becky sighs, "Not done with those crumbs yet."

And they tugged that tablecloth between them hard, Becky struggling to hold on while Aunt Marion tugged with such vigor Becky thought she was taking pleasure in pushing her around with a good excuse like it couldn't be helped. Becky's arm hurt for a while after that. They folded it together, Aunt Marion folding into her arms and leaving her with it. Tommy came whistling out of the house.

"C'mon," he said, taking her by the arm, "we'll drop it off at the laundry marked the spot," speaking in a Texas drawl so she could hardly keep from laughing.

Aunt Marion later complained, "They didn't do a good job."

And Becky saw a trace of the stain each time she set the table, but she covered it with a biscuit plate until Aunt Marion did it herself. Becky had to admit there was nothing then to cover.

Funny how people can turn even good things into tyrants...like learning and God and even being clean. Becky was frightened of clean-niks. They made her feel inferior if she had a spot or a wrinkle...or even worse...a criminal. Not that Aunt Marion ever said anything. Worse...she walked around setting an example. Becky plunged to make the bed while it was still warm with their bodies. Scrubbed the tub after a bath until she could almost see her face in it.

The town was disappointing. It had no promise in the distance. You couldn't take a subway to infinity for a nickel. Becky was used to a city with an out there that went on forever...and full of little places that held the world. You didn't have to travel if you were a New Yorker. The travelers came to you. All of Europe, Asia, and Africa around in microcosm...nations reduced to neighborhoods...all babbling strange tongues...and all foreign. Becky was used to foreign. Foreign was home. English was only real and warm and familiar when it was accented or broken, and tongues and eyes and arms and feet were all visibly connected...one didn't move without the other.

Tommy pointed, "You see that building over there...and there and there? That's where the town stops. You can see it all from here."

And he walked where the town stopped.

"And beyond the farms, that's all. Land and farms. You can travel here for days and see what you don't see in New York...land and sky. And all houses," he said proudly, "not like New York where you never see a big backyard."

'No,' she thought, 'you're all backyard down here.' There was an economy in the town...simple buildings, no waste...not even bureaucratic...no touches here and there of the necessary and the impractical...just for show...cravings and niches. Just the necessaries...a place for recording birth and death and a few places in between for some papers, auto licenses...things like that, doctors, lawyers, all in their little square boxes and grocers and butchers and fruiteries in theirs. Two concert halls, one in the park and one in the center of town, both built by the WPA...not because the town yearned for music but just to give the unemployed something to do. The grand sweep, the large hand, the majestic were beyond the challenge or competition. They were satisfied that nature had done it for them. The town was an adjunct, a necessary evil to be over and done with and they were careful not to let it forget itself and reach r things it had no right to. There were no skylines defined by buildings.

Tommy saying, "Aunt Marion always said it's against God and I believe her. Even churches are built at a respectful distance here. Humble, life they should be. Vulgar, in New York all those buildings clawing at the sky. Even buildings trying to outdo tranquility. We make a building because we need it...not to prove anything."

She'd never heard him talk so much.

"I never knew you hated the city so much," she said quietly.

"I didn't know it myself until now. Haven't home in so long, I forgot. Just seeing the grocer today made me think of things. Made me feel important just going in and saying 'Hello.' Without even buying anything...and you too, Becky."

She had to admit that all that 'Yes ma'am' and 'No ma'am' was unpleasant to the ears. The look of obsequiousness when he said 'Ma'am' talking show not rushing you out because there were customers. There was one war the South kept winning with the North, their charm, reduces us all to children clumsily learning 'thank you' and 'how nice to see you' and calling ladies 'ma'am,' instead of batting them out and waiting for someone to finish talking before we interrupt and the ladies gracefully feminine and the men courtly masculine. The Yankees shrivel in inferiority, meeting admitting his crudeness, then trying to ape the ways of the conquered and have been known, in time, to drawl. They seemed so confident, the men and women, all blonde and blue-eyed it seemed, sat in silence. Talking wasn't an urgent necessity. They ate slowly, like they weren't even hungry...not gorging stuffing. The desperate intensity between friends, lovers, relatives did not seem possible here. The faces were calm, void, impassable. Here, no one seemed touchable. She missed Poppa and Lottie and, most of all, the unknown streets in the city, yet to be found. With the known boundaries of a town circling around you, it seemed like a prison...worse...like...death...like being entombed... like spokes of a wheel, the town was, and they followed each spoke to it's end that afternoon and would start all over again tomorrow...a wheel going nowhere, just turning in on itself over and over.

Becky had never seen a town with an end before. It was scary.

Tommy said, "After the sea, I felt safe here. I know every tree and flower, every house, every stone. There's a place under the tree I used to hide things when I was a kid and I forgot about it. Yesterday when I was waiting for you, I looked and all still there in a little box under the ground, a dime, a curl of my own hair, a toenail clipping, don't know why I saved that, a postcard Aunt Marion sent when I was sick in the hospital."

Becky read, "Don't stay there too long, boy. Hedges need cutting."

"That was her way of saying she missed me. Aunt Marion was never good with love words. You have to look behind."

Becky wondered if he was looking behind and seeing things that weren't there. Becky didn't understand then that love comes in different kinds. It wouldn't matter anyway if she did. She didn't like that kind. Like money in the bank, you can't spend. Just know it's there, sitting in a vault, behind a dozen barriers, hiding itself.

And Tommy saying, like he read her mind, "Her love is like money in the bank. Feels good just knowing it's there. But to get back to what I was saying about the box. Things are still there where you left them. Not like where you come from. Not a house left standing you ever were in. All gone. You told me yourself...much less a box, a tree, or an old rock."

"That's true, but what's there now is more exciting than an old stone or a box. Big high rises, lots of people in them and hustle and bustle all the time."

"Suppose all we had in the world were high rises?"

"Suppose all we had in the world were boxes and stones?"

And they both laughed. Becky never fought to be right, and he never cared if she was. It was alright with him if she were smarter sometimes, but not with her if he was. She didn't like it but didn't say anything. It was good to have him win sometimes. He'd sent her otherwise.

Aunt Marion had a meal ready when they came home, roast beef, mashed potatoes with gravy, a small salad, white bread. Becky hated it all, small, trim helpings, Becky followed her timidly with a dish or two. They were always silent at the table. Aunt Marion thought it unsafe to eat and talk since a neighbor choked on a piece of meat a year ago while lecturing her son at the table. At the sink, her continued silence was grim. Becky, tortured, standing by wiping and stacking, waiting helplessly between dishes and silverware for the next offering.

"Did you like the meal?"

"Delicious!"

"I was just wondering."

On their way to bed, Tommy mumbling, "Why didn't you say something?" followed by a quick quip, "She was waiting for a compliment. Feels you're unappreciative if you don't compliment her on every meal."

"Especially you...coming from New York and all," he added.

"Does she know we ate meatloaf at home and porkchops by my parents and the rest in Chinese restaurants when we were in New York?"

"No, she doesn't, and I never thought to tell her. Come to think of it, I never saw her fussing so much with tablecloths and napkins and just so this and just so that."

And he laughed harder than she had ever heard him.

"Don't talk politics or she'll think you're a Communist and fumigate the house. Just let her keep on thinking you're something special."

"I do."

And he looked at her adoringly and took her hand. He hadn't cut his nails and they cut into her flesh where he squeezed, but she smiled and looked at him with equal adoration. He took her hand in between his, raised it to his mouth and kissed it lovingly. She could feel a roughness.

"Let me see your hand, Tommy."

He dropped it by his side. She pulled it up quickly and examined it...little white circles of peeling skin.

"I haven't been this scarred in years since I lied to Aunt Marion and played ball instead of going to church. But she never did, and I could hardly wait for next Sunday to go back to church and make up for it. I remember her being very pleased I left extra early. I can't do that with you, Becky. Truth is, I can't do what you want, and I'm afraid I'll never be able to make up for it. You'll go to school, Becky, but I don't know about me going anywhere but where I'm going. You expected coming here would make me brave or safe or something, so I'd never leave. Well...it hasn't."

His voice is distant now.

"I'm going...tomorrow morning."

She said nothing so he offered a timid, 'Maybe' and a hopeful 'Someday.'

"Someday," numbingly whispered and took his hand, putting the palm to her mouth, kissing it gently and putting it round her face.

"Don't. It's too rough. I'm afraid I'll hurt you."

She pressed harder. The marks were still there in the morning. Aunt Marion had them on her face, too, when he forgot and took her face in his hand and kissed her goodbye. They both lingered over those marks from time to time until they faded away. Aunt Marion, clean as she was, didn't even wash the spot. Dabbed only one side of her face with water. Becky wasn't that particular so hers faded first, and Becky let her have that satisfaction. After all, being a lonely young woman is still better than being a lonely old one.

Chapter Eighty-Five

The next morning, there was no smell of fresh coffee or the clapping of eggs on the side of a bowl being mixed in for scrambles, as Aunt Marion called them, nor was she peering into an open oven getting ready to put out the biscuits and gasping in pain as she burned her fingers piling them high on the plate and balancing them while they tottered, but somehow never fell on the way to the table. Only one time they tipped over and fell to the floor when Becky jumped up and offered to help. Becky just sat and watched over since, her heart jumping like it was a high wire act she was seeing...not just a biscuit...but that's how important Marion made it all seem. It wasn't until later Becky found out she made them from a mix.

Aunt Marion was sitting at the table near the window when Becky came down to join her. She was wearing an old cotton robe, one of those with tufts in lines and circles, limp and faded, careless everyday look of the old thing we wear in the house when no one's looking. The sun shone on her hair. It was frizzy, like an old sweater. She hadn't slicked it down like she always did. The table was a light green enamel one with two wings that snapped up and down. They were down now. She held the coffee cup in mid-air, her elbows propped on the table. Becky watched while she took a sip, turned her head, and stared out the window. Then, turning to Becky suddenly, she said 'Instant' and pointed to the left cupboard on the bottom shelf.

"You'll have to reheat the water. Eggs in the refrigerator. Help yourself. Pot's right there. Kettle broke."

"I'll just have some coffee, thank you."

Becky filled the pot and watched. At first, it was strangely comforting watching spurts of water start shooting their way to the top. Becky then becoming impatient until they finally burst into a lively clatter...while Aunt Marion watched, she measured the coffee, stirred, and put the spoon in the sink.

"Rinse it," Aunt Marion saying, "or the coffee will stick to the spoon."

Becky rinsed but some brown still stuck stubbornly to the tip. She took a piece of Brillo. Aunt Marion warning, "No scouring the silver."

Becky is desperate now, digging the embedded coffee out with her fingernail.

"No nails either," Aunt Marion firmer now.

"Get a glass from down the shelf. Put some water in it.

Becky did what she was told.

"Now, soak it, and when you see the water turn brown, take it out and wipe it."

"Can I drink my coffee while it's soaking?"

"Sure, why not?"

There was a big, black chip on Aunt Marion's side of the table. Scary. It was shaped like a dagger. There was always a tablecloth over it before.

"You ever do housework, Becky? Is that your real name, Becky? Not short for anything?"

"That's my real name."

"Just wondering."

"No, I was never taught to do housework."

"You're lucky. I was taught since I was eight years old and doing it all the time. I was learning but I never had anyone to do it for. Just helping, until Tommy. He needs so much mothering, poor boy. I do it, not because I like it that much, but to make up for my sister being taken away from him."

Looking hard at Becky now.

"And when he goes, that mothering goes with him. I don't know why. Not even interested in mothering my own self. You see, she was my older sister, always cared for me like I was her own little girl. There were so many of us, Momma couldn't mother us all, so we chose a youngling to be a momma to and an older one to be a baby to...and the one I played momma too...well...he got killed one day... just like that...went running after Poppa with something he forgot, and he was screaming after him, 'Wait Poppa!' They were building something, and he passed under one of those beams. It cut loose and fell on him with all that stuff on top of those beams."

Her head trembled and shook from side to side.

Becky jumped up, put a hand on her to comfort her.

"I'm so sorry."

She jerked it away quickly.

"Let's start mothering training."

Her face set firm.

"Mothering big people is not the same as mothering little ones. You shame big folks if you mother them like little ones. You want to learn Becky...mothering Tommy?!"

Becky thinking, 'not especially,' but saying, "Teach me."

Mothering, to Becky, was being a maid and sufferer, desperately in love with someone who doesn't love you, taking insult and offense. Degradation. Humiliation. Aunt Marion took a pencil and paper and listed his favorite foods.

"Corn pone, grits, hamburgers, fries..."

"Pork chops," Becky offered.

"He never liked them too much."

That night, Becky wrote a desperate letter, pleasant, sensible, calm on the surface, that she would like to have their own place so their lives could be what it was.

She quipped, "The walls here are so thin, when you kiss me goodnight, Aunt Marion throws a kiss and says goodnight, too. And besides," Becky mothering now, "I want to make us a home. Our home."

Dear Becky,

I can see from your letter that Aunt Marion's been giving you the 'he needs mothering' speech. I do, but not Aunt Marion's kind, biscuits, and darned socks and buttoned. You can take the sewing and cooking lessons if you want, but you don't have to put your heart in it. Stay with Aunt Marion while we're apart. I can save money that way. When I come home, we'll take a place for a month away. How about that? I think it's a great idea. Best of both worlds. You not alone in a strange place when I come home. Aunt Marion loves me a lot. She doesn't love you, but I hope she likes you. She told me she wants to... when she gets over being jealous. Said she'll try to make it soon. Like your mother loves you a lot and doesn't me. We all carry that into marriage. Someone who loves just one of us a lot. Your mother likes me now, doesn't she? So, Aunt Marion can too...in time.

From,

Tommy

Becky thought, 'Thank God for time.' It helps people who can't help themselves. But then, even time isn't reliable. I'm still worried about who likes who and who loves who like what I did when I was little. Still scarring not to be liked...no matter who or what...a cat or dog even...and still sulking like a child not to be. And it was all so confusing. Men liked her because they said she was pretty, and women didn't for the same reason. One's parents liked you smart, peers liked you dumb. One had to have a different hat for every occasion. Becky waited daily for a sign she was liked though she couldn't recognize it anyway if she saw it. Aunt Marion barely spoke at all with her tongue. Her higher purpose was reserved for Heaven. On earth, she was consumed with small purposes. Becky remained oblivious to most of them. And Aunt Marion seemed to be suspended in a condition of permanent waiting; silent, grim, churlish waiting.

As the weeks went by, Becky started school, had less and less time for mothering lessons. Becky never told anyone why she chose a Catholic school of social work. Becky was in the underbelly of Jewish life. The bearded Orthodox didn't even look at her as they hurried by; Becky in turn was ashamed of them, wondering about them, but never asking. Becky never even thought they were Jewish rich. Jewish was poor and poor was Jewish. And she was the poorest. There were Jewish doctors and lawyers somewhere out there, but they would have nothing to do with her.

Becky fled from being scorned by her own. She would lose herself in something bigger, something more benign. The church was like being close to a kind father who made her feel safe and protected, belonging, wanted for just being and a place to hide from the world in love and harmony. Becky needed to unburden herself of herself and take on a higher burden of limitless devotion and sacrifice. Not a baby. That was devotion to self since a baby was an extension of that self. Passion for the other. Becky offered herself to the Church. The first step in her offering...the school. Feeling scorned and abandoned by Jews, she went to the Christians. The pond where she was to be a big fish was an obscure school in the middle of a park, ivy covered, tradition, solid, like an English academy for boys. Becky had to discontinue her mothering lessons from the first day. She came home with a stack of books taller than she was, emerging from her room only to eat and then leaving the dishes. Sometimes, she found them where she left them the following day, Aunt Marion having cleared a small area and eating alone. Becky cleared a small space too and left the dishes. It was partly a habit. Mirele never required housework and partly Becky's frenzy to return the books...her mind so full of the written word, nothing else entered. She was oblivious to all other concerns and thought she had a right to service. After all, she was a student, wasn't she?

The tolerant, kindly, passive gentle attitude was nice from a distance. Here at the school, it annoyed and enraged her. The Dean Miles, dignified, gray haired, teaching the Organization of Communities. Consult them if you want to, lead them to act. Never force. Becky rose to her feet shouting the effectiveness and necessity of force, more because she could get attention and found academe weak, easy to show contempt, scorn and shock, so easy and satisfying she couldn't stop herself, until the class consisted of a debate between her and Dean Miles. She is shouting and ranting, to cover her feeling stupid, and contemptuous of his weakness when he tried to turn her wrath away with a soft word in class and later in a private conference. Her ideas were considered too radical. She was enjoying the notoriety, the attention, the drama of being the 'problem.' She turned to the students for militant agreement. They smiled politely and walked around her, whispering plans for the evening that never included her. Becky was the only Northerner in a class of Southerners. One Black was accepted in the school. She was the only one who talked to Becky on occasion. No one else. The others smiled at the black politely and walked around her too.

Mrs. Haus, teaching Case Work 1, sitting at the desk, looking the part, blonde, dull, lifeless hair round a numbed face with a fixed expression that never moved. It was arranged so it was perfectly detached, hands and elbows, too, both leaning on the table, hands under her chin, fingers intertwined loosely, uncomfortable, tight air of superiority, forced to press down any loose nerve endings that might be wandering about inside to mar the picture of perfect control.

But something else, too. The unsophisticated and provincial to match the pretension to all knowing. It sat like a mudpack on her face, like you could wipe it all off with a good rag...and Becky wanted to do just that. Get her down from the silly perch where she sat like a secretary bird. After all, Becky knew what it was to be a client of someone like that. 'Where is your mother, Becky?' 'You must release hostility from the client,' Mrs. Haus would say in that cold, flat monotone, slow voice.

Becky shot up her hand and spat out before she was permitted to talk, "After we are talking about pushbutton people or flesh and blood humans?!"

Mrs. Haus offered sentences and formulas like applying a scalpel where it hurts and watching the blood spurt, keeping the bucket right here and how many buckers does the client fill until you pronounce him well? Calm and composed while the client does what he's supposed to...releases whatever it is he's supposed to. Giving, giving, giving and Becky taking it all in, collecting, recording, leading, guiding, pushing, controlling, manipulating, certain, positive, while the client is uncertain, flopping about.

Becky said, "Tyranny and sadism is all it was in the guise of 'help.'"

The client, sinking more and more in deep water over his head, the caseworker watching and waiting until he's deemed ready to do without her. Becky wrote all this in a term paper and was called into the Dean to be chastised for her attitude.

In placement, doing her casework internship, she wrote, 'I had a cup of coffee with a client. The cup was cracked, the table dirty, filled with grapefruit rinds and pits, a baby with cereal over her face crying, four others running and screaming around the room, the client in a filthy house dream, too short, stocking knotted below the knee, pendulous breasts and stomach rolling under the housedress. Gagging, I drank the coffee. She told me her most private secrets. Client cathartic. All for just one cup of coffee.'

Into the Dean's office!

"Cup of coffee with a client?!" Mrs. Haus was shocked.

Dean Miles was composed. Becky thought he'd look calm even on his deathbed...accepting and all that...even then.

"You had 'coffee with a client,' it says here."

"Yes, I did."

"I must tell you that it's too subjective, too personal, accepting a service, putting yourself under obligation, more social than casework, even though it's called, 'Social Casework.'"

Becky, too upset to think of a reply, nodded disconsolate,

inwardly protesting, 'but how can you convince a person you're accepting them if you don't even have a cup of coffee with them?'

The other students surrounded her with questions when she came from the Dean...cats plunging into open drawers, they rummaged furiously, sated their curiosity, and scampered out. They talked to her only then. The rest of the time, she overheard conversations of restaurants and trips and invitations to homes. They left a little space sometimes for her to fit in but she stood numbly by while they exchanged giggles, conspiratorial and intimate memories and plans she couldn't share as if her loneliness bound them together even more, a background against which they fused more clearly and harmonies blended and disparate parts became whole. Together in pain, leaving someone out eased their loneliness. Exhilarated them. It united, bonded, made important. They were <u>somebody</u> because she <u>wasn't</u>. She and the black one who extended one dinner invitation to Becky, but she sidled out of it. Afraid to go into an all-black neighborhood by herself and was ashamed of it afterward. She tried to make up for it by sitting in the back of the bus with her the next day.

Lunch with Mrs. Haus and a visiting dignitary from another agency. Mrs. Haus saying, Becky is to visit the home of a boy who was adopted 13 years ago and tell him so. He is to hear it for the first time. The literature, Mrs. Haus says to do so and the visiting dignitary agrees. Becky asked again, incredulous.

"How old is he?"

"Thirteen."

"I won't tell him."

"Who pays attention to the literature, anyhow?"

Both snapping their wrists, gasping a hasty departure and Becky...into the Dean!

Becky saying, "But the literature is so...stilted...unnatural...full of phrases...not people...just high-faulting words strung together supposed to add up to people, but they don't add up!"

The next day, Becky visits a happy family and a contented boy with the Dean's orders to follow the literature.

Becky dutifully records the conversation with the family verbatim underscoring her recommendation, "Don't tell...ever!"

But compromising...the message delivered in the stilted *ad nauseam*, language of the <u>literature</u>.

In conference...God, how they loved that word.

Heads of the agency sitting around a large oval table listing the assets of rural clients...CW best saying, "One cow."

Mrs. Jenkins saying. "Two cows and so on around the table. Becky ever attended another conference and into the Dean!"

Becky saying, "What is there in common between these poor souls and such ridiculous talk?!"

In class, Mrs. Haus talking, "If there is a problem, what do you do, you send it to a committee."

Becky, "If you can't solve a problem, study it. Into the Dean!"

Becky goes to lunch with the clerks, spontaneous, witty, interesting, laughing at their superiors and their 'airs.'

Into the Dean.

Charge: Improper lunch companions. Not professional behavior.

Assignment: Baptist girl has illegitimate child to give up for adoption. Becky is to interview her before the court date. The child is given by the caseworker to the adoptive parents on order of the judge.

"Mother there, too?"

"Of course."

Becky interviews the girl, young, blonde, innocent, head bowed, facing the floor.

Becky saying, "You feel guilty about this, don't you?"

She nods her head.

"Well, sometimes we do things in a set of circumstances that are such that we can't do anything else. But afterwards, circumstances change, we realize our error and don't repeat it."

A sigh, "Oh, yes."

A crippling burden lifted from her pained heart. Into the Dean! He had said had condoned adultery. In a psychology book.

"I read it in an interview book."

"Not our book apparently, here, you learn you what we teach."

In court, Becky was holding the infant like it was a piece of fine China: the mother rushing over with open arms crying, "My baby! Give me my baby!"

And Becky giving...her tears and mother's tears falling on the child.

Becky contrite, helpless, wishing she weren't there, not knowing what to do, judging herself stupid, the world cruel, the mother unfortunate. The judge barks an order, and the mother hurls her arms obediently out, giving the child to the new mother who keeps her arms extended and the baby away from her like she wants to give it back. Mother is carried hysterically by her parents. The ashen faced foster parents stand numbed while the Judge drones on about the rights gained by them and lost by the mother. Even the child has a few rights. Becky leaves but the child is wailing as if to call her mother back and doesn't stop even when she's in the car on the way to her new home. The next morning, Becky, into the Dean!

"Too subjective," he said, reacting like that. "She couldn't exercise sufficient control for analysis and treatment," he said.

Becky testing, fortified by his weakness.

"Tell me about myself, Dean Miles. Maybe you know something I don't. I'll see myself differently from another point of view. Maybe it'll help me get along better in this school."

"Thank you for telling me."

And she concluded she'd pulled the wool over all their eyes. She didn't want them to know, and now despised them for their ignorance.

"They were wrong about everything," she concluded. Couldn't see through her at all, the way they pretended they could.

'It was all a lie. You couldn't know people at all. Too frightening, dibbling carelessly with their minds. Remember Pesach? How they worked with him, and it made no difference. It still doesn't. Made him worse maybe. He gave to them fancy titles and offices, conferences and they gave him reports, letters from relatives, a case folder, a few moments of sympathetic conversations, a patronizing pat on the back and strait jackets and barred windows and open toilets and visits from Momma and ice cream on Sunday and TB and black, sunken, hollow cheeks and death, at last, just for him. Not the file. That lives on forever. Modern immortality...the case folder. Imperative in this case. It was all that remained of him. Not that they wouldn't be glad to be rid of it. If they could, they'd have gone it up to Heaven with him.'

Dean Miles warning Becky now that she must do as she's told.

She attends a class taught by a priest.

He drones on, "You will see Mexican families sleeping together on the floor, all 10 of them, parents and 8 children, one blanket all over them."

Becky jumped up, "Why do they have so many children?!"

Into the Dean!

"We cannot pass you this semester, but you have a chance to try for another term."

Becky, feeling heroic, martyred, center stage, sacrificing for principles, the grand gesture... "I cannot, in good conscience accept a diploma from this school implying I accept what I've learned here. I don't and never will."

The next day she came to pick up her belongings in that school singing, 'Old caseworkers never die, they just fade away,' at the top of her lungs in the hallway. Later, the class came to her, one by one, told her how sorry they were for her and how they tried to intercede for her with the Dean. Suddenly, defeat was sweet. She'd won some affection and a place at the head of the class, in the very center, with martyrdom.

Before having the school, she stood, for a moment, near one of it's monuments. An idyllic setting. Bushes, and round them, flowers, bedecked like a spring hat. A small bridge, in the distance, over a pond, two ducks lazily floating round, the nuns, only their faces showing under a tight, white triangle above the eyes and a stiff collar below the chin, ambling together in silent devotion. The Brothers, also in black, taking their ease before evening prayer, watching one of God's creatures flutter its tiny wings bathing in the fountain. The Christian religion, humility, charity, brotherly love, poverty, hand in hand with the new: acceptance, understanding, compassion, insight. The priest folding his hands in the back, the caseworker in the front and jabbering together about her. She'd overhead them several times, deciding to rid themselves of her, not wanting Becky, even here. Not by God...or Man...or the two of them together. Not even by herself... participated in her own exile...and they let her.

Chapter Eighty-Six

They were sorry for her and pleaded her cause, guilty, remorseful, but not one of them offered a consoling invitation to break bread. They said they were sorry, shook hands and wished her luck and went on as always to meet each other in prearranged places she never saw and let her go home alone like nothing happened. Not even an exception in this case. She left the way she came...a stranger. Only at the end, like people behave when they see raggedy ones on corners with hands outstretched, extend a pitying hand as far as you can throw a coin, pass by quickly and forget as soon as you round the bend, waving and smiling a gleeful hello to a friend. <u>They went to their death singing</u>...those who dance to their own tune. Becky singing in a macabre dance of the humiliated, faces frozen in despair, stumbling alone on a black and shadow dance floor in ragged circles like an old drunk. <u>But you're waving the white plume, Becky</u>. Heart uplifted. Pride soothed. She was brave and special...even in a small pond. Becky learned her lesson well. Losing is a virtue. To have nothing is to have everything. Glory in defeat. Step over yourself, Becky, on the way to bigger losses, sacrifices, nobilities. Settling for being felt sorry for...like Poppa's revolutionary, significant, tragic, brave, cropped hair, facing the rifle of a firing squad, unflinching.

When she came home, Aunt Marion at the sink scraping potatoes, strangely, had the same look on her face as Becky. They both looked at each other pained and martyred...Aunt Marion saying, "This must be the millionth potato I've scraped. After all these years of inventing, you'd think man would come up with something that washes, peels, and cores them. Why do you think no one ever thought to do it?"

"Because inventions are done by men, I guess, and they don't peel and eye the damn things. We all have house working things we can't stand. I can't stand peeling!"

"Then why do you bother to eat them?"

"Because I love them."

Looking martyred again. The rumble of a truck sputtering to a stop in front of the door.

"Must be the egg man. See what he wants, Becky."

She attacked and cored, biting her lower lip and looking ferocious and shouting, "Who is it?" ...when it was too late.

A young man straddled the door, arms open, hands raised above his head, smiling, "How are y'all? You the new in-law of Miss Marion? I heard everything about you...a book reader, a student, very smart and, his eyes taking their full measure from head to toe, pretty as can be."

"Zat you Zeke?" Aunt Marion shouting.

He didn't answer but covered her from head to toe with another look...heavier this time.

"Hi," Becky managed a panicked smile and turned, leaving the door open.

"It's for you, Aunt Marion."

"Who is it?"

"It's eggs, just like you said."

Aunt Marion shouted, "Zeke!" and turned to find him behind her. She slapped him gently and threatened him with more. He stuck his face near her and dared her, turning the other cheek. She slapped him again.

"Now they're even," he said...and Marion laughed...hacking, loud, rasping, joyless and cruel."

"Introduce me."

"Becky, Tommy's wife..." pointedly emphasizing the word...wife.

"She's too pretty and smart for him," he said laughing, "He'll never keep her."

"Why?"

Aunt Marion eyes hardening her mouth even more, holding the smile stiff and firm.

"Me."

"You got to go through me, first." Still smiling. "And that aint easy, besides, I thought you were faithful to me."

"I am...faithful to all of you. Love one at a time...how many today Miss Marion?"

"A dozen."

He disappeared quickly and returned with the eggs. Aunt Marion bent her head, intent on counting and checking the eggs. He checked them with her, all business now, a weary look creeping over his face when he wasn't smiling or joking...and shy...seemed almost timid when he wasn't in the spotlight playing clown. Aunt Marion commanding now. She picked up the last egg and pronounced it, 'Cracked.'

"Yes ma'am," as he rushed out with the egg, bringing another one from the truck, cradling it as if it were rare China...holding it with thumb and forefinger, pinky extended while she peered at the egg.

"How much?"

"Twenty cents."

"Nineteen last week. Are the chickens striking? That's all you got working for you is the poor chickens so you can't plead high labor costs."

"Feed...going up."

"So put them on a diet. They won't know the difference."

Then, more talk about eggs and chickens and seed, the young man giving a sales pitch on the quality of his eggs and Aunt Marion enjoying his efforts to convince her.

Becky thinking, 'That's how he keeps his customers. Only man in years trying to please Aunt Marion. And he knew it. Probably cracked an egg or two himself so he could rush about trying to please them.'

"Gimme another dozen. I'll bake a cake today, I think."

"Yes, ma'am even more obsequious...and he returned with another dozen.

Becky watched him while he and Aunt Marion checked for cracks...as if he were a surgeon performing a serious operation. He had a boy's face, safe, simple, innocence that seemed to cling to him, though he was shrewd and cunning in business. Becky watched careful fingers touching the eggs gently. Her breasts tingled. It startled her. He looked up at her and stroked the egg with the tip of his fingers, looking at her with pleading in his eyes. He looked determined, the bones in his face, sharp, skin smooth and unlined, like he was never shaved. It was jarring like a boy in adolescence, waiting for the first stubble. Becky always thought it would be nice kissing someone who didn't maul your face with his beard. Now, she wasn't so sure. Marion's head still bent over the eggs, checking them over and over this time, the egg man adoring Becky over her head.

"Fine," Aunt Marion said, without raising her head. "See you next week."

"Yes, ma'am. And pleased to meet you, Becky."

Then mouthed over Aunt Marion's head, "Very pleased."

Becky shook her head up and down dumbly.

Aunt Marion turned her back on him and returned to the kitchen, calling out, "See you next week!"

"On the dot," he said and walked backwards towards the door, and facing Becky until he was out. The next day, when she went to the store to buy the paper, he was behind her. Waited all morning outside the house where he couldn't be seen and followed her. She picked up the paper and read.

He read over her shoulders and smiled, greeting her, "Hi."

She turned in surprise and quickly back again...mortified. She nearly touched his mouth. He went to the counter.

"Two coffees."

She heard the thud on the counter of two heavy mugs.

"Sorry," she said. "I have to run. See you."

And fled out, forgetting to pay for the paper.

He sat down on the corner, drinking first from his, then from the cup beside him.

He had turned to it, smiling, "Yes, Miss Becky, it is a nice day, isn't it?"

The steam curling from the coffees, he watched them come together, curling and uncurling...a dreamy look in his eyes...

"The flowers on Central Ave are beautiful...yes, the nights are chilly here...and...yes, I'll be glad to show you around," and silently, "you don't know how much."

The counterman was laughing so hard, seemingly not noticing the customer was serious, shaking his head and not smiling at the end. He applauded and thanked him.

Zeke paid him, "For the paper, too. Just like talking to some women. Seems like they ain't there."

"You're right," he called after him. And he flung the coffee viciously into the sink. It splattered all over the wall and came down in a brown stream."

"To hell with it! Let the boss take care of it! He does nothing but hand me a lousy paycheck anyway."

And then...chilling laughter.

"Talking to myself like that guy. And he thought he was kidding me!"

Zeke was in the store every day, the paper folded and paid for when Becky came to pick it up. She'd leave without a word. Tommy's letters were now growing more distant. 'He must be displeased she was thrown out of school,' she thought. Not even love now from Tommy and Aunt Marion looking at her like a criminal every time she came home without a paper...like she'd been to a tryst or something. Marion made sure Becky wasn't home when the egg man came. The neighbor heard the story from a neighbor, told it to Aunt Marion and Becky was now a flirt, adulteress, one of those from New York!

And Aunt Marion wrote:

Dear Tom,

I will make this letter brief and to the point. No sense beating around the bush. The neighbors were talking about Becky. Remember Zeke White? Well, he aint what his name says he is. Sends a hook out for all the ladies with his flirting ways and Becky's biting...or so I hear. I admit hearing not seeing, but it's close enough. I'm telling you so if you can come home real quick, come on.

Your aunt that loves you,

Aunt Marion

And he wrote back:

Dear Aunt Marion,

Can't come home, but you can be my eyes and ears. My trust in her is as strong as iron but it's not blind or deaf I must admit you've chinked it a little. I feel foolish now, even though there's so little going on. Can't help it. I'm that way. Guys taunting each other here all the time...rubbing it in...same old tired jokes about mice and cats and when I hear that joke now, there's little fires burning up inside me and spreading to my brain and hurting bad. Write to me as soon as you know anything more. I can't take it, but I have to.

You know I love you,

Tommy

And Becky reading the end of Tommy's letter first, looking for 'Love, Tommy...P. S I miss you,' and not finding it. 'Dear Tom' she wrote, then squeezed in 'Dearest Tom,' changed that to 'My Dear,' then angrily decided on 'Tom.' Trying not to heed the fear spreading while she wrote, she submitted in the end, 'Dearest Tom,' so he wouldn't be angrier with her than he was.

Dearest Tom,

It seems like I've let you down. Feels like I've started all over again being an immigrant like my parents. Coming to a strange country and not melting, like my Pa. He took his little town with him when he came, I took New York with me. It's like the first Negro in Russia for me. They took him on exhibition for everyone to see a black face. They'd never seen one before. They charged admission and the whole town came, my father told me, gaping and gasping, looking at the Negro's face from all sides, but staying at a safe distance. He was smarter than me. Didn't expect to be more than an oddity, but I did. I expected to be the center of respectful attention...not a barking dog that makes too much noise and the neighbor who poisons him feels a flush of sorry before the end, pats him on the head before he dies and he licks her hand, being grateful. I'll go back to New York and take psychology there. And they don't shock so easily, as you know. They're used to bursting, angry students preaching mayhem, taking them in stride. They don't murder politely, like here. I see it all now. I didn't before. In two years, I'll finish my studies, get a job here and be very quiet...I promise. And you'll come home, if you still want to.

All my love,
Becky
P.S I miss you terribly.

Dear Becky,

Sometimes we're too smart for our own good. Maybe that's what's happened here. I think your idea is a good one. San Antonio is no place for a woman alone. By the way, I won't be coming home next month as usual. They need me for special duty. I'll explain when I see you next, about three months from now. Too long a story and too boring and no time to get into it now. Have to rush, bye for now.

As ever,

Tommy

Becky sobbing, body shaking, begging, 'Tommy, please be nice.' Terrified, he's not being nice. Even if she was naughty, shouting, cantankerous, unpleasant, impossible, the world around her had to be nice...especially Tommy...even if she went with another man...even that...he should be forgiving and nice. 'Glad you came back, Pudgy.' And talking and holding her warm. To her...deep inside...that was the real test of love and she had to put him to it. Had to. Time going backwards, days going by with newspapers and dime store novels for her and...Aunt Marion...and listening while she sat crunching hard candy and reading. The sound of her rocker creaking was comforting sometimes. Other times, it seemed frenzied, shaking, her right foot pushing harder and harder as if it were on a piano pedal forcing sound faster and more violent until she'd suddenly drop the book in her lap, her head dropping to the side, breathing heavily, the rocker coming to a dead stop with her. Then she'd open her eyes, close the book, keeping her finger in it where her place was and move gently back and forth, soft as she could, not even a creak from the rocker, like it knew she wanted it to be quiet.

Aunt Marion had Becky buy the books for her when she went to buy the paper. Too ashamed to buy them herself. Becky was ashamed, too but she was curious to see what Aunt Marion saw in them. They weren't like in her day, when all the girls were goggle-eyed about the heroine wearing a towel. Tommy loved her wearing a towel. She did it all the time when she came from the bath. But she felt nothing. One little tingle, that fellow with the eggs, but mostly mind wanting. These new books were about women trembling and wanting, demanding the prince awaken them...Kinsey style. And Becky too, hungry now for awakening, like the book says. Becky would buy one, read it quickly first, then leave it on the rocker for Aunt Marion.

'Junk!' Aunt Marion would say every time she finished but ask Becky to pick up another a week later, 'just to see if this one is better...you can never tell.' And Becky would continue the charade. Too embarrassed not to. In those days honest talk was between people and books...not people and people. Becky made sure not even to look at Marion while she was reading. Not to stumble on the shame in her and Marion, too, looked away. Becky snapped the book shut when the front doorbell rang, as if there was a stranger peering over her shoulder at what she didn't want him to see.

One morning, Becky still lolling in bed, reading, the bell rang over and over again. It startled her. It's persistence rushing her down the stairs. Aunt Marion was out of the house. Just gone for a few minutes. Flinging the door open without asking who it is...Zeke, holding a diary against his chest so no one would see...just plucked from Aunt Marion's front yard.

"You letting us in?"

"Who...us?"

"Me and Miss Daisy," and he propped it's drooping head up with his finger, "Say hello to the lady, Miss Daisy. Don't be shy."

And he removed his finger and dropped it again.

"Shy! It wants to say hello and...will you do me the honor of meeting me this evening?"

"Go away."

"If not, I will stay here."

A tortured, "Alright, where?"

"Near the hall. Rhododendron bush. Large one. 8pm...front of Pelley Hall. Tell Aunt Marion you're attending this meeting."

He gave her a flyer.

"Suppose she wants to come?"

"She hates politicians and politics. Says they're all thieves and liars. She'll never come."

Nodding stiff and wooden as if she were someone else. He turned on one foot and pounded his back, prancing down the street, pretending to be a pony...like Tommy did when he was happy. Guilt rising like a sudden storm. She wanted to call after him that she had changed her mind, but the air was full of ears all around, clutching at strange sounds, molding them so their full fragrance touches them, 'the real opiate of the masses, Poppa,' scandal. Just one word amiss and they pounce on it, drugged with delicious expectation...somewhere. It seemed like Aunt Marion's, but she wasn't sure. She screamed, her strident voice rushing through the house, but it found nothing. 'Must be imagining,' she told herself, but didn't believe it. She told Aunt Marion. She was going to a meeting after dinner.

"Fine. Tell me all about it when you get home."

"You want to come with me?"

"What for? So, they can talk us into supporting them for four more years telling us how bad the other guy is and how good they are and not explaining how things are so bad when they been sitting behind the desk for all them years and they promised to improve everything the same way the other fellow did before them and nothing improved. How can they face us at all after wasting our time and money. Running again after lying to us the first time and being caught at it. If all their promises were true, the ones they've been telling us for years they're gonna do, there'd be nothing for them to improve. It'd all be perfect by now."

"You're right, but it's a good show."

"Yeah, it would be nice if they were honest about it and the curtain came down and then rubbed all the fake smiles off their faces and went home. Ain't no one can make life better, Becky."

And her face hardened, glazed with despair. She seemed to shrink before Becky's eyes.

"It gets better for a minute...or it doesn't. Stubborn like a damn pole cat. Can't make it do nothing!"

"But the government can make it better. Help people from the cradle to the grave."

"Them bums can't take care of anybody except themselves! Only take care of you in the cradle, is your momma. As for the grave, they'll put you in quick enough!"

"It's getting to be about that time, Aunt Marion."

"Go on. Enjoy yourself...and don't believe anything you hear! You ought to put some lipstick on, don't you think? You look so pale... no rouge, no nothing."

"I don't feel like it."

It was black outside...a night with no stars or moon. Becky slid behind the house and crouched under a light by the window, a mirror in one hand, she put lipstick on, rouge, powder on with the other then went slowly to Pelley Hall. His truck sputtered near the side entrance when she arrived, but he wasn't inside. She heard his voice behind her, 'Follow me,' and he took her hand, held it very tight and pushed her onto a small bench behind a huge, round bush.

"Wait here, I'll pick you up in a minute."

And he kissed her gently on the neck.

He begged, "I just want to hold you. Please wait."

All the fancies were gone now. Disappeared suddenly, without warning, the dreaming, the wanting, all gone. Just the same as always, a dead giving in, 'I'll wait.' She watched until he disappeared, running happy, revulsion turning in her belly. The large, round yellow lights of the truck glared straight at her as it rumbled past her, sputtering to a stop.

"Hop in."

She dragged her body, grown heavy with weariness, unable to lift it to the first step of the truck. He put out his arm and grabbed hers. Still not able to reach the first step. He jumped down and lifted her up, then sat panting by her side. She, stiff and rigid, silence between them, only the sound of his breathing when he lurched to a stop and the roar and rumble of the truck as it clacketed along a dark road. She could feel it, the moment they left the town, desolate, abandoned, alone, like a trap door opening into a black hole, the only light, the ribbons on the road from the headlights, scurrying of little animals in the dark, one terrible howl of one who wasn't quick enough, mosquitoes finding the light and whirring round and round in a macabre dance. <u>Watching Poppa remove his belt and not being able to do anything but stand there, froze, and hope it'll be over with quick, wouldn't dare move. And a degraded heap afterward of stinging bruises in humiliating places</u>. 'You were teaching me a lesson, Poppa. I forgot them all...all those lessons I was never supposed to forget...be good...even when I'm being bad...like now. Do what I'm told.

Last night she dreamed of an old game...

'May I take three baby steps, Poppa?'

'You may...when I say so.'

And she waited and waited, standing on one foot, the other raised and ready. Poppa took his time deciding and then, weary and aching, the foot came slowly and fearfully down.

Poppa raged, 'Not until I say so!'

She picked her foot up and it hung suspended again. Becky was shrinking, crouching against the door of the truck now, watching his profile in the dark, firm, commanding, purposeful, like a man looks when he's driving.

The big question choking her, 'Where are you taking me?!' becomes a soft, hesitant, 'are we going far?'

'Wait and you'll see.'

Shrunk and crouching again, like a terrified kitten in a corner with its tail curled around her facing a wall. Becky turned away from him, facing the black window. The truck whined to a stop, then bounced and sputtered, shaking them both up and down in their seats until the tears broke in Becky and it suddenly stopped, like it did what it set out to do and could lay quiet now.

'You crying, Becky?'

A strange face grieving over her...not clowning or insisting, so it looked kind.

'No,' ...trying to swallow her tears...choking, breathing hard.

'You scared, Becky?'

'No,' shaking uncontrollably.

'You wanna go home?'

Paralyzed, unable to say yes, looking helplessly at him pleading for mercy. He turned the key, made a loud zoom, pumping hard on the pedal with his foot.

Becky whispering, 'I'm alright now.'

Putting her hand on the key and gently turning it back. They were bouncing again when they sputtered to a spot. Both smiling while the truck bobbed up and down, drawing them closer.

"Do it again, Zeke."

And he turned the key. The truck banged and clacketed louder this time and she fell closer and closer until he could put an arm around her waist, her body shaking in his arms. He turned the key again and again, loving the touch of her, and she of him. Then he turned the key for the final time and moved away.

"I want you to know something. I'm a married man."

Stunned, she waited until her voice was calm.

"I am too. You know that."

"But I have children too, and brothers and sisters and parents... and I need you."

"Why? I thought people who had all that didn't need anybody else."

"I did, too...until I met you."

"What is it about me that you need?"

"I don't know yet, but something inside is aching to find out. I wanted to tell you here, right on this spot because this is where I'd come to dream, when I was little, of running away to the big city, New York especially...and I'd bring maps. I know all the streets and theatres and museums." He pulled out a big map, searchlight, "Where did you live, Becky? Show me." Excited now and moving the flashlight in a dizzying confusion of many lines. Becky could never read a map.

"Where is Brooklyn?" Zeke asking.

Pointing, "Here, that's what we're looking at." She plunked her finger on the spot. He circled it and put a 'B' in the middle.

"And where were you born?"

Another circle and more questions, "Where...?" And more and more circles.

"My secret picture of you, Becky. Dreamy. Happy. Now I'll give you one of me."

And he pulled out another map and made a circle.

"That's it, Becky, the whole circle. Born, lived, and dying there."

He turned quickly, slipped the maps under the seat, revved the motor again and again, though he didn't have to, like he was beating something out of himself, then a weary, "Time to go, Becky."

She didn't hear him, but she guessed that's what he said. The blackness seemed so different no longer magical, soft, secure, comfortable. Becky felt she could stay in this corner of the world for always and never go back. While they were on the road, Becky asked him to hand her the San Antonio map.

"Where is that place we stopped? I want to circle it." He stopped and wandered over the map with the light, searching.

"Here."

"Put a circle. I want to remember it always. My picture of you."

Chapter Eighty-Seven

She puts her head on his bony shoulders now and he drives, turning the wheel with one hand, the other around her waist. Her eyes turn to him like a child.

'Poppa, where do stars come from?'

'From me, Becky. I'm the star maker.'

And he'd say, 'See, here's one and another one. Follow them, Becky. Watch closely.'

'I can't Poppa.'

Then, his arm would shoot out high...as he could, 'There they are! See?'

And she believed Poppa was a star maker. For a long time, she believed.

"Can you make stars, Zeke?"

Talking now to the bottom of his chin, liking to watch his face, set, determined, fixed on the trivia like a silly child. He looked down for a moment, sweet, indulgent, protective look of a loving father.

"They're in your eyes, Becky. I see them there."

"But I mean up there, Zeke."

"Oh, that's easy. Anybody can do that. But your eyes, Becky. That's hard. Stars in them, now shining on me."

Becky cuddling closer, innocent, wide-eyed child-trust. He seemed sadder and more determined. Somehow, it pleased her, his being sad because of her.

"We'll be at Aunt Marion's soon. I'll have to let you off the corner."

He said it just like that, with nothing before or after. She jumped up, her body stiffened, her hands desperately smoothing wrinkles on her shirt that wouldn't go away...no matter how hard she pulled and tugged and pressed. Her chin was red with lipstick, her hair in an orgy of freedom on her head, standing up no matter how hard she ripped the comb through it. The goo she plastered it down with, long disappeared, the cowlicks ran wild. He stopped the truck for a moment. She stepped out terrified, holding tight to the step as she crawled down backwards, first one foot, then the other. Now just fat, ugly, clumsy, and humiliated. She fell on the side, picked herself up hurting and hobbled down the street.

He followed...saying after her, "Hi, pretty. Going somewhere? Can I give you a lift? See you tomorrow. Same place if you'll let me."

She nodded, still without daring to look at him, and he revved the motor. After 3am, Becky was excited and happy.

She hears his voice following her again, "Look at them two stars up there, Becky. They're gonna be there when you get home...just waiting to jump into your pretty eyes. Promise me you'll hurry upstairs, open them eyes real wide and look in the mirror quick while they're still showing themselves. You know how stars are, Becky. Have to find them before the clouds come and hide them. But you'll find them and keep them for me until tomorrow, won't you now?"

She nodded, her back still turned to him. The house was silent when she came in.

"That you, Becky?" Aunt Marion calling.

"It's me."

She crept up the stairs and quickly turned on the lights and pulled the shade down. She heard nothing. When the room was dark again, she was drifting into sleep, she could hear the gentle buzz of the motor.

"Goodnight Becky...my dearest Becky...goodnight."

She heard the truck rumbling away, listening very hard until only she could hear it. Then, suddenly, the light blazing in her eyes. Her head shot up. Aunt Marion standing at the door in an oversized cotton nightgown, her hair in pin curlers around her face.

"Just wanted to make sure it was you, Becky. Your voice sounded funny so I wasn't sure."

Becky pulled the sheet up, but not quick enough.

"The light...is hurting my eyes."

"Awful sorry, Becky."

Not a trace of anything but 'being sorry' in her voice. Becky was thrown off her guard. It's not necessary to have face to face talk in small towns. Whatever Aunt Marion wants to know she'll find out behind Becky's back. Like God's eyes...the town is everywhere. Aunt Marion had nothing to do but keep the kettle on the stove and wait for the story. She had the evidence.

"Seen it myself," she'd say.

"What, Aunt Marion?"

"Them eyes, full of wrongdoing...like the gals in the books she brings me, her face being all mouth like it was an offering."

"She couldn't have learned all that from books."

Aunt Marion's kindly, timid, protective eyes turned inward. The nights when all the town is sleeping or arguing, washing dishes, or having an after-dinner smoke or hitting children or beating wives or having one for the road, Aunt Marion would find a place in the park where the moonlight shone on lovers and sit quiet, hidden and watch and listen.

Just let Becky suffer with the maybes, while she waited to write to Tommy. Give her a wide berth. That was Aunt Marion's strategy. Plenty of room to maneuver herself into a corner.

"I'll be out tonight," she told Becky, "Out till late, so you do what you want, eat out, see the town, not much to see but ambling will take up some time and there's always the movies. Going on a trip with the church. Be home very late."

Becky's heart exploding, 'Free at last! Like being in my home! Close and open a door without preparing a face to say hello and goodbye!' Becky fled up the stairs clumping as hard as she could, put on heavy makeup, a dark, red mouth, shadows, and linings on her eyes and brushed the bangs on her forehead again and again until they fell on her face framing it just right, a careless sweep, soft and tender and a little devil-may-care and wicked. He was waiting in a small car near the bush where he couldn't be seen. She couldn't see his face, but she felt the heaviness, sadness, and fear in the air around him then touching her too.

Becky saying, "I can leave if you want me to. Maybe you're sorry about this. It's okay," leaning forward her hand on the door.

"Oh no!" his arm rushing forward, pulling her back, "Please don't go. You must know I've never done this before. Never wanted to. But I do now. I have to explain, and I want your answer. It has to be yours because you're nice and educated like no one I ever known before. I'm not one of those married men who 'loves his wife or doesn't, is understood too much or too little, needs adventure, new things, have to prove myself, something wrong with my wife, with me...' none of that. Don't judge me now Becky, please. Just listen. My wife is blind. I married her thinking it wouldn't make a difference. I loved her. I'd be her eyes and ears for her. For years it was alright, but then I wanted to travel, to see the world, to know something besides this wheel with it's few little spokes leading to nowhere from nothing. She said, 'Go with someone else. Go with someone who can see.' She must have known that's what I wanted. I wanted another pair of eyes looking at the wonder of the world with me. God forgive me, Becky. I wanted a woman I could see, and she could see me, and my wife knows that. I don't know how she knows, but she knows. All her life she lives in our house. Her mother gave it to us when she died. And the garden. 'And that's enough,' she says, 'of the world.' She wants no more of it. And the strange thing about all this, her I am with you, and that's all we can do is sit in the dark with each other like we're both blind. Both of us. And yet, you're the world out there, the big city, magic, books. She wouldn't read so she wouldn't yearn for things she couldn't see. She wanted to live like the whole world is blind and empty, so it wouldn't be that unbearable not seeing. We don't even have a radio...nothing. The children talk of nothing on the outside. She lives in a cocoon. The children...her mother and me raised them and loves them. She just birthed them. They hanker after her like I hankered, after my ma first, then Mary, my wife's name is Mary. Kids want maws for petting and loving, not pushing them away. The world is full of hankerers and pushers and we're hankering."

"What does she do all day?"

"Does what she can. Hands are always busy and her mind too with the same things her hands are, knitting and darning, fixing, and sewing. Damn it! I got two eyes! I gotta use them! Instead of me giving her light, she's taken it from me! She doesn't mean to, but that's what she's doing! Like living in a dark hole, quiet and black, like I'm a crab crawling out every morning and scurrying dutifully back in at night. my heart is broken for her like there's nothing left to break. What'll I do, Becky?"

"Forgive me for asking, but how come you married a blind woman," her voice treading gently over the question.

She could see muscle tightening in his face...snapping, quivering...jolting, memories knocking hard...

"If you can stand it. I'll tell you. It's a bad story. Very bad. Some of it, everyone knows. Some, only my Pa knows. And some, only I know...the rest, only Momma and...God. Here it goes. So, a little boy snuggles up to his mother and scurries right down again quick, hot whiskey breath in his nostrils, nausea clutching his stomach, angry eyes cutting, south sneering, bellowing, 'You're just like your Pa, always wanting, never giving.' He stretches out a clenched hand and opened it quick...an offering...eagerly, 'Here, Ma.' She lifts her head. 'What's that you got, boy?' 'A nickel. I found it and a whole...' She sends him reeling across the room, 'What am I gonna do with a nickel?! Cutesy, is all it is! Like your Pa, when he comes nuzzling and snuggling and give him what he wants, and I don't see him no more until he feels like it! Go out and play! Goodbye! Out! When you grow up, no one gonna have to tell you to play! Where's Daddy now?! I'll tell ya were, out playing!' 'What's he playing, Ma?' 'Round, that's what!' 'How you play that, Ma?' 'Round, that's what!' 'How you play that?' 'You'll find out someday. No more questions, you hear? Now, beat it!' insistent now, 'Why can't I stay with you?' I was crazy just to sit in her lap, my head on her big breast, both my hands on her big shoulders. She never let him, but this time he was determined. Sometimes, he wanted to lean the back of his head on her large, swollen belly and let it go up and down while she breathed, sitting snug between her heavy thighs, but she never let him. Her voice shrill, cutting now, "I don't want you touchin' me, ya hear?! Carried you for nine months for nothing! I wanted a girl. Them nine months was enough of carrying." "Just once, Momma...carry me...please." "You keep this up and they'll carry you...out...in a box!" He went to the ice box. Rotting fruit, peaches with brown circles and green fuzz. He searched and found one that's she'd cut the rotten part off. He tried again. "Here, Ma." She swept it out of his hand, snarled. "That's all I'm worth? A rotten peach?!" It rolled under her feet, and she pushed it away. It rolled back under feet, kept rolling back the more she pushed, and she jumped up in a terrible rage, stamped and mashed that peach with her foot, grinding it into the ground. "Stubborn! I'll teach ya." And she lost her balance, and her head came down on the heavy, wooden table behind her, hitting her optic nerve. She never saw again. The whole world got wiped out for her in one moment...and for me too.

She never came near me again. Wouldn't let me. Even as much as to touch her. If she heard as much as the creak of the floor under my foot, there'd be her cane clumping into another room. Couldn't even bear to breathe the same air with me. I tried to make it up, "I'll be your eyes, Momma." "I don't want yours."

I even blindfolded myself so I couldn't see, either. It just made me burn more and more with guilt and shame at what I'd done, knowing what blind is, groping and feeling and stumbling around. I couldn't go on with it. Never seeing a color. All the world, dark and gray. That was the hardest part. And I hated her, too, for still not letting me hold her hand and guide her down a stair. Would struggle alone as best she could herself. Sometimes, I could hear her scraping the floor with her shoes and me wanting to call out, "Can I help you, Ma?' But I didn't. Kept it all in. Can you imagine, hating her? Blind and all? Tried to teach her to read with her fingers, braille. Once, she let me trace her finger on the page. Snapped it away, "Who you kiddin'? That aint reading!" and she tore out the page. I made up my mind, then and there, I'll marry a blind girl and make up, one who'll let me be their eyes."

Becky asking, "But didn't you want someone who could love and love you?"

"That wasn't as important as giving back what I took. She was born on a farm, religious Baptist, lots of children, too many to feed all of them much. Mary couldn't read. I don't think they ever heard of braille in those one room schools, so she stayed home and helped with chores. I used to buy eggs from them, and Mary would put them in the box after her brother candled them. Never broke nary a one. I never had to flatter or court her. Just asked the family and they were glad to be rid of her. She said she wanted to know me first and we would sit on the porch, her hand on my face or mouth touching me while I talked, my eyes and all, the feel of the tips of her fingers caressing me. We'd sit in silence a lot, her just holding my hand and tracing the lines in my palm over and over with her finger. She liked that. And I'd try to tell her how the moon looked and the tree behind the shed and the flowers, but she wasn't interested, and she'd stop me. "Just you," she'd say. And I was so flattered. I didn't realize then. My god, what am I doing Becky?"

He crouched like a cornered animal, his head resting on her belly, the voice muffled now.

"Then, at the wedding ceremony, I whispered, "I'll be your eyes, Mary." "I don't want no eyes, Zeke," she told me, right there, our wedding night, while the minister was pronouncing us wed. And on our honeymoon, I was so proud of how I looked, muscles, powers, all over, I took her hand, put it nice and gentle on my arm, hardened my muscle, but her hand lay there frozen. I tried to touch her. "You're not blind," she said. "You don't know me with your hands, like living with a blind man, if you touch me." Her momma told her how babies come. We have two children. Twice, we've been close. She don't want no more children, she says."

Becky lifted his head from his lap.

"I want you to look at me while I'm talking, so you know I'm meaning what I'm saying truly and she proceeded to say words that sounded right, that soothed, that flowed natural as if from a hidden spring somewhere deep inside, but she wondered all the while if she believed what she was saying herself. But he seemed to. So she went on.

"What'll I do, Becky?"

"Nothing. You never know how you're gonna feel years after the day you make a promise...and she'll never see, and you can't make yourself not see. You tried, but you can't. You want a woman's adoring eyes looking into yours like you look into hers. You want to shout, 'Look,' to someone and she looks, sharing with you the delights of discovery. You want to live a little before you die. Gave your life away and you're sulking now because you want it back. Suddenly she wants to be home and unburdened, seeing his unreal, like she did before his confidence."

They were parked in a circle of trees. The moon was shining on her shoulder where her dress slipped. He traced the circle with his finger slowly, then down her breast. She pushed his finger away. He turned to her with a strange smile and dug both hands into her shoulders, so they hurt and forced her mouth to his.

It excited and repelled her and she spread both hands and pressed hard on his chest gasping, "Let me go," in broken syllables between her teeth while his mouth pressed stiff, harder, and harder, his knee over hers, forcing her legs apart.

She yielded, then resisted again. Turning and twisting, she inflamed him all the more. He held her hands in an iron grip while he prepared to enter her, his face full of love and wanting. Her body trembled against him, wanting too, then, a scream rising. He put his hand hard over her mouth. Her lower lip struggled free, and she bit hard on it while he took her again and again, ripping and tearing, maddened with hunger and pain...like a wounded beast...then breathing death out of his heart and body, and kissing her, exulting and grateful...she...numb and wooden as before. She would have been grateful. A fierce intellectual longing for loss of self, union with another, like the books said...for violence and formlessness, for passion that binds and shatters boundaries and makes one in one in mystical, breathless union of two. Maybe if she were broken and it was ripped out, exploding, tumultuous, wild, fierce, like rushing waters scattering all before them, then coming to rest...in benign stillness.

She yielded for an instant, then, searchlights intruding, "You alright, lady?"

The cool voice of a policeman.

"I'm alright."

"I think you better leave here. This place ain't safe. How come you're here. We got a complaint, 'Woman in Trouble.'"

Becky was mortified. He straightened his hair.

"Sure, we're leaving soon, officer."

Unbeknownst to them, a woman slid past them all in the dark and waited down the road. She was waving wildly.

"Wanna lift?"

"Yes," and she came toward them, headlights shining on her face, her eyes hungry like a woman crying to be taken in love, her mouth bloodied, in an agony of wanting, her face longing with ecstasy, begging, "Take me, Zeke, like you took her."

He sprung from the car, put his hand on her arm to steady her. She put his other hand on her breast and held it there, crying bitterly, "Forgive me, I'm so ashamed."

He lifted her gently.

"Let me be your eyes, Zeke. Not her."

Gently, "You were listening."

"I was."

She followed them and crouched under the door in the back of the car, then raised her head and peered through the window.

"And saw?"

"Everything."

"She has no right, Zeke. I've prayed to feel dry and shriveled as I look. You don't know how I've prayed. But I'm loving you, Zeke... warm and heavy and lots and lots like the prettiest girls there is and the youngest. You don't really think I'm a needing all those darn eggs," the words hurtling between sobs.

"We'd better go home now. Mary must listen to me and not hear me clumping into the house complaining about something like I usually do."

And he held Aunt Marion close, sitting her next to him while Becky sat smoldering in the back watching Aunt Marion sitting close and touching shoulders and cozying like they were an old married couple or something. Tomorrow she would be frightened and philosophizing about what she's come to. Nothing made a difference, neither Tom's courtliness, nor Zeke's primitive invasion, still numb...but tonight she would sulk, feel sorry for herself, and look out at the black vastness, the moon drifting through the clouds. There was a terrible secret between them now.

Not a binding, hidden tie, a well to draw from, a shiny place to touch and hold, a hidden treasure to put a glint in the eye, a place to return to together, over and over with eagerness and anticipation and love. Not that kind...but the other that scolds and darts eyes quickly far away with shame, as if we could fling the image as far as the eye could see as soon as it jolts our memory, and then scatters and disappears. Rushing to their room without a good night and then dreading the morning. Coming home, Becky is desperate to flee. Aunt Marion fervently praying she's gone. 'God grant me a miracle!' both opening their doors at the same time scorched with shame. They pass each other as if they were being tossed by a raging wind if they as much as glimpsed the other coming, each looking out their window for Zeke. One morning, two notes slipped under the door, one to Aunt Marion...one to Becky.

Dear Miss Marion,

I won't be delivering eggs here anymore. The company has changed my route. Hope you like the new man. He'll be calling and meeting you soon.

Dear Becky,

Forgive me.

Zeke

But they looked anyhow expecting that truck to come charging down the road and stop in front of the house sputtering.

Marion explaining, "He never had it fixed because it was a way of letting the ladies know he was coming so he wouldn't have to wait so long at the door. Some of them gussied themselves up for him, so while he sat in the truck bouncing and rocking, they had time for a setting their face in a smile and a final primp. Sold more eggs that way. Keep him here admiring if he thought they looked pretty. Otherwise, they'd be in a big hurry to get rid of him if they thought they looked ugly."

At first, they both looked out the window hopeful, then wistful, then, not at all, just listening. The house was divided with an invisible wall, so they seldom even passed each other. Becky ate in her room, each listening for the other's noise in the kitchen to stand before making her own meal...clattering plenty with pots and dishes so there would be no doubt, then clumping up the stairs. Two weeks of silence between them passed, the house without a human sound, laughter, arguing, hello, goodbye, not even a throat clearing, a cough, a sneeze. She was grateful for the sounds of nature, rain drumming on the windowpanes, thunder, lightning, crows cawing a raucous greeting in the morning. The house coming to life, protecting, shielding, like a big arm around her. They even took turns bounding down the stairs for the mail. As soon as they heard the clink of the slot in the door opening and closing, Aunt Marion first and then, Becky.

This morning, a letter from Tommy.

Dear Becky,

Just to let you know I'm coming home on the 18th, a week from now. We'll look for our own place then. Not fair to impose on Aunt Marion much longer. See you then.

Tom

Becky trembling. Letter rattling in her hand. <u>He knows</u>. Frightened... then angry. 'Leaving me alone with only an old lady for company who's a colossal bore at that. Becky turning on him like guilty people do when they're given a chance, the guilty victim turning on the innocent one...lashing and fuming and cruel in its devouring righteousness after being hungry for it so long. And then, the warm glow of compassion, 'He's lonely too,' and then reasoning back and forth, 'him and me, the pluses and minuses' and trying to be just and giving herself absolution for trying, at least, and then, the claiming of tights as if they were something owed, or uncontrollable. Life owes me something...or I can't help it, anyway. Becky ruled by the written world...craving to know what those books are talking about, passion especially...what Aunt Marion knows, shriveled, drab, stone faced, looking like a ghost in pink curlers. All that religion and all that ugliness still not enough to take the fire out of her and me, Becky, prettier, appealing, inviting, suggesting, free to pore over the forbidden banned, and married and knowing, and still not enough to put the fire out in me. Becky driven now. She had to know. No matter how many men, Tommy. Forgive me. No matter how many.

The Jewish passion that was given to God and revolution, study, ambition, and Talmud was now being spent on love. Midas of the heart, drawing in feelings and freedom...the end of millennia of feelings and can't feel. Doors flung wide open and can't take a step across the threshold. It's decreed...man is to walk with his tail between his legs and his tongue hanging out, humiliated and craving...no matter what. Taken, women beg to be loved...loved they beg to be taken.

Chapter Eighty-Eight

T he day of Tommy's arrival, Becky came down to the kitchen to find Aunt Marion in a flowered, new crisp robe bent over the table, a gleaming, white starched tablecloth over it now, and she's carefully placing silverware and flowers and humming a tune, the pink curlers out of her hair, combed and waved, kinky and shapeless, but 'as long as it had a wave to it,' she always said."Couldn't stand, thin, straight, stringy hair like mine if I don't frizz it up curling."

A taut, 'You're lucky,' to Becky when they were talking...long, wavy, auburn hair on Becky's head. She couldn't stand to be envied.

"My face is too small for it. Can't you see, I'm all hair?"

But nothing helped. Aunt Marion just looked martyred, and Becky looked worse...like she didn't appreciate her good luck. But now, Aunt Marion seemed perky...like life returned all at once...even humming a little. Yesterday, Becky passed her room. Marion accidentally left the door open. She was sitting on her bed, still, listless, the sunlight falling on a picture of Tommy's on her night table, her arm around it like it was real flesh and blood, her thin mouth open, pressed on his smiling one. Tommy innocent, smiling, unaware, snapping his hat off when she entered a room, rushing to open a door before her, watching his tongue.

"After all," he'd say, "Aunt Marion is a lady," a respectful tone in the very word...lady.

The crackle of bags, the gentle aroma of Marion's perfume and the smells of Tommy's favorite dishes waking up a kitchen that was lifeless until now.

"Can I help?" Becky said miserably...those few words kike jumping off a precipice, plunging in, then standing rigid, waiting for the anger that was just brimming, aching to spill over, to explode with the slightest touch, "Get out of my kitchen. Whore!"

And she stood trembling, tearing the wooden spoon out of the pot and holding it high, shaking with her and spattering drops on her freshly cleaned gleaming floor.

"Just because you got a pretty face, they're falling all over ya, those fool men. Well Tommy's mine! I reared him! And he's just on loan to you, that's all! I'm letting you borrow him!"

"You jealous of me?" Becky said quietly, pounded into submission, "Maybe you think I'm pretty. I don't. I think I'm ugly."

"You don't think! You reading and writing, that's all. No thinking and no feeling. You younglings don't know what feeling is! You talk about it plenty, but that's all! Talk! Yeah, I'm jealous of you. You've got something for the little pain you put out and I got nothing for the lot I put out! Nothing, ya hear? Even took Tommy away from me and Zeke, too. Took both of them!" Over and over howling in pain, "Both of them!"

Her back to Aunt Marion going down the hall and out the door, hearing, "Both of them!"

Behind the house, she collapsed on the cool grass, weary, emotionless, flat. 'I'm jealous of you, Aunt Marion, but you can't know that. What you're jealous of, you can see and talk about. What I'm jealous of, I can't even mention, not even in a whisper, a hint, or even a glance. You'll never know, Aunt Marion, how jealous I am.'

And she lay down and fell asleep until Tommy came home and found her there, kissed her and whispered, "Hi Pudgy."

She rubbed the sleep from her eyes, flung her arms around his beck, hugged him hard and was glad she, at least, had some lipstick on.

"I look a mess, Tommy."

"You do," teasing.

"I do?" She drew back, peeved.

"A beautiful mess. Most beautiful mess there is."

She hugged him again. It was the moment of forgetting and forgiving, like it always was when they first saw each other. The moment of triumph at the top of the hill until it all came tumbling down again.

"Dinner's ready," Aunt Marion called, a coy sickening sweetness.

They separated brusquely like an invisible hand grabbed them both by the back of the neck and thrust them forward rudely. Huge drops of rain suddenly pelting them. Aunt Marion strangely agitated, an innocent, girlish smile branded on her face, a flirtatious glance struggling with hate. A flash of lightning in the sky. On her face the struggle to reassemble itself once more into a new part, to a middle-aged nymphet.

Frantic, tearing the arid, empty years from her face, until it's moist and yielding. For a grotesque moment, they came together, an innocent eye and a thin, bitter mouth, the face twisting it's tortuous way and flitting quickly from one to the other, molding itself into bizarre forms until it settled into half laughing, half frowning, then lost it's way again, not knowing which way to go at all and hanging suspended, frozen, arched open eyes, stiff smile, twitching, slanted, scornful mouth.

From outside, she heard, "Coming."

Rushing out to meet him, eyes pleading, "I don't want to be a virgin anymore."

Tommy not noticing. Becky walking ahead in dread quiet, answering, "Me neither."

And she slipped Tommy's hand from her shoulder and hurried inside. Becky sat at the table watching for a sign of conspiracy between them, of guardedness or treachery, a signal, a look, a touch, or a passing glance. Nothing...not even a slight edge to his tone of voice. No connection between his mechanically worded letters and his adoring eyes shamelessly watching her...as if he was leaving forever. So embarrassed, she laughed hysterically, the fork trembling in her hand and gagging a few times. They both fussed over her anxiously.

She preferred that to the watching; Aunt Marion careful to meet out equal portions, not to play favorites, but she served him because 'he's a man.' Becky usually resented it, but not this time. There was a sense of security in the routine.

Nothing changed, even to, "You two can go now. I'll do the dishes myself."

Cheery like always. Becky not wanting to go for the first time. Aunt Marion knowing and insisting for the first time. Becky dutifully climbed up the stairs ahead of Tommy as if he were ordering her up to her room forthwith, to administer punishment. Stoic, forbearing, shuddered as she opened, then closed the door, forgetting, or not wanting to remember he was behind her.

He pushed it open before it snapped closed, laughing, "Hey Pudgy, locking me out already?"

The room was in blackness, a thin line of yellow light under the door. Marion's feet quickly passing. They both paused, staring down, until it passed, welcoming the dark. Then he held her, hard and hungry.

A whispered, "I miss you so much."

She stood stiff, as if to ward off a blow...her heart twisting with fear of angry words, recriminations, accusations, and soundless, guilty tears, not knowing what to reply, defenseless, beaten, trembling with hurt, racked. But there was only love in his touch. Her heart and body were softer now, tender, yielding. The argument was over... imprisoned in loneliness and silence. Suspicions bursting stings, hurling recriminations, and accusations into the naked light, then burrow down deep again, whimpering, denying, forgetting, then desperate whisperings and affirmations...love, love, love. The cocoon again of...love. Cautious letters that revealed more than he ever dated. And loving ones revealing more than she ever dared. Angry tears falling on Momma's forgiving breast, 'I forgive you, Tommy.'

Baby talk. Two children who frightened each other, clinging, each taking turns mothering and being mothered.

"Goodnight," in a little girl's creaky voice before falling asleep.

'Goodnight," a little boy's purring voice, warm, content.

Revulsion drifting into her heart for a moment and quickly driven out again, not to spoil, to jar, but it remained, lurking there.

Next morning, a harried whisper from Aunt Marion, "Don't worry. I'm saying nothing. I don't want you talking and him turning on the both of us, you hear?" Begging now...then hurrying past...and busying herself setting the table.

All month, Becky wanted to hear he was coming home to stay, but he only went through the motions, looking and circling ads for employers he never saw.

"A place of our own, Tom."

"You'll look when I'm gone...whatever you find is fine. I don't have the time."

And he'd go to the movies with the time he didn't have. Little suspicions squirming into center stage, demanding to be noticed. He doesn't want to move, and Aunt Marion doesn't want me out. Becky shaken, trapped, resentful.

Baby talking, "Becky homesick, Tommy. Wanna go home."

"Whatever you want, Becky," Tommy soft and frothy like cotton candy after they'd been close, gentle, misty, like soft rain, she, sleepy, honeyed, snuggled voice, "If we settle and get jobs here, can I bring my parents here like we planned?"

Brusque now. "I have enough relatives to support!"

And disentangling, turning his back, and leaving her bruised, shocked. The good Tommy tarnished. But the next day, the other

Tommy, dashing, suitcases out the door and sliding them down the hall.

"Tommy's marks," Aunt Marion said they were. She didn't mind, she said, indulgent. Becky jealous, her arms folded around her waist, tightening, digging her nails into her arms, straining to hold the pieces together before they break.

The cabdriver waves to Tommy as he runs out stumbling with the suitcase. They wave goodbye, Marion, and Becky. He rushes back, holds each by the hand, then drops them both at once, turns suddenly distant and walks quickly to the cab, jumping in and slamming the door decisively. He never looked back again, snapped his wrist, and looked at his watch intently. They looked at the rear window, waving to the back of his head. He never turned around. It snapped back just before disappearing around the corner. He was laughing. The house was empty, grieving and wounded, too. Lost its laughter. Marion's eye blurred with tears. Becky dry with hard decision. They turned from each other without a word.

"Going...always going," Aunt Marion sullen, demanding.

Becky surprised even herself, a snarl in her voice, attacking after Aunt Marion suddenly turned on her.

"Married a furriner, that's what he did...a good American marrying with a furriner. Ain't enough American girls in this land."

Aunt Marion wasn't prejudiced. She was just finding whatever she could at the moment and hurling it.

"And you can't even speak English! What you mean?"

"And what you mean bad?" Mimicking Becky's Brooklyn accent.

Becky turned and fled up the stairs in panic. The quick fire that rose in her retreated quickly, Becky cowering now in fear of it. Plunging around the room emptying drawers, struggling to free stubborn ones that refuse to yield and straightening and dusting the rooms until it was reduced to the bareness she found in the beginning. She straightened Tommy's picture on the bureau, closed the windows quickly, the sound pounding the house like hammers blows. Head bowed, body crouched, she crept softly down the stairs, shamed to be unwanted, to be cast out as undesirable. Into the street where all the solid citizens were ambling comfortably along, some brows slightly furrowed with small decisions.

Hurrying was considered common. Though they had to scuffle and scrounge and burrow like northerners to put a bean in the pot, it was done sub-rosa, the sleepless night, the extra drink, the beaten wife, the abused child. On the surface, calm, not even a ripple, unhurried...deadly.

"Howdy, Miss Becky."

She answers in a desperate nod, hurtling forward, going nowhere, a shortage of rooms in town. Just rushing away, willy-nilly discarding grimly the impulse to go back to Momma and Poppa, or be led by fortune...and circumstance, depend on the undependable. There was a brusque, inner stroke of the pen that blocked those alternatives, too desolate, both of them. By habit, she wandered into a candy store, small ads tacked on the board.

"Going somewhere?"

"No."

Dropping the suitcase on the floor with a thud.

"Just looking for a place to stay."

"You know of any?"

He shook his head, then checked the cards on the bulletin board.

"Here's one but you won't want that."

"Tell me," she said pleading.

He shook his head again, "Nope. I don't think..."

She struggled with waiting and obeying or insisting on a look for herself.

"Maybe this," he said, and checked again, her nerve endings hanging on every word, while he rubbed his chin and debated with himself. He had her in the palm of his hand...dangling, teasing.

Her eyes and mouth waiting, hoping, begging. The bell clanging...a customer.

'Hi, Bill."

He rushed over, all humble servant again.

"What can I do for ya?"

Then waited as if a sentence were about to be pronounced on him.

"I'll have a hamburger."

And then, the specifications. Becky tortuously waiting while they both debated, onions raw or cooked, well, medium or rare, cream or no cream and so forth and so on. He went into the kitchen and Becky scurried to the bulletin board, 'All rooms in a house for rent' in big, black letters. She memorized the address and fled the store before he returned.

The broker asking, suspicious, "For you, alone?"

But he was all smiles again when Becky said words like husband and school. Saying she was still going. After a big ceremony about looking for the keys so Becky would be worried and anxious and eager, which she was, she took her to the house. It was a big, old endless place that people were abandoning in those days, long before the passion to patch, rescue, and profit like it is now. Those were the days of other adjectives...inconvenient, impractical, uncomfortable...White Elephant...and assault by an army of wreckers. Those that escaped were now called romantic, poetic and assaulted now by an army of painters, plasterers, and hammerers. The last of the family owning this house had been long buried and abandoned the old woods of memory and decay. The vandals hadn't yet discovered it.

"But they will," the broker explained.

"That's why the estate is renting it. No one will buy it."

'Estate' ...sounded so intense. Impressive. Becky had no idea what it was. She wandered through the rooms and picked one, small, close to the bathroom, sparsely furnished, the old lady's room, untouched since she'd gone. The broker opened the bureau drawer. It was still full of her clothes...a faint whiff of perfume...pressed white slips, pink ribbons thread through them. The broker said he was sorry.

"That's alright. I'll live out of my suitcase for a while. How many rooms here?"

"17, I think," and she counted again and again on her fingers, trying to ascertain exactly.

'That's okay, never mind."

And later, Becky wandered through the house counting rooms and bathrooms and still wasn't sure. It was one of those houses. You could never be sure. It seemed like there were rooms and corners and anterooms and 'before and after' rooms, Becky called them, like each room had an introduction and a farewell before you entered another. That night, Becky fell asleep in a house that was all rooms and no people...and told herself not to be afraid...and she wasn't. After all, would Emma Goldman be afraid? Look what she suffered! Becky spent the next day in bed after buying every paper in town. No one knew where she was...even Tommy. Now she could do what she wanted. No one would know. She circled the 'Dance all night to your favorite tunes' ad, pressed her good dress on the bed.

Dressed and ready. When the door locked behind her, she stood hesitant and fearful. 'Who's gonna dance with me?' The empty, old house was desolate now, tossing her into the street and onto a passing bus. Near the hall, she could hear the violin playing old country reels and the hawker calling his incomprehensible instructions from the outside. Inside, just like the movies, round, checkered, tablecloths and a stardust floor. She chose a table. A young man rushed forward to help her with her chair.

"Can I have this dance?"

She rose quickly. In her haste, the chair fell. He picked it up and bowed and flourished with his hat so she wasn't shamed as she would have been. On the dance floor she stumbled, and couldn't move her feet quick enough.

At the end, he returned her to the table, said, "Thank you, ma'am," and asked her if he could join her at the table.

"I'm expecting someone," she lied.

"Sorry, ma'am," he said, "thank you," and hurried away, putting his arm around a girl near him and pushing her willingly to the dance floor. Becky watching enviously while he fancy danced her, swirling

her out and in and tricky steps and hops and in-between. But Becky
didn't want to settle just yet. There were so many others. He'd served
his purpose. Given her confidence. Coming toward her, a tall, bony
fellow, black hair, arms close by his side, dark, heavy shadow on his
face like he'd forgotten to shave, black, heavy eyebrows, high, sunken
cheeks, cold darting eyes, thin, determined, hard mouth, body jerking
from side to side as he walked. He bent over the table.

"How's about a dance?"

"Would you?"

A note of bitter sarcasm creeping in.

"Expecting disappointment?"

She wasn't sure. But he wasn't southern. Of that, she was sure.
Politeness was not one of his weapons. She nodded. He walked ahead
and she followed. In the middle of the dance floor, he turned and put
a stiff band on her back. He couldn't dance. Too rigid to follow
anything...even music. It had to follow him. He shuffled back and
forth, an arm's distance separating them. He smiled. Only the mouth.
Reluctant. Obliging. Ungiving smile. Just going through the motions.
Strange. More sinister when he smiled.

"My name is Irving. What's yours?"

"Becky."

"You're not from here, where are you from?"

"Brooklyn."

"I'm from the Bronx."

Exciting, gushing, "Really! I'm Jewish."

"Me too. I'm going to school."

"Me too."

"What are you studying?"

"Psychology?"

"Me too. I'm going for my Ph.D."

A quick look at her left hand, "Married?"

And dropped hands to his sides, drew back.

"Yes. Separated."

He returned but held her more at a distance.

Becky saying, "You remind me of someone."

He is parodying her in sing song, "Usually a man says that, doesn't he?"

"Now, who do I remind you of?" Biting, this time.

Without thinking, "My brother."

The words came tumbling out from that secret place inside, where they're curled up until their time comes.

"Really? What does he look like?"

"Did. He's gone now."

She could never say the word dead. It was too harsh, too callous, and unfeeling a word. He talked. A student at the university, just completed his M.A. What he wanted to be. All the Jewish sounding things she hasn't heard in years, even about politics and newspaper articles and books. He asked to take her home. She eagerly consented. He came to pick her up in his car, she sat entranced by his side while he whistled Stravinsky and sang the love duet from Tristan and Isolde so she could sing it with him, loving that part when the music comes crashing down after it builds and builds, each touching the other, louder, and louder, closer, and closer. The first time she'd sung with anyone since her father. Becky entranced...until the revelations came.

"I had a nervous breakdown two days ago, went to the hospital for a few hours, willed myself out of it. Willed myself well. Now I'm alright. I married a beautiful woman, and she betrayed me with everybody she could. I threw her out...and myself, too, I guess. But I found me again, you can be sure. Didn't throw too far."

And he went on.

"I'll be a very rich man someday. My mother was willed millions and when she dies, it all comes to me."

"That's where I live!"

"This is where you live?! You sure you're not kidding me?"

"I have a room here."

"Where?"

"I'll show you."

The moonlight coming through the window lighted their way while they groped along to her room. He slid along the walls with both hands upraised, his muscles bulging.

"You seem very strong."

"I was once a boxer."

Becky tingling. They came to the room. He sat down on the little bed. It collapsed under him.

"I'm sorry," he said flatly and turned it over and fixed it, still talking about his childhood.

"My father was a window washer. He was killed when I was young, fell from a window. They put us kids into an orphanage, all five of us. They were very cruel to us all."

Becky was protective now, wanting to heal and undo all the hurt and pain. Then he went on about the war.

"I was in the war, too. They sent a small group to the combat zones. I was in that group. Got lost in the jungle, one night, and ended up with dengue fever...for the rest of my life."

He sat beside her, stiff, looking at the wall.

"Place needs a painting, bad."

He was tired of himself now. Changing the subject...but just for a moment. More, after the war.

"Had a tough time when I got home from the war. Opened a restaurant and fell in love with the waitress. Driving her home one night, and didn't even see the pipes being carried, sticking out from the back of the truck in front of us. I went into them. She was killed instantly."

Rubbing his chin with his finger, flat, emotionless, like a child completing an assigned recitation.

"And I have this scar, see?"

It didn't even occur to her to ask why he was telling so much to a stranger. She wouldn't dare question or judge someone so smart. But she thought she might contend with him on politics, like she did with Poppa. That was a little scary, but she had to convince him she was smart, even if she wasn't. Else, how could she keep him? Convincing

Tommy, others, that was easy. He was the real test. Becky never paid much attention to order and connection. Words just flowed like attention to order and connection. Words just flowed like music and rose to a climax and faded. You just felt you were right and shouted loud enough until you convinced the other person...or like she did with Lottie...she agreed so she wouldn't be thought as dumb. But not with a man. If she wasn't smarter, she was pitiful dumb, like her mother. With Tommy she wasn't convinced. With Irving, she'd be convinced she was the smart one. She'd have the last word, like with Poppa. It wasn't just a man...but a special kind now. The test was harder.

When he kissed her goodnight, he pressed a cold mouth to hers and held his hands by his sides. Becky thought of the poetry of John Manley Hopkins...love...the freshest things deep down under...love deep down under...and she would find it and it would flower and be hers alone...like Heathcliff. He even looked like home and he would love her with the painful, anguished devoted love she read and dreamed about. And he'd understand her too. A psychologist. He'd know what she was thinking and feeling and forgive, not judge. Be her ideal father, knowing what was on her mind. Sing with her like Poppa. And rich too, someday. Imagine going back to Dorothy's grocery store on West 3rd Street in a limousine, the wife of Dr. Taylor...and what would Momma say? Jewish and learned! In a haze of hope and dreams, romantic fancy of limitless love, victory, and respect and...pleasing Momma...Becky neglected to notice that Irving was insane. The iron girders he was riveting down desperately deep in his brain to hold fast, firm and ordered...the floor that as pressing to break it's fragile bounds, flow over and drown him in all that pain... the savagery on his back in the orphanage, the humiliation, helplessness and abandonment, his thoughts now checked with the same hovering caution as the road, not letting a careless word slip in. the world was a careless, unpredictable, disorderly place. Logic was the only refuge; safe, secure, orderly.

The war and its maiming of his body, the mind torn with guilt over a lost, careless moment. Only the academy remained intact...the progression of cold ideas moving smoothly. To Becky, logic was a severe, cold, disciplinaries, a weapon that had nothing to do with hungry people and worker's rights and all the decadent things she'd never questioned. There was a time when minds battled, not bodies... yet. In this brief meeting, the lines were clearly drawn. But then, Becky's fancied, he would indulge her and love her, patronizing sometimes, but she loved that, to be spoken to like a little girl, not taken seriously when she was terribly wrong. Pronounced cute. He'd be above really competing of trying to outsmart her. A psychologist, after all. Becky's dreams grew fatter and fatter, sinking their teeth into her and not letting her go. Irving...the current versions of the prince come to rescue her. Every age has one, after all, doesn't it?

Chapter Eighty-Nine

Tommy had frightened her, suddenly turning again, hit, and run like before. A stranger without magic, the haze of unreality, becomes an enemy. The WASP cowboy, the uniformed gentleman marches off alone in the sunset. But Tommy turns on the lady first, then leaves with honor. Tommy deserts and abandons and doesn't keep a promise. Man as God must keep his promise...or the illusion of keeping a promise. Tommy's word had fallen from etched in stone to dust in the hand. Becky depended on the Word and the Promise...and the power of an old dream bursting through disappointment and resentment.

'I've met Heathcliff, Momma...and he's Jewish, you hear, and rich and he'll be a doctor and a psychologist and he whistles Stravinsky and he talks and talks and talks and looks like Pesach...not only has his hollow, haunted restless face, but the spirit, a fire raging inside and stiff like a wary tiger with the strain of it being forced down and about to burst. So exciting Ma, after all that calm. And he hates the world Momma...like Heathcliff...he'll only love me. The Bohemian lover of the world, disdainer of possession and property, lusting to possess and be possessed by one who disdains the world she wants so much to save and is doing nothing about saving. He'll love me cause we'll go to school together. I'll sacrifice and prove he can trust me, and I'll love him like no one else ever has. The dreams were rushing in from all the distant places where they'd been, Pesach from years, and Heathcliff from decades and Momma's from centuries and Becky rushed on heedlessly and whirled around the maypole, giddy, ecstatic. She'd make a flower bloom in the desert. Bring forth lush and green vines and tender grapes, force death to release it's hold and return grudgingly, slowly, painfully to life what it mercilessly wrenched so many years ago. Give back what I took...Pesach Persie. If it was decreed Becky would have children, they were not to be born from life, but from death. To succeed where Momma failed.'

And then, the mountain came tumbling down.

'But what will he be doing with me...a chubby nobody from West 5th Street.'

Squirming inside again.

'May I take a baby step?'

'No, you may not. Not. Not.'

'But I'll let you take a giant step.'

Becky lying prostrate.

'On me...Heathcliff Irving. See?'

'I don't want to.'

'Pretty please.'

Sulking, angry, 'Leave me alone.'

Becky shrinking. Wretched. A sudden rustling and banging on the wall...then a knock on the door. Flinging it open, 'Howdy,' ...an extraordinarily handsome man.

"I'm the neighbor next door. Just moved in, care to share a cup of tea? I have no coffee."

"Why...yes."

And she followed him into his room. Not a sock or necktie strewn anywhere, though he'd just moved in.

"You're beautiful," he said, "please sit on this chair."

And he unfolded an old bridge chair near the window where the flower weeds had grown high, and the sun made a square on the floor.

"Like you're a painting in a golden frame," he said, "just right... the flowers framing her behind the window.

"Are you an artist?"

"No, I'm an actor. Didn't you see me in the Sean O'Casey play at church? The Plough and the Stars."

Reddening, "No."

"Sorry. I didn't mean to ask you an embarrassing question like you committed a crime. I just meant I have free tickets if you want to."

"I want to."

"That's how we get an audience mostly. It's called 'Paper the House.'"

Becky tingling. Whatever happens now, she was in the world... her version, that is. Another dream stepping off screen and into the living room. Meeting an <u>actor</u>. No one in the movies did prosaic things for a living. They were all journalists or detectives or singers or actors and all handsome and beautiful. He was wearing a white sweater with a blue trim, and corduroy trousers, easy, confident, in command of himself, moving with ease and grace, talking like Roosevelt, clear, grounded, perfect English...like she never heard close by. Eager blue eyes attending only to her. What did actresses do when the leading man gazed at her like that?

They only showed the profile so you couldn't really tell where they were looking. Becky looked down. At least, she tried to. He knelt and followed her eyes, so she had to face him.

"Is it that I'm so good looking you're afraid you'll turn to dust if you look at me? You don't have to worry. No Goddess up there in Olympia IS in love with me so you'll have to make her jealous and you'll be terribly punished if you as much as look at me."

Becky's chin dropped closer to her chest.

"Forgive me," he pleaded, putting his finger under her chin, "didn't mean to make you uncomfortable. But that's no excuse. Most of the meanness in the world is the 'brick falling on the head' type and that's all we can do is stand over the bloody mess and say we're sorry."

Becky thought, 'A performance, only for her, on command, like for a queen. But it was real, too. Acting and real getting so mixed up now, she couldn't tell the difference. That was scary. The movie generation crossing an invisible line. Life imitating art, like Oscar Wilde said. But Poppa wasn't a movie generation, and he was over the line, too. But every generation has its fakers. Poppa and Momma had the Jewish stage. With Tommy, she knew calm real, gentle real, tender real...<u>dead</u> real. How can anyone ever know what people really are if they're given so many choices? Didn't Werner start a wave of suicides? The obsession with find the real from Know Thyself must have started with giving man a dramatic alternative to his being that seemed nothing to the drama being played out before him...from the Bible to Odysseus and King Lear...to the drama of fail- ure...even Willie Loman. The world worships success and rises to it's feet for failures...depends how it's done.'

Becky never trusted the actor in Poppa and discovered she couldn't trust the gentleness in Tommy. Perhaps...the coldness in Irving. But this was unnerving. Not to be able to tell when he was on and off stage. Real was very important to Becky after all of Poppa's faking. 'Why not a pleasant faker? The question never occurred to her. Better a jovial faker, than a real maniac, no Becky?' Becky answered all the questions before asking. Of all the questions Becky asked of life, she never asked that one. Every generation sees it's hapless people on goose chases...The Living God, Communion with the Dead, now...it was the Real and Love and several others that had the Becky's' leaping and searching, burrowing, and clutching. 'Every fool has his followers,' Spinoza said. Becky was flopping about in a wild dash for the real and discarding it the minute she found it. It was too dull...too ordinary, too real. Weighed down under a fancy and trying to hurl it over the mountain into reality.

"OK, the tea is ready. Sugar...one lump or two?"

Shaking her head violently, "No lumps."

A thread dangling from each cup. Becky couldn't stand people who used one bag for two cups. Little things like that. Very important.

He brought the cup to her. She stirred and the thread fell in, cardboard and all. She looked up helplessly and quickly down again. He could tell if she was acting, too. He couldn't be fooled. Becky couldn't bear to be caught acting. Sometimes, she wasn't even sure if she was or not. But he would be. The overhead fan was blowing her hair and dress and she tried to keep her blowing dress down with one hand, while it ballooned stubbornly the more, she tried to pin it down, the hair blowing in her face.

"Ah, me lady," he said, and he took the clattering tea and cup out of her hands.

"Let not the winds of Heaven visit your face too roughly, becoming very Shakespeare an assuming a formal stance while he flicked the snap, and the fan whirled slower and slower to a stop. The heat made breathing hard. He raised his arm, his leg apart, like Cyrano about to give a lecture on his nose, wiggling from side to side, setting himself just right and beginning the famous speech... 'No toady...no...' he'd chosen rightly. Though he was too pretty for the role, he knew what her would please. Instinctively, they knew. His face like Lord Bryon with graying hair, but without the pessimism or sophistication or depraved worldliness, light skinned, kindly open face that knew neither reserve nor suspicion and his large eyes and mouth so full and tender, it could have been a woman's. his body was neither lean nor hard looking, like he looked in the mirror, not to flex his muscles but because he had to, for a final okay, or to practice a role. His stomach protruded a little, but he didn't seem to mind. His shirt was buttoned carefully, so his chest wasn't exposed. For an actor, he seemed very conservative. She applauded widely when he finished Cyrano's speech...for two reasons.

He was so good, and she was so flattered. For the rest of the day, she hid behind talk of politics and human nature...and drank her tea head up. Whenever silence threatened, she read another soliloquy from Cyrano, and they laughed and laughed.

"You read now," he said.

"Me?"

He didn't press on. She was grateful for that. He knew when to stop. The next few days they had lunch together and tea. They spent hours together. He touched her hand only once...when he was Cyrano, talking to Roxanne, just because he couldn't stand Cyrano being that chaste! Then one night, a candlelight dinner, cheese and salads in the deli, paper plates, homemade gourmet. She couldn't see him touching his face, lowering his eyes, painful sigh and his hands clenching and unclenching.

"You've never asked me if I'm married, Becky. I appreciate that. I was once. Had a beautiful wife. Dark eyes and long, lovely hair...like you...good hair and all...like you. At first, I knocked on your door and to be neighborly. Then when I saw you, I had to know you."

Desperation in his voice now frightening Becky.

"I don't know how to tell you this, Becky, but I must. Like having to cleanse my heart before God. I have to do it before you and not because it needs cleaning because I did anything. It's because it seems like I have. It's harder that way. Even if I were told I didn't, I wouldn't believe. It's like faith in God...this faith in your own evil. Remembering now....no matter what...we were happy...Joy and I... Joy...her name was...would you believe it? I left her in the morning with a pencil in her mouth, figuring and counting, sitting at the kitchen table, surrounded by papers, sorting, and piling and bouncing them on the table, just to make a neat bunch neater. Goodbye Joy, I said, and blew two kisses when I left. Goodbye, she called out to me and smiled and thumped a bunch of papers hard on the table twice, like she was blowing something back to me, too. And that's how we parted. Like we always did. Me, taking part of her with me, and her left with part of me I left behind. And I came home the same way I always do. She'd open the door and I'd sneak the flowers around the bend just like it was a peace offering though there was no reason to be offering. We never had a war, and I could feel her cheek on my hand, so she brushed her face on them. Then I'd open the door wide enough, so she'd come around and kiss me and I'd smell those flowers on her cheeks; sweet, fresh, like her smile. This time, I opened the door, put the flowers round like always. I waited. Maybe she hadn't heard. Then my arm started aching. So, I opened the door wide. She wasn't in the hall or the parlor. I ran into the bedroom. She was lying down, her head on the pillow. When I came closer, I could see right away, her eyes were shut in death. A black gate she'd closed tight around herself that no one could ever open...a bottle of whiskey, empty pill bottles by her side. Somehow, she knew how to mate them, so they were deadly. I thought we shared everything. What else didn't we share? I dread to think how much was there I never saw or heard? I don't know. There was no note. She died the way she was born...without explanation. Do you think I was to blame, Becky? Tell me," pleading now.

He ached to be told the truth, so he'd be told a lie over and over again.

"No, Irving. Of course not. You're not to blame."

But the fear was rising. She was blaming him. The hapless victims of the victim are pilloried all their lives. They must have done something. She excused herself early. Said she had to search for a job. The next morning, he knocked but she didn't answer. That night, she waited until she heard him leaving, then decided to go to the dance where she met Irving. She saw him as soon as she came in. He was dancing with another girl, his chin firmly jutting over her shoulder, his body bent like he was keeping it as far and pure as he possibly could. He saw her when he was bringing the girl back to the table, but he did not acknowledge her. She realized why later. A man was standing behind Becky's chair, unbeknownst to her, his hands on the back of it, and bending over her like he was with her. He whispered, "The next dance."

She turned around and looked into a smiling face, dark skin and glowing white teeth, coal black hair and black eyes...a Mexican. She nodded with her head turned and cricked her neck. Dancing the whole time in miserable pain but smiling all the while...answering the same questions. The one question unanswered...asked in innuendos...testing his charm...the look in his eye, the touch of his hand and watching carefully, while he seemed unaware and entranced. And Becky watched, too, while she glittered and bubbled in a rush of flowing spontaneity. Nothing in her eyes. Nothing in his. Alive and sparkling without...a dead caution within...unmoving...still...mustn't jump too quick...too easy...timing...when to take...when to give. An old want...still pushing...to be close without marching rigid to a duty. Becky still did not know and was made to crave with the desperation that men have torn the earth and the seas, seeking, and burrowing and having to find. And now, women are being taunted by the sirens. Nirvana was in the magic of man. And you haven't <u>lived</u>...until... Becky's worst fear of <u>never having lived</u>. Mama said living was giving, so she gave...and living is learning so she learned...and Poppa said living is rebelling and fighting so she rebelled and fought a little...not much but...some. And the books psychologists said living was <u>being a woman</u>. All men saying what women need they told women they had to have babies to fulfill themselves. But that got expensive and burdensome. Told them not to work and that got too expensive and burdensome. So, they search around for something else where they're indispensable, necessary, and needed...and found it. But they dug a hole for themselves too. Hearing now that they're not loving enough.

"My first name is Pancho, and my middle name is Villa...you know, like the rebel."

"I know."

"You do?! American girls don't, as a rule."

He let her go and tap danced around her, arching his back an clicking his heels and sweeping an invisible, black brimmed hat from her head and grabbing her with the other hand, and putting his face close to hers while she bent fat back like the Mexican ladies with long, black hair who danced a taunting courtship and submitted in the end, falling to the floor, the man over her...victorious. They sat down after the dance...Becky wanting him at first, with the feminine craving for a new hat and thinking she found a true man...alive, vital...then...the flooding hope that makes men tremble when they plunge deep in the earth's surface and make it yield treasure...at last. She left her hands clenched in her lap so he wouldn't see them tremble. But he did. And she saw that he did and the self-satisfied smirk that flitted quickly across his face. And the nausea came to Becky and the deadness and the trying hard to go backward a moment in time and failing and the determination to plod and see...maybe.

"Can I take you home?"

She got up without answering and he followed...eager now and obeisant, rushing with the groveling air of a new servant. His car door slammed shut with brisky finality, his mind seemingly elsewhere. She slumped in the seat...the clouds and moon as blue as they whisked by. She numbly directed him in monosyllables. Left...right...next corner. He screeched to a stop.

"You live here? With family?"

"No. Alone." He turned to look at her.

"Why so glum? Smile," he coaxed her. She showed him her teeth.

"Pretty teeth. All perfect, I bet."

"How do you know?"

"I'm a dental student. I know my teeth."

She closed her mouth tight.

"Let me see. They're beautiful."

She opened her mouth wide.

"More. More," laughing now.

"So, I can really see," and she burst out laughing.

He looked so funny staring at the teeth inside her mouth.

"A treasure. You're so lucky."

"You have nice ones too."

"Just in the front."

"Well, that's where it matters."

Becky never believed Latin lovers could talk about teeth and molars.

"Do you have a cold drink in the house?"

"I think so."

"Would you mind? I'm very dry."

Becky walked stolidly into the house, her face frozen like a mask, drained of will and still clinging tenaciously to a 'maybe.' He closed the door behind her and took her hand before she could put on the light, pulling her to him, embraced her hand with one hand holding her firmly and decisively in place and was loosening his belt with the other. She could hear the horrible clanking and shuddered. He couldn't wait until he's undressed, pushing her down on the bed, two gruff impatient hands, groping hands, pulling down her underthings with one swift, crude sweep. She stood numb, stepping out of one leg, then the other and he invaded her with cold determination, like he was drilling a tooth, his trousers still on and his belt dancing above his face until he collapsed and rolled over on his side, panting heavy. She turned from him and covered herself with the sheet and sat on the bed, staring at the window, her hands clutching and unclutching the side of the bed. He hadn't even kissed her. He suddenly jumped off our bed and switched on the light, snapping his wrist to look at his watch.

"Late! I must go! Early class in the morning. Heavy exam and I still haven't studied."

His face looked mean, now, and bloated. Self-loathing creeping over her now. He looked so trim all dressed, natty jacket, stiff, starched, white collar, stroking his hair into place with hand and comb, admiring himself in the mirror. Becky, the one undressed and left...in a demeaned position. It's one of the male's tricks degrading women that way, standing in front of her dressed and in a hurry while she's undressed with no place to go.

"When can I see you again?" Door half open and one foot out... Becky still holding the sheet in front of her.

A wooden, "I'll let you know. I don't know just now."

"Call me..." and he threw a slip of paper on the bureau, smiled broadly, and bounced out the door. Becky curled into a ball like a wounded animal...a scream inside...Ma and Pa and Lottie, doctors, professors, columnists, women's libbers... 'if this is living, I want to die.' Three days later, a call on the hall phone. A 'how about tonight' call. They grew surlier as the excuses mounted. Becky smiles back, much like a tired mother being kicked by a child in temper tantrum, not even feeling the pain anymore. Just letting it happen. Without anger, patient indulgence until the storm passes.

Chapter Ninety

Alone, she attended the play of the next-door neighbor. He turned to her from the stage. At intermission, Pancho Villa accosted her in the lobby.

"Would she see him again...when...when...when?"

Irving found them, just to say a brittle hello. A girl waving at him, wildly. He ignored her until he was ready. I'll call you, he said to her...and a stiff wave back, more of an army salute, then a greeting. And later, Zeke's truck was waiting near the house. He jumped down lightly. A night to remember.

"How did you find me?"

"The coffee shop. He told me right away, but I waited until I forgave myself. Easy to heap on a lot of excuses when you must...and I had to, Becky...wanting so much to see you."

She drew back, not from fear, just an old habit, jumping away from a person at first. Anybody. Didn't matter...even Momma if she came too near too quick.

"Don't be afraid. I won't hurt you. Not a step further. I'm staying right here."

He brushed his foot around in a circle.

"Unless you say I can move out of it."

"You can move out of it."

Enjoying his mortification and self-laceration. Liking him like that. Feeling sorry and all over...but standing like a jack in the box, waiting for her to set him free.

"You wanted me too much. How can I blame you for that?"

He sunk to his knees...head in his hands. She stepped into the circle and bent down with him, took his hands away from his face, cupping her hands over it, a gentle pressure and he followed her up. They stood looking at each other in loving, tender silence.

"Why did you leave Aunt Marion, Becky? I would have been content, for the rest of my life, to meet you in Bill's coffee shop, even count eggs at Aunt Marion's and love you when you let me."

If she hadn't met Irving, she might have considered it. Becky was grateful for just being flattered, wanted until then, but he filled her head with big ideas that were now, for the first time, possible. And being a wife? She wanted to try that. Just to see if she could. There was a lurking suspicion in her head that she scorned it because she couldn't...not a real one. Part time girlfriend, playing house with Tommy was all she'd been able to manage until now.

Girls whipping her into being a clown, a beggar, men adoring, wanting, turning her into a queen...for a moment, at least. And when the star falls to earth, once brilliant in the heavens, now ugly, scarred, misshapen, distorted, cavernous rock.

"I can't stay at Aunt Marion's, but chickens don't care where you bring their eggs and I won't have to sneak out to the coffee shop anymore if I'm not there. Besides, you can now ring my bell without a bunch of eggs in your hand."

"That's a good first step. I'm leaving with the family on vacation for a month and when I come back..."

His eyes closed and his face warm and glowing with love. Becky slid away and left him there alone in his circle. He stood rooted on the spot until her footsteps faded and he couldn't hear the crunch of earth and stones under her feet and he sprang into the truck happy.

In later years, she saw herself as two people...one clinging to moonbeams and moments, magic and brief interludes, parting and coming together, of making a religion of transience...and the other... hurtling herself willingly into domestic drudgery, into reality...and both a severe test...being an eternal date...being a dutiful wife...taking care of another person...really...not just courting and negligees and feeding the vanities. Always an invisible standard poised above her head what it was to be a woman...really...and clutching desperate to catch that slippery, volatile contradictory tyrant and batter him down once and for all and not able to and not even asking whether being it made any sense at all or how you really know when you were one. Just being ruthlessly driven by the slogan of the day...and collecting all the parts that go into it, careful not to leave anything out, and hoping they finally add up to, what she would finally call... WOMAN...the same desperate men had calling themselves...MAN. Not enough, just being born, one or the other. Never has been. The ancients had their ordeals and rites of passage and we have ours. Except ours is hopelessly convoluted, muddled, and unclear. Theirs was brief and to the point. The men went through fire and had a son. The woman just had to have a son. Strange, Becky never included that as proving anything. She thought it was stupid to create problems for yourself when you had a choice not to...motherhood degenerating women into cows and screamers, robbing them of all femininity, poetry, softness of nature, gentility, mystique. The final degradation.

Chapter Ninety-One

In the morning, a note slipped under her door from Fred.

Dear Becky,

You've been avoiding me lately and I think I know why. You're scared of me, thinking that I'm really not a nice person. But I am truly. You're one of these people who thinks niceness really hides evil and evil hides niceness. You'll be very hurt, someday, making judgments with such a simple equation...just looking for opposites...the insanity behind sanity and vice-versa. Sometimes you do look in the water and it's clear all the way down...and muddy, too, is slime all the way down, no matter how deep you're plunging, head and heart, that's what you'll find. The troupe is leaving in an hour for the road. I will knock twice, before I go, to say goodbye. You don't have to open the door if you don't want to. Just want you to know who's knocking and why.

Love,

Fred

P.S I looked for your backstage yesterday, but you didn't come. Hope you liked me.

More love,

Fred

Becky heard him knocking but didn't answer. She was too shy for goodbyes, sometimes.

"Bye Becky," a knock, "Dear, darling, love, Becky," he whispered.

She could hear his suitcase clumping down the stairs after him. Wouldn't dare stand near the window to watch him. He might suddenly turn and see her and know, for sure, she was intentionally playing possum. Couldn't bear him to know. Heard a neighbor shouting, 'Hop in,' give him a lift to the train station.

The car door banged and sped away. Becky cautiously opened and peered out. Then, into his room. There's a desolate bareness about a room that's just been deserted. Round balls of crumpled paper forming a circle around the paper basket. She bent down and smoothed a few. They were different versions of the note he sent her, finally settling on one. A brown circle on the windowsill where he drank his last cup of coffee. The bureau drawers were left open. A black sock dangling. He'd forgotten it. She picked it up for a closer look, not knowing why. It had a big hole in the toe. He'd left it on purpose. She put it in her pocket. 'Good for rags,' men's socks, dusting, especially. She fingered the sock in her pocket. She thought of an old neighbor, the squeaky sound of her washing line every morning, her head out of the window with the clothespins between her teeth, big, black socks neatly paired, each one topped by a pin of its own.

Mirele in wonder, didn't know how she had the patience pairing and pinning all morning. Small, checkered, plaid ones also with their own pin. Seemed degrading to Becky then, doing a man's dirty laundry. She never would! To this day, she never touched Tommy's laundry. Except at Aunt Marion's. She'd grab it out of his hand and insist on doing it herself. Even pressed his socks. Becky was once taken into the basement and shown the double sink. 'Did your wife do your socks, Fred?' Funny, the things you wonder about.

Giselle and Celyphids, the ladies who tip-toed on the points of pink slippers, and the hands that troubadour sang their songs to, and poets their poems, to...do they do men's wash. Did they? Read from Cyrano and O'Casey and Wordsworth and Keats, entrance with the music of your voice and give a humble, grateful bow while applauded. Then, when the show was over, she was wrestling with a pile of shorts and socks. What would Roxanne have done if she married Fred? Would Cyrano do his own socks? Interesting, isn't it? It was still poetic for Cyrano to be killing a hundred men...but wash one sock?! Inconceivable! Forgive me Fred for running away when you needed me to trust you, stand tall and be your friend. It was like you told me you killed once, and I was afraid you'd kill me again. It would be nice to smell the coffee coming under my door in the morning, knowing you'll be fussing and waiting for me, and ask me every morning, 'Sugar?' though I always say no.

And then taking a piece of your cookie after watching the crispy crumbs falling and digging my fingers hard against them so they stick and licking them and going back for me and you insisting, 'Come on, have a piece,' and breaking a chunk and more crumbs falling, and me always saying, 'I shouldn't. Too fattening.' You are saying, 'A little piece won't hurt.' And so, I went every morning. A haze around us. You broke the bubble, Fred. Took away the soft and pink and light brought the blackness in. You did it to us. Had me wondering if you did it to her, too. Thought you were so safe with me, so comfortable that you could, and it would be alright. But you misjudged Max. I'll become a sock washer too, though I don't know how. That's what you're telling me, isn't it? And she took it out of her pocket and draped it over the open bureau where she found it. Roxanne's argument with Cyrano, 'Why didn't you tell me?' And Becky's 'Why did you?' She was musing the best of the past without being mired in what it becomes. Better that way. Much better. Even better, maybe, no <u>was</u>, no <u>becoming</u>, nothing to lose, terror in losing and watching, vanish...the haze. With Irving, sock washing from the beginning, nothing to lose, something to gain. The hall phone rang.

"Hi Beck, it's Irv."

A stiff attempt at jauntiness from one who is unaccustomed, an alien lightness to hide the heavy straining underneath, just his voice alone, tension, a danger alert. Watch every word, every gesture or the floodgates will open, scorn, abuse, criticism, contempt. All deserved. She'd be found wanting.

"How about the beach today?"

"OK."

"Pick you up in an hour."

"OK."

The whole day, they argued about politics. Irving was a Jew who was <u>not</u> a Communist. Becky couldn't believe there was such a person.

"You're not being logical Beck," he said, with that cold, staccato, whipping tone in his voice...and worse, "not even knowledgeable!"

Becky reeling from both assaults, especially the second. He'd caught her. She'd gotten by on a few phrases and compliant agreement for so long.

Fearing she was stupid, ignorant, she became even more strident, shouting, "Why shouldn't people share the wealth?"

"Why should they?"

"So, you wouldn't have people starving on one hand and people glutted on the other!"

"The world is the way it is because people want it that way!"

"They want to starve?"

"No, they want to glut! There's always shadows on the other side. Nothing exists without a shadow. Everything brings with it an antithesis. Remember Hegel? No matter what system, it falls in the 'be kind to your neighbor' department. They've all been tried."

"No, they haven't!"

"Let's go home," a vicious order, "mine, not yours."

In the car, both were still wearing their bathing suits. He drove in grim, tight-jawed, silence. Becky not daring to say a word and intrude, her legs sticking to the seat, she kept ripping them up, hurting herself each time, but still not daring to utter a sound.

They draw up to a white, frame and brick bungalow, the grounds neat in the front like a starched, green apron, bounded by a white, picket fence and roses winding their way in graceful bends and curves. Irving stepped out of the car. A tiny man, with a hose turned on the ground, his stepfather, commanding a stream of water, small knobs for knees on bone thin legs, a tiny face, huge nose, a small blonde mustache. Irving told her that he shut his mouth and didn't interfere in any family business. Italian. A sweet, gentle old man. He stopped the hose immediately and extended a hand. Irving hadn't expected to see him.

"I'm going," he said, "late already. Your mother is waiting. Nice to meet you."

And he ran off. He waved goodbye from the car.

Becky wondered, 'Why is he in such a hurry? He's always late and always in a hurry, can't figure that out. How a person used to rush is always late. Italians, I guess. Can't be on time, they say. But generalizations are invidious.' Becky always generalized.

"Why?"

"Too many exceptions."

"It proves the rule, doesn't it?"

Venomous now.

"How can it? An exception disproves the rule."

He opened the door. First house she'd ever been to that looked so homey. Two red, glass lamps on a bureau in front of a large mirror on a dark, mahogany well-oiled buffet, a deep oriental carpet, a solid dining room with six soft heavy chairs and a lace tablecloth. Living and dining room...a sofa and two chairs in a little grouping on the left, a shiny, white kitchen, and a bed with a white, colonial bedspread and big, shiny bureaus rubbed and polished so they shone, glass perfume bottles and little pictures in glass frames of children and grandchildren. Becky didn't dare touch a thing, just stood there gawking at those lamps. Someday she'd have two, just like that at the end of the room so you could see them as you walk in, like they were here.

"Beautiful," Becky said, in hushed tones, in this room she spoke quite somehow.

He turned to face her, a stiff tight grin on his face, his taunting hollow cheeks in a cast iron mold and staring. She guessed he wanted to kiss her. She fancied there were emotions breaking through and showing her love, real deep love for the first time. She put an arm around his waist, then the other and embraced him warmly while his arms hung limp behind her, just where she put them, without moving. She hugged him, his body stone rigid, like his face. She put her mouth to his and he bent to kiss hers, tight-lipped, briefly touching and drawing back and bending down again, touching her mouth, and leaving it there, like one leaves an imprint on a mirror. A thin, bony hand touched her breast and sped away to the safety of her waist, then touched her again, limp, and lifeless, like his hands were pinned to his body...a puppet, a marionette, or a machine. She was even more convinced, 'You have to dig deep to find, Becky. But I suppose a trap door opens and you're flung down into a black hole and you batter your fists until they're bloody and you wear them until it breaks and your knees crawling on the hard ground and the damp wet on your tears and no one hears? Then what, Becky? Impossible.'

She was sure he held the secret. There was a look now of terrible laughter in his face, soundless, only the look of death smirking, derisive. She wanted to tear that look away, put her hand on and off like she was juggling hats, first one, then the other, like a child discovering noses and eyes for the first time.

"Peek-a-boo!" she laughed, mirthless. clumsy, nervous laugh.

"Don't play games. I don't like games."

And he pulled down the straps of her bathing suit. She stood in front of him passive, her breasts white, exposed, under a circle of red on her chest. She sat down on the bed, arms propped and slanted behind her, so she looked thinner. Becky was embarrassed at the little rolls her waist and stomach made when she sat down naturally. Shame rose and was quickly pressed down again.

"Stand up again," he said.

She stood close to him, looking away while he tugged and pulled at the suit. She helped a little, twisting and turning until it fell to her feet. His face was still stiff, but a hint of a smile. His eyes closed, gripping her shoulders, laying her down on the bed. She could feel his body trembling. He entered her quickly. She watched his face. It was alone in a cold, distant, contentment, as if she weren't there at all. She kissed him before they separated. He let her, dutifully leaving his mouth on hers until he fell from her body and lay by her side. She waited for his arm around her waist, a loving word, but he wasn't even breathing hard, or weary like men are after making love. His eyes alert and watchful, staring at the window. A fly buzzing, desperate to get out.

He pulled out a newspaper out from under the bed, rolled it up, sprung to the window, opened it. The fly dashed away with firm determination in the opposite direction, protesting as it hopped from wall to wall, away from Irving's attempt to help.

"Shut up!" he screamed, "I can't stand that infernal buzzing."

He dropped the paper, cupping his ears and shutting his eyes tight as if the sound would come through them as well. He picked up the paper, rolled it again and struck, louder and hard each time. It eluded him until it suddenly fell from exhaustion or fright. She never knew which. It lay on its back, the legs wiggling content with satisfaction while it struggled, until its legs stood stiff in mid-air. He turned it over with the tip of the paper and flung it out the window.

"When I was a kid I used to have a cork with the center hollowed out and pins all around for bars, depending on how long they fly buzzed and annoyed me, I'd sentence it to jail, the longer the buzzing, the longer the sentence and if they insisted to put their dirty selves on me and they'd still insist on harassing me, I'd put them in and never let them out," he muttered savagely, "I will not be defied!"

Becky, her body outside her will now, jumped up in shock, then fell on the bed again, giddy and shaking, head up, legs apart, staring at the shadow of a lead trembling on the wall. He seemed a blur, then becoming clearer, the haze vanishing, she felt strange, like she'd been somewhere and returned to a cold, violent stranger straddling the room like a Colossus. Naked power set on his intent face. Man-God that she would stay at the right hand of...he's fighting flies, Becky... foolish girl. Doesn't matter. It's the spirit...the fist clamped tight and shaking in the air. Even a fly has to straighten up and do turning, understanding, humble, Becky thrilled to the vengeful, the haters, the arrogant, the leaders, the tyrants hungry for blood and power and backs bent to serve and care...men and women....and they found those who were waiting for the chance. Even Becky...the rebel, the revolutionary, Marxist, Women's lib-nick before her time.

'How does a stubborn, 'I won't,' convert itself? Snapping and jumping into place like a Mexican bean, into an 'I will,'...want to... must...let me...please?'

From the muted, soft color of misty, ethereal romance, from a marriage narrowed to anticipation and yearning in the future and a brief, intense present to this, some peculiar meshing of the contradictions and tangled lines in Becky's life, she found herself wanting to do the real, daily things, at least, thinking she did...helping him through school, to make up for no children. She still stood fast on that. That would be the life bond, instead...since it would be something only, they would share, and he'd be indebted to her forever for her sacrifice and help.

She would touch the love in him. And so, she replaced another fantasy for the hate she lived in already. A Jewish millionaire doctor to thumb her nose at the world, have them groveling instead of sneering, and a husband at home like everybody. There was always a yearning in Becky to be like everybody, though she recoiled in terror at everybody's life around her. But still, she thought she was a failure and that she couldn't live it. Smarter than everybody and dumber, was how she put it. Oh yes, and something else. He should be very smart, but she should win every argument...like she did with Poppa, and he should be nice about it and proud, like Poppa was...not to turn on her like Pa did on Ma. The blood still froze in her heart when she thought about it and she shriveled inside like she was beaten and weeping hot, shamed tears, her bent finger digging in her eye like she wanted to hurt herself more and seeing bright colors in her eye and rubbing it harder just to see the colors.

He broke in with, "Let's take a shower, Beck. You like you're dazed by the heat."

He jumped in, she behind him.

The soap fell and slid out of her hand each time until he bent down, picked it up, turned his back and handed it to her over his shoulder saying, "Do my back."

Tommy would say that too and turn, 'Now my chest,' he'd say, wanting to love her, touched by the smooth feel of her soapy hand on his body and kissing her long under the water. She loved it, kissing under a torrent of water and thought Irving would turn, too. But he didn't, just walked off. She watched the white foam retreat under the force of the water. He jumped out of the tub, grabbed a towel, and vigorously slapped and rubbed hand and foot making strange sounds all the time with his mouth, gasping and grunting, while she stood there, water pouring on her back...and watching.

He slammed the bathroom door and left her in the tub without a parting word. She finished quickly. There was only one towel...his... wet.

She did the best she could with it, then shouted, "You have another towel?"

He slid one through the door while she draped the shower curtain around her, suddenly shy, both of them. She put on her bathing suit. It was still damp and clammy. He was natty, now, starched, white pants, and bright, yellow shirt. A slight grin, scornful by habit.

"I'll take you home as soon as you dress," he said.

The door opened and she heard the crackling of bags.

"Help me, Irving."

He sprang to the door. She heard a woman's voice, "Heavy Irving, be careful! The bag is wet on the bottom. See? And the soda bottle is coming through."

"I'll have to empty it right there. Becky, bring a towel," he shouted, "in the hall closet."

She opened the nearest closet she ever saw and took one from the blue pile. They were stacked in colors. Irving, holding the treacherous bag said quickly, "My mother. Momma, Becky."

She nodded at Becky and grabbed the towel from her hand and removed rolls, eggs, and soda.

"Now get another bag, Irving."

"Why didn't you get one in the first place?" Snapping at her angrily.

"I was nervous not to dirty the carpet, so I wanted to do the fastest thing first," apologetically.

"Never use your head! First, you walk out with a load like this without asking for a double bag, then, you go from bad to worse!"

Her face twitched, but she said nothing. He was chastising her like she was a dumb child, and he was an impatient father. Becky thought he would have continued berating her but stopped because she was there, but he continued muttering against the store.

"What's the matter with these markets?! Haven't they learned anything?! What hope is there for a world that hasn't even learned what to do with a bag?!"

His mother shook her head silently, in agreement with him. It didn't help. Only seemed to invite him to go on. She didn't even look at Becky for a sign of support. Only a stoic look on her face, waiting for it to end, and looking down abashed, like she deserved it.

"I bet you don't even have another bag," he screamed.

She shook her head.

"We'll have to carry it from the kitchen, piece by piece!"

He grabbed eggs and grapefruit. Gave Becky lettuce and a big onion and his mother picked up the milk. It leaked white spots on the rug on the way to the kitchen. She never noticed until she put the milk down and saw the white lines streaming down her dress. She rushed to the bathroom to splash water on them and returned to the kitchen with round circles of water all over the front of her dress. She fell down a chair gasping for breath.

"Can't take the heat," she said, flapping her hand up and down in front of her face to move the heavy air around. She was a very heavy woman, her stomach and breasts hanging over her thighs so that she had no lap. Her face, round and flabby and chalk white, not from fear, but like life had gone out of it a long time ago and left a faded, blood-less, limp mask. She looked up at Becky permanently fixed in a narrow, suspicious, searching glare. Her wide nostrils flared in and out as she breathed and her body bent, her legs spread apart, she stared silently at Becky, panting, her mouth open like a sweltering dog.

Becky rushed for the paper in the bedroom that Irving used to attack the fly, and waved it up and down wildly, fanning his mother. She straightened up her head and body fell back over the chair.

"That feels good," she said.

Becky waved harder and harder until her hand hurt.

"Here, Irving," Becky said, "I can't go anymore."

Sarcastic, "she'll be alright. Enough now, Ma. Can't be that bad," and to Becky, "Air conditioner broke, we have to bring the fan down from the attic."

"Introduce me, won't you Irving?"

Smiling now, "Of course. Ma," the edge gone in his voice, "I want you to meet Becky. Becky, Ma. Eva, but you can call her Ma."

"Pleased to meet you," then forcing herself, wretchedly uncom-fortable, to say, 'Ma.'

Humiliating, this familiarity she didn't feel. Her hair, we used to call dirty blonde, now frizzy, tiny waves on her head, proud she doesn't need a perm. Becky thought she was displeased with her, but she couldn't really tell. It seemed to Becky she looked like that all the time, like she was wearing a hair shirt or had a nail in her shoe. Faces like that always frightened Becky, made her aching to oblige, to please, anything to see a smile. Eva said nothing about being pleased to meet her. Not even a meaningless, 'How do you do?' 'Would you like something to eat?' And without waiting for an answer, she struggled out of the chair, her dress, crinkled made a bell-shaped curve in the back, exposing folds of flesh that hung above her knees. Becky looked away embarrassed and revolted.

Irving said, "Let's leave her alone in the kitchen," and led her into the dining room.

Becky heard the heavy shuffling between kitchen table, sink and refrigerator, chopping, scraping. She set the table, making several trips back and forth. Becky made no offer to help. Irving told her to sit down. She was too intimidated to defy him. Eva plunked a heavy bottle on the side of Irving's plate, the bread on the other, brought his food plate first, then Becky's. She noticed Irving's plate had a bigger piece of cold chicken on it than hers. Eva patiently skinned and boned it for him.

Perfunctorily, she offered, "Want a piece?"

Becky nodded. She took a piece from Irving.

Becky hastily added, "Thank you," and thinking, 'a woman reminding me of my place and worse, I'm scurrying into it. Can hardly wait, standing on my hind legs like a squirrel, paws bowed, tail curled, begging...for permission to keep scurrying.'

A memory.

Momma dutifully standing at attention at the table, body crooked, head straight up, her bad leg dangling by her side...waiting... and Poppa passing judgment to her...and always the same, 'Can't cook like my mother,' and he turned his hand one way, then the other so hard, he'd snap his wrist. She quietly took his hand in hers and massaged it until a surly, impatient order to leave him alone, already. And Becky, degraded, hurt, swearing, 'Never! Not me!'

And now she was praying, 'Irving, make it me.' The past hovering over her defying her to undo millennia of tradition with a few harsh words and decisions. Bred for service like a lap dog, she was let out for a while, now running back home where she'll tear at a leash when the master permits. With Tommy, the ritual romance was now empty, boring and the unspoken future hanging in the air, not being talked about, but there, like a dread disease. Sickening, touching a naked nerve. Just to think about it...filthy drapes, the rancid smell of sour milk in the air, food dribbling down the mouth of a red-faced squalling baby, accompanying the ear-splitting insistent cries banging a Mickey Mouse cup on the table and linoleum floors with black, worn patches and tracks, strewn with the debris of living things who are careless and a woman who's tired. Old food, colorless room with just the necessities. Fanny looking for the broken chips of the last cup the baby broke and scared to go barefoot. One of the comforts of home, going barefoot.

'Can't remember any furniture in Fanny's house, just babies stamping around the house with dirty diapers, banging pots and pans, and she's staring out the window not seeing or hearing and me no help, just sitting and staring too. No pictures, knick-knacks...life's unadorned and a future...a mountain of suppers and dinners, lunches and breakfasts and exile in a blank corner of the world with baby talk, no talk of neighbors clacketing about their babies and competing with mine. Theirs did it all earlier, the first word, the first step. And, after all that, to be like I was to Ma...nasty, abusive, offensive. Carrying on about not asking to be born as if they gave me permission to be impossible. Wasn't her fault. We weren't available to each other for a prior consultation. Becky flinched, just thinking about it.

Mirele was assaulted and abandoned by both children. Poverty, disorder, punishment, death, and desertion. Tyranny, too, Momma. First Poppa, then Pesach, then me, now Poppa again. And the bosses, Momma. How they complained, it was never clean enough, while they sunned and bathed themselves all day and came home to judge and rub fingers on your work. Go to school you said, so I did. So, they tyrannized and judged and humiliated like your boss, the boss in the shop. A boss is a boss. So, what's left for me, Momma? but to serve a leader whose interests are infinite, not one like Tommy who hides a small square and Irving will talk to me, Momma. can't live without talk. I'll cook and be afraid and wait for me to love me, just me, in all the world. And while I'm waiting, we'll be learning together in a garret. That's romance enough for now. To Becky, life was looking forward. To Tommy, life was not looking at all.'

To Becky, freedom was someday having pride...with Irving... instead of being ashamed for the rest of her life with Tommy. Married a goy...for nothing. No forgiveness or allowances made. Can't survive in the Jewish world without being <u>something</u>. Not a student, a scholar, a lawyer, a doctor, not Jewish enough, kosher enough...never enough...the demands were too high. Never enough, it seems to Becky. But now, she was answering the call. She was impatient to be rid of silence, baby talk. He was even losing his looks, his hair going, a pot belly. She was glad to retain a Christian name. Forman...just as nice as Hall. But what makes you imagine he'll want you at all? She was sure he would. She'd make herself necessary, like the old-fashioned women did with their cooking and button sewing. Women always did that, knowing how to sidle into a man's life so she became an addiction. Of course, one has to be able to know how to choose wisely. Instinctively, Becky avoided the non-addictive types. Like nurturing a near dead plant, coaxing a tiny bud to life and watching life slowly take over. Becky could hardly wait. He needed her already...to feed a cold lust and his pride.

Becky was beautiful...he liked being seen with her. She could tell how he held her hand a little firmer when a head turned and he caught him, turning his head at the same time. But he was suspicious, too, and angry.

"Beauty betrays," he said, "can't help it."

"Were you ever in business, Mrs. Forman? I don't know why, but you seem like a business type."

Her eyes, shrewd, calculating, "Yes, as a matter of fact, I was. In hats. I made plenty, don't worry. A fool I wasn't. For two ribbons and a veil they paid, and for a real hat," she waved her hand, "well, you can imagine...she wasn't like Momma...a pushover, naïve, eager to please...anything...Becky should be well. Money. No money. Didn't matter. What's money? To the lady in hats...plenty. Showing it off, calculating it, hoarding it, but, most of all, hardness."

Mama, shrewd, manipulative and cruel too, but Momma's were naïve calculators not honed in the world of real-politics, in the service of innocence and purity and high standards in a small, circumscribed non-world. In the little circle of people who touched her, manipulation for personal gain was unknown to her. She was out of the world; Eva was in it. Becky couldn't deal with it. It frightened her.

Chapter Ninety-Two

Driving her home, she waited to hear when he would see her again, straining, her heart knocking hard.

"When is your husband coming home now?"

"He's not," she lied, "we're separated."

"Getting a divorce?"

"Yes."

"When?"

"Soon."

The car stopped suddenly, in front of her house. She opened the car door, hesitating, got out very slowly, as if it were a major, physical feat, groaning, as she crawled out, first one foot, then the other, then leaving the door open and standing there.

"Close the door!" he shouted and sped away...without even a goodbye.

She turned wistfully toward Aunt Marion. Two weeks since she had been there. Mail from Tommy must be piling and they're wondering where she is. Time to come out of hiding.

Aunt Marion wasn't home when she got there. A note for the milkman, not to deliver. She would be away for a month. Sunday newspaper thrown on the porch, still in the rubber band. The mailbox with one letter for her with Tommy. An electric and gas bill for Aunt Marion. Becky sat on the porch, sun in her eyes, squinting.

She opened the letter from Tommy. A check fell out, money for the rent...first of the month. And read ...

Dear Becky,

A brief letter...must run. I'm going to try to stay home with you this time. Heard about a good job. Meanwhile, I want you to learn to drive. You need to have a car in Texas. I bought one in New York, and they'll be delivering it to you on the first. You have a month to learn how to drive. Please...learn. Aunt Marion says you moved. Still waiting for a word from you with the new address the mail is slow because of tropical storms.

Love always,

Tom

In two weeks, she learned to drive and took her test. Passed the first time. The car came. It was a mint, green chevy. She scratched it the first time out, squeezing into a garage behind the house. Tommy still didn't know where she was, and she didn't want to tell him. But now that the fancy she'd built with Irving came tumbling down, she was resigned to a decision to include her address in the next letter.

Dear Tom,

I wrote you my address, but it must have gotten lost. Here it is again. Thank you for the car and for thinking about coming home to stay. Even thinking, I'm grateful for.

Love,

Becky

Now she didn't want him coming home. The marks on the calendar were for the free days remaining, not marking time until she saw him, like it used to be.

A week later, a postcard from Irving.

As you can see I'm in Dallas. See you when I return.

Yours,

Irving

She slept all night with the card under her pillow and didn't mail the letter with her address to Tommy...and weaving fancies around Irving's card... 'yours...and mine,' she thought, 'that's what it really means. That's what he's telling me.'

Strange how she turned against everything she trusted and yearned for once...even peace at any cost and harmony. Irving and she fought bitterly every day, he is overpowering her with the volume and intensity of his voice alone. 'This was real life for the first time, contending with a real person.' The psychologists said hate and battle and contention were real. For years, it seemed to her now, life itself was an exclusive circle she was kept out of or kept herself out of. Becky fled from the raucous struggle at home to polite curtsying, flowing gowns in gossamer and pink mood, white clouds and rainbows and gentle flowers bending to a soft breeze, caressed by gentle rains.

Love, smooth and sweet, without a wave or ripple, never a storm or hint of discord. Some of us can make the high leap to that thin wire. Becky couldn't. The wrangling was too deep. It was home, lived and living. The other had never been lived...imagined, pretended but never lived, the heart and blood full of familiar ways that had to be trod over and over, nerve ending attuned to a certain kind of pain and thirsting for it. And savagery aided and abetted by the new learning. Niceness, a mask, a fake and dangerous...cause underneath more than the obvious. With Irving, it was all exposed. Safer, that way. Nothing mysterious, lurking. How much more bloodletting and scarring was visited on hapless couples by the professionals prodding to 'let it all out.' 'Healthy,' they said, while declaring civility, poetry, manners, delicacy, to be 'sick.' Marriages and civilization itself, crumbling into health. And Becky, tumbling along, following the calamity of normal family life with it's aiming for the jugular. Only Momma and Poppa no longer had any. Pogroms, depressions and the ingenuity of nature, pounding on them relentlessly, experimenting with various varieties of misfortunes of mankind had torn it out of them so that their arguing wounds were minor in comparison and fell on hard, veinless, nerveless sounding boars. But Becky had a jugular...the result of softer living...one particularly alert, easily reached and ripped...exposed. But Becky didn't know the difference. Nature makes no allowances for differences, sometimes. Careless, sloppy, Becky forced to fight an old war with no weapons, no protection, undefended...just a terrible need to have the last word, and about to pay a terrible need to have the last word, and about to pay a terrible price for it. Irving was not a Poppa. Fighting with him, she was Momma. She'd grown up and changed places and kept squeezing Becky into Momma's place. Life with a man, for Becky, was one long debate that she'd be winning, though she wasn't really equipped, maybe with feelings, but certainly not, with words. Her heart just knew his head was wrong and he screamed because he couldn't stand her insisting, he's wrong without a logical string of words to convince him and she shouted because she felt the logic was wrong. Momma and Poppa with college diplomas. How little they mattered, after all, these degrees. But Becky still hoped for the ideal father. Hoping and hoping...on Irving.

"The Russian government means well," she'd say.

They want peace but they're ringed around by American missiles. The rich in America are threatened by communism. They want Russia in shambles, so they can enslave the working man again."

Irving enraged and pounding on the steering wheel, "How do you know what goes on in government?! How can anyone know when they sit in secret rooms having secret conversations?!"

Becky repeated her arguments so long, they'd become a faith, "Everyone knows what I say is true!"

"How do you know?! Have you asked everyone?!"

Politics had suddenly become a science. It had been Becky's romance and Irving was not romantic. He looked like one and Becky struggled to fit the morbid, cutting gaze and grim purpose in his face with the dark eyes and cheekbones and didn't notice that they conflicted with each other...couldn't...or wouldn't. The words finally ceased to matter. A terrible silence or both drumming fingers. They were like two dumb, blind men tapping canes, louder and faster, angrier and harder, gazing past each other, making helpless motions just to make them and listening in silence, for the other. Sometimes Irving would stop. Sometimes Becky. Too tired to go on. A day or two would pass. They had no contact with each other. Then Becky listened for his call.

And finally, "Hello, it's Irv. I'll be over in an hour."

Then it was three days or four...the silence. She decided to call home.

Chapter Ninety-Three

"Ma, it's Becky."

An anguished sobbing, "Poppa's gone! Two days already. The funeral..."

And she couldn't go on.

"I'm coming home, Ma! Right away!"

"Come home, Becky."

She hung up.

Becky embracing and clutching the phone like it was still there because it carried her voice a minute ago. 'Momma, Poppa, forgive me. I wasn't there. At my own father's funeral,' her fingers making long, streaky smudges, digging harder and harder into the black box and the tears flowing down and round the horn where she talked and falling in the coin box making a little pool, and her head moving up and down with her sobs on the metal plate until it ached. The coin box filled again and again, and she emptied it with her finger, watching the tears fall to the floor in small dirty flops, and smearing them with her foot in ugly streaks, making angry, grotesque designs. Self-loathing savaged into the grim lines as if to be etched there forever.

The phone sprang to life again. So close, the ring seemed assaultive.

A cheery, "It's me Irving."

"My father died. Momma just told me. I called home."

"When?"

"Day before yesterday."

"I'll be right there."

He hung up. When she opened the door, he had the look on him of a man hurt in a football huddle, body bent, eyes wide open, serious and alert, calculating to attack. He put a cold, limp arm on her waist and stood stiff and rigid as always. He was uncomfortable burdened with her tragedy. She didn't mean that much to him or didn't know her long enough to have her thrust this on him. He resented it. She could feel it...demanding too much from him before he was ready. She was sure there would have been more from him if he knew her longer, if they were closer, but she wanted more anyhow, though she felt she really wasn't entitled. She put her head on his shoulder, careful at first, not to weep too hard, but the tears overflowed on his clean shirt.

She jumped away, "I'm sorry."

He looked down and up again, quickly.

"Let's sit down," without an edge in his voice, but firm, holding his arm out while she leaned on him, stumbling to the chair, her body bent, moving slow and labored, like an old woman. He couldn't refuse her now, even if he wanted to. He moved to sit down on the bed. He fell on his lap and cradled her head on his shoulder near his stiff neck, eyes looking away. He put one arm around her, then the other. She pretended he was comforting her while she rocked back and forth. This was his sorrow before. Now, it was hers. She wondered how long she could yield to herself and draw from him. It would be unbearable now, the sting of his impatience. She reached around and took both his hands in hers, making a wide arc with his arms, putting one down as far from her as she could, then the other and slid from his lap to the floor. She wanted to lean her head on his leg but wouldn't dare. She hoped he'd put a hand on her shoulder, but he didn't. She regretted putting his arm so far behind her. She would put his hand near her now if she could.

It would have been nice, talking quietly while her fingers curled in and out of his. She suddenly felt a sharp pain in her shoulder. His left hand fell, palm upwards, on the side of her neck. He turned it around and left it there, squeezing occasionally, abrupt and sharp. She left it there, grateful.

"You going back home, Becky?"

"Soon as I can."

Softly, "Good," and squeezed her neck, "I'm going to school there. We'll go together. I'll drive. They've accepted me for my Ph.D."

Numbness creeping over her now. Separating from the pain, as if she suddenly turned a corner and left it all behind, living, being...the body being merciful to itself, spreading it's own tender blanket, a drug, hypnotizing, protecting. They sat in a gray light of a waning day, sober tones of a momentary truce between them. His voice, friendly and relaxed, welcome now. She listened for the words, neutral for the first time.

He talked without rancor and said, a little gladness rising, "We'll have more than we ever had. Poppa's death made them friends at last, if just for a moment."

'Thank you, Poppa.'

And she wept again, her body leaning on his hard leg. The room was black now. She turned his eyes to him but couldn't see his face. She dug her nails into his legs, not meaning to. They weren't long, but she knew they hurt. He never moved and sat very still. His muscles cramped, aching, but he never moved, not once, until she was silent once again. She pulled herself up, holding on to his arms and touched his face with her mouth. He turned his mouth to hers and she kissed him. He was trembling, undressing her while she stood there, limp, not helping but uncomplaining. And he stood up, left her standing there naked while he undressed. She was embarrassed, though he couldn't see her and covered herself with her hands. He put his closed mouth to hers and held it there. Then he put her on the bed and took her without love and she let him because she was grateful. Then he turned his face to the wall and fell asleep and she put her arms around his body and her breasts on his back, touching him so it wouldn't be so lonely falling asleep. And more. Nudging the flower to bloom in the desert. Make him used to, then wanting, then not able to do without, then giving so much she couldn't even begin to imagine. Her head tilted, her body curled, the lips parted, receiving, like a child at mother's breast clinging in dark, smothering warm sinking into drowsy, helpless numbness. He tossed suddenly, brusquely, stabbing his elbow in her mouth brutally. She didn't cry out. He was in a deep sleep. She wouldn't dare him.

A memory.

Eager clambering on Poppa's lap and sitting there, dangling her legs and watching her feet swinging back and forth and counting. The most she ever made was three good swings, back and forth, before he'd rudely shrug her off. She'd try to pick a good mood when he was happy so he'd let her stay, but she found out the mood never mattered. He didn't like to play like that. He'd set her down and walk away, like he didn't even know her. It was awful. Like he'd hit her. Worse, even. That happy, good feeling turned hard...humiliated, thrown away like an old rag when she was begging, 'I want to fall asleep on your lap, Poppa,' timidly. An angry dismissal, 'Laps are not for sleeping.'

Quivering with embarrassment though no one there to see, mouth clenched hard in pain, the long, dark, lonely hours until the morning...and Irving...breathing calmly beside her...shattering...even in sleep, a stranger, her eyes looking on him with caution, hate and fear. She turned her head away from him waiting, hoping, groveling, but his arm, close, but not touching, lay unmoved. Then she curved her back ever so slightly to feel the tips of his fingers on her, the open hand flung at his side. It was too desolate. Not touching, just empty dark all around. In the morning, she rolled her body round to fit into his and his arm stiffly followed. She took him with a woman's taking... performing. The wanting and the sighing like stage props making thunder and lightning. The unreal reaching out and touching the real; the audience hearts racing like it's the real thing, taking too. Then, he took her...with the self-satisfied smile, then a purposeful stare, like Tommy, like he was still alone with himself...and she too, alone with herself. But she had to make friends again, and hoping maybe this time, burrowing hard in stubborn rock, and finding the ground yielding...but there was nothing...just the bareness of a cold dawn.

A thin, lifeless, dutiful pat several times on the shoulder then, "We'd better rush. Too many things to do if we're gonna leave in a couple of days."

Smashing into the soft underbelly with booted feet and grinding hard with soft words, but bloodless and impatient.

"Hurry up, let's go. We have to do a million things to leave tomorrow."

He was all business and efficiency now. She hurried up.

He ordered, "Pack all your things and come with me. Tomorrow, morning, early, we go."

"What will I do with the car?"

He didn't answer. She didn't press. He put her in the car.

"Follow me."

They drove to a permanent parking garage and left it there until further notice. It was a relief to be rid of a burden. She was too frightened to drive it to New York. They left the next morning, luggage piled so high behind them. He couldn't see the back window. He assured her it was alright. She believed him. He was God. A cold, stern, unyielding argumentative one, but God, nevertheless, to whom she sacrificed, groveled and prayed. And then there were those times when, sinking deep down, she touched Momma and reared up, gnashing teeth and spitting fumes, grasping for the last word and waiting for the silence that never came...never once. Snarling and biting the air, punching out the crisp and pointed words that wound her into tightening noose of vagaries, then fear creeping in, then desperate for safety, she crumpled into a mortified, rebellious, sulking silence. He was her test. Life examining and judging, deciding whether she can enter. Strange, how she looked at life the same as death...Irving at the gate, testing, probing, deeming her worthy or unworthy.

When they arrived in New York, he drove her home. She pointed to the faceless anonymity of housing projects everywhere. Somehow, you knew these were buildings for the poor, cubicle windows, not a patch of color, a flower, or a shrub anywhere, the meanness of poverty even in the brick of the building, ground into the first stone and covering these houses inside and out like a shroud. They hurry by quickly, those more fortunate, without knowing why.

"You live there?"

A familiar exclamation from the past. The car door clicked open and slammed shut so hard it startled.

He pulled her bags out, threw them on the floor panting, "Shall I carry them up?"

Screaming, "No, I'd rather not!"

He dropped them, kissed her cheek, "See ya," waved, a stiff smile, cool, friendly, sardonic, untrusting.

Waving back, "See ya," desolate, as he churned the motor, whizzing away. She wanted to shout after him but couldn't. the old pain reaching for her now, 'Poppa's gone, and I wasn't there.'

A cold wind blowing dirt in circles round her feet, bubble gum wrappers and wrinkled cigarette packs gathering in a small pile between her legs. She put them closer together, tight, so nothing moved, imprisoning them and listening while they crackled, then she parted her legs and watched them scurrying away free swept by the wind into the air.

She watched them free and flying, then bent her head resigned, straining under the weight of the bag. A small wad blown back by the wind, strikes her on the head. She goes on doggedly, narrowing her eyes, the dust whirring about the head now, stinging.

Up the stairs, plopping the bag on one at a time, then following it up and plopping in on the next one...one stair at a time, until she stands at the door, banging and crying, "Ma!"

The door opens, her tears almost blinding, "Tommy! What are you doing here? Where's Momma?"

"She's out shopping for me."

He embraced her hard, put her head on his chest, held her, soothing, comforting. She parted from him, pushing gently but firmly.

"Let's sit down."

He sat beside her, his eyes all loving compassion.

"I was here the day your father died. Your mother locked the door and put the gas on. We had to break it down. Tried to kill herself, Becky. It was awful."

"You saved her life, Tommy. She was grateful," distant and ashamed.

He touched her hand; she drew it away. Couldn't bear his touching her. Wanted him away from her, kind, tender, cloying, owing him everything. Even Momma's life and inside a tempestuous, demanding, shrieking child, "Go away from me!"

Tommy was death, too. Death is still around in this house, keeping her from life. Irving was life and pleasing Momma, too. Especially now. She had to please her. Her heart filled with rage and hate and he, in all innocence, warm and begging.

"I thought you were mad at me, Tommy."

"I was, but now I'm not."

"Why not?"

"It was terrible not knowing where you were, Becky, not hearing from you. I thought, for sure, you left me and were never coming back, and I was hurting terribly."

"And how did you get back here?"

"I flew! I dreamed one night, I saw you through a glass window and I hollered, Becky, louder and louder and you never turned around and I wanted you to, so hard, and I banged and hollered so you'd hear and I was desperate hoping, at least, you were hearing me, but you didn't turn, no matter. That's all I wanted for you to turn and look at me, nothing else."

He put his finger under her chin, "That's all I want now."

She held her head down firm, his fingers pressing. Sound of shuffling feet at the door.

"It's Momma, I'll get it."

He jumps up.

She could hear Momma's voice insisting, "No," to Tommy urging, "Let me help you, it's too heavy for you."

They both came in tugging a bag. She's hidden behind Tommy. He rests the bag from her and put it down.

"Beckele!"

She hobbles around Tommy and sits down by her side, looking hard at her.

"You alright? Let me see."

But she doesn't seem to be seeing, looking as hard as she might.

Becky puts Mirele's head on her shoulder, "You, Momma? how are you?"

"How can I be? Alone, now."

And her body shaking hard with more grief that it could hold, exploding inside, and Becky holding tight as if there'd be nothing left if she did. There are moments when mother becomes child and child becomes mother. This was one of them. But Momma wasn't one to let Becky have more than one moment. She pulled back gently and leaned back on the sofa, breathing hard until there were no more tears.

"I'll fix you something to eat, you must be hungry."

"I'll help you, Momma."

Becky opened the fridge door. Tommy had emptied the bag... everything neatly, in order, unlike Momma who threw everything willy-nilly, and it was always a jumble, searching and looking and moving and rearranging just to find a stick of butter behind a bottle of milk.

"Look how nice Tommy did the refrigerator, Ma. Look, how nice."

Mirele's face tightened into a stern, stubborn, knot...still unforgiving.

The next morning, Becky found Tommy's order in the fridge as if it were deliberately placed precariously, and behind it, the apples and pears, butter and cheese ripped out of their places and thrown helter-skelter in a jumble that once was familiar but not angry and spiteful. 'It doesn't matter, Tommy, what you do, how hard you try, to her, you're still a goy. Each time I hope, put my heart in her hand, she crushes it with just a look. I die a little, but not enough to stop hoping and trying harder, but this time is the last. You win, Ma.'

Becky never told Tommy how much it mattered to Ma, what he was. Telling and honest talk was still so scary, the words lay silent and unborn, not hinted at, or even thought about. Words that had to crawl through shame and trembling to no purpose. Conversion? Never. Becky wouldn't dare ask. After all, hadn't she always claimed religion wasn't important? How could she raise the issue now? And she never raised it with Momma neither. Because she was too embarrassed to ask him. As if changing one's mind in this question was ridiculous, scornful. Becky hung out tenaciously to Poppa's teaching, 'a person should be accepted as they are.'

"We're doing our dance, singing our song, two step shuffle, a bow and one foot raised in the air behind us, arms spread out, eager smile. Were we good, Momma? Did you like us? Say you did?"

That knotted face, stern, grim, silent.

"It's all over Tommy. Momma doesn't like the act. No matter what. Bending, twisting, shuffling, sawing me, sawing her. You'd still be a goy, Tommy, that's all."

Poor man never even heard the word. He'd accidentally stepped into history and wouldn't have understood what all the fuss was about even if he were told. Why... if even Becky couldn't understand.

"People are people, Momma. All the same."

"Goyim aren't people. They're goyim."

"But they have eyes like a Jew and a mouth like a Jew..." all Shakespeare's eloquence flowing, in defense now of goyim.

"But they're goyim...hands and arms that put swords into Jewish babies. I saw myself! With my own two eyes," pounding her finger hard against her temple, "that's people?"

"But Tommy couldn't do anything like that!"

"Ask me. I know what they can do. I don't want to hear that they're people!"

It was Friday night, she told Tommy she was sorry and she forgot pork chops. Tommy read the paper while she lit the candles and prayed. He told her several times he didn't believe in it, heated and firm like he was being debated, though he wasn't, like there was someone inside fighting and he was fighting back. Becky wanted them both, Momma deep in fervent talk with God, and Tommy on the sofa pulling the paper with a thud. Then, Momma served dinner. He came to the table, chicken soup with matzo balls. He had told her before that he didn't like boiled chicken. She must have forgotten.

Chapter Ninety-Four

Time for bed, Becky saying with a wan, distant smile; Tommy hovering behind. And in the darkness, the anxious question, the first, timid step, the kindly soft, seemingly all merciful, all forgiving words that touch, melt, invite, beseech, lay a soft carpet, open a loving door and beckon, and the unwary tumble to the gentle snare and a door clang hard behind them. Confession for which there is no penance or absolution. A quiet answer is like a cannon exploding, the victim reeling and plotting vengeance and both sides armed and bristling. The beginning of the end when 'I love you' becomes 'what's the matter?' Three little words...one of bright beginning, the other, the standard reply, 'nothing' or worse.

"I want a separation, Tommy."

The harder word was still in the throat. She couldn't say divorce. And shrinking from the eruption to come.

His face struggling with anger and fear of losing and then, the plea, "Don't leave me, Pudgy. How can you not love me?"

Jumping up suddenly, the hurt exploding in him.

"Of course, you do. You don't know your own mind...your father and all!"

'He's right. I don't know my own mind. What I wanted so very hard once I don't want, just as hard, now. Has nothing to do with mind.'

"Being with you now is like being in the sea, those soft, mushy jellyfish crawling up and down your arms and legs and stomach and tearing on yourself all over, desperate to get away. Wish I could rub a lamp and you'd disappear."

"You can't do this, Pudgy. I won't let you!"

The words were strangers to him. They sounded forced and unnatural. Sulking, pouting, running...but not demanding and ordering. His face puckered in the dark. She could see it, clear in her mind, how he looked then; a small boy, hurt, angry, bewildered.

Becky lay stiff as far as she could away from him. The hand he'd reached out to her, carefully put back between them so it was not near her. He moved it towards her again. She moved it away. Both near the edge, Becky unable to move without teetering over or touching him, and he, only his arm resting on the empty space by his side. She never turned to him. He woke in the morning to the light touch of the sun on his face, blinking. He thought he was dreaming, not sure where he was. Home was still strange to him. Her arms were hanging over the side of the bed. He reached over and placed one, then the other, tight by her side. It fell soon again. He reached over and held it gently, so she wouldn't fall over. She turned with a moan and struck him hard, as her arm fell on his throat. He turned swiftly away in pain. She woke and saw him huddled in a corner.

"Something wrong, Tommy?"

"Nothing."

Her hand throbbing, "Did I hurt you?"

"A little," waiting for her to reach over and comfort him.

Crisp, "When are you leaving, Tommy?"

"Today. In an hour."

"I'll help you pack."

"You don't have to bother."

She'd always stood by watching, hoping the clock would stop, while he hopped about gathering and folding the final two boxes he always favored sitting down hard on the luggage and the goodbye kiss as he dashed out the door, as if he came home to complete an assigned task, had done a job to his satisfaction, puffed and pleased. Becky, lonely and yearning the moment he shut the door on their time together and she counted his last footstep on the stairs. Sometimes, he paused for a moment, and she hoped it meant he wasn't taking that final step, but he always did. Now, his folding and neat, careful fitting and tucked seemed eternal. She'd never realized he took so long.

An agony of waiting and finally, the clank of buckles, the bang on the floor when he lifted it and threw it down again pronouncing it, "Heavier all the time."

At the door, "Write to me, Becky. Just tell me you love me. Write it on a little piece of paper every day. Nothing else. Me, too. I'll write to you every day."

"And what else, Tommy?"

"What else is there?"

"I thought you'd come home, someday, and we'd live a normal life."

"I don't think you really wanted one, Becky. You told me, so many times, over those Chinese dinner tables, how you wanted a man who came and went...to keep the romance alive. I was just doing what you wanted me to, that's all."

Eyes panicked, begging, craving.

"Guess I did mix you up, Tommy, but...the missing got so hard."

Hope springing, "Pudgy! You'll see. you'll miss me and you'll call and this time I'll come running, swimming if I have to, flying, walking on water."

"That's easy, coming and going, Tommy, but will you stay? Not saying now, I want you to, but if I did, would you? You'll get so tired of me, you'll beg me to go, and I'll tell you I'll think about it and I won't really."

"Thanks Becky. I have something to hope for now."

She let him go with hope, knowing there wasn't any. This time she didn't listen for his foot on the stairs. The sobs were coming. She forced them back before Momma woke and hovered and worried and made her more miserable.

"Where's Tommy?" her first question.

"He left already. Forgot to say goodbye," she replied

When Becky was little she hated to be leaving anywhere, Momma saying 'Say goodbye' and Becky shrinking with shame every time and couldn't say it and Momma nagging and nagging until she did. To this day, Becky couldn't say goodbye without shriveling and hurrying away as fast as she could...but Ma never cared if someone didn't say it to her. She had no pride or principles about that. There'd been a picture of them both on the dresser, her and Tommy.

"Where is that picture, Momma?"

"What picture?" And she hobbled out.

Becky found it a week later, only half of it. Just Becky's face. It was torn in half. Just Becky's face. It was torn in half. Tommy's picture was gone. Becky shuddered, and that night, she wrote her last letter to Tommy. Seemed simple, brief, even sweet, but underneath impatient, hit and run, savage. She wrote quickly, then hurled it into the mailbox, pounding clanging the lid several times hard, just to make sure.

Dear Tom,

(Not dearest Tommy like before, he noticed that right away, sent a chill through him. Stiffened, frightened, on guard, he held the letter far away as he could, his arms outstretched, squinting, he read)

First, let me quickly say what I have to. Please believe me that I want to be kind, but I can't. There is no nice way, scratching away with a pen and digging into your heart, scribbling on anyhow things. I'm getting a divorce. I don't love you. I can't help saying, that's how it is. I can see your dear face now, dazed and wondering why, and crying too, maybe, because you're hurting.

Forgive me,

Becky

She expected they'd be friends, like the movie where the leading man is such a gentleman about it all, even when the leading lady chooses a rival. But from Irving, she expected Heathcliff and Don Jose, passionate, possessive, Jewish scholar, guiding her with a firm hand letting her win in debate, deferring like a man should, as a gentleman, not stooping to win a debate with a woman and whistle Stravinsky. Like men who divide women into sweet and pure in the kitchen and wanton temptress in the boudoir, Becky divided men into her own categories, images that remained in her head, another's unreality that became her reality, and down dee, the memory of a boy, dark, brooding, angry violent face searching it's like, and Momma's pushing, 'Live Becky,' making life seem like a leaky vessel. Rush it to shore or you'll sink and drown. Momma had said, 'Live Becky' and to take life wherever she could, sneaking up and taking away, but tempting and leaving her ravenous. Taking it away, like Tommy was now, like he did with his comings and goings and promises and maybes and now with his pleas not to leave him. For what? To stay with him...so he has someone to post a letter to? And visit between movies until he's ready to stare out at the sea again? Damn it! She'd seen a lawyer. Not to get anything. Just to know how to go about it, getting a divorce. She'd passed Korngold and Colucci, Attorneys at Law, many times. A dark brown painted door that stood a jar and wouldn't close, creaky banister, staircase with brown, worn patches on the rug, a sign on the bathroom door, 'Out of Order' and near it a sign, Matrimonial-Criminal-Immigration...in large, black letters. Pushcart lawyers. They do everything. Whatever they can get. She knocked on the door marked, 'Korngold.'

"Come in."

An empty desk. No secretary. He was at his desk on the phone and waved her way.

"A few minutes."

He kept his word, "Sit down. My name is Korngold. Yours?"

He extended his hand, she thought he must be the ugliest man she ever saw.

Largemouth splattered across a face square as a box, jutting chin and nose with flaring nostrils, blonde hair that stood straight on his head.

"What's it all about?" he barked, superior, arrogant, and waving a foul chair.

"I don't want to be married anymore."

"If all the people that felt that way ended up here, I'd have to close off the Pacific Ocean and put up a sign. Korngold and Colucci. Specific, "Why are you here?"

"I want a divorce," the word trembled in her mouth.

"OK. You just passed your first hurdle. The word is out. Now we can talk. What you got?"

And he wrote, 'HOUSEHOLD GOODS.'

"Nothing. We lived with my mother and father and rented a furnished place and lived with his aunt. We never had a place of our own."

"Not even a painting, a doodad, or a plate? Because the reason I ask, if you have something, take it right away. Hide it, before he gets his hands on it."

And he rolled his cigar from one side of his mouth to the other, giving her a look all shrews and practical, certain, with not a trace of doubt that he stood on firm, justifiable ground...and waiting...like he'd just sprouted the wisdom of wisdoms, an air about him of solid right-eousness.

Becky was shocked. Grubby, grimy, grabbing...from Tommy?!

"We have no things. Just never thought about them...never thought about them at all, as a matter of fact. Oh, we looked in windows, everybody does, but not with any real wanting. Things like that never mattered."

"Jewelry?"

He spat the word out and waited. She stretched out her third finger, left hand and pointed to her wedding ring.

"Bank accounts, vaults, that would have to be cleaned out today."

"Nothing to clean," she mumbled.

"So, what do you want?"

"A divorce, I told you."

"That's all?"

"What else is there?"

"Alimony."

His head nodding up and down…

"For five years being a devoted wife," in a pious tone like he was addressing the judge, trying the case.

"No."

Enjoying being noble and self-sacrificing now, he thought, and later, when it's too late, she'll come tearing in here, feeling done in, spiteful, wanting her due and so on or maybe there's another guy. They're always in a big hurry tearing out of one hole in a big rush to fall into another.

"New York law is a one-year wait."

"Too long. I want it right away."

He rolled his cigar back and forth again.

"You'll have to go to Alabama."

"Fine."

You'll pay me a fee for referring you to a lawyer down there and pay him for drawing up the papers. About a hundred dollars, all in all."

"I'll bring the money next week." She rose to go.

"Not yet! Wait a minute."

And he wrote, 'GROUNDS.'

"Why do you want a divorce?"

His salacious eyes behind puffy lids scrounging for what he called the 'meat and potatoes' part.

"I don't know where to begin."

They never did.

He plunged in, the cigar trembling in his mouth, "Bed?"

His head was not moving, still…like a stalking cat…waiting…his brain clicking…too much, too little, too dull, one other, others?

"No." Humiliated. Head averted.

"Then what?"

"He wants children. I don't."

"How long is he out at sea at a stretch?"

"Three months."

He wrote, 'Desertion.'

"Yes, that's fine."

"He has to agree."

"I think he will."

"Next time you come, I'll need some money and no thinking. You'll have to know so we can get started."

He got up and extended his hand. His way of turning out.

A young woman sitting there too, at the attorney's desk being lectured, miserable, biting her nails, a nasal, guttural, Brooklyn-ese voice shouting, "I know these guys. If you don't go home now and clean the place out of all the paintings and silverware, there'll be nothing left, you hear?! Don't be stupid! Hire a truck and get it out of there now!"

Tearful, "But I can't do that to him."

Pressing on, "You got to or you'll be sorry!"

Becky fled down the stairs and, on the way home, turned her mind to getting 100 dollars...where and how.

A letter waiting for her when she arrived home. A federal agent advising Mrs. Bromsky her disability funds as the recipient, Poppa, is deceased. And another letter, that since Mr. Bromsky left 5,000, which she never knew she had and Becky as Executrix, which she never knew she was and didn't know what that was anyhow, had to visit Surrogate's Court to collect the money. And...a letter from the management at the housing project that Momma was to vacate her apartment as soon as possible for a smaller one, since there was now only one person in the apartment, instead of two.

She was given five days to make arrangements or she could no longer consider herself as a tenant.

"It's alright," Momma said, "I'll work. And I don't need so many rooms. I'll move."

"Momma, I have something to tell you," and she talked of Irving.

"I'm glad," her eyes shining. "He's Jewish. Tell me, he wants you Becky, you think?"

"I think."

"No, we'll hope. Everybody owes themselves a little hope."

The telephone rang. Momma answered.

"I'll get her."

Whispering, "It's Irving, Becky. Sounds like a nice boy."

"Are you alright?"

"Yes."

"Your mother?"

"She, too. You want to meet her maybe?"

"I'll be there tonight."

And he hung up.

Momma put on the one black dress for fancy that she always wore for important occasions with a Woolworth pin at the beck because it was too low. Not really, but she thought so. When Becky opened the door for him, she smiled and stood at attention, like she always did when he was showing respect. He gave his slight, cruel, ironic smile and sat down without invitation.

"Ma, Irving, Irving, Ma."

She nodded and kept smiling.

"I know you're hungry. You should excuse me."

He nodded. They sat silent while Momma clanked and stirred, shuffling from table to stove until she invited them to the table. Not everything she made could fit on the bridge table, so they moved it near the sink and put the platter of mashed potatoes and string beans and salad on the drainboard.

"You from New York?"

"Bronx."

"I've never been there. Is it nice?"

"Very nice."

"You go to school?"

"I'm going for my Doctorate in Psychology."

"Becky told me you are such a smart man. What is that... psychology?"

Becky interrupts, "You know what that is, Ma. I told you myself."

"I know, but I want to hear from him and hear what he says."

Irving lecturing now... "It's the study of the mind, how people interact with each other and themselves..."

Momma not understanding and humbled even more and mumbling, "People what is crazy...like Becky told me?"

Annoyed, impatient, "That too, we got to go now. I'm sorry. We're late for a show. Nice to meet you," and he fled out the door, Becky following.

Momma shouting, "Come again."

The door slammed hard on her words.

"Where are we going, Irving?"

"Nowhere. I want to be alone now...with you. I've said all I have to say to your mother. I'm staying with a friend. He's out till 10 and it's 8 now. We have to run."

He opened the door on her side, and jumped into the other side.

She stood at the open door, "I'm not coming."

"Why not?"

His face contorted, desperate with impatience, angry, shouting so several passersby turned their heads, "So come in, at least, and sit the hell down so we'll talk."

Her will bent by temper and insistence, obeisant and compliant now, she sits down, staring ahead, her face turned from him.

"What's the matter, Becky?"

"What's going to be with us? I'm just nothing to you, a night's entertainment, that's all. Cheap."

"Are you kidding or something?"

Screaming and pounding the steering of the wheel, "Of course, I love you and want to marry you, but with what? I have no money!"

Pulling both linings out of his pockets.

"I have money. Poppa left Momma 5,000 dollars. I didn't know that until today."

He talked on and on about the future, how he would revolutionize the field. Becky thought he must be a genius.

"Becky, would you live with me for a while so we can see how we get along?"

"I will," heavy and meaningful, like they were standing before a preacher getting married.

Talking later to Momma, trembling, ashamed, "he wants to live with me first, but he has no money. How can we help him?"

"Take the money, Beckele. Take it and be happy. What do I need it for?"

Pressing the bank book in Becky's hand.

Becky protesting. She insisting and insisting, "I'll take it on one condition. You come live with us as soon as we're able."

"I'll come Beckele. I'll come. Don't worry."

But Becky didn't know if she really meant it to placate.

"Alright, ma. You win. I'll take it."

"That's good, Beckele," her voice sleepy now, her head falling back on the sofa, her mouth open, her hand sliding from Becky's and she fell asleep.

Becky thought, 'Still taking care, Momma. where'd you learn, to take so much care? From your Momma? She never did. From Poppa? He couldn't.' Like a bird. Who teaches it? Caring until she wears herself out...or even dies sometimes...from that kind of taking care. She looked so frail and small now, the taking-care, two pairs of strong, firm, agile limbs and brains leaning on her, taking and she's still giving, eager, willing, as if she could scrub floors and rub spigots forever.

"How long can you go on like this, working?"

"Hard as a rock," she answered, pounding her stomach, smiling proud rushing out the door...taking care...not to keep the customer waiting.

Chapter Ninety-Five

The phone ringing. Mr. Bowles, the lawyer who handled Poppa's disability case.

"Let me take care of your affairs now. Let me help you."

"No."

'How could she tell him Poppa had saved $5,000 when he always pleaded poverty? Shame the dead? Show he's a liar?'

"You sure? You won't know what to do. Let me help."

"No, thank you."

"Do what you want!"

He was furious.

Mirele asking, "Who was it, Becky?"

"Nobody."

"Why do you look so bad? Like you were hit in the stomach? Why are you holding yourself?"

"I'm not holding myself."

She dropped her arms from around her waist and straightened up quickly.

"I'm not holding myself," but she was.

"Irving called. He wants you for something important. He said you should call him here."

She'd left out a number.

"Ma, 5-346...346 what?! Can't you see there's a number missing?! Why don't you listen, Ma? You never listen!"

"Why are you screaming? You have no shame for the people? They should hear you?"

"I'm scared to lose him. Don't you see, he'll wait somewhere and I'm not calling back and he'll get mad and won't call again ever! You can't forget a number, Ma! Not a number! NEVER!"

And she pounded the wall with her first like Momma used to. On a tightrope, just one misstep, and a terrible plunge into nothing. She didn't hear the knock on the front door, Momma shuffling into her room.

"It's Irving, Beckele. He's at the door. I should tell him to come in...or no?"

Mortified. Calmed. "Tell him what you want."

"I'll tell him what you want."

Becky remained silent. Mirele went to the door to let him in.

"Sit down, Becky's coming. You want a drink?"

"What you got?"

"Water...milk."

"I'll have some milk."

She washed a glass, holding it up to the light and turning it several times. He watched her silently. She sniffed the milk, then poured enough to fill the glass halfway, pounded the container several times, one drop, then another.

"Sorry, finish."

"Careful. You'll get wax in the milk from those containers."

"Sorry."

She hobbled quickly to serve him on the sofa, her eyes riveted on the glass of milk. Setting it down, her hand trembling, a drop spilled on his pants. He took the glass from her looking scornful. She hobbled to the closet, took a clean rag, plunged it in cold water and was anxiously rubbing the spot when Becky came in and saw Irving with his arms up, helpless, waiting and watching while she rubbed.

"Irving!"

Becky takes the milk from his hand.

"That's enough, Ma."

Irving thanked her while looking down at the big, round circle she made on his pants.

"Do you think the circle will go away, Becky, when it dries?"

"Sure, it will."

"You sure?"

"Yes, I'm sure."

But she wasn't really. Just hoping very hard it wouldn't leave a mark.

'Why was Momma so dumb? Just two minutes alone and making a mess already!'

He stood up. The pants stuck to his leg, clammy, where the circle was.

"Damn it!" and he stamped his foot.

Momma and Becky were frightened. He gulped the milk to the last drop, holding the glass over his yawning mouth upside now. Becky watched the drops trickle and fall...one...then two, then he held the glass out toward Momma nonchalantly. She hobbled over and took it from him.

"You want more? I'm sorry."

Shamed, sighing heavy, her face hard, eyes looking in, like she was beating herself raw. He stood up and slapped himself on the back and side like he was pounding the dust out of a rug...Becky wondered why he did that.

"Let's go Becky, I have something to show you."

"Don't you want to wait until it dries?"

"The car's outside. I'll rush in. nobody will see. Besides, I want to talk to you."

"I have to dress better."

"Don't bother. Not where I'm going. Sorry, I couldn't wait for your call. Had to rush out right away. You'll see why later. But you can use that number if you need to reach me in an emergency."

"Where is it Momma? Where did you put it?"

"Don't worry, I'll give it to you again."

Becky never learned what mattered and didn't matter to people. Some people never do. Things were always suddenly mattering very much or not mattering at all. Whim and caprice, never predictable, mattering and not mattering, long as she could remember...with everyone. Together near the car door. She, nearer than he.

He said, "I'll get it," and swiftly extended a hand.

She jerked it open herself, just to show him she's different. Not necessary...outdated rituals. She thought he'd like that. Silly, standing in front of a door and not lifting a hand to open it. First time he'd ever done that. She wondered if he was testing her or some-thing. Hate tearing out of him, sudden and staying in his eyes like a fever.

"I can't bear those silly women who stand there waiting!"

Becky was glad she did what she did. He seemed sick about things like that. But that's alright. She'd make him well. Hating every-one. Loving just her. She'd hoped for that more than anything, never once wondering why she turned aside the love of those who love and lusted after the love of those who hate. An exclusive club, maybe... having a special place no one else has, being loved especially hard like no one else can, an idea fixed in her head. Hate, an impenetrable door that admits only one and treasures there that no one will ever know but her. Hatred...a stronger bond than love when it's turned inside out.

A hundred years ago, a lonely old maid wrote of a dark, brooding, hating man who loved. And a poor, tormented, hating boy, dark and brooding, too, with madness...hate ravaging his poor, thin body, and confused brain so he struck out and innocence. Ghosts of real and unreal...finding each other...melding into one. Irving talking of numbers and research findings and lines and dashes and Becky seeing only the tormented gypsy on the moor, loving the dead as he had the living.... and a tortured brother who knew nothing of love at all.

"I'm not loved," he said.

Never used the word before or after. The force of Becky's images was as powerful and compelling as the parent's pressure on young ladies to marry right...in the generations before her. It made little difference. One tyrant was replaced by another. Becky had her own private tyranny and the fates were sitting around the bargaining table negotiating her dowry....in this case, sacrifice, hurt and fear, the vanity she called 'love' table in this marriage. That was the loco-parentis today...luck and chance.

"What do you want to talk about?" she ventured, always hesitant to ask questions. Still raising her hand first, still being seen and not heard, still thinking, 'May I?'

He told her right away. His directness offended her. He should have shuffled from one foot to the other and removed his hat in his attitude, in his voice...or she was not a lady. What was a lady now? Not morality, certainly...it was narrowed down to whether she was paid or not for her attention. It was unendurable to Becky that she should not be considered a lady, to be thrust into a humiliating cate-gory at the hint of the slightest fall from grace. Becky had never expe-rienced it, but it was strange, that fear inside, Momma's finger pointing, a dire warning, not to be called 'cheap.' But Becky was kins and the men were grateful. Cheap...was a hurtful word, hurled at women by men who looked down at their humiliation before them and couldn't bear it, so they made public the humiliation heaped on them in private...and called the women cheap...the whole cursed lot of them. But Becky didn't know that. She just lived in dread of being boring, unloving, ungiving, silly, not living, being lonely...or cheap.

Whichever way she chose, there was a burning judgement to be imposed. The age-old weapon of the male to meet that of the female. She could lure him but would pay for it dearly.

"I told you I want us to live together, and I want it to be soon," in crisp, metallic tones like he was giving a research paper.

"Sounds like a good idea."

'Companionate marriage,' she thought, 'like Bertrand Russell the philosopher said.

She suggested it herself in one of her show-off moments, glowing and sparkling with new, innovative ideas, like life was a debating society. In a way, she wanted it, too.

If they didn't get along, they'd separate, with no one interfering.

Poppa once tol her these were not new ideas. They had communes in his day. Socialist freedom...no bourgeoise weddings...but...the feelings were not socialist like the ideas and there was much jealousy, quarreling, possessiveness and wrangling over mine and yours as the non-Socialists. And besides, to Becky, being somebody was being different. That you could be an unnoticed nobody being different had never occurred to her.

"And the money. When will you have it?"

"I have it now."

"I found a place for us. I have one month's rent. Next month, you'll pay."

Becky was glad to.

"Sure." Warm, happy, "I'll pay."

'The yellow fingers of Mr. Baker behind the counter. The candy was behind the round dome of glass, so you could see but not touch. The sign said, 'Don't poke the window,' but the kids couldn't help it. Their fingerprints were all over it. Begging Poppa until he stopped hammering, put his hand behind his black striped apron and pulled out a dime. Her little friend waiting, 'Buy us, Becky,' eager fingers and sparkling eyes. She led them and they followed meekly. 'I want... I want...I want...that...and...that!' And she put her dime in the yellow fingers, and they'd scamper out and leave her and he'd part the curtain and disappear behind it, leaving her, too. The hard door closed behind her clanging and into the lonely street. She ran home and asked Poppa for another dime. 'Think I'm made of money?' Then she'd play with the cat, force him on her lap and pet him until he couldn't stand it and ran away one day. He didn't like petting. She always remembered that moment when the dime was shining in Poppa's long, outstretched hand, and the joy bursting when she'd see the girls on the corner and she'd show them the dime and they'd all be nice, getting all around her and making her feel like a queen all over. That was the moment on top of the mountain. Like an old dream she had…running with a fist full of dollars and a man turns and meets her, deep sobs coming out of his shaking body, bone thin, hollow cheeks, gaunt. 'Take them,' she says, 'Please take them,' and throws them into his cupped hands.'

A forlorn, weak smile slides gently over his face. His hands clenched tight, he raises them over her head and embraces her and she looks at him through eyes blurred with tears.

"Don't be afraid. I'll take care now and you'll love me for always and always."

He took his arms from around her, stuffed the money in his pockets and turned away, a trail of crumpled bills falling behind him. And she turned away, too. One backward glance and she saw him return, greedily sweeping them up again, after some that were scurrying down the street…waiting, then seeming to elude him as he pounced on them, his face sweating and grotesque.

He whispers in her ear, "Run, Becky," the crumpled bills flying around her feet now in circles.

He snarls, "Pick them up, damn you!"

And he clamps her neck and pushes her down and spins her around and round, her palm grazing the hard ground until it's raw and bloodied. A few bills in her hand. He pulls her up by the hair, bends her head back and wrenches the bills from her grasp and counts.

"Not enough, Becky," he snarls.

"I'll be back tomorrow."

"I'll be here," she whispers.

A little friend passes by paddling a red wagon with a long, wooden handle.

"Hop in," she says to the man.

In the wagon he curls up, knees pressed against his chest, her friend cranking and pushing the squeaky handle up and down, the wagon tottering under his weight, the little girl groaning. He sits calm. The rocking of the wagon comforts and lulls. Inside him, the quiet purring of a baby that's just been fed.

One bill forgotten, left unnoticed. Becky watched the wind driving it on. It struck a corner and wedged it there, clinging until an angry blast tore it out into the open and pushed it on, faster this time and even more determined. Becky watched it, until it was swept around a corner and disappeared. Night dreams weaving into the day and making the days unreal, too. It means he'll always be back. Caring and him needing. That's what Momma taught her.

"What happens when they can take care of themselves?"

"Even if it looks like that they can always use a little more and somebody to give them, especially money."

"But Irving will have millions someday, so he won't need me."

"By then, it'll be too late. He'll need you for other reasons, like Poppa needed. He doesn't feel well...or he needs to holler at somebody...or he needs somebody should holler on him."

Irving stopped the car.

"The apartment I found for us."

A conspiratorial tone as if somebody was listening.

"It's a basement in a two-family house with a landlord on top, but it looks like a nightclub, a bar and everything."

Excited, "Let's see!"

"The landlord asked only one question, 'Are you Jewish? This was our party room," he said.

Becky had never seen a party room before. It was like the movies...a Jewish home with a bar...making an arc from one side of the room to the other with fancy sounding names, but empty, lined with shelves. The floor creaked under the worn carpet. Becky walked shyly around, not daring to investigate closets.

"Look around Mrs. Schneider," the landlord shouted, "don't be ashamed."

He flung open the closest doors and struggled with the bathroom that refused to open because it was stuck with new paint. The landlord tugged, reddening, his foot on the wall for leverage. It shook but remained firm.

"Let me."

Irving pulling. It resisted him, too. The landlord wedged a knife in, and it flew open. You could see the bar from where they were standing, a Castro convertible, an early American bureau, the drapes slipping on and off the top of it from the wind. It didn't fit the bar. The landlord opened the Castro, pounded on the mattress, pronounced it, 'good as gold.'

"Sit down please."

She sat and could feel the metal spring on the back of her knees, the thin mattress, its coils popping. When she rose, there were red circles on her thighs.

The landlord saying, "What did I tell you? Comfortable."

The mattress had black and white stripes like prison wear.

The landlord's wife climbed down the stairs, "You'll need a lamp."

She was carrying a tall, brown stick with a red shade that was tippling, the plug falling down the stairs behind her.

"There," she said...a dim light peering out from under the shade, a little circle on the ceiling with tiny spokes where the light shone through the top.

That night, just the little lamp shining. Blackness all around. Irving's fingers dipping in and out of the shadows while he talked on and on of things she didn't understand, the tedium of numbers and curves, lifeless, colorless, touchable, practical and she spread her fingers under the light and stared hard at them while the rest of her remained in the shadows and she bent her fingers and dug in and spread them out and counted the spaces, the forefinger of one hand jumping between the fingers of the other and far into the night until he fell back on the bed exhausted and she shut the lamp and fell down, too. And so, it went. Night after night. Becky drugged while listening. Irving struggled to convince her and himself too, that he was a genius. He wanted so hard to be one. Becky was won over. Took away the hurt and shame of all the years and put a shiny haze on the future. But the present was a grim pendulum between fear of displeasing and hoping not to. Like the little band of believers who sell all their belongings and stand on a hill and wait for the Messiah... sure He's coming...this time.

Chapter Ninety-Six

Sometimes, listening was hard. Blank dashes inside her head where words should have been, so she groped for sound and nodded or smiled, whatever felt right, but she could only hide for so long until he sensed she might be faking.

A cutting, pressing block, then, "You're blocking!"

Whining, "I'm not."

"What did I say?"

Her mind scrambled desperate to remember. in times like these, not a word came trembling in.

"Answer m-e-e-e!"

"I think it's a good idea."

Pursuing, "What is?! What? What? What is it?"

Becky dulled. Like a beaten child. Submitting without protest. Waiting until it's over and done with. Blocking! A shameful plea of guilty inside and outside, a mouth shut tight, denying.

Timid innocence begging mercy, "Blocking! Remember Becky?"

'Huddled innocence, bruised and shaking? Then why are you still hiding in terror behind it? Useless then. Why not useless now? Never safe, Becky. Not then. Not now. Can't ever trust innocence. It doesn't protect. There is no appeal. And he? Cold, unbending rage, still battering, hard, untouched, as if she could order her mind the way he ordered his statistical curves and numbers.'

"A determinist who believes in Free Will," she told him at other times, in the morning, when she felt strong and wanted to be smarter than he, have the last word like she did with Poppa.

If she listened with argument, he'd think she was dumb, and so would she, and listening with argument convinced him she was dumb, and not listening enraged him. The common Jewishness was never even discussed. It was just there. Both psychologists. The same interests. And it was there, they tore the hardest. He for precision. She for the mystery and complexity of understanding. They made no sense to each other. In music, she loved melody, to dream and dance to. He sang Stravinsky, she discovered because he hated, he said, with such savagery, sentimental mush like Strauss waltzes...which she loved. Made her shudder to think someone didn't. She never thought it possible. Becky had peace, once with a stranger with home she had nothing in common...tender breakfasts and loving nights. Above all, a dull peace. And now, tormented things in common. And both are frightening. How she feared losing Tommy in the days she wanted and the fear of losing Tommy in the days she wanted him and the fear of displeasing Irving. But with Irving, still the dream of happiness ever after. With Tommy no, the resentment of barring her from paradise...stronger than fear and suffering, the myth of Heaven on Earth. Why the most miserable creature clings to life and endures. Someday...it'll all be worth it. With Frank, she'd arrived at her *someday* and found it wanting, empty, disappointing.

Water glinting, sparkling like diamonds at a distance. And then, nothing in your grasp and other mental intellectualism that Irving was writing and researching and talking on and on about. It never occurred to either one of them to have a drink there. It was just a way station between the kitchenette and dining room table and they both sat down on a stool at the bar if they were having a heated discussion and Irving had to sound on something then and there to make a point often criticizing his professors. He loved to do that. No one was smart as he. He couldn't stand not being the smartest person in the world. He wanted to be Freud. Maybe somewhere, he really thought he would be.

Irving was right. Becky wasn't listening. But that's why they're all still around. Catholics, Communists, Socialists, Jews, marriage, and children. Nobody was listening. Not on Earth. Not God. Not Heaven. Imagine coming there, and they're waiting, too, for someone to listen...somewhere else. Maybe they're just born again when they get there, starting all over again, getting to heaven and waiting to be born to get out of it. What else could there be? Becky couldn't even imagine a place where people weren't looking forward. They must begin again from the beginning...like fruits and flowers. Coming home and wandering again. That's people. Heaven is only a way station, like everything else God made. She wondered what it would be like, the other heavens...after Irving became Heathcliff and Freud and Rockefeller and God. Exciting, just thinking about it.

Nothing to think about with Tommy. It all happened. And she wasn't ready yet to live in the past. There wasn't enough of it. Too skimpy. She only had so much that was alive in her and all of it was pushing for tomorrow. Nothing left for anything else. Becky feared living and not living. A greedy grabbing now or it may be too late... or letting it all go because it's too much trouble struggling to get it. And hold it when you do. Becky clutching onto Irving. A bigger fear was not living. Tommy was not living, and she was too young to die. A soldier's last furlough, everyone dying around him, or never really lived at all, he gets wildly drunk, has orgies of eating, beds women and has babies. Becky felt death and dying and not living at all around her. She was fulfilling a mandate. Mirele's. To live. Becky filled the order, though it was killing her to do it. She thought about life all the time, examining and concluding and going on like she hasn't examined it at all. Schopenhauer had no faith in promises.

"You're not listening," he was telling her, too.

Mirele looked forceful and determined, legs standing in their uneven rhythm with purpose.

"He's calling and calling. Too much calling. Why are you not telling him nothing? Tell him. He's calling three o'clock," he said.

The phone rings. There he is," with sulking resignation.

"So, be on a fire?"

"He saved your life, Ma?"

"So far, they took so many, so they saved one."

She remained unforgiving.

Becky trembling. Guilt.

"All the rules and formulas for life aren't telling you how to TELL SUCH A THING."

'She was from the age of hiding and, even in the age of telling, how do you tell such a thing?'

And cracking through the shy, obeisant, hat-in-hand, thin voice of Becky's is Tommy's cold righteousness, "So you came by plane from Texas, did you? You were with another guy, and you stole it, my car, both of you. That's a crime. Interstate theft of a vehicle. First, the FBI is coming after you and then, my lawyer," craven, pleading now, Becky's fear of government.

An older fear through the generations. Poppa's fear.

And shock, "You're doing this to me?!"

The self now judging innocent hatred as it had judged guilty, so quickly swayed, the conscience. Tommy, a stranger now, and Becky pleading and sobbing, the words hacked out and struggling.

"To me, you're doing this? Please, Tommy. Please, Poppa. Please."

And knuckles digging deep in her neck, pushing her down to more humiliation and pain and afraid of pain and begging for mercy... and it was never given...from Momma, Poppa, Irving and now...even Tommy. Made them stronger and colder, than begging. But the Beckys' can't help begging. They beg for love, for mercy, for attention, for love, for reward, and when they get a beggar punishment, it looks like they asked for it, but they didn't. It is just because they're beggars, that's all. Worse...craven ones. He hung up. Becky's head and body bent, pain forcing her mouth open like a fist struck inside, anguish rising in her and standing firm and still. Like a giant wave about to break.

Mirele shouting, "Becky?"

She reached her hand out to the door and slammed it shut. Mirele answered by slamming the front door on her way out. There was a deadly quiet in the house, as if the street were suddenly emptied of all the shouts and greetings and horns. Even the air was still. The house, so full of neighbors shouting to children who bounded down the stairs three at a time, babies crying in mother's arms. All still, like the world around me fell asleep or died was whisked away by a mysterious unknown, a magic spell, a stranger, or a wizard. In the stillness, the pain grew, turning in on itself. It had nothing to run to.

Turning on the bed, twisting and writhing, digging her nails, like claws, into the pillows, "Help me, Ma! M-a-a!"

'Becky, good girl, quiet girl, well-behaved, never in any trouble, and now...a thief, hunted by the FBI. Tommy sullen and vengeful like she was an evil stranger, or worse, a hateful wife, looked down upon. The movies taught her you could leave a brief note and be friends afterward. Everyone walked out like ladies and gentlemen.'

"Put you in jail!" He said that before hanging up.

The ways of wounded male pride were unknown to Becky. She'd been scorned many times but had never known this fury. The sulking run-away child with the trembling lips, maybe, hoping to make someone sorry or frightened and be brought back again. But that's all. It could be said that Tommy's vanity was deeper than Becky's love. The first time he hit her with a callow announcement, she'd planned a safety net to protect herself. Sad she would collect a diploma in one hand and say goodbye with the other. More and more grotesque now...the happy endings. Tommy's hearty laughter, mocking tears, Irving's dry smile. She'd never seen him laugh. Remember Momma saying, 'Smile, Becky. She never laughed then, either.' It was as hard as saying goodbye.

She still couldn't smile for the camera or face the moment of parting. Clutching the bedpost now, as if it were human and moaning until she fell asleep. She woke to find Irving grinning over her in the dark. In the dim light of the streetlamp, his arms straddling her on each side, his body arched, his weight heavy and bearing down on her, the only warmth that diffident smile, almost a smirk, but not quite. Hovering over her like the shadow of a huge black evil bird, he fumbled with her clothing, she helped him mechanically, robot-like, without pretense or struggle, without wanting magic or playing the game. When she woke alone, it seemed like a nightmare, but a comforting one. Someone to help her after all. But with the light of morning, the terror returned.

"Ma!"

"I'm in a hurry, what do you want? I have to go to work!"

"Irving was here last night. I didn't mean to wake you, so I went to sleep myself. He stayed a while and left. For how long, I don't know. A while."

"Did he come into my room?"

"I don't know. I heard him take off his shoes with a good hock on the floor and then I don't know. I fell asleep right away."

Becky sorting images, wanting them both to be unreal. Degradation, both of them. Tommy and Irving. Another voice on the phone now. An important one. Man having a job and doing it. Official. Confident. Hard. Metallic. WASP America commanding immigrants who preach overthrow of the government and are afraid of it. As long as it was something without a voice. Just called the government, she could deal with it. Something far away and unreal. But when it had a voice and looked like a man...

The phone trembled in Becky's hand. She agreed before he finished the sentence.

"Yes, I'll meet you," her head bobbing up and down like a top on water.

"Yes, yes, yes, of course yes."

She would have to put her heart to the knife if he asked her.

"Of course. Of course. Of course."

In the restaurant, he was sitting at the table when she arrived and rose to greet her, extending a thin, manicured hand, pumping her hand once, a jerky, definitive, assertive one, the friends-for-life type and sliding deftly back in while she clumsily shook the table, struggling into the narrow booth, the space between the table and the seat.

He did have to say a word to enhance his importance. Showing his credentials, he pulled his card from an inside pocket, Wellesley Deal meet Becky Bromsky. Just his name, the way he took the card out of his pocket with aplomb and tucked it back in with such class...a slow arc of the left hand, two tugs inside his jacket, starched cuff showing at the rim of the sleeve when it slid up, and the watch...the hands gold and gleaming and...no numbers. Becky'd never seen a watch like that. 'How can you tell the time without numbers?' But there was more of nature's bounty bestowed on him...tall, handsome, trim, graying hair at the temples, friendly, like Fred Astaire or Warren Williams. Just looking at him, Becky would admit, confess.

The image inspired confidence and terrified. The rest was easy. Seemed like a silly joke. The government's crack investigators who were created for Dillingers, Capones and Murder Inc. even bothering to waste time talking to a bumbling, naïve girl who, sort of lost an automobile through carelessness, imperviousness to things practical and material...or plain stupid about both.

'How do people see people,' she wondered. Couldn't really believe she was sitting there, the shy, little girl who hid in the dark on a laundry bag not to meet her uncle, the teacher. Mirele's daughter, that wouldn't steal a word from someone else's paper. That stole only once...at 8 years old...a fountain pen whose point went in and out at a turn and she yearned for it. Then one day, the girl who owned it was out. She'd left the pen in her desk and Becky took it...and was guilty about it ever since. And Momma, giving things to whoever consented to take them from her and Poppa's socialism... 'Absurd,' he said, 'to want automobiles, houses, and children. To want anything, even steam heat and refrigerators. The WASP's had done a good job. The Ethical Marxist of Gronow, and Lidow and Suvalk were confined to one place and the children thought the whole world was Jewish Socialists who argued and debated their whole life about socialism but agreed capitalists were bad and money and things.' What was he seeing, Becky, Mr. FBI? He told Tommy later, in a voice tough and hard boiled, like he knew evil well and nothing could be put over on him, not the voice he used on Becky, warm, friendly, you can trust me. T

Tommy's detective found the truth already. She admitted coming North with a boyfriend, in his car, but he didn't believe it. He was paid not to believe and loved it. Life was so much simpler that way and controllable. Becky blind to evil. He, blind to good. To him, Becky was a bum who betrayed her husband, stole his car and run off with the boyfriend.

To Becky, "Oh yes, thank you so much for your time."

"My time?!"

Becky felt safe, comforted. Important to make her feel that way. So, she'll be careless.

To Tommy, "We'll keep an eye on them."

Sooner or later...he winked the rest of the sentence, pounding his fist into his palm.

When she told Irving, he smiled and told her not to worry. Even laughed for the first time. Something he liked about it all...the scent of battle.

"You're not afraid?"

"Of what? We didn't do anything."

She still had not told him the truth...Tommy and she had not agreed to a divorce. She told him she took a plane home.

Irving pressed on, "So, tell me, what are you afraid of?"

"Nothing."

Becky had always been a frightened person. She lied; they all do. No one can accept the truth. That's why they were so frightened.

Beginning with parents, children learn the first time they tell the truth...lured into it with a promise of forgiveness, then punishment after it's fettered out. So they got frightened of it and lie and keep lying. Truths get worse when you get bigger so you get more frightened to tell, so the lies get bigger. Irving was a man of war and Becky a pacifier. She could never see how anyone could like battling. It scared her so. That was one of their problems; Becky forcing him into a peace he couldn't stand...and her not knowing it.

'After all, everyone wanted peace, didn't they?'

Chapter Ninety-Seven

Mirele, insisting she call every day and twice a day, confronting her like a criminal if she missed a day. Worse than a criminal! Much worse. Every day she was reminded of her crime. And every day, she was at risk of committing another one. In Momma's hand, the telephone was a glutton that needed constant feeding.

"I'm alone you know, Beckele."

"I know! I know!"

"So?!"

And Irving, "Calling your mother again? Christ's sake! Enough is enough!"

"Someday, maybe she'll live with us, so she won't be so lonely and clutching."

"What?! You crazy or something?! Live with who? What?!"

The argument, the questions, died in her throat.

"What she did for you!"

But Becky could defend a point on top of a mountain, not herself. Momma bludgeoned her with that for years, what she did for Becky, and she couldn't possibly use it on anyone else. Becky swore she'd never. And besides, it wouldn't make him grateful, only angrier, like it made her. So she sat beside him in the car, twisting in quiet torment, giving in, a limp, frightened kitten, tossed from hand to hand and back again.

Mirele had what she called a lawyer letter from Tommy. It said 'Esq' on the address, so she knew what that was. Becky once explained it to her.

'Arrangements have been made for you to secure an Alabama divorce. Two days must be spent in residence. See Mr. Dalby, Attorney. He will meet you at the station. Divorce final in 60 days.' Becky thought he didn't have to mention alimony. It would never have asked him for that.

'The Southern gentleman lawyer was charming, trotted out all his manners and then some, for Becky, then waited to see the effect. Blushing, giggling, discomforted, those Northern gals. Made them easy for bedding. They were so dumb. We sent them Negroes and kept our charm. Though they got the good end of the deal. They'll know better soon.'

He excused himself to 'call the wife.' He always did that so they wouldn't get any ideas. Women divorcing are funny. Getting the hell and can't wait to find another gate to open and rush into it again. He was whatever he sensed they wanted, mild-tempered, comforting, patient, wise to some. Strong, commanding, tough to others. They all thought he was the answer. So he made his call...just to let them know, though he enjoyed being the answer for a while. As the evening wore on, he felt them adjusting to the new time schedule. Not a forever answer, just one for now. The lonely hours in a hotel room.

"A little dinner, darling?"

"Why not?"

Then holding onto him for another hour, then another, not close the door behind her in an empty hotel room. Didn't matter the flowered chintz and wallpaper so it all looked so homey. They tried, but it was still like crossing a threshold into nothingness, like a spare room in the house that was never used, just made up like someday might me.

A room everyone avoided going into. Not even a human breath in the air, everything tight and tucked in, stiff and straight like a picture in House and Garden. All furniture and no people and even the careless touch contrived...a book carefully left open without one page with a bent corner, not a paperback with a loose page or a chair with a shirt hanging on the back of it or a bureau drawer where nothing can be found though it seems, you straightened it a thousand times. How grim those empty drawers in hotel rooms that she never dared put anything in for fear she's forgot it in there. Whoever remembers to open bureau drawers when you're leaving someplace in a hurry. Becky dreaded returning to that room, turning, and twisting in a strange bed, desolate, asking herself over and over, 'What have I done with my life?' And answering, 'It's what I'm going to do!' The rush of excitement. Becky could hardly wait. 'Life with Tommy...petty, small, a man of little imagination, petty purposes, and tiny aims, taking life in baby steps.

'May I take a giant step? You may. Shall! Must! Must! Will... maybe. If you'll have me.'

Like all shy people, Becky was ashamed it should show. Too shy to be shy. Becky blamed the system. Capitalism made a virtue of pushy, brash, self-confident, arrogant, sell yourself. Becky thought she was born at the wrong time. 'Don't be shy!' she was warned over and over again. 'Why not?' She always wondered.

Mr. Southern Charm wanted her to dissolve into shy tittering, struggling with painful inferiority until she wavered and succumbed. But Becky had learned to hide well that she was a victim, that anyone could make her tremble, run, and hide inside, especially southern charm. For the life of her, she couldn't remember his name, then or after if she was too easy he'd scorn her, or if she wasn't, he'd laugh at her, not much of a woman though she appears like one. She couldn't fool one such as him. He knew too many women before her. She'd disappoint him. And so she bantered and quipped and finally, as the elevator door closed between them, she caught a glimpse of his plead-ing, insistent eyes and flirtatious mouth turned hateful, surly, enraged. He looked like a Southern politician without his props, cigar, brandy, hat, or audience. Alone...with the election returns. A loser.

An hour later, she heard a soft rap on the door, put the covers over her head and didn't reply. She could hear his heavy breathing through the door. Terrifying. The sound of a stranger lusting. She didn't even dare move. When she heard the elevator door slide to a close, she pulled her arm out from where it had been under her stom-ach. It was tingling...and she let it fall limp, swinging it back and forth, clenching and unclenching her fist until she collapsed in a dreamless sleep and woke up the next morning wondering where, until she remembered, bounded to the keyhole, and peered through it, focusing with one eye until she could see well. He wasn't there.

But she draped a towel on the doorknob...just in case. She heard nothing from him the next day and he left without a goodbye. Two months later, certified mail, blue papers stipulating clearly the marriage was null and void, the language, legalese, cold, precise. Nothing holy or poetic about divorce. God was not involved as He was in the beginning for Becky.

"The papers are here Irving."

"Well, let's get married then."

"You have to propose."

"I did, didn't I?"

How could she forget that screaming proposal under pressure, like she was beating it out of him, "Soon as my exam is over. A week from then."

He pulled out the calendar, snapping the pages smartly. She silently named the months as he flipped them, staccato, a military drill, like the crack of a whip inside, then silence, his finger moving.

"Get me a pencil."

She couldn't find one.

"Damn it! Three college degrees in the house, and not one pencil!"

She plunged her hand quickly into her makeup case and scrounge for her eyebrow pencil. She could feel it sliding between her fingers, gripped it hard and rested it out from the corner where it was wedded...a small red stub.

He said, "Needs sharpening," and drew a circle, then resting his hand on it, smudging the page, his hands brown.

"A mess! Find a damn pencil. For God's sake! No efficiency in this house!

True, she was disordered and messy. It looked like a search, but it wasn't. Just going through the motions to appease and pacify. She submitted to his discipline. Though she needed it that way. She lifted the same things, looking under them over and over. Had to be there, but it wasn't. Each time, she thought she remembered she'd exactly put it there in this drawer, the pencils and pens, or under the book she'd last underlined. She opened the drawer over and over and peered in the darkness, looking under the book again and again. Aimless motions to appease and pacify.

"Is that what you call looking for?! Associate! Associate! What did we learn about memory?!"

"But I've associated and it's not there where I've associated!"

"Has to be!"

"It's not!"

"Let's not follow the course, logically. When did you last use the pencil?"

"To underline...and it's not in the book."

"Before that."

"To make a shopping list."

"What kind?"

Scorn. Impatience growing. Patronizing. Drunk with power.

"Grocery."

"Ah! Getting somewhere at last! Where?!," in a sarcastic tone, poised for effect.

Humbled, "On the table."

Cutting, "Let's look at the table."

He put his hand under her elbow as if he were taking her to a ball...mock, exaggerated courtesy. Then, separating the bread from the potatoes, "Oila! The pencil!"

Freed, it rolled bouncing and rattling to the floor. He watched as it fell and rolled under the radiator. She fell to her knees, swept the floor under it with her hand and pulled out the pencil, small clumps of dust still clinging to it. A light breeze coming through the window, the gray glob of dust shook gently, then blown away, floating in air, falling on his sleeve, trembling like a bubble before it pops open and disappears like it never was. She watched like they were one, trembling, too. He flayed the air violently as if a sock still clung to him.

"It's just a piece of dust, Irving."

"Minimizing doesn't change a thing! The place is filthy! When was the last time you touched the bottom of that radiator with a broom?!"

"I'm not a maid!"

"You don't have to be a maid to clean! I'm not asking you to clean someone else's house for pay! That's a maid.! But your own, that's cleanliness! And you know what that's next to, so I'm putting you in excellent company."

"You can't say that I'm not, can you."

And he put his right arm to his breast, his thumb through invisible suspenders and pacing back and forth with large strides...an attorney summing up before the jury.

"Momma's a maid, Irving. To me it's degrading to be dirty and degrading to clean," whispering now, a plea for sympathy.

"So, you'll be dirty all your life just because your mother was a maid? Is that logical?!"

That word stabbing again, one of the best in his arsenal...ripping, shredding, reducing. He always caught her somehow, not being logical...when she didn't expect it. It exasperated him that she wasn't, made her stutter and babble helplessly inside...that she wasn't...logical. He was frightened by disorder and she by order. Seemed so silly, she never told anyone.

Something ominous about opening a bureau drawer and finding stacks of gleaming, white squares, piled in perfect straight lines, the spaces between seem equal, one to the other, like they were measured with a ruler, "very important those spaces," he said, as if daring them to move, the shirts and shorts and black ovals, the socks. Never even piled them so high, they topped over.

"The spaces," he said, "that's the secret."

She could never figure out why. Once, she'd seen his mother's sewing drawer, threads all standing straight in rows of matched colors, needles tucked neatly in their pouches...not spools of thread with needles stuck carelessly in them, with clumps of loose, multicolored threads entwined so they could be untangled and bare spools she's never thrown out despite intentions and resolutions, like Becky's drawer. And letting buttons dangle until there were just a few threads hanging and then, the safety pins because she couldn't stand sewing.

She put the pencil under her dress and wiped it clean. He bent down and took it from her, returning to the calendar, brow furrowed, eyes burrowing into the numbers. He raised a hand and waved her over with the pencil.

"C'mon let's finish our wedding plans."

"Help me up. My foot fell asleep."

He helped her up gruffly and left her standing to pound, shake and straighten her skirt. Just biding time. Embarrassed, to be that close to what she wanted. She always was.

A tender memory, now. Tommy would never pick her up and rudely part, turning to other business before she was on her feet, still staggering and steadying herself and having to lean on a chair alone. It would be the beginning of a close and tender time, a loving time...like the movies. It hurt then, losing. She never thought it would.

Irving circled a June wedding.

Becky saying, "That's so nice," and putting an affectionate hand on his neck.

"What's so nice about it? Be specific," always speaking in glittering generalities, his favorite subject...general semantics and misuse of language, "You're not communicating!"

"Good God! Can't I make a simple comment without worrying about communicating?!"

"We can't relate to each other without communicating!"

"All we do is talk about relating, without ever relating!"

"Now, what does that mean?!"

Another one of his specialties, 'what do you mean by...' 'you have to clarify from abstract to particular!' 'Now, what is it that's nice? The day, the month, the circle...what?!'

"It feels nice! Feel! Feel! Feel!" pounding her heart with her fist.

"Think! Think! Think!" jabbing his finger into his head.

"I don't know," she mumbled, defeated.

"I thought so," softly, satisfied now.

"Now, how's about Zimmerman's Hungarian restaurant? They have a chapel there, too."

She was about to say, 'that's nice,' but didn't.

She just nodded, her tongue stiff in her head, not daring even to look at him, head bent, and eyes glued to the calendar...and venturing, "You're not sure of the date yet?"

"No, it's only tentative."

Anger rises again, "How can I be sure without checking with them first?"

How he loved checking and verifying.

It was a small wedding, with five couples. Becky's cousin and her husband, a man who called her to the table to where he was sitting from wherever she was to butter his bread. Stanley loved center stage and even competed with the groom for attention, insisting he give Becky away since her father was gone. Irving didn't like him, so he refused. They had such a terrible fight, the rabbi had to intervene to separate them. Irving was so enraged he stamped his foot on the glass so hard that Becky instinctively put her hand to her eyes, afraid it would fly all over. He put the ring on her finger, shaking so she feared Irving would leap from the chuppah and attack.

Irving, his eyes jumping wild when he distractedly said, "I do," and giving her a quick kiss, brushing her mouth with his when they were pronounced man and wife.

Ma sat at the dinner table staring blankly into nowhere. She wore black gloves for some reason known only to her and ate with them on. She'd forgotten to take them off. But no one told her. Either they didn't notice or didn't want to embarrass her by saying anything. Maybe she wanted them on after all. But it was never mentioned then or ever after by anybody. But it told Becky, more than anything, how far-gone Momma was. A table-hopping photographer took a wedding picture that came out then and there. Becky kept it rolled in the closet. Never showed it to anyone. She was ashamed of Momma's gloves.

Chapter Ninety-Eight

He's hard to live with sometimes, Momma...hollers, hard to live with being shrunk and crouching then jumping to a high corner like a frightened animal and watching him searching in the dark, for the prey, frantic and brutal, then finding, and sudden hammer blows, swift, cutting, staggering, confused, blind and reeling.

"Straighten up, why don't you?"

"But you holler, too. I see how you talk about the President and you not letting him finish and your mouth. He thinks he's so smart in psychology and you make him like he's dumb, laughing at him and everything. A person has to be a little quiet and listen sometimes."

"But that's the only time I can talk to him. Only time I have some courage, and besides, I just have to. I don't know why. I have to disagree with him on those things."

"On everything, Becky, maybe? Like you used to when you were little? You want to go out? No, you said. You want to stay home maybe? No, you said. Up was no and down was no. I couldn't stand it, I'll tell you that."

Becky quips, "Two Jews together, Momma. they disagree with themselves if no one else is around."

"They didn't get along too well with the Christians, either Becky, remember."

And her face froze hard.

"But he picks on me for nothing, Ma."

Whining, desperate tone, begging agreement.

"When he finishes school, Becky," soft, reassuring, certain, "he'll be different. Not so nervous, when he has his doctor's diploma."

Becky couldn't go on...taking Momma's dream and throwing it high in the air and watching it, shining and bright in the sky, then came crashing down in front of her.

"Look at it close, Momma. Hard and cold and gray, like death. Pesach and Poppa gone, really gone and no one to sacrifice for, no one learning or going to school. All the years Pesach missed, the Talmud scholar he never was. Irving is now the brother and the son.

Becky never even dared ask, 'Did Pesach ever holler Momma, at you, at Poppa?' And it never occurred to her to ask, 'Where is he buried, Momma?' It was such a secret mystery, like it was kept by God. So, Becky grasped at images, the black hair, the high cheek-bones, the face, grim, shadowed with dark anger, bits and pieces of memories making a collage, fragments becoming whole again with excuses, blame and reasons for being. Irving theme over and over, reductio ad absurdum, that he pondered like it was eternal truth.

"A circle tending to a close, Becky. That little gap, Becky. That curved line that closes in on itself, but not quite. You're used to seeing it closed, he'd say."

And he'd draw an open circle.

"How you draw it for me, Becky."

And she'd close it, like he wanted.

"You see!" excited, like he was rushing with the flame to the top of Mt. Olympus with the Gods truth found at lost, as he phrased it in, "an incomplete circle tending to close. You see, Becky, man finds meaning where there is none."

"Just carelessness, Irving. Habits are hard to break...then I think, we're both right. Me and Momma carelessly put meaning where there is none and we can't help it."

A weary, resigned conclusion. 'People have been doing that with life for centuries. Putting meaning where there is none. So why not you and me, Momma?' She'd wait until school was over. Maybe then, it will be different, like Momma says.

"Why are you so nervous, Irving, tense, on edge all the time, like you're ready to burst like a volcano, sudden and murderous, making me feel guilty if I'm not committing a crime?"

"But you are!"

"Always insisting to be right, when you're wrong!"

"So, what's wrong with saying, once in a while, I'm right?!"

"Do you learn nothing?! There is no absolute wrong and right. Semantics, remember?! you are again using the logic of the excluded middle!"

She'd forgotten a basic rule in the structure of language, his favorite topic...a thing can be both wrong and right. Irving stressed both, through tight, exasperated teeth. Becky thinking, 'Seems so silly, all that fuss about excluded middles.' A slight grin, an arrogance flitting across her face, a brief instant of proud and haughty reign.

He shouts, "Stupid!"

Her eyes glared at his thin, bony hands and the dark curly hair on them. Nausea. Fear. Help me Momma. I'm frightened. He crouched like a boxer. One punch in the air, then another in a phantom fight, sprinting in short steps back and forth across the room.

"I'm leaving!"

"Don't you dare! Don't leave me!"

He grabbed her hand as she fled out the door, pleading, "Don't leave me. It's the school's work, Becky. When it's over, I won't be testy. Believe me. That's what it is."

Softly, Becky believed him. She kissed him, but the softness was not in his mouth or in his hands.

"Quiet, Becky."

The voice quiet now, not soft. She wished she didn't know the difference.

"The freshest things deep down under," Mr. Hopkins said.

Once Becky believed it had to be. This belief was Becky's odyssey, her titling windmills, her Holy Grail, Her Promised Land, her pearl in the oyster, finding the deep down under. Finders' keepers. She believed that too. It was the reward for finding...keeping. Ancient man sacrificed his children for the Gods, and modern man himself, for his children. Deeper than food and drink and love in the covenant with the Gods, the sacrificing though it didn't rain, and the sons were given and the sons of sons and fathers were given and mothers and wives and husbands and that myth still hypnotizes, luring its victims on. They're plunging, headlong and eager, full, and warm and giving, arms and bodies, blood and years, youth and age, life itself and grateful that the other is merciful and takes it. Becky prepared herself for sacrifice. There was no one to hold her hand, not even God. Those who have are encouraged to indulge themselves more and those who have not...to sacrifice, to renounce even more than life has deprived them of, and they ache to do it. Abraham was to sacrifice his only son. 'Did God want Pesach, Ma? Maybe you angered Him by not being willing? He wants everything, Ma.'

"I gave it to him, Becky."

"He wants more. Now he wants me too."

"I know, Becky. So go! So quick!"

"I'm going, Momma. As quick as I can."

So, Becky carried her dowry, her small repertoire into the marriage...all she knew of real life, sacrificing, doing without, talking all the time, going to school, giving money to others as generously as you can. Irving was not pleased. Not enough. If he wasn't pleased, she wasn't pleased, so she tried harder and the more she tried, the more he found to displease him. It amused him to watch her. 'Does it amuse you to see me running and frantic, like a trapped animal, breathing hard for a breath of air and shutting the trap door in my face and listening while I scuffle round and round, pounding my body against the wall is a desperate futile struggle to get out, and each time I'm on one side, taunting me with the other and shutting it in my face soon as I get there, so I run faster in smaller and smaller circles. Blaming myself each time you let in a ray of light then close it dark again. But next time...

Irving explaining, "My thesis, Becky. You don't seem to understand," and he'd hold her captive explaining until dawn came.

Desolate hours for Becky, being awake when no one else was. But Irving didn't mind at all. As long as he had an audience. She learned how to answer without understanding, to agree without knowing. But she was scornful and in awe, too, of his bell curves and statistical particularities. How could he understand such things?! She couldn't even imagine. But they had no mystery or magic, poetry, or intuition.

He'd scream, "Nonsense to all that. Nothing exists you can't verify!"

"But...the imagination, music, poetry, the sublime, the spiritual!"

"All there in the brain. We'll find out someday...where and how."

"I wish they wouldn't."

"Why not?"

"You see...you don't respect my work!"

"Not really!"

Becky plunged and scrambled in the box again.

"What has one thing got to do with another? There are many sides to people. I just wish they'd leave a few of them untouched and unseen and unexplained."

"Then what in the world are you doing with someone whose whole life is seeing and explaining as much as we can. You want to go back to faith healing and incantations?"

"Just maybe one little something, Irving?"

"The whole is in a small part! Haven't you learned that yet, by God?! Nothing learned from me?!"

The following week she told him her M.A thesis was 'Closure and Fascism.'

"Good," he said, "very pleased."

An hour later she heard him shouting that the kitchen was mess.

"The spigots aren't clean! I like clean spigots!"

Becky welcomed the big sacrifices she'd made. She resented the little ones, if he didn't cook or if the place wasn't clean enough. Her ideas needed pruning...more concrete, visible referents...as he put it. He considered her lack of interest in material things demeaning, typical of the background that spawned her.

"You're still a peasant," he told her.

Becky attributed his fussy attitudes to his work. When he received his diplomas imagined a loving heart and spirit, a tender and generous hand and maybe an 'I love you' once in a while. How fortunate are the non-givers, those around the grateful for a kind word carelessly thrown and quickly taken back, unlike the givers who hold their heart in hand while the non-giver asks, 'Is that all?' Then they turn away, the givers, guilty they haven't done enough. The world is quick to appreciate a crumb from the non-giver remembering and grateful. While, on the offering of givers, the page is quickly turned and forgotten. The pages were turning quickly now, but Becky was sure it would soon be over. The five birthday cards he's given her were the tenderest sentiment he'd ever expressed. 'Love, Irving.' Irving still like a brief acquaintance with her. Becky still hoped, 'We'll get to know each other, Irving.'

She was the only one he even wrote that, too. Made her feel special. Feel he was sincere. Only world haters could really love one. Somehow, in Becky's mind, those who loved the world couldn't love their wife. She just thought so, without ever wondering why love should suddenly begin or stop with the wife, why love was a matter of opposites, flipping over and turning to hate when it stepped over a doorstep. Irving was a world hater.

Somewhere, deep inside, she thought he had to love her. Becky couldn't conceive of a person who couldn't love. She could imagine people without hate, spite, revenge, jealousy...but not without love. There was simply no such thing.

The first day after graduation she followed him from room to room like a faithful dog.

"What do you want, Becky? You're suffocating me. Cut it out."

That night he took her as always, nothing new, nothing special, nothing changed. As always, his head turned, hugging the pillow. As always, Becky grateful to be wanted, hoping to be kissed.

Momma said, "Wait until he gets a job."

So, he got a job, teacher of Psych 1 in a university. Nothing changed.

"We're invited to a New Year's Eve party, Becky. Professor Douglas, that blonde, blue-eyed handsome fellow. Remember him? You met him once."

"I do remember Irving. How can I forget?"

'He never stopped looking at me the whole time. I was so flustered and uncomfortable you thought it was the heat and told me to stop fidgeting.'

"He has a pretty wife, I was told, Irving."

"You jealous?"

It would please him to think she was...but...she wasn't. Above such emotions, she always thought, and a noble sentiment quickly followed.

"If you want someone else, take her. What can I do?"

Irving jolting her out of her reverie.

"Answer me! You're not even jealous? What would you do if I wanted another woman?"

"If you claim to love a person, you put their happiness before your own."

"Sounds like nobility, but it really isn't. It means you don't care. Did Othello care for Desdemona? Did Don Jose care for Carmen? Yes...they cared! Saying, 'it's been nice to know you, like Carole Lombard said to William Powell, in those pictures you were weaned on, is that caring?!"

"You don't believe anyone can be noble."

"Did you ever know jealousy or hate...revenge or spite welling up and shaking you and driving so hard there's little breath left for anything else? No turning away no matter how hard you try to free yourself from what must be done? Caring so much that heart and mind bend, and madness breaks through? You ever cared that much, Becky?! Hurting so much you could kill? Of course not! The beggar brags how he'd give all his money to the poor if he ever had any...that is...until he has it. Then he hoards and clutches and counts like everyone else. You can be sure he won't nobly give it away if someone else will be happier to have it in his pocket. That you can understand, can't you? Non-materialistic that you claim to be...but a person? The torment of love...means it's not an easy, convenient emotion. Clap your hands and it's gone. A gentleman's agreement with a lady. Do you love me, Becky?"

She nods.

"And you still say you wouldn't be jealous of another woman?"

She shakes her head no.

"Then how can you love me?"

"You're angry with me because I won't storm and bash about, make you hate me, clutching, demanding and then killing you!"

"Yes, if you could bear it!"

"You mean you're mad because I can't imagine killing you?"

"Yes! Believe it or not, I am!"

Coy now, "Can you imagine killing me?"

"I won't give you the satisfaction!"

"Why on earth should it satisfy me to think you'd kill me?!"

"Think about it if you can, even though it's no use if you can't feel it."

"I think it hurts vanity, that's all."

"You mean like someone saying, 'your wife's ugly or I don't like your suit?'"

"No, there's a difference."

"What's the difference? That's the point."

"It's not just anything. It's Othello killing Desdemona, Don Jose killing Carmen, Medea killing her children and Oedipus blinding himself. Anna Karenina killed herself. For someone so obsessed with love, it's astounding how you're missing the titanic passion underneath all these love stories, thinking you're noble to be so bereft and claiming to love!"

Irving brooded and lamented for two days about Becky's arrogance, the shallow nobility she called 'love' ...until the night of the party when his spirits lifted.

Professor Douglas was everything Irving wasn't. This was not a practiced charm imposed on clumsy abruptness locked in with shame and rushing out of the underground from time to time when the guard is overwhelmed, only to be pushed down as quickly and rudely as it erupted. Professor Douglas was used to charm. He didn't put it on like an ill-fitting garment and squeezed into it uncomfortably when the occasion demanded. He knew nothing else since he was born but grace and gentle manner, slow pace, and a ready smile, not clumsy and eager but...easy. Everything about Professor Douglas was unhurried but commanding.

A quintessential WASP. You wanted him to take charge. His patrician air inspired confidence...destroyed Becky's. Of immense assistance was his good looks, aided and abetted by his joie-de-vivre. The professor was a happy man! There was no sign on his face of titanic inner struggles stiffening his body, narrowing his eyes. He'd never known the kind of shame that annihilated him daily and made him play someone else. He'd never had to change the way he said his "A's." The family had a big house in Connecticut. He had a big apartment here, furnished with the family's antiques that they had for generations...mothers...not mommas.

As the evening wore on, he drank more and was more charming than ever, witty, taking Becky by the hand and spinning her around the room. She tripped over her feet a few times. He returned her to Irving, blushing and thanked him profusely for letting him dance with her. Her hand was to her chest. She was breathing hard. He offered her a drink. She declined, pointing to the drink she was nursing a whole night to be courteous. She took one sip and frowned as she always did. It tasted to her like medicine. She hated liquor. He pressed on.

"Have a fresh one."

But he made no offer to Irving, who was talking ceaselessly about closure to a male guest glazed eyes with boredom. Irving didn't notice. Becky was painfully uncomfortable, but glowing. Professor Douglas sat down beside her, wedging himself in the small space between her and the arm of the sofa. She wanted to jump away but didn't want to hurt his feelings. Instead, he bounced up, bowed with a flourish, and asked her to dance, didn't wait for an answer, pulled her up and held her close. Becky would've refused him anyhow. She couldn't say no and hurt him. Her body was stiff and arched like the kisses at the door when she was single. He was in a state of euphoria. Becky worried about not being able to follow him gracefully and stepping on his foot, and his body touching hers when it was forbidden, especially for a married woman. The lights dimmed. The year was drawing to a close, the music soft and dreamy, the Professor standing in one spot, swaying with her now, as if they were alone. And Becky's senses clouded and shaded imperceptibly into a romantic mist. She moved closer to him. His hand was on her back, not forcing now, but soft, insistent, warm, full, and giving. That's how life begins, with loving hands and bodies touching and holding.

Before speech, a baby's cry for hands and arms and breasts, fear melting, the haze of snuggle-comfort. Hypnotic, Momma giving her breast and baby her mouth, secret, tender union, one with each other...again.

He touched her mouth. There were no tingles down her back, nor blood, heat and burst of passion. He, perhaps. But not she. Then, warmth pouring into her from his mouth on hers, soft, sweet, cuddle warm. The lights snapped on. New Year's bursting in on them, horns blowing, glass breaking. It seemed natural, their kissing under the mistletoe. No one noticed. They were kissing, too in the embarrassed, frenetic way people do on festive occasions, forcing gaiety because they're drunk...except Irving...who was letting himself be kissed, his face full of red lipstick from the women's mouths and Mrs. Douglas's face, set, intent, unsmiling, letting itself be kissed, too.

A small boy comes sleepily rubbing his eyes, tugging at the Professor's pants, "Daddy, daddy, kiss me Happy New Year."

He bends down, lifts him in the air, kisses him long and hard, "Happy New Year!"

The boy turns back again and looks up at Becky, "You're not Mommy. Daddy. I thought you were kissing Mommy."

"It's New Year's, son. Everybody kisses everybody!"

"Why aren't you kissing Mommy?"

"I did Willie."

The boy turns his eyes to Becky, "Can I kiss you 'Happy New Year' too? You're so pretty. Can I? Can I? Can I?"

Becky bent down and felt his mouth on her cheek.

"Now the other side," she said, "so you wouldn't make this one jealous."

Irving cuts in, "That's what you worried about...a jealous cheekbone?"

The boy gave her a quick peck and scampered away. Irving scared him and Becky, too. There was scolding in his voice, with a 'wait until I get you home' anger a boy knows so well.

"Get your coat Becky! We're leaving now!"

A brutal command whispered through tight teeth, Becky running like a dutiful child into the bedroom where the coats lay heaped on each other. She searches slowly, silently begging for time.

He storms in, "Why are you so damned slow?!"

And flinging the coats in air, hurtling down like people falling to their deaths from high places. He was flinging them as high as he could...one after the other...in a frenzied rhythm. As one fell, he threw another in the air at the same time. He didn't even notice his own near hers. She caught them both as they fell into her arms.

"These are ours you're flinging around now, Irving. I guess you didn't notice. Are you tired? A timorous plea in her eyes.

"No! Why should I be tired? The evening's just begun!"

Chapter Ninety-Nine

They walked home in silence. Just the rattling of the keys he held in his dance. Nervous habit. Jiggling those keys. He liked that sound. Comforted him. But it unnerved her. "Maybe that's why it comforts you," she once told him, "because it discomforts everyone else...especially me." 'Maybe.' Tonight, he shook them very hard, swinging in and out of his palm. The bulb was out in the hallway. It was very dark. The matches he lit went out before he could find the lock to the door. His body tensing now, behind him growling numb with terror.

"Hold the match damn it!"

It burned her finger, but she held it. Wouldn't let go. Too afraid to.

"Alright, Becky. I have it now."

He closed the door behind them and drew the latch. It was such a final sweep. Like the door clanging in a prison.

A voice crying inside now, "Run! Now!"

She pulled the latch back...he slid it shut again. Back and forth... the timid sweep of hers, the determined one of his. And then he stood in front of the door...friendly...that thin smile on his face.

"Let's stop being foolish now, Becky. Let's be friends huh?"

He patted her arm twice...stiff...mechanical. Nausea. Repelling that touch. But she was always friendly the instant he was.

"What would you like, Irving?" eager to please.

He followed her into the kitchen. She'd forgotten to buy soda. Smelled the milk. It was sour.

"Would you like some water?"

"With ice cubes."

How she hated struggling with that tray! He knew that. Watched her pounding, her fingers frozen. They all fell in a heap in the sink.

He said, "They're dirty now. Try the other tray."

More pounding until she managed to wrest out three ice cubes intact. He clinked the keys round and around.

"Like the keys jangling, Irving."

"Yes. It helps me think."

A paternal indulgent tone, now, "So tell me, why did you embarrass me like that? Kissing him...and...like that...in front of everyone."

Becky, eager to trust, make friends again, stumble into an honest confession.

"I wanted a little warmth. I wanted a kiss mostly. More than I thought I did. It just came over me...like anger does...with you."

"You're defending your action."

Becky had never heard anyone say they're wrong. Didn't how to herself. Was like being annihilated to say such a thing. She never learned you could just say it cold and unfeeling as a ploy and win over the opposition. They'll defend you, then. She went on defending herself.

"You're still defending yourself!"

He put the glass down and stood over her.

"Why can't you admit it for once?! How you disgraced me in front of everybody?!"

She fell into the trap he laid for her. He seemed pliant and pleading, 'Trust me, Becky' on his face. She trusted.

"I shamed you in public and you shamed me in private."

He sprung, like a beast out of hiding.

"How can you be ashamed when there's no one to see?! The whole faculty was there looking at my betrayal! I wasn't even the last to know! Not even that mercy! I was the first! Good God! Don't you see that? Don't you see how you touch my mouth and run away like it's something unclean? How do I shame thee? Let me count my ways! Shame is indifferent to its audience. It matters not to who it is. Burns just the same...for your eyes and mine."

"It's not the same! How dare you say that?! I have to face a hundred eyes tomorrow, you have to face two...mine!"

"You're shouting so they can hear you in the next room. Lower your voice."

He raised it louder. "That's what you're worried about?"

It was.

Becky shriveled.

"Please, Irving, let's stop. Maybe it's better we separate. Hurting each other so much. Bringing shame. I just needed to be kissed, that's all. I didn't know how much."

"And if I needed to?! How would you feel about my splattering that need all over his living room like you did and now you think you're leaving. Abandoning me!"

He barred the door.

"Let me out please."

"You're not going anywhere!"

His body bent like a boxer. In his black eyes, savage cunning.

Every nerve taunt, alert. Becky cornered, shrunk to nothing but fear, pleading, crying, "Let me out, Irving, PLEASE!" But held at bay until the morning, eyes darting wild, her body jumping from side to side and his following hers, leaping handily in front of her from one foot to the other, that dry smile mocking her and, time to time, a terrible howl, "You're abandoning me!"

Becky is in terror of staying and not staying.

"Alright, I won't go."

Relaxing against the door, his head rolling from side to side, that smile still on his face, "I thought so...now undress yourself and get into bed."

He pointed to the bathroom, "Not in there. Here. In front of me. Everything. I want to see you...naked as a plucked chicken...and ready for me. He got you ready. I get the prize. He did the work for nothing. I did nothing. He can be jealous of me now."

Becky undressing...crying and undressing. Afraid not to.

He turned her around in front of him...talking to the professor at the party, "You'd give anything to see this, wouldn't you?"

She looked down. Her stomach quivering. She'd always been ashamed of her stomach. Never stood before him like this so he could see. She always managed to hide it a little, thinking he didn't see when she stood close, touching her body with his. The lights shone cruelly and mercilessly on her. Her head sinking now and cupping her hands over her face in a desperate attempt at modesty.

"Stand up straight and put your hands above your head!"

A lame attempt, limp arms slowly raise, bent an elbow.

"Higher!"

She stretched before him.

"Straighter!"

She arched her back.

"That's better! Now...bend over."

And he put his hand on the back on her neck...pushed her down and took her like an animal in heat. She fell on the bed crying. He wrapped himself in the sheet tight, so it was between them, and rolled over leaving her exposed.

"Stop crying. I want to sleep. You're making too much noise, damn it!"

"I'm cold. I need to cover myself."

"Damn it!"

He unwrapped himself, angrily picked up her clothing from the floor and threw the on her back...

"Your dress! Slip! Brasserie! And panties! Cover yourself with that!"

A memory:

"What do you know about Mirele? Stupid!"

Becky preening, "I know everything, Poppa."

"Take a bow, Becky. Do it right now. Down. Down."

Becky choking on his two fingers digging deep in the back of her throat.

"You have to know how to hold your head up high. But, more than that, you have to know how to bend it down. Bend, Becky, bend."

"I am, Poppa. See?"

And she'd touch the floor with the palm of her hands, and her dress falls and hangs over her face, so it's all dark inside, and her muffled voice saying, "See, Poppa? See?"

And the belt stinging and Poppa's voice cutting, "Not good enough, Becky! Lower! I said, not good enough!"

A strangled voice, "I'm sorry, Poppa."

Hugging the wooden floor with her open mouth, taut with pain, soundless.

"Now, it's right, Becky. Be smart."

"Yes, Poppa."

"Now, bow Becky. Be good."

"Yes Poppa."

End of memory.

It was getting colder. She wrapped the slip around her waist and shoulders. When he turned to fall asleep, she carefully dared to put a bit of the sheet around her, until he turned again violently, snatching it away from her. Fearing to wake him, she searched for her overcoat in the dark, stumbled over it on the floor where he'd thrown it, and went back to bed. He found her the next morning, lying beside him, wearing her overcoat. She heard him waking, but pretended to be asleep, fearing he was still vengeful, waiting for her to awaken so he could attack again...a cruel word, a hard look, cutting, accusing.

She heard the zipper closing on his briefcase, four quick, concise strokes. He closed the door gently, tip-toed down the hall, stepping over the creaky broads, careful not to wake her. He wanted to be friends again. She could tell.

A memory.

'Leave now! The courage to run...now!'

Oh, if only...she told Mirele a little...not enough so her dream crumbled...but enough for her to say, 'stay a while.' Like it was a wind howling in the distance...not near enough to come crashing in, breaking, or tearing. Just enough to warn and scare.

"Be nice, Becky. Be good, Becky," ...at first. And then, a week later.

The worried questions, 'so when are you going back? He doesn't want you?'

'Never, Momma.'

End of memory.

The dark, cold streets, wind cutting through a thin coat, the long, lonely walk home from the subway, Irving following her in the car, his hand on the horn, insistent, now promising, warm, comfortable. Now.

The lonely nights waiting for Momma to come home from work, empty mornings with the smell of fried bread the only sign of her having been there. A hurried breakfast she made for Becky before scurrying out the door. Sometimes, Becky woke and heard her frantic shuffling before falling back to sleep. Mornings are always a desperate time for the poor...frantic juggling of precious minutes, fighting for the bathroom, cursing the time hurrying away from you. 'If you just had time for one more lousy cup of coffee. Not asking for much!' If you're not working, the morning is desolate. Hours long and interminable. No need to set the clock anymore, but you wake up at that lousy hour anyway. Becky hated mornings. How does a person who never questions the daily grind have someone who does nothing but? Becky argued incessantly with nature that gave her a sense of beauty and surrounded her with ugliness...the fates that doomed Mirele to the torments of Sisyphus when she had defied no one, not people, certainly not God. She was proud the women let her do their scrubbing and cleaning then drink their coffee and give them advice. And Poppa? How she missed him, too. Whatever it was, that's the way it's supposed to be. To Becky, nothing was right, 'the way it was supposed to be.' Only the way it could be.

Every night, the insistent call from Irving.

"You hurt me, Becky, and you're killing me, now. Please come home."

She'd hang up and not answer no matter how many times it rang and rang, scaring her as if he was with her...until it stopped.

And Mirele, "It's a pity on him, Becky. All alone like this."

"And me, Momma?"

"You have me."

"And you, Momma, without me, you're telling me all this time, you have nothing. And with me, now what do you have?"

"Nothing, if you're not happy, Becky. What's wrong?"

"You'd find an excuse for him if I told you. You'd say he works too hard."

That was always her excuse. Poppa was upset because he didn't work or upset because he worked too hard.

"You have to be patient, Becky. You have to understand."

Becky understood. It hurt him more than it hurt her. She decided to go home.

"Don't you hate him, Becky for what he did to you. Those who hate find excuses as readily and handily as those who don't."

"How can I? He's a sick, poor man. He needs me."

Memories grow tender and hazy, lulled to sleep by the mercies, and then, the coup de grace, the pleading, the battering of the will, wispy and fragile as it is, and finally, delusion...hope, "Tomorrow will be different."

Mirele gives orders as she shuffles in and out of Becky's room, "Take your scarf and gloves," and picks her things and piling. Becky still hated to hang things up. Becky wasn't even listening now, Momma's words disappearing as she looked for shoes under the bed, the words getting lost there.

"Where's your hat?"

"I don't need it now. Forget it. I'm late already."

Becky tense now, watching the clock. Irving hated lateness. Momma was frightened too.

"Go, go now! Hurry!"

Helping Becky balance a purse, a shopping bag full of her clothing and a bag of fruit, he should have something to eat.

"Wait a minute!"

"What Ma?! For god's sake!"

The bag digging into her arm, the fruit bag slipping, bent and desperate holding on, Mirele standing straight like a child for inspection, arms at her side, feet close together, the lamp one limp, suspended, her kind words piercing, "You'll call, Beckele, huh?"

She nods her head and struggles with the doorknob while Mirele watches. Her hand slips and slips again.

"Ma! Let me out!"

"I'm sorry, Becky. It sticks sometimes..."

And she jiggles the lock until it springs open. Becky rakes long steps down the dark hallway, guided by the lights from the open door behind her, an acute sense of Momma watching her making her rush all the more. The bag broke and the fruit tumbled down the stairs after her, Momma picking them up and holding them in her dress all the way up the stairs shouting, "Wait! I'll get you another bag!"

Becky rushed on. On the table, propped up on a milk bottle was a card, 'Happy Birthday. Love, Irving' A shy kiss on the cheek from him. She put her purse on the table. Worry creeping in.

"Where are your things? Aren't you staying?"

"Oh my god! I must have dropped it! Carrying both in one hand, I didn't realize! Maybe I left it on the train!"

"Careless! How could you do that?! Not thinking!"

She was sorry already, 'I should have never come home.'

Chapter One Hundred

P eople making dreams...making nightmares.

"Still wearing your hat, Becky," Irving, shy, awkward now, not Don Jose...yearning, jealous, pleading, fire and wanting from a coy, flirtatious temptress.

That's what she dreamed would happen. Not an Irving standing at stiff attention, like a doorman waiting to serve and reminding her about the hat. She bent down to remove her shoe. It was new, uncomfortable, it rolled under a chair. He picked it up and carefully brushed it with the side of his arm.

"Shall I help you unpack?"

"Don't bother," quick to reassure him she can do it herself...not to burden.

"Just a few things, it can wait."

"Shall I put a suitcase in the closet?"

"No, leave it where I can see it so I can remember to unpack."

"Why not now?"

"Too tired to be bothered."

"You want it there, don't you, just in case you change your mind."

"No," she lied, "in case you change yours."

"I'll make sure neither one of us will," and he turned it over and emptied it on the bed.

She gathered them again, threw them in the suitcase, snapped it shut.

"Later, not now."

"When?"

"I don't know when."

"Why?"

"I don't know why. I just have to see it standing in the middle of the floor like it is."

"Come here, Becky."

He takes her by the hand.

"Let's forget about that for now. I'm not thinking about that night anymore."

"But I am."

"Why? No one said a word to me about it, or blamed you, or pitied me."

"That's what I was afraid of. All you remember is my disgracing you."

"What else was there? Our private argument...between you and me. You let the world in. I didn't. That's the crime...letting the world in. like my first wife," twitching and glaring now... "letting them laugh at me. I didn't do that to you and me. No one laughing. No one knowing I'm not man enough to please a woman...keep her. You want everyone knowing you're not a woman?! The little shame and blows to the pride we give each other...so what? I don't like your house-cleaning. You don't like how I blow in your ear. So what?! The four walls are bloodied with ugly words but that's all...from me. It goes no further. It's natural. People living with each other destroy and degrade...but...the world out there, where I make my bread and butter...where I need to be looked up to....to rob me of my dignity there again?! First her...then you!"

"Do we drop our pride the minute we close our door, Irving?"

"Of course, why not? Who do we have to be proud to...you to me and me to you? What do I do, play the crowd pleaser all day and all night, too? I come home to you every night and you to me...and I want to know where your beauty marks and warts are, your private curves and corners that no one can see but me...and that's not my pride...that's because I need something special at home no one else knows."

"Why are you so concerned about the privacy of beauty marks and care nothing about exposing arguments, venom, rage, hate, insult...all the hell of domestic quarrels to the neighbors?"

"Don't be silly. No one hears me."

"It's unfair. You're saying it doesn't matter how we degrade each other in private as long as we save face in public."

"I'm saying more than that. There is no degradation in private... just living together. It shouldn't degrade you that I say you won't learn to cook a decent meal or clean a spigot."

"You're saying I'm too sensitive."

"That's right."

"Would it degrade you if I told you didn't know how to kiss me, love me? That you're cold and unfeeling? Is that degrading or just living together?"

"That's neither. That's your problem. Plenty of women out there who don't agree with you," screaming now, "Get out of here!"

She reached for the luggage. He jumped in front of it before she could reach it.

"Where do you think you're going?! Sit down!"

She fell on the floor where she was standing.

"That's better."

"How do these 'plenty of women' know not to agree with me? Have you been toying with my public pride, perhaps?"

"I can't help it if students get crushes."

"You said women."

"It's a matter of definition. To me, they're women."

"And I?"

"You're an older woman. They're younger women."

"Why quibble about women and pride? Do we or don't we get along?"

"A matter of definition. What's 'getting along?' What I want is simple...a home...definition: warm...food...clean...companionable. That's real. that's what I want. And what do you want? Courting and fearing the fate of the courted...Anna Karenina, Madame Bovary... and trying to avenge them both my being Carmen while I'm supposed to be Don Jose and Heathcliff. All those little students straining to invent profound questions to put to me after class have the same dreams. It's impossible now for a door man, don't you see? Not enough to go out there and drag home a slayed dragon or two. I can do that...another promotion, another paper published...but how do I turn myself into a gypsy beggar striding the moors obsessed only with you and getting a PHD at the same time or...should I be a fool like Don Jose and give up my career and destroy you in a passion killing. Passion, that is, that you're reading about and seeing in the movies and they're always Italians or Frenchmen...never American Jewish boys discussing socialism with their leftist wives and fighting about Marx and Trotsky. What do you want from me, Becky? I'm a real human being fighting with ghosts. Someone imagined them and you're in love with them...and with me because I resemble them... eyes, cheekbones, God knows what...but you don't love me. You're waiting for me to be something that has no referent? Did you ever touch or feel a Heathcliff? By God, Becky, just go around telling everyone they have no feelings? I wonder...did you ever find anyone who does? Yourself maybe?"

"No, not even myself."

"Waiting for me to perform miracles, I guess. Both waiting to touch the fire inside, so to speak?"

"I suppose."

"Let's just leave each other alone to do the best we can, Becky. I'll kiss you, 'Hello' That's a good beginning."

She rose and pounded her skirt because she was embarrassed how he was staring at her and... 'to kiss someone because you're asked?! It's just supposed to happen. Acutely and painfully conscious, she lifted her face. He tried hard this time, pressing his mouth down on hers until it hurt, but that melted the tight humiliation. Feeling sorry for him now. And hope.

Now that Momma was nice after thrashing her; still firm, still determined, purposive...and Poppa, too, but her friend Evelyn was nice afterward and Becky thought it would last forever but it didn't... Becky still hoping it'll last forever...still hadn't learned...it didn't. still inching her way to the same dark places testing, asking forgiveness, not finding it...still looking to make Momma glad and Poppa too, and Lottie and Leona. All the people mad at her, she had to make glad... even those who weren't glad to begin with, like Pesach-Persie...like Irving. He was never glad to begin with. Becky is still waiting to be glad...afraid to be mad.

"Never leave you, Irving," she was promising now. Sure, he'll be glad, forever. But a moment ago, it seemed like he'd be mad. Forever. The circle turned and turned, Becky pleading, searching, begging, raging and each time, the rock on top of the mountain, now resting, it seems, forever. Becky was confident now.

"Irving, you're not serious about clean spigots, are you?"

"Why not?"

"Because I'm not a spigot cleaner!"

"Still haven't learned!"

And he thrusts her away like it was death touching him.

"And what else aren't you? I want children and you aren't the mother type, a good dinner and you aren't a cook, a little help with my thesis and you aren't a typist, a good debate and I tell you that you aren't a good thinker!"

He was waiting now. She was cornered. Condemned.

'Anonymous grocery bags propped up against the door and the donor ran away. Momma is proud. Nobody knows. No one is supposed to know. It didn't even occur to her to say such a thing. Becky had no defense attorney. Prisoner at the dock stands mute. Someone else, maybe, had to say you did good. Not you, Becky.'

"When do you grow up?"

Irving, cold, intent, waiting for even a murmur so he can plunge in again. She didn't care.

"I'm leaving now. Class in 10 minutes...if I can imagine making sense after this. Be back in an hour."

She left a note, 'Leaving. Not coming back. Called Leona and asked if I could stay with her. She said, 'Yes, come on over.'

On the way there, Becky sniffling turned into a heavy cold. Leona raved when she arrived. Just had a new baby. Came home to an empty icebox which her mother neglected to fill, David came home drunk, pants torn, rambling, falling on the floor, no use to her at all, her mother, David, and Becky too. David came out drunk, fighting. Becky fled. Better to go back home. They didn't even know she left. It was 2AM. All she wanted was a place to lie down until the morning or until she was well. She rang the bell...heard a scuffling inside, a woman's voice.

She pounded the door hard.

"It's me."

And heard, "Just a moment."

He opened the door slightly.

"There's someone here."

"I'll turn my back and let her go out. I won't look."

More scuffling and then, "It's alright, Becky. Come on in."

"I'm leaving tomorrow. I'll find a place."

"Aren't you jealous? She's a student at the university. Pure, sweet...I can break her in the way I want her."

"Not at all jealous. Really. Relieved, as a matter of fact. Someone to take care of you."

"You're really untouchable, aren't you, Becky? Leave me without so much as a look back until I give in begging...not missing me, not even a call in the wee hours of the morning before dawn when one would think you might be lonely...nice and easy for you...not desperate like me, shaking with pain and giving in...calling, begging... please Becky come home. Not wanting children, to please me, to serve me, relieve me of pain, massage and soothe me, tell me, once in a while. I'm right. To come home because you have a cold...not a heartache and not even be jealous that I've turned to another woman...and it's me that's cold?! Won't even make me a cup of tea, for God's sake!"

"But...20 cups a night?! turning around every minute to hear you say, 'Tea' like a bell ringing like one of your conditioned rabbits."

"That's what I was reduced to! I couldn't believe my luck! I said 'Tea' and something happened."

"You ordered and I hopped."

"Let's say, I asked you and you responded like a woman. Worst of all, Becky, you're playing a man's game. The chase excites you. The conquest bores. Marry so you're not humiliated being single. Marry the doctor and get respect and status without the work. You're lazy, Becky, and maybe a little dumb, too, superficial, easily bored, empty and it's all painted over with a fine brush how you sacrificed seeing me through school. You're settling for too little, Becky...sympathy and nobility you think you'll be getting. They'll think you're a fool, too, but you like that...as long as they think you're a noble fool. Still playing for an audience hungry for applause. Can't be alone in the spotlight if you're like everyone else. Emma Goldman, on stage, I don't need Becky. I'll tell you the scenario now. No one understands that now you have married potential, you don't want it. A Jewish Ph.D. with money. You had it all and it's nothing much once you have it, is it. Just bickering and nagging and waiting too long for that pot of gold at the end of a long road of pain and terror, neither of which, I might add, I have any patience with. I'll help you with the suitcase when you're ready."

That night, she returned to Doyle's bar. A sailor looking like Tommy, blonde, blue-eyed. Shy again.

"You're pretty, you know that?"

Shyer, her hands trembling, he held one, then the other, and sat silent, just holding her two hands in his. She pulled them away, brusque, still feeling the warmth of him...like no one else...ever.

"I have to go now."

He followed her out. Just before the door, spun her around, kissed her deep, like a lover's lost and found again. Yet, they'd never love. Her cheek settling on his chest, listening for his heartbeat. He turned her gently round and slipped a note in her pocket, 'call me.'

She walked away, unsteady, in a daze, slowly at first, then rushing on.

Irving is still awake, "Where were you?"

"Looking."

"At this hour?"

"Did you find anything?"

"A hotel I guess."

"I guess."

"You guess? Don't you know?"

"I know, Irving. Now, I know."

"For sure?"

"Without a doubt."

The next morning, she found a place in an hour. Irving helped her carry the suitcase, a few books, and left. He worried about the lock and warned her several times to be careful. It was a bare room with cheap, colonial furniture, old brown walls, a bed with a striped mattress in the corner, a bathroom with a pull chain. She wanted the hot plate, but he said he needed it, so she didn't insist. The restaurant, across the street, flashed red on her arm. The paper drapes, flowered, tore in her hand when she pushed them aside. They forgot to put a bulb. She sat down in the dark, the red flashing on and off on her head...and cried. Again, to the window. Couples, hand to hand, in and out of the restaurant. A payphone in the hall, she called Herbie.

"I'll be right down. No problem."

He cheerfully rearranged the furniture.

"There!" he said and sat down on the bare mattress. He turned his mouth and arms to her with his body. He loved her the way she wanted, all eyes and mouth and arms...and left her. After a week, ashamed he couldn't give her more. She insisted she didn't want to anymore. He didn't believe her. She missed him when he'd gone... more than Irving. More than anybody. The real reason he left. She knew. Like Irving said, 'You're cold, Becky.' Nestling, snuggling, hungry for love and taking.

"Too late, Becky, for Momma."

That last night, curling to his breast, teeth sucking hard, it hurt, but he let her, cradling her bent body, and nestling his head like a baby, she whispers, he pats, "There, there, now," until she succumbed to the soft, dark haze. He was gone when she woke without a word.

A note years later, 'I can still feel them sometimes, the tiny round my breast. No, I haven't forgotten.'

She hadn't either. But it was so nice to know he hadn't either.

Chapter One Hundred One

What did she remember from the marriage?

Social evenings:

"You talk too much Becky. I'm supposed to be the man."

"Alright then, I won't talk at all."

A silent resolution. Then going home, "Why didn't you say anything all evening?"

"You told me not to talk. Can't be pleased, ever!"

'No use. He wants to be displeased. What'd you do with a need to please?'

The screaming and blasting...without words now...in memory... just fear...jumping startled, silent battering for which there is no protection, no visible scars, no preparations...a sudden flash...terror rushing in, dashing wildly everywhere, afraid even of itself, scurrying madly until it's swept into it's corner again with the first kind word. And then, no comfort even with a kind word...realizing...yesterday is like tomorrow...death of hope...remembering yesterdays and waiting for them to come again. And they did. Over and over.

Becky saying, "I think women are more normal than men."

"What do you mean, normal?"

"You know what I meant."

"No, I don't."

"You feel what normal is."

Becky insisted, so did he.

"Shut up!" she continued.

He slapped her in the mouth, in the dark in the car and continued screaming. It was a bad habit she had of having to have the last word. And he, too.

"You wanted to be treated like a man...debating...but like a woman. I should let you win."

"Of course."

Liberation. Work. Two college degrees and no job, but one on welfare. Now, Becky's the investigator...irony...poor still taking care of poor. A savage superior...dictatorial, watching every cent of the city's money. An old woman applies for help. She cannot account for the money she spent on a bird cage, Becky sent back and forth for an accounting. The old woman dies. Case closed. Court for wayward adolescent girls shouting if she arrives at 9:01... Ma and Pa terror, 'Heads will roll around here!' Marriage terror...now...job terror... 'The head rollers will find out...she was not following rules. Every day a new crisis. Adolescent girls were not obeying rules. Becky thought they were too strict. She bent them. Conspiring with the girls against the court.

She was supposed to look the part, "Prop up your elbows, have your hands meet in mid-air, just under your chin, deepen the voice, slow the tongue and look distant, calm, mature, studied, objective."

Later, the style changed... "Rap, jive, bounce, bounce. Don't bring up. You get down."

Becky out of step. Unteachable. Becky wrote her own text as she went along. The words just came, flowed, like lovers, springing easily, magically between her and the unfortunate client, just flashed and sparkled for a moment, hypnotizing, disappearing in an instant from memory but remaining deep inside...to heal. Becky was considered a 'good worker.' Crime: Girl reported in shorts.

Becky defending, "Girl is suicidal."

"Oh."

No promotion. Becky is Emma Goldman in miniature and Sacco and Vanzetti and Ma and Pa and B in movies...happiness in poverty and struggle and smiling through pain and rich is cold and heartless and miserable and frighteningly sophisticated and finally, Will Shakespeare, 'How futile seem to me all the uses of this world her colleagues...timorous, careful...was promoted.' Becky was happy for her...wearing proudly her selflessness and idealism...like standing before the world receiving a medal of honor for purity of purpose. And then, accusing herself, 'Alone above the herd. Vanity, vanity, all is vanity.' And defending herself, 'Better that kind than any other.; both her good and evil were continuously on the dock. She suspected her evil was excused quicker by the conscience, but never took accounting.

After hours, bringing a baby home from the hospital.

Having to find a home, clothing. Hours of researching, buying...in terrible heat...frantic haste...then slinking home at 9 instead of 6 and Irving springs as she opens the door, "Where have you been?! Why didn't you call!"

Timid explanation. Guilty now.

And he... "It is not sufficient! Nothing is! No excuse! Should have called!"

"Didn't think of it."

"Further evidence of her selfishness!"

She's rescuing the helpless and the homelessness and he's deaf to everything but a phone call. Nothing more demanding or tearing than righteousness opposed, unrelenting, unforgiving, deaf, blind. He'd given her his concern. How dare she give another her conscience?! Her concern?! For each other, nothing left now but venomous, cruel, repeating of the question in the mind, 'How can she do this to me,' and she asks, 'How can he?' and answers, 'He's right. Why didn't I call?'

Both learned words of war...none of peace, diplomacy, charm, flattery, obeisance. Pain twisting, bending his head, breathing hard like a man in heat of passion, so thick and heavy she could almost touch it...around him like a dense fog. Watching and succumbing to the weight of it and running when it turned menacing.

"Watching me! Like a rabbit in the bush and running as soon as my back is turned!"

That thin, snuggly little reflex you call fear. You don't even know what fear is. I know what it is. Alone in the jungle at night, nothing to do but close your eyes tighter and roll yourself into a ball even when a twig cracks or the moon hides behind clouds and it's darker than ever. Hurting your little feelings with an unkind tone...mind you...not even a word, God forbid, and you're slithering out the door already.

"But I'm afraid all the time...even when you're nice...then I'm afraid you won't be."

"Of me?!"

"I'm a woman, Irving."

"Hiding behind that again?! Dragging out that old sword? Women built the Burman road through China, and they didn't faint at the sight of blood."

"Never hear from you, strangely, than you suffer more because you're a woman, feel more because you're a woman."

That was true. He suffered more...but that was expected. Meant he loved her. Was supposed to suffer. 'Didn't Heathcliff? Life should be only, 'Hello' 'Goodbye' meetings, partings, the in-between, worse, no dramatic beginnings, surprise endings.'

"The clients, I'm afraid of them, too. Don't know what to do with them. So mysterious, so complicated and me...groping. Not just you. Afraid of people."

"Then what are you doing with me?"

"Thought you'd comfort and protect me. Sacrificed for you, didn't I? no one more merciless than the helpless seeking mercy.

Because that's all you have to offer, isn't it? No children, no cooking, no cleaning, no nursing, no tending, no taking rage meant for others, no family, no status, no friends, a revolutionary without revolution and no courage if there was one. But you couldn't count. The new psychology is charts and graphs and numbers. So he counted for you...his name is invisible behind yours in the Master's Diploma."

"You should publish it," the teacher said.

"I will," she lied.

Could barely understand it herself. 'Don't be greedy Becky. You might be found out.'

They each have a guilty secret. Irving doctoring his numbers on the Doctoral thesis swore her to secrecy, too. She couldn't bear to look at her own work. Found it stupid, really, a sham, a front. But he could look at him with pride.

"Silly stuff. What did all those numbers have to do with a person?"

And she said so once. It was wifely to respect his work. She couldn't, alone or with others. She didn't know how to be with another, hugging the spotlight and having to have the last word, needing always to be told she's right. Ashamed to play second fiddle in the living room before the guests. I should have practiced how to debate with a husband in private and in public.

'It wouldn't have mattered Becky, don't you see? Life cannot tolerate formulas. Stealthily, it creates new and unforeseen dilemmas. Man is hurled against himself no matter what. In this case, the home breaker is, 'Premature Closure or Why Man has Intolerance of Unfinished Tasks,' ...Irving's thesis.

"We have a pained set of vanities, Becky, that we settled for so little."

"You, little?"

"Not when we found each other, Becky, but now, after all the pounding, I can't bear looking at you looking at me and vice-versa and vice-versa. We're ashamed what we see now, small, shrunken, shriveled, an embarrassment, and me puffing myself up higher each time and hollering more to drag that image up to where it was before and you hollering more to drag that image up to where it was before and you hollering back to do the same so you can look at yourself and me at mine. But I'll stay with the shame, because I can't stand the abandonment."

He hacked the steering wheel with his clenched fist, breathing heavily.

"I'm not abandoning you, you're pushing me out."

"I'm pushing...but not out. I'm pushing because I'm a pusher."

Despairing, philosophical, "What's the use, Irving?"

"None, but I can't lose, you know."

More pounding in the dark on the wheel. He loved to trap her in the car, at night, smothered in blackness. His little cell, like the flies he trapped. She was like one of them, and yet, unlike them. They buzzed and struggled against the bars, beating themselves round and round, desperate to escape, while Becky just sat there hollow and shaking.

"I'd released them when they'd served their sentence depending on how much time they spent making a pest of themselves."

'When am I to be released, Irving. I want to know, now.'

He read her mind, "You want to run now."

So frightened, she stopped even thinking.

"I like to frighten you, Becky. Not because I'm cruel, like you think, but because I can't get any other feeling out of you, so I've contented myself with that, for now. But the minute you're not frightened, you get over-confident...like that fly. When I'd first let him out, he flew to the window hopping around frantically to escape...so I'd open the window to oblige and damn if he didn't decide to come right back and I'd have to chase him all over again. Just like you, Becky. I give you a small taste of peace, just so I can catch my breath, if nothing else, and you're right back again in the same old place, like a slum kid when the cop turns his back, sneaking and conniving once again, a sullen, 'I didn't do it, Mister,' soft, compliant, 'You, too,

Irving. You're always defending yourself.' You see what I mean Becky!"

This time the car was near enough to a main street. She snapped the door open quickly, fell, lifted herself and scurried away. He followed beside her, while she ran.

"Next Friday, Becky, 'The Convention.' I'll see you there, Room 412. Shouting with horns blaring behind him, 412...repeating 412."

Ashamed, she turned and shouted, "Room 412!"

And kept running. He followed slowly, the headlights on the car, two grim searchlights a few paces ahead of her, mocking. She ran faster but they outpaced her. Then, they made an arc and disappeared. A piece of paper flung out of the car landed at her feet. She picked it up. She read it by the light of a store window.

"Room 412! Don't forget!"

At the convention, there was a party in Room 412 when she arrived, Irving in heavy concentration, listening hard and shaking his head in agreement, "Becky, I want you to meet Hal Keacher. You know him. I quote him again and again in my work and yours."

Becky was more frightened of this man than she was of Irving. 'Those few moments I wasn't afraid of you, sharing my humor with someone else at your expense, free and heady with joy doing as I please like I'm a child and you're a smaller one and I can do whatever I want with you. With this man, she would pretend not to worry about her fear, see him like a child, frightened, and she, the comforter and she wouldn't be afraid. A famous man, she expected his eyes to be roving, looking for someone else more important. Everyone did that at conventions, said, 'Hello' with a distant look in the eye and running way to someone else. Everyone's eyes were rolling in their heads.

She heard him saying, "I want to dance with your wife."

His voice, warm, he waltzed her away, Irving face still frozen, with the look of respect. And she, panicked, hides behind a mask of a quick repartee, playing Tallulah and Greta Garbo, hiding behind the skirts of strangers. Playing flirt, tease, elfin, mysterious...and he loved it. How unlike Irving...running for cover from a trace of womanly wiles.

"I'm like a shadow," she said, ephemeral, mysterious, "If you don't look quickly, I'm gone," and she snapped her fingers.

"Where are you staying?"

"Under a tree...in the arms of Morpheus, with a loaf of bread... waiting."

"For me," an indulgent, caressing smile, "you're with beneath the vine?"

"Without the jug of wine. I don't like it."

"Me, neither."

He didn't take her teasing seriously. Just a woman. She liked that. Not competing with her. Like he was above that/ he'd let her win. Have the last word. What difference did it make? He didn't have to watch the score every minute like ticker tape. He knew and didn't have to be reminded who and what he was. He made it so easy, strutting and fretting before him...femme fatale...ingenue...she went through the whole repertoire. He loved it. Inviting her to best him, to flirt and tease and toy with him. And they talked seriously...of young radicals in the party, and his eyes not lonely and lost now but light and giving and from somewhere down deep words bursting from pain of joy, 'you remind me of my youth!'

They went out on the balcony and stood in the farthest corner, he behind her, touching her ear with his mouth...clumsy.

"Kiss me, just once," whispered, but his voice was so deep, heads turned round and looked but it was too dark to see their faces. She offered her mouth and saw Irving in the doorway watching with a grim sneer on his face.

To him, "Would you mind returning my wife?"

To her, "Do you mind being returned?"

"One more dance and you can have her."

He pulled her on the dance floor. Irving following...watching.

Becky saying, "We're separated, but he won't let go."

"Of hurting you or loving you?"

"Hurting me."

"I thought so. Missing the feel of your soft neck between his hands."

"I thought you only miss what you love? I do."

Looking at her, blue eyes wide open like a good father looking at a cooing child...adoring, besotted...like the Christian martyrs take a last look at Heaven...grateful for the chance to die...and find God.

And she, perky, bubbling, saucy, "I'll see you at the next convention."

A throw away sentence to close the last act. The smile and bounce lingered until she met Irving, grim and stony, waiting for her.

"Whore!" and he spat at her. "My lawyer will call!"

A wailing inside, crumbling, butterflies in her eyes scattering quickly, the mask gone and shame flooding over everything.

She never went to the next convention. Though, surely, he never gave her a second thought. But she attended the following year...after her divorce. After all, she might meet someone. He was there in the hotel lobby. The mask again gave her courage. She tapped him playfully on the back. He turned and fell against the wall.

"I rushed back from Europe to see you at the last convention. Where were you?"

He took her hand, looked to everyone like he was saying, 'Hello,' but she knew, to her, he was saying, 'I love you.'

Chapter One Hundred Two

What kind of vanity, Becky? Money, love, honor. The last of the most insidious. It takes all. Gives sparingly. Sacco-Vanzetti, Emma Goldman, and Cyrano with his white plume. The unreal still real competing with voices of relatives pressing, 'Make a settlement for when he gets the money. The MONEY!' The noble answer, 'What right do I have? The marriage failed. What has that got to do with money? Money...still the soil-er, the degrader.'

"I'm not a whore. No one can buy and sell me. Like Marx says, 'I'm not a commodity...to be bought and sold like an automobile. No price tags hanging on my back.'"

In a burst of noble pride and glutinous martyrdom, head erect and shoulders forward, she marched proudly into the shame of poverty. 'Why didn't you pluck life when it was dangling there before you, juicy, fat and giving. Just had to let it fall into your lap, find the hollow of your apron like ripe apples and they'd be magic, burst open and...freedom with respect. Yes Ma'am. No Ma'am. Never again having to shyly ask, 'How much is it?' and watch contempt spread over the sales girl's face. Cyrano had honor with pride. His poverty with fear and respect. No match for him, Becky. What's the difference between the white plume that glows for all time and the one that wilts and sags and never raises its head? Drooping and bending and hanging its head like its owner, graying and yellowing without notice and mocked...even by me. What's the difference that makes a difference?'

Becky will not be forgiven for living in a dingy room in tatters in the middle of life and the end, like she was in the beginning. The page that has her name will quickly be turned. But on Cyrano, they linger. Because you can't be a little Cyrano, a fraction of Vanzetti, and a drop of Emma. Dreams were too big and the fear was bigger. When the man says, 'Those protestors who continue to sit will go to jail,' you get up, Becky. But that's not it, either. Outclasses Becky. Wanting membership in an exclusive club. Giving up what's easy, Becky...not freedom but security in life. And even if you didn't. Even in this exclusive club, there are those who arrive and are counted and those who slip through unnoticed, their sacrifices, nobilities, falling off their shoulders and sliding into oblivion, like Momma...and even worse...held in contempt. For her non-materials, now, only the dead applauded. The living called her a fool. Becky, too, joined those ranks years later. But now, drunk with the need to throw it all away...

Money was evil and everyone loved it and was greedy for it and prostrated themselves and begged and cheated and lied for it...but she was different. 'You'll be laughed and dismissed by everyone someday.' Doesn't matter. Becky restricted her world to where she began. Nothing else was real...the Roads in Grapes of Wraths, Paul Robeson and Old Man River, Poppa...no house, cars, or children, Will Shakespeare...

'How futile, seems to me, to all the uses of this world.' Cyrano renounced so much, not to today. Becky left Irving not today. And for money?! Especially...never...ever!'

But...unequipped for the honest life with glory, the dishonest one with safety, Becky clung tenacious to a few guideposts whose end was tragedy, noble tragedy, to be sure, but tragedy, nevertheless.

Becky embraced and loved the lost man and woman, too, and was determined to be one of them. After all, claiming a million, anyone can do that, but…give it up…renounce it, only Becky can do that. The pain of being a loner is easier if it's a significant one. To her, that was significant. The happy death of the martyr…singing on the way to the firing squad! Any reasonable facsimile, Becky. Be brave! Renounce! Revolt!

Irving was only too glad Becky remarried. She went to see his lawyer, arrived exactly on time, accepted 50 dollars a month to pay back the 5,000 dollars he owed her…and would never ask for another penny…

"Of course not," petulant and proud. A grin on the lawyer's face, full, satisfied, like he'd just finished a good meal and was reaching for his cigar.

"And something else, too, Becky. Remember? Herbie…the new neighbor…a communist who married a Black and she threw him out. The party did, too, because he divorced her…wouldn't plead his way back into the house. He pleaded, but she refused. 'Didn't plead hard enough,' the party said."

He cooked, served, and waited on Becky hand and foot. He adored her even more.

He begged, "Don't fight for the money. It will harm you in the end."

"I won't. Of course not."

Herb's father was rich, but he worked in a factory, like Marx said a good communist must do. Brilliant in mathematics, but he left school for the nobility of work, like Marx said. He told Becky his father threw him out and disinherited him. He was very proud of that. Becky wheeled on his kindness and tolerance, time in her life, like a fist in the face…he served her all the more and she hated him all the more.

"Stop talking about all this abuse, Herbie."

"Why not? I love you."

'So, this was love, abuse or being abused.'

Irving came one night, unexpectedly. Sat on a chair, stiff, staring, drumming his fingers on the wooden arm of a chair, looking angry, like he always did, and Becky watched, fearfully wondering when he would leave, why he came, and being ever so polite. Not asking for the money...was it nobility or lack of courage? She watched the blood pulsing in his dark, unshaven cheek.

'Does it really make such a difference? Yes...one has to account to oneself. That's the new God, now. He's moved inside the head, watching, and weighing, and judging, and finding...wanting meticulous and demanding accounting, more than the Other One, busy with someone else, sometimes...but this one cannot be swayed or diverted. He's just yours alone, Becky. No one and nothing else to be seeing or hearing...just you. Like being in a solitary cell with your own special guard staring in through the bars, watching all the time. So how come you do wrong, Becky, with him watching all the time? Because he's tricky. No fun for him if you're good all the time. So, he'll open the door and let you free, telling you, you deserve it. He needs a rest from watching and you need a rest from being watched and what was bad seems good. You touch temptation, then wallow in it...and suddenly, there he is again, madder than ever, slamming you in that cell again, shutting the door tight and watching. He is no match for vanity. Is quickly overcome. Vanishes...but knows it won't be for long. Feeding the pride is a sumptuous banquet...heady, but short lived. The raggedy petticoat shows before long. He waits. Knows you're like a trained dog...pawing the ground to be let out and scrambling back in yourself when the time is up.'

"I'm going to the Psychology convention. Herbie missed the last one. I'd like to see this one."

"Of course."

At the convention, people mill about in the hotel lobby, carrying lecture calendars and rushing about with a sense of purpose, playing important roles. Seemed like every other man had a Freudian beard and spectacles. They looked like boys playing at being grown up. No wisdom in those faces earned from years of suffering, soul searching.

These had a diploma in Life and didn't even know the difference. All bland, confident security...instant, wisdom...the book stalls all crowded. 'Like America,' Becky thought, 'the business of psychology is business.'

In front of her, a familiar back.

He turned, "You!" flushed, startled, excited, and fell against a pillar.

"Where were you at the last convention? You said you'd be there, remember? I rushed back from Paris, where I was teaching, to a guest lecturer and looked for you...at the convention...until the last day. I was so sure you'd be there! God, how I looked! Let me see you for dinner. Meet me here."

And he counted the fourth pillar from the center.

"I have to go now. At 6. Right here. Remember!"

She met him accidentally, before dinner, at one of the parties. He introduced her to all the big names in the field, those she'd seen under their book titles, in footnotes and on radio, only. One had written a bestseller. They both followed her everywhere. The man in the bestseller was not the same as the one speaking to her now.

"Why don't you come to my room? We'll make love to Brahms's Symphony. You look like an old girlfriend of mine that had several orgasms to his 4th symphony. In his books, he was tolerant, wise, soft, tough, cruel...like a petty hood in 'B' films. But...he was famous...and many a psychologist lost his wife to him for a few hours at these conventions and one...for a lifetime."

Becky feared him, but she could brag, in later years, that he wanted her and capped it off with, "I didn't want him."

Too frightened on his caustic tongue. He never knew it...knowing nothing about women. Fame was his matchmaker. At dinner, she nibbled slowly, a sharp contrast to the hurried gobbling she did at home, alone. She was twice miserable now, acutely self-conscious, never realized before how long was the distance from plate to mouth.

Trying hard to be clever, witty, intellectual, confident, and making it all seem so spontaneous...natural...the revolutionary Greta

Garbo, a minx with mystery. It was all thrown into the hopper...all varieties of woman she'd seen double featured for a dime plus the YCL club on the corner. Again, they talked of Earl Browder and very carefully...his work.

"They're different," he said, "communists and fascists."

"No, the same. Did you ever ready Trotsky, 'The Revolutionary Betrayed?'"

"I haven't. Would you send me the book?"

"I will."

"It's alright if you know something I don't know. I always learn from my students something I don't know."

She grew bolder and taunted him, feeling her power and testing his strength with coyness, flirtatious cruelty, tossing her head in mock indignation. He pleaded for her to turn and look at him again. A whole feminine repertoire that lay buried, suddenly spilling over. a man wanting her to be this fantasy woman and revelling it. But even he couldn't touch that hard fear...he would find her stupid.

An indulgent, loving smile, she grew bolder...and more frightened.

"You're so strong," he said, "so confident."

The fear was growing. A sudden feverish outpouring from him now, looking deep inside and digging his fingernails into the palm of his hand.

"You remind me of my youth!"

A boy's face looks up at her and she wants to laugh. His loving makes her bold, witty, a versatile and engaging performer...but not loving back...they will talk madness now, he with desire, she with fear...until fear touches him, too. And then he will be sober and staid and clear thinking. Now, only Becky is filled with fear images. She observes while seeming not to. Behind the shield, it's easier to take the blow. He looks at her with wonder. She looks back with caution.

He tells her, "I'm a mortgaged personality."

"I make no demands," she says, and he thinks that's glorious.

She knows it's time to run before she is politely asked to leave.

All of life was a test she was to fail. Unconditional love with conditions waiting...if not to set by the other, then set by oneself. With total freedom from someone she saw as an authority, she was a frightened pretender, but an engaging one, having no faith, at all, it exists. The troubadours and poets were no match for the past, the philosopher's reality. There was never a B film on a happy marriage. She'd settle for being a momentary pleasure...be grateful for it as long as she could be one...grateful it searched and found you looking up and ready...eager and waiting to be found once more. It taunts and teases, points, dashes, darts, and the face is turned away, playing the game now...uncaring, indifferent, and carelessly dancing away... untouched by wanting, by not wanting, caring, or not caring. Then the rain comes, heavy drops running over her in streams, and she stands and waits until it's done with her. The price to pay for a moment of light. You have to die willing to pay and pay...and Becky willing...the heavens venting themselves on the sacrificial heads of all the payers...loving the poor the most...they give so much for so little.

Heaven is an old hand at collecting...and Becky's at paying...a contract stretching from the past to infinity. The rich, on the other hand...dance on the mountain all the time, angling only for the center of the rainbow...some of them even born with it...the very center... colored, sweet, warm, uplifting, treasured by awed eyes and excited, eager, painting fingers. Just being, Becky...is all they had to do. Just be...and figure what to do with so much...how many balls, how many loves and how ungrateful, how ignoble...without asking or deserving. Not figure, like you, Becky, how to justify and balance and pay for so little.

The bitterness gives way to truth, at last. Memory cleared now of fear, pride, the need to please and she sees the flat mouth, the clumsy scratchy hands, seldom cut his fingernails for some reason, the empty hollowness at the bottom of a deep, warm voice. Pain and missing and yearning, but no passion. Warmth in voice and eyes, but not mouth and touch. In her, passion pretended, in him...lust...clouded with tenderness. She can't wait to turn to another. And one night, a call ripping her out of sleep.

"Becky, I told my wife about us. I love you!"

Becky had already met somebody...at a dance at Columbia University's International House...one of a group of young unemployed sent here to keep them busy...unemployed street wanderers, café habitues, compulsive flirts and potential troublemakers. They were middle class school dropouts...studying trade unionism in a country with mass unemployment and all members of the Socialist Party. They attended a course being given at Columbia, then traveled around the country meeting dignitaries and, of course, had very little spending money...the whole affair was a charade engineered by politicians at home who were pocketing all the funds they could that were supposedly allotted for this purpose.

Becky forced herself to 'casually' drop in alone, playing a woman of mystery. They went to her room. For the first time, she drank too much. They never turned the lights on. He wanted it that way, too. Sweet, boy's kisses...touching forbidden places, timorously, then warm caressing and...parting from him brusquely...the fear and shame spreading, not finding words but twisting her body so it rolls from side to side. He was serious, now. Knew she was troubled. And while she writhed in terror...that he'd take her and leave her...not being wanted anymore...though, even now, she could feel his adoration flowing over her...comforting...pleasing. He stood still...waiting... hovering eyes concerned. Waited until she rose and closed her arms around him pressing her breasts to his body, then daring to look at him in awe and wonder and kissing long and hard.

Then, how wonderful, his voice weaving round her, "I know it now, Becky, I don't love my wife. She's a wonderful woman. I love you, Becky."

And she loved Becky as his voice went on adoring her, but, for him, she felt nothing...though he thought she did. The days following, at the convention, dashing from lecture to lecture, party to party, so exciting to have a secret...all those important people, and he searched only for her. Everywhere, he was somewhere...looking. It was the most titillating game of her life.

To him, "You are my life," he told her...and thought he was hers.

Took it for granted. Never once asked, 'Do you love me?'

He loved her and never doubted she did love him. She didn't love him and doubted he did love her. The unloving suffer...with or without...love. Loving meant losing...only being loved meant keeping... Anna and Madame Bovary and Momma.

Harry Fonte...he sat behind her, his warm hand on her shoulder in the dark.

"Among all those people, only I exist for him. Everyone is seeking him out and he's seeking me."

Vanity of vanities. Becky glowed. Her pride stroked and warmed to bursting. But how long could she play blissful lover, sparkling companion, lost in a daze of romance and magic, wanting, desiring, lusting, raping, overcome...when she didn't want him at all? She was grateful the last day had come. She demanded the ultimate from him...a tortured yearning...desperate missing in her absence but doubted that could be. Summer romance and all that. He'd get busy with his work and forget. Important things will take over...

'Much more important than me. Pupils, classes, children...work... five nights of loving and talking love...Becky taking, and he is giving... telling them both to sleep after they'd loved. That was best of all... being in a cocoon of arms and words...snuggling...safe...pillowed in darkness. If only she could stay here, forever hidden...his voice remote, as if he were talking to a distant dream.

Parting time, now. Jerky movements...brusque and spasmodic. Putting a hand out to touch her and puzzling it back...the sound of shaving, water running and scraping, picking up underwear all over the floor where it was hastily thrown and his lingering over and intimate of hers, kissing it with his eyes closed as if it were her mouth, draping it gently on a chair and desperately darting away. The last kiss with pain, his hands clawing her back.

"Hurt me, too," he pleads, "let me feel your pain on me," and he opens his shirt, and she scrapes his chest with her nails.

His face flushed and vulnerable, "I love you, Becky."

She turned her away as he rushed out the door. Outside, his face settles again into the familiar...joyless...purposeful. He passed a colleague in the hall who fawned at him. He nodded. The old rhythm back again, quiet, paced, regular, routine, glazed, ordered, dead. Her head, full of images...what she told him...what he told her of his father...a religious fanatic. He left home at 16 and never returned. And of her father...the good parts only, slightly exaggerated...a worker intellectual.

"Then you'd be interested in Eric Hoffer...I'll send you his book," he told her.

A writer who was a worker-intellectual, not exactly in his league, but she never said so. She promised to send 'The Revolutionary Betrayed.' A week later, she sent hers without a word. He sent him a long letter.

The day she came home, the door was open, Herbie, in her apartment, painting, standing on a stepladder, slowly, carefully doing what he was told. He didn't know she came in.

"Good heavens!" she spat out at him brutally, "Aren't you finished yet?! Get out!" hateful, now, "Get out!"

"Please, Becky, tell me...what have I done?"

Desperate to hurt him, be alone with memories, "I've had an affair!"

"I don't care! Just love me a little...or let me love you. Let me, Becky, please. I love you so."

"Get out!"

A cold, hate, frightening, even to her.

"I'll close my eyes and count to ten."

Hands cupped over her eyes, a merciless staccato, one, two, three, four, five...she separated her second and third finger and peeked around. He was gone...without a word...without a sound. She didn't even hear the door open and close.

Every morning, she found a note under her door. She picked it up like it was something foul, diseased, contaminated...and flung it in the basket. He assumed grotesque shapes...disgusting...like a squealing, slimy, wriggling new baby. Herbie shamed her...small, thin, Becky's strong arms winding round him, his trembling body like a frail woman, a footman, a lackey, loving her with a wife's love, tending, serving, pleasing, submitting...giving in...giving in...and she...power flowing over her...a burst dam and he, holding on like a small branch in a tumultuous whirl as it sweeps over him. And he spins and spins and spins in a helpless round. His footsteps on the stair in the morning, he'd pause and turn, thinking whether or not to knock on her door. She froze, paralyzed, until she heard his foot on the stair again. She didn't hear the scrap of paper under the door anymore. That was a relief.

Becky's vanity rushed right in. 'The wanted is wanting me,' and Becky not daring to want or it's all over...a fearful eye on tomorrow while she's arrogantly picking and choosing...when men 'found her out' or worse...she bores. Terror of that word! Shame...deep and black inside...calling the tune...and Becky dancing and dancing...afraid of the tyranny of a husband...repelled by the passivity of a wife. Shame kills and Becky struggles while vanity pitifully tries to breathe life into a dream, a vision, not a hope...never a hope. Wouldn't dare, Becky. Wouldn't even dare.

Chapter One Hundred Three

"Every relationship has its own life," slim philosophy now... Man looking dapper in his suit and saying a patronizing goodbye to you to your matted hair and wrinkled nightgown, face swollen with sleep, mascara, now, the dark smudges under your eyes.

She'd told him that right away in the beginning. Man was hungrily after a moonbeam, he grasps for a fleeting second...grasping, to free himself.

"Discovery now, Becky. When a woman dilly-dallies, man clutches at permanence and she struggles to free herself from the hand around her breast. He would leave, going back to dry, dusty days, positioned, and known, like prisoners...steady, calm, reasonable, measured. He looked at her...awe in his eyes...like early man first looked at his world...frightening, awesome miracles everywhere...and on her face...shrinking to a distant immeasurable point...where only pain burns and burns in a vast nothing like the earth's beginning... where nothing touches...nothing grows, nothing changes. Becky took him like a man...biting his breast and scarring his body, hungering, and needing. And when they are loved, she'd become a child woman, grateful to him for having loved her...and he was then...the man... talking love...half dreaming...half awake...his deep, powerful voice soft and soothing now...joy, contentment making him tender...child with her father...the tip of her nose drawing a heart in the hair of his chest spelling his name and her name and drawing an arrow. Moonlight touching the pillow, she could see his eyes...filled with happiness...and she wanted to laugh. Tried hard not to. He looked so... foolish. She attacked him again with what he thought was passion and was ready to go her way when the time came, thinking, 'I'll never see you again,' and he thinking, 'I can't live without you,' and neither knowing what the other thought after telling each other how they were like one, how much they loved each other.

Becky saying, 'Me too,' when he could see her, and 'I love you,' in the dark after they had loved...forcing herself but making it sound natural.

He'd plead, 'Tell me you love me, Becky.'

Momma urging, 'Say goodbye Becky, say hello. Say, say, say!'

The words hardened in her throat, 'I can't Mama.'

'Say, Becky, say!'

The words holding tighter inside stubborn...the mouth leaden. Wanting to turn and run, but Momma's arms grab her, 'Say Becky,' her face reddening. Head down, all eyes of her...waiting, her body taut, she forces a strained and tortured whisper, 'Bye.'

Warm eyes looking down at her, a tinge of sadness. She likes that. His yearning for her even more. Becky like being a secret sadness in the heart. Better an excited anticipation, the rush of love, warm and eager, subsiding into glow and haze, tenderness and talk of beauty, colored in poetry, hushed in sound, misty, and fading into despair... not of each other, but of life...and then...gathering again into the deep of love and stillness. Sometimes a burst of pain from him, a loud railing against rending and parting and Becky in silent, compassion... waiting until the storm inside is stilled.

And once, a moment of impatience...scarring, "I don't need a debater, Becky! You just have to be I'll do. You be."

"I'm not smart enough for you."

He was impatient with her for the first time. One doesn't stick a pin in an idol; tamper with a goddess.

"You're perfect," he told her, and he had to believe it...always.

The guilt...three children and a helpless wife...he wore it like a hair shirt.

"My father was a Hasid. I wore curls as a child. He was terrifying...more than God...and I heard of His vengeance every day. He read to me from the Old Testament...God avenging the perfidious people He chose that betrayed him over and over and the penalty for not obeying His commandments. And now, I don't believe in God, but I fear Him. Strange, isn't it. Becky, how my father loved the vengeful God. I think that's the part he loved best because he was a vengeful man. God validated his cruelty."

Becky lived without ever asking the question, "How about your Momma?"

He'd talk in the darkness after loving, her breast so small it fit snug in the palm of his hand, talking of the past in the safety of the present...Becky feeling more and more special...their cocoon being filled with more and more secrets, heavy with the hidden aloneness that seems timeless and other worldly and safe...safe...safe...until the morning breaks...parting...and his words are pain filled and hers... weary...not letting in hurt or wanting...despair...or clinging...and feeling alright. After all, he's not bored or impatient. Missing, yearning is so much better, isn't it. He's looking back rather than forward...like she's something to escape from. Then suddenly, aloneness, like a trap gate springing open...and plunging into desolation...the hideaway is now banishment and exile. She grabs a phone to talk to the desk clerk...anyone...just to hear a voice. He went home in a car with others. She thought it was like a summer romance, fading when the familiar surrounds him again...and old meanings firm again...habit...the dresser...the bed...even the alarm clock.

Florence said, "Dinner's ready."

The Chairman dropped in for a chat, the younger, the middle and the oldest interrupting, "You'll have to...you must...we need..."

And the student's hero worshipping and wanting from their Gods...as always.

'A mortgaged personality, Becky,' he once said to himself. And then, to her, goodbye, my gypsy friend who danced with me on clouds...and not wanting or asking...just helping me fly. And if I soar so high in the heavens that not even you can see me, I know you'll wave me on...not because you want to, but because the farther I go, the closer you'll be to me. Only you can understand that. And if I'm faint of heart and fall to earth with a broken wing and shattered heart, I'll be caged again, and everyone will delight in my meager fluttering until I'm declared well enough to smash against all the familiar windows. An open window now, Becky and I don't know what to do with it. First, the distant revelations. Then, more immediate ones followed. His wife was one of the leaders in the Communist party when he first met her. She loved a black man before she married him. I'd come home to a woman looking far away...seeing him. I shouldn't have succeeded so early in this life. Working so hard, I wouldn't have noticed. She never succeeded, came to conventions, or anywhere else that we could be alone...far away from children, friends, chores, the things that excuse and interfere, push off for another time all the unsaid words and unwept tears, and look at, not past each other. She said, 'The door needs mending, the laundry needs doing, the man from the electric company is coming,' Me, 'get rid of those damn slippers!' She, 'but they're comfortable.'

Despite herself, Becky's leg snaps up and she looks, takes a quick, admiring glance at the feathered, high heeled mules she is wearing for now and will discard as soon as he leaves, for the comfortable ones she usually wears, the backs pushed down and the insole curling. The hushed whisper of love though there's no one else to hear, 'Goodbye, Becky, my friend, my companion, my dearest love, goodbye...for now.'

He left quickly, like people do when they desperately want to stay. And for her, there was no parting...memories that she could snuggle in warm, like a pillow, with both arms tight around them...joy in thinking he's hurting for her and wanting him in that pain. Then musing, 'I'm in a place to hide for you. Nothing more than that...and you're a place that feels important for me. Goodbye forever, my friend for a little while, that I am amused, and you'll occasionally remember and at other times...a stab of grating memory. A party of pretty, young students at the convention, many of his class. Not feeling his eyes on her back, she turned quickly, seeing the face of a man having his vanity stroked, gay flirtatious laughter surrounding him...and he fled from her, to each one of them. Later, sullen, morose, alone in his room, he put an arm around her, concerned and question-ing, 'What's the matter, Becky?' Impetuous words flailing about, 'You're just a flirt!" Sated with pride then, soothing words comforting, 'Just friends and students, Becky, means nothing.' And more sulking until she had punished him enough and was afraid to go on for fear he would get angry. But now, she'd be on guard, watching. A man wanted by all those women; he was not to be trusted. He'd say, 'I can't marry you. I want you to find something.' A scarring nobility. But Becky summoned the leaden acceptance that entombs...grateful for memories made and content to sit huddled in a corner with an after image.

Even philosophy has its classes...one for the poor... 'A jug of wine, a lot of bread and thou beneath the bough is happiness enough.' A moment of joy in a lifetime of despair is happiness enough, the little bit, the crumb, the light on the top of the mountain coming down and touching your face for a moment before it flies up again to her trem-bling nerve ends, holding them fast. A quick look at her nails, the fingers stiff in front of her examination. Ashamed of them. Polished in a hurry on her way out the door, red globs clinging to the cuticles... sloppy, uneven...and a defiant, 'I don't care!' burning inside with caring.

A whisper in her ear, "Vant to danz?"

She turned...black hair, black eyes, and white teeth...confident, suave, careless joy and a hint of cynicism expecting disappointment... well prepared for it...laughing. Becky, enchanted and intimidated, matched his ease and brightness with hers. He held her very close. Small, thin, and bony, the body of a small boy, the face of a man. She asked him name.

"Orlando Guarducci."

"What?"

He repeated it slowly several times and laughed. Becky had never known such laughter, pure and free, bubbling, and sensuous...open and happy. She asked where he was from.

"Siena," he said.

A place she'd never heard of.

"Where is that?"

"Near Florence."

"What do you do?"

"Nothing. But someday maybe I'll go back to school. You see, I have a small forehead. I was always told that meant I have no brains."

"Oh no!"

And she shook her head vigorously. When they finally left the dance hall it was bitter cold. He insisted on accompanying her home.

He talked of the Socialist Party and Becky froze while he stopped to make his points, but she loved it...hearing him say, "Bella between political monologues on convoluted Italian politics," that she could barely follow.

"Where do you come from?" he asked, out of the blue.

Proudly she said, "My parents were Russians..." and then softly, "Jewish, that's what I am...no matter where I come from."

"We don't pay attention in Italy. We don't know whose Jew and not Jew...all the same...makes no difference. We don't even think about it like here...this one Jew...this one not Jew. They are so religious in America? In Italy, a lot of us don't even go to church...but we need the priest for when we are born, when we die...things like that. I come from the Red Belt in Tuscany. We have a Communist mayor. It was after the McCarthy period...when people were so frightened of being suspected of Communist sympathies that they'd thrown out copies of the works of Karl Marx, surreptitiously read PM, a radical newspaper. How easily and naturally he mentioned the word 'Communist' like it was not a disease or the mark of a traitor. It was the style then among the 'Progressives.' America...synonyms for greedy, heartless, capitalist, anti-intellectual, anti-human, empty, naïve, primitive...all adding up to anti-Communist. The European...who...with his so-called 'political sophistication and worldliness had embroiled himself in a war destroying millions of hapless people and had to be rescued by 'McCarthy' and a vanishing world. Measured tone now, hands stiff at sides, on laps, and measured talk of studies and numbers and passions poured, and bottles poured and bottled in small theorems, history reduced to cases and become a virtue to be detached, uninvolved, controlled, not overreacting. And here he was, waving arms dancing smoothly in graceful rhythm with eyes and face, words, and body. Loving not learned from books, but naturally from father to son, and wisdom not stoic and memorized from the current fashionable text but lived and carried through time and generations. From him, Becky thought she would learn to know and feel, if only she was good enough, if only he liked her, didn't find her lacking. The other didn't because they knew no better, but he knew. She'd be the only woman in the country with a man from Siena. Everyone would be charmed, intrigued and envious. Americans were obsequious now to foreigners, now that they're traveling and tourist-ing and clumsily copying...awkwardly raising eyebrows and throwing hands about... with that look on their faces that people have when talking to children...pantomiming, mimicking, straining to look extra-friendly and generally appearing foolish. The American struggles as much with the Italian vowel as an oriental struggling with the English L, only the oriental doesn't sound so stagey.

Becky still believed...the printed word and the screen. Still too young to believe nothing. Some things took turns, waiting to be believed, and others hung on with tenacity. Some were dismissed, but not many. Becky was a believer...but a strange one...arguing the other side like a knee jerk reflex. Her opinion depended on time and mood and who was talking and what he was saying. But the person mattered mostly. She couldn't stand certain types of people no matter what they said...opinionated, arrogant, defensive, argumentative, and never logical...like Irving cuttingly lamented and viciously despaired. The nouveau academician...like the nouveau riche showing his riches, strutting, and shaming...cold passion or none at all. And here, she thought, this man from Siena was the 'natural' man. Herbie would accept anything. She couldn't accept that and yet demanded it from someone who would set limits she imagined they left. Never anything uttered. She couldn't take a word, a hint of criticism. The need to please had to come from her...not the demand from him. If he made himself nothing, her everything, he became nothing, too and she stamped and crushed and listened for a moan, a whisper of protest...nothing. The contempt grew, flamed into hate, and busted into violence. Unconditional love is unbearable to the human psyche. From the beginning, it cries, then feeds, then turns and beats its mother's breasts with its tiny fists and if it's still held with soft murmurings of love it twists its little body and howls in terrible pain, but no one hears. He beats again and again...frenzied, more frantic and no one feels.

Someone shouts, "No! And it fears and knows life is there... protecting...and it's bigger and we fear it. We have to fear from then on or we feel alone. Just someone being there doesn't matter. We don't fear them. Fear them punishing...we run...fear them protecting, we try to please...and that's loving...trying to please and fearing you can't. the rest is being loved...they're trying to please and fearing they can't. both of you doing the same thing...then you can say you love one another. For now, that was the thinking she'd done on love. While taking her home on the subway to Brooklyn, he talked and talked, and she listened. No studied pulling of words from an ungiving mouth. Words sweeping up and around...electric... sparkling...like Poppa's used to...life crackling in that dingy train. He stopped only when the screeching was so bad, they both put their fingers in their ears and laughed until it was over...soundless, but the joy was in their faces. The others looking deadpan...like in a coma... dazed and comatose from subway shock...they remained impassive, expressionless, untouched...but Becky caressed every moment, holding on like it would suddenly vanish. She'd seen so much laughter without joy. When they raced out of the train hand and hand, a flash of shame...how small and skinny he was. Then he vanished, just as quickly. Looking at him in one way, his face seemed broad and very handsome, and when seen in another way, slim and homely. She forced herself to look at him in that way, from that angle...dark and exciting...to hold on to enchantment. How different the foreigner seemed to us now. During the war, Americans bragged how they could have the Italian woman for a pair of stockings and all the little Orlando's begged for chocolate bars. How they were laughed at and mocked, and every American soldier was a plutocrat with a chocolate bar. But now, the little boys are grown and being called 'Latin lovers.'

He was from an old culture stepped in love, love, love. He would teach her everything.

"Everybody in my town belongs to a club since they're little boys. I saw many things there. I trust no one...man or woman. Married women having affairs with married men send their children playing in the club, calling another man 'Father' the husband...not the lover... and things go on as usual...like nothing happened. I'm too jealous for that," Becky was thrilled.

'They were really that sophisticated?! A man forgiving and forgetting the ultimate betrayal?! How little she knew...how people really are. Learning already.'

They were still talking in the street outside the door and up the stairs without interrupting the conversation. She made a point.

"You're right," he said.

She'd never heard anyone say that and...without pain. On the contrary, with respect. He'd left school in the 10th grade...and spent the days playing pinball machines, and the nights arguing politics in cafes or flirting with girls. He laughed as he said that his whole body laughed too, the hands graceful, flourishing with a dramatic sweep... and his walk...sensuous, lithe. You could even see from the back that it was an assured, continental...just the way he walked.

Inside her apartment, the talk became more personal. They laughed at me when I was little. I thought I'd never grow. In my country, you got out with a girl, and you're engaged. At a dance, parents sit around the hall, watching their daughters. And even more serious.

"I love my town, but the people are very cruel."

She exempted him from that class. He seemed so gentle. And more than that, she did it automatically, without thinking. Made an exception, exception, excused, isolated. He was a victim. He lived out of town as a little boy and had to raise his hat passing a city boy. He left school when the teacher laughed at him...and called him 'peasant,' he was lazy, uninterested, not serious, and therefore there was no sense in continuing. He came here on impulse, just for a lark. He knew the head of the program. It was a chance to visit America, to learn something perhaps, getting off the street for a while anyway.

"Shrewd, the Italians," he said, "so shrewd, that they out-shrewd each other. The program took them from the farms and streets, the poor unemployed and near-do-wells and decided to send them to America. Maybe they'll find something to do there. Dump them on American Italians. But the American Italians, he suspected, wanted to dump them back where they came from. Where PHDs are bus drivers, they do desperate things. Even the Socialists, my party, couldn't think of anything better than that. For us it's okay...putting up a front...a show...like the war we fought in Ethiopia. Mussolini strutting like he's a conqueror, armed to the teeth with ships that are painted and rusted, old, and useless underneath. In Ethiopia, putting gasoline bottles in the ground and pretending they're landmines. When the war was declared against the Allies, we stood dumb, not a sound in the square."

"I thought the Italians were militaristic."

"Only Mussolini's chin. Show...that's all. All show."

"But suppose it's a war for a good cause?"

"I run anyway."

"Then you're a coward."

"Yes, I am. I don't like war. If I have to die, I want to die in bed of old age, with arms and legs and teeth, if I'm lucky."

Then in Italian he said, "Come here, Vieni qui. Let me look at you, Bella."

And he traced her eyes and cheekbones and mouth with his finger. Caressing her back with his hand, he held her closer, looking warm, hard, studying.

"I talk to my friends at home like this, but to no one else. It's been a long time."

And he brushed her mouth lightly with his and kissed her.

He drew back and said, "You don't know how to kiss," and kissed her again.

She tried to follow his tongue but couldn't. she still didn't know how to kiss. The men she knew were more innocent than she. They followed her! She watched for a sign he was disappointed. She managed a wan smile, masking the humiliation.

Holding her face like it's fragile, his thumb moving slowly on her face, "You have such sad eyes," he said his voice caressing, compassion, warm and comforting...and on his face a look of tending...grieving. Gathering her face now in both hands, his body bending over hers.

"You must have suffered so much," his eyes misty with sadness.

The summer is coming to this dark, wintry earth, suddenly and without warning. It was that kind of miracle...those words...touching a secret place in the heart and nesting there. Not words hurting and battering, defending, and accusing...alienating, separating...not knowing.

"I'm frightened, Momma."

"I know mien kind. Momma's heart and ours are one heart. No

one had ever known before...like all God's men need adoring eyes to gaze upon them."

"Lead me in thy truth and teach me."

Little Gods now are leading and teaching. Faith trembling now, fickle, and fragile...the rock has turned diaphanous, gossamer, resting on one word and swept away another...a touch, a glance, a moment in time, memory. Becky's faith lighting on him.

Suddenly, he shoved a rude hand under her dress, caressed her neck and ear with a gentle touch, whispered, "Bellissima," and it was all over so quickly.

She waited for the explosion in him, in her. It hadn't come, but something else...a mystical, romantic haze. This, she thought, was love...truly. Now, she knew.

"You are a Buena," he whispered.

She was 'good.' She had pleased him. And he turned and fell asleep. She indulged him. 'He's tired, poor man.' Remembering for a fleeting moment, the long kisses after love, the warm words pouring round her far into the night. but it didn't matter. The new God never disappoints...even when he does. The others fall into disfavor and the new ones into the soft lap of excuse and forgiveness. The humble penitent is never wrong. He is always right. And whoever is deemed the all-knowing is everything and we are nothing. Becky leaned on one elbow and looked at him quietly sleeping...black hair falling in bangs over his forehead, the face boyish, but sensuous and uncaring. Why is uncaring so appealing to the caring? And not needing to the needy?

When he left in the early morning hours, he said, "See you tomorrow."

It carried her through the day. She touched the place on the pillow where his head had been, sliding her finger in and out of the ridges and the circle and tenderly kissing the place, smiling to the memory of his laughter, sparkling, like the river at night with moonbeams dancing. Then, another memory, hard, unyielding...to time...to life.

A young boy, the face black with the dark shadows of madness in the brain, black eyes burning with the scream inside...and dying. An unlived life waiting still...revenge for taking his, Becky...devouring yours. Behind the image of one face...another...round and round, circling as if they were the same...He...and Pesach-Persie. She would do anything for him. He had only to ask.

Chapter One Hundred Four

A rainy night and she's waiting by the window...feeling foolish; the nine o'clock date with him becoming 10:30. Giving up now and seeing his hat under the streetlamp. He looked so tiny in that coat. Repulsion darting quickly in and out... banished by the smile, the accent, the nearness...then it tips like magic. Becky, the magician pulling love out of a hand and not knowing it.

"The painting is beautiful. Repeat after me, children," and splashing the canvas with broad strokes where the cracks show, "class, repeat after me, 'the painting is beautiful and...how do you spell beautiful? O-r-l-a-n-d-o. you hear, repeat after me, O-r-l-a-n-d-o."

Becky's smile at the door, accepting and ready to understand.

"I was cooking dinner for everybody."

'Charming' she thought. He went quickly to the bed and swept the sheet with the palm of his hand.

"Checking to see if it's warm on both sides I'm very jealous, you see."

It was exciting to see real feelings in such times...anger, jealousy... ironed out into understanding. Acceptance...or nothing at all. Void.

Poor pretend for the rich and rich for the poor. Sleeping on the floor in the Village, then going home to the folks on weekends. The appeal if Negro and Mafia...craving to see a human being experienced, a genuine emotion that hasn't been flattened by reason, battered by training, rooted out by analysts, shamed out by status, class, professionalism, Waspism, Americanism.

Milt was a man who suffered over her. A somebody who was known to the world and Becky on top of it because he only loved her...but the pride would forbid her thinking she loved him cause, since he was somebody, he would drop her in a minute. Becky was always making such pronouncements. Balancing on a fragile trapeze on one foot...the fall waiting. The romantic has to hold on to suffering and knows she can't. How would he look, the sufferer, the morning after...a harsh light snapped on in a dark room...two faces bloated, sated, tired...out of magic, out of wanting, out of struggle, out of love. The marriage license curls in the drawer. Tormenting the lover with nagging and reprisal, desperate to touch that delightful pain again, but it's gone. Orlando had no suffering. Nothing to lose and regain. Nothing to miss. With him, she was Goddess on Earth with trembling feet of clay.

Every night, Orlando stood over her little hot plate and cooked. Milt didn't. No Jewish man she'd ever known...cooked! And one night, he confided he hoped to go to school, study science, find a cure for cancer. A rush of noble impulse in her blood...fantasy...immortality...helping...helping...helping...a Nobel Prize at hand. That would stop the question, 'How could you marry a man who is nothing?' And so, it was forming...another alliance...based on buried memory still pressing...fantasy...cooking...and unattainably...

"You'll grow tired of me," he told her, "You'll grow tired of me."

She listened in silence. Liking the feeling she was too much for him. Needing the confidence more than he. Being an American...that was given to him...like being rich or famous. With him, she had a given, for the first time in her life...and being educated. Not knowing, he thought her diploma from a university whose name had to be recited twice and whose response was a dropped face and changed subject, was worthy of respect. She loved his laughter, the laughter of a child she never knew as a child, bubbling, spontaneous and...now discomforting. She didn't know how to have that kind of fun...she tried when she was little but knew only the sadness to be left out of the game, grateful for the times she was let in, and afraid she'd be put out. No room for fun in those games...just pleasing, so she'd be kept on. To him, she became the all-knowing mother, friend, sister...his words. He'd gorge himself on a banquet of giving like she'd never known...then leaving her, he'd be hungry, and she'd be waiting. He left for home saying he loved her.

All she could reply was, "Me too."

Some weeks later, a stunning few words, 'For you. I'll give up my Siena,' he'd written on the back of the picture. Loyalty to a place? Something she'd never known and knew now that she missed. She was brought up with messages...hate...your country, city, neighborhood. Run like a trapped animal from corner to corner.

"No one leaves Siena," he'd said, "you live and die there."

"The same house too?"

"Of course."

Others could forget themselves, bursting open like new life in the spring...laughing. Becky plodded sincerely when sincerity was a bore...out of place. She smiled too...trying...not able to join, giggling on the sideline though she was in the center. Told to draw a picture of a person, she made one of a girl with her hands tied behind her back... immoveable...ungiving. Unused to fun, she pretended gayety... sarcasm, sophistication, wisecracks...the wit of the outsider...but never the freedom of joy.

He loved to play silly games. She found them foolish but wouldn't let on when she played with others. In him, strangely, it was charming. She tried and felt the pains of shame lifting, the walls cracking a little, but repairing and hardening after Poppa and Momma scorning, she tried to read him her underlined paragraphs in books she'd been reading and wanted to share with him. He listened, but politely. She would have liked more interest. 'In time,' she thought...and set that aside for changing.

They'd visited a friend with two young children. He became a child with them. Becky had never seen anyone have fun with children before. Disciplining, lecturing, discussing...never playing... having fun. Poppa took her piggy bank sometime. That was all. But she couldn't see his face and she laughed alone, and he did, too. Smiled a little, that's all. She told him she didn't want children. He set that aside for changing. 'Be serious,' they told him, 'Not serious enough,' 'Laugh,' they told her. Too serious. Not laughing enough. He felt secure in her seriousness, and she strained to join in his laughing. And the war inside continued. Status doesn't count, but it does. Profession doesn't count, but it does. The TV set she never put on was snapped on while eating and stayed on. 'Relaxing,' she thought... and undemanding. A relief not to have to live up the expectation to be intelligent when you really weren't. Just able to shine for a moment...if that. All glitter and no substance. She gave up music after reading a biography of Mozart and academia after Irving. Passing an examination in logic was what being with an intellectual was all about. And besides, there was something in her that craved someone who could just live for the moment without doing, striving...just savor the sweetness, with an arm around her, of doing or saying...nothing... and if there were words to be said, she was always right, always smart...not the tongue trembling, touching a mine every time it trips on a word out of place and has to submit to harsh judgment...loud, boisterous, swift, cruel, cutting, discouraging talk, and demanding she 'say something!'

Orlando's becoming a doctor with no problem. How many fools plodded into the limelight? The world would forgive her marrying '*a talaner**,' after all, if he was to become a doctor...besides, it would postpone the day of reckoning...or maybe erase it all together, 'a wife without children is no wife, no marriage, a sin against God and man.'

____

* ***Talaner – Yiddish for Italian***

Maybe she could make up for it? Do penance? Substitute a diploma for a baby? His doubts...whether she was good enough for him made him unattainable. And she had to have him. Forever, the little girl standing by the sidelines, aching, craving. What was dumb wanting then, becomes an anguish now...just wanting to be inside. Being wanted by the disinterested, the face turners, the finger rubbers smirking and shaming...then scorning them in time. Scorned and scorning, a circle round and round of giving and receiving a bitter beginning and end...Orlando now was the symbol of forbidden paradise, the gate that wouldn't open. She was tugging very hard behind the calm, benign façade when he left. She thought it would be forever but said it was nice and thanked him for the memory. She was still stunned to be remembered...wanted. The gate had to be crashed again and again. Each time it clanged shut behind a man's back it seemed like he'd never turn around again. There was no high drama the night before he left. Didn't even say he loved her.

"I don't want to be alone," he said, "I'll miss you. You are the only person who ever said nice things to me like I'm really enough."

She laughed despite the despair. He meant to say, 'unique.' She told him he was accenting the wrong syllable...and, too embarrassed to tell him what he'd say in words, she used innuendo and unfinished sentences and he understood and laughed, too.

Then holding her hand very tight, he said, "I will lose you. I know it. You are too much for me," he repeated.

And Becky thought she wasn't enough for anybody. She watched him under the dull lamplight, his little gray rain hat sitting atop his head like a pancake. He never looked up until he crossed the street... and looking down at the subway stairs he waved. She waved back from the window, then he ran across the street again, put both hands to his mouth...then...flinging his arms wide open hard again and again blowing kisses. She did, too, until he turned again and disappeared into the blackness. She waved again and again, waving at no one, her head pressed to the window...but he was gone, and she turned wearily to the bed, the sheets crumpled where he'd thrown them.

He'd remember her sweetly...then he would forget. She was philoso-phizing, numbing...starting now, becoming a memory...she had to. Like a summer romance. He'd forget her as soon as his feet touched home.

And then, a month went by, and 10 letters arrived...one for every day on the ship. He found writing easier to do than telling.

"I miss you. I love you. I will tell my parents about you. I'll tell them I want to marry you if you'll have me. I dream too much. Too high. But dreams have no walls. Forgive me that I take such liberties. I know you are too much for me."

Stunned. Like the first day of spring after a long hard winter. Seemed it would never come again. A miracle every time.

"Write to me every day," he pleaded.

She determined she would...and told him in the tenth letter that it was alright to speak to his parents. She waited that long, let him think she was too much for him...better than too little.

At work...9:01...the boss is shouting, "Heads will roll around here! Lateness will not be tolerated!"

As soon as Becky saw the arrow pointing in the corridor to rooms 1600-1609, her room among them, hers, the spirit tightened. Without a job, starve your belly. With a job, starve your pride. Waiting still for the other...to crack the whip and command...even the lover to love... remembered...the evenings with Orlando. The letters still came from Milt...evenly spaced, balanced, the letters straight up in one direc-tion...like his life had been...purposive, direct, linear, stable. Not one higher than the rest, more to the right than the left...not one, sudden, unpredictable, moment...open, clear, honest, legible. Nothing super-fluous...like Becky. Her sudden shifts slanting in all directions, confused, ambivalent, torn, not able to steer a steady course even with a pen.

And Orlando...flourishes, curlicues, unnecessaries, trimmings, flowing free. By comparison, Milt was losing. He sent copies of letters to professional meetings...just to meet her...scheduling them in New York as an excuse to leave home. They were acceptable and above suspicion. Becky's bruised vanity stroked and tended, was glowing...wanting more...but not too much...just enough to make memory and yearning and keep the shadows at bay. Orlando was necessary to keep her from clutching at Milt. Being dignified, rational, limiting her sites, tuned to reality...not wanting and wanting...the infinity of fine tunings to keep a finger on the dike...take the pleasure...keep out the flood of pain. Keep him wanting...not you, Becky. Never you. The crush of pride...the worst...the bottom. Don't go before the fall. It is the fall...when you feel the subtle turn round the corner...weeks between letters, days between calls. Man can't love what he has...only what's someone else's, what he's losing, what he once had.

It was all over when he said, "I can't marry you, Becky."

She decided then, she never would. He erred badly. First, assuming she would want to. Then, making up his mind, instead of waiting for her to make up hers...as if hers was assumed. Tactical errors that were now impossible to repair. Her pride forbade her.

How easily we forget the anguish in the search to find the dream. We make new comparisons and review old fears the dreams made no allowance for. But then, the haze...drunk on being wanted. Every day a coronation...the willing subject pleasing...mocking, teasing, being amusing. Power is new so she wields it ignorantly, clumsily, fearfully. Men read Machiavelli. Women have no such guidelines.

The last letter he was coming in for a conference in a month. She planned for the day. The phone was silent now. The hours came and went. No one is coming through the door. The habits of romance...a drug like liquor and cigarettes, sweets, home cooking and shopping. Needing a replacement. The man's voice...warm, honeyed, loving. Midnight calls when he couldn't sleep, and she couldn't either. Her sleepy voice caressing the sweet power of his...the needing of his... Milt calling now as the days grew nearer...the habits of love...slim pegs on which precariously dangled confidence, pride...even sanity. She stares out a grimy window...the grim yellow glare of lamplight on the gray, lonely street. Other frightened, lonely eyes staring out of dark windows, too...waiting...for calls...for sleep, for the bell to ring...

for a caller, a neighbor...something. The wind moves a naked branch. It knocks on her window. She dreamed later it was a messenger, tapping messages to the lonely, and suddenly there were lights shining in all the windows, excitement in the air as window after window snapped open and people shouting, 'Hello!' and hands reaching out across courtyards. And then, all was quiet. She waited for the sound again...the branch knocking on her window...then the sky blazed with light and she heard a crackling. She rushed to the window. It was hanging limp...waving back and forth...a last goodbye. She waved back. The jagged edge of another branch like an upraised arm menacing the sky. Another cracking, the wind cutting, but it held firm to the last when it gave up the struggle and splintered into a thousand pieces. The next morning, she watched the crowd off to work, being herded into the city's dead underground.

The branch rolled and clung to a curb until a boy picked it up and used it to swat bushes and trunks of trees on the way. Becky was in the habit now of listening...for the telephone...a knock on the window...the tap on the door...something to make a final visit at night and tuck her in...something binding to life...before submitting to nothingness.

She'd read somewhere that you can love two men at once. Two can feed your vanity as well as one...worship, grovel, adore, suffer. I was reading it somewhere.

In memory now and still frightened. Every day the threat of being banished from paradise...stopped by him...stopped by her...the women's game that's lost by lifting the veil...found wanting...naked, alone, and ashamed. Not the edict of God or a betrayal. Nothing as dramatic as that or as world shaking. Just a slight turn somewhere deep inside...a change of mood...unplanned, unforeseen. Impatience, boredom, a nervous edge in a once adoring voice. How long be a dream? He'd stay a month, he said. It would be difficult, but she'd try...perky, exciting, rapacious, bursting, tender, being irresistible. For a person basically lethargic, shy, lazy, it was a tall order...a strain that had to be controlled by time. It could not go on. Just so many performances and this play had to close...to be sweetly remembered in memory. To be scorned in the having or yearned for the losing, bickered with in the present or revered in the past. Becky made a romantic choice. The anguish...watching the magic...drop by drop... fall into a sea of neglect, indifference, boorishness. The curtain always came down when the wedding was over. She was not smart enough. He'd find out and she'd be banished...not for tasting the tree of knowledge but for not tasting enough. Paradise now was hungering and filling oneself on that tree...being God...being Goddess. And you will have no other Gods before and after me. But you will...before and after and all at once. And changing and interchanging...abandoning and coming back to. Only these Gods we pull down from the heavens and plunder the heart, see it breaking, carelessly letting the pieces fall where they may, not even staying to dry the tears...just our own when we've fallen from Grace...and we search for other Gods, and they search for us. Easier, right now being Orlando's Goddess. There wasn't the terror of being found lacking and judged, stupid, ill-informed. To him, she was the Goddess of Knowledge...to Milt, the Goddess of Love.

It was comforting to know that he knew it was a brief interlude. She wanted it that way. Wouldn't have a man with three children and preferred to see him go when the time came. He'd want her more and more. Men begging as if she were a life giver. Becky liked it that way. She preferred being Cathy to Heathcliff...never Anna Karenina or Madame Bovary. And she liked to bring men down from their podiums and lecterns and spotlights to their knees adoring her, being playthings, amusements, tormented as her whim dictated. She liked power over the powerful. Needing to be courted and terrified. Needing to run and hide and terrified, too. Torn between fear of needing and fear of loneliness. The desperate beating of bird's wings...wanting to fly and not being able to leave the ground...not trusting man yet needing him. Minutes before he comes the frantic questions in her mind, beating at the bars like a caged, frenzied animal throwing itself again and again at the same place unbending...

ungiving...like Becky's fear of love turning...yet searching it again and again. She'd turn from it herself. But not him. He mustn't turn. From marriage, yes...love no. He must have changed his mind already. Come to tell her it's all over. must be sensible. Was nice while it lasted. Prepared, defended, a sweet calm masking the panic, she flings open the door. He stands smiling benignly, adoring, large innocent warm eyes...the look of a man besotted with pleasure at the sight of his newborn baby in his wife's arms...innocent awe of a heavenly miracle...protective nurturing of the weak and helpless...not being able to move or talk...just stand mute, looking at each other...like gazing at the sun...too bright...too glaring. Then, his arms around her...and hers around him hugging hard. And in the deep professional voice that folded round her.

He said, "I love you, Becky."

She hid her surprise by hugging him harder...he never knew she doubted and feared. Said he loved her strength and confidence. Becky just needed a cue to play the part. This one was easy. Poppa had prepared her. Emma...the revolutionary, the Anarchist...the first Emma in her life before Bovary...Poppa's Emma...Goldman.

Chapter One Hundred Five

It was like meeting yourself anew every day and not believing... the self-suspended and a blank other...hearing and seeing a stranger in a strange land...watching a drama unfolding of which you are not a part...yet...are a part...the world given...we receive...tasting, touching, gazing...taking...taking...taking...and giving, too...tending the sick and helpless...but in passion suffering... we stand stiff...like frightened animals in a strange jungle...watching, listening...wary even of the crack of a twig. She watched and listened in wonder and awe as his words flowed and flowed...caressing... stroking...love words...poetry words...of love and yearning and finding...and aching still. After they'd loved he had a fleeing image of a white horse, pure and swift with large wings, high in the air.

"Flying Becky, you, and me, on that horse. And all the world's eyes looking up and seeing and saying, 'Look!' Oh my god, Becky, what am I to do?! I want you to be my wife! How can I leave Lenore and my children?!"

Desperate, anguished...like a man in a dark tomb scratching, digging, strangling or breath. Becky numb with shock...searching for and finding and not believing.

A flashback.

Rosele had turned from the warmth of Basha and opened the door to a dark, vast, desolate loneliness. The village was asleep. Rosele's huddled little figure moved hurriedly on an empty stage. She looked to the moon to guide her. At night and alone, she was frightened, though she knew every little path and stream, the hills, the forks in the road. She found little comfort in chiding herself. Don't be a fool. The devil is too busy to bother with me yet. Did she think he had nothing else to do but look for her on the edge of Batyevka, on a dark night? There were more important people he could find more easily. She was too small for him to bother with and too insignificant. But still she trembled. Roselle often talked with the Devil. It was her secret. He had already come into her life once. She didn't think he'd come again for a long time. Roselle had paid for her sins long before she knew she had any. She tried hard to be as good as she could, so she could remind him from time to time that he had no claim on her.

Little Roselle, they called her. She was so tiny. At age three, she was orphaned, when the Cossacks came yelping through the town with blood curdling screams, swinging their whips and sabers. Everyone went hiding under the bed. They had no trouble finding her parents, her brothers, and sisters, but she was so tiny, she was overlooked. When the quiet descended again, she peeked out cautiously, a piercing howl exploded from her poor body as she fled out the door and into the street, leaving a trail of blood behind her.

Back to the present.

A voice begs, urges, insists...

"Take my hand, take it...take it. For God's sake, my sake, your sake!"

"No, thank you."

It will never move, that hand and heart and tongue. Spring will never come in. The ground is frozen hard, numbed with too many winters...shame, hurt, fear...and it glazed over.

Painted vivid colors on a blank screen and believed when the show was on because the audience wanted to...and Milt wanted to...

asking and answering his own questions, 'You do love me. You would marry me if...' Her silence was... 'Yes.' And strangely, he pained, suffered, anguished...but didn't feel. His hands, mouth, arms, body... wooden. Just the heart...like a lone star in a black heaven, and the tongue circling her round and round with words of pain and love. The God became a clumsy child and underneath her knowing, power, disenchantment, contempt. Taking him one night as he came through the door...pretending the wanting...lusting. And his sweet, naïve believing...his happiness brimming. Unwanted...but he could still want and feel wanted. A man can. Becky couldn't. The waters had closed over.

'I love you loving me...but I don't love you.'

And not telling because he won't believe, won't hear, and because she needs him loving her. Learning status, respect...nothing... compared to the strength of myth. Will Orlando, too, feel nothing? If he did, it would be her fault. With Milt, it was his fault. Latins knew.

The vanity of men to make their women idols...goddesses...to rob the heavens and take them for themselves...then to fear being dethroned, themselves. And remember, Becky, when the Gods were bored, they discarded handily and found another. Becky lived in terror of being found boring. She was a jester, clown, read paragraphs from books, poems, played music, danced, amused, entranced, and watched the calendar counting days. Her repertoire was thinning.

"No one would believe," he said, "a whole month together...no friends...just two of us and so exciting. I could go on like this forever."

She knew better. It couldn't go on like this forever. Divorce his wife, marry her, and love and live again...the gray pallor of routine, stultifying habit...fatigue and complaining...a flat, inactive, unruffled present. And the children...hurt, scowling, accusing. The guilt, Becky, watching it stab and clutch at him...the Hasidic finger grown big and bludgeoning now, whipping a sinning son, his back bent under the lash, beating himself, too now, arguing his case like an old Talmudist...like he taught his classes, now...weighing and balancing... life lived...on the one hand. Not lived...on the other. Was there an argument? There was! The little boy with side curls studying and being tyrannized by an exacting father who never even thought to be tempted to step over the line.

"A mortgaged personality is what I am," Milt derided himself, "old religionists scourging themselves for God. Old Socialists scourging themselves for Man. A new fight looming now for love and happiness. No equipment, preparation, weapons...innocents floundering...wide-eyed and gullible...like a child entering a new classroom for the first time and no one to tell him, 'Take off your hat, sit down, take out your pencil, fold your hands. Behave.'"

He didn't know how to behave...to her...to his wife and children.

"I'm a teacher and I don't know. The new scribes...Freud and Fromm...free love...free...free...free. The circle turns. Moses comes down from the mountain and finds the Golden Calf worshiped once again. Tantalus...with a Jewish conscience. The Jew in a titanic struggle with the Mosaic Law. And Becky choosing between hurts. The Lith commandment, 'Thou shalt not hurt.' Who will hurt the least? Orlando won. Still, she will give him everything. He will live in her shadow...not she in his. With Milt, she pictured being hostess at dinner and conversation later...her head nodding, agreeing, listening mostly...to Milt. How can I be quiet now? Needing to be the center... provoke...contend...be Emma Goldman...without a revolution. And never telling of hurt. Silent...keeping everything to herself...till last night. Becky was relieved. Thirty days and nights she had kept him amused.

Leben Kunstler, he called her.

"An artist in living, no one would ever believe," he said, "no friends, no invitations. What would happen after?"

Becky was silent. Another black fear buried. She was looking at him from a distance now...as if he was mad...fevered.

An illness that will pass. And, after the wedding, when the clouds lifted, seeing and knowing for the first time...and turning away...rejecting, "What have I done?!"

And the children turned, "What have you done?! No match for

the Jewish conscience...home and needing...poised against passion, happiness on earth. The mortgage must be paid. 'Don't pay the price, Miltie, because I can't.'

"Becky is a good girl, Mrs. Bromsky."

And now, three savaged children...sulking, condemning, hating. Desire bending his will, and he is ending hers...but both characters standing rigid and inflexible...wanting praise still...for being good. Good is not doing what is forbidden...as well. Give in...release...but don't break the family.

"No practice, Milt, dividing yourself. Hurled into sophistication from naivete without preparation and not knowing how to slip and slide, manage and maneuver the passions, so everything stays in place...I love you," meaning one love, one you, one I.

He told how he'd rock his son Johnathan to sleep until his arm was tired. One of us. A tab of jealousy. He talked of Christmas.

"A lonely time for me. I hate it. She left me alone when we were courting...every Christmas. Never explained why. But I knew. She was seeing him. Every Christmas I'll see you, Becky," and later he said, "if we marry, Becky, I'll have to go home every holiday."

'And I'll be alone.'

Silent, fearful, touching of the future.

"The children, Becky. You know how it is. I miss them."

'I'd rather you missed me.'

"You understand how it is. I have to go home. They need me."

Weak helpless them, and the strong independent him. The rock on which they're all leaning. If it goes sliding down the mountain, 'I'm leaving too, Miltie.' Letters from Orlando every day with proposals. Silence.

"I'm going to Italy to marry him."

"I understand Becky."

And when his suitcase was packed, the bare room was stripped...even of memories...just like it was in the beginning. He fled out the door, like he always did and an hour later, a phone call.

Milt...a desperate voice demanding, "Don't marry him! Promise me!"

"I promise."

"Don't go!"

"I won't."

"Wait for me."

"I will."

She hung up thinking, 'Proof...he wants me when he's losing me. If I stay, I will lose him. Alone here in a furnished room, while he struggles to make peace with them and himself...or marry him and see him turn. With Orlando...no titanic struggle...splitting the heavens, pursuing stars, and opening his hand and finding it empty...a flicker of disappointment, annoyance...the ordinaries...degradation to her of, 'Hang up my coat, sew a button, clean the place, will you change a sheet,' and 'what's for supper?' just one and the love bubble bursting.'

Dulled, leveled, being a wife. She felt important being the other woman. A wife whom he didn't love...preferring her whom he did. Forbidden, she was loved even more. As the wife provoked guilt, he resented her. She stroked the fire even more, being an obstacle. He was crazed and she was used to his being that way. The simple order of life would mean she was no longer loved. That was not bearable... Milt coming in the door and saying, 'I'm tired.' Gone...the yearning pain...the expectation...the bursting pleasure.

"Life is never boring with you," he quoted his wife as saying. She'd never known this kind of excitement with him. Nothing to compare or remember.

"She helped me with my book," he said.

That clinched it. 'Smarter than me,' Becky thought, 'I'm leaving.'

Chapter One Hundred Six

A week later, struggling down the stairs with her suitcase, having discontinued the phone service from 1pm and it was almost that now, and her ship ticket in hand, she was on her way, when the phone rang. She knew it was Milt. He'd be insisting again. It was too late to find out. She was glad of that. The phone stopped ringing. Her life in that room was over. And another memory.

Milt testing, "My wife said you want to marry me because of who I am."

'How dare he! Never! Never! The ultimate humbling...that test. Not trusting...not knowing me. And putting me in a secondary position! She remembered saying she could have had others, equal or higher. He'd seen that at the convention, hadn't he? But it was a weak defense. That's what everyone would think.'

Becky lumped with ordinary women. She'd show them. He and his wife. A female Cyrano...going out with her white plume. Of the flood of words...thousands whispered across tables...or holding hands in the streets...or whispered at night on pillows...only a few remained...the frightening ones, carrying the message, clear and burning, 'Don't marry him!'

'Without Momma, Poppa, or God to make our decisions, we clutch to a few words, listen to fears, pride, humiliation, a few images, listing happy and unhappy and gambling where we think we have the least to lose. Orlando...I'll have him forever. He'll owe me. Milt...I'll owe him. And always too lazy. It has to keep itself. With Milt, she would have to work at it. With Orlando, it just be...without consciousness of time...worry...masking...hiding...under all the moments. Spontaneity, joy, ecstasy, bubbling...all battling against the pull downwards...hers that she knows of and his that she doesn't. She often wondered how the lady who was exchanged for a throne lived the life of a lover. Becky couldn't imagine. What would happen to them if love dies?'

On the ship she wrote Milt every day and yearned...and had a shipboard romance with Enzo Guarducci...a married man with three children who couldn't speak a word of English and all they could do was make motions to each other. She was enchanted when he removed his elbow from the dinner table, so she could rest hers, putting his elbow on and off until she understood. He pleaded for a kiss on the deck in the moonlight. She refused, but looked smitten, anyhow. The wife and children were waiting tearfully at the deck to greet him, and he eagerly introduced Becky. She was stunned, embarrassed, clumsy, managed a faint smile, nodded her head, and fled. Orlando was waiting, too. A shining laugh and body, bowing up and down gracefully, hiding embarrassment. Happiness, joy, carefree... refreshing...after all that Jewish rage, morbidity, sadness...a titanic struggling with conscience.

Then, sitting on a park bench at night, he proposed marriage, pleading, "I don't want to be alone."

She'd connived and tricked...made him used to a life at home with the same woman...same room...same bed. She knew it would become a habit he couldn't break...a new kind of loneliness...losing all that. He said he would go to school, find a cure for disease and she believed. Saving a life...helping mankind...immortality!

And drawing both men in was her playing all calm, all accepting, all giving, non-demanding mother. More dangerous than the witch woman or the virgin...the woman who knows our weaknesses and accepts them mercifully, compassionately...or turns them into strengths...so we delude ourselves into needing her to cling to our delusions as she needs ours to cling to hers.

The wedding cost 25 dollars and his sister bought the ring. His father served the meal in his restaurant and a poem to the bride was readied by an old man. Orlando's father bought the bride a gift, a small gold pin with two flowers that meant 'faithful forever.' Orlando didn't have the money for a gift. His father looked like a gentry: tall, handsome, graceful, warm, mild mannered. He shopped, cooked, and waited on Becky like a queen, putting the plate down in front of her with a flourish, a beaming smile as he served Becky first.

Mother, primitive, gross, hard tongue, but also serving Becky, washing, cooking, pressing...even her stockings. Becky was 'someone' being American...just having been to college...didn't matter which one. His father was broken hearted when Orlando left school, now, he was proud. But another desperate need. Becky...wanting so much to help. He was going to lose his home. Swindled by his son in law. Couldn't pay the mortgage. Becky would provide. There were six enormous rooms. Becky's at the very end and two boarders in-between on the way to the bathroom. She tiptoed at night, not to wake them.

The gay laughing, carefree Italian...another gone awry...punctured...when she met his friends. Piero...his mother, a frail, subservient woman, who was a drug addict. His father, a tyrant.

The apartment, huge and gloomy, in the center of town, the home of a wealthy man. His son, away at school in Florence, had been unable to graduate for 10 years. He couldn't pass his orals. The boy lived in a drafty little room with no heat, his father so stingy, he was always threatening to discontinue paying the rent. Viero, married to a beauty, invited Becky and Orlando to dinner. Servants, candles, a plate for everything, damask and silk and soft carpets. After dinner, Orlando and he had a private conversation in the car going home which she could not understand. Then, Orlando consulted her proudly.

'That's his love for me, too,' she thought, 'status.' And then philosophized with the usual summing up of 'that's life.' She to him...what an irony...money and status. She realized now she was buying him, but...what else could she really do. She had nothing else really. Big fish in a small pond. Playing that game, now. She'd found a small pond. Becky advising, and Orlando proudly translating. Sad faced young man, never smiling. Becky stunned to hear he never loved his wife, had to marry her, and made her pregnant. He didn't say, but Becky knew. He loved another. Becky said in time he'd love...wife and child...though she knew she lied...but they both believed her.

Enzo, slim, high cheekbones, sensuous, sensitive face, sensuous body, lithe like a ballet dancer. He was an artist who worked as a civil servant. He was a communist who had several breakdowns. Worked for the cause with such dedication, he developed TB. A true idealist, not a scholar, never heard of Trotsky, a dreamer. 'True freedom,' Becky thought, 'a communist in government!'

He was married to a short, homely woman, whose parents were so strict, he had to court her by mail. She always looked unhappy. He was a womanizer...even had one or two serious affairs. Becky wondered how he came to marry such a homely girl. Orlando wondered, too, but never dared ask. But it was the type who needed a secure love...always waited while he dallied then returned home... grateful to have him.

Orlando's sister, after a 13-year engagement, married a man who became a wife beater, screaming in the house all the time, and had two children who screamed too, every time Becky entered their house, reinforcing her determination not to have children. 'Didn't

Orlando mind the ruckus?' The answer was chilling, he didn't. On the contrary, he took pleasure in the wild, noisy stomping while Becky crazed and hating stood helplessly by. Becky delegated the children's problem to time. Wouldn't think about it. Couldn't.

Another friend, Fusco, the plumber. A girl he loved dropped him after she saw him walking through the main street carrying a toilet... though handsome, manly, black eyes and hair, warm, spontaneous. The women didn't want him. More particular than Becky. Can you imagine?!

Cesare...rich, handsome, married a rich Dutch girl. He was a member of Parliament, now living in Rome. In America, he was a scorned lover. Threatened to jump off a building and was talked out of suicide by the desperate pleas of friends. Here, he talks to his wife, like the jaded Italians, men in an Italian movie, 'I'll be home late tonight,' he says. The desperation of the betrayed woman now turned to weary scorn on his wife's face. Her head bowed, ashamed.

'How late will you be?'

'Don't know.'

She had told Becky that she attended Columbia when she was in New York, loved the city and the theater. Rome, in comparison, was empty and boring. Becky tried to impress, criticizing the city, praising Rome, "That's ridiculous," she said, cutting.

Becky hurt...silenced...unwittingly offered herself as a scapegoat and was accepted and used. A face full of innocent trust...slapped, eager to please...slapped...wanting praise...slapped...friendship... slapped...approval...slapped...slapped...slapped. It took years for Becky to realize women were jealous of her. Slapped by Becky, she slapped back. She was stocky and homely...the Dutch girl and who can accept superiority without complaining. The users...the needers...deferred. And the Italians...part of their deception and manipulation...deferring. Becky didn't know. She lapped it up. Loved it.

Meanwhile, Milt's letters in Genoa, Paris. Not picked up. She didn't even know they were there. His stories frightened her, too. The academic community...adultery...gluttony...passion for football. Another myth exploded. No happiness anywhere?

To Venice on their honeymoon Becky was paying. They saw a movie 'Cabiria's Night,' the story of an exploited prostitute. He was very sad when he left the movie.

When they returned to the hotel, he said, "I'm a procurer, like the one in the picture. My brother-in-law calls me one because I'm taking money from you."

Becky was shocked.

"Makes no difference where the money comes from. We each do whatever we can."

She believed before the movement made it acceptable. Becky, her mother, her grandmother did women's lib all by themselves. They had to. Momma and Grandma slaves at home and the marketplace... like today. But Becky decided she would be a slave in the market-place, but at home, freedom, and dignity. That was important.

At night, they walked the streets with his friends, sat in cafes.

"What do you talk about every night?" she asked him.

"The same thing," he said. and underneath the respect...Becky shrinking...the fat, little rejected girl...daughter of a domestic and a shoemaker who shrank to laborer. No amount of polishing could clean out that 'damned spot.' She fell back to the same place time and time again...and curled herself into a ball...like an old photo that's been hidden and rolled for too long. It springs and bends no matter how hard we pull and push. By habit, shriveling, shrinking...running towards the dark at the end of the tunnel. Only rescuing someone else lifted a little for a brief time. Being dependent on a superior...like a mother to a child. That's why people have children...God and Goddess for a little while. Becky started with the adult child...but child he was...and Man...couldn't do without her. She was the center of his life, he said. Becky needed to be that important. Not behind careers...children. No one more jealous...possessive...than Becky.

Images flooding...Orlando's father when he had gone shopping and bought a chicken for lunch to please her. Pulling it triumphant out of the bag with feathers still on it. And later, around the table, the stability and order she never had, the family feeling of home...she never had.

And in Paris, visiting her uncle. He had tickets for the Opera Comique. Orlando insisted on eating first, so they missed the ballet. How her uncle sneered at his shallow values. And how she burned with humiliation.

The new job was waiting for her in New Hampshire. A party at the house of Dr. Kraus, who obtained the job for her. The lady boss chided her, calling her Kraus's divorcee, and threatening to work her hard, take it out of her hide. She worked for her as a psychology intern. The next day, fleeing back to New York to ignominious slavery again and grateful for it. 'The workhorse of the department.' The tradition of service to continue, Momma a domestic and Becky a civil one.

And finally, Orlando, looking down on himself and whispering, "Kiss it, love it."

He had a name he called it, Giuseppe, and laughed. She kissed his body all over, the best she thought how and then back to his mouth. He turned away.

In the dark, she heard him say, "Giuseppe is not happy. You've hurt him."

And he surrounded her with 'I love you,' and car amia, Bella, Bellissima, the words of love and the songs of love. At a dance the friends dance with her in turn like a princess at the ball, and he held her close, the descent was swift. She went from an adored, unattainable princess on the dance floor to a woman performing sexual exercises at home...that's how it felt.

'It's my fault,' she thought. She had no feelings. The night before she left to go back to America, she was devastated. She didn't know how to kiss, touch, and love him. Then he described someone in the past who did know how...that was his power over her. She could not please him. Didn't know how. She was sympathetic to his weakness. He was scornful of hers. But when he kissed her hand again and again, waited on her, served her, looked long and sad into her eyes, and then waved to her until the last minute she was enchanted again. In that dingy room in a seedy hotel in New York when he said, 'te amo, cara bambina.'

It didn't matter then and nothing else mattered now. He was beautiful. He would join her in America in six months after he got his visa. She left in a haze. She would rescue him and his parents. He'd be hers forever. Never mind that he played slot machines every night. She thought that was because he hadn't developed himself and he liked childish fun. She needed that after Irving's leaden mobility every moment. Whatever he did was charming. This was the age of the Italians. Spontaneity, childishness, naturalness, anti-intellectually. Becky was following fashion and didn't know it. When she arrived in New Hampshire, a call from Milt.

"Did you marry him?!"

"Yes."

"Did you receive my mail?"

"No."

"Wrote to you all over Europe! I'm leaving my wife! You must come!"

"I'll break your heart."

"You must come!"

No longer in command of her will, she fled to Michigan. He met her at the airport, took her to an apartment he'd secured for her. Tried to love her and couldn't. He was breaking down. Guilt. Desperate to keep Becky, he'd left his wife. Becky knew now, he had to go back, so she sent him home and found herself alone once again, without a job, a husband, or a friend.

"Forgive me, Becky," he pleaded.

And she did...because he loved her and was suffering for the not me. Be kind to evil and to love...just seeing the need to have. The world's oldest marketplace...desiring and discarding. Women knew it all the time...the lust for possession...the hungering for the breast...the exile of man hungering for a woman. The eternal Tantalus. If the

Gods, for one moment flooded him with the sweet juices. Temptation in his grasp, let him drink until he succumbed to it's sweetness and looked at it with numb, sated eyes, taking the few remaining in his hand and flinging them as far as he could see, and when they splintered in purple clouds anguished, beckoning, he doesn't even bother to look up.

Chapter One Hundred Seven

Milt said she was strong and independent...not like his wife. She secretly loved those comparisons...as he did... her comparisons with Irving. Not like Irving...this...not like Irving...that. Comparisons told her what to be like. She listened for clues...she would be whatever the wife wasn't. The list of fears, so long, so deep, Becky lost sight and sound of them...so many...so glaring...they blinded and numbed...and pretended they weren't there until Becky believed them gone...except for the tremble...the panic that shook her now and then...startling and unnerving like a sudden noise in the dark...clutching the guilt to her chest and listening...then a sudden bravado...the jump into the dark...the search...the pursuit... Becky feared phones, interviews, bosses...the job. She made the call and left the same day. They needed an intern now.

It was the age of permissiveness...the new tyrants. Let them do what they want...children...animals. Those who could not do what they want...workers, the poor, and parents...the new underclass.

Mr. Silver, head psychologist, lived in an assembly line spirit level...two boxy rooms split by four-by-four stairs and six boxes above. Bare furniture in the living room except for a chair where the little girls were hanging from the bottom, so as not to impede the jumping, racing, screaming. When bis wife opened the door, Mr. Silver was on all fours, bring ridden like a horse by the youngest who was marching him smartly...giddy-yapping and slapping him fore and aft and pulling on his tie from the back of his neck...jerking him to the right, to the left, and digging his heels in when the mood came upon him to knock his father with both heels as hard as he could.

Mr. Silver smiled, proud that he was such a good father...and motioned Becky to the chair...the circles of metal springs bulging...the creak of Becky as she sat down...and squeaking until she settled herself in. Then sitting very still, too embarrassed to be squeaking on.

He was a short, fat man, round all over, his bald cheeks in a perfect circle, all belly hanging from hip to chest.

The child clambered down and fled past Becky into the kitchen... then...a whining tantrum...the foot slamming into the floor, the refrigerator door shut with a bang.

"Ma! No Flunkies!"

Becky listened for an answer...but there was none. Then again... an angry "No Flunkies!"

And the screen door squeaking open hanging shut with such force, Becky shuddered...then heard the boy calling, "Hey Joe, wanna play?"

Then Mr. Silver got up, slapped his hand on his trousers, and extended a hand to Becky, "You see, we run a free house here," and he sat down on a wooden chair he took from the kitchen that needed tightening.

He rocked back and forth in it, Becky afraid he would fall. Then Mrs. Silver hurriedly put on her coat, "Be right back!"

More creaking and banging of the screen door and Mr. Silver turning to her now, "Tell me about yourself."

She told him...the resume self...the 'good in print' self.

"And how are you related to Milton?"

A content calm on his face like a well-fed drowsy baby...a face that never responded to life...like a Buddha watching...but untouched.

Mrs. Silver returns, flinging her coat on a kitchen chair with such force, it falls over. She leaves it there. Later, struggling with a heavy tray she returns, "Coffee?"

Becky nods.

"And have a Flinkie. Chocolate. They're very good. Just came in from the bakery. Take one," and hands it to her.

Mrs. Silver forgot to get napkins at the store. Becky takes a bite... not asking...so she won't embarrass her. Mr. Silver takes three...also takes a bite. Now, Becky and he have crumbs on their faces. He doesn't mind. Becky stands the feel of them on then on her face...and rolls the tip of her tongue around, but she can't reach and stretches the point of it until it aches, but there are still a few sticking... stubborn.

"You'll start tomorrow," he says.

Becky trembling...like she always does when she wants something so hard and...gets it. He shakes her hand. The interview is over. Mrs. Silver joins them, gulping coffee and a 'flinkie' wipes her mouth with an apron and shakes Becky's hand, saying how nice it was to meet her. When she is out of the door, she wipes her mouth with her sleeve when no one's looking. And repeatedly in her head, 'I have a job!' The happiness brimming...and the fear...too. 'Can I do it? The fear, as always...to have...and not to have. Dance to your own tune.' Becky dancing...to the beat of circumstances. Orlando tugging at her with, 'I miss you' letters...the poetry, the lift, the smile, the gait, the ark magic in his face...and Milt...weekends in the motel room...the pull of his suffering and pained happiness...the boyish trust...his looking up with naked eyes to one who couldn't bear to be adored... frightening to be a goddess...frightening not to. The calm, all understanding earth mother...raping, desiring...loving...lusting, child trust, innocent, adoring goddess. When she once lamented, she wasn't intelligent enough, he didn't need a debater.

"I can talk to my friends."

He was in no comparison with Irving and how much comparison with Orlando? How much did the comparisons matter after all?

Milt insisting, "You're not going back to him. You're mine!" And then, "But how can I leave a helpless woman with three children?"

'Amazing,' she thought, 'once a leader of a communist cell and now...helpless? Impossible to break the tie of helpless and helper. The need they have for each other...the guilt when the helpless cord pulls too tight...when the helpless in the helper reaches for his helper...and is drowning in a bigger sea. She feels him pulling away and clutches harder begging...and the rescuer has to choose...her or me...the rescuer now drowning, too.'

"Help me, Becky," and Becky, unable.

"Come with me."

"I can't."

"Don't come with me."

"I can't."

"Guilty about her, the children and you, Becky."

The woman and children free from choice and decision, the lonely anguish of making a terrible decision and not making it. Love words, to promise words, to strength words, and brave ones.

The weekend that begins with, "I'll leave her," and ends with, "I can't."

And then, "the revelations...deranged sisters, a tyrannical, Hasidic father, a non-being mother...and running away from them all at a tender age. Becky trying to picture the little boy with curls and felt her enchantment curling at the edges, shrinking. The man was not a God, now...a Prince, a Heathcliff...just a little boy with large, blue tortured eyes that look numb on the world and think and reason the pain away in Talmud classes; still now weighing the questions in both hands, needing answers. It didn't matter. If you didn't find one, you find another equation. But not this time. The answer, Becky. I must have one, now...still two hands."

Becky expected the ever-turning circle. That didn't matter. Keeping him enchanting those two days. That mattered. He feared losing her...all of life...fear. When that goes, love goes. That's why there is no love in marriage...the fear gone. No love in a lover...the fear gone. Fear...and you run from love. No fear...love runs. Becky chose running.

More revelations. His friends...compulsive eaters, promiscuous wives, one...a beauty who scarred her face...couldn't take the guilt anymore. A Jewish goddess who couldn't play Circe...no matter how much Freud and Kings approved. It was hard now to repair the conscience like a new hemline. It wouldn't give. There was no tradition of lovers and mistresses to give...only romance and weddings and doing one's duty. Becky wanting to be a mistress...suspend time...the suffering of passionate love and being unattainable always.

"But I can't take the pain anymore, Becky."

And Becky thinking, 'Take it! There is nothing on the other side! How you worship the word faith, in, of all things me?! Only God can handle being God. And He lost believers. So how can man or woman...the years fell away as he came close...the detached, fumbling child...and she played 'let's pretend.' And when he left, the daily letters...not a day filled with him now. And not tanking on the day of decision. Where does one point to oneself? What does one do? A life outside life...living between lover and love letters. Where else was she loved...wanted...important! Outside of life. But just for a moment. It had not permanence. It was like the pain of performing, the fear, the terrifying anticipation...for the moment of applause. Only as good as your last concert, play, book. Only as good as your last weekend. The sudden turn, the abrupt end...expecting that each week, like fragile things do.'

That's how she saw love...momentary, sleight of hand...disappearing...like magic does...and illusion. And more revelations. Friends in academe who were obsessed with football. A male friend of his visited every night to talk with his wife and a black lover in the past of whom she still dreamed. She never wanted to go to conventions with him. Now she did. But he, no longer interested. And one night, saying 'Becky,' in his sleep. She wouldn't want to be in his wife's place. It was truly a marriage in her mind...numb, indifferent...guilt, criticism, and friction endure...not love. At the first sign of all those permanents, it shrivels, hides and the dying begins.

The strange characters at work...a lesbian director, late middle age who had two treatments for the patients...lobotomy or shock therapy. The poor soul was wheeled in to a room full of 'ists,' psychologists, psychiatrists for observation...and after then wheeled out, at which point a census was taken and around the room each responded, 'lobotomy, lobotomy, lobotomy,' or 'shock therapy' another round robin across the room. The patient waiting in the hall for a sea of expert opinions to add to their torment to a brain that knew too much of pain already. It broke through the barriers and sent off their thin little protectors crashing in air in pieces...then find where they'd fallen and put them all together with less care than squeezing a ship into a bottle. Shock it all back together again or cut the frayed edges but altogether.

Stucker...the psychologist with a tic criticizing, "You talk with your hands," his face arrogant with professional disapproval.

And Becky countering with, "I'll give up anything to be a credit to my profession, but not myself."

The Jew who quoted Freud had become him, the analysis waiting for the patient before he walked in.

And the morning, Stucker saying, "You know, Becky, I attended a party last night and found myself talking like you."

And Becky countering with, "Of course, you're a chameleon. Heaven knows who you'll be tomorrow."

And Mr. Stern...a Brooklyn Jew who spoke with a Southern accent.

And Dr. Jones with huge pictures of his girlfriend all over his bathroom and Dr. Kargas, a Hungarian psychiatrist who said, "It's good there are so many sick people. We can make a living."

And Becky countering, "Imagine a world without them, all healthy, normal and me in relief. I'd prefer that. And suppose you became one of them, would it please your tortured soul to be giving them a living? If it ever happens, I hope you don't come across someone like you."

And the test...Becky giving her opinion of a patient's problem with others giving theirs...stiff mouthed females competing with her diagnosis...love never mentioned by any one of them...just Freudian symbols mechanically interpreted. A picture of a young girl it is seen leaning against a post...and interpretations are exchanged of this picture drawn by a patient.

Becky interpretation...the girl is job hunting, daydreaming, escaping to the movies...Stucker screaming, "You're wrong and took a phrase from Freud to prove he is 'right.'"

The following morning, Becky's first patient, a young girl who tried to hurt herself. Becky is interviewing Mr. Stern saying, "I never saw an interview that wonderful with an adolescent girl."

For the first time, Becky making breakfast for her and Milt explaining, "I can't cook."

An authoritarian dictates in his voice for the first time, "You'll learn."

It cut the cord. The following Monday, she resigned, packed and fled...leaving the naked face of pain...the heavy sadness of his guilt the future of dead, domestic days, failing from the pedestal and submitting...from Goddess women to drudge woman, panic to please woman, to mother woman...regretting, the magic dying, a frenzied tossing and gnashing and then...the crush of admitting, "We, too, unloved, rejected, glad you're going, packing of suitcases, parting in shame...unwanted. Better to leave...wanted...missed, yearned for, searched, suffering, loving, heart aching, hands reaching out and not finding. Not to be found lacking, imperfect, untidy, boring, usual. Not to be found. To remain a memory, that's why we hurt the one we love...so we know they love us...still...the ache...anguish...that's love. But the burden is too heavy for her to carry, so she throws it back into memory. And chose the one she could bear to lose, the lesser love...an inferior...would look up to her...always...true freedom...each doing what they do best."

She would work and send him to school. He would cook. She would avoid children on this pretext as long as she could. The diploma would make her acceptable.

With superiors, every day, the fear...needing to prove oneself once again and again. How much reading, chattering, intelligent listening...and remaining spirit... for how long...not even a noisy yawn interfering with the poetic, spiritual air. Gian was spirit and flesh. The body was not new to an old culture that was still primitive and didn't have to struggle through the Talmud, the Ten Commandments, Freud. They had been set aside for centuries when necessary or inconvenient. The People of the Book didn't know how or which book to follow...so they followed a bit of each and the books warred with each other savagely in the deep of the heart and the twists and turns, accommodations and determinations, games and considerations of the mind.

And it all came to a head in a simple sentence...the fates battering Becky back to the poor humble nothingness from which she came... the poorest girl on the block, And married, to have, to hold, to sacrifice...to be afraid of mind or body, she chose body even to peek at those books that demystified and despiritualized, deformed and dehumanized, degraded. It would come from mind...like it was supposed to...the knowing.

And like the mind, too...the feeling of knowing nothing and will never know. Too scarring...and the other scarring, too. But still, the knowing Goddess, the all feeling Venus...the faith...with ones...it will go, and with the others it never will. Such is the power of the helpless, the inferior and the dependent. And unique, the only woman with a man from Siena. Fear makes unreason and the reason too.

People calling Momma dumb... and turning to me. Becky never recovered. Momma was proud, but Becky was ashamed of her. Poppa always said, "What does she know?" And she agreed, proud that he knew. Mann turns a woman into that... being judged. Judging the mind... judging the cooking. Demanding satisfaction. Becky couldn't... wouldn't. And something else, too. Pursuing the unreal...

the dream...the fancy in her head. And when her fancy was joined by another, she fled, Becky could only dream alone.

It was raining the night she met Gian at the airport. Like nothing intervened the callousness with which the secret lay...close, quiet another life...closed. He looked so small, a gray flat rain-hat on his head shrinking him even more. The gray raincoat tied tight around his slim body too long for him, a trace of repulsion and shame quickly pressed down deep like it never was. He was struggling with two massive suitcases. She waited until he turned and saw her. He quickly dropped them, and the brilliant, glowing smile spread on his face, sparkling the light in her eyes, quickening the heart. They were strangers... unfamiliar ones... not the familiar strangers they've seen before.

"Cara Bella!" He embraced her, the sensuous face, exciting, touching, but awkwardness and fear now, too.

'Momma, you weren't afraid. Why am I? When did men and women get so afraid of each other you weren't, and Aunt Rose and Cousin Leah. But I am. And men chase after me and love me and adore me and I am prettier and smarter, so why am I so afraid and feel uglier and dumber. The church says give me the child the first five years and I have him forever. And Mr. Freud says, inferiority and shame, too, is that the overwhelming question now what to do with humanity: there are women who create to destroy and women who create from the destruction of other women?'

Becky was one of those, the explorer who found the treasure under the mud and debris, and sculpted, molded, a Pygmalion to a male... subservient, and fearing her creation... but less than if he was ready-made... a light unto himself, and she is sitting in his reflection. Becky was not a reflector. On the stage, the fear gone, and the exhibitionism takes over. The light shines on her, and he is lost in the darkness with the others. At home, when he gets her alone... berating, accusing, sulking, pain talk those hurts...but Gian would not. He would let her have centerstage and watch in the darkness proud of his applause joining the others. They talked about ordinary things. He had a friend who reserved a room in a lady's house for them. Tonight, they ate at home in the room on a hot plate. He loved without suffering, gloom, guilt, and the assault of heavy, dark tones, ponderous, dark shadows, on a river of words. His body, frail and thin. In her strong, powerful hold, he seemed a small boy, his voice, thin, joy, and laughter, wanting to break through under the seriousness of love, but he seemed in himself, tune to his own pleasure, not with her, and still, the illusion clung. Even with him at a distance, but she blamed herself and not him. With Milt, she blamed him. Looking forward to no demands, relaxing in front of TV... The demands coming from her... Not another. No great questions, passions, or loves.

Life was easier when he jumped out of bed with a light spring, announcing, "We have to eat."

He left her in bed with a 'Cara' and went to the market, returning with a cooked chicken in a can and a new pot, paper, plates, and plastic spoons. And it was such fun, the first meal was like 'it happened one night.' Only she didn't have a millionaire mansion to return to. The movies had taught her poverty was fun and ignominy and discomfort was fun, and she was having a grand time not being rich and bored, cold, and nasty and critical, and scornful, and betrayed like the rich are. Becky was deliriously happy. She didn't know any better... comparing life with Irving... with Milt...this was bliss.

Chapter One Hundred Eight

Trying desperately to have fun when she didn't know how... trying to be one of the gang...to belong...still trying...not to be so serious...another mandate...freedom. Shunted hither and yon by mandates...and bowed by them and thinking 'You're free after all.'

Tradition...saved from the labor of Sisyphus, not to have to choose between one or another. Too frightened to stay up there for more than a minute...grateful to be hurling down again. 'Goodbye, Milt. Just to totter a moment on the pinnacle was all I was able to do. Forgive me.'

Enzo, Becky started again, from the bottom of the mountain. Emma Goldman in a new guise and not seeing signs, and not wanting to face the challenge of his life...so she wouldn't have to face hers. He was the new life, and...living...to fight the dying...not to die without having lived...like Pesach.

'Live, Becky,' Momma said, not dreaming of the strange distortions it would come to mean. All the mandates...sacrifice...not to be a maid...not by materialistic pursuits. Be rich. Don't be rich. Poor, don't be poor, be different, romantic, respected, loved, gracious, a home, the meal on the table with someone, never to be left and Becky, the boss, now that lived only to please and inferior. A month later, he took a high school equivalency test and passed.

"You passed," meeting him outside the school full of confidence and a beaming smile, "you passed high."

"If I failed, I would leave," he said, "No one ever had confidence in me before."

And she would prop up, tend, see him grow...like, watching the first clumsy step of a baby and waiting for the other. He was learning to walk again, and Becky, waiting... suspended...until he takes the second step.

Floor scrubbing, and washing dishes, sitting up nights, doing his term papers, and working in a welfare office and giving him all her pay...that wasn't Momma, but cooking and sewing buttons, and being hostess that was degrading. Working and housework certain, kinds that wasn't. Becky couldn't hire a girl to do the housework. No patience to watch her cleaning...and too much guilt...Frank was constantly around it seemed, and his presence subtly increased.

One night he drove her home. It was winter, dark, early. He suddenly grabbed her, kissed her violently and passionately, and it was met by her with the eruption of a violent desire she had never felt before. The struggle was eternal now Becky missed the frustrated, love, unattainable, the gnashing and desperate, twisting, and turning in a closed circle, and being reached for desperately and drowning blithely away each time only to be hunted and yearning for even more desperately than before the secret meetings and letters with double entendre sent to famous people Names and meant for her. And he had his charms, the academic conversations, and the anxiety of a grade. He was smart enough not to be worried about boring him. He was never bored. He was content to eat a good meal that he cooked and then sit with his arm around her, watching TV, not even reading the drama of the conversation. Obsessional like she had all her life, twisting and turning and talking, talking, talking once it's decided that's that he'd say Becky decided only to undecided and all the trapped words festered with swing then panicked, tortured, and degraded talking now alone and not talking no restaurants no plays no concerts. Gian is not interested.

Becky limited her life to mothering, but a smiling disposition, except for exposure moments loud sudden, but without hate even fuming as a matter of fact, and no demands for cleanliness or service she paid the bills, made him a graduation party, and sent him to school for a PHD. She would avoid the issue as long as she could and then she refused to think about it the boredom setting in Becky yearning for the drama without substances, better than shallow, but the halo she adored, and looked up to in childlike wonder was still there when he smiled and looked at her from a certain angle very handsome, but everything faded.

She wrote a letter to Milt. Discrete, asking in many words, 'How was he?' His letters came to the office, lifted her pride and gave her something to look forward to and give her a secret life that made her feel important. The secret he yearned to see her and they arranged a meeting.

She greeted him as always simulating, excitement and passion. He still loved her, and the force and flood of words, loving, accusing, and Becky surprised, still loving her? And she was ready with the excuses of the chronically unconvinced the best of because he didn't really know her because they weren't married because he didn't really know her, because it was always a brief encounter because she performed ecstasy and excitement to feed his pride, because she fed his illusions, because she adored him in childlike wonder, and she did all men, and she was a loner isolated, didn't know how to love because she couldn't compare herself to others only with fancies heroines, and nothing in advancing to go home leave him, looking at her with the wide open adoring eyes, and opening the door of her home, and guilt battering needing to wash the magic moments Feeling only unclean. Then standing in the tub, watching the water rising and looking for a sign head to mouth scratching biting scars of passion there are more. All dead.

Becky. Gian. Milt. Mill had a heart full of warmth and pain that never turns to passion the lips that look from a distance, the mouth not the body that hand that touches another. And Gian too, joy and sparkle both the bubble of a child that never sobered, grew, deepened, a peck and a limp handshake. Becky unloving, but needing know this, but Gian and Milt...loving, but didn't their lies. The difference between men and women. A woman knows who is owed with his heart. Mann doesn't know if the woman is or is he himself is suffering his joy, his anticipation, his pride deludes him.

The woman does not have the comfort of delusions, so she waits and doesn't even know she's waiting until a big room at work, and all men are all admiring, and Becky still not knowing she is beautiful and making Becky sparkling, gay and flirtatious. The dark heavy man in the corner, largemouth, deep, dark eyes heavily withdrawn. Sometimes he'd buy coffee for them both then call her and say \$.10 Miss Taylor and she beautifully pay the dime on the desk and talked while he stood frozen, nodding, asserting on occasion.

He reported the cases, and sometimes he'd send a message to the judge who was demanding to see her on a case. She dropped everything and ran up the stairs without even waiting for the elevator to arrive, panting and breathless, and he tell her the judge changed his mind one day she used his coffee pot, broke the top, he accused her of carelessness. Didn't remember doing it, but was guilt stricken. One cold night, he offered to give her a lift. She accepted the next day accompanying her to lunch. She teetered on the ice and rested her hand on his arm. He bent it to accommodate her. She could feel him trembling. She had wanted to be his friend standing aloof, but attentive, commanding a view of the whole room. He'd watch her and she'd perform the naïve Sweet friendly, warm, and giving naïve coquette. Vein she was, but she was grateful still a new and surprising experience being popular in a room full of men. She walked into a welcome every morning from a dozen smiling eyes all except Frank never smiling, firm, rigid, unbending, hard, but available, always available for lunch, coffee, and talk. Never had so much company so steady even if she visited a neighbor, she felt timid, uncertain imposing or she was told to leave but not Frank her first steady friend. She never thought it's strange or stingy that he calls and demands his '$.10 Miss Taylor.' But he kept his distance driving home one night in the rain. He asked suppose a person is afraid what can he do if he's frightened, Becky, not daring to ask what he was afraid of, but she sent it was her too frightened to ashamed to shy and asking Becky if she knew about her, and if she was a good mother, knowing all, if he needed an answer, desperately from her, she too frightened to answer seriously to step past the boundary into seriousness with him, showing the heaviness like it all mattered, and yet not believing that she could really be important to anyone or that anyone would want her or think her pretty or smart.

"Are you afraid of something?" A long pause, then whispering "Or just afraid?"

"We're all afraid that's what life is fear I can understand you being afraid of life is frightening from the beginning to the end, afraid to live, afraid to die the human condition."

That night she tucked candies into her bag, and the next day she read him her under linings, 'the absurdity of life, and what to do with the absurd.' She loved it, sad, poetic, unhappiness, that she lifted with words and chatter, and just being.

Every month the letters from Milt - detached logical controlled sentences as intellectuals talk of love. Others, talking of emotion and experience. Gian plays his role until it plays him, and then is him authentic and real emotion, and feeling impulse intention and the senses, body free from the tyranny of the mind thoughts from the tyranny of logic, free as waves, and flood and fire. Milt logical even when he suffered in anguished and Becky knowing only love when it was pain. Momma pain. Poppa pain. Always looked for pain and suffering, and when it was gone, the love was gone. 'I look forward to a normal life,' Gian said once.

No more partings and pain gone love gone. From significant to insignificance from being one to being nothing from perfect to having nothing from romantic pain to domestic pain from living life, hard, making love, reciting poems, dinner, and cafés, the amusements of theocracy romance, and then the obsessions of the middle class, the practical and the impractical habit and familiarity the man who measures statistical correlations, is not a packed the flood of the practical and mundane habit and familiarity. in the middle class swooped into and romance was out of style living in a haze in magic of one on one a circle of rainbows ethereal mystical the hush after love, and never knowing the Blair of a car horn a paycheck the clang of the time clock bill to the pound, or to be late for looking for, and he by the scribbling by the midnight lamp, while she sleeps above an arm, slung, over and pillow and staring at the cracked light under the door.

Becky feared death any death, and it was always just around the corner. Becky was always racing with it just a step ahead the last meeting parting dinner and phone call always the last morning, the crack of light under the door, and waiting for an instance to bear, the door closed softly, and the roar of the motor the job has claimed him the long hours night and mornings alone the studies and career, and just hovering with all the including and something dies with Becky world to conquer. And she asked him to pick up some bread on the way home and every night she waited while he bought bread only Frank, the only Christian in her life who loved her because they were more than their own people a sense of misery about him and a thick wall privacy so impenetrable that Becky did not dare ask a personal question like the sorcerer's apprentice. The dream stops suddenly when she came home to the heavy blanket duty silence the aloneness of quiet contentment when this is still the press to talk, but she could be quiet now, and welcomed it. She was also tired of talk the restlessness of the day nothing left at night.

Becky needed obsessive rumination. She is digging into his heart and him digging into her drama, a film every night to keep tension, excitement flowing between them instead of emotionless living.

And home being there no testing no judging no negatives the

living room held only as a set Becky panicked when it broke down. What would they do until it was fixed with degrees between them.

"You're strong, Becky," Gian said.

"You're fragile," Frank said.

No one ever knew that not even Becky herself. Then she started paying attention to all the twinges of pain and hurt. She lived with a voice, the tone of a voice that was bruising every day slipped out of her out the door into an avalanche of a flood of hertz, big and little, and had been devouring erasing, then wiping them out quickly. A daily battle of hollering and protecting when the issues were outside of herself, still playing the rebel cause she had to where else would all that pain go? The assault especially of, the detached and careful, that abandoned, never joined, and left her alone when she needed them. And Frank, the hating and retreating, the bureaucrat, criminal in his liberating, born from fear. The followers of principle are seldom principles, except for the leader.

"You're too serious," he'd tell her, "You need to have more fun."

After Irving, she loved his laughter, but hated stupid activities like the beach, camping, and tennis boating. She got tickets to concerts, but he attended without enthusiasm. And during the day, reading and waiting to delight in sharing a well-turned phrase on wisdom, or witness from the master.

Sometimes she would take a beer home, thinking he wasn't picking her up that night. To Becky late meant never. She never took things for granted at times she had the feeling his car was behind the bus and her silent phone call at night. Frank? The thought terrified her. So, it was a relief when Gian announced, 'We have to go to Italy to see my parents they're getting old.'

Frank was beginning to frighten her not what she knew he did but what she imagined she told Frank the following day. He wished her a good trip and questioned when she was leaving and how long she would be gone. When they came home, she found a note in the box after he had gone to work it said, 'Welcome home - Frank.' it frightened her a little that he was there in their absence. Something ominous about that, though it seems so innocent.

Once this was a Newland, dreaming, exploring man as the wanderer, the visionary the restlessness, whether he was searching for new lands or old memories, he knew not a new woman here and there, without bending ties. Searches, wanders, explorers, conquerors, and now women. To fall in love with every appealing man and they fall in love with her everywhere because she is now everywhere. And like we avoid the foods and places that are disease and discomforted, we avoid the people to, and choose what we think is livable juggling and juggling love tempered by fear now of the real and mysterious memories, hiding in the dark of the mind, and sending smoke signals to baffle and mislead. What was there to explore and conquer then? Women more immoral than men. They could spread their greed to other things. But women are just focused, mainly on men, the new life, and living to fight the dying not to die without having lived like Pesach. Live, Becky. That's what Momma always said. Not even imagining the strange distortions it would come to me, knowing no other, but what it meant now, all the mandates to sacrifice not to be a maid, not to have children, but to go to school, marry, a Jewish doctor, and not be mistreated or abused.

Chapter One Hundred Nine

Frank was gone. They said he went on vacation for a week, a twinge of pain, seeing the dusk empty. Lunch without him, missing the bread. She was looking for his car. She thought he saw it, but it turned, Seems like in profile, maybe? She stared hard, but it was too dark to tell. She expected him to be waiting when she came off the bus. But he wasn't. It hurt a little. She wasn't prepared for the pain.

He surprised her at home, a call, Gian saying, "Hello, hello, hello, hello!"

And again, the phone rings.

Gian answers 'Hello, hello, hello!'

No answer. Strange. Becky was puzzled and frightened.

"We'll have to change our number."

Every morning she found she was looking for him, and loneliness was deepening. The following week sitting with her head down, she didn't look up, shuffling behind papers on the desk, and suddenly, very shy, both alone in the room, where there was usually light. Becky pauses her head when someone else enters. Then, others, one by one greeting her from a circle around her, and then Frank to join the circle, but standing silent. She looks coy and smiles. He smiles, too, a stiff, cold, strange smile with dead eyes, and he walks away. He leaves before lunch. She goes with the others facing the door.

He walks in the lunchroom after they're all seated and sits facing her, but talking to everyone else, but her.

He looks handsome for the first time, a feeling of power and steadfastness about him and then suddenly his voice asking, "So did you enjoy your vacation, Becky? Where did you go?"

Questions, assaulting, probing in military repetition, "Would you go back again soon?"

He waits. Silence and repeated, and with urgency now the demand from o to 10 he repeated.

Becky replies. And he says, "Are you sure?"

Becky, suddenly playful now. Dodging, teasing, withdrawing, feeling the advantage is hers, now. He ceased to be important, just like that.

"As sure, as anyone can be about anything," sparkling, devil in this coffee shop on a bench with a long table, a dark basement paper on the floor but just He to Becky company at lunch, belonging, men, admiring her, sparking conversation.

The ghetto Jew, once removed to Brooklyn. After lunch, the pills, high blood pressure, diabetes, heartburn, probation officers, the scape-goats of the department, judge, clients, lawyers, blame someone the probation department, kill the messenger when the news is no good. The reports are no good. The department couldn't solve the crime problem. Change the report, Becky considered the best probation officer, but still was a big fish in a little pond and hating and ashamed of the little pond. Becky, being humiliated every time she said a probation officer like it was a woman's fate to be humiliated by a husband, and now a job. Gian was a desperate effort to make the peasant a doctor, and then perhaps acceptable to the Jewish world. She couldn't imagine him being without her and it pleased her to think of the guilt to carry all his life if he didn't. Frank mentioned offhandedly that he was going on vacation on Monday.

She never realized how she looked forward to Monday morning. Now nothing to look forward to. A desolate walk into the office and facing her empty desk and at the end of the day looking for the car to be driving up. She missed him and '$.10 Miss Taylor.'

The day he was supposed to come back, that, eager lightness again, the care getting dressed, the rushing to the office.

"Hi Frank!" a deer smile from her and a stiff one from him she wanted to ask so many questions.

"Did he go anywhere? Why not?"

Becky never had an interest in where people went, but now he was never animated smiled, but not with his life. A little group chosen among the rest, Becky was finally chosen, and then the slow hesitant rising to face duty again, and the parting, and the end of commander, ship and freedom, and the beginning again of explaining, accountability, why she did this, and that, apologizing, accounting, explaining, mortified, puzzled, confused, but looking very professional, complacent, obedient, well, disciplined, on time, unclear about the contradictory rules of the hour, never knowing Where shouting and accusing will come from and when, the goal, keep us imbalanced only lunch was balanced. When she was seated at that long bench, and surrounded by laughter, and or the causes that made history that day, she talk that make them all feel superior and important, and all things they didn't feel, and have before when they were working with people, tired and unwilling, and forced to ask the same questions and fill the same boxes, you're only one step above him, Becky. Both city friends, both on the dull. 'He's one match above the unemployment line and you are one notch above. He didn't worry. You did.'

The big room was in a gray building that looked older than it was because of neglect. Fancy criminals, even have fancy rooms, hushed, so clean and full of remain statues, and the slum dwellers have theirs too, the dirt ground into the marble walls, the darkness in the ravenous buildings, where man and boys have straightened their hats and sat their faces, so that they can go out the same day they came in.

The population exploded, and the building could not keep up. It became a justice factory and store owners became cautious and politicians were smugly satisfied. Another closet to put a judge, one of their own. The halls beckoned, the grimy windows that were never washed, clients lined the halls with their stories. The eyes held close, looking, innocent, appealing to the heart. Abusive husbands, beaten wives, the family court, where there was no family, just battling wounds, winners, and losers, and ultimately all losers.

Chapter One Hundred Ten

The first moments of love in this whole story. If only we can grasp and hold it without ever having to look back and remember. The intelligence struggles – succumbs, the heart suffers, lies, anguished, shame, the signals faint and return again, like the moon and a nest of dark clouds and linger forever. One word, a gesture, a brief smile, the turn of an eye, a word at the wrong moment like a flood, hungry, water reaches for and devours a young sprig.

The pained, 'I love you,' whispered in anguish in the darkness as quickly as the shamed, 'I love you, too,' and the wanting and staring helplessly mute, a mystic silence that must not ever be broken by a word. The hushed quiet, the silence caresses, protects and separates a small loving circle, secure in it's aloneness.

Then, the shattering, forced out of the circle, still wanting, craving, and facing, leaving by her own door. Guilty now and ashamed. The happy, eager, smiling face of Gian.

The dear greeting – 'Preziosa, Cara Carrisima,' a kiss hello, and the mouth still warm from another and for the first time, trying to force her tight mouth to be fuller, softer, receiving, taking. He sits back, looks at her bewildered.

"What are you doing, Cara?"

"Nothing, why? Something wrong?"

He smiles again, "Let's move, Cara."

He takes her by the hand and dances her into the kitchen, lifts the lid from the pot and pronounces it, 'Delicious.'

She sits through dinner, miserable. And then, grateful for the first time, the TV. She goes to bed smiling, nestles her head on his chest and then turns to the wall for the first time. Like a small boy with that chest. She was now fault-finding. He was a boy, rather than a benevolent father. The eruption of a violent desire, a huge chest, a full warm, feeling passionate, mouth, huge hands that encompass and hold, warm, protecting man – compared with admiration, novelty, pretense, maternal care, idealism, fun, invidiousness, emptiness, Italian style.

The job-loving, frightening, demeaning Frank, put excitement, enchantment in her days. No more leader, unwilling, feet slodding to work. No contest. Guilt and passion. The desperate tension of wanting and not having a home, having and not wanting.

Woman's fear is the knowledge of her temporariness. How many of them feel the stability of a piece of property that they will be loved and fought for to the end. Rather she feels like prey...hunted, conquered, discarded. Being wanted, suffered, and anguished over then being all to being nothing. Then she yearns for the wanting she once knew. 'I'm wanted therefore I am, imagined, sought after, dreamed of, tormenting, tantalizing, therefore, I am. If a man suffers over me grandly therefore I am. If he tires of me, I am not.' In that sad and worshiping drama, ladder heavy, Frank's adoring whisper, the desperate hunger of I am, and in the sweet affection of Gian's, '<u>I am not</u>.'

She had to be the first to go and had to get a stamp to return her clothes. She faced many frustrations, tramping from office to office in Italy only to be told she would have to come back the next day. Then the day after, to get a stamp, finally, Becky threatened to blow the building if she didn't get her stamp. Finally, after days passed, Gian appealed to a friend, an official who fulfilled the requirements to get her stamp to get her clothing in Italy and she was still fuming but now she received the gently flowing Italian graciousness to comfort her from her tantrums or low servants do to a spoiled rich lady. It seems the head of the office appeared dressed like an admiral and playing the part – an air of significant authority, aloof, silence, and then a spending on their faces and each saying, rushing to please her.

The papers, examinations all passed, years passed of TV and school, like he was a growing boy. Becky lives in Bert and Russel's compassionate marriage, forever on the school campus. And, as he obtained his degree there was the gentle nudge for another and another, after all if he became a doctor, maybe she'd be forgiven that he's not Jewish, and that he's short and skinny, it life becomes real, no matter what honors along the way, like a little ball fall into holes, wiggles around and settles itself in one, at last. He was, but she wasn't.

The pain and the hurt when he came down the mountain would destroy her. But Becky never realized how destroyed she was already. The next morning when he would turn from life, she didn't exist, back and forth between wanting and fear.

And Frank pressed, "I want to know you," she was holy with a voice so deep, warm, and loving to which Gian's light gentleness was no match. Frank was powerful, overcoming and conquering. A desperate, fierce, longing in one, and sweet affection from the other. Passion filled, moments in love and chore-ridden days in the other.

Becky was resting. Gian had to finish his schooling for his Ph.D. So he could get a job in Europe and return to his parents, so Becky's responsibility would be fulfilled. She had wrested him from his country and family. She owed him.

Every morning Frank took her to lunch now in his car in the park and she was coming home later and later. Life was now interesting. Frank had introduced her to the world of secret meetings, romantic, intrigue, and frustrated love. Better wanting and earning than sitting safe and dying and withering with habit and time and not noticing, the one you once lived for, the site of, and not looking forward to the first eager kiss in a dark hallway, or an old car. Nothing pleases you more and you find fault with everything, especially the love you married, bitter taste, ashes in the mouth, bored.

The first day you leave for a vacation with a lover. She earned to spend a day and night and morning, let the car go and never stop. The confinement of time and space heightened the intensity, until he begged once more for a little time together just to be alone, without eyes looking, to close the door behind them and sit somewhere alone and hold hands. Six months and never alone. Kissing, touching, he was a religious Catholic raised at a Catholic school. His father was violent. His mother, long suffering. Many times, he separated them, holding the door against an enraged, father, threatening to get her. He brought a cat home, and his father threw it out. He was an only child who had no friends, just a few Jewish ones that he liked. Now he was a lover, had no one. His family was a tempestuous lot who raged him maliciously, one day and avoided him the next.

At age ten, she declared there was no use in people or in living and turned from the world. He had a picture of himself at age eleven – angry, sullen. He had no picture of himself smiling. Never laughed, even now, with joy, just a sardonic smile, with rage, not sadness, determined to survive, to live, even though he hated it.

As if someone was determined he shouldn't. It was an act of rebellion, rather than an affirmation of life. At Catholic school, the nuns tormented him. A gullible boy he was, terrified to return to school on Monday, not to be banished to hell before he had a chance to confess an impure thought. He loved Jewish people because they were kind and hated his own. He was in his mid-30s. Becky never knew if he had a girlfriend. He never said. She never asked him. But she wondered and really didn't want to know. She was very jealous. Even in the past. Becky was his only love, his only friend. She wanted it that way. Becky couldn't bear another love in a man's life, not even a friend, or could either because of a memory, Pesach. He had no friends. Only with men she had ever known. What it means to be the first, the only.

She was terrified and careful. If the car broke down, he calmly repaired it, never shouting in traffic, never shouting at Becky, never even raising his voice, caressing her with loving words, hurtful, brilliant, perfect. He never doubted or questioned her. Never talked about the ordinary or practical like Gian. And that she loved. Philosophy, his major in college abstractions, poetry, deep thoughts, each by them instead of Gian.

Eating was the main high point of the evening at home and Gian was contributing to his own disaster without knowing it. Unwittingly he was the barrier that made the romance, the unrequited, passion, and obsession with the both of them. Poor, half less innocent man, the center of hiding and subterfuge guilt, plotting and turmoil of which he has even been aware of.

Frank said he didn't want children and would wait for forever just to be with her in any way. Becky loved loyalty but never had any of it. Feared he left it she wasn't perfect, any precarious moment, shifting moved and she feared she'd be found wanting. Gian was loyal in thinking to a wavering constant like Becky, flopping like a sheet in the wind.

Both, too embarrassed now. The clothes on their backs made them strangers again. Finding familiarity uncomfortable. He insists she pose for a picture outside the door. Her face is twisted like it's a sunny day, but it's cloudy and he records her shame, forever. She will always hate that picture. It was not a happy time. People don't generally take pictures of unpleasant moments, but he does. With his dark suit on, the side of his face, showing strong, he appeals again. Overcome by the guilt of not wanting to leave, the pain returning of wanting to hold, of yearning, for someone who is not gone, wanting to hold more time, and the joy of knowing he suffers, and for Becky, needed longing, and wanting, coming together and parting, having and not having, being lost, and found again. Hell, and heaven, all in one, the ultimate dream. The strings on which human life is intensely played, and for which he yearns to light the fire in the deepest heart. And so, she was torn between yearning to be with and without. And with Gian, yearning to be without and with guilt, panic, loss, fear, not passion. Months past. He and Becky were together often. Like Samson, looking at Delilah before she blended him. Heathcliff's tyranny at a distance had her terrified nearby. There he was wanting to see her on weekends, Saturday morning, he insisted. Gian wouldn't let her. He seemed to suspect, but unsure, she went to buy a paper. A quick call, quiet and frightened.

"He won't let me go. Frank, I'm coming."

"Don't."

"I'm coming!"

Gian banging at the door, "Let me in!"

"I'm not letting you go!"

Protecting Frank, pushing the door against his father furious.

Gian, "What do you want? Who is he, Becky?"

Two of them conniving. Fantasy and reality.

Gian, "Stay away from my wife! I'll kill you!"

Becky collapses on the floor, not able to face the confrontation. Frank leaves as Gian is picking her up.

"What is this?!"

He looked concerned, but strangely calm. No remorse, no ugly scenes, no jealous tantrums, no pain in Gian's voice or the face. Becky startled but grateful and slightly upset that the scene she feared was not even slightly enacted.

"Tell him not to bother you again, OK?"

Calm, a little distant. He never mentioned it again. The incident was buried like it never happened, but Becky wondered what if it did or felt like when his faith shattered into 1 million glistening pieces struck by a rock thrown carelessly, and how did he not dwell and remember and repeat and dig and probe to heat all her pain by scarring her again and again showing the jagged edge of trust when it's battered and broken and turns mocking, cutting, unsettled. There are those who ask no questions, turn their face, and plot their own betrayal when this time arrives. Gian waited.

Becky, "No, not at all," she mumbled, and suddenly feared Frank and wanted to get away from him. His force was too much for her.

She had picked him well, she thought. He would spend his life stargazing, that star in Becky. She would always be too much for him. She could take liberties. But he couldn't. After all, who would interest him after Becky? How to handle the terror alone and the shame of not being alone and the pain of missing the domestic habit of Gian. They tampered her office; he couldn't find her. She missed his letters and his missing her. Made her feel important just being wanted, praised, desperately, and loved. Solidity is a transitory memory in yesterday and forever.

She sent a note from where she was.

"I'm here if you still want to see me."

At the height of wanting, her not wanting, disappearing, and returning, having to be a beggar again, and expecting to be coldly dismissed. But she gambled on the fantasy. She counted the days for arrival and return of mail. On the exact day an envelope arrived with the familiar handwriting.

Counting the days to the convention. Longing to see you.

Love you,

Milt

She was sorry already and self-judging. Guilty about Gian. Becky Bromsky, the little girl, lonely, rejected, and now this?!

Frank wanted her to be in his room. Everyone had left. Petrified, shy, she had behind a warm embrace and deep kissing, and not being able to let him go.

"Let me take a look at you," he said lovingly and warmly.

She smiled an endearing smile, and suddenly wanted to flee. His large eyes, naïve, submitting dreaming and dreaming, stubborn persisting. When and why not a word in so long from him.

"I met someone else I wanted to marry, then you came back to me. I dropped her and ran back to you. I can't live up to Frank or down to Gian," beating himself up, "what am I doing here? Tell me, Becky."

Becky tries to play wise, "Stay away from here, once and for all," not returning to her between women, "Don't go back," she whispers.

"You're right," he says, "now tell me about you," he asks.

Close in a chair, she loves the feel of shoulders, chest, arms. She tells him about Gian who loves me no matter what she gives the messages of demanding unconditional surrender as a test of love. He understands. Becky understands, both the understanding of love, and that the wonders of love can survive understanding. Both laughed.

The world is meaningless in both, but both charm and bend the wheel. The two parts of Becky to hide from the world, to take from the world and teach him to hide or let him take her to the sun with him, when it's too bright for blinking. Becky's mines scurry back into hiding. Guilty about Gian. How can she leave him, and he'll have his Ph.D. Things had to end right with proper goodbye speeches. One doesn't fly into the night and leave home. Gian had no warning, there was no one else he suspected, their marriage for him was fine. How could she just leave a note? She had to finish this. She was guilty over his parents, took him from them, but she made them proud. Took him from playing games all day and made him a professional scholar, made them proud. And besides, she didn't want him now. He'd come when he wanted her. She wished he'd leave. Otherwise, no sense going on to marry a student who shared his interest in the scientific, the statistical, the social studies.

Frank decided he would be happy with her, but his cold, intellectual part of him prevented him from giving his heart. She put a letter from him in her dark and later discarded it. She was now solving her endless confusions by objectifying them, demanding, for instance, Gian's heart, in comparison to Frank's, was cold, distant. She really felt he had none. He was all personality and charm. The demands of the unloved can never he not. No one knew that. Tom had given up the struggle. Gian just met it by not recognizing it still an unanswered question in the heart. 'You'll wait forever,' she thought she would.

A letter arrives from Gian:

You've lived without me for a long time – too long. You'll be hearing from my attorney as soon as I learn to live without you. When you read this, I shall be where I belong, in my country. Where I can bear the pain that you've inflicted on me while I end this marriage if you can call it that...at this time. Thank you for the good times...the beautiful, the wonderful times, but the pain has become unbearable when I am not loved. You can arrange for legal proceedings. Mine will be brief and to the point. Nothing to do if I am no longer loveable. But you will always be in my heart.

Gian

The paper was spotted with tears. But then, she realized, she was weeping for him, but not for herself.

She shouted, "Free! At last! From the Dictates of the heart, she was free! At last!"

She paused and thought, passion, doubting, philosophical, a cynical smile at self.

THE END

www.ingramcontent.com/pod-product-compliance
Lightning Source LLC
Chambersburg PA
CBHW020503110726
47899CB00004B/1049